SAMSON DUKE

STAN—
BY PROXY FOR MY
FRIEND, SEYMOUR, WHO I'M SURE
WILL SIGN THIS COPY OF HIS
BOOK LATER — SANDY AND
I WISH YOU A SPEEDY &
COMPLETE RECOVERY FROM
ALL OF YOUR PRESENT
PROBLEMS.

Bud

by Seymour Kern

THE GOLDEN SCALPEL

SAMSON DUKE

SAMSON DUKE

a novel

Seymour Kern

Sherbourne Press, Inc. / Los Angeles

FIRST PRINTING
ISBN 0–8202–0096–4
Library of Congress Catalog Card Number 75–182520

Typography by Shirley Shipley
Composed, printed, and bound in the United States
of America by
The Colonial Press Inc., Clinton, Mass.

To Jessie

If I had my life to live all over again
I'd get a license to steal.

LUCKY LUCIANO

1929

CHAPTER ONE

The compartment was cool-green and the train began to move without a sound, first slow then gathering speed until the waving figures on the platform began to blur and disappear as the car plunged into the tunnel. As the train passed 125th Street and then Yonkers, he watched from the window and saw the river and its green shores, then Peekskill flashed by and Beacon and Pough-keepsie. It was hard to believe he was on his way, roots pulled, being conveyed to the country's other end.

For a year his aunt had been writing from Los Angeles, plead-ing for him to come, painting waving palms, a blue sky one could actually see, and everyday there was sun, warm and good to feel, better than a tonic. But his bones were young, New York winters were easy to bear, and you didn't mind sweating through an Au-gust, when, standing before the Times Building you looked up Broadway, a belch of fire in the dark, framed in neon and pounded by a million feet, a bauble encrusted with palaces of con-crete and steel, flicker and sputter and snakes of light, a Gomor-rah and the castle in a dream. There are nightmares too, and they're not all woven in sleep. The past week had been just that.

He tried to read but could not concentrate, turned to the scenery that began to change from lush countryside to squat dirty towns ringed by neon that turned to ugly grotesques as night came. The first dinner gong sounded and he walked through the cars to the diner. By the time he finished his meal the car was full and he returned to his compartment. It was early but it had been a long day, so many events crowded it and the days preceding it; he could no longer relate the happenings to their proper sequence in time.

Standing before the mirror he brushed his teeth and examined his face. Even in the dim light of the compartment the muted features mocked him. The shadows were cruel that night: the aquiline nose dipped and the eyes appeared closer together, almost converging on his bridge; the part of him without fault, a broad forehead, was lost in the poor light. He finished his preparations and crawled into the berth. Closing his eyes, he tried to block his thoughts but they began to whirl in his head like dervishes, insistent, demanding, tearing down the barriers he had attempted to set up and the events of the past days began to flash through his mind like pictures off a reel. It was no use. His head was full and, faced with the images, tumbling, kaleidoscopic, he found himself struggling to separate and put them in their proper place.

He was walking through a tiny park, a seamy oasis set aside long ago and now surrounded by stacked tenements. A few elderly persons were still on the scarred and chipped benches as if too tired to make it back to their flats after the long hot day. The grass was burned, the paths littered with Eskimo Pie wrappers, stained hot dog buns, Jewish rye, Italian bread, and heaping trash cans. As the sun's last sliver teetered on the horizon and sunk, silhouetting the trees and buildings around the park, and the stink of the Bronx wafted and assailed, he began to have doubts and he remembered wondering if he was headed for the right place. But he had no choice, it had to be done, that was certain, and done without delay. You did not buy an abortion cheap on Park Avenue. Why did he look for bargains at such a time? He was buying it for himself as well as for Rita. Wasn't she tied to him like an anchor to a ship?

He was consulting a piece of paper on which he had written an address. The number was on Seabury Place, a few blocks from the little park. Rita had given it to him; it was where her girl friend had it done, and if Rita did not mind why should he?

Samson Dukins, idiot, penny pincher, asshole! He knew it would be reasonable but not that low. That should have been the tipoff! Fifty bucks to abort on a kitchen table, stick out your neck for years in jail or maybe worse if the girl didn't make it! He should have known; a fat Hungarian who performed with a hickory stick in a dingy flat, and her husband, grinning, half-toothed, the goddamned agent with whom he made the deal. And it wasn't that he was broke. He had forty thousand dollars laying in banks —more than most men see in a lifetime—enough to buy a fancy doctor and pay his fees for a year.

The wheel noises were no longer a clack but the pounding of a sledge on an anvil and his thoughts were compounding fear and anger. He paced the room puffing the cigarette to a sputter and rang for the porter. He knew he could not sleep that night. Ordering a pot of coffee, he fell into the chair and closed his eyes. Thoughts began to tumble in his head and he fought to forget and they sorted out and he saw Rita waiting for him when he returned from the Hungarian. She was at the window of his apartment, the curtains pulled aside, and she was scanning the street. Rita had the door open before he could finger the bell. He told her about the plans, mentioned the fact that the woman had been a midwife, had delivered a thousand babies in the old country her husband had said, and assured her there was nothing to fear.

"Delivering babies is easy," she said. "It's with God's help."

"Look, I met the woman. She seems capable."

She gripped his arm. "Sam, why can't we get married?"

"I thought it was settled." She released his arm and began to sob. He put his arm around her. "I never gave you reason to believe we would get married. Jesus, Rita, I'm only twenty-one. I'm not ready." She moved away from him. "We've gone over this a dozen times. It's no use." She was seated now, hunched over, biting her nails, her eyes puffed and full of fear, and as he watched all his feelings for her disappeared. If she had that baby, he wasn't going to be around to claim it. "I'll pay whatever it costs," he told her. "But I can't go through it for you!"

"I'm afraid!" she cried out.

"There's nothing to be afraid of. It's simple . . . like pulling a tooth."

"That's what you think!" she flared as she jumped up. "My girl friend had it done by that fat old lady who made her leave right away. She was bleeding. For two days she was bleeding!"

"But she was all right, wasn't she?"

"Oh, Sam, I'm so scared!"

"I can't force you. If you want the baby, go ahead. But it's going to be all yours." He brushed by her, went into the bathroom, and slammed the door. He needed time to think. If she did not have that abortion he would leave her, disappear. He buttoned his fly and returned to the room. Rita seemed calmer now, resigned, and he spoke to her reassuringly. "The whole thing takes a few minutes. I'll be with you all the time."

She crushed her cigarette. "I guess there's nothing more I can say."

"There isn't."

"When do we have to be there?"

"Ten o'clock tomorrow night. Be here at nine and we'll take a cab." She gathered her things. "You'll see." He led her to the door. "Everything will be all right."

The train seemed to be gathering speed, its whistle was insistent, the wheels sounded a clamor driving his thoughts from his head. Samson Dukins slipped into his clothes and entered the narrow passage. There might be people in the club car, someone he could talk to and maybe the fat Hungarian and Rita would disappear and the last few days would blur until all his thoughts and concentration would never bring them back in focus. The lounge was empty; he bought a bottle of Ramshead from the porter and returned to his compartment. Opening the pint he took a long shot, chased it with Coke, and started to undress. His belly began to warm and it was working on his head. By the time he slipped into his pajamas he was thinking of that California sun and the wavy palms and then he took another shot and he thought about Aunt Annie and remembered her auburn hair and the dancing flecks in her eyes, always lighted, alive, full of the only love he ever really had. The Coke was gone now, he was drinking straight and it didn't sting anymore, just warmed. Everything related to time and space and New York was ten hours and five hundred miles away and soon three thousand and that was a continent and the event's shadows had limitations and were soon swallowed in space. The horizon was curved and when you reached the crest and went over the other side you could no longer see what you left behind, only the mind's eye could bring it in focus.

He grabbed the bottle, took another swallow, staggered, and fell into the chair. Getting up carefully, he stood before the mirror and admired the broad forehead. The aquiline nose was proud like a Roman's and the eyes deep-set and glittering. He lit a cigarette, inhaled, became dizzy, crushed it in an ashtray, stumbled backwards, and landed in the chair. Why shouldn't he think about what happened the past few days? Why not! There was time and space on his side growing every minute that ticked by and if he thought it out to the bitter end it would be finished, done with and he could file it away forever. Get it over with! He closed his eyes and picked up a thread and then another and began to weave.

Rita was huddled in a corner of the cab as they wove their way through traffic in the direction of a hotel on Fifty-eighth Street. He wasn't going to take her back to his apartment, just in case, telling Rita that his landlady was a snooper with rigid views on morality. Rita remained in the cab as he took her suitcase, registered under a fictitious name, deposited the bag in the room, and returned to the taxi. They headed for the address in the Bronx.

He had the cab stop half a block away. It was better not to draw attention to their arrival at the building. As he took Rita's arm and they began to walk he felt her body tremble. Her steps began to falter and she leaned against him. By the time they reached the door of the flat he felt all of her weight against him and he almost had to carry her inside. The husband was dressed for the occasion and though he wore no tie his hair was combed and a closely shaven face shone in the lamplight. Rita was no longer able to move without aid and after passing the money the woman appeared and hustled Rita off to the kitchen.

The husband sat by the kitchen door like a sentry. Minutes dragged. Then he heard a piercing scream, jumped from his seat, retreated back from the angry glare of the husband. Now there were faint sobs and then the door opened and the fat Hungarian beckoned him. He found Rita slumped in a chair, her head fallen forward, her chin resting on her chest. He went to her side and gently lifted her head. She appeared in shock as half-open eyes stared at him without recognition from an ashen face. Her hair was matted with sweat that poured from her forehead down the sides of her cheeks to her neck. The woman took a half-filled glass of brandy and forced it through Rita's lips. She gasped, moaned, and her head slumped forward again. The husband pushed Samson aside and passed a bottle of smelling salts under Rita's nose. Her head twisted, she shuddered, and started to cry. This seemed to be what they were waiting for as they lifted her from the seat by the arms and led her from the room.

"Taxi is waiting downstairs," the man said. "Take her now." He handed Samson the bottle of salts.

"Don't worry. I'll drive carefully," the cabbie said. Rita had fallen against Samson as they drove off.

Soon it became apparent that in addition to a state of shock, she was drunk. The woman had forced more of the brandy on her than he had imagined. Clinging to him, Rita sobbed violently, stopped, looked up at him, smiled foolishly through tears, and resumed her crying. By the time they reached the hotel she had cursed the woman, included him, recanted, annoyed him with slobbering affection, then succumbed to a drunken belligerence. He guided her through the lobby of the hotel, propped her up in the elevator, and almost had to carry her to the room. He removed her shoes and outer clothing, got her into bed, and in a few minutes she was asleep.

Why didn't he put a couple of hundred bucks in an envelope with a farewell note and leave? The worst was over, she was sleeping peacefully. Women survive these things, most do anyway. Less than one in a hundred run into trouble. Up to that moment he had done more than the average guy. Who takes them by the hand, leads them there and back? Nobody, except an idiot like Sam Dukins! And did he ever get a guarantee it was him?

The bottle of bourbon was almost empty and he drained the last few drops. Then he rang for the porter. The man came prepared, the bottle was slipped from an inside pocket, and the money was palmed. Samson cut the liquor with water, added an ice cube, and sipped the drink slowly.

No, he did not run out of that hotel room. He took a post at the window as Rita slept and looked out on a narrow shaft. He had been in the room over two hours and though she was sleeping and there were no outward signs of hemorrhaging, she kept twisting and tossing, crying out unintelligibly. He approached the bed. She seemed to be rousing as her lips parted and appeared to be forming words. He leaned over hoping to catch what she was saying. She opened her eyes and he drew back. There was a puzzled expression on her face. She gripped his arm.

"Am I all right?" she whispered.

"You're fine." He managed a smile.

She passed a hand across her brow. "Such a headache. There's aspirin in my purse."

He rummaged through her bag, found the aspirin. She propped herself on an elbow, swallowed the tablets, greedily drank the water he gave her. Then she sank to the pillow and closed her eyes. He lifted the sheet carefully and looked at the spot between her legs. A wad of sanitary napkins lay bunched around her crotch, but no sign of blood. She was sleeping again, he covered her, and returned to his seat at the window.

He spiked the drink with more bourbon and took a long pull from the glass. Pushing himself out of the chair he stood before the mirror, shifting his position until most of his face was in the shadow and only the forehead appeared prominently. He held up the glass toasting his image, took a sip, and then hurled the remainder at the mirror as he cried out "Fool! Goddamn fool!" She had been asleep, there were no signs of bleeding and instead of getting the hell out and disappearing he hung on. God, he was asking for trouble! So he sat by the window in the lousy room and dozed until a dirty gray dawn barely lighting the shaft greeted him when he awoke with a start. He heard sounds from the bathroom and water running. The bed was empty. He crossed the room and knocked on the door. At first there was no response but he knocked again and heard her voice.

"Stay out!" she cried.

He put his ear to the door. "Is there anything I can do?" he said.

"Just stay out!"

He was about to demand entrance when the door opened. She was clutching a towel around her waist and her eyes were sunk in a face that was dead white. She started to say something, hesitated, then shook her head as if dismissing it and walked to the bed. Through the open door he saw a pile of her underclothing soaking in the sink. As he approached the bed she crawled under the sheet and pulled it to her chin.

"How do you feel?" he asked.

She shook her head slowly from side to side as she looked at him and did not say a word.

"Is everything all right?" he insisted.

She finally spoke. "Are you worried?"

"Of course!" he exploded. "This was an ordeal for me too."

"Well, it's over now. I flushed your baby down the toilet a few minutes ago. And you slept through it."

"I sat up most of the night," he protested. "I just dozed. Why didn't you wake me?"

She turned and buried her face in the pillow. It was over, the worst part, and nothing else mattered. "I imagine you want to stay in bed for the rest of the day. Let me bring up some food."

"I can't eat. Bring some coffee and a box of Kotex."

When he reached the street he found it muggy as fat clouds drifted lazily in a leaden sky. The all-night drugstore on the corner was open and the smell of fresh coffee reminded him he was hungry. He ate a breakfast and some of the tensions stripped away. When he returned to the room, Rita was sitting up in bed. She had put on some makeup and brushed her hair. For a fleeting moment his old feeling for her returned, then rapidly disappeared. He managed a smile, handed her the coffee and placed the Kotex on the table beside the bed.

Now he had to get away. He could smell the blood and Rita's looks were piteous. The pale light in the room emanating from the cheerless shaft seemed to cover everything with a gray shroud. And he needed time to think. Vagrant thoughts had been fleeting through his mind and were now proffering like a temptress and beginning to form and shape. Whatever contract he had with New York had expired. He had quit his job a month before; a thankless task collecting tenement rents for a pious old fart who handled the buildings for a family who had been living in Paris for a generation. It wasn't easy and every once in a while a delinquent tenant got nasty and in the year he was on the job he collected one shiner, a bloody nose, and a sprained hand. He would have quit long ago—the pay was low—but a few months before he had devised a way to double his income with a little juggling. Then the bookkeeping system was changed and he was back to the low wages. So, there was nothing to keep him in Manhattan, not a piece of ass or a filled till and trains were leaving every day for the West, and the only person who gave a damn about him had been calling from California for a year.

He ran a hand over his beard and turned to Rita. "I'd like to leave for awhile. Just to my apartment to shave and change clothes."

"How long will you be?"

"A couple of hours."

"Get back as soon as you can. I don't want to be alone."

After a hot bath, shave, and clean clothes he felt better and returned. What little composure he had left her with had disappeared.

"Thank God you're here! I started to flow right after you left. It's like someone turned on a faucet. I don't know what to do!" she cried. She pointed to the Kotex. "I've gone through half the box!"

Before he could say another word she leaped from the bed with a cry and rushed to the bathroom. The towel with which she was wrapped was stained with blood and a stream ran down her leg. He followed but she slammed the door in his face and the lock clicked. Then he heard her. . . .

"Mary, Mother of God, please help me . . . !"

He pounded on the door. "Rita, let me in!"

"Oh, my sweet Jesus . . . !"

"Open the door!"

"Sam, Sam . . . !"

"Rita, open that door!"

"Sam. . . ." Her voice trailed off.

The train's whistle was shrill, the cars strained, the engine puffed. They rounded a curve and took a hill. Samson Dukins tipped the bottle of Ramshead and swallowed a straight drink. Then he became rigid and stared ahead, afraid any motion would release the thoughts that had been raging through his head for days. He was drunk and the pain of the present filled his head, crowding out the past and blocking the future. The train was going too fast and the lurches were quakes; wheels were spinning inside his head and engine smoke filled the room. He took a step, found no floor, and felt a sharp pain in his head as he caromed from the wall to the berth. For a long while he lay on his back, pain jabbing his head, everything crowded out of his mind as the ceiling spun and he concentrated on stopping it. Now the room was a giant mixer and he was the center and his guts were being whirled . . . faster and faster . . . they were tearing, couldn't hold on . . . it was no use! The hot stinking vomit gushed from his throat through his mouth and nose, covered his chin, trailed his neck, and matted the hairs of his chest. For a few moments he was relieved; then from the bottom of him there seemed to be a quake and it heaved and he croaked as a thin stream of bile spurted through his teeth and dribbled down his chin. The stench in the compartment was unbearable as he rolled toward the window and tried to pry it open. It would not budge. He fell back on the pillow and moaned as the ceiling began to spin again; the train started to sway as his guts churned, depositing what seemed to be their lining in a puddle as he leaned over the berth. Though his head still pounded and he felt weak there was relief from the nausea and he struggled to his feet.

He had to get out of the stinking clothes, the room, the smell! Ashamed of his condition, the mess, saturated with filth, he rang for the porter. There was no choice, he needed new bedding, even a new mattress and pillow and the rug was soaked. By the time the porter answered his call he had stripped off his clothes, washed his body and put on a robe.

"I'm sorry, George," he said, handing him a five dollar bill. "It was the last drink," he went on forcing a grin. "Anyway, change everything, the mattress too. I'll be in the smoker at the end of the car." The man said nothing, just shook his head as Dukins left.

The smoker was empty; he settled in the window seat and lit a cigarette.

Again he closed his eyes and the hotel room came into focus. Though he panicked when Rita screamed, he was still convinced he did the smart thing. Fleeing the hotel he'd gone to the nearest booth, looked up the name of a doctor whose office was close and called him. He told the physician he was calling for his wife who was having a miscarriage and hemorrhaging. They were visiting from out of town he said, gave him the address of the hotel and number of the room. The doctor told him to keep his wife in bed with her legs propped and said he would be right over.

There were few tracks to cover. He had no close friends, few acquaintances; he would not be missed. Months before he'd cashed in all the stocks Aunt Annie had invested his money in when his parents had died and she'd sold the New Brunswick farm. He had seen carloadings drop, production fall off, employment decrease, and some pretty smart men were writing about the market bottoming out before the end of 1929.

By two o'clock that day nothing was dangling; everything he owned was on his back, in two suitcases, and in cashier's checks nestling in his wallet. At Grand Central Station he bought a ticket to the coast. Before leaving he put a two hundred dollar money order and a short note in an envelope and mailed it to Rita at her residence at the "Y."

The porter brought the coffee and as he sipped it he suddenly realized he had made a colossal mistake. That foolish note! It was an admission he was a party to an abortion. If she died he nailed himself as a party to it. It could be manslaughter! Everything else had been handled so well; the doctor didn't know his name, he signed the hotel register with an alias, the Hungarians were given no name and nobody knew where he was headed. He even gave another name when he bought his railroad ticket. Why in hell didn't he just send the money? Rita would know who it came from. Why did he have to explain?

He left the smoker and made his way back to the compartment, but the strong smell of the disinfectant mingled with the sour smell of the vomit and his nausea surged again. Returning to the smoking compartment with a blanket, he curled up on the seat and spent the night sleeping fitfully until awakened by two men shaving.

Back in his compartment, the pain in his head raged dull and steady and his insides felt scooped out and he was bone dry. He shaved and dressed, made his way to the diner, and ate a large breakfast washed down with a pot of coffee. Packing his bags he returned to the club car and stared out the window as the landscape began to change, towns sprouted, grew larger and then linked, knitting into the sprawling suburbs that sprang from the cramped guts of the great city.

During the hour wait in Chicago he wired his aunt the time of his arrival and combed the New York papers for an item about Rita. There was nothing. Boarding the train he found his compartment and settled by the window as the train began to pull away from the station.

The train crossed the Mississippi where it curled near Moline, then touched Davenport and Oskaloosa and dipped to Kansas City. It sped across the plains. The country widened and grew taller, humped to the Great Divide. Then Samson saw majestic mountains pasteled against a glorious New Mexico sky and soon the great canyon and forests and the green of California after Mojave's dust and sand, weed and brush. The country was vast, broader than he had dreamed; distance multiplied time, New York was a week ago, a month. Rita was a shadow.

The train pulled into the station with a final shudder, gasped, and stopped. His aunt was waving excitedly, running toward him as he left the platform. Her auburn hair was close-cropped in a boyish bob and she looked ten years younger than when he saw her last. Then she had him in her arms. "You've grown!" Holding him at arm's length, her eyes filled. "You've actually grown," she repeated, taking his arm. "I thought you stopped years ago."

"You look wonderful, Aunt Annie. The bob makes you look younger."

She looked at him, eyes smiling, and hugged his arm. She still clung to him as he got his bags and they settled in a cab. The driver wove through narrow streets crowded with small warehouses and entered a square. She kept holding his hand tight as if he would get away, and then leaned forward to the driver. "Take the Third Street tunnel, it's shorter. When you get to Western

Avenue, turn south." Then she faced Samson and seemed to pour out everything at once; the accumulation could no longer be contained. "I missed you, Sam. It's beautiful out here. I love it. Every day it's like this. Sun all the time. But it's been a long year. Lonely." She sighed. "I'm so happy you decided to come out. I live on the south side of town. You get more for your money there. It's pretty though. You'll see. I have a cottage. I'm so glad you're here. You'll love it, Sam, I know you will. No frost, wet shoes, slush. And you can *see* the sky. It's like it was on the farm only it's a city with everything one would want." She squeezed him, stroked, and patted him.

At Western Avenue, they turned south and Aunt Annie continued. "It's part of Los Angeles, really. It's called Gardena. Don't you think it's a pretty name? I bought the cottage. Didn't pay much and only a small down."

Aunt Annie went on and he half-listened as he became aware of the city. The downtown area surprised him, a runty Manhattan and the size of a corner of it, it's tallest buildings thirteen stories with the exception of the new City Hall, zoned for twice the allowable height. As they left the center the city flattened, and there were the palms, tall and wavy with tops like tousled heads, some with trunks that looked like elephant hide and others squatting like giant pineapples. Little houses were pistachio and pink and stark white and you *could* see the sky, the total blue of it, and to the north a huge sign HOLLYWOODLAND clung to enormous black hills dotted with houses that in the distance seemed hung on the hills like toys. Everything was new and fresh like something just made.

Samson's thoughts vaulted the mountains and the rivers and all the distance between himself and the dreary room that opened to the shaft. Suppose Rita bled to death and they traced him? He had to find out what happened. Either Rita was dead or near it or his panic and hers bore no relationship to the facts. The bleeding could have been normal, could have stopped long before the doctor arrived and at this moment, Rita could be back at the "Y" lamenting his departure, delighted with her recovery and planning how to spend the two hundred bucks. As the taxi pulled up before a stucco box fringed with red tile at the roof, an idea occurred that could record the outcome indelibly. Call Rita. Call person to person at the "Y." If she came to the phone, he would know she recovered, he could hang up and she would never know who called. On the other hand if she died or was in the hospital he would be told.

Aunt Annie paid the cabbie as he carried his bags to the front of the house. Trying not to show impatience, he followed her about the tiny home as she detailed every item of transition she had effected since buying it. The former owner had let it go to pot, and she'd done it over completely. If it hadn't been for the orange tree he saw through the living room window, he'd have sworn he was back in Brooklyn. Aunt Annie had had all her things shipped out from the east, and although the rooms here formed a square instead of running along a hallway, they were about the same size and shape as the ones they'd shared in Brooklyn. She'd even managed to find a wallpaper with tiny rosebuds and another with bunches of grapes, almost duplicating the ones adorning the living room and one of the bedrooms of the Brooklyn flat. In the kitchen was the final touch, the Grogan & Sons calendar, "All Kinds of Insurance," hanging above the table, its picture of a thorned and haloed Christ looking Samson straight in the eye.

"I don't know what I'd have done without my things," she said. "It was like I brought part of you and friends along with me." She took his hand and led him to the rear yard. A huge avocado tree shaded one entire corner. There was an orange and a lemon tree, some tropical plants he'd never seen before, and the evenly edged beds were filled with roses and camellias. "You should have seen the yard when I took over, Sam. The weeds were so high you couldn't find the trees."

Samson complimented her on the house and yard, and alibied the need for a walk. "Three days on the train, Aunt Annie. I'm stiff."

"Don't go too far. I'll have lunch ready when you get back."

Out on Western Avenue he found a corner drugstore and a booth, placed a person-to-person call to the "Y" and heard the familiar voice at the switchboard answer. "Miss Rand is not in."

"Can she be reached at another number?"

"No."

"When do you expect her back?"

"I'm sorry, we do not have that information."

He could get nowhere, and headed back to the house, agitated. His favorite light meal awaited him as he entered the kitchen, but it did not offer him relief. He sat down to scrambled eggs, Heinz baked beans, an uncut tomato (which he'd eat like an apple), and a glass of milk. On a separate plate, Aunt Annie offered two Oreo Creme cookies. "We get the same brands out here."

Samson ate everything while she talked of her happiness having him in California. He'd probably want to live alone, she speculated, but a room would always be available here for him.

The hours passed quickly and when he looked at his watch again, it was nearly three—six o'clock New York time. Again, he edged out to the drugstore telephone.

The same metallic voice answered at the "Y," but this time, there was encouragement. "Just a minute," it said, and he felt his heart begin to pound, and then he heard Rita's voice. "Hello?"

It was done. He was free. Off the hook.

"Hello?"

All he had to do was hang up.

"Hello," she was still saying, and he answered.

"Hello, Rita. This is Sam."

Her voice came through low, even. "Where are you?"

He started to lie, then realized she could check with the operator. "California." He'd really put distance between them. "I'm on my way to Australia. Leaving tomorrow."

"Australia?"

"That's right. How you feeling, Rita?"

"A lot you care."

"If I didn't care I wouldn't be calling. I sent the doctor, didn't I? And the money. Did you get the money?"

"Thanks for nothing."

"What do you mean, nothing?"

"The doctor put an ice pack on me, told me to stay in bed and keep my legs up. That cost one hundred dollars. The other hundred went to keep him from reporting me to the police."

"The bastard!"

"You're a bigger one! And something else. You're an ugly bastard. I'm glad I don't have to see you again."

"Rita . . . !"

"I hope you croak!"

She hung up and he stared at the phone, started to leave, then pulled the receiver from the hook and shouted into the mouthpiece. "You little bitch! I did you a favor from the beginning. Do you hear? What makes you so good? A lousy wop waitress, who lives at the 'Y!' " He slammed the receiver and rushed from the booth. He'd show her—show them all!

CHAPTER TWO

Within a few months after Samson Dukins arrived in Los Angeles the avalanche was on its way. The stock market bottomed out and that proved to be the gunshot crack to start it. Overnight, hopes became as slim as margins. He had been in a brokerage house in the financial district on Spring Street, dabbling with short-selling when the irrepressible wave struck.

His broker had been on the job only a few weeks after two years as a runner and board boy. The agitation of the market had rubbed off his thin layer of polish and what had been an urbane manner a week earlier collapsed with the plummeting averages. Each time Dukins would sell a lot short the broker would look at him as the perpetrator of the board's decline. Samson began to notice others, customers' men and clients who for the past week seemed to be preparing for the final act.

Their uneasiness, punctuated by an occasional outcry, now became shrill, strident. The bottom was opening and it looked like everything was falling through, collars were open, sleeves rolled, cries of anguish filled the room, telephones were working, the

28

brokers shouting into receivers with eyes riveted on the board. Every clack of the ticker brought new groans. Tape was strewn on the floor like twisted guts; it was a nightmare now, the end of roseate dreams, bedlam, madness, tears, remorse as the paper profits were curling to ashes. Wedged in a corner as they milled wild-eyed about him, Dukins watched with fascination. A man, seated near him, shirtsleeved and sweaty, was pounding his thigh with a fist like a railbird urging a horse. "God, let it close!" he shouted. "Let it close!" Soon the cry spread through the room. Samson looked at his watch. Five minutes to go before the market's end. The room became stifling and he moved along a wall to an open window. The boys on the board had given up, no longer able to keep pace. Finally there was a hush and then a few shouts. For a moment the only noise in the room was the clack of the tickers and the ringing phones. Then, as if regaining their senses, the voices rose and hell was loose. Dukins pushed through the crowd, found his way to the street, and headed toward home. He was out of the market, and had made enough during the past weeks by selling short to live on for a year.

He could not wait to get home to Aunt Annie. "You should have seen them," he said when she greeted him at the door. "It was like somebody turned the world upside down and their money fell out of their pockets." He felt exultant, ecstatic, wanted to shout. "I told you it was coming. Any fool could have seen it months ago. The signs were all there: farm income dropping, carloadings sliding, unemployment." He grabbed hold of her and whirled her about the room.

Puffing, she eased out of his arms and fell into a chair, looking up at him and smiling sadly. "You're smart, Sam. I've got to admit. And we're lucky. But what about all those people?"

"That's their problem, not ours. We got cash, a scarce commodity." He paced the room with gesticulating hands as if plucking his thoughts from the air. "Every dollar we have is worth a helluva lot more than it was yesterday. Wait'll you see what it will buy, Aunt Annie. Maybe all the things you ever dreamed you wanted." She watched silently as he toured the room like something caged that had a rendezvous and needed to escape. "I dreamed about a day like this," he went on. "It's like pulling a royal flush in the biggest pot of the night. Everybody's tapped out and you go home with it all." He stopped short and looked down at her. "Do you realize what it means?"

She nodded, smiled, and rose. "I'm ready for tea. How about you?"

He followed her into the kitchen about to expound further when he sensed her lack of enthusiasm. Didn't she realize what had happened? Didn't she care? Is this what she wanted out of life: a lousy bungalow and a yard to putter in, three meals a day, and a ride on Sunday? Well, it wasn't what he was going to settle for and the sooner he got out of her orbit the better. He would see her often and they would be close but he wanted a place of his own, an apartment where he could take a dame if he found one, where he could be alone when he wished.

Aunt Annie poured the tea, set out graham crackers and jelly and he joined her at the table. He came directly to the point. "I've got some plans," he began. "I'm going to get an apartment. It'll be in the neighborhood so we can see each other often."

"I think it's a good plan, Sam."

"It has nothing to do with you and me."

"I understand." She patted his hand.

"And I'm going to work. I've laid around long enough."

"When will you move?"

"I'll look this weekend."

He checked the ads in the Sunday *Times*, marked half a dozen and started out. Most of the offerings were in rundown buildings that already showed the marks of a business depression; long vacant with worn furniture and sour smelling carpets they offered no enticement.

Near the end of the day, ready to quit and try again he ran across a well-kept building with manicured lawns and new paint that shone like a well-scrubbed face in a bevy of filthy urchins. He was greeted by an attractive woman behind the desk. "I'm Gloria Tuberville," she said extending a hand. When he released it, her fingers sliding from his, he thought they lingered longer than they should. It was easy to make a decision when she showed him a freshly done apartment on the quiet side of the building.

Seated in a tiny office beyond the desk he looked her over as she wrote out the tenant's agreement and inventory. She had a nose almost too small for her full round face, a slightly plump figure and appeared to be in her thirties. However, there was the freshness about her of a young girl clinging to the last of the baby fat instead of a matron piling on weight. She finished writing, looked up, and handed him the sheet.

"You can read it if you wish. The fine print, I mean."

It was a standard apartment month-to-month lease contract. He read the first paragraph, signed, and handed it to her.

"It looks all right," he said, making out a check and then told her he was going to move in that afternoon.

He hoped Aunt Annie would not think he was rushing things. She came in from the garden as he entered the kitchen. It must have been the look on his face; expectation, excitement, because before he could blurt it out she exclaimed:

"You've found a place. And you like it."

"How did you know?"

She put a flame under the kettle and reached for the cannister of tea. "Sit down, Sam. We'll have sort of a parting drink." Arranging her chair so that she faced him squarely, she started to talk. "Sometimes I think you don't give me enough credit." He started to protest but she held up a hand. "It's true, and I don't blame you. With the exception of reading books on chicken raising when I was young and married, and glancing at the paper now and then the rest of my education came from the Testament and the Missal. And that I took with a grain and only went to church once in a while to keep a toe in." He tried to interrupt again and she reached across and placed a finger to his lips. "I've been listening to you for a few months, doing little talking back. Hear me out." The kettle began to wheeze and he waited as she poured the tea, took a sip, and went on. "I watched you from a puling infant until a year or so ago. When you love someone you're always looking for signs on their face, the way they talk, even how they walk. And I got a good memory." She smiled. "Guess I should have dipped into books. A lot of what I read might have stuck. I knew every time you lied when you were growing up. And every time you stole from my purse was written on your face for me to see."

"It wasn't as often as you think," he said. "I can count the times."

"So can I. And I'm not complaining. I'm just telling you so you'll know that everything there is to learn is not in books. You told me so yourself when you quit the university after a year."

Samson remembered that year. A rehashing of old ideas by low-salaried academicians walled in by books, their lives smothered by semantics they repeated like parrots. It was one thing to understand Plato's "Allegory of the Cave," and another to escape from it by the force of one's wit and will. By the end of the first semester, after taking courses in philosophy and economics as well as literature and history, he realized that organized education was not providing him what he wanted. "You're right, Aunt Annie. Half the stuff they dished out I had no use for. Now I read what I want and need."

"I never learned a taste for reading," she said, "but there's lessons in living and I've had them for nearly fifty years. I don't know much, but I know this: one has got to receive and give love, and for that, I'm thankful to you." She whipped out a handkerchief and daubed at her eye. Samson went to her side and placed an arm about her. "You sound like I'm going off to a war or something equally disastrous. I'm only a couple of miles away. I'll see you as often as you like."

She patted the hand he had about her and he returned to his seat. Dry-eyed now, she refilled their cups and a smile wreathed her face. A shaft of sunlight speared the room lighting the top of her head, dust motes floating in its beam; in it, her auburn hair tinted to copper. "I'm happy you're getting a place of your own,

Sam. You need a life without meddling. And to tell you the truth, I'm looking forward to my own privacy."

"That's the way I feel, Auntie," he said. "If you'll help me, I'll be out of your way in no time." His suitcases were packed, a few books and other items were put in a carton, and he carried them to his three-year-old Packard. He wanted no tears, kissed her hurriedly on the cheek, told her he'd see her in a day or two, and drove off.

By early evening, he was moved in, completing the last of his unpacking when he heard a knock at the door. It was Gloria Tuberville, and as she entered, she surveyed the apartment with a practiced eye. "You'll need another lamp," she said. "I'll have one here in the morning." She walked into the kitchen and Samson followed, watching as she inspected the contents of the drawers. "There's only service for four in here. If you need more, let me know."

"I don't plan on entertaining for a while."

When they returned to the living room, he noticed she'd changed her dress. A gaily flowered sheath was pasted to her curves. She sank into a chair. "Mind if I sit a while? I've been on the go all day. Sunday is usually hectic. Lots of lookers and only part-time relief on the desk."

He assured her it would be a pleasure and at her insistence went on with his unpacking. He was in the little dressing room folding a shirt when she joined him. "You men," she said, punctuating their helplessness with a flip of her hand, as she took the shirt from him, folded and patted it before placing it in the drawer where she seemed to caress it in place. "I don't understand," she said, straightening up. "I've had two husbands and no matter how I tried I couldn't teach either to fold a shirt." She pulled at her dress which had crawled above her knees when she stooped before the dresser, and then, smoothing the top by running both hands over her breasts, she brushed past him. He got a whiff of strong perfume.

"No one ever showed me," he said.

"You've never been married?"

"Never."

She sighed. "It's a big adjustment."

Settling on the couch, she crossed her legs. Her dress crawled up far enough to expose a wide area of thigh. "It's a matter of learning to give and take—marriage, that is," she began. "The strange part is that one must be a taker as well as a giver."

Samson took a chair, angling it to get the best view of her legs.

"That was my problem," she said. "With one *and* two."

He looked at her questioningly.

"My husbands. Listen," she said, half-rising, "I'm boring you. Here you're just getting settled and I . . . ."

"No, no," he hastened to assure her, "I'm interested."

She smiled at him gratefully and she sat back. "Anyway, as I was saying, everybody has certain needs. Some people are more filled than others and need a vessel in which to pour."

"That's very well put."

"It's like warmth and cold, friendliness and loneliness." She stopped, raised her hand as if to pluck another example out of the air and then sighed. "I'm sure you know what I mean."

"I certainly do. In fact, your being here is an example."

Her face lighted. "What do you mean?"

"I'm new in the city. It is lonely, and you're being friendly."

"I'm so glad," she said, leaned forward and her dress slid half-way up her leg. She made a vain attempt to pull it down and settled back. For a moment neither of them said a word. Then she began with the stock questions Southern Californians reserve for one another.

"Where are you from?"

"New York."

"I've always wanted to go there. I'm from Illinois. Springfield. It's the capital."

He nodded.

"Your first trip?"

"Yes."

"How do you like it?"

He told her he loved it.

"That's unusual," she said. "Most people have to make one trip back east before they really appreciate California."

"I don't know why."

"They have family and friends back east," she explained. "After a while you miss them. Everybody has to go back once." She pulled at her skirt which returned his eyes to her legs.

"Have you been back?" he asked.

"Twice. The first time was when my mother got sick and the last was when I separated from Charley. He was my last husband. I threw him out but he wouldn't leave me alone. I'd come home from work—I worked in a department store then—and there he was. In the middle of the night the phone would ring, it was him. I couldn't get any rest. Finally, I quit my job and decided to go back east." She uncrossed her legs and switched and during the maneuver flashed a piece of thigh almost up to the crotch.

"Did you get your divorce there?"

"No, out here." She started to question him about himself and he answered vaguely. There was nothing about his life he cared to tell her. Somehow, he felt he'd make better headway if he suggested his loneliness was complete.

By this time Gloria gave up all attempts to put her dress in place. He sat and admired the exposure with undisguised pleasure. Now, there were long pauses in their conversation. The game became so intense that he developed a hard-on and had to keep shifting in his seat to keep it from showing. He was about to rush the couch and take her right there, when the telephone rang shrilly.

"It can't be for me," he said. If he stood up his prick would have stuck out like a jib. She went to the phone. It was the desk calling for her. Somebody wanted to see an apartment. She left at once, whispering a goodbye.

The following day she shopped for him, filling the refrigerator and shelves with staples. On the third night she invited him to her apartment for dinner. It was her day off, she explained, the only time she could entertain without being interrupted.

Gloria greeted him with a warm smile, led him to a small bar in the corner of the room, and handed him a drink.

"I hope you like bourbon and Coke," she said. "It was all I could get."

"My favorite," he said. They clicked glasses and he took a long swallow. The bourbon was barely diluted.

"Sit down and make yourself comfortable," she said, "while I get the hors d'oeuvres."

He watched her as she went into the kitchen, her behind jiggling in tight pajamas. She returned with a tray, set it down before the couch, and joined him.

She would get up from time to time to look in at the dinner and to mix their rapidly disappearing drinks. An hour passed and he found himself unable to resist her ministrations. She had propped a pillow behind him, suggested he remove his shoes, insisted on undoing the laces, and, just before they sat down to dinner, had thoroughly massaged a tightening she noticed in the back of his neck.

After a skillfully prepared meal, he found himself standing behind her as she was at the sink readying to do the dishes. He decided to turn on the radio and get some dance music. Once he got her in his arms he was certain the rest would be easy. As she turned to leave the room his hand brushed her behind accidentally. She whirled around, grabbed a towel, dried her hands and flung herself into his arms.

"Oh, Darling!" she cried.

Within seconds they were in the bedroom. Her skill and speed amazed him. She flicked off the spread and with one hand folded it perfectly as she began to unbutton the top of her blouse with the other. In a flash the covers were pulled back and the shades were drawn. By the time he had removed his tie, she had all of her clothing off except a black teddy. He shivered with excitement as he fumbled with the buttons of his shirt. She rushed to his side. "Let me," she implored.

She forced him to lie down on the bed and started to pull his clothes off with the abandon of a child opening a gift. Unbuttoning his pants, she yanked them off, and tossed them to the floor. He tried to take off his shorts, but she would have none of it, slapping his hand playfully as she shucked them off. Eyeing his nakedness as he tried to squirm under the covers, she dropped her shoulder straps and with her hips supporting the garment at the waist she jumped in bed beside him.

Whatever Gloria lacked in imagination she made up in total concentration and sheer energy. So completely would she give herself up to the act that at times when he attempted a casual conversation during the periods of rest she would not hear him and would start the game again.

Two or three times he made a move to get up and dress only to find himself pinned by her arm or a leg. Finally, at one in the morning he caught her dozing. Grabbing his clothes, he found his way to the living room and managed to escape.

During the next two months his appetite was matched only by her eagerness and with the exception of running down some tax delinquent sales and playing around the edges of the stock market, he spent his energy recklessly. He would be awakened in his apartment in the morning by the rustle of silk as she undressed before his bed, making just enough noise to arouse him. She would dramatize the moment. Using her own brand of vulgarisms, she would proceed with a monologue, carrying on the entire conversation with questions. Her favorite theme was "mama" and "papa" talk.

"What is papa going to do to mama?"

Knowing by now that she liked to do the whole thing he would not answer. She would continue. "Is papa going to let mama play with his thing?"

By this time she would be stripped to her teddies which were always on until the last and fastened with two buttons at her crotch.

He still would not answer.

Then she would talk about her boobs, and he would let her go on until she involved her box, her bush, and her behind. By that time they would be properly aroused and she would jump into

bed and have him unbutton her teddies, the final preparatory ritual. Then she would hand him his only line. "Now, what is papa
going to do to mama?"

"Fuck mama!"

If he would drop in for an afternoon cup of coffee she would
have him in bed before it cooled.

He saw Aunt Annie two or three times a week, had her over to
his apartment a few times, always on the days when he knew
Gloria was to be away. He began to note a change in his aunt, at
first subtle, then overt. It was her grooming: more lipstick, higher
heels, and the use of a scent. He suspected she was seeing someone but in spite of his curiosity he refrained from questioning her.
In all the years he had known her she had never been out with a
man and though he was puzzled about her celibacy it was never
discussed. Aunt Annie was attractive and well formed, had
chances which she always declined; the few times he tried to discuss it with her, she would switch the subject curtly, almost angrily. He wanted her married, settled, wanted to be free of any
obligations her old age might present, and if something was working he would do nothing to upset it.

Soon, Gloria's demands began to exceed his supply. Samson
began to realize that nothing is free. Some things are paid for on
delivery, on others one is given time plus carrying charges. Gloria
was extending credit and the bill was beginning to pile up. He
started to avoid her, no longer able to keep the pace. And he
began to understand the plight of Charley, marveling that he
lasted three years and was not surprised that her first husband was
counted out in as many months.

For days he dodged her, leaving the building when he knew
she would not be at the desk. He spent nights at the movies or
Aunt Annie's, sneaking back to the apartment in the early morning hours. After a week of eluding her, she nabbed him one night,
entering the apartment with her pass key after he had ignored her
persistent knock. She switched on the light and stood before the
bed. Drowsy and irritated, he threw back the covers and crawled

out of bed. Her clumsy attempts to conceal her drunkenness only made it more apparent, and by the time her manner had changed from polite inquiry to his whereabouts during the past few days to a demand for an explanation to tearful protestations of love and then to hysterics, he asked her to leave.

She started to undress.

"If you open another button, I'll never see you again."

She dropped her hands and started to sway, grabbing the back of the chair for support. He put on a robe. "Look," he said, "you had a little too much. Let's talk about it in the morning." His hand was on her arm and she began to caress it. He brushed it off. "Listen to me. I'm tired, dog-tired. I want nothing in the world this minute than to get in that bed and sleep. Alone."

She was swaying again and having difficulty focusing her eyes. "I love you."

He finally convinced her she could express her love best by letting him get a night's sleep and promised to discuss it in the morning. The following morning she was at his door after breakfast and apologized. He did not see her for a week.

Returning one evening after spending the day running down a false lead on a delinquent tax sale, he found a note from Gloria in his box. In a businesslike tone, it asked him to call her immediately on a matter that might be of interest. She greeted him at the door of her apartment with her usual warmth but with none of the intimate overtones, and though on guard he sensed that her immediate project had nothing to do with fornication.

"I ran into a friend of mine today," she began. "Bob Kinder." She described a real-estate broker to whom she supplied occasional leads for which she would get a finder's fee. "He's opened a new office and has a desk for another salesman. I told him about you."

"Is it a big office?" he asked.

"Just two other salesmen."

"What did you tell him about me?"

"Just that you're young, energetic, intelligent."

"Thank you."

"You're all that, Sam." It was said meltingly and he turned the conversation back to business.

He asked her about Kinder. "All I know is, he's smart. Everybody's starving in the business and he seems to be making it." Kinder was an oldtimer, had been in the business about thirty years, knew everybody in town and once was a vice president of the realty board. She fumbled in her purse and removed a card. "Call him at this number. He'll be expecting you."

The office was in a store on Western Avenue in Gardena. The front was partitioned from the rear by a paneled wall and had a pair of desks along each side, two of which were occupied. Both men barely looked up when he entered. He heard a loud voice coming from behind the partition and then a receiver slam and a moment later, a small man, slightly bent, seemed to spring into the room, shouting.

"Didn't I tell you to get the wife!"

One of the men swiveled around.

"What happened?" he asked.

The little man advanced, his jaw jutting. "The deal went down the drain, that's what happened!"

"But the husband said. . . ."

"That he'd get his wife's signature," the little man mimicked.

"That's right."

"Well he didn't. Because that was your job." Now he waved a finger under the man's nose. "How many times have I told you to get the wife signed up?"

"But she wasn't home and the husband said. . . ."

"Aah!" He waved his hand in disgust and turned to Samson. "I guess you're Dukins."

Samson nodded.

"Go in," he said, pointing to the private office.

Kinder came in a moment later and slid into a high-backed chair behind an oversized desk where he seemed to crouch like a giant toad, his eyes darting nervously as he spoke in a high raspy voice.

"Thank God, you're young," he began. "Not like those two out there."

Samson was a little embarrassed, sure that the men had heard.

Apparently, Kinder's anger had not cooled because now he shouted. "Notice the fat one?" he said, referring to the one he had talked to. "Sits and stares all day. That goddamn long-distance stare." His voice rose even louder. "He's looking way off to the twenties!" Then he switched suddenly and turned to him. "Are you broke?"

"Well, I. . . ."

"Good. I like hungry salesmen. They produce! Walsh, out there," he said, waving a hand, "and the other one too, Benjamin, they've got a few bucks yet. Left over from the boom days. They'll fatten their asses in those chairs until it's gone."

By this time, although he could not help admire the aggressiveness of Kinder, he began to question Gloria's recommendation. If Kinder's office provided opportunities it would have attracted a different breed of salesmen. Walsh seemed beaten and the other one, Benjamin, though a little younger, had ignored the entire outburst as though he did not have the energy to react. Samson had made up his mind to get out as gracefully as he could when he heard the front door open and close. Kinder jumped up, ran into the front room, then returned to his desk. "They left," he said. Then he looked at Dukins for a long moment and started to talk as if he had just read his mind. "I'm fifty-two years old. When I was your age I could take my time. Now, all day long I look for short cuts. The first thing you and I are going to do is to put all the cards on the table, face up. There's no bluffing that way and the game goes fast. You're wondering about Walsh and Benjamin. They've been with me over fifteen years and until a year ago did pretty well. Also, they're my friends and as long as I got an extra desk they can sit around and warm their behinds. Walsh used to be the best lot man in town and Benjamin's the whitest Jew I ever met." He stopped talking for a moment and then shot a question. "You got enough to carry you six months?"

There was something in his tone and manner that rekindled Samson's interest. "I can manage," he said.

"You got a good car?"

"Almost new."

Now Kinder leaned forward, almost rising from his seat and kept waving a finger as he spoke. "There's no salary in this business, no draw, only a desk and a telephone. You get fifty per cent of the commission. But, if you do everything I tell you, exactly as I tell you, and work your ass off seven days a week, and nights if you have to, in a few months you'll be making more money than you know what to do with." He sat back.

Kinder was saying the things Samson wanted to hear. "I'm ready."

Kinder pushed back his chair and stood up. "Be here tomorrow at nine o'clock."

When he arrived the following morning, Bob Kinder was in his office; Walsh and Benjamin had not arrived. He was assigned one of the desks, made out his application for a temporary salesman's license, and handed it to Kinder for his signature. He read it over and looked up at him with surprise.

"Born in 1908? That makes you only twenty-two."

"I'm still twenty-one," he corrected.

"You look older."

"I guess that's an asset."

"As long as you feel like twenty-one," he said. He signed the form and asked him to be seated. "For the first few weeks," he began, "all you're going to do is follow me around. When I look at a property you'll go with me, if I meet a client I want you there. I work with a lot of brokers, you'll get to meet them, and if I'm not around, Walsh and Benjamin will take you along. And ask questions . . . a helluva lot of questions."

By the end of the two weeks Samson had acquired a speaking knowledge of the business. Though many of the terms were confusing, he learned about values in the area from Crenshaw to La Brea and Imperial to Slauson, met a half-dozen brokers, all much older, and he stored away their real-estate talk. When he was not with Kinder he sought out Al Walsh and Joe Benjamin. Although they answered his questions readily they would turn every conversation to the deals of the past and it soon became evident they wanted no part of the present and would not think about the future.

Walsh, who suffered from diabetes, brought his lunch, which he spread out on a table in the rear of the office and attacked hungrily at the stroke of noon every day, stressing each time the necessity of eating punctually. Benjamin appeared as sound as a rock but his wife would call him two or three times a day to inquire about his state of health. A small man, the size of Kinder, he had a large wife who babied him—Kinder once explained—because they had no children of their own. Also, she would come to the office two or three times a week to bring him a clean handkerchief he forgot or with vitamin pills he neglected to take, making him an easy butt for Kinder's jibes.

By this time it became evident to Samson that Walsh and Benjamin were just looking for crumbs and would be no competition. It was also becoming quite clear that Kinder needed him as much as he did the older man. There wasn't another young man around with enough money to carry himself and the older men were either deadbeats or in business for themselves. Impatient to get started, he approached Kinder one evening about a month after he had started. "I'd like to begin," he said.

Kinder reached in his desk and removed a book which listed all the properties in the area, giving the names and addresses of each owner. "Go through this," he said, handing it to Dukins. "List the names of all the owners who live on their property."

Samson flipped the numbered pages and noted there were over a hundred. "The whole book?"

"Every page."

"Then what?"

"You're going to call on ten a day, seventy a week, over three hundred a month." His voice started to rise. "In a year you'll talk to thirty-six hundred owners and know more about this area than all the stumblebum brokers in town!" He stood up and grabbed the book from Samson's hand, holding it high above his head like a torch, shaking it as he shouted. "Only ten a day!" He slammed the book on the desk. "You live one day at a time, that's all!"

"All right, I'll call on ten a day. What do I say?"

All his anger gone, Kinder smiled. "Easy," he said, waving a hand. "You ring the bell." He indicated the action with a finger. "A woman will answer. The husband is usually at work." He was acting it out and enjoying it. "Good day, you say, addressing her by name as you hand her your card. I represent the Robert Kinder Company. We're in the neighborhood, you know." He smiled ingratiatingly.

"Never mind the introduction. I can handle that."

He ignored Samson's interruption. "Is your property for sale?" he said.

"No," Samson said, curtly, jumping into the woman's role.

Kinder went on with the game. "Perhaps you're interested in buying something? We have many choice listings."

"I have no money," he said, his voice freezing.

"That's just it," Kinder said, smiling broadly. "You don't need any."

"What do you mean?" Samson asked, suspiciously.

"We have many clients like yourself. They own other property but have no money. They want to change their position and we might get them to trade their property for yours."

"Then what?" Samson asked.

"If she's interested she'll let you in. Get all the dope on her property. Amount of mortgage if it isn't clear, taxes, size of lot, income if any, everything. Find out what her husband does. Maybe they'll trade for something larger and add cash."

Now Samson filled in. "If she wants to sell try to get the listing and tie it up. If she wants to buy, find out what."

"Exactly. If you make the ten calls a day," he said slowly, "and keep it up," he added, "you'll have more listings, more prospects, than all the big-assed brokers in this area put together. You'll have all of them working for you," he said, leaning back.

Samson went home that night and listed over a hundred names

to call upon. Determined to do a thorough job he bought a thick notebook, devoted a page to each name, which would give him room for a full description of the property and every fact that might be of aid. Then he took a small card file, indexed it for every day of the month so that each day's duties or call-backs would be at hand. He was so absorbed in the work that he did not hear Gloria's knock and looked up to find her standing by his side dangling the passkey from a finger.

"You must have slipped in awfully fast," she said. "I was at the desk and didn't see you." Her businesslike attitude of the past week was missing. In fact, the dress she wore was tighter and shorter than any she had worn and to be sure there was no misunderstanding she ran a finger gently up the back of his neck.

His first impulse was to ignore her invitation, plead work and ease her out, but the touch of her hand brought the heat. He slid his hand up her leg, felt the smooth hot meat of her thighs as they crossed to grip him, and before he could drop the pencil he held in the other hand, she had her dress pulled over her head and her pussy was inches from his face. They were on the floor in a flash.

It was more than an hour before they finally separated and rolled apart. The room was dark and he could hear her heavy breathing and then she began to whimper and he became conscious of the room, the hard floor and the parts of him that hurt where she had dug and bit and then the unfinished work on the table and tomorrow and the days after and his capitulation that night and that it had to end!

He must have dozed, for when he awoke it was near midnight and Gloria was gone.

The following morning firmed his decision to break off with Gloria for good. In spite of hours of sleep he barely had enough energy to crawl out of bed and a close inspection revealed bruises from his lips down. As he started to shave he realized she had spared nothing; even an eye was puffed. It had to end. "Ten calls a day, seventy a week," in Kinder's raspy voice kept going over in his head and nothing was going to stop him, not pleasure, not even Gloria's brand.

Refreshed after a shower, he gathered his notebook and papers and, after calling the office and telling Kinder he was starting from home, he went on his way.

Determined to stay ahead, he made eighty calls by the end of the first week. They filled all his days and half the nights, some requiring an evening visit to meet the husband. He kept notes on everyone who appeared interested in doing business; when to call back, bits of information to refresh his memory, items of a personal nature worth remembering on his next call.

One woman told him of a gall-bladder operation her husband was to undergo. He called to find out how he was. Another told him of a first grandchild that was due to arrive any minute and that the sale of her house had to await the event. He was told of a divorce and a silver anniversary to be celebrated and one widow in her fifties tried to load him up on sherry as she paraded before him in her living room barely concealing a broad beam and huge breasts beneath a sheer dressing gown. But many were prospects, some wanting to buy, some to sell and others to think it over. By the end of the first week he weeded out and ended up with a dozen live ones. During that time he was spared the necessity of warding off Gloria. He figured she was marshaling her forces or giving him a chance to refuel.

The second week was more difficult; keeping in contact with the old ones and calling on the new. He talked it over with Kinder and was told to turn some of the leads over to Walsh and Benjamin. He would share in the commission if a deal was made. By the end of the third week the work began to pay off. He'd tied up a four-unit apartment house near Vermont Avenue and ran into a hot prospect for a six unit. Her name was Mrs. Ginsburg and after two calls she made it clear that although Mr. Ginsburg, who worked in the garment industry, made the money, she handled it. During his third meeting with her, she made a remark that was so upsetting all his thoughts jumped the track upon which they had been concentrating and forayed wildly into the past. They were parked in front of her house and just before she opened the door to leave she turned to him and with a knowing expression said, "Dukins. Dukins. Maybe you changed your name?"

Momentarily surprised at the question, the full realization of its import struck him. She took him for a member of the tribe! A Jew! In Jersey on the farm and all the years in Brooklyn he had been called everything but never that. Melted in with Italians and Poles, Irish and Slavs with whom he was dragged to church on occasion by a part-time Catholic aunt, his ethnic origin had never been questioned. And he was always with the leaders when they ventured forth for a shot at the neighborhood Jews. Sure, his nose had a hook, but so did Joe Valenti's and Wally Zvaleko's, and not far above Father Kelly's collar, his nose dipped like a crow's. Samson's first impulse was to deny Mrs. Ginsburg's remark, but swiftly calculating the advantage of her speculation, he found himself giving her a knowing smile.

"It's not I got anything against it, you understand," she assured him. "You from New York?"

"New Jersey."

"Jersey, New York, the same thing. Morris, that's my husband, and me come from New York."

He smiled and shook his head as if to convey their new rapport. She left that day assuring him she meant business and would await his call if anything came up that he thought was a good buy.

As he drove home the thought of the woman's remark eroded the exultation he first experienced in latching on to a qualified prospect. Mrs. Ginsburg was no fool, in fact more astute than most buyers he had met, and the fact that she took him for a Jew drove all other thoughts from his mind.

In the apartment he rushed to the mirror and examined his face carefully. His hair was black, which he supposed could be characteristic of a Jew, but his eyes were blue, hardly a Semitic color. Could it be his lips he wondered as he traced their fullness with a finger? Was it possible he was a Jew? After all, he did not know his real parents. So he had a hooked nose, but so do Popes and German generals and American Presidents. Julie Horwitz, a kid he went to school with, had red hair, a turned-up nose and freckles. He was as Irish as Aunt Annie always believed and Mrs. Ginsburg was creating an image she wanted. Then he remembered a course he had taken at the university on ethnic groups and there it was; he had the black hair of a Greek, an Italian, a Black Irish, a Russian, Pole, or Cypriot, the blue eyes of an Englishman, Scandinavian or German, and the complexion of a Spaniard, Frenchman, sun-tanned Finn, or a Brazilian. It was true, it was what the book said, what anthropologists knew, but you don't meet them on golf courses, country clubs and when you're negotiating on real-estate deals. He took another look into the mirror, pushed the tip of his nose up, flattened out the bridge in his mind and his face was transformed. Grabbing the morning *Times* he leafed through the pages until he found what he was looking for, an ad that seemed to be in the paper every day. He clipped out the one-inch ad showing a male and female profile before and after, under which a caption stated "Why Be Unsightly? Noses Reconstructed. Dr. James Gantner." There was an address on Hollywood Boulevard and a phone number.

The reason for Mrs. Ginsburg's interest in his ancestry became evident the following week. He made an appointment to show her a couple of new listings and when he picked her up she introduced him to her daughter, a slight girl about twenty who followed them reluctantly to the car. Seated in the front seat beside him, Mrs. Ginsburg kept turning to the girl in the rear, making every effort to draw her into the conversation.

"Mr. Dukins is from Jersey," she said.

He heard the girl mutter an acknowledgment.

"Ruthie is going to college," she went on. "A commercial course."

He said something about its practicality.

"Typing, shorthand," Mrs. Ginsburg went on. "After all it's a depression. A girl should help a husband."

Through the rearview mirror, he saw Ruthie squirm. They came to the first building near Century and Western and he pulled up at the curb. Taking out his listing book he read off the figures as Mrs. Ginsburg appraised the building with a critical eye.

"Needs paint."

"Just the stucco."

"The trim too."

"A couple of hundred dollars," he said.

"Here, let me see the figures," she said, grabbing his book. After making some notes of her own on a crumpled piece of paper she removed from her pocket, she shook her head and told him to drive on. The next building was a few blocks away. It was impressive; authentic Spanish with deep arches and heavy balconies across the front that had just been painted. Mrs. Ginsburg turned to Ruthie.

"Do you like it?"

Ruthie rose slightly from her seat and looked at it blankly. "I don't know, Ma."

"You should take an interest," Mrs. Ginsburg said, and then, looking directly at Dukins, "after all, it'll be yours some day."

"Please, Ma." Ruthie said.

It would be a long time, Samson thought, looking at Mrs. Ginsburg's sturdy peasant frame and remembering her firm man-step walk.

He could not interest her in anything that afternoon but had a feeling hers would be his first deal. He had everything on his side. She wanted to buy, she felt that the market had reached the low point, and she had something to sell and he looked like a helluva prospect.

The following day Mrs. Ginsburg called him at the office. "Sammy," she began, "how would you like a Friday night dinner?"

He decided to play the role and accepted. He wanted that deal.

Arriving at seven o'clock he met Mr. Ginsburg for the first time. A little man, almost as short as his wife, it soon became obvious he lived only by her direction. He would look for a sign from her before he would begin to speak and stop short in the middle of his conversation whenever she opened her mouth. She did most of the talking, telling Dukins how hard they both worked. The house where they lived was free and clear; they had fifteen thousand to invest plus a little extra for emergencies. She had a rich brother in New York, a dress manufacturer who was a bachelor and Ruth was his favorite niece.

"I understand he's going out with a chorus girl who wants to marry him," Mr. Ginsburg put in.

Ruthie giggled.

"He'll never marry," Mrs. Ginsburg snapped.

"He's not that smart," Mr. Ginsburg said, under his breath.

"He's my brother! I should know!" Mrs. Ginsburg shouted and then turned to Samson. "He's not the marrying kind."

Realizing the evening was getting out of hand, Dukins pacified her and praised her cooking. Although Mrs. Ginsburg calmed down, she did not address Mr. Ginsburg directly for the rest of the evening. By eleven o'clock, after dancing a few times with Ruthie, who clung to him listlessly during the wail of some records Mrs. Ginsburg had insisted on playing, he left, promising to call in a few days.

The following Sunday he ran into a building he knew she could not turn down. It was where she wanted it, priced below the market, and the terms were perfect. When he told Kinder about it, the older man said, "If she doesn't buy it, she's only a looker and you can forget her." Samson called her and told her just that, and made an appointment to show it to her on Monday. She saw the value immediately and gave him a deposit without consulting her husband. He put the deal in escrow the following day and closed it so rapidly Mrs. Ginsburg's campaign to make him part of the package never got beyond a luncheon to "cele-brate" to which Ruthie was dragged, after which Dukins evaded her successfully.

Though the commission on the Ginsburg deal was only a few hundred dollars it opened up Samson's career. Now he was a pro. So rare were sales that the news spread throughout the area before the transaction was out of escrow. Most of the versions were exaggerated. Nevertheless, other brokers began to contact him and even Walsh and Benjamin seemed roused and started to pound the phones and check the ads. Kinder made the most of it and rode them hard, and when a week later a listing of Samson's was sold by another broker, he stepped up his lashings.

Encouraged by his success, Samson added another feature to his system. Talking Kinder into hiring a girl from a secretarial school for one day a week, he followed up every promising call with a letter thanking each prospect for the time they gave him and telling them not to hesitate to call on him at any time they decided to change their real-estate position.

So completely had his work taken over his life that he managed to stay clear of Gloria. If he was not spending his energy elsewhere she would have undoubtedly brought him down at every attempt.

He soon realized it would be impossible to keep the pace he had set. There were times when he became so exhausted he would doze while driving and once fell asleep while Kinder was talking to him in the office. Kinder had to shout to wake him. "How long do you think you can go on?"

"I guess I've been going too fast."

"Like sixty, that's what. You got a long way, you got to pace yourself. Look, I said I like hungry salesmen and you're sure it. But how much does it take to feed you?" Kinder began to enumerate on his fingers. "You got one deal made, one in escrow, a dozen prospects, you're full of piss and everything and best of all," he went on, "you're a lousy twenty-one."

"I'll slow down," Samson promised.

"It's not enough. You got to have fun too, relax. Girls, do you know any girls?"

Samson smiled. "I get enough of that."

"I bet you do," Kinder said, almost wistfully. "Anyway, how about golf?"

"Haven't played in a couple of months."

"Take a day off, once a week. Go to Griffith Park. You need it. And you'll meet people there, prospects. Brokers, too."

He did not go to the golf course at the park but took an afternoon off once a week at a driving range and took lessons. He was still a beginner, and though he had good coordination he lacked experience, and realizing the importance of the game for business contacts he had no intention playing the courses until he perfected it.

Better acquainted with the city now, and after months in the business, Samson Dukins began to realize that the neighborhoods in which he was operating would never afford him the opportunities he was seeking. The sales were small, the clients not affluent and the best one could hope for would be a good living. The city had a fat side: the Wilshire district, Beverly Hills and the communities west. Not only were the sales larger but the money was there, the fish were big and Gardena and the south part of Los Angeles were where the minnows lived. He had a plan for a major change and decided to discuss it with Aunt Annie. It began to formulate after his meeting with Mrs. Ginsburg, and it was not until now, with experience behind him, that he was ready to put it into action.

CHAPTER THREE

His visits with Aunt Annie were usually confined to Sunday brunches and the evenings when he sought escape from Gloria. However, they would swap calls once or twice during a week. Though he was certain now she was dabbling with a man, no mention had been made of it and he decided the time had come for inquiries. Certain that her lack of experience could make her vulnerable he was determined to put a hand in before her emotions got an upper hand. Annie was far from unattractive. The addition of her bank account, which rated high at depression prices, made her an exceptional buy on the marital market. But she wasn't going to be easy pickings, not with him around, and if he had anything to say the lucky man was going to put up loot for loot. Aunt Annie's pride was only matched by her stubbornness and this latter trait became most effective at the slightest opposition, so he'd have to be careful.

She had just returned from church when he arrived that Sunday. "It looks you're back into the fold," he greeted her.

"Just the past few months. One gets lonely and you do meet people."

"Anybody interesting?" he said, casually.

There was silence as she worked at the sink, her back toward him. Then she turned, smiled slightly, wiped her hands on her apron, and seated herself at the table. She lit a cigarette before she spoke.

"As a matter of fact, there is someone. I met him at Mass a couple of months ago." Flustered, she patted her hair in place and crushed her cigarette. "We've been to a couple of movies and went for a few rides."

His head was bursting with questions; the man's age, marital status (he wasn't going to have her running around with a married man), and most important his financial condition, but he restrained himself and waited for her to continue. "It's nothing serious, Sam. Just a friend." He waited. "He's a widower. Happens to come from Brooklyn originally. Not far from where we lived."

"What does he do?" he finally ventured.

A smile spread across her face, lighted her eyes and then she began to chuckle. "You'd never believe it."

"What's so funny?"

"He's an undertaker." Her eyes were on his face, searching it for a reaction.

Instantly, a dour-faced, cadaverous figure in black appeared in his mind, speaking in sorrowful tones as he waved pasty-white clammy hands. Dismissing the image, he managed to smile. "There have to be undertakers."

She rose and returned to her task at the sink. "I guess you're right." There was a moment of silence and then she almost whispered. "He also owns part of a cemetery."

Undertaking was a good business, he was sure, steady, depression-proof. But the man was more than an undertaker, he sold a package. The man interested him and Samson sensed he needed a boost.

"What's wrong with an undertaker?"

"What's wrong!"

"Yes, what's wrong?" He was prepared to defend the profession to the hilt. "They're needed, aren't they? What would you do without them?" he challenged.

"They also need grave diggers . . . and executioners!" She stopped for a moment as if looking for more odious comparisons. "And they need garbage collectors and street cleaners, don't they?"

This was an opportunity; a man with money, a foolproof business, a well-heeled suitor with plenty to spare. Also, he had the feeling she wanted to be convinced. "I think we're missing the point," he said. "The *man* is important, not the work he does. It takes courage and conviction to be in that profession. In a way I admire him."

She began to set the table. "It's just that nobody likes an undertaker. I never knew a soul who knew one, socially that is."

"That's silly, Aunt Annie," he said, "I'm sure they have families, friends, belong to organizations." He took a long chance. "I'm sure he isn't tall and skinny with a long black coat and clammy hands, smelling of formaldehyde."

Wrinkling her nose in disgust, she laughed. "He's nothing like that. In fact he looks like he can be anything: a banker, even a real-estate broker. You'll probably like him."

"I'm sure I will," he said enthusiastically.

"He'd like to meet you. We talked about it this morning. There's a place out the beach called Paul's. It's on the pier. Mr. Baldwin would like to take us there for lunch next Sunday."

Samson agreed, and then questioned her about Mr. Baldwin. She told him that Harry Baldwin was fifty-five years old, had migrated from Brooklyn some years after his wife's death. He was forced to sell an undertaking business in Brooklyn that was started by his father because of a chronic case of asthma that finally put him to bed. The California climate was all he needed to restore him to health. Purchasing an established parlor from an estate, he expanded it and later with another man subdivided two hundred acres in the San Fernando Valley into cemetary plots.

"It's called Hallowed Hills."

"I've seen it advertised," Samson said. "On bus-stop benches and billboards. It's some operation! 'Give us your loved ones. We will give perpetual care.' "

They ate in silence and his mind turned to his own plans and the discussion of them with Aunt Annie. The move he planned was a big one, a qualitative change in his pattern. Although he was going ahead regardless, he would feel better with her blessing.

He sipped his coffee watching her carefully brew her tea, a ritual he remembered from his childhood: the tea pinched from the cannister by a thumb and forefinger long exercised in the rite, the pouring of the boiling water into the flowered pot—the one heirloom she possessed—the wait for the brew, and the filling of the cup after a quick inspection of the contents and the sweetish smell that rose with the steam. As he watched he wondered about this woman, an aunt by chance who brought to his life nothing less than one with the proper parental credentials could ask for. He realized that since he could remember, all of her acts, the pattern of her life, was designed to fulfill the role of his care she so willingly undertook.

He rarely thought of his origin, and when he did he felt like an amorphous blob, slipped into life through the backdoor. Whoever his parents were, he imagined, he'd come along at a time when they had no choice but to leave him (bundled well he was told), on a bench of the Myrtle Avenue station where he was found and brought to a Catholic institution who handled these matters discreetly. Turned over to a devout middle-aged couple who were childless, he lived with them until he was eight, when they died in quick succession. They had moved to a chicken farm in New Brunswick which they owned with Aunt Annie, his mother's widowed sister, where they lived until shortly after his parents death.

It was more than her approval he wished now for his plans, it was her support and her consent. He brought the teapot into the living room, set it on a table, lit her cigarette, and settled in a chair beside her.

"I want to talk to you about something, Aunt Annie," he began. She settled back. Now he found himself at a loss for words. "I don't know how to begin."

"Say it out, Sam."

He told her about the office, his successes, and the limitations the area provided. He had ideas, big ones, and Gardena was no place to test them. Los Angeles was a large city, but not in one piece, and since he was starting on a career he wanted to move over to the piece that contained the wealth. She thought it was an excellent idea to work in the Wilshire district, the west part of town, and saw nothing to stop him. Nothing would, he told her, but he wanted to start with a new image. Then he told her about Mrs. Ginsburg.

"You have no idea what it is to be taken for a Jew. All of a sudden you feel barriers are being set up and you are less than you are."

"But that's silly, Sam," she said, setting the teacup on the table. "I've known Jewish people. They're no different than anyone else."

"Most people think differently, Aunt Annie."

"They're wrong."

"There's a lot that's wrong, but I don't intend spending my life correcting it."

"That woman, Mrs. Ginsburg, it was just her idea. No one before thought you were a Jew."

He turned his head, putting his profile on display. "Look at this nose. If there ever was a Jew nose, this is it."

"Sam, a lot of people have noses like yours. Do you remember Father Kelly?"

"Sure I do. But everybody knew he was Irish and a priest. I have no label except my face and I don't like it." He got up and paced the floor. "I won't live with it. There's no reason to."

She went to him and put an arm about his shoulder. "What can you do about it? Cut it off? You're as Irish as your name. I always said so."

He slid from her arm and returned to his seat. "That's another thing, my name. It's not really mine. All my life I never had a choice, parents, name, face. Everything was an accident. The only thing I ever got that I really wanted was you." If there had been any hesitation to his plans, they now were dispelled. The rage, the bitterness, vaulted the protective covering of her love and it poured. He remembered the lies he told the kids on the block, the lies in school, the fantasies he wove during hot sweaty nights when he could not sleep, the curses he heaped on the two who were responsible for his being, the sting of shame when he made up a father, even described him, and the emptiness he felt when he told the tale.

He was on his feet now and his aunt sat looking up at him with bewilderment. "I don't like the way I was born. Now I have a choice. I'm getting a new name and a new face! Here, look at this." He whipped out the ad he had placed in his wallet weeks before. As his aunt read it, he went on. "And I decided on a name. Samson Duke!" As he said it aloud it sounded good. The tongue flicked it from the palate, it was imperious and it fit. He grabbed the ad and returned it to his wallet. "I'm quitting my job and moving back with you. The minute the surgery is done and the nose is healed, I'll move out and get an apartment on the other side of town."

Aunt Annie finally spoke. "I can see nothing wrong in changing your name, if you like the other one better. I guess Duke sounds more refined than Dukins. But Sam, your face. . . ." She shook her head. "Somehow it seems wrong. It's what God gave you, not man."

"What's God got to do with it! It's genes, chromosomes. They can be imperfect like a lot of things on this earth. And if Dr. Gantner can improve on Nature, I'm sure going to give him the chance."

"Suppose it doesn't turn out?"

He cupped his nose and ran his hand down the length of it. "Anything will be an improvement. I want a new name and a new nose. Is that too much to ask?"

She turned and took his hands. "I'll have to admit that all of this is a shock. But if that is what you want I guess you should do it. This doctor, is he the best?"

"I don't know. I'm calling tomorrow for an appointment. See what he says, what he sounds like."

He spent the rest of the day with Aunt Annie, took her to a movie that night, and by the time he left for his apartment was certain she was an ally as she cautioned him again to check the doctor carefully and in parting called him Mr. Duke with an admission that the name at least was an improvement.

Dr. Gantner's office on Hollywood Boulevard across from Grauman's Chinese Theatre exuded stability and confidence. The reception room was high-ceilinged, a ribbon of yellowed oak rimmed the top of the wall, matching a wainscoting between which forest green walls tastefully hung with a few Spy's and old prints blended with a thick-padded dark red carpeting. Two student lamps on side tables added the final touch to what could have been the rectory of a cardinal or the waiting room in a Swiss bank. No less impressive was the rest of the suite: an attractive nurse in a crisp gown with a low modulated voice, precise and confident, a fluorescent-lighted surgery stark white with enameled cabinets and stainless steel, and a consultation room the size of a library in a fine home with book-lined walls, framed diplomas, and paintings with the blended woods and colors of the reception room, added to which were deep leather chairs, a massive walnut desk, and a bust of Lincoln pedestaled in a corner by the window.

By the time Samson met the doctor his history had been taken by the nurse. He'd filled out a form: name, address, occupation, and annual income. The surgery had been priced and any doubts or qualms had been totally dispelled. The doctor's smile was warm, creasing a strong face beneath a shock of thick graying hair. His nose was so perfectly formed it seemed chiseled. After a hasty examination, a critical look at Samson's profile, and an assurance that with his broad forehead and good cheek bones the new nose would be as natural as if he carried it all his life, an appointment was made for the following week and he was turned back to the nurse who snapped a half-dozen pictures side view and front and ushered him out. Samson Duke left the building happier than he had ever been in his life. And the new name he had given the nurse, hearing it used by a stranger for the first time, added the final luster to the image that already possessed his mind.

His campaign chartered, he went about executing each move with precision. First he had to rid himself of Gloria. He packed his things the night before, moved out on her day off, and left her a note with a check for the rent and a promise to get in touch with her. Leaving Kinder was another matter; it could not be done without a confrontation, he needed the older man's signature when he was ready to transfer his license. Besides, he had a vested interest in a half-dozen pending deals.

He got to the office in the morning, before the usual arrival time of Walsh and Benjamin, and waited about a half-hour before Kinder came in.

The older man was sorting the mail as Samson stood in front of the desk and waited. Kinder finally lit a cigarette and leaned back.

"I want to talk to you, Bob."

"Don't look so serious."

Samson tried a smile, failed, and came directly to the point. "I'm leaving."

For a few moments, Kinder said nothing, just watched the end of his cigarette. Then he crushed it in the tray and kept grinding it as he looked up. "You haven't got a broker's license."

"I'm going to take the next exam."

"What's wrong? What's the complaint? You've done all right here."

"I've done fine and I have you to thank. But eventually a man wants to be on his own."

"To be honest, Sam, I don't think you're ready."

"I'll manage."

Kinder leaned forward. "Maybe you don't like the cut. Suppose we change it. Sixty-forty." He sat back and smiled. Samson's look gave no encouragement and before he could answer, Kinder raised the ante. "I tell you what: we'll make it seventy-thirty." Now he rose and smiled as if the thing was settled.

"It isn't the cut. I just want to be on my own."

Kinder smiled again but it did not conceal his anxiety and Samson realized how much he meant to the office. During the months he was there the only deals that were made were his, he had infused a semblance of life into Walsh and Benjamin and Kinder himself seemed to have a new head of steam. He returned to his seat, tapped a pencil on the desk nervously, stopped, tossed it aside and then spoke. "I tell you what I'll do. Take a desk for twenty a month, get your broker's license and be your own boss."

"I don't want a desk. I want an office, like this," Samson said, waving a hand around the room. "Furthermore, I'm moving to the west part of town; the Wilshire district. Look, Bob," he said, leaning over the desk, putting as much sincerity into his voice as he could, "don't think I'm not appreciative of what you've done. And believe me I'll never forget it. It's just that I know the town now, I've looked it over and I want to get established on the other side. You've been here all your life, you know everyone, it's where you belong. With me it's different. I'm getting started and I want it to be where I think it will work best." He straightened up. "It's that simple."

"I guess your mind is made up."

He told Kinder he would leave in a couple of days. They agreed that any deals he was working on would be made through the office. All listings he brought in he was to share in if a deal was made.

He left exhilarated. He was on his own, would soon have a license and be on an equal footing with any broker in town. More than equal, he thought. He had cash, lots of it, and Aunt Annie had more and he could buy and sell as well as make commissions and by God he was young and had steam and before the country got off its ass he would have his share!

Already moved in with Aunt Annie, he visited an attorney,

made the preliminary arrangements to have his name changed legally and spent the remainder of the week cruising the Wilshire district, Beverly Hills, as far west as Brentwood, acquainting himself with the parts of the city where he was to cast his lot. From La Brea west the city began to thin out; Beverly Hills, the domain of Will Rogers, Pickford and Fairbanks. Its stately trees shading a few fine homes north and south of Sunset Boulevard supported a small business community on Beverly Drive. The Los Angeles Country Club and the new Fox studios comprised a couple of miles of open areas reaching to the border of Westwood Village where the Janss family's fief was developing, designed, village fashion, around the new campus of the University of California in Los Angeles. Then the open spaces broadened, dotted with the estates of Bel Air and Holmby Hills on to Brentwood, beyond which most of the land lay pastoral and untouched to Santa Monica, and the ocean. It was the natural path of development, he was sure, the farthest distance from the city center and the slums, land of small forests, canyons and rolling hills, smells and vistas of the sea.

Swept by his enthusiasm, Aunt Annie added encouragement to his plans and by the time Sunday morning came around, the day they were to lunch with Harry Baldwin, she had allied herself so thoroughly that she announced her intention to introduce him to Mr. Baldwin as Mr. Duke, and that he was having nose surgery the following week to correct a severe break he'd sustained as a little boy.

Mr. Baldwin was to pick them up at one. Aunt Annie went to a late Mass and returned at noon. Over a pot of tea, she prepared Samson for Mr. Baldwin. "He's a little loud and sort of pushy. But he is just a friend, not a beau, and don't you forget it." Then she went into the bedroom to change her clothes.

At one, an enormous Cadillac sedan pulled up at the curb. Rushing from his post at the window, Samson warned of Baldwin's arrival. He moved to the door and opened it directly after Baldwin rang the bell. A bear of a man, Baldwin seemed to bounce into the room. Simultaneously shifting a package he held under his right arm, he extended his hand. Samson took it and felt Baldwin clamp down with great pressure. "You're Sam."

Removing a felt hat, which he wore in spite of a warm day, he swept the band with his sleeve and set it on the Victrola, placing the package beside it. He rubbed his hands, looked around, seated himself in Aunt Annie's rocker, and eyed Samson across the room. "I understand you're in real estate."

Samson nodded.

"I'm sort of in it myself. Land, that is." He got up, seemed to spring from the chair, and walked to the window, looked out and then facing the room he rocked on the balls of his feet with hands clasped behind him. He ignored Samson, appeared deep in thought as he stared at the ceiling.

Samson examined him carefully. Although shorter than he first imagined, Baldwin was a huge man, not stout in the usual manner, but padded evenly, no part of him protruding. The fat layered his belly, ran flush up to his chest, tapered around his neck, seemed to keep its thickness down his back, and settled in his behind which was flat but very wide. Not a part of him was flabby, he was just thick.

He pulled a watch from his vest, looked at the time and replaced it. He walked to the window again. This time he opened it, stuck his head out and shouted, "Get away from that car, you kids!" He shook his fist and Samson heard shouts from the street. Whirling about, Mr. Baldwin ran out the door. Samson rushed to the window. The car was emptying. Three boys scrambled in all directions as Mr. Baldwin reached the street.

Aunt Annie rushed into the room. "What happened?"

"It's nothing. Just some kids. I guess they never saw a car like that before."

"He uses it in funerals," Aunt Annie said.

They heard Mr. Baldwin's steps and Aunt Annie went to the door. "I hope they did no damage, Mr. Baldwin."

He was shaking her hand awkwardly. Regaining his composure, he brushed it off lightly and came into the room. "This is for you," he said, handing her the package he had brought. "Open it." She obeyed as the two men watched.

"It's lovely!" she exclaimed and removed a half-dozen lace doilies from a tissue wrapping. She thanked him with her best smile.

"Suppose we go," he said, brushing the hat band once again with his sleeve and placing it on his head. Aunt Annie reached for her purse and gloves and they left the house.

Whatever notions Samson had about undertakers were dispelled that day. He was always certain they were as tales and rumor described: thin-lipped and dour, uncommunicative, mysterious, handmaiden to God or the Devil, idolator of the Angel of Death, loners who took up residence next to or on the upper floor of their mortuaries, friendly only to crones and freaks, baseball umpires and sleazy politicians. Harry Baldwin was none of these; he was hearty as Falstaff, gusty, alive, a total negation of any alliance with death.

The car they drove off in was a seven-passenger funeral limousine, upholstered in fine leather, and floored with a thick gray carpet. Seated in the rear, Samson sunk himself in its luxury as they drove along Wilshire Boulevard toward the beach. At Paul's, the maitre d' greeted Mr. Baldwin by name and led them to a table overlooking the sea. With a flourish, Baldwin waved the menu aside.

"Order what you please," he said. "They'll prepare it." Samson tried unsuccessfully to think of a dish he had heard of but never tried. Aunt Annie appeared to be thinking too.

"May I make some suggestions?" Mr. Baldwin said. He started on appetizers and worked through soups and salads to main dishes, his large, chocolate-covered eyes glistening as he recited a litany of exotic foods.

"Just a cup of chowder and broiled filet of sole for me," Aunt Annie decided.

"Is that all?" Baldwin seemed stunned.

"It's all I can eat," she apologized.

Baldwin shook his head and turned to Samson. Determined to please him, Samson ordered oysters on the half-shell, a bowl of chowder and lobster thermidor. Mr. Baldwin seemed to glow with satisfaction. After placing their orders he explained that on Sunday he forsook breakfast and only took one meal. Then Baldwin ordered a large bucket of steamed clams, a boiled fish, steak with mashed potatoes, and a pitcher of beer.

While Aunt Annie nibbled at her food, Samson saw her watch as Mr. Baldwin swallowed at least fifty clams. Then he boned the fish with surgical deftness, coated it with ketchup, and washed it down with half the pitcher of beer in a few short moments. Without a pause he infused thick chunks of butter into the mashed potatoes, then attacked the steak with businesslike sawing motions. He did not say a word throughout the entire meal; he was in constant motion wielding the knife and fork, reaching for the breadbasket, pouring more beer, and, after every mouthful, drawing the napkin across his chin. Finished at last, Baldwin watched balefully as the waiter cleared. With the dishes removed he returned to life. "Now for dessert."

"I'll have orange sherbet," Aunt Annie said. "And some tea." As if sure of more enthusiasm, Baldwin turned to Samson, who did not disappoint him. Earlier, his eye had caught a glimpse of a cut of strawberry shortcake out of the corner of his eye. It was as big as a catcher's mitt. When he ordered it, Mr. Baldwin glowed paternally.

"We'll make it two," he said winking.

Nothing was said during dessert. By now Samson could sense Aunt Annie's coolness and made every effort to compensate for it by a display of enthusiasm. He praised the meal, complimented Baldwin's selections, and ignored Aunt Annie's glare. When at length Mr. Baldwin excused himself and headed for the men's room, Aunt Annie turned on him. "You were almost as bad as he was. You both ate like pigs!"

"I just wanted to be sociable. Does he always eat this way?"

"I hope not. Anyway, don't butter him up. And I know what you're thinking. But just remember, I'll do the picking and choosing. Do you understand?"

She would make the decision all right but he would be sure to be on hand if she needed a shove. Baldwin's cut might be a little rough but he wasn't an imitation.

Now Mr. Baldwin approached the table with a big smile as he puffed on a double claro cigar, pushing its torpedo shape in and out through pursed lips, wetting it to the middle. By the time Aunt Annie had gathered her things, he paid the check, tipped the waiter, and they were bowed out the door.

The sky had clouded, and the Sunday bathers were leaving the beach. Trudging with camp stools and umbrellas, shopping bags with leftovers and with small children tugging at skirts and sleeves, perched on shoulders and dragged by their hands, they swarmed toward the parking lots.

As they drove toward the amusement park, Samson could see the familiar forms like ghostly etchings against the sky; the huge skeletal of the roller coaster, a giant Erector-set configuration perched on the end of the pier, banners fluttering from slender poles atop the cupolas adorning the buildings and rising above it all, the Ferris wheel with its swinging gondolas.

The sun began to peep from the barrier of clouds and the car pulled to the curb. Mr. Baldwin turned to Aunt Annie.

"Suppose we walk around a bit."

Before she could protest, Samson leaped from the car and opened her door. She got out with hardly concealed irritation. They strolled to the end of the pier and started back and then Mr. Baldwin put his prowess on display. At a shooting gallery he drew a crowd shattering pipes and ducks as they walked off with two Kewpie dolls, a Grand Canyon pillow, and a doorstop shaped like the Los Angeles City Hall. At the baseball throw, Mr. Baldwin caused the operator to groan as he swept away row after row of pyramided bottles, adding a Chinese doll and a real clock to their loot. Samson contented himself with watching and carrying the booty. By this time Aunt Annie began to thaw and joined the fun. She played the Races and pinball machine, squealing with delight when she won, rode the Whip, and screamed and laughed through the Crazy House. After three times around on the scooters and a roller-coaster ride, on which she had to be coaxed, all her natural good humor and warmth returned. It was growing dark as they headed for the car. Passing a hot dog stand, Aunt Annie paused.

"I'm a little hungry," she confessed.

Mr. Baldwin beamed. "I knew it. You didn't eat at lunch." He led them up to the counter.

Although pleased with the turn of events and sure that Mr. Baldwin had closed a tactical gap, Samson watched with apprehension as he began to order. Baldwin's eyes were wide as he asked for five hot dogs. Samson noticed a shadow cross Aunt Annie's face. However, her good humor must have been well entrenched. As Mr. Baldwin devoured three franks in the time they ate one apiece her frown disappeared and her smile returned.

Whatever energy or reserves Mr. Baldwin possessed now seemed depleted. As they walked toward the car, Samson noticed that his step no longer had a bounce and his shoulders drooped. He turned to Samson as they reached the limousine.

"Would you care to drive?"

Samson slid behind the wheel as Mr. Baldwin and Aunt Annie settled in the corners of the rear seat and through the mirror he saw the older man lean back and close his eyes, his face sagged with exhaustion. When they reached Aunt Annie's house, Mr. Baldwin declined an invitation for tea, climbed into the car and drove off.

After piling the prizes on the couch, Samson removed his jacket and tie and kicked off his shoes. He wanted to talk about Mr. Baldwin. "Sure is a nice man. One would never guess he's an undertaker."

Aunt Annie flopped into a chair and lit a cigarette. "He's loud and he's pushy. And today I found out he's a glutton."

"He's a big man. They require more food."

"He was *once* a little boy. Probably skinny too. What else but eating made him that big?" She flicked her ashes and her stubborn look wreathed her face. "Anyway, I don't want to talk about Mr. Baldwin anymore. Now, leave me alone."

As he watched her, Samson realized she had remained content all during the years, nourishing herself with memories of her short marriage. He recalled her telling him about that marriage one night when they first moved to Brooklyn. They were in the kitchen, she was drinking her tea and he the cup of cocoa he usually had before bed. Her eyes began to moisten as she told him about Fred, how much in love they were, and that he died in just two years from spinal meningitis.

"We had just moved to the farm six months before. It was Fred's dream. He had made the down payment from the pennies we both saved. I worked in a laundry in Brooklyn and he was with the city in the Park Department. Every night he would come home from work with books from the library. They were on farming, mainly chicken raising. How he would study!" she exclaimed. "I guess he read every chicken book in the library."

"What kind of a man was he, Aunt Annie? I mean, what did he look like?"

"He was a small man. Had the blackest hair and bluest eyes you've ever seen. They were like a child's." Then she stopped talking and looked at Samson for a moment. "You know," she went on, "the color of your hair and eyes are just like his. You're a bigger man but there's a resemblance." Then they talked about the Church. "Fred was a good Catholic, but he took it with a grain. When he passed my faith took a turn. It's never been the same."

Then she told him why she never remarried. "I was asked but they never measured up. Once I promised a man and backed down a week before we were to be married. I didn't have the feeling for him. I was just lonely, but it wasn't enough. I guess I'm not the kind that can do things part way. I'm not too educated, and I don't know much. But I know myself. And when I do something, I have to do it thorough."

But it was different now, he was sure, as he watched her half-dozing in the chair, across a country from the farm and their Brooklyn home at an age when dreams are limited by time and loneliness touches the border of panic. Baldwin's company, maybe not the best, would surely be a wiser choice than reliance on faded memories and fainter hopes.

CHAPTER FOUR

Long before the swelling had gone down and the purple shiners disappeared, Samson had Dr. Gantner permanently installed as an object of worship. On the day the larger bandages were removed a small strip of plaster was placed over the bridge of the nose. Samson saw the result for the first time as the nurse fixed the mirrors to cover all angles. The doctor stood aside, smiling with satisfaction and Samson experienced the exultation of a rebirth. The nose swept from the bridge straight to flaring nostrils. It seemed to broaden his face, widen the space between his eyes, and even square his jaw. It was majestic! Days before, even bandaged the result was hinted, but Samson would not permit himself to give way to the delirium of joy. Now, the promise was a fact. He was handsome! Groping for words of gratitude, he fumbled, his throat lumped, and he felt his eyes moisten as he gripped Dr. Gantner's hand. Assured the prognosis was perfect, that the final result held greater promise with the reduction of the swelling he left the office, walked down Hollywood Boulevard casting side glances at every plate glass window, containing with effort the greatest happiness he had ever felt. He wanted to shout, kick his heels, dance, as he headed for his car. He began to run, piled into the vehicle and sped home. Never in his life was he surer of himself; the change of his name, the new face, the move to the west side . . . the decision to come to California. Wait until Aunt Annie saw him!

She was in the living room as he burst into the house. Removing his dark glasses, he stood in the middle of the room and turned slowly as she surveyed him. For a long moment she didn't say a word, just looked, then she gripped her handkerchief and brought it to her eyes and finally swept him in her arms.

"Sam, oh, Sam, I can't believe it!" She held him at arms' length, dabbed at her eyes and stepped back. "You're so different, your face is changed. You're handsome!"

His jubilation and elation were no longer contained. They poured from his throat as he threw his head back and roared. "I told you!" he cried out. "Nothing is God's will!" He grabbed his aunt and whirled her about. "That goes for everything, Aunt Annie. We don't have to accept a damn thing!" He led her to the kitchen. "Come on, let's celebrate. A pot of tea!" She seemed unable to take her eyes off him as she found the kettle, turning from the sink as it filled, placed it on the stove, looked again, reached for the tea cannister and finally fell into the chair and just stared.

"Don't take *all* the credit from the Lord, Sam. The doctor got his power somewhere, and anyway, you had a fine face to work with."

Samson Duke sipped at his tea, grinned with satisfaction. His image was new and perfect. Tomorrow he would begin a new life.

Within two weeks all the perceptible swelling had disappeared. Dr. Gantner cautioned Samson to treat the nose with care for a few months and dismissed him. Now, with the discoloration gone, and the strip of plaster removed, Samson set about to find an apartment. He settled on a comfortable furnished double just off Wilshire near Western Avenue and moved in on a Sunday after a tearful parting with Aunt Annie. Deciding to move slowly before locating himself in an office, he spent his days checking the values in the area.

He was determined to locate on Wilshire Boulevard, and, starting from Western Avenue he combed everything west to La Brea. With a few exceptions, a block or two of store fronts and a couple of multistoried buildings, all the street was improved with old residences, most dating from the early part of the century. Some housed original occupants, others now owned by mortgage companies, were being used by dentists, physicians, chiropractors, and real-estate men working out of former living rooms, bedrooms, and even kitchens. He made a list of all the vacancies, spoke to a dozen landlords and kept looking.

In the meantime he began taking daily golf lessons at a driving range and one day toward the end of a month ventured to the public course at Griffith Park. Nervous at first, unsure of his game, he asked the starter to place him with a foursome who lied about but never broke a hundred. He filled in with two doctors and a pharmacist who seemed more concerned with discussing medical economics than with the game and found himself low man at the end of the round. After a half-dozen games and another series of lessons, he eliminated his slice, began driving a long ball and brought his score down to the nineties. Confident now, he felt prepared to play with anyone and early one morning walked to the tee and introduced himself to the three men who were swinging their clubs as they waited to begin. Two were friends and the third man was a single like himself. They paired off from the other twosome and by the time they reached the third hole he discovered that Art Jennings was a real-estate broker with offices on Wilshire Boulevard a few blocks from Samson's apartment, that he played with a regular threesome once a week, was getting in an extra game that day and would be delighted if Samson wanted to join him in his regular game the following morning.

"Why not meet me at my office at eight o'clock?" Jennings suggested when they parted.

His office was in an old house on Wilshire a few blocks west of Western. Two-storied and frame, it's second story bulging with fat bays, the roof line scalloped with crenulations, it represented an incongruous combination of Norman and Victorian, topping an early Californian's dream of Gothic. He had the master lease and had converted the rooms into offices which he rented to brokers who worked alone. His own office, formerly the living room, occupied one half of the lower floor and was separated from a rear porch by French doors. Contrasting Jennings' personal neatness it was the most cluttered office Samson had ever seen. The desk was piled with manila folders, littered with papers, a huge tarnished Victorian inkstand, battered cotton golf balls, pencils, erasers, and a large bowl filled with hard candies. A couch lined each wall and a leather chair, cracked with age, and matching ottoman filled a corner. Beside it a low table overflowed with magazines. At least a dozen golf trophies lined the mantel below a half-dozen plaques that circled a hunting scene in a gilt frame.

Though Samson tried to make his inspection seem casual, Jennings noticed it. "One of these days I'll get this place straightened up, Sam. Anyway," he said, brushing aside a pile of papers on his desk from which he extracted a fountain pen, "I know where everything is." He took a package of new golf balls from a box on the mantel and they left.

They drove in Jennings' car, a late model Lincoln sedan, long and black and highly polished. Somehow it suited him and Samson could not imagine Jennings driving anything smaller or less elegant. Samson sat beside him, caught his profile, and saw signs of middle age that his full face did not reveal: the pouch of fat hanging below the chin, deeply etched wrinkles about his eyes, and the corner droop of his mouth that would soon work its way down the side of his face. He turned to Samson. "Did you say your office was in Gardena?"

"It was. I left there. I'm looking around."

"Got your broker's license?"

"A salesman's. I'm taking the broker's exam next month."

There was silence for awhile and then Jennings said, "The brokers we're playing with, Al Lifton and Roy Phillips, are good men. Al's a Jew, had some kike name like Lipshutz or something. Changed it a few years ago. Said it was because of the kids. Anyway, he's married to Harry Finkelstein's daughter."

"Who's he?"

"Either the luckiest bastard in town or the smartest. He had a big wholesale meat company and was in the market up to his ears. A year before the crash he got a heart attack and the doctor told him to quit. It scared the hell out of him so he sold his business, all of his stock, plunked the cash in a bank and took a trip around the world. By the time he got back the bottom dropped out and all he had was *gelt*. Now he buys and sells, makes loans to the boys, and has a finger in every deal in town. Everything has to go through Al. I've known Finkelstein for twenty years, long before Al married in. But you know those Jews. Everything stays in the family."

"They're sure close."

"The funny thing is that Al and Finkelstein hate each other's guts. I guess the old man wanted his daughter to marry a doctor or something. Anyway, he treats Al like shit."

They were nearing the park and Samson asked about the other member of their foursome.

"Roy Phillips. Wait'll you see him. Barely five feet. Even ladies' clubs are too long for him. He had to have them made special. His brother is a naval commander in San Diego. I met him once and would you believe it, he's six feet tall."

They had pulled into the parking lot and headed for the clubhouse. A small man came running up to them, shouting at Jennings, his face livid with rage. "You sonofabitch, you're always late! We were up ten minutes ago and had to let two foursomes play through."

Jennings looked at his watch. "I guess I'm slow."

"That goddamn watch is always slow!"

"Anyway, meet Sam Duke," Jennings said. "Roy Phillips."

Samson extended his hand and Phillips tried to crush it. They changed shoes and met Al Lifton at the tee. His ball was up and he was swinging his club. Tall and thin with tiny black eyes and a huge hooked nose, he acknowledged the introduction without a trace of a smile.

"We usually make a team bet," Jennings said. "A dollar a hole with carry-overs." He asked Samson his handicap.

"I'm a beginner. I'll be lucky if I break a hundred."

"That puts you in Roy's class. Al and I shoot about the same game."

"When he cheats," Lifton put in.

Jennings ignored the remark and it was decided that he and Samson would team up against the other two and they would adjust after the first nine.

Lifton teed off first. He had a smooth easy swing and hit the ball far down the fairway with a tail-end hook. Samson was next and sliced into the rough. Phillips stepped up, took about six practice swings, topped the ball, and swore. Jennings drove near Lifton and they started on their way.

As the morning wore on it became obvious that business alone brought the three together. Jennings bullied them both, Phillips snapped like a terrier, and Lifton's resentment was barely disguised. They screamed and cursed at one another; the two accused Jennings of cheating and Samson saw some evidence of this as he continually improved his lies.

Only when they discussed real estate was there harmony. Finkelstein's name came up in the discussions and every time it was mentioned, Lifton followed it with "the sonofabitch" to the delight of the other two. Samson was like a spectator and as the day wore on he began to realize he had been in real estate the hard way, he was doing the shovel work, the digging; these men were picking up the gems without dirtying their hands. They rarely worked on commissions, got the choice listings from other brokers, optioned or bought them and that was where Lifton came in. Finkelstein would put up the money on any deal that looked good and split the profits fifty-fifty. In other instances he would lend them nearly all the money and take back a second trust deed at high rates of interest and big bonuses.

Before parting, they all agreed to meet the same time next week. Jennings and Samson stopped for lunch and during the meal Samson started to question him about Finkelstein. "He's got a good deal," he began, "just sits on his ass and it rolls in."

"When he doesn't buy your deal to split the profit and lends you the money on a second mortgage, how does it work?"

"He charges ten per cent per annum on the mortgage plus a bonus," Jennings explained. "That part is under the table in cash."

"How much of a bonus?"

"If you want a one-year loan it's fifteen per cent. Then he adds five per cent for each additional six months. He won't make a loan for more than two years."

Samson calculated swiftly. "You mean if he makes a two-year loan he collects twenty-five per cent under the table in addition to the ten per cent each year?"

"That's right."

"It looks like Finkelstein's got a monopoly," Samson concluded.

Jennings mouth was full and he shook his head negatively as he finished swallowing. "He's got plenty of competition."

"The others' rates the same?"

"Not by a long shot. Harry's a gentleman. I guess he figures being a Jew he's got to take it easy. They do that sometimes, you know. You should meet some of the others. You'd think they were Israelites, too. One guy, Ralph Taylor, rams it in like Finkelstein but then he breaks it off. Same interest, same bonus, and after he creams the deal, he grabs twenty-five per cent of your profits. Then there's an outfit in Pasadena, fancy lawyers, a firm with a long name I can't remember. They prettied it up. Say, you need ten thousand dollars to put down on an apartment house." Jennings had a pencil out and was writing on the tablecloth. "The note reads six per cent per annum and is for one year.

They make you pay it back in twelve equal installments like on a car. But," he went on, punctuating the air with his pencil, "they have a monthly service charge. Three per cent of the full ten thousand payable every thirty days. I figured it up once. They get about a hundred per cent interest each year." He threw his pencil on the table.

"What if you sell the building the first month and pay off the whole loan?"

"That's the kicker. There's no payoff privilege for six months."

As they drove back to the office Samson's head was full of figures, multiplying the cash he had in the bank then adding and multiplying again until the zeros began adding onto the end until they disappeared over the edge of his mind's eye. Then another thought occurred to him. "There must be a fat profit in these deals if you can afford to pay so much for the money."

"Only if you can find sleepers. The insurance companies and banks are foreclosing all over the place. They own half the town right now and they're dying to unload. You've got to be careful though," he cautioned. He started to say something else and stopped abruptly. It appeared he sensed that Samson had pumped him enough.

On the drive home he sifted everything he had learned that day. Jennings and the others had the formula. It might not be the best but was an improvement over what he had been doing. Kinder made a living, no more, and he put in long hours doing it. Samson was not so sure how Kinder would have done if he did not have him or someone like him ringing doorbells seven days a week, halfway round the clock. Well, he wasn't broke, and if what Jennings said about tight money was true, he was in a position to put money to work and not have to sweat. Maybe now was the time. If the Finkelsteins' and the Taylors' and the bunch in Pasadena and others like them had their dollars working like an army, what was wrong with him doing the same?

Then it came to him. There was an in-between position, one that Jennings and the lenders did not hold. Jennings borrowed the money because he didn't have it and the lenders loaned because they did not want to work or could not. But why lend money to Jennings if a deal was good? All he did was find property. Samson would have to put up all or nearly all of the down payment to get the high interest. However, if he found the deal and bought it himself, he could take the whole pot.

By the time he arrived home he made his decision. He would settle somewhere in an office, do brokerage, and keep eyes open for that sleeper Jennings talked about. Now was the time; property could go no lower and when a bottom was reached, any move had to be up.

When Samson met Jennings the following week and they headed for the golf course, Jennings told him that Al Lifton could not make it. "Ralph Thompson's joining us. Used to be in the trust department of the Pacific Bank downtown. Now he manages their branch on Western."

From the moment Thompson got into the car until they reached Griffith Park, Jennings ignored Samson and directed all his charm to the older man. In his middle fifties and wearing a perpetual smile that played about his mouth with none of the merriment appearing in his flat gray eyes, he hardly spoke, nodding and grunting his answers. By the time they reached the clubhouse, Jennings had inquired about his health, assured him he looked better than he ever did, praised his golf game and completed his courtship by presenting him with a dozen golf balls he took from the glove compartment. "They've got your initials on them, Ralph," he said as Thompson fumbled with the box.

Thompson examined them without a word.

Roy Phillips was waiting and they teed off. This time there was no talk of a team bet as Jennings and Thompson arranged a large bet between themselves with Art giving the banker three strokes on the first nine. Thompson played like a pro and by the time they reached the tenth tee had won seven holes.

Though he made every effort to listen in on their conversation Samson was only able to pick up bits as they huddled on the fairways and tees. However, he picked enough to inform him that managing a bank was a sideline and that Thompson's fingers were still rummaging in the bank's trust department. By the time they finished the game and reached the clubhouse it became evident that some of the "sleepers" Jennings spoke of came from Pacific Bank.

The following day he called the bank and made an appointment to see Thompson. He was surprised by an unusual warmth as Thompson ushered him to his desk. Samson praised his game and got down to business. He decided not to reveal the amount of money he had. With conditions the way they were, he could be tapped for personal loans. If he bought a building with his own funds it would be difficult to participate in commission since he would be considered a principal.

"I want to open an account," he began. "It isn't much now." He handed him a cashier's check for a thousand dollars, made out the cards, ordered a checkbook, and as he got up to go, turned to Thompson as if with an afterthought. "How would you handle a trust account?"

"What do you mean?"

"An estate in the east, sort of family. They want me to look around for some good buys in real estate. Thought it would be better to have the money on hand. I expect a large check, maybe thirty or forty thousand dollars." Thompson could not hide his surprise. "I don't want to co-mingle it with my funds."

"You're right," Thompson said, "it should be in a trust account." He had an arm about his shoulder as he escorted Samson to the door.

"One thing," Samson said. "The account is to be confidential."

"Naturally."

He waited a week and opened the account with thirty thousand, leaving the balance he had in another bank. The following day he received a call from his attorney telling him that the hearing for his name change was scheduled for the end of the month. This was what he was waiting for; now he could take his broker's examination.

He went through the exam in two of the four hours allowed, and after finishing, called Art Jennings and asked him to dinner.

They arranged to meet in Jennings' office before going to the restaurant. Art greeted Samson with a tray, set with glasses, ice, and a bottle of liquor. It soon became apparent to Samson that Ralph Thompson's tongue had jarred loose after Samson's large deposit; all this spurred Jennings' interest, which began to evolve toward patronage as he recommended restaurants, suggested tailors for Samson to visit, and insisted that Samson make no move in real estate without consulting him first.

"It'll have to be bourbon," Jennings apologized, thrusting a generous glass at Samson. "My druggist ran out of other prescriptions."

"I'll take it in a tall glass of water," Samson said. "Still can't drink it straight." He proposed a toast. "To deals."

"Lots of them."

Jennings downed his shot, refilled it and settled back in the chair. Samson lit a cigarette. "We got some time. I made it for eight at Perino's."

Rolling the glass between his fingers and holding it up to the light, Jennings said, "It's a lousy shame. Prohibition, I mean. Nobody's stopped drinking, the stuff costs twice as much and the wop bootleggers are making all the money."

"I guess I'm too young to know what it was like before."

"How old are you?"

He was about to blurt the truth then changed his mind. "Old enough to vote," he said. "Where are you from, Art? Originally, I mean."

"Kentucky. A little town near Louisville. I was a country boy. Pulled out early. Only went back once to see my father buried."

"Come straight out here?"

"No. A lot of places first. Ended up in Boston. Came out here after the war." He poured another drink in a tall glass and filled it with water. Sitting back, he stared ahead in silence and Samson got the feeling he'd said all he was going to tell.

He decided to talk about himself, careful to remember his story so that future references to it would fit. He told him his mother died when he was young and that he was brought up by an aunt.

His father sort of drifted, he said, remarried and died a few years back. Knowing that Thompson repeated all he had told him, he explained that a long-term trust had been set up by a relative and that he was a minor beneficiary. "My aunt is co-executor and I guess I'm her favorite." He smiled modestly. "She talked them into investing some money in Los Angeles real estate." Jennings said nothing, just sat sipping his drink. "All this is confidential, Art. I don't want the boys to know. They'd treat me like a client and I have to make a living selling." Now he leaned forward and put as much sincerity into his voice as he could. "Ralph Thompson knows. And you."

"You can trust me, Sam." Then he told Sam, "I've got a daughter your age, lives near Boston with her grandmother." The sentence ended with a tone of finality. "The way things worked out, I haven't seen her much."

"Her mother alive?"

"She died when Beck was a year old."

After dinner, Jennings asked him to return to his office. Ushering him into an upstairs room he switched on the light.

"How do you like it?"

It was large, almost as big as Jennings', sparsely furnished with a cheap desk, a few wooden chairs, and a worn couch.

"It's all right. Could use some paint and a new carpet."

"It'll be available in thirty to sixty days. The rent is cheap. Thirty-five a month. I'll paint but you'll have to put in the carpet."

"You just made a deal, Art. Thanks."

Nothing fit his plans more perfectly; a setup in a nest of pros, an address on Wilshire Boulevard, time to get his license from Sacramento, and to orient himself to the area and its real-estate values. As he drove home he pictured the room and furnished it in his mind; leather chairs and a walnut desk, a typewriter and a file and print-covered walls and a lamp or two and beneath it all a carpet thick as a wad of bills.

Aunt Annie called the following morning, complained at not seeing him for two weeks, and invited him for dinner that night.

He knew she was seeing Harry Baldwin but had no idea what progress was being made. If she would marry, relieve him of her future care, there would be nothing ahead but forward progress. Baldwin could tire of pursuit, read rejection in delay, and a rich widower, always in demand, can be picked off without warning. Aunt Annie had to be made to understand. By now she might be more vulnerable to loneliness than to the adjustments of marriage and he had a lot to say about both and she was going to listen.

They had finished dinner, were at the dishes and she still had not mentioned Harry Baldwin, and he realized something was wrong. Just then the phone rang. She answered, her voice laced with ice. "My mind is made up, Harry. It'll do no good to come over." She listened a moment and then added, "Suit yourself." She hung up.

"Aren't things going well?" he ventured.

"For Harry Baldwin, not for me."

"What happened?"

"It isn't any one thing. It's little things, lots of them and they add up wrong." Now she seemed to be appealing for corroboration. "He has to have his own way. Oh, he's good to me, I suppose. Taking me to shows and dinners and buying things. Maybe that's it. He's spent so much money he wants a return. Well, I can pay for my shows and buy my dinners, and I don't have to watch him eat. Stuffing himself like a pig. And the other night after dinner . . . you know what he was doing?" she challenged. "All at the same time? He was caressing his belly with one hand as he forced the food through his teeth with a hissing sound and picked the wax out of his ear with a toothpick. I could have died! Huh," she said with disgust as she flung herself into the chair, "and he talks about spiritual values."

"But these are only habits."

"Habits! They're part of him like the skin on his back. And that business he's in." Her face contorted with disgust. "He's always talking about it . . . a job he did that day, a smile he put on his face, how they all look better dead than alive. He still does embalming, just to keep a hand in he says, even though he has two working full time. It's disgusting and I'm sick of him and death."

Samson ventured feebly. "It is his business, after all. And he has his good points. Don't you think he deserves another chance?"

"He's had all the chances he's paid for."

He was about to reply when there was a knock on the door. Her flustered attempts at tidying up as she smoothed the front of her dress and tucked strayed hairs could have been a reflex but he prayed it was not. When she hurriedly surveyed herself in a mirror and rushed to the piano top for her purse and removed a rough puff and dabbed her cheeks, his hopes soared.

Though Mr. Baldwin was well equipped with conciliatory weapons, he lost the initial encounter as she looked past a huge bunch of her favorites, tea roses, a box of candy tucked under an arm, and a heroic attempt at a broad smile. "I'm tired, Harry," she said, "I am going to bed. If you want you can visit with Sam." He eased past her, advanced into the room, and deposited his offerings on the table. Retaining his smile he shook Samson's hand warmly.

"Haven't seen you since we were at the beach. Hoped you'd drop by the mortuary."

"I intend to," he said, watching Aunt Annie out of the corner of his eye. It was the last thing he wanted to do, but he had no intentions of permitting a natural distaste from interfering with his plans.

Aunt Annie wavered at the door for a moment then approached the table. Eying the flowers, she swept them up as if reluctant to leave them to die and carried them into the kitchen. Baldwin settled in the rocker, still wearing a vestige of his smile. He clipped a cigar and lit it. Aunt Annie returned with the roses fanned out in a large vase and placed them in the center of the table. She spoke with a shade of warmth. "I'm really tired, Harry. You'll have to excuse me."

Without another word she walked out as he rose to bow stiffly. Now he grabbed the overstuffed chair and by the way he settled

into it, wriggling to a comfortable position and placing the ashtray "just right," Samson knew he was prepared to stay. There
was something pathetic about the big man; it was evident it would
have been a relief to leave, nurse his rejection without a witness,
but to do so would not only be embarrassing but an admission of
defeat. Samson's anger at his aunt was directed less by her cruel
treatment than by her inability to see the advantages this man
offered. Well, he was going to patch Baldwin's ego if it took all
night. He started by asking Mr. Baldwin about himself.

"How do you have time for all those things?" he said, pointing
to a bevy of emblems dangling from a chain strung across his
chest.

Baldwin contemplated the end of his cigar. Now, he brightened, drew deeply on the cigar, released the smoke lazily, and
smiled. "I make time." He fingered the Elk's tooth socketed in a
gold band. He displayed it for inspection. "It's from a real elk."
He dropped it into place. "I'm a Moose and a Lion, too." He
sighed. "Of course, most important is the Knights. Headed it last
year. Sort of chairman of the board now."

Samson shook his head admiringly, opened the box of candy
Baldwin had brought and they started on the first layer. Baldwin
licked a chocolaty finger. "People don't realize that when an hour
is lost it's gone forever." Now, he jabbed with his cigar as he
made each point, warming to the conversation. "Time is all we've
got. Some use it, some don't. And believe me, Sam, you can't
waste a minute. You never know when God reaches out for you.
When that time comes you've got to be ready even if you're
nipped in the bud." He sighed. "I've turned all kinds over to the
Lord; people I knew, friends. And there were plenty in the lot
who did a lot of wishing and little working." The cigar was removed from his jaw, now his face was benign. "Rewards are
given by the Mother of God. The gifts of Heaven. One gets all
that's due when he arrives." They reached for a candy together.
Baldwin settled back eying the cream as he bit into it. "If he's
earned it, that is," he concluded licking the chocolate from his
upper lip with a fat tongue.

For awhile neither said a thing. Baldwin appeared somnolent as if lulled by the power of his words and Samson pretended a silent reverence as his thoughts tilted with Baldwin's pontifications.

Samson was not impious, believed in God, but believed in the practical side of religion rather than the spiritual which he thought too speculative. The dealing in futures, particularly in the Catholic faith was the kind of gambling he meant to avoid. The meek may inherit the earth, and the dogmas, whose explanations the faithful are told are to be found in Heaven, might provide ample justification for those who embrace the canon of blind faith, but he liked to see around a corner before he made a turn. He liked to play it safe, and though the possibility of rewards after death may prove valid, he believed in gathering gifts and goods here on earth in case the promises for the hereafter should fail to materialize.

"I never thought about it that way, Mr. Baldwin," he began. "I imagine undertaking gives one a different perspective. We all face death but try not to think about it. You are forced never to forget it."

His philosophic bid opened the gates and Baldwin's thoughts poured through. With the proper amount of immodesty he likened his profession to that of the physician who delivers life, adding that the final journey also has to do with life and actually was more important since the ascent after deliverance was for eternity. The profession, he went on, demanded forbearance because of the associations in man's mind.

"There are too many jokes about undertakers," he said, sadly. "Far too many."

Samson agreed, was about to turn the conversation to the real-estate end of the burying business when Aunt Annie appeared clutching her robe tightly around her throat. Though she seemed ready for bed her makeup was still on and every hair was in place. Baldwin pushed himself from the chair with an effort.

"I guess we're keeping you up," he said apologetically.

"It's just that I'd feel better locking up after."

Baldwin swept up his hat, beamed his face with a smile and was at the door. "I'll call you tomorrow, Annie." He hesitated. "If I may." She nodded and he turned to Samson. "I meant to tell you . . . your nose they repaired. You look like an actor." At that moment, Samson would have ridden his hearse and followed him to Hell.

"Thank you. I guess the doctor did a good job."

"Perfect," Baldwin said, shaking his head admiringly. He was about to leave, and turned. "I'd like to make a date to show you around the parlor."

"Anytime."

"Tomorrow? For lunch?"

"I'll be there at noon."

Aunt Annie had the kettle on the stove and Samson joined her in the kitchen. "Tea or cocoa?"

"Tea."

She set out the cups, crackers and jam and joined him at the table. "What were you two talking about?"

"About things. Real estate, his business."

"It's his whole life. He never stops talking about it. You'd think when he's away he'd want to forget."

"I don't care what he does. I like him. Just compare him with what's available. I don't understand you."

"Maybe I don't understand myself," she confessed. "I know Harry Baldwin's intentions are good." She shrugged. "But I've been independent for a long time. I had chances. Not many, but I had chances." She shook her head solemnly. "Some women reach out for anything. I'm just not that kind. Sometimes I wish I was. Maybe I'm looking for things that don't exist. But they're real to me and I'm not giving up." She was pouring the tea now.

He decided to avoid the center of resistance and maneuver the flank. "That's up to you Aunt Annie. I like him. And I'm new out here, need contacts. Mr. Baldwin's got them, I'm sure."

"What good are they? They're all dead."

"It's no use talking. You're just prejudiced."

"Prejudiced am I! I never feel alone with him. It's like we always got company. It's like he's working for Gabriel and the

Devil and they're always in contact. Sometimes when I leave him and get in bed I hear noises, voices. . . . Oh, I know it's in my head. But I hear them! And then I think of him in that room getting them ready, up to his elbows in it . . . I get sick. And if Harry Baldwin thinks he'll find favor with me by warming up to you, he'd better save his time." She lit a Wings and puffed it furiously.

"You got it twisted. I'm warming up to him. He doesn't need me."

"That's your business. And it might be fair to let him know that any favors he extends is just between you two. Not for the right to call me."

"You mean you won't see him anymore?"

She rose. "I didn't say that. Now go and let me lock up."

That's all he wanted to hear.

Above a gate a wooden trellis supported a neat sign on which "Baldwin Funeral Parlor" was spelled out in gold letters. Opening the gate he proceeded along the walk, the sound of crunching gravel beneath his feet. Though he had a cool detachment toward death he shivered a bit as he mounted the steps. He was admitted by a middle-aged woman who ushered him into a darkly paneled room, told him to wait and closed the door. The only source of light filtered through two stained-glass windows that occupied the corners of one wall. He selected a comfortable chair that faced the door and surveyed the room. It was severe, neat and sparsely furnished. Next to his seat was a large desk in front of a dark leather chair and on another wall a long library table with a lamp in its center, a chair at each end making up the rest of the furnishings. The walls, covered with a raspberry-colored silk, were bare and on the floor two small throw rugs lay diagonally across the dark parquet.

As Samson sat, straining his ears for a sound from the rest of the house to be reassured that life lurked there as well as death, the door flew open and Harry Baldwin burst into the room. A broad smile and hearty pat on the back contrasted sharply with the subdued decor and his somber dress.

"Hope you haven't been waiting long. Had a bit of business to finish." Speculating on its nature, Samson allowed himself to be led from the room to the entry hall. They mounted the stairs and Baldwin explained. "Let me show you the quarters upstairs and then we'll take a tour."

Two long darkly paneled halls led from the landing. Facing Samson and covering the entire wall was a huge tapestry depicting what appeared to be a Roman funeral procession replete with musicians, buffoons, and jesters preceding the body, lying face up on a couch, followed by torch bearers and milling throngs. At the end of the hall they entered a large room. The sun, streaming through the pairs of French windows that faced the street lighted it like a flare. All over the walls and in glass-enclosed cabinets were paintings and prints, figures and urns relating to the funeral.

"How do you like it?" Baldwin said, beaming as he seated himself behind a kidney-shaped desk in the corner of the room.

"It's fascinating," Samson admitted as he looked around.

"I'll be with you in a minute," Baldwin said, "just have to get this note off."

Samson moved about examining the collection. Every item had been carefully labeled. On one wall surrounding a beautiful replica of the Gold Mask of Tutankhamen were small reproductions of Canopic jars, a chest for the same purpose and varied drawings of Egyptian rites. Dominating another grouping was an engraving of Hogarth's Funeral Scene from "The Harlot's Progress" and in a pot-bellied glass case a death mask and a half-dozen painted urns of Greek original rested on a velvet shelf.

"That's finished," Baldwin said, sealing the envelope and sweeping the room with a wave of his hand. "Those were the days," he said. "The pagan knew how to bury. There were pageants . . . colorful, and imaginative, too." He crossed the room and pointed to a large print of a procession. "That's Queen Elizabeth's funeral. Seventeenth century. Even *then* they knew how. Look at it. It was a spectacle! Today," he went on sadly, "it's somber."

"Have you had Aunt Annie here?"

"Lord, no! To be honest with you, Sam, I know she hates my work. So I talk about it as little as possible. She refuses to understand the importance of the profession. And the consequences if it didn't exist. I confess I love it. Not because it deals with death but in spite of it." As he talked he tidied up, changing things around on the top of the desk as if they were chessmen and each move was a gambit. He pushed a glass inkstand off center and brought a tiny jeweled casket in its place, placed an empty spindle to one side and slid a box of pen nibs against its base. He put the last item, a paperweight fashioned from a coffin handle in place and sat back in his seat. "I'll never forget when I was a little boy," he went on. "Couldn't have been more than ten. My father was putting up a guest. He was passing through and spent a few days. It was E. Z. Ghant, Jr." He stopped a moment as if to allow the full import of what he had said sink in. Samson regretted his ignorance as to Mr. Ghant's identity. "He was the dean of modern embalmers! Self-taught, too. That was the remarkable thing. He had a feel for it few men ever possessed. Undertaking requires a rare touch. Only one in ten thousand have it."

Samson found himself agreeing with the observation.

"There are times when I'm not sure I'm fitted," Baldwin said seriously. "Everybody isn't a Ghant. I was in embalming school when my father died and I had to rush home to the business. It was a three-month course and I had been in school four weeks. I never went back. Had to complete the course by correspondence. It took in a lot."

"What did it cover?"

"Anatomy, bacteriology, contagious diseases. Also physiology and chemistry."

Samson was impressed.

Baldwin sighed. "People have no idea of an undertaker's background."

At that moment, a slight bent-over figure walked in. After being introduced to Samson he blinked nervously and asked Baldwin if he could see him alone for a moment.

"What is it, Finney? You can talk in front of Mr. Duke."

"It's O'Conner." Though his tone suggested a disturbance his tiny eyes were twinkling behind rimless glasses.

"Mr. Finney is our embalmer," Baldwin hastened to explain. Then he turned to the little man. "What's wrong?"

Finney hesitated, appeared to shrug slightly. "I can't get the face right."

"What's wrong with it?" Baldwin said.

"He looks angry."

"Did you leave the teeth in?"

"No."

"Didn't I tell you to use the teeth when you can?"

"But they don't fit," Finney protested. "I don't know how he chewed."

"All right," Baldwin said, wearily. He turned to Samson. "I'll just be a few minutes. Why don't you make a reservation for lunch? Any place you want." He left with Finney and Samson called Perino's for a reservation then seated himself behind the desk and waited, toying with the objects on its surface. Aunt Annie was right; Harry Baldwin didn't look like an undertaker. That is, not until today. He was certain that if she spent an hour in Baldwin's Parlor and witnessed the sheer love he had for the work his chances with her would be as dead as the merchandise he handled. Somehow, he imagined Baldwin directing his business from a desk with the same detachment a packing house executive would exhibit toward carcasses he ships. He was in it, it was depression-proof and he made it pay. However, it was obvious his interest extended beyond the balance sheet; he loved the grisly thing. Well, he could not change Baldwin nor his aunt's nature but he sure in hell was going to do all he could to see to it that she never set a foot in the Parlor. At least until after a wedding ceremony.

After about a fifteen-minute wait, Baldwin strode into the room followed by Mr. Finney. He was speaking over his shoulder.

"Now you see what I mean?"

"I guess I should have thought of it myself," Finney answered. "Just a couple of sutures on the inside of the lips," Baldwin went on.

"I get you," Finney said.

Now Baldwin waved a warning finger. "Remember, use the draw stitch, not the figure eight. Here," he said, going to the desk and drawing a diagram which he showed to the embalmer. "Study it," he concluded, as he folded the paper and gave it to Mr. Finney who looked at it for a moment, shook his head sagely and started to leave. "One more thing," Baldwin said. "You use too much wintergreen in the fluid. I've told you a dozen times. Use a little lavender or rosemary. O'Conner smells like a wad of gum."

"I'll remember," Finney said and left. Baldwin's eyes followed him. "One of the best in the business," he said as the door slammed shut. "You should see what he's turned out. Masterpieces! But, God, he's slow. You'd think I paid him by the hour. He lingers, and lingers."

By this time, Samson was racking his brain for an excuse to bow out of the lunch. He knew he couldn't eat a thing, wasn't sure when he could eat a meal next. As he groped for an excuse the phone rang. Baldwin swept it from the desk with the motion one would employ in trapping a fly and in solemn tones started to talk.

"This is Mr. Baldwin speaking."

His head rocked up and down as his face wore no expression.

"Try to calm yourself, Mrs. Reagan."

His eyelids closed as if weighted.

"When did he depart?"

He pulled a watch and consulted it.

"Did Dr. Spalding leave you a sedative?"

Pulling a fountain pen from his jacket, he clamped it between his teeth and unscrewed the cap with his free hand. He made notes on a pad.

"There is nothing for you to do."

His fingers drummed the desk.

"It's the Lord's will."

He stood up and pushed back the chair.

"I'll be there within the hour." He hung up and turned to Samson. "It's an old friend. I'm afraid I'll have to handle it myself." He draped an arm about Samson's shoulder as he led him to the door. "You've got a rain check for lunch. I know you understand." Samson was out of the room in seconds, negotiated the stairs two at a time and on reaching the street ran to his car.

CHAPTER FIVE

A s he waited for the vacancy in Jennings' building, Samson spent a good deal of time with the older man. They played golf a half-dozen times and dined together often. Since the first night they had dinner he was only able to pull out a few additional pieces of Jennings' background. One evening, however, after they had eaten and returned to the office for a drink and talk an incident occurred that opened Jennings wide. The phone rang as they got settled and Samson knew immediately it was Jennings' wife. The heated conversation ended when Jennings slammed the receiver after telling her he would get home when he damned pleased.

Still furious, he turned to Samson. "Don't make the mistakes I did!"

"We all make them."

"Not like mine," Jennings said. "I'm ingenious. Goddamned ingenious!"

"Is that why you left Kentucky?"

Jennings considered for a moment. "No," he said. That wasn't a mistake. I slugged a sadistic bastard of a teacher, cut out of school, figured what the hell, and kept right on going. It took me two day's walking, but I got to Louisville."

"Is that where you stayed?"

"Just a couple of days, then I moved on. For a year I kept going. Memphis, Nashville, then south to Atlanta and finally over to Raleigh. Never had trouble finding work, Sam. I was big and strong and I guess I was cheap. Anyway, after a year of shoveling horseshit on farms, hauling coal and ice, washing dishes and working on roads, I got fed up. So I headed north to Boston where I had an uncle, my mother's brother."

Samson knew Jennings was wound up now. "I guess Uncle Charley was expecting me. He sure didn't look surprised when I popped in. I told him I wanted to stay, that I wasn't going home. My aunt and he agreed to take me in and the next day I went to work in a restaurant he owned in Cambridge. Around the corner from Harvard and the Square. I worked there four years.

"I guess sometimes a man can't control what happens to him. It seems some people gravitate one way and some another. Maybe we give off signals too, sort of leave a trail. All I know is if you'd shake a tree near where I was standing nothing but dames would fall out." He was grinning now, trying as hard as he could to look and sound modest. "I don't want to sound like I'm bragging, Sam. But I guess I was what you could call good-looking. Tall, then. Didn't have this gut," he slapped at the roll of flab edging over his belt. "Had all my hair, and . . . well, I guess I must have been a sight." He paused and a smile touched a corner of his mouth.

Samson watched him and saw the lean young face now puffed with fat, the firm jaw that now dropped like a sack and the gray-green eyes beneath a once full shock of hair, buried now and looking like dark seeds in layers of wrinkled flesh.

Jennings sighed and continued. "Anyway, I had more ass in those days than most get in a lifetime. All them girls from the college. I guess they thought they were changing their luck. You know, with a guy from across the track. I slipped them all what they were after. I found out that high-class coozies were no different from the other kind—sometimes not as good. Until one day. . . .

"It was like lightning, Sam. She walked in, sat at the counter, looked up as I waited for her order and we connected. She came in the next day and the day after and then I started taking her out. Talk about a physical attraction—whew!" he marveled. "We never had enough of each other.

"When summer came she went with her family to their place at the Cape. I got a letter every day. Sizzlers. Then one day I got a phone call. It was from Beck, that was her name. Her folks were going back to town for a few days. She was going to be alone. I hustled up there and we never left the house. Right after that it happened."

Samson knew what was coming. "She got pregnant, and you got married."

"Before you could say Kentucky. And that," he said, leaning forward, "was my first mistake. You'd think I learned. Not a chance. More times than I like to think about, I made it legal. Marrying when all along I could have had it without a preacher." He heaved a sigh. "Anyway, Beck told her parents right away and I got a call from her father. He said he thought we should have an immediate conference. Beck hadn't told me much about her folks and was I in for a surprise.

"The house was a three-story gray thing in a swank neighborhood. Had ancestors hanging from every wall from the entry to the attic and not a smiling face in the lot," he laughed. "Boy, you should have seen that bunch when I walked in. Mrs. Hamilton was sitting on the edge of the couch stiff and cold like she was done in stone. Beck was standing at attention beside her and Mr. Hamilton was at the fireplace with one arm on the mantel. He was a little guy and I swear he was standing on his toes. Nobody moved a muscle until the servant shut the door. Then it began." Art started to shake his head.

"It was the damnedest thing, Sam. Everything went so smooth it was like it was rehearsed. You'd think old man Hamilton had a daughter knocked up every month. He got off his toes and walked to the center of the room. 'I'll be brief and to the point,' he began. Mrs. Hamilton didn't move a muscle and Beck began to cry. He turned around, looked at her and she stopped. Then he went on, laying it out like a campaign. He said a lot of things like family, reputation, and the usual stuff. Then he told me when we were going to be married, how it was to be done, and where we were going to live. He made it sound like I wasn't being roped into the family but that I was being allowed in, sort of knighted or something. He was a lawyer and compelling. Instead of turning to run, which is what I wanted to do, I found myself shaking my head in agreement to everything he said. I guess it was like in the army, like a private taking orders from a general. Before I left that day I had a wedding date, a new place to live, and a position instead of a job.

"I'd be lying if I told you I was too unhappy about the whole thing. I liked Beck well enough, and we sure hit it off in bed and selling real estate was better than wiping greasy spoons. That's what the old man did. Got me in the real-estate business. He said something like I had to be elevated from my present work and since I had no other training but did have a good appearance he thought real estate was the thing. Also, he had a friend in the business and would see to it I got set up."

Jennings went on to say that things worked out better than he expected. After his marriage his in-laws warmed up a bit and by the time the baby was born they were on fairly good terms.

"Everything worked out fine. I was even making money in real estate. Guess I had a flair. Then, in the middle of one night, Beck woke up complaining of a pain in her stomach. She had been having them for days but never so severe. We called the doctor and had her in the hospital in an hour. She died a couple of days later from a busted appendix."

For a while they both said nothing. Samson felt that no comment he could make would be as expressive as a reverent silence. Finally, Jennings sighed and continued.

"My father-in-law called another family conference. Mrs. Hamilton sat on the edge of the same couch, and he stood by the fireplace. This one was even shorter and more to the point. Little Beck was entitled to advantages I could not give, and they had a big home and would hire a nurse and I could visit anytime. It was settled. I was only twenty-one. How could I bring up a baby?"

Samson assured him he not only did the right thing but that it was an unselfish act. Before they parted Jennings made him promise to discuss with no one what he told him that night. From then on they were in touch with each other almost every day.

It was not long before the trust account at Ralph Thompson's bank lured a sleeper. Less than a month after Samson opened it, Thompson called, inviting him to lunch. Cautiously, he got down to business after Samson made it clear his appreciation would be more than verbal. The bank was putting a thirty-unit apartment house on Union Drive up for sale. A brochure was to be sent to the brokers in a week but it could be disposed of prior to publication if a deal was submitted that was in line with the trust department's idea of a fair offer. On the morning after their luncheon Samson picked up a prospectus. Though rundown, the price and terms justified spending the money necessary for rehabilitation. He made the offer as directed and the acceptance was confirmed the following day. They opened an escrow and the deal was recorded in a week. Thompson got a new golf bag with a hundred-dollar bill clipped to a note.

On the morning he became the official owner, Samson was down at the building to take possession. He inspected the outside, made notes on work to be done, and went in. To the left of the lobby was a small room furnished with two faded and torn overstuffed chairs separated by an equally dilapidated couch. Over a mahogany mantel that framed a false fireplace there was a Remington print in a cheap frame and in a corner, a desk was between a table that contained old magazines and a lamp with a parchment shade that tilted on its base. The wallpaper was gray with dirt and peeling in jagged strips. On the right of the entry was a dark oak counter, gashed and initialed, a row of wooden mail slots, an old desk scattered with papers, a ledger, and a dusty typewriter. All about him was the smell of stale sweat, dirty clothes, and garbage.

He hit the bell on the counter. Minutes later the manager lumbered out. He had been on his day off the week before when Samson made a quick check of the building and they had not met. Big, beefy, about forty, he appeared to have been yanked from bed by the bell. His face was covered with a dark stubble peppered with gray, long strands of thinned hair laid in all directions across a half-bald head that he scratched vigorously with one hand as he snapped his suspenders in place with the other. He had no shirt on and a yellowish flannel undergarment, half-buttoned, exposed a hairy chest.

"Did the bank call you?" Samson greeted him.

He blinked a couple of times, seemed to rummage through his thoughts, then he smiled and a hand shot out and clasped Samson's.

"You must be the new owner. I'm Jack Delaney."

"That's right. I took title this morning."

"Sorry, Mr. Duke, but I didn't expect you yet. It's kinda early."

He led Samson into his apartment, where the smells were more intense, the stink of home brew stronger than the rest. Clearing the only chair of a bundle of dirty clothes, he then moved helplessly about the room trying to tidy an unmade bed, a table littered with cigarette butts, beer bottles, and a crumpled newspaper. Then, glancing over his shoulder to the tiny kitchen just off the room to a sink piled high with dirty dishes, he threw up his hands in despair and flopped on the bed.

"I should have been ready for you," he said, shaking his head. "Had a friend in last night for dinner. Didn't get a chance to clean up."

Samson forced a smile, his mind made up to fire Delaney as soon as he pumped him about the building and its operation.

Delaney rose, selected a shirt from the closet. "There's so much work around the building one hardly gets time to clean his own apartment," he explained.

Samson removed a pad from his briefcase and started to question him. "What type of tenants do you have, Mr. Delaney?"

"Well," he began, rubbing his chin. "We got a few permanents. They been here for years. Mostly old ladies and men living alone. Some get pensions. Others get checks from their kids. They pay on the nose and no trouble. Then we got the others. In and out, in and out. Dishwashers, winos, a waitress or two. Those I gotta watch. I get the rent every week, sometimes even twice. You can't let them get into you for more than a week. If you do they'll skip and you're out." He rapped the table with a huge fist. "Knock wood, I've been here two years and nobody's left owing the bank a dime."

Remembering his experience with tenants and the kind he had to deal with it occurred to him that in spite of his first impression, Delaney might be what the building required. He questioned him further. "How many vacancies do you have now?"

He rapped the table again. "Not a one. Rented the only vacancy last night. You see, Mr. Duke, I got an advantage over the other buildings in the neighborhood."

"What's that?"

"I ain't afraid to handle certain kind of tenants. What I mean is, that if a guy comes in looking and he's a little loaded I'll rent to him. Provided, of course, he comes up with the money. The other buildings have women managers. They're afraid of these stiffs. So they turn them down. And then you get a dame, maybe she's a hooker and maybe she ain't. All I tell them is I don't care what they do, but just keep it quiet."

Samson made no comment and asked to be taken through the building. He was only able to see a few apartments since most of the tenants were at home but was pleasantly surprised to find them better furnished and cleaner than Delaney's. By this time he decided to keep him on until he found more reason than untidyness to make a change. After acquainting him with the method he required for keeping the records he left, more pleased with the buy than he had anticipated.

It had been nearly a year since the crash and in spite of Hoover's pleas for confidence, the country was heaving with a sickening lurch and what had been ripples were now swells. Farm income and carloadings were down sharply, suicides were up, so were bankruptcies and unemployment. Rooms were to be had for a dollar a day and mortgage bonds for a dime on the dollar, and there were no takers. The humor was grim and newspapers and billboards, magazines and radio talked about "a stiff upper lip" and "prosperity around the corner."

Though Samson felt the bottom had not been reached and prices had not yet flattened out, he was certain enough panic had been generated to enable one with a good eye and cash to ferret out the low apples. And he could afford to wait. It was apparent that the building and Delaney were a perfect match. After the first month there were still no vacancies and it looked like there would be a large net spendable. Though he climbed on Delaney for his untidiness he never pressed beyond the point where he felt there would be resistance. In the meantime Delaney would not let him paint or buy a piece of furniture.

"You would be throwing your money away, Mr. Duke," he told him one day when he had inspected a vacancy that had just come up. "If you paint and put up silk curtains and lay a bearskin rug you won't get a nickel more rent. They're bums and pensioners and they ain't got it."

On a morning in early December Samson received a call from Jennings telling him that the office would be ready the following day. His furniture was selected and ready for delivery, the carpet was waiting to be installed. By the following Monday he had the office painted, the carpet laid, and he moved in.

If he had chartered the real-estate business like a mathematician, engaged a wizard to calculate, and a good genie took his hand he could not have entered a lusher compound than Jennings' building. Unlike Walsh and Benjamin and even Bob Kinder, the men about him now took lessons from the past without wallowing in sticky nostalgia. He suspected that the mire of the Depression, which had knocked out the front-runners, was providing them with a footing more to their liking. They were using latent talents easy-dollar days never called upon. Realizing they were shrewd and not to be trusted, he found himself sharpening his own resourcefulness.

The real-estate firm of O'Connell and Ritchie had similar offices across the hall, and downstairs in what had once been the dining room of the old house G. B. Ward had set up an operation using a converted kitchen as an office for a secretary.

Phillips specialized in apartment houses; Cal O'Connell and George Ritchie ran a general business dealing with widows only. Their leads came from the obituary columns and they worked as a team with O'Connell doing the courting and Ritchie the leg work. A disease had wiped Cal O'Connell's body clean of hair, even to eyebrows and sideburns, which a clever wigmaker had replaced with sets that defied detection. The eyebrows were arched giving him a thoughtful expression and above them an iron-gray hairpiece with a soft wave and trim sideburns matched a mustache. He always wore dark expensive suits, was never without a boutonniere and pince-nez which had no correction but gave him a professional look. Never out of character, he always spoke in the hushed tones one hears at funerals or in the presence of a bereaved. In contrast, Ritchie, a stocky man with unruly hair and a total disregard for dress, was loud and vulgar and continually made course jokes about his partner's conquests.

G. B. Ward floated into Los Angeles in the middle twenties after a dozen years of rainbow chasing, selling Texas oil leases and Florida swampland, and settled in the real-estate business. Originally from a little town in west Texas, he combined a drawl with urbanity effectively, dressing for the role in tailor-made suits, a string tie, and a wide-brimmed hat with a narrow band. In spite of an aura of expansiveness and skill at check-grabbing he squeezed the last cent from a deal with malignant determination. His first job in Los Angeles was in the loan department of an insurance company. When the Depression hit, he took over the liquidation of the properties they were acquiring in foreclosure.

After months of dumping buildings to speculators, for which he received a small salary and a little graft, Ward decided he was on the wrong side. Quitting his job he set himself up in business and began using his contacts for his own account.

His office, almost as large as Jennings', was furnished like the library of a fine old house. One wall was covered by a map of the United States, with Texas occupying all but a third of the area. A big man, though disproportionate in size, with great quantities of flesh that hung loosely from his large bones as if he had been dipped and hung from his behind with everything running to a rounded belly, he had a full head of honey-colored wavy hair, which was always faultlessly oiled in place. This he cared for a dozen times a day with a comb he would whip from an inside pocket.

At first, Samson's appearance in the building brought a chilly reception from these tenants. O'Connell and Ritchie would keep their office door shut at all times, would cover listings they had on their desks, and suspend all telephone conversations when he was present. Roy Phillips, who by this time knew all about his trust account at Thompson's bank, did not know whether to treat him as a competitor or a client, and Ward ignored him completely. After a few weeks, he made a small deal with Phillips, bought a second trust deed at a discount from O'Connell and Ritchie, which they had taken for a commission, and got drunk with Ward one night in the company of Art Jennings. His acceptance was beginning.

Whether it was a change of heart or the effects of his own strategy, it appeared to Samson that Aunt Annie's attitude toward Harry Baldwin was beginning to undergo a qualitative change. During the evenings he spent with the two, Samson detected in his aunt's actions more than an attempt at civility. She was trying to please now and the evidence was many-coursed, carefully prepared dinners at the bungalow during which Baldwin's gorging and compliments of her cooking brought forth the affectations of modesty becoming to a good cook.

Her personal grooming, always neat but without distinction, now seemed geared to the better of her gifts. Her bob and shingle was always trim, the cut of a dress or blouse contoured the fine breasts and hips, and clung rather than covered all the other parts that would please the eye. Aunt Annie had turned the corner, he was sure, and though the end of the road was not in sight, Samson was damn sure where it would lead. Any lingering doubts were dispelled one night after the three of them had finished dinner. As Baldwin fished out a cigar, the doorbell rang. The visitor was Father Keenan of St. Julius, who had been invited for coffee and dessert. Surprised at the warm reception tendered the priest by his aunt, it became obvious to Samson by the end of the evening that Father Keenan was a frequent guest and that Aunt Annie's secularism had been halted. She appeared to be leaning back toward the Church on the strong arm of the priest. Knowing Aunt Annie's past feelings toward the Church, Samson was certain she had assumed her new role to be able to harmonize with the environment of enthusiastic religiosity in which Harry Baldwin was encompassed. He also learned that evening how generous Baldwin's contributions to St. Julius were, and how he, in turn, was the favored undertaker of the parish. The barter, Samson was sure, was not unprofitable.

Attended by Aunt Annie over cigars and coffee, Father Keenan directed the conversation deftly with Jesuitical skill. A youngish man with a disarming, pugnacious look, he was a baseball fan and a lover of earthy things. He combined Hollywood star talk with quotations from the missal, mild anticleric jokes, and even a ventured remark on the inconsistencies of certain Church dogma.

There was no doubt in Samson's mind that Father Keenan was guiding Aunt Annie with great care. Not once during the evening did Father Keenan question Samson on his church affiliations, but it was apparent he was preparing that terrain for a future assault. "The practice of religion," he pontificated, "must emanate from a strong need and desire from within—an accumulation of faith that would eventually lead to worship." Aunt Annie listened, not with the rapture of a firm believer, but with the intensity of a seeker of truth. After the coffee pot was emptied and the cigars reduced to ashes, Father Keenan rose to thank Aunt Annie for her hospitality. "I'll look forward to seeing you tomorrow morning at the early Mass." At the door just before departing he told Samson he hoped to meet him again very soon. Within a few minutes, Harry Baldwin eulogized the meal, complimented Aunt Annie on her new dress, and arranged to meet her for lunch the following day. Then he, too, left.

Samson was about to question Aunt Annie on her plans for marriage, the extent of her involvement with the Church, but she turned to him and placed a hand on his arm. "I'm very tired, Sam."

He started to ask for a few minutes more, but there was something in her look that told him she knew his mind, read it, and wanted no questions. It was as if she had decided on a course, was not certain of it, and wanted to feel her way without a push.

He decided as he drove home the deal between his aunt and Harry Baldwin was near closing. But there was always the danger of overselling. Going to weekly Mass and confession were fine, but if church attendance became a daily rite and Aunt Annie displayed other manifestations of fervor, Baldwin might suspect a show for his benefit. Then the allure of the chase might alter. After all, nothing adds more to a woman's desirability than the barrier to be scaled to her bed. He was going to stick close and see to it that this deal wasn't lost in escrow.

Although the new nose, with the magic it wrought to his ego and the adornment to his face, had been effective, Samson nevertheless found himself avoiding opportunities to campaign for the consummate piece of ass. It was as if the new wings were good to look at but untried, and to test them unsuccessfully would be more than he wished to chance. There was time, he figured; the right moment could not be far off. When it came he would know it and sense it. The risk of failure would be minimized. But in the meantime the juices were always flowing and were evident at night when he would lay fingering a stiff prick and in the morning when he would awaken with a hard-on. So, when Gloria called him at his office one morning explaining she reached him through Bob Kinder, purring a "let bygones be bygones" tune, and tickling his groin with an outright statement that she needed to be fucked, he made a date for that night and counted the minutes until he knocked at her apartment door.

After an enthusiastic endorsement of the result of the nose repair which produced such joy it almost brought him to tears, she swept aside all preliminaries and went for the target. Five minutes after he came into the room she grabbed his cock, which showed through his pants like a rod, led him to the bed, and proceeded to savor him like a condemned person would a last meal. All his previous experiences including those with Gloria became puerile compared to that night's exercises. Aided by her insatiable appetite, his imagination transcended all former bounds and unrestrained he touched upon areas of eroticism his most wanton thoughts never imagined. Even when he buried his new nose inside her cunt (a thing he swore he would never do), sniffing and licking like mad as she twirled around to find his cock with her mouth, his fired mind groped for an even rarer experience.

They lay together all that night, dozing off near dawn. When he finally arose it was ten o'clock and after showering hastily he dressed and left without a word. Feeling drugged and aching all over, he made his way to his apartment, fell into bed, and slept until early the following morning. When he arrived at his office that day there was a message from Gloria. Her tone was subdued when he reached her, she thanked him for the evening, and pressed for another date. Still battered, the furthest thing from his mind was a rematch. He was in a new business now and it needed all of his energies. He made a vague promise of a future date and said he would call the following week; her tone began to edge with petulance and then a bit of anger and she hung up.

Observing the operation of the other men in the building, Samson realized that Jennings' method was the most successful and he soon learned that system. Instead of working on one building at a time like the others, he would gather together listings from a dozen brokers, mail them to offices all over the city, and count on the law of averages to bring him deals. In this way his sources of listings were unlimited. He needed no buyers of his own and rarely had to show a property. It was a wholesale business and he was the middleman.

Rather than rely on mailings, Samson decided to refine Jennings' operation. He chartered a daily route and made each round once a week. Visiting a half-dozen brokers in the eastern part of the area in the morning, he would take what listings they were willing to submit, ask them what they were looking for, and make careful notes of their needs. After lunch he would canvass the western section of the city as far as Brentwood and do the same. Unlike Jennings, who would submit properties he had never seen, Samson made it his business to inspect every property he thought had merit. By the end of two months he was in contact with over fifty offices and found himself barely able to keep up with the action.

In spite of his vast personal contacts, he noted that Art Jennings, who relied on random exposure, was still making more deals and larger ones with only half the effort. Samson found himself on the phone continually, making appointments, showing buildings, and applying every ounce of effort he could produce, only to see deal after deal bog down and finally peter out for one reason or another. Cornering Jennings one evening, he decided to talk to him. It was after six and everyone else had left.

"Teacher," he began, falling into the chair beside his desk, "I need some advice."

"Better make it quick," Jennings said, looking at his watch. "My wife is due any minute. We're going to dinner."

"I make more phone calls, put in more miles driving, show more buildings than all of you put together and somehow I can't close a deal."

"You're doing all right."

"Not for seven days a week, ten hours a day."

Jennings looked at Samson thoughtfully for a moment. "Did you ever go fishing?" he asked.

"Yeah, when I was a kid, off the end of the pier."

"How did you do?"

"Sometimes good, sometimes not so good. What's that got to do with it?"

Jennings was enjoying himself now. Lighting a cigarette he sank to the back of his chair and rocked back and forth. "When I go fishing I always use two poles. I'd use ten if I had as many hands. But when I get a nibble on one I let go of the other and play the sucker until I sink the hook. When that live one comes along you must be able to feel it—sense it—smell it even. That's when you dump the others and close in. Of course it takes a lot of experience to develop the feel."

"And I guess you think you've got it," Samson said, falling into his mood.

Jennings held up both hands and spread his fingers, looking at them admiringly. "The ends of all of them tingle with it." All Jennings told him was the obvious. The real moves, gambits, he would have to find out for himself.

Samson was about to reply when he heard the front door open and shut, the clack of a woman's heels on the tiled entry. He turned to the entrance and stepping into its frame was an exquisitely dressed beautiful young girl. Long black hair framed an olive-tinted oval-shaped face, all of it flowed to a delicate throat below which a low-cut black dress revealed the edges of her breasts. He just stared and Jennings broke the moment of silence.

"Come in, come in," he said, with impatience.

She had been poised at the entrance and stepped into the room as if descending a pedestal. Without rising, and indicating her with a wave of his hand, Jennings introduced her. "My wife. Sam Duke."

"How do you do," she said, softly, fingering her gloves nervously. He thought he detected a trace of an accent.

On his feet he acknowledged the introduction, when Jennings rose and looked at his watch. "I guess we'd better go."

"Your dinner this evening, Art. Is it private?"

Jennings shrugged. "No, why?"

"I've nothing to do. And I owe you a dinner. How about you and Mrs. Jennings being my guests?"

Jennings slapped his shoulder affectionately. "Sure, why not. Where do you want to go?"

"Where would you care to eat, Mrs. Jennings?"

"Any place will do."

"I like Perino's," Jennings said. "Let's go."

They were placed in a corner booth and she was seated between them. Though he made every effort to keep the conversation alive with Art, Samson could not keep his eyes off her. All his attempts to draw her into the conversation were rewarded with fragmented answers and cold glances. He did learn, however, that she was born in Mexico City where her family still lived and that she graduated from the Marlborough School for Girls in Los Angeles and had been living in the city for seven years. Jennings kept talking about business, ignoring her completely. Samson kept an ear open but his mind and eyes on Mrs. Jennings.

The effect of meeting Art's wife was disturbing. None of his plans had provisions for serious emotional involvement, surely not with the wife of a man whose kite he was still tailing. As he drove home from the restaurant that night, with all the rationality he could summon cautioning him to forget the lady, he found himself providing ready answers to other questions that occupied his mind tantalizingly.

Mrs. Jennings was the most exciting woman he had ever met. Art obviously did not love or even care for her. Did he not slam the receiver and tell her he would be home when he goddamned pleased? Of course, it could have been a burst of anger, meaning nothing. But he did chase around and his treatment of his wife in the restaurant showed neither love nor affection. What about Mrs. Jennings? Even if Jennings loved her, what were her feelings toward him? She hardly smiled all evening, they barely addressed one another, and Samson got the feeling when they parted she was happy for his company—damn happy—and would look forward to seeing him again. Also, he would be immodest if he ignored the fact he was tall, now good-looking and half Art's age. As old as Mrs. Jennings.

He was in his apartment now, settled in his big chair, his feet were on the ottoman and his eyes were closed. Her face was before him, floating and blurred, and then it stopped and her eyes were sad and then she smiled and they lit up and her lips parted and began to move as if she were trying to speak and he found himself muttering, trying to think of her name. He opened his eyes and realized he did not know. It was not mentioned all evening. Or was it, and did he forget? No, he would remember.

The phone rang and he jumped up. It was Gloria. He answered coldly.

"You don't have to be so nasty," she said.

"I'm sorry."

"You sure can turn it on and off."

"I said I'm sorry."

There was a moment's silence. "Just wanted to say hello. See how you were."

"I'm fine. How are you?"

"Fine."

Another long silence. Then an idea began to formulate. "Are you busy tomorrow?" he asked.

"I'm free."

"How about coming to my apartment? You've never seen it. We can have a couple of drinks and go out to dinner."

She was delighted.

The following day he arranged to have lunch with Art. Avoiding any mention of the evening before or his wife he began to talk about Gloria.

"How would you like to do me a favor, Art, and get yourself the greatest piece of ass you ever had at the same time?"

At first Jennings eyed him suspiciously and then an uncontrollable smile spread across his face. "What's she got, the clap?"

Samson laughed.

"It's no gag," he said, and told the story of Gloria. Jennings listened, his face forged into a grin. "It's just that I've had enough and don't know how to get rid of her. And I know you can handle the situation a lot better than I."

"How old is she?"

"In her early thirties."

"Blonde, brunette?"

"Blonde."

"Nice body?"

"Perfect. Especially if you like them a little plump," he said, thinking of Mrs. Jennings' slender figure.

"Who doesn't. Nice tits?"

"If you like big ones. Can you get out tonight?"

"Of course," Jennings said, without hesitation.

"She'll be at my apartment at seven. We're supposed to have a few drinks and go to dinner. Get there a little after seven. Say, you just dropped in for a drink."

"Then what?"

"We'll all be drinking. She gets loaded pretty fast. I'll pretend to be drunk and be nasty . . . say something she won't like. Just enough to get her sore. You jump to her defense. I get angrier and tell you both to get the hell out. She's got her own apartment and the rest is up to you."

Gloria reached the apartment a few minutes before seven and by the time Art arrived she was coddling a glow in the middle of the second drink. Jennings insisted on leaving the moment he saw Samson had company, did such a thorough job of it that he had Samson pulling him away from the door as Gloria came to his aid.

"I didn't mean to interrupt anything," Jennings said, permitting himself to be escorted to a little bar Samson had set up.

"You're not interrupting a thing," Gloria said.

Samson poured Jennings a stiff drink, barely covered the bottom of his own glass and filled them with water. Gloria and Samson went to the couch and Art sat on the edge of a chair across the room, a foolish grin on his face.

"Are you in real estate too, Mr. Jennings?" Gloria asked.

"He's the best broker in town," Samson said.

"Far from it, Mrs. Tuberville."

"He's just modest, Gloria."

She rattled the ice cubes in her glass which she always did to signal for a refill. This time he poured two shots before putting in the Coke. Art was looking at her with open admiration and Gloria was smiling back at him. Samson handed her the drink and decided to get on with it, fearful that if it was delayed too long she would be too drunk to fight. "Sip this one slowly," he said. "It's all you're going to get."

She took the glass from his hand with an angry gesture and gulped it. "You're giving Mr. Jennings the impression I can't hold my liquor," she said. She added threateningly, "Aren't you?"

"Yeah . . ." Art drawled.

"It's not that," Samson said. He waved a hand as if brushing it off.

Art started to work fast. Crossing the room he grabbed the seat on the couch next to Gloria, put his hand about her shoulder and looked up at Samson belligerently.

"I'm sure, Mrs. Tuberville knows when she's had enough."

"Gloria," she said, turning to him with a smile.

"I'm sure Gloria knows when she's had enough."

She shook her head emphatically.

"All right," Samson said, throwing up his hands.

"He always does that, Mr. Jennings."

Jennings' hand was around her shoulder. "Why don't you fix yourself another drink, Sam, and relax."

"I've had enough."

"Well I haven't," he said, handing him his glass.

"Fix it yourself," Samson said, and stalked out of the room. He figured he would stay away for a few minutes and give Jennings time to work on her. As he waited in the bedroom he thought of Art's wife. He would have given anything to have been with her at that moment and here was her husband slobbering over Gloria like a dog passing up a steak for scraps.

When he returned to the room, Gloria was in the center of the floor executing a feeble shimmy and Art was applauding enthusiastically.

"She can really do it!" he said, looking up excitedly. Encouraged, Gloria went at it more energetically and succeeded in converting the dance to a series of bumps and grinds. Art grabbed her about the waist and they waltzed around the room. Breathless, Gloria stopped, reeled and would have fallen if Art had not held her up. She looked at him a little sheepishly, grinned, he smiled back, and they both started to laugh without control.

Now Samson was not sure whether Art was putting on a superb performance or was really drunk. He decided to finish it. "Don't you think you've both had enough!" he shouted.

They froze, Art stepped in front of Gloria and faced him. He gave him a smile and a wink. "No one tells me when I've had enough," he began. Now he was poking Samson's chest. "I make that decision."

"He's always like that," Gloria said, coming out from behind him. "Giving orders." She was glaring at him.

"You keep quiet," Samson said, pointing a warning finger.

"Don't you talk to her that way!" Art said.

"If you don't like the way I talk," Samson said, walking up to him threateningly, "you can get the hell out!" Then he whirled on Gloria. "And that goes for you too!"

She spun on her heel, grabbed her coat from the back of the chair, and headed for the door. Art opened it, followed, and slammed their way out. Samson poured himself a drink and toasted Mrs. Jennings.

Art Jennings was up the stairs and in Samson's office the moment he arrived the following morning. Grinning, and pacing the room like a restless stud, he recounted the whole evening. "What a night, what a night! The greatest piece I ever had. One of the greatest anyway. I picked up a couple of hamburgers and French fries at Simon's Drive-In and we went straight to her apartment. She couldn't wait! We had the sandwiches in bed and went to work. That dame can't get enough! On the bed, on the floor, and then we went into the kitchen for coffee and I swear she got me on the table. Then we got some music and started to dance— without a stitch on—and before you know it we were at it again." He stopped his pacing before Samson's desk. "I swear to God, Sam, I never got it so many times in one night in my life."

"I told you. . . ."

"Anyway," Art went on, "I gotta tell you something. Don't feel bad about palming her off on me." Samson started to protest, but he went on. "I don't mean you, I mean her feelings. Please don't get me wrong, Sam. I don't mean I'm a better man or anything like that. But she told me that you and she were through, and that she was up in your place last night like visiting a friend and that I shouldn't feel like I broke up anything."

"You didn't break up a thing."

"I'm resting up and going back," Jennings said, rubbing his hands. He pirouetted out of the room.

During the next few weeks Samson learned that Mrs. Jennings' name was Paula. He called their apartment several times, asking for Art when he was sure Jennings was not at home, embellished the image she had of him and soon they were addressing each other by first names. Also, he made it very clear he was looking forward to their next meeting. Though he sensed a reticence at first, their conversations later tended to linger and finally he was certain she had invested interest in his hopes. Night after night he would look at his mirror for traces of his former image, the sharp-faced visage stripped of ego. It still lurked behind the new façade but it was shadowy now, blotted by Dr. Gantner's creation. Damnit, Paula saw only what existed not what was before! She was going to be the test, the acid for his mettle and he was damn sure it would be unresisting.

Whether Aunt Annie's passion was disguised or real it manifested itself with action. She lent herself to every arm of the Church; the ladies auxiliary, nurse's aide, a mother at the Catholic orphanage, lay assistant to the mother superior at the local convent, and alto in the choir. Harry Baldwin's look was beatific and Father Keenan acted as if he had pocketed a convert. Every time Samson visited his aunt the priest seemed to be there. At first, Samson was delighted, certain now that the Baldwin-Boyle nuptials were not far off. One night, the wisdom of his matchmaking became questionable. He was present when the priest, Harry Baldwin, and his aunt comprised an ad hoc committee to which he was invited to celebrate the dedication of the Annie Boyle room at Catholic Hospital. A bottle of wine was donated by Father Keenan (procured from the church cellar), and consumed during a meatless Friday night dinner that Aunt Annie had prepared with her usual skill. It wasn't until after the meal when their bellies were warmed by the wine before Samson learned the extent of his aunt's generosity.

"It isn't often a woman of your meager means makes such a contribution," the priest said lifting his glass for a toast.

Harry Baldwin looked proud.

The priest lowered his glass and smacked his lips.

Samson looked at his aunt, to Baldwin, and then the priest. "What is the cost of a room?"

Father Keenan beamed. "Five thousand dollars."

Samson smiled and then calculated quickly. Aunt Annie had about fifty thousand dollars in the savings and loan association. The contribution represented ten per cent of her net worth. Enough to live on for two years. He looked at the two men and then at his aunt who sat with bowed head looking as humble as a novice. Could he have been wrong? Could Harry Baldwin have been nothing but bait to lure Aunt Annie's small fortune into the sticky hands of the Church? Was he a professional Catholic! Was his aunt mad? Or was this gesture the final gambit to lure Harry Baldwin into marriage. Now he was not sure who held the trumps and named the game. Of course if she married the undertaker it made no difference. He must be worth a fortune. But suppose it did not come off and her feelings toward the Church were genuine. The sons of bitches could siphon off her last cent! Aunt Annie could become a dead-broke fanatic handed over to him to support.

He looked at the faces of the three of them hoping for a sign. The priest radiated contentment, the look of a winner in his grin. His aunt and the undertaker were eyeing each other with joy, her hand on the table trapped by his paw.

Father Keenan poured a round of wine emptying the bottle, leaned back as he sipped contentedly and then turned to Baldwin. "I think now is as good a time as any to give you a bit of news." Baldwin released Aunt Annie's hand and looked at the priest expectantly. Father Keenan looked at Aunt Annie then at Samson in an obvious move to rivet their attention and continued. "I did not want to tell you yet, but it seems a certainty." Harry Baldwin placed the wine glass on the table and leaned forward. The priest smiled mysteriously, slowly sipped the wine, wiped his lips carefully with a napkin and then wreathed his face with a solemn look. "I was at the chancery today. Bishop Cassidy is proposing you for papal knighthood."

All the fat in Harry Baldwin's face shifted into a smile. He shook his head, seemed unable to speak, then blurted, "I can't believe it! I just can't believe it!" He turned to Aunt Annie and took both of her hands. "I can't tell you what this means to me, Annie. They've only conferred two knighthoods through our chancery in three years. Howie Brandon down at the bank and Sam Tuttle at Empire Iron and Steel. Now me!" He leaned back, overcome.

"When will we know, Father?" Aunt Annie asked.

"It'll take awhile. Maybe a few months. A petition is sent to an agent in Rome. He presents it to the Cardinal Chancellor of the Orders."

"What order is it?" Aunt Annie asked.

"St. Gregory."

She turned to Baldwin. "I'm so happy for you, Harry."

"It will mean so much to us," he told her.

Samson wondered how much it would mean and then addressed the priest.

"What do they do?" he asked.

"Who?"

"In Rome. With the petition."

"It's processed. They investigate to see if the nominee is worthy."

"I'm sure he deserves it, Father," Aunt Annie blurted.

"I'm sure he does," Father Keenan said.

Though Samson knew nothing of papal knighthood he assumed it carried with it certain responsibilities. And he realized that Aunt Annie's role as Mrs. Baldwin would have to be supported by full-hearted adherence to the Church. Lip service would no longer be accepted as a substitute for attendance or skepticism for belief. He left that night unable to determine whether the events he witnessed forecast joy or despair. If Harry Baldwin's generosity was as expansive in marriage as in courtship he had nothing to fear; on the other hand if after nabbing Aunt Annie he displayed a tight fist there could be trouble ahead. It looked like Father Keenan had a bead on the finish line and was hustling.

When Samson arrived at his office the following morning he found the priest waiting for him.

"Was in the neighborhood. Thought I'd visit. That is, if you have a few minutes."

Samson assured him he had some time and the priest followed him to the office. After commenting on the attractiveness of the room and the apparent success of one so young, the priest settled in a chair, bit the end of his cigar, and came directly to the point.

"I'll be brief, Samson," he began, seeming to savor the use of the full name. "It appears that your aunt and Harry Baldwin will marry. A blessing, I may add, for my old friend." Samson was watching him carefully, studying the face for the true import of his words. The most expressive feature of the priest's was eluding, for he had busy brows that swirled about his eyes which always seemed to be in hiding. "It was not difficult to lead your aunt back to the True Faith," he continued. "She was in darkness and only needed light. Her transformation is a joy to me."

"She has changed," Samson said.

"For the better you can be sure." Ignoring Samson's lack of confirmation, Father Keenan continued. "However, all this is evident and is not what I wish to discuss." He raised his brows and his eyes tuned to a modest smile. "I'm here to try to herd a stray."

Though Samson knew what he meant he looked at the older man with surprise. He was not going to make it easy for the priest, wasn't going to make anything easy for him. "I don't understand," he said.

Father Keenan took time to light his cigar. "Papal knighthood is the highest honor the Church can confer on the laity. That Harry Baldwin will be so honored is almost a certainty. He has earned it. However, soon you will be one of the family. To be honest, Samson, I am here to ask for and confer a favor."

"If there is anything I can do I would be happy to," Sam asserted.

The priest studied him for a moment, as if evaluating the extent of his sincerity. Samson relaxed, certain he had the priest on the defensive. "There is something you can do. For yourself and the faith. And my reward will be your everlasting piety."

"Just what is it?"

Samson could see that his feigned confusion was beginning to anger the priest. No longer smiling, Father Keenan went on, suggested that Samson's heretical tendencies were disturbing to Mr. Baldwin and to his aunt as well. Samson assured him that he had a misconception of his religious leanings and that his hesitation was motivated by a cautiousness he found himself incapable of displacing with blind faith, and that once convinced with proof of the dogmas he felt had not been explained his devotion might become impervious to secular assault. He delivered this with a serious face, accenting it with a tone that suggested a plea for clarification. By God, he was enjoying himself. If Father Keenan thought he was a pushover it was apparent by the look on his face that his mind had been changed. He watched him calmly as the Father eyed him for a moment, bit into his cigar, and spoke. "What are the answers you want?" he asked, smiling again.

Samson decided to ask the important question and proceeded with a careful formulation. "Although I am sure that the existence of God is incontrovertible, it has never been explained to me."

Father Keenan eyed him with a pitying look and then, as if resigned to dealing with a raw heretic, proceeded. "Would it not be easy to worship God if evidence of His existence was indisputable?"

Samson agreed it would be simpler.

"Simpler, yes. But without faith."

"I don't understand."

"God, in His goodness wants Himself served through faith. Without it where would the worshiper derive the glory of serving Him without proof of His existence?"

"But if the worship of God is desirable and He wishes all men to pay Him homage, why doesn't He reveal Himself to those who doubt His existence?"

"To do as you suggest would only deprive man of the faith that is necessary to comprehend the virginity of Holy Mary, the infallibility of the Holy Father, and other mysteries of the True Church that are beyond human understanding." He sat back and eyed Samson carefully.

Samson pretended to think upon the words. The conversation had gone far enough. He had no desire to antagonize the priest. Aunt Annie's dilemma was not yet resolved and until it was, he wanted Father Keenan fighting for his soul with some assurance of success.

"You've given me something to think about, Father," he said, rising.

Father Keenan seemed pleased, shook his hand warmly. "Perhaps after you attend Mass some day, we'll talk more."

He was clever, Samson thought. Aunt Annie was no match for him. Well, she could remain in the Church, marry Baldwin or not; but one thing he was certain of: her money was his legacy, not theirs. And he was going to make damned sure it remained that way. He would see her immediately, nail down his rights, then there could be a free-for-all for her soul.

As he passed Art Jennings' office on his way out he heard him talking on the phone and realized the conversation was with Paula. "There are some papers for you to sign. They're at the escrow department at the Bank of America on Hollywood Boulevard. No, I can't bring them home. They've got to be signed by noon. Be there at eleven." Samson slipped out the front door. Aunt Annie could wait.

Reaching the bank a little before eleven he saw her entering the escrow booth and waited until she came out. Her smile was instant. Encouraged, he invited her to lunch. She hesitated, then accepted, and they headed down Hollywood Boulevard for Musso's. The noon crowd had not yet arrived and they settled in a rear booth. Not a word had been said since they left the bank and he sensed an air of anxiety about her.

"You seem worried."

She lowered her eyes. "Sometimes lunches can't be explained."

"I'll tell Art I bumped into you."

"Please," she cautioned, reaching out and touching his hand. "Promise me you won't."

"Is he that jealous?" he said, laughing.

She shook her head and sighed. "He doesn't have to know."

"I won't say a word," he assured her, delighted she was capable of deception. She appeared to relax a little and unbuttoned a light coat she was wearing, released her arms and draped it about her shoulders. He found it difficult to take his eyes from her exquisite throat and expanse of breast exposed by the low-cut dresses she seemed to fancy. They ordered and he decided to waste no time and find out as much about her as he could. He wove his questions casually with tales of himself.

"I always wanted to visit Mexico," he said. "Even when I was a kid back in New York."

"It's a beautiful country, but very poor."

"I guess all countries are poor right now."

She shook her head. "You do not know poverty in America."

"Did you live in Mexico City?"

"No. Cuernavaca."

"What does your father do?"

"He was in politics. He's dead," she added sadly.

He changed the subject and made up stories about his childhood. She began to question him about New York with the excitement of a child wrangling a favorite tale from an adult.

"I've wanted to go there more than any other place."

Now that she was more at ease he turned the conversation to where he wanted it. "How long have you been married to Art?" he asked.

"Four years."

"You must have been pretty young," he said. "You and I are about the same age," he added.

"I was nineteen." They were on their coffee now and she was stirring the cup absently.

"Art's a great guy," he said, smiling. "How did you meet him?"

"He knew my father. They met once in La Paz. Art was on a fishing trip, I think. My father came to Los Angeles a lot on business. They became friends. We met when I came to Los Angeles to school."

She looked at her watch. "I must go," she said, abruptly.

He walked her to the parking lot and stood beside the car as she got in. "I'm looking forward to this again."

Withdrawing her hand from his, she went off without saying a word.

By the time he pulled in front of Aunt Annie's he had gone

over every moment of the lunch with Paula and read into them all the promise he hoped for.

As he entered the house, Aunt Annie was coming in from the garden carrying a bunch of roses. There was something about the contrast between the fresh picked flowers she held to her breast and her appearance that startled him. He had always thought of her as ageless, no different than the image of his first memory of her. Though her hair had become sprinkled with gray, it had been so gradual it passed unnoticed. Now, as she walked through the kitchen clutching the blossoms, her face unmade, his attention was caught by a slower step and sagging breasts. When she reached the parlor and began to arrange the flowers in a vase, a ray of sunlight speared the room and he examined her face. There were wrinkles he had never seen, lines bitten deep along the sides of her mouth, pinching her face and wearying it. Even her voice, always a ring, was dull.

He asked if she were ill.

She looked at him with surprise. "No, why?"

He shrugged. "You look tired."

"Did you ever feel," she said, "that the hill wasn't worth the climb?"

He looked at her, puzzled.

"I *am* tired. It seems I've been treading water all my life." She sighed. "I want to put my feet on solid ground." She walked into the kitchen and he followed. "I'm tired of fighting for what I want—for what I believe is right." She put a kettle on for her tea. "Next birthday I'll be forty-eight. You're gone. I don't want to live alone any longer." She closed her eyes as if shutting out the prospect. Then she looked at him for a long moment. "Harry wants to get married. Right after he's made a Knight of St. Gregory. Wants our honeymoon to be sort of a celebration."

"That's wonderful!" he cried, embracing her. "He's a great guy!"

She patted his cheek. "I guess he is. Anyway it's the only alternative. I've got a lot of changing to do. The Church is very important to Harry. With what is going to happen, it will be his whole life. And it will have to be mine."

"But how do you feel about it? That is, do you believe?"

"I'm trying hard. I have to believe in something. The Church is as good as I have found."

"There is nothing wrong with it, Aunt Annie." Now he came to the point. "But you have to be practical. That contribution you made for instance. It was a fine gesture, but you have to put a limit." Then he laughed lightly. "You know the Church. They'll take all they can get."

"What better thing can I do with my money? Sick people, children? Anyway, Harry has enough for both of us."

"But you have to think of yourself. Suppose . . . well, suppose the marriage doesn't work. It happens, you know," he hastened to add. "What then?"

She patted his arm. "I'll make it work. I know Harry by now. With all his faults we'll get along. Anyway, it's all settled. I've agreed to join my money with Harry's. He plans to retire soon, sell out, and we'll work together and give to the Church."

He panicked. That money was his. It would have been when she was gone. Now it was going into a pot along with Baldwin's. And if she died first? Samson ran the risk of being cut off without a dime! It was a lot of money. Thoughts began to prowl his mind like caged wild animals. What a fool he had been!

"You can't do it!" he blurted.

She looked at him with surprise. "Can't do what?"

"I won't let you put your money in with Harry Baldwin's. You've got to be protected. Anything can happen. Anything!" She shook her head in bewilderment. He took her by the arms. "Listen to me . . . tell Harry Baldwin the money is invested . . . with me . . . in a building, that you can't get it right away. He'll understand. That'll give you time . . . to see what happens . . . if everything is all right. I have a trust account. You can give me the money, it'll be safe and then when you're sure of everything you can do what you want."

"But I *am* sure."

"You're not! You're buying yourself companionship and the Church is getting a legacy." Now he tried another tack. "Harry Baldwin should worship you if you came to him in rags. Damnit, Aunt Annie, you don't have to buy a husband!"

She looked at him with horror and ran into the parlor. He followed. Realizing he might have gone too far he now spoke softly. "I'm only thinking of you. You're not sure of the Church, you're not sure of Harry Baldwin. Why give up what you've taken a lifetime to accumulate?"

"I am sure of Harry. As for the Church . . . it's really all I have."

He was about to tell her she had him but even the thought rang false. There was no use, his aunt's stubbornness always took on sinew when pressure increased.

From then on, Samson stayed close, visiting her two and three times a week, waiting for an opening. He neglected his business, almost forgot about Paula.

Aunt Annie seemed to be slipping into a state of euphoria, her spirit diminishing with her new dependence. She never missed a day in Church, read the missal constantly, her reference to God was more frequent and was accompanied by a tone of veneration she had never displayed. A feeling of helplessness came over Samson as he watched her, drifting slowly beyond his reach.

And Harry Baldwin was a different man, too. His piety was now a garment he never removed, as if to do so would reveal a chink in the armor of his religiosity. He trapped his beads like a monk, carrying them wherever he went sighing Our Father's and Hail Mary's through the day. His eyes held the fever of a holy man. Long before he could reasonably expect to hear from Rome, he would call Father Keenan at least once a day.

Finally, Samson stopped going to the house. Watching them was too painful, his impending loss too traumatic. He kept in touch by phone and buried himself in a press of business activity.

He had opened an escrow for the purchase of a ten-unit bungalow court in Hollywood and had been stalling the final approval of the inventory and rent statement. The seller, three installments behind on his mortgage payments and threatened with foreclosure, had been calling Samson daily, pleading for the approvals. Samson used every stalling tactic he knew as he waited for a resale through the same escrow Cal O'Connell was near ready to close. Unless Cal made that deal Samson had no intention of completing the purchase. The building was rundown and half-vacant. Cal's client was to trade a clear home in Santa Monica for the equity in the bungalow court. Cal had a buyer for the house for six thousand, was paying Samson thirty-five hundred, and was picking up the difference for himself. Cal's client, an old lady anxious to close the deal, was unable to do so until the final probate of her husband's will. This was expected momentarily and Samson had been hounding O'Connell daily as he waited for the word. He nabbed him one morning after hanging up on his seller who had stopped pleading and was threatening. O'Connell was at his desk, adjusting a fresh flower in his lapel.

"We'll probably hear today," he said.

"My seller is ready to pull out of the deal," Samson said.

Without a word, O'Connell picked up the phone and dialed. Eyes closed O'Connell started to speak. "Good morning, Mrs. Fraser," he crooned. "Cal O'Connell." He smiled sweetly. "You *did* recognize my voice?" He looked bored. "I've been thinking of you too. I enjoyed the evening too. Look, Mrs. Fraser, have you heard from the attorney?" He sat up and his eyes lighted. "This morning? That's wonderful. I was worried about your losing the deal." He looked at his watch. "I'll bring the agreement out within an hour." Disappointment spread across his face. "All day? How about this evening? Can I come out this evening?" He listened for a few moments. "All right. At nine tomorrow morning. For breakfast." He hung up. "She can go ahead. The attorney just called. I'm seeing her in the morning."

"When do you think we can close?"

"My end is set up. I've already got her house cashed out through an escrow in Santa Monica."

"What about the mechanics?"

"The seller of the bungalow court deeds his property to you. He gets twenty-five hundred dollars for that. You deed it to Mrs. Fraser then she deeds the house to you, okay? Then you sell the house to me for thirty-five hundred dollars and I in turn sell the house to my buyer for six thousand." He rubbed his hands. "Everything falls into place neatly. Mrs. Fraser ends up with the equity in the bungalow court. Your man gets his price. My man gets the house. You end up with a thousand profit, and I make twenty-five hundred. Simple." He rummaged through a folder on his desk and handed Samson a sheet of paper. "Here's Mrs. Fraser's full name and the legal description of her house. Get it to the escrow and have them draw all the documents. Meet me at her house tomorrow morning at nine. We'll have breakfast." He gave Samson the address and Samson left for the bank. Though O'Connell was making more than twice as much as he, Samson could hardly resent it. He'd been romancing the old lady for a month and had the buyer for her house. All Samson did was put up a hundred dollars option money.

O'Connell's car was pulling up in front of the house when Samson arrived the following morning. It was a rambling one-story bungalow set far back from the street. A well-groomed garden, shaded by a pair of live-oaks and a huge pepper tree, was set off by a white fence that encircled the entire property. On a long, narrow porch, a couple of rockers and a swing were almost hidden by a series of hanging plants strung across the front. He handed Cal the papers and they headed for the door.

The usual somberness of O'Connell's dress was set off that morning with a dark gray hat snapped rakishly at the side which matched a pair of gloves he carried in his hand together with a tiny bunch of violets.

"Let me do the talking," he cautioned, as he rang the bell. They waited a long time and then the door opened. At first Samson could not see Mrs. Fraser, who was obscured by the gloom of a darkly paneled entry. It was not until he entered and his eyes became accustomed to the unlighted hall that he saw a shrunken figure, topped by frizzled blonde hair, teetering on a pair of high heels. O'Connell took her hand and bent from the waist.

"Good morning, Mrs. Fraser. You look as fresh as these," he said, handing her the bunch of violets.

She took them and smiled coquettishly, and then, seeing Samson for the first time, stepped back gripping the flowers nervously.

"This is my associate, Mr. Duke."

He muttered an acknowledgment. O'Connell sniffed the air like a beagle. "Mmm, that coffee smells good."

Mrs. Fraser led them to a small breakfast room, heavily curtained and darkened, that was separated from the kitchen by a pair of cupboards lined with potted plants. The table was set for two, she hastily placed a third setting and went into the kitchen.

"I brought Mr. Duke with me to take the signed papers to the escrow," O'Connell called out. "Then we can visit." He began to remove the papers from his case.

Mrs. Fraser came into the room, looked at Samson, shifted a nervous glance to O'Connell, and then, wetting her shriveled lips began to speak.

"Mr. O'Connell, I must talk to you. Something has happened."

Cal, who was shuffling the papers, placed them on the table and looked up at her. "What is it, Mrs. Fraser?" he asked softly.

"I had a dream last night, Mr. O'Connell."

"A dream, Mrs. Fraser?"

She shook her head. "I don't remember it all. But somewhere in it, God came to me."

"God?"

"Yes." She was looking upward now. "He was talking to me. At first I couldn't hear what he was saying." She lowered her head.

"Then what happened?"

"He came closer and then I heard it clear."

Cal cleared his throat. "What did God say, Mrs. Fraser?"

"He told me not to make the deal," she said sadly.

For a single instant, O'Connell's eyes showed shock. His face turned white, then, just as quickly he became composed and his color returned.

"I'm sorry. . . ." Mrs. Fraser was muttering. "I'm sorry. . . ."

Now, O'Connell was smiling broadly and reached across the table and took her hand. "Mrs. Fraser," he said. "I have wonderful news for you."

"Yes . . . ?"

He was stroking her hand. "I had a dream, too, last night. It was after yours. And God came and told me to tell you he changed his mind." He gave her hand a final pat and sat back, smiling.

For a moment she looked at him as if trying to comprehend and then her face lit up with all the life she could muster. "Oh, Mr. O'Connell, are you sure?"

"Never more sure in my life!"

"I'm so happy," she said. "I did so want to make this deal." She turned to Samson. "And I didn't want to disappoint Mr. O'Connell." She headed for the kitchen. Samson was so overcome with admiration he couldn't say a word.

In a few minutes Mrs. Fraser returned with a pot of coffee, freshly made biscuits, and a dish of marmalade and jams which she placed in the center of the table.

"Mr. Duke's had his breakfast," O'Connell said. "Why don't we get the papers signed now so he can be off to the bank?" He fanned them out and handed her a pen. She began to scratch her name on each document as he held a finger to the space. "We'll have a leisurely breakfast when it's finished," he added. He snatched the papers when the last one was signed and Samson was on his way. He delivered them before noon and returned to the office. O'Connell was already there. Samson walked up to his desk and extended his hand.

"You were great!"

George Ritchie was slouched in a chair cleaning his nails. "That one was a cinch."

"What do you mean, a cinch?"

"Dreamers are easy."

"She was telling me about her dreams for weeks," O'Connell said. "It didn't come as a complete surprise."

"When they rely on fortune tellers, astrologers, tea leaves, and even coffee grounds," Ritchie said, "that's when it gets tough."

O'Connell chuckled. "The toughest one I ever had was a spiritualist. She'd go to a seance once a week and communicate with her dead husband. Remember that one?" he said, turning to Ritchie.

"That was a beauty. We were taking in ten clear lots in Brentwood for a lousy two-thousand-dollar equity in a dump on Alvarado Street."

"Every time I'd get her ready to sign up," O'Connell went on, "she'd get another message. It went on for weeks. Finally, she called me up one morning after a session with the medium and told me the deal was off. Her dead husband said he didn't like the deal and he didn't like me, either. Since I never met the man when he was walking around and didn't know a soul in the spirit world, I got suspicious."

Ritchie interrupted. "The goddamn medium had a real-estate license and was working through an office on La Brea. Can you imagine anyone digging up deals that way!"

Later that day Samson sauntered into Art Jennings' office and found him on the phone. He had the same foolish grin on his face he'd had that day he'd sat across from Gloria in Samson's apartment. Jennings cupped the mouthpiece with his hand. "It's Gloria." He waved Samson to a seat. As he listened, the grin became broader and soon the first sounds of a chuckle came from his throat. Reaching for a cigarette with one hand, he beckoned Samson for a light. He took a drag, almost choked, crushed the cigarette in the tray, the grin disappeared and a strange look spread across his face. "Save it," he said, his voice hoarse. "Be ready noon on Friday." He hung up, for a moment seemed oblivious to Samson's presence, then turned to him. "Do you know what she was doing?"

"What?"

"Giving me a preview of coming attractions. Got herself undressed, flopped on her back, had my hand on her boob, her hand on my cock, and if you hadn't come in I would have fucked her on the telephone!" He rubbed his hands. "What a dame! I'm taking her away for the weekend. Told Paula I have to go to San Francisco on a deal." He was grinning like a kid on his way to a circus.

The following Friday, Samson watched as Jennings left for the day, just before noon. Quitting the office at five, Samson went home, showered, and dressed carefully. At a few minutes before six he was ringing the doorbell at Jennings' apartment. Paula greeted him with a look of surprise and after a moment's hesitation invited him in.

"I've been trying to reach Art all afternoon," he said. "Thought I'd catch him home."

The living room was richly furnished in period French. With the exception of a massive desk that must have been Art's touch, everything else was delicate: slender-legged tables and figurines, silk and down, pinks and powder blues, frothy curtains, and a graceful spinet.

Samson sank into the thick cushions of the sofa and lit a cigarette before Paula overcame her initial surprise.

"Do you mind if I wait?"

She was standing in the center of the room with a puzzled expression. "But, Art's not home. He's not coming home."

"Where is he?"

"San Francisco on a deal."

Samson stood up. "I guess my business will have to wait. When did he say he'd be back?"

"Sunday night, I think . . . or Monday morning." Paula followed him to the door.

He had his hand on the knob, then took her arm and led her back into the room. "I want to ask you a favor."

"What is it, Sam?"

"Do you mind if I sit down?"

"No, please."

He went back to the sofa and she joined him, sitting on the far end with her hands folded in her lap.

"I closed a big deal yesterday and owe myself a celebration. I hate eating alone. Would you have dinner with me?"

She lowered her head and stared at her hands. "I can't," she whispered.

"Why?"

"I'm married, Sam, that's why," she said, looking up at him.

"What's that got to do with it? I'm a friend of the family. I'll tell Art I came by to see him, didn't know he was out of town, found you alone, and took you to dinner. What's wrong with that?"

"You can't tell Art," she said.

"Then you'll come?"

"I didn't say that."

He reached over and took her hand. "Is there anything wrong in having dinner with a friend?" Her eyes were on him. "Come on," he pleaded. "Join me for dinner."

"Where will we go?"

"Any place you say."

She hesitated and he pressed on. "There's a place near the beach. Nobody ever goes there. It's not fancy but the food's good. Do you like fish?" She nodded. "The best fish in town. And you don't have to dress. Just anything." There was a hesitation, then a smile.

"Give me about twenty minutes," she said. "There's a drink in the kitchen cupboard." He found the bourbon, poured himself a drink and then thought about Art. What a fool! Leaving this for Gloria's boobs and her slobbering kisses, crying jags, and hangovers. Returning to the living room he poked his head through the doorway and called down the hall.

"Can I fix you a drink?"

"There's some sherry in the kitchen," she called back. "I'll have a glass." He found the wine and brought the drink to the bedroom door.

It was a warm night as they sped down Sunset Boulevard and headed for the beach. Below, the city began to turn on its lights, to the north the mountains were already etched in black, and ahead, the western sky still glowed from the last of the sun. Dressed in a simple suit, flat-heeled shoes and a beret, Paula looked like a schoolgirl in a uniform.

He reached over and she allowed him to take her hand. All during the drive neither said a word.

The restaurant jutted over the sand. The tide was high and the building shuddered as each wave crashed against the pilings. Two spotlights, beamed from the edge of the roof, shone on the surf as it swirled around a mass of rocks and then rushed in eddies back to the sea. It was nearly eleven o'clock and they were the last customers. He'd paid the check earlier and the waiter left. Now the owner turned off the sign and was in the kitchen cleaning up. As they left, Samson put his hand around her waist while they walked to the car.

All during the dinner they had skirted the edges of their thoughts and talked of generalities. Then he began to probe, question her. She was evasive at first, her answers were short, curt, but then the story came—all of it—and by the time they left the restaurant she told him what he wanted to know.

Driving home, she sat close, her head on his shoulder. The scent of her was all about him—perfumed hair, the subtle smell of her skin—and her hand stroked his like the brush of a wing. They drove in silence and he began to arrange the pieces of her story and those parts about Art that were new.

All her life she had been protected. When her father died he left a large family and with the exception of a small income from property in Cuernavaca, barely enough for them to exist. She was in her last year in the Marlborough School. On learning of her father's death, she'd turned to Art, the only adult she knew in the

States. He was kind and protective. He paid for her trip to the funeral and was on hand when she returned. Soon she was graduated and the time came for a decision. Mexico offered little and Art was standing by. They were married shortly afterward and Art brought her mother up for the wedding. It was a little shocking, she confessed, that day they stood before the altar with her mother at her side. She was a beauty, too, and three years younger than Art. There was no honeymoon and her mother stayed with them for two weeks and returned to Cuernavaca.

It was not until they were married a few months before Art told her about his first marriage and his daughter in the east. She also learned there were two other marriages that ended in divorce. This she found out one night during a heated argument. "And they were both younger than you!" Art had shouted. One was only eighteen.

They pulled up in front of the apartment and as he turned to get out of the car she drew him back, circled his neck with her arms and kissed him. Her mouth was open. He found her tongue and her body trembled. Now she dug her fingers into his neck and began to sob.

"Paula . . . let's go inside."

She pushed herself from him and buried her face in her hands.

"Paula, listen to me . . ."

She looked up.

"Let me take you in," he said, putting his hand on her arm. She shook it off and reached in her purse for a handkerchief. "Let's go inside," he repeated softly.

"Don't even take me to the door."

"Why?"

She was calmer now. "Because we'll both be sorry."

"For what? Feeling this way and doing something about it?"

"And what comes after that, Sam?"

"What do you mean?"

"After tonight, and other nights."

He grabbed her arms and turning her toward him, "I don't know what comes afterward. And I don't care."

She twisted from him. "But I do."

"Why don't you give yourself a break?"

"A break?"

"Sure. For once in your life—just once—do something you feel like doing." He started to reach for her and she was out of the car. She slammed the door and poked her head through the window.

"Don't be angry with me, Sam. I'd like to have you come in. And I'd like to see you tomorrow and the day after." She shook her head. "But it won't work." Then she was gone.

Laden with groceries for a banquet breakfast he was there before nine the next day. He was not going to give her time to cool or think. There would be no doubt in her mind about his intentions. He began to suspect there would be conditions and he was prepared to negotiate.

Paula met him at the door clad in a long robe. Her hair fell below her shoulders and her face shone without makeup. "I thought you'd like a little breakfast." He extended the bags of food. She hesitated a moment, clutched her robe about her throat, and stepped aside without a word. He headed for the kitchen. She stood in the doorway as he emptied the packages on the table. Now he turned to her.

"Did you sleep well last night?" he began.

"I didn't sleep at all."

"You look so lovely."

She dropped into a chair wearily and looked up at him. "Why did you come, Sam?"

"I couldn't stay away."

"You'll have to go."

"I'm not leaving."

She walked into the living room and he followed. All her listlessness seemed stripped as she turned and faced him. "I want you to leave now."

"Didn't last night mean anything?"

"I didn't close my eyes. I thought about every minute of it."
She was clutching her robe in tight fists. "Thought of what might
have happened and was sorry it didn't. At midnight I wanted to
call your apartment. Then I thought some more. Then I was
afraid."

"Of what?"

She just looked at him, shaking her head.

He saw the round edge of her breast, the shimmering satin of
her nightgown. Grabbing her arms he drew her close. She began
to struggle and he gripped her tighter. "I want to feel and not
think. All my life I've done it the other way." She tried to push
him away. "You've done the same. Reasoned yourself into a marriage, and what have you got? Damnit, you've used your head all
your life!" She stopped struggling. "Feel, Paula. Christ, feel for
the first time!" He had his hands under her robe and felt the soft
flesh as she pressed against him.

He did not leave the apartment until five o'clock the following
morning. As he drove home, the eastern sky was tinted gold, the
smell of the new day mingled with the scent of Paula that was all
about him. All his previous conceptions of women were shattered.
She would rise from the bed and whirl in a dance, her satin body
aglow in the soft light. Then she would croon a sad Spanish song
and then she would become gay and beat a wild step and her head
would sway and her hair would flow and finally she would return
to the bed and lie beside him and her breasts would rise and fall as
she panted and he smelled her sweet hot breath. It was as if all her
life she had prepared for this night.

He awoke late Sunday afternoon and called the apartment. Art
answered the phone, friendly and gay. After offering a logical excuse for the call, Samson hung up satisfied Art knew nothing. On
Monday morning Art cornered him in his office and gave a detailed account of his weekend. Gloria had surpassed all previous
performances. After thanking him again for the introduction, Art
went off to his own office. Moments later the phone rang. It was
Paula. "Can you talk?"

"Just a moment." Samson closed the door.

"Do you love me?"

"I do."

"Say it."

"I love you."

"I must see you, Sam."

"We'll arrange something."

"When?"

There was a knock and Roy Phillips came in.

"I'll have to call you later," he said, guardedly.

Phillips sank into the big chair in front of the desk and lit a cigarette. Somehow, he looked smaller that morning as he slumped and his head slid below the top. The phone rang again.

"Why did you hang up?"

"I have someone in the office," he said coldly. "I'll call you later."

"When?"

He found it difficult to keep an edge of impatience out of his tone. "Later."

She hung up without a word and though he tried to hide his irritability, Phillips noticed it. "Women. They sure get in your craw."

Samson shrugged.

"They're wonderful," Phillips said grimly, "until you marry them. Put them on your payroll—for life. Then they give you a kid. That's their insurance." He half rose in the chair to reach for the ashtray on the desk then he settled back, burrowing himself in a corner.

"You must have had a rough weekend," Samson said.

It looked as though he was going to talk about it then he shrugged. "How about your apartment house down on Union?"

"What about it?"

"Is it for sale?"

"Never thought about it."

Roy stood up and all of him stretched as far as his muscles would permit. He ended up at attention, his jaw pointed upward and only his eyes looked down at Samson. He shook a finger.

"Don't fall in love with a piece of real estate," he warned. "It's for buying and selling."

"Okay. It's for sale. At the right price."

Phillips took a pad from the desk, talking as he wrote. "You bought the building for thirty thousand with three thousand down. That left a twenty-seven thousand first."

He was disturbed at Roy's knowledge of the exact price and terms. Then he realized Phillips and Ralph Thompson were old friends.

"All right," Samson admitted. "That's what I paid." He looked him straight in the eye. "Now add a thousand for fixing up."

Roy looked at him suspiciously. "What did you do?"

"Paint, furniture, a couple of carpets, plumbing. It adds up."

For a moment it looked as if he was going to dispute the figure. "So you're in it for four thousand." He slumped back in the chair with the pad on his knee. Samson watched as he compiled the figures hurriedly. He finished, studied them for a moment and looked up. "I got a guy from Porterville. A Yugoslav or something. He's got two lots in Fresno and twenty acres of almonds in Paso Robles. Free and clear. He says the whole thing's worth twenty. Wants to trade it all for an apartment house equity in L.A."

The deal with O'Connell gave Samson an idea how lucrative a trade could be. This time he had no intention of ending up on the short end. He decided to start dealing like a hog.

"If that's what it's worth I guess I can take it in and pay a commission."

He could see Phillips' anger mount, tint his face the color of brick, the jaw muscles knot and then his lips formed a smile and his face relaxed. His eyes remained malevolent.

"The town is for sale. The whole town. Buyers are different. They're scarce. When you latch on to one you got to romance him. Go on the make. This Bohunk came in town three days ago and answered my ad. First, I found out he likes *schnapps* and after we loaded up for a whole day and half the night, he got heated up. There's no ass in Porterville, strange ass, that is, and he wanted some bad. I got him laid. It wasn't easy. He's wall-eyed and he's got a big brush mustache stiff with snot and he's smelly and his plates hurt so he took them out and his gums looked raw and rotten. I took him to two cathouses and they turned him down. I found a hungry hooker in a third who took him on for a bonus. Last night I put the slob to bed and had to come in smiling this morning when I took him to breakfast. I'm going to sell him a building. But not for a commission."

He lit a cigarette, settled back and closed his eyes as if to erase the memory of the past two days. Samson watched him for a few moments.

"What do you want?" he finally asked.

"First of all," Roy began, "his property isn't worth twenty thousand. You can bet on that. This guy's no fool. He's shrewd like all those foreigners. Without looking at the stuff you can bet it's not worth more than ten. You can usually get half of what they're asking. I figure we'll split fifty-fifty above your cost."

"If we get ten thousand, my four comes off the top, then we split the six?"

"That's right."

He only owned the building a few months. Would more than double his money. And the whole town *was* for sale.

"What happens if the property isn't worth ten?"

"I'll get him to fatten the offer or we won't make the deal."

He gave Roy all the figures on the building, called Delaney, and told him to show the building when Phillips came with his client. Roy made an appointment to pick up his client that afternoon, and left. He locked the door and called Paula.

"I'm in the same building with your husband," he began. "He's in and out of my office all day. And if it isn't Art, it's Roy Phillips or Ward or any one of a dozen others who might know you. If I don't talk it's because I can't."

"I'm sorry. I understand. It's just that I've got to see you."

The urgency in her tone disturbed him. "Is there anything wrong?"

There was a long silence.

"What is it, Paula?"

"I don't know . . . I'm confused . . . I must talk to you."

"I'll call you in the morning and we'll arrange something."

She hung up after exacting his promise to call before ten. He left for the Union Drive building. It was important that Delaney show it properly. And he knew Delaney wouldn't be enthused if he thought he was selling himself out of a job.

Delaney met him in a state of depression suitably accented with a two-day stubble, bleary eyes and a dirty undershirt.

"You look like hell," Samson said, eyeing the untidy apartment and the usual sinkful.

He groaned and sank into a chair. "I guess I gotta be truthful."

"Go ahead."

"Well . . . selling the building. It came like a shock."

"Every building's for sale."

He shifted in his seat. "I thought maybe this one wasn't. I work hard, Mr. Duke, and I know the building's paying."

He put as much reassurance into a smile as he could. "I don't know whether you know it, Jack, but you're doomed to work for me a long time."

He gave Samson a puzzled look.

"That's right," Samson went on. "And now's as good a time as any to talk about it."

Delaney started to empty an overfilled ashtray, pick up littered clothes and finally ran a hand over his cheeks as if discovering his beard for the first time.

"Never mind all that now," Samson said. "Just sit down and listen."

Delaney sat in the chair, clasped his hands and stuck them between his knees and looked up at Samson like an obedient child.

"I'm going to own a lot of buildings. They'll all need managers. And I want one man to supervise them."

Delaney buttoned the top of his shirt and covered one cheek with a hand as if to hide the growth.

"You can be a great manager and even a better supervisor." Samson continued. "Except for this." His hand swept the room.

"I know, I know," Delaney broke in. "It's sloppy and I am too. But I'm up all hours taking care of things . . . checkouts, cleaning apartments, handling drunks. You don't know what it's like, Mr. Duke. Just the other night a guy left one of the hookers. He was roaring drunk. It was three A.M. I caught him in the lobby and couldn't quiet him down. Finally I had to kick him in the nuts and drag him a block. I couldn't have the cops find him in front of this building."

"I understand. And I appreciate what you've done."

"Get me a building with some class and you won't know me. What can a guy do here? Everybody's a bum."

"I'll have another building before this is out of escrow," he promised.

Delaney muttered his thanks and Samson explained about Phillips' man. "The minute I leave I want you to shave, clean up, and tidy the apartment."

"Don't worry," Delaney said grinning.

"Only show the best units. Tell him the others are occupied by day sleepers. Show him the roof but keep him out of the basement. It stinks. Oh, yes, one other thing," he said, as he got up to leave. "Tell him we rent to hookers."

"Tell him *what?*"

"And tell him we don't let them stay unless they're friendly to the management."

Delaney grinned. "I getcha."

Roy Phillips burst into Samson's office shortly before five, waving a sales agreement. "If I close this deal I'm giving your manager a hundred bucks!"

"What happened?"

"The building was rattier than I thought. After we saw two apartments my man was tugging my sleeve. He wanted out. We were standing by a corner apartment and Delaney turned to my man. 'This is one of the nicer ones,' he said, 'but I can't show it. A woman lives alone. She's a day sleeper.' My man asked what she does. 'She's a whore,' Delaney said. Just like that. Then he went on to say there were two more in the building and when my man asked about the cops, Delaney said they did nothing if things were kept quiet. Then came the clincher. He turns to my man and says that instead of charging them higher rent which most apartments do, he and the owner take it out in trade."

"To hear Delaney, it sounded like you and he were getting it twice a day! Anyway," he said, kissing the agreement, "I signed him up in front of the building."

"When are you going to check his property?"

"I'm leaving the first thing in the morning. Probably get back Thursday or Friday. We got a deal somewhere along the line. That old bastard is going to have a hard-on for a week just thinking about the building."

The moment he was gone Samson called Ralph Thompson. He told him the Union Drive building might be sold and to keep his eye open for another deal.

"I got one right now," Thompson reported. "But it's big. Seventy units. Near the Ambassador Hotel."

"How much cash does it take?"

Thompson told him to drop by for all the figures.

When Samson arrived Thompson's usually expressionless eyes were alive. First, he told Samson, the situation was a little unusual. He would be functioning as an individual, not in behalf of the bank. Certain information he'd managed to secure put him in a position of being helpful. Although he was acting in an ethical manner some people might interpret it otherwise. Samson assured him of his understanding, and then Thompson handed him a setup of the building. It was on Harvard Boulevard, a short block from Wilshire. Five stories of reinforced concrete construction and one of the finest properties in the area. It had earthquake bands, the furnishings were like new and most of the apartments had been recently painted. About a year before, the bank had made the owner a hundred-and-seventy-five-thousand-dollar loan. He was a big manufacturer and for years could have borrowed a hundred thousand or more unsecured. But this time he was a little shaky, and the bank had insisted on taking a mortgage on the building. His business blew up, the building was under foreclosure and the bank had installed a receiver.

"The man is flat," Thompson summed up. "Lost everything."

"When is the foreclosure sale?"

"Not for months. But that isn't the way, Sam. If we wait for the sale every speculator in town will be bidding. I talked to Charley Courtney in the loan department. Told him I might have someone to get the bank off the hook. God knows they want out. We've more buildings now than we can handle."

"Would they carry the same loan if I bought the owner's interest?"

"That's what I have in mind. Charley thought they might if the new owner was responsible and the bank got a token amount on account."

"How much?"

"Five thousand should do it, Sam."

"What do you think the owner would take for his equity?"

"He's real low. Twenty-five hundred would look big right now." He knew Thompson wasn't handing him that equity for seventy-five hundred dollars wrapped up in a long-term bank loan. "What other costs?" he asked.

"He still owes six thousand on the furniture. It has to be paid off. There'll be another five thousand. In cash." Samson looked up questioningly. "For miscellaneous items," Thompson said. "I'll handle them personally."

"When does that have to be paid?"

"The day you get possession."

Samson requested until the following day to think it over, and left. Within two hours he'd inspected the building, found it in perfect condition and returned to his office. It was noon.

Ritchie met him at the head of the stairs. "Your phone's been ringing off the hook."

He remembered Paula and his promise to call before ten. The phone rang as he was about to dial. He barely recognized her voice.

"Why didn't you call?"

"I got tied up."

"I must see you . . . today."

He calmed her down and agreed to meet her at three o'clock at a restaurant on Sunset Boulevard. Now he turned to the building figures. If the bank would give him a long-term loan and he could maintain eighty per cent occupancy it could leave about six hundred a month net spendable. True, the investment of eighteen thousand five hundred was large, but if he was going to move, now was the time. It was the best building he had seen since he had been in the business. And he did not want to lose Delaney. He was rough but Samson was certain he would take a polish. He was a worker and could be trusted. However, his immediate problem was to get rid of the Union Drive building. If Roy Phillips' deal did not go through and he made his deal with Thompson he decided to dump Union Drive at the best possible price. It would not operate without Delaney, whom he wanted for the larger building. He called Ralph Thompson and told him to proceed. Then he went over his finances and realized even if he did not dispose of the Union Drive building he would have a twenty-five thousand cushion after purchasing the new building.

Paula was at the restaurant when he arrived. When he joined her in a corner booth, she gripped his hand in both of hers and for a few moments just looked at him and said nothing.

"Can we order now?" she said, "I haven't eaten all day."

He beckoned to a waiter and then asked her if anything was wrong.

"I just wanted to see you."

He pecked her cheek. "You don't know what it's like in the office," he said. "People coming and going all the time . . . ."

"I know. I shouldn't have called so many times. But I had to talk to you . . . see you."

When the food arrived, Paula nibbled on a sandwich and pushed the plate away. "I can't eat. Just coffee, please."

He watched her as she sipped the black coffee and thought of the night in her bed. He ran his hand along her thigh. She put the cup down almost upsetting it and turned to him.

"Please, let's go."

He drove up Beachwood Drive and headed for the hills. As they climbed higher the city began to spread below. An August sun was only half sunk in a cloudless sky and by the time they reached a flat summit just below the Hollywoodland sign they could see the ocean shimmering at the city's edge and Catalina in the middle of a blue frame. Facing the car to the view he turned off the engine. In an instant, she was in his arms, found his lips and with half-open mouth, tongued and bit him as her hand found his fly. Without a word they scrambled to the back seat and tore at each other's clothes. She gripped him, cried out, and then almost smothered him as her mouth covered his and her arms caught him like a vise.

They dressed in silence and returned to the front seat. She sat apart from him staring out the window and tears began to stream down her cheeks. What if this went on display in a showdown with Art? He was drawn to her more than to any other woman and if marriage was in his plans she would be difficult to resist. But he had no such intentions and if he did he would not cart off a wife of a friend whose business relationship he needed.

She was looking at him now. The tears were gone, she was struggling to smile.

"Do you want to go now?"

She shook her head. "Not yet," she whispered.

He lit a cigarette. The sun was lower, nearer the sea, almost balanced on the top of it. They watched it without a word. She began to speak.

"I must tell you something. You're the only other man I have been with. I was a virgin when I married," she went on. "I didn't know what to expect. No one told me. The first night I was torn." She closed her eyes. "The pain was terrible. My mother was staying with me. I tried to talk to her the next morning but it was impossible. My husband was angry." She shrugged. "I don't know why. Soon the pain was gone but there was always fear. It never stopped. To this day he's loathsome."

"Why didn't you leave him?"

She smiled sadly. "For what? A small town in Mexico where there'll be another man like Art? He'll want a lot of babies and go every day to his *casa chiquita* and his mistress."

"Why Mexico?"

"What would I do here? I went to a fancy school. They prepare you only to be waited upon. Oh, I can sew and cook a little. And maybe look pretty."

"You can learn things," he protested. "Typing, maybe sell, or become a receptionist."

She shook her head. "With all the people out of work, what do they need with me? Anyway, I do not want this. I want to be a wife."

She leaned over and kissed him, then withdrew and brushed his cheek with a finger as she looked into his eyes. "I found out what it is to love. This is what I want."

He realized at once his position must be made clear. "I never met a woman more exciting than you," he began. "We all have plans," he continued. "Some we can control and others we can't." She withdrew to the window and looked at him without expression. "I am no different," he said. "Someday I want to get married. I have things to do first."

She reached into her purse for a handkerchief, making every effort to control herself. "Do you think I can carry on this way with you?"

He shook his head. "I hadn't thought it out."

"Well, I can't." Her voice raised. "I have felt things I never knew existed." She buried her face in her hands. He took her wrist and she twisted it from his grasp. She looked up. "Do you know what it will be like now? When Art touches me!"

"I'm sorry, Paula."

"Sorry! Why did you come after me? To sleep with me once, maybe twice? To see what it would be like? To try something new!"

"I thought no such thing. From the first time I met you I knew I couldn't stay away if I wanted to. Does there have to be a guarantee of marriage?"

She reached across and slapped his face as hard as she could. Without a word he started the car, slammed it into gear and headed for the hill. Winding down the mountain at top speed with tires howling at the turns, he reached Sunset and pulled beside her car in the parking lot. She ran to her car and he drove off.

CHAPTER SIX

It was no use, he couldn't sleep. He got out of bed, settled in a chair, and lit a cigarette. Obviously, if he'd known the results of his actions with Aunt Annie then, he would have acted differently. So, looking ahead should have been the dictum. And, Christ, there was evidence all over the place! The day he met Father Keenan he should have *known* Aunt Annie was outmatched. That priest wasn't putting in overtime just to bring her salvation. He'd save her soul, but the price was going to be high and if you don't pay for it on the installment plan here on earth they grabbed a lump sum in the end to pay your passage out of Hell. Now, it was so clear. And Paula. She was in a trap, locked tight. So what did he do? Instead of dangling a key (even a vague promise of marriage would have fit the lock), he made it too clear he was not on the market.

He made a pot of cocoa and brought it in the living room. There was no desire to sleep now, he was wide awake, alert. The thick sweet liquid tasted good and as he sipped it slowly his thoughts began to revolve around a solution. With Paula it would be simple: a change of tune, add a few lyrics, keep her hoping. Aunt Annie, however, might be round the bend and out of sight. The priest already had her praying for her own soul and the road back from that power was difficult. Harry Baldwin was as pious as a monk now, and reaching for a papal coronet. What could return his aunt to secularism? Harry Baldwin's refusal to marry? Perhaps. But in despair she might be driven even closer to the Church. What if she decided not to marry? That was better, he thought; it would be a sign of strength, independence—an indication she could act without a crutch. And it would be a blow to Father Keenan who was working on a package deal. That was the key.

Returning to bed, he sifted his thoughts and then a lurking idea began to grow. At first he rejected it as something he dared not risk. But as every plan fell one by one, he smothered his fear and examined it carefully. The plan was simple, had few parts, needed no confederates, and there was little that could go wrong.

Rising early, he went to the office, took care of the mail, and was at the downtown library when it opened. What he sought was not in the *Catholic Encyclopedia on Papal Knighthood*, but in a definitive work by an obscure priest. He gathered all the information he needed, crowded notes on a piece of paper, and within an hour his research was complete. His next move was to determine if Bishop Cassidy was in the city and would be in his office for the next few days. A call to the Chancery took care of that. Bishop Cassidy was indeed here and kept office hours daily.

It was an hour before noon when he left the library and found a stationery store where he purchased writing paper and envelopes. Returning to the library, he found a quiet corner and started to compose a letter to His Excellency, the bishop. He wrote slowly and with great care. After three drafts he finished. The typing room was crowded when he entered. He reserved a machine and went to lunch. Returning in half an hour he began to type the letter he had written.

Your Excellency:

Please read this letter carefully. It contains information I
am sure you would want in your possession in connection
with a petition to Rome for the nomination of a Mr. Harry
Baldwin of St. Julius for papal knighthood.

I too, am a member of Father Keenan's church and have
lived in the parish for over thirty years. My devotion has
been constant guiding me in the path of the Lord and providing me with the peace of mind so generously bestowed
by Him and Jesus Christ, His Son.

A few weeks ago, however, when Mr. Baldwin's nomination became known, I was confronted for the first time with
a decision I found unable to resolve with the assurance I was
acting for the good of my Church and in a manner of a pious
man. Torn between reason, which told me to right a wrong,
and faith in the judgment of my bishop and priest, I found
myself confronted with a difficult choice. Finally, I decided
to write and give you what facts I had, certain if they were
not already in your possession, you would desire them. On
the other hand, if all I am about to reveal was known prior to
the nomination of Mr. Baldwin and in spite of it his devotion
made him deserving of the great honor I would feel I had
done my duty and could accept the decision of my Church
with complete faith.

I have known and admired Mr. Baldwin for a long time.
His stature in our community is deserved and though some
have said he has used his religious contacts to aid his business
I am certain the ends he desires are in concert with good intentions and the well-being of the parish. The fact that his
material rewards are great should in no way detract from his
Christian charity. There are those that have been critical of
his business methods, claiming that the ownership of a cemetery in addition to an undertaking establishment is a greedy
attempt to monopolize the commercialism in death. Though
I am in the minority, it is not with these activities that I find
fault. It is with his personal life that I am concerned.

The private affairs of a widower provide wild speculation, most of which contains little flattery and less truth. For months I ignored the tales that circulated our parish, certain that in the telling and retelling, what had become unspeakable debauchery was surely no more than an innocent flirtation. However, when Mr. Baldwin was selected for honor by Your Excellency, I felt duty-bound to pick up the threads of rumor and follow them to their origin. I confess I was not prepared for my discovery.

The woman involved (I should say girl, for she was barely twenty), was hard to track down. After much conscientious effort, I was able to locate her living with a family in a small town in Northern California with everything provided for her comfort during the confinement. Also, generous arrangements had been made for the young woman's fresh start in a distant city. The baby was to remain with the couple in whose home she was staying, to be brought up as their own. I must say that the whole incident was handled in a Christian manner and in view of the circumstances, one could hardly ask for more.

My one regret is the withholding of my identity. This is necessary for the protection of the large family with which I am blessed. To involve them without consultation would not be fair and to spread my information further would be an injustice to Mr. Baldwin.

Yours most sincerely,
A devoted parishioner.

P.S. I thought it proper that the authorities in Rome have a complete file. I sent them a copy of this letter.

The reference to Rome was untrue. He would have liked nothing better than to have had this added insurance but did not know to whom he should write to in the Holy City. A call to the Chancery would give him precisely the information he wanted but that was too risky. He was forced to rely on the bishop's judgment, and if it was influenced by a personal relationship with Baldwin, the postscript in the letter would surely cause the prelate to set aside relations with the laity for more important ecclesiastic ties.

Samson mailed the letter at the post office within the parish and returned to his office. Though satisfied with what he had done and certain he had no other choice, nevertheless he felt uneasy. He was counting on the Church's discretion in these matters, hoping they would halt the proceedings without confronting Harry Baldwin with his letter. It seemed to him they would wish to avoid an airing of what might prove embarrassing for themselves and their nominee. If his guess was wrong and the bishop's ties with Baldwin were closer than he supposed and he would elect to defend his judgment against an anonymous accusation, it was possible that with no positive proof, Mr. Baldwin would emerge a martyred Knight. Samson dismissed these thoughts.

He felt the results would be swift if the plan worked. There was no telling from what direction they would come, nor what form they would take, but its force would be shattering, and, if his calculations were correct, would cause Harry Baldwin to reexamine the cost of his devotion in the light of its rewards. If he were denied the papal knighthood, Samson felt sure the crushing blow could quench his religious fervor. In more optimistic moments, Samson dreamed of Baldwin's bitterness extinguishing his religiosity completely. There was nothing to do now but wait and go about his business.

The phone rang early the following morning. He twisted from the covers and looked at the clock. A little after six. Roy Phillips' voice, angry and insistent, stripped his drowsiness.

"Be in your office at eleven."

"Where are you?"

"Porterville, I'm leaving now."

"What happened?"

"I'll tell you when I see you." Phillips hung up without another word and Samson rolled back under the covers. Roy sounded angry enough to have lost the deal. On the other hand, Roy was always angry. He tossed for awhile and then unable to get back to sleep he dressed and went to the office. Ward's door was open and he saw him hunched over his desk poring over the ads. They had not talked to each other much since he had moved in and had yet to make a deal together. Ward did very little brokerage, just bought and sold.

"Just getting in or haven't you gone home yet?" Samson called out.

Ward put the paper down, reached for a comb on the desk and ran it through his hair. "Come in, come in," he said. "I'm an early riser. Get here every morning before eight." He wiped off some hair oil that streaked his scalp, and picked up the paper as Samson took a seat. "Look at this," he said, slapping it with the back of his hand. "That guy, Roosevelt, in New York, proposing to raise twenty million for relief. The whole trouble in this country is people don't want to work. Listening to those damn red agitators whippin' up a storm." He leaned forward and his eyes narrowed. "If I had my way I'd string them up. Every damn one of them! I don't understand them in Washington, Hoover or the whole lot of them. Pleading and coddling. If it was up to me I'd get out the army. Huh, food and relief."

"I guess you've got to feed people," Samson ventured.

"Feed's for cattle. Make them work. Look at Mussolini." His face wrinkled shrewdly. "There's a man with the right idea."

Samson had heard Ward's ideas before. Although he agreed with some of his premises, Samson could not go along with the pat solutions. He started to leave.

"And don't forget one other thing," Ward said, waving a finger.

"What's that?"

"The yellow peril. I tell you, Sam," he said, "someday those Japs and Chinks are taking over. And when they do, God help us."

He was at the door. "How about you and me making a deal?"

"I'm ready."

"You got a minute?"

Samson returned to the seat. Ward rummaged through a pile of papers on the desk and pulled out a sheet. "Here's a sixteen-unit I just bought. I'm a little short. Need two-thousand second for a year."

Samson looked over the setup. "I'll pay ten per cent and a bonus," Ward offered.

"How much of a bonus?"

Ward scratched his head with a finger, careful not to muss his hair. "Two, maybe three points."

Samson scanned the figures again and shook his head.

"You won't find a better loan," Ward persisted.

"All right," Samson said. "But I've got to have ten points."

"That's a lot to soak a neighbor."

"Money's scarce."

Ward looked at Samson for a moment then hunched his shoulders. "The escrow's at Thompson's bank. When can you put up the money?"

"Whenever you're ready." Samson was at the door. "One more thing. I want a ninety-day prepayment penalty."

Ward got up and flung an arm around his shoulder. "C'mon, Sam. Lay off the penalty."

"Why?"

"Well it's . . . you know, it's a little rough."

"I agreed to make the loan without seeing the building. Somebody else would horse you around for a week. You know that."

"But ten points *and* a penalty?"

"You probably won't pay it off before the year anyway. So don't worry about it. Open the escrow. I'll put up the money today."

Not a bad start he thought as he reached his office. The two thousand would net him nearly twenty-five per cent within a year. And if Roy squeezes out a deal and Thompson's man is hungry enough the day could finish fatter than a prize hog.

He heard footsteps on the stairs and knew it was Phillips before he burst into the room. His collar was open and his tie was stuck in his breast pocket. His mouth was working furiously, biting out his words and his usually clean-shaven face was covered with a dark stubble. As he leaned over the desk Samson got a whiff of booze. "I drove eight hundred miles, burned out a set of bearings, and get my ass nicked by a bedbug in a lousy hotel to find out that a stinking Yugoslavian tried to screw me!"

"Calm down."

"Calm down!" He banged the desk with a fist. "I'll calm down. You know when? When I tie his balls!" He started to pace the room. "He said his property was worth twenty." He swung around. "You remember?" Samson nodded. "I figured it for ten. Right?" Samson agreed. "Do you know what it's really worth?" He crossed the room and gripped the edge of the desk with both hands looking down at Samson. "The best offer I could get was six! Three thousand for the twenty acres and three for the lots."

"Sit down," Samson said. "We'll figure something out." He calculated quickly. The six thousand gave him his four and two to split with Roy. Ordinarily he wouldn't consider it. Now he was anxious. "Do you think you can raise him?" he asked.

Roy was slumped in the chair. "I don't know."

"The way it stands we got two thousand to split."

"I'm not making this deal for a thousand dollars. I wined that pig and dined him, wiped his puke, and got him fucked. Not for a thousand dollars." Roy paced the room. "Driving down I got a wild idea." He seemed to be talking to himself. "Maybe it'll work." Reaching for the phone he dialed the operator and put in a person to person call to Porterville. He cupped the receiver as he waited. "I pulled this once before and almost made it. Maybe this time I'll push it over."

"Mr. Bukovich. This is Roy Phillips. Just got back." He shook his head. "The owner was with me and I'm afraid you're in trouble." Samson could hear the other man's voice. "That's what I said," Roy went on. "Trouble. You told me your property was worth twenty thousand. Right? Well it's only worth twelve thousand." Bukovich must have protested, as Roy shook his head impatiently. "Never mind all that," he broke in. "Just listen to me and listen carefully. First, I want to know one thing. Are you an American citizen? Yes, that's what I said." Roy was listening and shaking his head emphatically. "That's what I thought," he said, smiling triumphantly. "Not even first papers." He was beaming now and the voice at the other end grew so loud he was forced to hold the receiver from his ear. He spoke again—slowly. "We're going to give you a break. Instead of making you put up the difference we're going to split it. Unless you're in my office before noon on Monday with an additional four thousand dollars in a cashier's check ready to go to escrow, I'm going straight to the immigration office." He listened for another moment and hung up.

"What did he say?"

"He was practically speechless." He felt his face. "I'd better get home and clean up."

"What do you think he'll do?"

"I don't know. But something tells me we got an edge now."

Ralph Thompson came by the office later that day with a letter giving Samson an option to purchase the equity for twenty-five hundred dollars provided he exercised it on or before noon of the following Tuesday.

"I just can't give him the money," Samson said. "I need a title report. There could be a dozen liens in back of the bank's loan."

"The bank got a report. It's clean except for the six thousand owed on the furniture."

"And my loan is set with the bank?"

"I'll have the papers by the end of the week," Thompson promised. Before he left he made arrangements to see the manager of the building over the weekend.

Delaney met him in front of the building on Sunday. In place of his usual attire, he wore a neat but faded suit with a new shirt and tie as bright and dramatic as a sunset. He stood before Samson as if for inspection wearing a foolish grin.

"You look fine," Samson said. "But you need a new wardrobe. You're a little out of date."

Delaney looked down at his shoes. "I got this outfit when I got out of the navy."

The manager was expecting them. Her apartment, just off the lobby, faced the street and he saw a curtain drop in place as they went in the front door. She was a frail woman, almost seventy he judged, with silver hair and a narrow pinched face. Although she wore no glasses, it was apparent she wasn't seeing much beyond the length of her nose. "I guess you're Mr. Duke," she said.

Since he did not know when Delaney would take over and wanted all her cooperation, he told her the old owner had recommended her highly and that he had no plans to make a change in management. They spent an hour going through the building, went over the mechanics of the heating and refrigeration systems, discussed the tenants, her method of collecting rents and making deposits.

"What do you think?" he asked Delaney as they reached the street.

"It's some building," he said, shaking his head admiringly.

They got into the car and Samson turned to him. "We got a few things to straighten out."

"What do you mean?"

"I mean when I got something on my mind I'll say it. I want you to do the same."

"I've always been honest with you, Mr. Duke."

"First of all call me Sam. Second, take every stitch of clothes you've got and burn them. I want you to look like a businessman, not a sailor on leave. When we close the Union Drive deal go to Pestere's in Beverly Hills and tell them to sell you a couple of outfits. Include shoes," he said, looking down at the orangy cracked pair Delaney had on. "Let *them* select everything."

"Sounds like a lot of money, Sam."

"It's an investment."

"You're the boss."

"Don't forget that," he emphasized. "I know you're a cocks-man, Delaney, that's your business. But it's my business who's gettin' screwed in the manager's apartment. It's my business when there's all night drinking and hollering broads."

"It's not been that bad, Sam."

"I can't have it in the building, Jack. We'll arrange for you to take off one day a week. Twenty-four hours. Find yourself a dame with her own apartment or rent a room. But not in that building. Not even once."

"All right," he said. "It's a deal. And don't you worry."

On Monday morning while Samson and Phillips waited, he persuaded Phillips to agree that if Bukovich did not show up, they'd make the original deal. It was nearly eleven o'clock and he was just getting ready to leave again when he saw Phillips' face light up. Turning around, he saw a dirty little man enter timidly as Roy got up from his desk to greet him. In spite of the August heat, he wore a battered felt hat with a faded maroon band which he removed and fingered nervously as he advanced into the room. The skin under thinning hair was paste white contrasting sharply with a weathered face. He wore a dark blue shirt that had a sweat-stained collar and a greenish raveling tie and when he approached Samson with extended hand, Samson got a whiff of dried shit. He moved nearer the open window as Mr. Bukovich took the chair beside Roy's desk.

Roy's face wore a rare smile as he began to talk. "You're making a good deal, Mr. Bukovich. Like I told you, if Mr. Duke's mother and father didn't sell their farm back east to come out here to live on a ranch there wouldn't be a chance."

Although hearing about his parents and their farm for the first time Samson managed a smiling acknowledgment.

Mr. Bukovich cleared his throat. "How many acres they have?"

"Eighty," Samson said.

"What they grow?" he said, his eyes lighting with interest.

"Tomatoes," he said, remembering row upon row of them in and around New Brunswick.

Bukovich looked at him blankly and Samson wondered if he said the wrong thing.

"Anyway," Roy said, "they'll be growing almonds soon. Right, Mr. Bukovich?"

He shook his head and tried a smile which barely lit his face. Roy leaned forward, planted his elbows on the desk, clasped his hands on which he cradled his chin and asked Mr. Bukovich if he brought the money. For a long moment Bukovich looked at Roy. Roy was motionless. Bukovich's lips began to move but there was no sound. Roy kept smiling. Finally, Bukovich sighed, reached into his back pocket and pulled out a worn billfold from which he took a crisp cashier's check.

"It's in my name," he said. "I will endorse it."

Roy leaped from the chair. "Let's go right to the escrow." He took Bukovich by the arm. "You can come down a little later and sign your papers," he said, turning to Samson.

They left and Samson went to his office. He started to make a call when the door opened and Bukovich came into the room followed by Roy who was signaling with a frantic affirmative shaking of his head.

"I forgot one thing, Mr. Duke," Bukovich said. "The manager will stay to work for me?"

"Absolutely. And he's a good one too."

"I need someone who knows the building. I cannot take care of it. Can only come once in a while from Porterville."

"You have nothing to worry about. Mr. Delaney will take care of everything." He attempted a broad grin and his upper plate was missing and Samson got a view of the gums Roy complained about.

The moment they left, Samson called Delaney, and told him to keep his mouth shut about leaving.

"But when the time comes how do I tell him?"

"If you can't figure that one out you won't have a new job."

About an hour later, he received a call from Roy. "Tonight, we celebrate!" he shouted. "It's signed and sealed. Boy, you should have seen him. He didn't read a document. Just scratched his name on everything we gave him. I swear, Sam, I could have given him an order for his own deportation and he'd have signed that, too. Don't make a date tonight because I'm taking you out."

Samson did not relish the engagement, but thought it best to accept. The few times he'd been present when Roy was celebrating, he found him to be a nasty drunk and a bore. With each drink, Phillips' face would become redder, his voice louder and more snarly, and a large vein snaked its way across his forehead, swelling as though it would pop.

Samson went to the escrow after lunch, found everything in order, and signed. Roy lunged into the office a bit after five, well on his way, his face flushed, the smell of whisky reaching Samson across the room. Roy stood in the center of the office, feet spread, hands on hips. "I got us two dames," he announced triumphantly, "and two quarts of bourbon, and we're going to use your apartment."

"Who are the girls?"

"Mine's a blonde, tall and like this," he said, describing a bass violin with his hands. "I got you a brunette." He made the same motion.

Samson had hopes of a quick dinner and an early departure. "Can't we forget the girls?"

"Are you crazy! What's a celebration without dames?" He looked at his watch. "We pick them up at six."

"What do they do?"

"They work at the title company." He winked and punched Samson's arm playfully.

Samson tried once more. "Can't you call that end of it off, Roy?" He smiled. "Let's do the town alone. See what happens. It's more fun that way."

"What can happen that we ain't got in the bag? It's all fixed. They're coming to your apartment to get loaded and laid."

It was no use. "Where do you want to take them to dinner?"

"I don't. I've got enough trouble at home without being seen at a restaurant with a dame. We'll get sandwiches or something. Take them to the apartment. Anyway," he said, swaying a little, "who in hell wants to eat?"

It was almost five-thirty. "Okay," Samson said. "You get the girls. In the meantime I'll get the food and straighten the place up."

"Good idea." At the door he turned and shouted, "Two bottles and two broads coming up!"

Loading up with bread, meats, and salads at the delicatessen he drove home, tidied up the apartment, shaved, changed his shirt, and belted a straight shot. He was becoming excited at the prospect of meeting a strange girl, tried to form a conception in his mind, remembered what Roy had said, that his was a brunette and curvy. He found himself thinking of Rita and then Paula and saw black eyes, big and slanted, and snow-white skin and hand-sized breasts with straight out nipples and a soft behind good to feel and a patch of hair, black and fine to the touch. What the hell! He had something to celebrate too! He took another drink. And maybe Bishop Cassidy was reading that letter at this very minute and having second thoughts.

Phillips didn't bother to knock. The blonde in back of him stood a full head over him and she was curvy but Roy's arms didn't spread far enough. She almost filled the doorway. Samson could not see what was in back of her but was sure of a brunette counterpart. Would a cow like that trot around with a friend who was right-sized? Not if she had a brain in her head. She stepped aside and he felt his face draw into a smile. The girl was petite, almost tiny, and her mouth was sensuous and her eyes were dark and bright and bold too and her breasts popped out just right and he led her into the room and slapped her behind and it felt great.

Her name was Helen and Roy's girl was called Alice. Roy pulled out a bottle and held it high above his head waving it, chanting drunkenly looking like a gnome at a bacchanal. Alice stood over him, towering, menacing, and snatched the first drink he poured. It was obvious they had a head start. Someone turned on the radio and Helen kicked off her shoes and started to dance alone. Samson grabbed her and started to twirl around the room. Her head barely reached his chin as her hand crept to the back of his neck. Someone shouted for food and he went into the kitchen. Helen followed and they tore open the bags, made sandwiches and put up a pot of coffee. Then they were all in the kitchen, a drink in one hand, food in the other and Roy had Alice against the wall pushing into her feverishly as she looked over his head with a vacant stare. Samson put his arm around Helen and half-dragged her to the living room and they flopped on the couch. She was all over him with her mouth her teeth and her hands and he was beginning to feel his prick stiffen and then somebody handed them a drink and they sat up and the music got louder and Alice was in the middle of the floor doing a dance and they all applauded and urged her on as Roy took his tie off, then his shirt and joined her, dancing about the room like a terrier leading a Saint Bernard.

He raised his head off the couch and twisted around to look at the luminous hands on the clock. The room was pitch dark and it felt like midnight. It had been more than an hour since Roy and Alice had gone into the bedroom and Helen and he had gotten at each other on the couch. They had fallen asleep and now his head was about to burst and he could smell cigarette butts, stale whisky, and delicatessen garbage and Helen was lying naked beside him. He wanted desperately to be alone. He started to tap Helen on the shoulder when he heard voices from the bedroom. At first he could not distinguish the words but soon they came loud and clear. Roy was shouting.

"Say that again and I'll belt you. Do you hear!"

Alice's voice was closer now. "Shrimp!" she shrieked.

Samson bounded off the couch and Helen rolled to the floor. Switching on a light he found his shorts and pants in a pile on the floor, struggled into them, and then heard a scream and the sound of blows. Rushing into the bedroom, he found Roy and Alice, completely nude swinging at each other wildly. Roy, his head down, was roaring like an animal. Alice, huge breasts swinging, was trying vainly to fend him off. She fell backwards onto the bed and as he leaped towards her, she kicked him in the groin with all her force. He screamed in pain and crumpled to the floor. Samson grabbed her, pushed her into the bathroom, and called for Helen.

"Get her dressed and the hell out of here!" Roy was still on the floor when he returned to the bedroom and though he was groaning Samson was certain he was out cold. He picked him up and placed him on the bed as the phone rang. It was the desk.

"You'll have to keep it quiet, Mr. Duke."

"It'll be quiet."

"It better be. Your neighbor threatened to call the police."

Helen was standing in the middle of the room buttoning her blouse. Alice was sobbing as she pulled on her clothes, her hair was disheveled and Samson noticed the beginning of a shiner under one eye, a bloody stain under her nose. Dressed, she straightened up to her full height and glared at him. "I hope I ruined the little bastard!"

Samson was cold sober. He grabbed her by the arm. "Listen to me carefully," he said. "I don't know what happened in that room and I don't care. If I ever hear a word of this repeated or if anybody gets the stupid idea to go to the police I'll see to it that you'll lose your job."

She twisted her arm from his grasp. "I'll lose it anyway." She touched her eye gingerly. "How can I go to work like this?"

"Tell them you're sick."

"It'll take a week, maybe two to heal."

"Tell them you're very sick." He turned to Helen. "Get her home. If there are any doctor bills I'll pay them."

"What about my salary? They don't pay when you're sick."

"I'll pay that too. Now get the hell out of here!" he said, pushing her toward the door.

"Don't shove, I'm going."

He heard Roy groan. They left and he went into the bedroom. Roy was sitting on the edge of the bed struggling with a towel trying to fit it around his crotch. He looked up and Samson could see he was still drunk.

"She got me square in the nuts. They feel like they've been crushed." His face screwed with hate. "If I could walk I'd get that bitch tonight and kill her." He reached for the bottle on the table and the towel fell to the floor. Ignoring it, he poured a drink and tossed it down. He looked up at Samson. "I can't get the towel cold enough. Got any ice cubes?"

Samson emptied the ice trays from the refrigerator, filled a bowl and returned to the room. Roy dumped them on the towel, folded it and placed it gingerly on the spot and propped himself up. Then he reached for the bottle. Samson grabbed it and set it on the dresser.

"You've had enough."

"Give it to me."

"Not a chance."

Roy tried to rise and sank back with a groan. "Wait'll I lay my hands on that broad."

As Samson looked at him still drunk, his short legs and hairy barrel-chest reminding him of an ape, he was overwhelmed with disgust. He grabbed the bottle from the dresser, poured its contents down the sink and came back into the room.

"What did you do with it?" Roy whined.

"You've had enough for one night. Wait until the nuts feel better, then get dressed, and get to hell out of here."

"I can't move. It even hurts when I breathe."

"Then why in hell didn't you pick a fight with someone your own size!"

"The bigger they are the more they're my size. Do you hear!" His face contorted and his chest began to heave. "They can't be big enough. Not even you, you bastard!" He tried to rise and take a swing. Samson pushed his face down until he was half-smothered in the pillow as he flailed wildly with his arms. Suddenly, Roy stopped struggling, his body went limp, his whole frame shuddered, and he began to sob. As Samson watched him, all the tensions of that day and of the night that had been bottled up by the drinking closed in like a vise. The ache in his head began to pound. He went into the bathroom, doused his face with cold water, and swallowed two aspirin.

Roy's sobbing became fitful now and the hand with which he had covered his face fell to his side. He turned his head and looked at Samson for a long time without saying a word.

"Can I get you anything, Roy?"

"A drink."

Samson got a full bottle that was in the kitchen, filled a glass generously, and placed it in Roy's hand. He looked at Samson gratefully and started to sip it slowly. "Light a cigarette for me, Sam." He took a deep drag, closed his eyes and then opened them. "Funny thing about drinking," he said. "You get tight until you feel another drink will put you out. Then something happens. You seem to level off. Then you take another and everything clears."

Samson looked at the clock. It was after one. Then he looked at Roy. He was burrowing his ass into the mattress like he was settling down, holding the drink high above his head with one hand as if keeping it out of reach, and propping himself with the other. A gust of wind flapped the shade and Samson felt a chill. Wrapping himself in a robe he went into the kitchen and put some coffee on the stove. Might as well write off the night's sleep. Roy wasn't going anywhere, not with swollen balls and a new drunk starting. Outside of screwing Samson could never take a couch for more than a short nap. When the coffee boiled he filled a cup and sipped it black. The aspirin was beginning to work and when he returned to the bedroom the headache was dulled. "Want some?" he asked, offering Roy his cup.

"Never change my brand." He drained the glass and poured another. "Guess you'll have to put me up."

"How about your wife?"

"What about her?"

"Don't you have to call her?"

"What for? My wife and I are out of touch. Not in communication." He held the drink up, swirled the contents and then stared over the edge. "We got married on Armistice Day, 1918. It wasn't that we were celebrating the end of the war or my getting out of the service, cause I never did make it. Just an inch too small." He took a long sip. "Celeste wanted our anniversary on a holiday. We were talking about Christmas that year. Then the war ended unexpectedly. We were living in San Diego and went to a party at Coronado. A friend of Celeste's. Her husband was stationed at North Island. He was a chief in the paymaster's office. The booze flowed and the food came cheap from navy lockers and the party lasted all night."

Samson got up to shut the window and Roy stopped talking until he returned to the seat.

"Did you ever have a dream?" he continued, "that you were holding onto something tight, something you wanted bad, and you were surrounded and hands were reaching out to take it?"

He nodded.

"Well, anyway, it was like that. Instead of the party petering out it got bigger. There were rumors that the war was over but it wasn't official yet. Everybody kept going like they had to be higher than a kite and celebrating when the word came. Soon it looked like the whole fleet was in that house. For hours I was like crazy keeping my eye on Celeste. Even a slob looks good in a uniform." He stopped to fill his glass. "It was like everybody was working up to an orgasm. Like the world was coming to an end and not a beginning. There was humping on every bed in the house and the couches were filled and the chairs and those with standing room were at each other against the wall. I felt that Celeste was slipping through my fingers and that it would be forever. Then the word came that it was over. I punched a big sailor who made a grab for her and dragged her out of the house. We got married a couple of hours later in Tijuana, dead drunk."

He shifted his position and groaned, then reached under the covers and adjusted the towel. He looked up and Samson could see he was very drunk. Samson got up.

Roy's words slurred now. "Where you going?"

"We'd better get some sleep. I'll try the couch."

165

"Don't go, Sam."
"Why not save it for the morning?"
"I gotta tell you now. Please!"
"All right."
He closed his eyes and went on, his words rolling over sobs and at times spitting out in anger. He told him how they settled down in San Diego in a little house in Mission Hills. He was selling land, business was good and he was making lots of money. It brought them a big car, a bigger house, expensive clothes for Celeste and they were in the navy crowd. Top brass this time. Commanders and even captains. And he matched drinks with the best, played high stakes poker and took up golf. He could buy and sell them all. Then Celeste started staying out late nights and once when he came home near dawn from a card game she was not there. He waited by the window watching and in the early morning a car pulled up across the street. The man was an officer he knew, the husband of one of her friends. He was very tall and blond. She tried to lie when he met her at the door but he did not listen. He slapped her until he knocked her down. She moved out that day and a month later they were back together. He had asked to be forgiven and took her back with no terms.

It took a long time for the break to mend but eventually it did and when she told him one day that she was pregnant everything seemed healed. The baby, a son, filled in all the empty places. And then Celeste got fed up with San Diego and wanted to move, insisted in fact, and he closed his office and within a month they were settled in Los Angeles. The infant was a year old.

Roy got out of bed and walked open-legged to the bathroom. Returning, he sat on the edge of the bed.

"When you're with someone every day you hardly see the change. Even with a kid."

Samson agreed.

"Did you ever see my wife, Sam?"

"No."

"She's my size. And she's got black hair and dark brown eyes."

"Sounds pretty," he managed to say.

"She is pretty." He crawled back into bed, reached for the glass and gulped the drink. "When my son was seven years old we sent him away to camp. It was one of those places with rules. The parents can't visit all summer. It was the first time I had been away from him for more than a full day. Finally, it was after Labor Day and we went downtown to meet him at the bus. The kids came streaming out and it seemed like he was never going to get off. Then I saw him. He was on the top step of the bus and waving. He looked like he was six feet tall and the sun all summer must have bleached his hair because I noticed for the first time it was blond."

It was nearly three o'clock. "What about some sleep now," Samson said.

Roy ignored him. "Tom is now thirteen and he's over six feet tall and his hair never turned darker than that summer."

"All kids don't look like their parents," Samson said. "Some look like uncles, grandfathers, go back generations. And some don't look like anybody you know."

"Sure. That's what Celeste always says." He was too drunk to hold on to the glass and it slipped from his grasp to the floor. He rolled over on his side and Samson turned off the lights.

Dozing for a couple of hours Samson got up at six. His head ached again and his mouth was woolly. The room stank. Filled ashtrays and spilled drinks covered the tables and the floor, half-eaten sandwiches and pickles and crumbled potato chips were everywhere and in the center of the room a dark stain circled an overturned coffee cup. The kitchen was like an overflowed garbage can. In the bedroom, Roy was on his back snoring. After a cold shower, Samson dressed and left the apartment. It was too early to go to the office so he decided on the beach to clear his head before breakfasting somewhere in Santa Monica. He walked along the palisades park, and then on to the pier. A few early morning fishermen dangled poles, overhead some gulls wheeled lazily in search of their own breakfast, and out in the bay a navy ship, gray against the horizon, churned southward.

As Samson walked, he thought of Roy and wondered if the little man would remember his long, drunken soliloquy. He hoped not; he had no wish to share that kind of intimate relationship with the man. Then he made a mental note: confine all future contacts with Roy to business.

By the time he got to the office, his head had cleared and he was ready for work. The deed on the new building had been recorded that morning and he was now the legal owner. Since it would be a few weeks before Delaney could take over, Samson decided to see the old manager immediately; she needed to know that all rents collected from now on belonged to him. When the time came, he'd give her two weeks' salary and move her out. Anyway, Delaney would handle that.

By the end of the week Samson closed the deal with the bank on the new loan, and met Ralph Thompson to turn over the five thousand in cash at his suite on the top floor of a large apartment house overlooking the Midwood Country Club. Sitting in the living room, from which they could see the broad fairways and carpetlike greens that spread over a hundred acres in the heart of the city's best residential area, Thompson slid the envelope of money in his breast pocket without counting it. Samson was at the window looking out on the course.

"Did you ever play it?" Thompson asked.

"No."

"I'll have you as my guest."

"I didn't know you were a member."

"My one luxury, but I have no family." He shrugged. "I guess I can afford it."

"I hear it's a great course."

"Best in the city. Maybe in the country. And they keep the wrong people out."

Art Jennings had told him once that Midwood's restrictions were so carefully maintained that a member, exposed as a Jew who had been converted, was forced to resign. It had prestige all right, and membership was a ticket to the dress circle.

"There'll be two memberships up for sale. Poor devils haven't paid dues for a year. I'm on the committee and have a few favors coming."

"I'd appreciate it, Ralph."

Thompson went to a desk and took out a form. "You might fill out an application. Take one back to the office for Art. He's been waiting for this for a year."

It was a double-page questionnaire and Thompson said every item had to be answered. "My recommendation will go a long way. But the committee wants an answer to every question."

That night Samson went over the application carefully. They forgot nothing: mother, father, when and where they were born, the country from which the family originated, church affiliations, schools attended and a combination of questions one might expect for a job at Fort Knox or a private audience with the Pope. They plugged the hole on conversions with an asterisk on religion and a footnote indicating that the faith they were inquiring about was the one "born into." He decided to make his background so respectable that anyone questioning his desirability would be considered impudent. So, he became a third generation American of English, Irish, and Dutch ancestry, steeped in Presbyterianism, a product of two prep schools and Columbia University. His birthplace became Groton and his last New York address was an impressive one in Gramercy Park. He made a copy of all the questions and answers and committed the important ones to memory. The following morning he delivered the application to Thompson and asked him to look it over. Thompson read it and his face beamed.

"There'll be no question," he said, smiling. "I might have a little problem with Art, but not with this," he went on slapping the form with the back of his hand.

Samson asked him about the membership fee.

"Only five hundred dollars. Used to run as high as ten thousand."

If they checked the information concerning his past he would be washed out in a flash; on the other hand if he told the truth he knew he would never be considered. So, he had to take that chance. And there was Aunt Annie and Harry Baldwin; they knew enough about him to get him blackballed anywhere. He would have to talk to his aunt; she would understand and keep her mouth shut. There was always the possibility that Harry Baldwin knew a member of the club but it was unlikely. The undertaker ran with a different pack, churchmen and the laity, embalmers and cemetery plot salesmen and Samson had a feeling that Midwood's prejudices covered a wide field and that Catholics and undertakers would not be considered with favor. In any event, there was no other way, and Los Angeles was a big city, large enough to establish two identities and keep them far apart.

Back at his office he found a message from Aunt Annie. Her level of excitement when he reached her indicated that word from Rome might be on its way. "Be here tomorrow night. Harry's coming over. I'm making a dinner. Sort of a celebration."

Samson could barely conceal his disappointment. "He got it?"

"Not yet. But the news may come at any hour. Anyway, it's my birthday. You probably forgot."

"I was coming over tomorrow to surprise you," he lied. After he hung up he wondered if his letter had gone astray. Or perhaps the bishop got it, labeled it crackpot, and tossed it into the wastebasket. Perhaps there was more to papal knighthood than he knew. After all, Harry Baldwin could be worth more to the Church dead than alive. Perhaps the honor was sort of a payment in advance. In any case there was nothing to do but wait and hope that Mr. Baldwin's euphoria was circumstantial and that the letter had done its job.

On his way to Aunt Annie's the following day, he stopped at a local jeweler, bought a fine necklace of seed pearls, and had it gift wrapped after inserting an appropriate card. Harry Baldwin had not yet arrived and after acknowledging the gift with a gush of

tears, Aunt Annie went into the kitchen to complete the preparations. A few minutes later he heard an insistent toot of a horn,
poked his head out the door and saw Baldwin emerge from the
car and beckon. The rear seat was filled with packages. As Samson carted in a large suit box, and a round hatbox, Baldwin followed with two overfilled grocery bags and a bunch of roses. He
was beaming; Samson had never seen him happier. He almost ran
toward the house looking like a large bird ready to soar. Aunt
Annie was at the door, he pecked her cheek and then stepped
back as his arm shot out handing her the roses. She hugged them
to her breast and they followed her into the living room. Taking
the suit box from Samson and placing it on the Victrola, he
grabbed the hatbox, and gave it to Aunt Annie. She handed Samson the flowers and started to open it.

"I hope it fits," Baldwin said. "It'll make you look like a picture."

It was a large hat of fine white straw with a garland of small
flowers about the crown. She ran to the mirror, placed it carefully
on her head, then stepped back to survey herself. Her pleasure
was evident as she turned and traced his cheek lightly with her
fingers.

"It'll go with a wedding dress," he said.

"It's lovely, Harry."

He clapped his hands and rubbed them together. "How about a
toast?" He looked at Aunt Annie, seeking her approval. "I
brought a little something." Reaching in one of the bags he removed a bottle of bourbon. "By prescription," he explained and
winked.

She brought out the glasses and he poured three shots. Glass
held high, he toasted her birthday, downed his drink, refilled the
glass and started to empty the contents of the bags. There was another bottle of bourbon, canned delicacies, and pungent imported
cheeses. As Aunt Annie carried them all to the kitchen Baldwin
finished his drink and stretched out in the easy chair.

Though Samson suspected Baldwin hit the bottle now and
then, he was surprised to see him guzzle in front of her. His nor-

mally florid face was now tinged in deeper tones and the color spread to his neck. An aura of nervous tension crackled from him. Samson watched as he poured another drink, gasp, and down it in a swallow. Aunt Annie called Samson from the kitchen. He carried out a large tray on which she had placed slices of cheese, Greek olives, a mound of goose liver, and small squares of black bread. They all began to eat with gusto and Samson found himself caught up with the fever. Baldwin poured another round, gulped his shot, and pulled a slim package from his inside coat pocket.

"For your birthday, my dear," he said, handing it to Aunt Annie, his face a broad grin as she untied the ribbon carefully. "I hope you like it."

Opening a flat jewelry box, she removed a finely wrought silver crucifix that dangled from a chain of tiny opals.

"It's old," he roared. "Belonged to a cardinal. Sixteenth century!" Aunt Annie seemed unable to speak, just shook her head as he took them from her and placed them around her neck. She fingered the cross as Harry Baldwin sat back after downing his drink. "Do you like it?"

"It's lovely," she whispered.

The undertaker's joy was more than could be contained. He was chortling now, out of control, slapping his knee with a hammy hand and rocking back and forth. "The birthday party isn't over!" he exclaimed and withdrew another package from his pocket. This one was long and round as a sausage. Removing a gay outside wrapper, Aunt Annie extracted a rolled-up parchment tied with a black ribbon. She looked at Baldwin. "Open it, open it!" he cried.

Samson watched as she slipped off the ribbon and unrolled the document. She started to read and at first her face wore a puzzled look, then she shook her head with disbelief, and handed the document to Samson. It was a deed to a cemetery plot in Hallowed Hills, made out to Annie Boyle, hand-drawn in ancient block print, signed by Baldwin and his partner, corporate sealed, and notarized. Samson looked up. Baldwin wasn't smiling and if the

expression on Aunt Annie's face was a reflection of her thoughts
it seemed possible that the letter to the bishop might have been
unnecessary, that Father Keenan's efforts at her conversion had
been nullified and that the undertaker was about to be thrown out
on his ass.

"How could you!" Aunt Annie rose and tore the paper from
Samson's hand. Samson stood up and withdrew behind his chair;
Baldwin's face was no mask for his confusion as it worked convul-
sively and he seemed unable to speak. "Can't you forget your
business! Can't you forget death!" She flung the deed on the
table, picked up her drink, and swallowed it.

Baldwin poured and downed a shot faster than Samson had
ever seen it executed, and whined as he spoke. "We all have to go
someday, Annie, dear. It's a fact." She turned her back to him.
He pushed his bulk from the chair and reached out to touch her
shoulder. She shuddered and he withdrew his hand. "It's the loveliest spot in Hallowed Hills. Right under an old oak." She whirled
on him. "Harry, you're sick! You're closer to death than you are
to life. Sometimes I think you want to die. Maybe to get those rewards in Heaven. Well, I don't!" She ran into the kitchen and
Baldwin followed, pleading all the way. "I meant well. I didn't
understand. We'll tear it up and forget about it." Samson stood at
the kitchen door watching, itching to make an observation that
would further aggravate the situation. Before he could think of
something to say, his aunt's fire banked and Baldwin got back in
the running. "Harry, you've got to understand how I feel about
these things," she said more gently, as the undertaker stood at her
side almost bleating with joy. The booze had him unhinged, he
was whimpering. "I know, I know. I promise you nothing like it
will happen again." He grabbed her hand. "You'll see," he said,
reading her face for a sign of forgiveness.

"All right," she finally said. "We'll forget it." Then she smiled
and Samson was certain Baldwin was going to fall to his knees.
She led him back to the living room, he grabbed the deed, tore it
to pieces, threw them in the air and they both laughed.

Now they were at dinner, finishing each course to loud praises from Baldwin. By the time the tea had cooled and the crumbs were swept, the single candle Aunt Annie had placed in the center of the table was sputtering near its end. Samson watched as Baldwin snuffed it with his fingers as if reluctant to see it die. His spirits appeared to have sagged but soon revived as he laced his cup with bourbon, mixing it generously with the fresh tea Aunt Annie had poured. Samson saw her start to speak and then shrug as she cleared the last of the table and went into the kitchen. Baldwin rose unsteadily and followed her and although Samson's back was turned he knew the undertaker's hands were playing as he heard her snap at him. Baldwin returned to the parlor wearing a foolish grin as Samson went into the kitchen to help with the dishes.

In a few minutes Baldwin appeared in the doorway holding the large box he had brought. "I got a surprise," he said, patting it, unable to control a broad smile.

Aunt Annie dried her hands and followed him as he backed into the parlor. Samson watched from the kitchen.

"What is it, Harry?"

Now his face had a mysterious look as he kept backing into the room as she followed, holding up the box as if it were bait.

"I saw Howie Brandon today," he said, placing the box on the table and patting it. He looked at it with so much feeling Samson almost expected Mr. Brandon to pop out.

As he started to untie the string Samson came into the room. Aunt Annie stood with arms folded and her mouth drawn as if defying him to surprise her. He fumbled with the knots and then with a flourish swept the lid off the box. Neatly folded and wrapped in tissue were the vestments of a Knight of St. Gregory. From a flat case that rested on top he removed the medallion, a red enameled Maltese Cross suspended from a yellow bordered red ribbon. A small white center was engraved with a likeness of St. George and on its back the motto "Pro Deo et Principe."

"What does it mean?" Samson asked, as Baldwin read it in solemn tones.

"For God and Prince," he said; his voice choked.

"Let's see the other things," Aunt Annie said.

He started to remove the contents handling each item as one would the Infant Jesus. The dresscoat was of dark green, open in front and covered on chest and back with embroideries in the form of oak leaves. He placed it carefully on the back of a chair as Aunt Annie fingered it admiringly.

"What lovely handiwork," she exclaimed.

"It's made in Rome by the cardinals' tailors."

Samson could not help admire the white trousers with silver side stripes and bicornered hat.

"It's quite an outfit," he said as he displayed the last item, a knightly sword that completed the vestments.

"Is Mr. Brandon lending it to you for the ceremony?" Aunt Annie asked.

"Oh no," he said, as he held the dress coat in front of him as if trying it for size. "He loaned it to me for tonight. Just to show you."

"Why don't you try it on?" she suggested.

"Do you think I should?"

"Go ahead," she said.

The undertaker poured himself a steadying drink and downed it in a gulp. Removing his jacket, he slid into the garment and with Aunt Annie's help hung the medal around his neck. The last drink removed any trace of sobriety. Strapping the sword around his waist, Baldwin puffed up and started to pace the room, reeling and gesticulating like a lusty ecclesiastic in a *Decameron* tale. Samson grabbed him as he nearly fell after knocking over the lamp, and led him to a chair. Aunt Annie ran to the kitchen and returned in a few moments with a mug of steaming tea.

"Drink this!" she commanded, "and stay put."

Baldwin gripped the mug with trembling hands, slumped in the chair, and started to sip the hot brew. The telephone rang. Baldwin bolted forward nearly tripping on the sword and sloshing tea as he clutched at the ringing instrument. "Hullo," he slurred, and then, as if revived by an electric charge, he was stripped of his indolence. "Yes, Father Keenan! Yes, Father, I'm listening."

As he did so, a puzzled expression spread across his face, then changed to utter incomprehension. "You say he just called?" Baldwin started to shake his head slowly, as if negating what he had just heard. Then, at length, he roared. "But *why?*" The sword had shifted to the front and caught between his legs. He pushed at it violently. "He's got to tell me *why!*" Spittle was beginning to form on the corners of his mouth and his eyes rolled in his head. "That isn't enough. There has to be more. I demand an explanation! Do you hear me?"

He listened another moment, Samson heard a click at the other end, and Baldwin slowly replaced the receiver. Aunt Annie helped him to the chair as Samson backed out and went into Aunt Annie's bedroom. It wasn't only that he couldn't bear to watch, it was that Aunt Annie usually read him right, and this was no time to test her powers of observation. For a fleeting moment he felt sorry for what he had done as he sat on the edge of the bed with the door open and listened to them in the living room. Aunt Annie was speaking softly, consoling Baldwin, but Samson could not distinguish her words.

Then he heard Baldwin, loud and clear. "They turned me down. And for no reasons!"

Samson left the bedroom and went into the hall, getting as close to the living room as he could without being seen.

"Just what *did* Father Keenan say?" Aunt Annie was asking.

"The bishop called. Said he got a communication from Rome. Just that I was turned down."

"Steady yourself," Aunt Annie said. "Take this."

Samson imagined she was giving him another drink. For a few moments there was silence. Then he heard the chair creak, as Baldwin arose, and then his steps as he paced the floor. He kept repeating, "I don't understand. I don't understand."

"Maybe there's a mistake," Aunt Annie offered.

"Oh, no. The Church doesn't make this kind of a mistake."

"Maybe if you speak to the bishop? Or write to Rome?"

"They thought of that too. Father Keenan said I'm to speak to no one and forget it. The Lord has strange ways, I think he said."

"It's true, Harry."

"Well, I don't like them. Do you hear?"

"Harry!"

"I don't care!" he shouted. "After all I've done."

"Please, Harry."

"It's easy for you," he went on, "but I've got to face people."

"You've had enough to drink," Aunt Annie said. "Quite enough."

"Leave me alone," he said angrily.

"I might do just that!"

"Oh, my God!" Baldwin intoned a woeful petition. "How could they do this to me?"

"Come here," Aunt Annie said kindly. "Sit by me."

His heavy steps moved across the room and then there was silence. For a long time Samson heard nothing and was about to move to a position where he could see when he heard Aunt Annie cry out, "Harry, don't!"

"Please, Annie. Please."

"You're drunk!"

Samson heard a scuffle, Aunt Annie screamed. Rushing into the room he saw her running from Baldwin, the top of her dress torn and part of her breast exposed. Baldwin lurched, tripped over the sword and fell to his knees.

Aunt Annie shot past Samson into the hall screaming hysterically. "Get him out of here! Get him out!" She reached her room and slammed the door.

Samson approached tentatively, then helped him to his feet. The undertaker was dazed. The scabbard of the sword was bent, the corner of his mouth was bleeding where the hilt must have struck him as he fell. His lips were working as if he was trying to speak. Slowly, dreamlike, he began taking off the dresscoat and undoing the sword. After placing the vestments in their box, he picked up his own jacket, hefted the large package and tottered out of the house without uttering a word.

It was the end, Samson thought, as he prepared to leave. Aunt Annie would have to write the epilogue, but he was damn sure the undertaker would have no part in it. He straightened up the house, left her a note saying he would call in the morning, and went home.

When he called the following day Aunt Annie refused to discuss the incident. Later, when he visited her, he got the impression she was experiencing great relief. The undertaker's efforts at a reconciliation—phone calls, flowers, and gifts—were ignored and she resisted all efforts of Father Keenan to see her. At length, Baldwin gave up, Father Keenan persisted a bit longer without success, and it was not long before Aunt Annie was fully recovered. There were scars, Samson was sure, but they were well hidden and soon faded. She referred to the entire incident only to make such points as, "there's an awful lot of truth in a bottle of bourbon," and "if I was unlucky I would have married the guy," and then she congratulated herself on her good fortune and credited "the luck of the Irish." Soon her resiliency returned all her bounce.

CHAPTER SEVEN

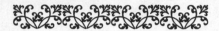

Nearly a month after they had applied for membership Samson and Art Jennings were notified of their acceptance by Midwood Country Club. Ralph Thompson broke the news, and they lunched that day in the club dining room with him, played a round of golf together, and afterward met at the bar. Everyone had his own bottle labeled with his name, tucked under the counter.

As Samson looked about he thought of the pine-floored kitchen of the New Brunswick farm, the chicken shit that always ringed his father's shoes, his thick fingers and dirty nails, and later the dreary Brooklyn flat. Now seated at a table in the birch-paneled room, a forest-green carpet cushioned Samson's feet; there was shiny brass, the crystal sparkled, and the smells were good. Soon, Art Jennings became drunk, his voice boomed and when he laughed his fat jiggled and Samson was reminded of the fat Hungarian in the Bronx and her husband—scrawny, his monkey face screwed, the creases filled with dirt—and then Rita and the hotel toilet streaked with blood. The picture blurred and faded as he got a whiff of a good cigar and saw the tree-lined fairway through the window and a Negro waiter was at his side, bowing, and the past blotted out. He felt like a coin that just got flipped. It was heads-up now.

Ralph looked at his watch. "I have time for one more."

"What's the rush?" Jennings said. "Let's have dinner. The three of us."

"I'd like to," Ralph said. "But someone is joining me."

"A woman?" Jennings smirked.

"As a matter of fact it's Miss Wilson from the bank."

"I tell you what," Art said. "Suppose I call Paula." He slapped Ralph on the back. "We'll make it a night." He turned to Samson. "How about it?"

Samson saw Thompson hesitate and was certain the banker wanted to be alone. Also, if he saw Paula again it would have to be under different conditions. "I'm afraid I can't make it, Art."

Jennings pounded his back. "C'mon." Then he turned to Ralph. "I know Willy. She'll like Paula."

Thompson had no choice. He asked Samson to stay, a plea in his tone. Maybe it was best this way, Samson thought. The presence of others would take the strain off and he did want to see Paula. He agreed and Art went out to call.

"I didn't want to intrude," he said the moment Art left.

"You're not intruding. When Art's drunk I don't argue with him."

Jennings returned and said Paula would be in a cab within an hour. Miss Wilson soon joined them and Samson found himself watching the clock across the room. Ralph had another bottle set up and by the time Art was paged to meet Paula at the entry, their party had become the noisiest in the bar. Samson managed to nurse his drink, and when Paula approached their table his head was clear.

The moment their eyes met he knew that she was told he was going to be there. He searched her face for a trace of surprise and found nothing but a faint smile tinged with amusement, as if knowing the meeting would disturb him and enjoying every moment of it. All the images of her he carried in his mind during the past few weeks were poor copies. Her hair seemed darker, a shiny blue-black, her eyes were larger and her skin, set off by a green dress, was glowing pearl. When she sat next to him, deliberately it seemed, he felt as warm as if their bodies had touched.

During the meal she barely looked at him and did not address him. Once or twice she nodded to remarks he made, and then returned her attention to Miss Wilson. Though they had stopped drinking, it appeared that Art was getting drunker. His eyes kept circling the room looking for a familiar face; he'd waved and grinned foolishly.

Once the meal was over, Samson saw Ralph look around like a trapped man for an exit. He caught Miss Wilson's eye and Samson knew the time had come to break it up. Calling the waiter, he signed the check in spite of Art's fumbling protests, and announced he had to leave. Jennings rose and almost fell. Samson rushed to his side and found an empty flask lying at his feet.

"Suppose we take him home," Ralph said.

"Don't bother," Paula said. "I'll handle him."

Jennings slumped in his seat.

"You and Willy go on. Let me take care of this," Samson said.

Thompson hesitated a brief moment, protested feebly, but left with a grateful nod at Samson.

Paula looked at Art with disgust. "I guess I'll need your help."

"Art drove down with me," he volunteered. "His car's at the office."

They got him to Samson's car, put him in the back seat without saying a word. All the feelings he had when they first met returned, more intense now, an accumulation. She sat beside him, looking straight ahead. Samson reached for her hand, which was resting on the seat beside him. For a moment it did not respond, then it turned and gripped his. They pulled up at the curb in front of Jennings' house. A groan came from the back seat. They both turned, looked at the inert mass, and got out of the car.

Samson dragged Art into the bedroom, dropped him on the bed, and removed his shoes.

Paula was in the living room and came into his arms the moment he entered. He left her sleeping on the couch at midnight and slipped out the front door.

Art came into his office at noon the following day. "I don't know how Paula would have managed without you."

"You were kind of heavy," Samson said guardedly.

"Can't remember a thing after you paid the check."

"You must have killed a quart."

"I really celebrated. Anyway, thanks." He left and Samson called Paula. Her voice was more cheerful than he had ever known it. "I had the best night's sleep in a month."

"When can I see you?"

"Whenever you wish."

With careful planning that could be often. Art was always under his nose, and he would even get an advance notice of an out-of-town jaunt. As he hung up the phone and started to clear his desk he thought about the past few months. Every hook he baited had brought a catch. His net worth had been increased by commissions, there was a profit on one building and the acquisition of another. He had gotten rid of Gloria, Paula was available, and most important, he had become a member of the club. And all the while, all about him, in the city and in the country, millions were scrambling for jobs, any kind, enough to eat and a place to live. Even his membership in Midwood was once owned by a chump who could only make it when the going was good.

During the following months he discovered that even the established had rotten timbers. The club became home and office and he managed to get there every day. He saw more memberships change hands as those who were hanging on dropped and were replaced by an eager waiting list. The members who had it a long time, inherited estates, bonds and blue chip stocks all paid for, had only to tighten their belts, but those who'd made it in the twenties riding high on thin equities went down the drain. A few still clung to their holdings, stalled mortgage holders and borrowed from friends, hoping desperately for a turn in the economy. In the beginning when the bottom slipped from under the market and it was thought a temporary adjustment, the members closed ranks, accommodated the losers with personal loans and moratoriums on dues and assessments. Now with the bite getting bigger and the cost of carrying the club shifting to fewer shoulders, the sounds of pity became rumblings of discontent and soon after a cry to dump the nonpaying freight. By the time Samson had joined up there were no more tears. It was pay-up-or-get-out. As memberships became available the admittance rules relaxed and a bank account carried the weight. Though a surface camaraderie was observed, the old-timers kept to themselves. He remained apart from both cliques putting himself in a position to deal with either.

As Samson was leaving his office, he saw Aunt Annie coming up the steps. He hustled her through the entry hall, into his room, and closed the door. Until then he had managed to keep her away in spite of the fact she had asked a dozen times to see his office. He had every excuse to keep her tucked away in Gardena. The old nose had disappeared and so had Dukins. And his ancestry had been embroidered. Though Aunt Annie did not look like a peasant, she was rough-cut and miscast for a role in his tale. As she looked about the room admiringly he wondered how to get her out without being seen.

"I won't be long, Sam," she said, removing her gloves and hat as she seated herself. "Don't worry."

"Why should I be worried?"

She ignored his question. "I invited myself today because I couldn't wait any longer for an invitation. And I'd like to see your apartment while I'm at it. Is it close?"

"Just a few blocks. Why don't we go there now?" he said, standing up.

"Let me rest a bit. It was a long walk from the bus." After a few moments of careful observation, nodding approval at an Atwater Kent radio and a handsome table on which Samson stocked copies of the Los Angeles *Times*' classified ads, his weekend "bible," she began to pull her gloves on slowly and reached for her hat. He took her arm and led her from the room, made the street without bumping into anyone, and drove her to his apartment. After inspecting it carefully, fingering the drapes, trying the couch and the chair and even bouncing on the bed, they left and he carefully chose an elegant tearoom on Wilshire where he stood no chance of being recognized. After lunch he drove her home. She was restless, she told him, found long hours between chores with little to do. "I've energy for much more than is laid out for me. And it's a pity it's going to waste."

An idea flashed in his head. It would keep her busy, freeze her money, and he wouldn't have to worry about it dribbling away. "Let me find you a good buy in an apartment house. It will be a fine investment and you can manage it. That'll give you plenty to do."

"With things like they are, people poor, unable to pay rent. . . ." She laughed. "Can you picture me kicking a poor devil out?"

"It doesn't have to be that kind of a building. We'll find one in Beverly Hills or someplace like it. Everybody isn't broke, you know."

"No, I'm not the landlord type, Sam."

He began to argue with her but she would not budge and he reminded her that he was a landlord and that it paid four times what she got in the savings and loan.

During the following weeks he kept in touch with her by phone but found no time to visit her. Aunt Annie was not only pleasant about it, there seemed to be a tone of relief in her voice when he declined her dinner invitations.

From a club member in dues difficulties, Samson acquired two more smaller buildings, placed them under Delaney's supervision, and discovered that his estimation of the man had aimed low. The more work Delaney had the more time he found, as though each project tapped new sources of energy. His limited imagination made it impossible for any manager to innovate a method of his own. He had his ways and they worked and to change them would be unthinkable. Anyway, the buildings were full and Samson wasn't going to tamper with perfection.

Since he was buying when everyone was selling there was talk about him at the club and somebody started the rumor that he was a "Duke," a member of the southern tobacco family. Samson said or did nothing to discourage the stories.

As Samson's activities flourished, a series of events in Art Jennings' life made Paula available to Samson as often as he wished. After a violent argument with Gloria resulting from her insistence that Jennings see her more often he gave her up, fired his secretary, and hired a young girl he had met weeks before. On the day she came to work, Art sat in Samson's office gloating over his coup.

"Is there any reason you shouldn't have it around when you want it? And on the payroll too?"

Samson could see his point.

"And it's a helluva lot cheaper. I get laid, letters typed, some bookkeeping even if it's a little sloppy, all for sixteen dollars a week."

She was young, could not have been more than twenty, and though she had a fine figure her face was plain, course grained, and she never smiled. She would answer calls in a monotone, hunched over her typewriter as if the effort was painful, took dictation in longhand, and when Art was not in the office sat at his desk smoking incessantly and reading magazines.

"She's not much to look at," Art admitted. "But she's great in the hay. Loves it. And she lives alone in a hotel room on Sixth Street. It's sure convenient."

When Samson had time he would have Paula meet him at his apartment where they would spend the afternoon. On the nights

Art would stay out, they would go to dinner and on one occasion when Art took the weekend off they drove to Santa Barbara for a night.

Though Paula accepted his decision about marrying and never brought it up directly, her feelings were always bristling under the surface of their conversation. At times she would flare up for no apparent reason, then simmer down to a state of depression. On other occasions she would discuss marriage in general, investing it with the good life of companionship opposing the lonely existence. Samson would listen and say nothing. The conversations were becoming more frequent and he realized sooner or later she would take another shot at pinning him down.

During the presidential campaign, he began to see her less. The club had become a Hoover headquarters right after the nomination in June and Samson was named cochairman of the Ways and Means Committee. Though he maintained his preference for the President over Roosevelt, who had swamped Al Smith at the Democratic convention, his choice had more to do with fitting in than enthusiasm for Hoover. He did not know much about Roosevelt but could see nothing in Hoover's projections that might bring the country out of the Depression.

In spite of his feelings, however, he worked hard and gave life to the committee that the chairman headed in name only. The work brought him in contact with the wives of the members who were active in the campaign. One morning he received a call from the head of the women's division asking for an appointment to discuss a fund-raising affair she was planning.

"I'll be at the club," she said. "Can we have lunch?"

He made the date and tried to remember what he had heard about her husband, Eugene Botsford. He recalled a casual meeting, could not recall a face to go with the Botsford name, but knew he was an attorney heavily involved in real estate.

He was pleasantly surprised when an attractive woman looking to be in her late twenties rose to greet him from a corner table in the dining room. His frank appraisal as they seated brought a burst of laughter.

"You look like you expected an old dowager, Mr. Duke."

"Not exactly," he hedged.

"Well, I'm older than I look." She examined him. "I imagine you are too."

They settled down to business and he listened and watched her. She had a fresh beauty, fine features, highlighted by exquisite eyes beneath brows that tilted upwards giving her a look of eagerness. What impressed him most was her self-assurance and poise. As she enfolded her plans he half-listened and found himself wondering about her husband and her relationship with him.

She interrupted his thoughts. "You don't seem to be listening. You've agreed to everything. I need advice, Mr. Duke."

"You've arranged everything perfectly."

"Except the main attraction. We need a name that will pull. Perhaps a movie star." She named a few, known to be active Republicans and he told her he would try to line up one immediately.

Nearly a week later he went to the club for nine holes before going to the office. There was no one about and he decided to practice putting until someone showed up. He heard his name and Grace Botsford approached, dressed for golf and carrying a putter. "Looking for a game?" she asked.

"As a matter of fact I was."

"Do you mind a twosome with a lady?"

They teed off and if he had any fear of her slowing down his game they were dispelled when she hit the first ball. She had a grooved-swing and the ball sailed two hundred yards down the fairway. By the fourth hole she had him three down.

"I don't want you to tell anyone about this," he said, as they reached the fifth tee.

"Don't worry about it. I can beat half the men in the club. I've been playing since I was a child."

Somehow she gave him the feeling he didn't belong, was an uncut stone needing a polish. But then his game warmed up and he took the next two holes and she dubbed a few shots and he belonged again and figured a lot of polish was rubbed on with a dollar bill.

They finished nine holes and after showers she joined him for brunch. They parted and made a date for another game. They played a week later and a week after that and then twice a week. He learned that her husband had been syndicating deals with clients and friends, was in quite a few large apartment houses and had dealt in first mortgage bonds.

One day after finishing at the club he walked her to the car. "I'd like to take you to lunch," he said.

"You have been taking me to lunch."

"I don't mean at the club."

There was a moment's hesitation. "How about the day after tomorrow?"

He agreed to pick her up at the hairdressers at noon.

Returning to his office, he worked until evening, then decided to surprise Aunt Annie, whom he hadn't seen in weeks. He did not reach the house in Gardena until after seven. Walking in, he found his aunt and a strange man finishing their dinner. The last of a bottle of wine, a wedge of golden provolone cheese, and a bowl of fruit were in the center of the table as they sipped black coffee from tiny cups. As Aunt Annie rose to introduce him, tucking her stray hairs, an action she always indulged in when flustered, Samson had a feeling he had stumbled upon something that had been hidden from him. "This is Mr. Marcotulli, Sam," she said, fingering a lock as she held it in place.

The man bowed his head and muttered a greeting so softly he could not distinguish a word.

"Mr. Marcotulli is a neighbor. Lives up the street with the Rizzos," she said, looking at the seated man as if to confirm her explanation.

"That's right," he said, in that strange soft tone, distinguished this time by a strong Italian accent.

Samson had never heard of the Rizzos, did not know his aunt was intimate with anyone in the neighborhood. Now he felt like an intruder, decided to stay a few minutes, leave gracefully and get the full story from Aunt Annie in the morning. Smiling at Mr. Marcotulli, he turned to her. "Was in the neighborhood, thought I would drop by for a few moments."

"Have you had supper?"

"I'm not hungry."

"Some fruit perhaps? Maybe some cheese?" Mr. Marcotulli asked, smiling. "Good Italian cheese?"

"Come on, Sam," Aunt Annie said, seeming to have regained her composure. "Let me get you something."

He saw no reason for not finding out about Mr. Marcotulli first hand. Besides, he was hungry.

Aunt Annie went into the kitchen as he seated himself at the table. Mr. Marcotulli was deep in thought as he pared an apple. Samson watched as the delicate hands, handling the knife with incredible skill, peeled the skin as he twirled the apple, ending with a spiral intact which he held up for a moment and then let fall to the table. They both watched it curl up and then lie still like an expiring snake. He quartered the apple, placed it on a dish with a piece of cheese and offered it. Then he poured a water glass full of wine and placed it in front of Samson as Aunt Annie came in bearing a salami sandwich and a glass of milk.

"He doesn't drink wine!" she cried out.

"It is good with food," Mr. Marcotulli said.

"Well, he's not used to it."

"Aunt Annie, I'm not a child anymore."

Mr. Marcotulli tossed his head back and laughed and the soft graying ringlets that covered it in a marvelous thick disarray, danced as his frame shook.

"What are you laughing at?" Aunt Annie demanded, unable to contain a smile.

Marcotulli straightened up and looked at her, a pair of wide-set eyes staring amusedly from his long hollowed face. "Wine is squeezed from grapes. Milk is squeezed from cow. What is wrong with grape?"

"Oh, Danny," she said, raising her hands in mock despair.

He wondered how long she had been calling him by his first name.

He smiled and turned to Samson. "Your aunt, she change my name to Irish."

"What is your name?"

"Dante."

"Danny's easier, that's all," she said. "And it ain't Irish."

"Oh, I like it, Annie," he said. "I like it much."

If there was any doubt in his mind about their relationship, it was dispelled when she ruffled his hair playfully.

"Come," she said, "you and Sam do the dishes while I straighten up."

He rose from the chair, surprising Samson by his height. As he sat, his shoulders slumped, he gave the impression of being no more than average size. Even stooped, he was close to six feet. He cleared the table and insisted on washing. "Anyway, you finish sandwich. Is good for my hands," he explained, extending them, palms up, the long fingers stained at the tips.

"What kind of work do you do?"

"Cigarmaker."

"Where do you work?"

"I work for Buckeye. Third Street, near Broadway."

"Buckeye?"

He turned, leaving his hands resting in the water. "Buckeye is a little man. Used to be cigarmaker. Now has small place with three, four workers."

"Do you work in a window?"

"No," he said, as he resumed washing. "But I've worked in window."

He was scrubbing a pot now as he hummed an unfamiliar tune and Samson, still munching the sandwich, dried the dishes silently. He began to wonder how far this thing had gone and whether Aunt Annie's secrecy or his preoccupation had kept him ignorant of its existence.

Depositing the last dish on the drainboard with a flourish, Marcotulli dried his hands as Aunt Annie came in. She was dressed to go out and with hands on hips surveyed the kitchen.

"I see you had Danny washing."

"He wanted to."

"I like it better," he said, rolling his shirt sleeves down and linking the cuffs.

"We have to leave," she said. "I didn't know you were coming."

"I have to go anyway." He started to ask her where they were going and decided against it. There was something about her air that suggested it was part of the secret.

Donning a long, dark overcoat and a battered black fedora which he wore like an old-time actor, Mr. Marcotulli took Aunt Annie's arm, and they left.

One thing was certain, his aunt's relationship with the Italian was not casual and if that was the case, Samson wanted to know all about him. He was obviously broke; every piece of clothing he wore looked like they were handed down and Samson was damn sure cigarmaking had no future. He could not understand what she saw in the man. Oh, he was sort of attractive, and his manner, foreign though it was, had some charm, but where were the things that tied people together? Being Italian Samson figured he was Catholic. Could it be that, another crack at religion, escorted this time in another style, a tall, thin swashbuckler instead of a slab of lard? One thing worried him; he hoped it wasn't physical attraction, infatuation . . . love.

The following morning he popped in at Aunt Annie's just as she sat down to breakfast.

"This is a surprise," she said pointedly. "No work today?"

"Sure. Just thought I'd drop in. After all, I haven't seen you in some time. And last night . . ."

"We did have an appointment."

He poured a cup of tea and joined her at the table. "Your friend, Mr. Marcotulli. He seems to be a nice man."

Her mouth was full of food and she nodded.

"How long have you known him?"

"About a month."

"How did you meet him?"

"At Mrs. Rizzo's." She had taken a last bite, a sip of tea and then eyed him. She started to laugh. "You're sitting there like you're about to bust."

"What do you mean?"

Now she laughed aloud and he finally joined in.

"All right, so I want to know all about him. Is there anything wrong?"

"Nothing. What do you want to know?"

"Well . . . you know . . . all about him."

She lit a cigarette, puffed a few times, and for a moment did not speak. Then, very seriously she began. "One day I saw Mrs. Rizzo in the grocery. We used to just say hello. This time we talked and she invited me in. There was nothing else so I went. I met her kids and Mr. Rizzo. They were nice and treated me like I belonged. I never met people like that before, Sam. They were warm. It was like. . . . I don't know how to explain. . . . maybe like I had a family." Her eyes lingered on him for a moment. "You're all I've got, Sam. I get cold sometimes when I think if something happens. Your moving away or. . . ."

He assured her he was going nowhere and brought the conversation back to Danny. "When did you meet him?"

"It was one night when I went to a meeting with Angie and Tony. That's Mr. and Mrs. Rizzo," she explained.

"Meeting?"

"Yes." She was looking at him steadily, a little defiantly. "In a hall on Eighth Street, downtown. There were speeches. They were raising money for the Scottsboro Boys."

"The Scottsboro Boys! They're criminals."

"They're innocent," she said firmly.

"That's not what I hear."

"From who?"

"I read, don't I?"

"What do you read?"

"The newspapers!" He was shouting now.

"You mean the lying capitalistic press!"

"Aunt Annie, what are you saying? You sound like an anarchist."

"Maybe that's not a bad thing to sound like."

"You're joking. Anarchists want to overthrow the government. They're dangerous!"

Aunt Annie jumped to her feet and shouted back. "How do you know! Did you ever meet an anarchist? Do you know what they believe in?"

"Aunt Annie, you must be crazy! *Everybody* knows what they believe in."

"What does *everybody* know?" she said, standing over him defiantly.

"They don't believe in government. They cause strikes. And they're all foreigners."

"That's what I thought," she said contemptuously. "You don't know a thing. You just wait here," she said, and rushed out of the room. She returned with both hands clutching fistfuls of booklets which she slammed on the table before him. "Here," she demanded. "Read these and *then* tell me you know about anarchism."

He spread them out, over a dozen pamphlets: "Anarchism: What It Really Stands For," by Emma Goldman; "Psychology of Political Violence" and "Marriage and Love," by the same woman; "The Wage System" by Peter Kropotkin; another containing his ideas on "The Historic Role of the State"; others on "Patriotism and the Conquest of Bread"; and finally some tracts by two with the unlikely names of Voltairine de Cleyre and Hippolyte Havel.

He looked up at her. "You read these?"

"Every word."

Though he only had a fleeting moment to scan the booklets it seemed that to understand their contents would require more than a few years in school and a home course in chicken raising. Aunt Annie had common sense but sure in hell wasn't ready for a sudden leap into higher learning. With the exception of the Bible, all of her study had been confined to the daily paper and two cookbooks. As he watched her standing over him, her face alive with excitement, it was evident that, contained in the infection of anarchism, was an elixir that transported her to a state of ecstasy.

His concern was not with her new interest but the power of its grip. No sense to any further discussion until he had read the pamphlets, he reasoned, then gathered them up, assured her he would go over them carefully, and left.

"You'll find a new world, Sam," she called out after him.

By the end of that day, he finished the last of the unbelievable polemics and realized his earlier battle with her involvement in the Church had been a local skirmish compared to the one he now faced. Although not easy to fight, promises made for the hereafter can find strong opposition in desires for the present, but when utopia is offered to be enjoyed here on earth, its a siren-call hard to resist.

By God, the Church was in business for a long time and he knocked them out of the box and he was damn sure a dead-broke cigarmaker with a new religion would be a cinch. But his aunt was vulnerable, had a big heart and a bank account.

The situation with his aunt and Dante, which had persisted in his thoughts, still rankled at the outer edges as he drove to meet Grace Botsford for the luncheon he had planned so carefully. Picking her up, they headed for an out-of-the-way place he knew, a small French restaurant in Santa Monica.

From the moment she got into the car she began to talk about the election. It was a month away and all the polls showed Roosevelt ahead. She could not understand how people could vote for the man. "If he wins, the country will go down the road to socialism."

"He sure talks that way," Samson said.

"Sam, he just *can't* win."

He laughed. "You sound as if I can do something about it."

"I wish somebody could. He's a traitor to his class."

"On the other hand, if things get much worse there would be anarchy." He thought of Dante and his kind and how delighted they would be, and wondered what would happen if they took over. Somehow, it struck him as amusing and he started to laugh.

"It isn't funny," she said angrily.

"I wasn't laughing at that. It was something else. Something silly. Anyway," he went on seriously, "things have been getting worse since the Crash. Hoover has tried everything. Nothing seems to work."

"You sound like a damn Democrat."

"I'm a good Republican. But I'd like to hear a little different talk from Washington these days."

"What kind of talk?" she challenged.

"Hoover should be making promises. Let him talk about a give-away."

"You mean a takeaway," she said. "Like that Socialist, Huey Long, said a couple of months ago. Get rid of the millionaires!"

"That's campaign promises. Everybody forgets them after the election. But they get votes. And that's what Hoover needs."

"But he's not Huey Long. Hoover is an honest man. His promises will have to be kept."

"Just a few. Voters have poor memories."

"Suppose you're wrong. He could be pressured into giving up all the rights we've fought so hard for."

"Sometimes you have to give up a little to keep a big chunk. If this thing goes on there could be a rebellion. It could mean riots and guns. God knows what. They could take away everything a man has."

"What do you think Roosevelt will do? Just that. Do you know, Gene is so frightened of what that man will do he's talking of leaving the country!"

Samson had not arranged the luncheon to talk politics and decided to turn the conversation around. "If he leaves you will go with him?"

"Of course."

"I wouldn't want you to leave."

That brought a smile and he edged closer. Then he got a look at her other side, the part that didn't show, as she told him of her girlhood in Philadelphia, the only child of a physician and how they finally let her go to Los Angeles, and of her meeting with Gene Botsford.

"He was thirty-five and I was twenty-two. It was what I needed. Even after two years away from home I was frightened. All my life every decision had been made for me." She nodded slowly. "My parents meant well, but it would have been better if they'd propped me up the moment I could stand and given me a push."

"I was luckier," he said. And then he dressed his past with wealthy parents, a broken home, and being raised by a maiden aunt who had not relied on a push, but rather a sound kick.

"You were fortunate," her hand was resting in his now and their thighs were touching. Then she told him about her marriage. "Gene's family were prominent in Pasadena. Their home on Orange Grove Avenue was very large. There were hundreds of guests. We left on a three-month honeymoon to Europe and returned to find a wedding present. It was the home we now occupy. A gift from my father-in-law furnished by my parents."

"Generous."

She shook her head emphatically as she lit a cigarette. "It was appalling! It was *my* home and I wasn't consulted. But it was what I needed to wake me up. The house was a smaller edition of Gene's parents' in Pasadena and the furniture looked as if it had been carted out from Philadelphia."

"What did you do?"

"Something happened to me. It was as if I had never seen myself and suddenly there I was in full view for the first time. I hated my dependence and knew if I did not take a stand then, I never would." She smiled. "We moved to a hotel. I called a dealer and sold everything in the house. Stripped it to the walls and then had it redecorated my way. I refurnished. It took me a whole year but I got what I wanted. I tell you, it was like being set free."

"It took a lot of courage."

"Just the first step. Then it was easy."

When he left her that day he realized that his interest in women in the past had centered around one drive. To be able to talk to a woman, exchange ideas, enjoy her company out of bed, was new.

Art Jennings and his secretary were leaving the building when he reached his office. From the way they were hooked, arm-in-arm, he knew they were headed for her room and a late night. Being with Grace Botsford had primed him. He called Paula.

Her voice was edged with anger. "I thought you disappeared."

He realized he hadn't spoken to her in a couple of weeks. "It's been the campaign. Day and night."

She made a nasty remark about Hoover. Ignoring it, he asked if she could get out that night.

"Sure, why not. Art called awhile ago. He said something about the club, an appointment and a few other things I didn't bother to listen to."

"How about my apartment. I'll get a couple of steaks."

When she got there and greeted him without a smile he realized how much he had neglected her. Until he'd met Grace Botsford he managed to see her once or twice a week. He soothed her, asked for forgiveness, said that the election meant a lot and took so much time.

"You could have called," she said. Now there was a trace of a smile and soon her anger disappeared. She stayed until midnight.

During the next few days he called Aunt Annie a half-dozen times and there was no answer. On Saturday morning he arrived at her home before nine. Although she greeted him with a kiss, he noted a coolness. Dumping the pamphlets she had given him on the table he told her he had read them and wanted to discuss them. Her look was hostile.

"Don't you want to talk about them?"

"I'll listen."

He chose his words with care. "The ultimate end these people seek is admirable, but they're bucking the true nature of man. They'll never succeed. Utopian dreams are just dreams, Aunt Annie. They never did work and they never will work."

"Why not?" she demanded. "Because you say so?"

"No. Because all history has proven it so. If you took all the wealth of the country and divided it equally, within a short time a small elite would have it all again."

She screamed. "You mean the international cartels, the finance capitalists, the exploiters of man! They'd be wiped out! You talk that way because you're one of them." She was puffing on a cigarette and looking at him with a hint of contempt.

She sure learned the jargon, he figured, and had the fire of the novice, but she was operating on passion, not facts, and he knew damn well that Mr. Marcotulli was supplying the charge. To oppose her with logic would be useless and to hurl rhetoric in the face of hers would be like screaming at the wind. She did not have a slight infection but the whole disease and it looked like it was going to take a lot of curing. She stood in the middle of the room now, hands on hips and legs spread apart.

"Aunt Annie," he began, "How can you accuse me of being one of them?" He shrugged. "I'm a little man. I work hard. Suppose I own a building or two."

"The worst exploiter is the landlord. He produces nothing."

Now he thought about her money laying in the savings and loan producing interest without any effort on her part. He wondered what she thought about money multiplying itself but wasn't going to ask.

"What do you call a producer?" he asked.

"A man who works with his hands . . . a man who makes useful things." She headed for the kitchen. "How about tea?"

"Make it coffee this time. Strong." He followed her. "What about a man who produces with his brain? Say a lawyer."

"There would be no need for lawyers in the new society."

"All right then, a doctor."

"He's a healer."

"But he doesn't produce with his hands."

"Yes he does."

Then he ran through engineers, architects, and teachers and got the same answer. By this time they were seated at the table sipping the hot drinks. She seemed to soften now and asked if he wanted eggs or pancakes. He declined and went on. "Look," he said. "Some of the most important contributions are made without the use of hands. There are philosophers, thinkers, planners."

"Are you comparing yourself with them?"

"I'm not, I was just saying. . . ."

She laid a hand on his arm. "Sam, dear, you contribute nothing. Somebody built the building you own, somebody manages it and collects the rents and all you do is sit on your behind after putting the money in the bank."

Mr. Marcotulli must have been doing some fast talking because Aunt Annie hadn't originated those lines. It was bad enough filling his aunt's head with anarchistic nonsense, but now it looked like he was being alienated as well.

"I guess the only way you and I are going to get along is for me to sell my buildings and get a job digging ditches."

She laughed. "I don't expect anything like that. You'll probably end up owning a hundred buildings, and we'll always get along, no matter what." She reached over and pecked his cheek. "But for the first time in my life I know what's right. And I'm going to spend the rest of it fighting."

"And there'll be no hard feelings?"

"Never. Except if you try to stop me, Samson."

"Don't you try to change me, either."

"It's a deal," she said.

When he left that day he was disturbed, certain the Italian was drawn to his aunt because of her money. What else could there be? Sure she was attractive but there were a lot of good-looking widows around, and unless they were honeyed-up with a bank account they didn't attract flies. And it looked like the cigarmaker had some education—more than a little—and Aunt Annie knew nothing. So, they had nothing in common except that which usually makes a match: a plump, attractive widow with money and a lean, hungry suitor.

Betting became heavy a week before election. The polls indicated a Roosevelt victory and the gamblers were laying as much as three-to-one. In spite of it the club was flooded with Hoover money; so much so that bets were being offered at two-to-one and less, and even money that Hoover would carry California. In spite of his sympathy, Samson was convinced that the Republicans did not have a chance. To take their bets would put him on the outside and to win would make it worse. But he felt he could not pass up a sure thing.

A few days before the election he had joined a gathering at the bar. Within a few minutes he added to the chorus that Hoover could not lose, affirmed that the polls were working for the Democrats and patted one member on the back when he predicted that Norman Thomas would siphon enough votes from the Democrats to defeat them.

"Three-to-one," someone said. "They must be crazy!"

"It's all talk!" another shouted. "I'd like to see the color of their money."

"I'd like to make a big bet," one man said. "Three-to-one or two-to-one If that man gets in he'll have all our money anyway." He was Teddy Hofstedter, a stockbroker who had inherited a profitable business from his father. In his early thirties, with a round face and belly, he was known for his German sympathies. On a tour of Germany the year before he had met Hitler and since, sported a square mustache.

"I know a hot Democrat, Hoff," Samson said. "I know I can get two-to-one, maybe better. But he wants a big bet. About ten thousand. I'd take a thousand of it."

Hofstedter pushed his way through the crowd and grabbed Samson's arm. "I'll take the rest. All he wants. Try to get better than two-to-one." Others insisted on taking a thousand each. Hofstedter relinquished grudgingly. "I'll let you know tomorrow," Samson said.

"And I want the cash put up." Hofstedter shouted as Samson walked off.

"Will you trust me to hold the stakes?"

"Of course I will. And you'll get mine the minute you tell me it's a bet." The other bettors agreed. Samson was to hold the stakes.

He called Hofstedter the following day and told him he had a bet. "Ten thousand at two-to-one. Couldn't do better."

"Did you tell him about the polls?" Hofstedter insisted.

"He told me to bet the magazine."

"All right. He's got a bet. I'll guarantee it all and collect from the others. Do you want my money?"

"I'll get his but I don't need yours, Hoff." He was so sure Hoover couldn't make it to the gate he decided to sweeten the pot. "He gave me twelve hundred to a thousand on California," he said. "It's got to go Republican."

"It's a cinch," Hofstedter said.

"I figure it is, too. Do you want half the action?"

"I sure do. Thanks a lot, Sam."

A few minutes after he hung up, Hofstedter called back. "Who's the sucker we're betting with?"

For a reason he could never understand only one name came to his mind. "His name is Marcotulli."

"What!"

"An Italian. He's related to the Guastis," he added hastily. "Old California family. Vineyards."

"It's going to take a lot of grapes to pay off," he roared.

"That's what I told him, Hoff." He wished he had doubled the bet.

By ten o'clock on election night even the most enthusiastic Republicans knew they had backed a loser. The victory celebration at the club had turned into a dirge and Samson found it difficult, going from group to group, to match the stunned looks and unsmiling faces as he contemplated the quick forty-five hundred he was to collect from Hofstedter. He had all he could do to wreathe his face with bewilderment and pain and shake his head in disbelief. He joined a party in the bar where Grace Botsford sat pulling at a wet handkerchief. He got a good look at her husband for the first time. Slightly stooped with rimless glasses pinched to his nose, he looked like one of Samson's dusty old professors. A halfdozen others slumped at a table and the talk was depressed. Grace looked up as he approached, tried a smile, mumbled a few introductions including one to her husband and lapsed into gloom.

"I guess we're in for it now," Samson said. "Word is, Roosevelt's going to nationalize all businesses."

Voices rose in agreement.

"The banks, too."

". . . a Jew in the White House."

"A Jew?"

"The family name was Rosenfeld."

"I didn't know."

"Sure."

"Wait until the market opens tomorrow. . . ."

"It'll bottom out."

He moved to the edge of the group. If this kind of panic prevails, he thought, there will be more bargains and bigger ones. Every bit of common sense told him you could not sell the country short. Was there a better one, a richer one, a better place to go? And if they were right and the whole thing went under, what difference would it make? Their dollars would be worthless, their properties taken over, and even their lives would be in jeopardy. He knew what Dante would do if he got control. His apartments would become housing projects and Midwood a rest home for over-aged cigarmakers and they would all be *comrades* and Emma Goldman and Farrar and Kropotkin would look at you from the face of a dollar bill. Everything a man sweated for would be divvied up.

Outside on the veranda it was cool. A breeze tinged with jasmine whipped the dried branches of a eucalyptus, in the distance the fairways were black stretches and on their edges he could see the lights of the houses and above them the sky was inked out and higher up it was shot with stars. Nobody was about as he sat down and lit a cigarette. Through the door he could hear the radio still blaring the returns and a babble of voices drifted from the bar. He thought of Grace Botsford and her husband and the frightened men in the other room. He got the feeling that a new game was about to begin, with a fresh deck and different rules. Until now he had been walking cautiously, testing the surface before each step, looking to the older, more experienced to show him the way. He had lied to everyone about his age; a label of inexperience, ineptitude, unreliability, and then thought of Jennings with his young wife and younger girl friend attaching himself to youth, and Roy Phillips, runty and full of gin and Ralph Thompson tied to the bank, too old to stand on his own, and Bob Kinder begging him to stay, and the half-dead Walsh and Lifton, and it was clear that youth was the chips they had all lost. Where was the clear thinking, vigor, power to absorb? Isn't the mind clearest, sharpest, at twenty? And the store of energy, not drawn on by ulcers and hypertension, hardening of the arteries and coronaries? By God, youth wasn't a liability! It's drive could be a steamroller!

He arranged to meet Teddy Hofstedter at the club the following evening. Teddy had collected on the bet from the others; now he handed Samson a check made out for forty-five hundred dollars.

"Fill it in," he said. "I can't even spell a dago name."

"He came around early today, Hoff. I already paid him. Put it in my name." Hofstedter borrowed his pen and completed the check as he shook his head.

"It's not Hoover's loss that scares me, it's the landslide. It looks like he only took six states."

Samson had his bottle brought to the table and poured the drinks. "What difference does it make? We lost. That's what counts."

Hofstedter pulled his chair closer, leaned forward and lowered his voice. "It's a sign. The Jews and Commies have taken over the big-city machines as well as the federal government." His face was so close Samson noticed that the top of his squared mustache was penciled in. "Something's got to be done."

"What can you do?"

"Hitler saw it coming in Germany. The Jews and Commies taking over."

"But Hitler lost out in the elections the other day."

"Only a temporary setback, only temporary."

Samson saw Grace walking toward their table. As she joined them for a drink, Hofstedter seemed irritated by her presence. Anxious to be rid of him, Samson got Grace down to committee business. "Have you the final tabulation?" he asked her.

"That's what I want to talk to you about," she said. Samson caught the barest glint in her eye.

"This could be dull for you, Hoff. Will you excuse us?"

Hofstedter rose grudgingly and left.

"You're too bright," Samson said. "My mind was read before I opened my mouth."

"Anyone would want to get rid of Teddy. He's obnoxious. And that disgusting mustache." She made a face.

"Anyway, I owe you something. How about dinner some night?"

"How about tonight? Gene's off to a meeting and I was going to eat alone."

"Not any more. Where do we go?"

"I have to run home and tuck my son in. Suppose I meet you at Perino's," she looked at her watch, "say at seven."

As he drove home he began to plan strategy. There was no doubt in his mind that Grace was as eager as he. She had too much at stake to jeopardize her position by being seen alone with him for a senseless flirtation. But he could make no mistakes. She wasn't the kind he could take to a hotel, and he realized his apartment was ordinary, cheap. For some time he'd been thinking about moving to a larger, unfurnished flat. Hofstedter's easy pickings was a windfall and more than enough to furnish and decorate elegantly. He decided to look for a place without delay.

Arriving at Perino's early, he selected the darkest corner he could find. She joined him a little after seven.

"Did you have them lower the lights for you?" she said.

"For us."

Her answer was to move closer. They ordered dinner. He brought up the apartment idea and asked if she would help him find a suitable one and furnish it.

"I wouldn't think of it!"

"Why not?"

"Well, it's like . . . it's like a naughty tale of de Maupassant . . . or Balzac." His look was so serious she burst out laughing. "It really isn't that bad, Sam, but it can be misunderstood."

"By whom?"

"Others. And you."

"I don't get it. I meet a woman of excellent taste, solicit her advice, and she suggests triangles and intimate relations." He shook his head solemnly.

"I guess I deserve that. But the truth is I feel guilty about being here with you." He started to protest. "Not what you think," she interrupted. "Gene and I always had the kind of relationship that permitted me luncheons and dinners with men friends. He's been busy these past years and I've been alone often. But until tonight my dinners were with Gene's friends, mutual friends. And that's all it was, just visits. I enjoy business, find it exciting, Gene and I discuss it all the time. I know all his affairs."

He wondered about her last remark. Could it be that financial interests were the only thing she and her husband had in common? Or was he reading too much into circumstances, the difference in their ages, her husband's unattractiveness and that the fact that they were out together and alone?

"Gene's not a jealous man," she said. "I can tell him anything. I intended to tell him about tonight, but . . ." she hesitated. "I'm beginning to think I won't and it bothers me."

"I'm bothered too."

"What do you mean?"

"When we first met I found every moment with you stimulating. Talking to you, exchanging ideas. Didn't even mind the beatings at golf." He moved closer. "You're lovely, but that was only part of the attraction. I found you interesting to talk to, more than with most men. Now I must make a confession. Soon I knew I was kidding myself." He took her hand and forced her to face him. "I've never been out with a married woman before. I've never felt like this."

She reached in her purse and removed a mirror, found a lipstick, and drew it across her mouth, ran a finger under each eye as if to smooth a line and then lit a cigarette and puffed it slowly.

"I hardly know you," she said, moving from him. "You're so much younger than I. I'm thirty-four and you can't be more than twenty-seven or eight."

"Remember, I'm older than I look."

"Everybody at the club is talking about you, Sam," she said, changing the subject abruptly.

"About me?"

"You're young and rich and bright. You own apartment houses that are full when everyone else has vacancies. You're modest and never use the weight of your family name."

"The Dukes would probably deny I'm family." Now he changed the topic quickly. "Don't believe everything you hear. I'm not young, really dull, just look bright, my name was Dukin or something like that and I changed it to Duke because I thought it fitted my face and my buildings are filled with deadbeats." She laughed and then looked at her watch.

"It's getting late and if I'm not going to tell Gene where I was I had better get home before he does."

The parking lot was deserted. He slid into the seat beside her and pulled her toward him. She pushed at him for a moment and then came into his arms. Her lips were warm and moist and her arm about his neck squeezed like a vise and her tongue flicked against his and then she cried out and pushed him from her with such force that he fell against the door.

"Please go. Please!"

He walked to his car as she drove off. She didn't look back.

A half-hour later he was home mulling over plans for the new apartment and thinking about Grace and those last minutes with her. The phone rang. It was Paula.

"I've been calling all night. Are you still campaigning?"

"I was cleaning up loose ends."

Her voice was edgy. "I'm glad your Hoover lost."

"Is that what you called to tell me?"

"No. I just thought you should be the first to know."

"Know what?"

"That I'm going to have a baby."

For an agonizing moment he said nothing. He needed time to think!

"I had the test. Got the result today."

"Have you told Art?"

"He has nothing to do with it."

"How can you be so sure it's me?"

"Because I haven't let him touch me for months."

"Suppose we meet tomorrow, darling," he said, as tenderly as he could.

"Where?"

He suggested his apartment. She agreed to be there at eleven. Tossing all that night, unable to sleep, his thoughts grappling with fantasies, shattering bizarres; Paula hounding, demanding, haunting and a cuckolded Art Jennings confronting him, he welcomed a gray dawn and dragged himself out of bed. He went to his office, cleared his desk of urgent matters and was back at the apartment a few minutes before Paula arrived.

She looked elegant and calmer than he had ever seen her. Removing a pair of gloves slowly, she commented on his appearance, made the observation that the campaign had trimmed him a bit, examined a new painting he had bought, and then sat down. There was an air about her of confidence. He waited for her to speak.

She smiled. "Well, what are we going to do?"

"It's up to you."

"What do you mean?"

"Do you want to get rid of it?"

"An abortion!"

He nodded.

"I wouldn't think of it. It would be murder! I may not be a good Catholic, but I haven't strayed that far."

He shifted. "I didn't think you would. Just thought I'd mention it." He joined her on the couch. For a moment he looked at her and then put all the sincerity he could into his voice. "I thought about it all night and think I have a solution." She closed her hands over his. "We'll get married. But it will have to be handled carefully."

She was smiling now and her eyes were moist. "Oh, Sam. . . . I'll tell Art tonight."

"That'll ruin everything."

Her grip on his hand loosened.

"Look, Paula. I want that baby as much as you do. But I want to be able to support it, give it everything. If the word gets around I've been having an affair with a friend's wife and she's pregnant. . . ." He rose and waved his hands with a gesture of despair. "Well, if that happened I might as well give up everything and move out of the city." He turned and faced her. "Every friend and contact I have knows Art. I'd be thrown out of the club and barred in every office in town." Fear and uncertainty began to cloud her face. He waited a moment until it got a good hold. "You're going to tell Art. Right away. But he's got to think it's his child."

"I don't know what you're getting at, Sam. If I did what you say he'd never believe it."

"He's got to believe it."

"But I haven't let him touch me. I told you!"

"How many times has he come home drunk in the past few months?"

She shuddered.

"Tell him it must have been one of those times. He'd never know the difference. Tell him he blacked out. It's happened to him before. I know it will work," he insisted, and went on. "It's his child. He's happy and the baby is born. By this time your life becomes intolerable. He's been cheating and you know it. You fight. You want a divorce. Then you turn to me, one of your few friends and I can't let you down. I even tell Art that you came to me, there was nobody else, and I'm lending support. He might even appreciate it. After all, you have a child to worry about. His child. After the divorce I start seeing you and in the usual course of events we fall in love. We get married and I legally adopt the baby. You see, Paula, it's simple."

"Simple?"

"Sure," he said.

"Simple," she repeated. "Convincing a man a baby is his that isn't." He started to interrupt, but she went on. "Spending a pregnancy with a man I despise!"

He got the feeling he was losing control and tried to interrupt but she ignored him, then stopped and looked at him shrewdly, suspiciously. "What if you change your mind?"

"About what?"

"Marrying me."

"How could I, darling?"

The moment the words were out he knew they weren't in the right key, rang too sincere. The look that went with them should have contained more hurt, indignation. He waited. Anything he said now could be the wrong thing.

She watched him a few moments longer as if enjoying his discomfort. "You know, I almost believed you." He started to protest but could only get to the beginning of an injured look. "Don't even try. I know you're lying. It's all over your face and it's sickening."

"Now you listen. . . ."

"You listen! I'm going home and tell Art how you slept with me the first time in his bed the weekend he was away. And the times in your apartment and the night in Santa Barbara. And the night on the couch. When we brought him home drunk. Remember?" She seemed to be enjoying herself.

"Suppose I deny everything?"

She got up. "Just try."

"You'd better wait, Paula. I only touched you once. Do you hear? Only once." She was at the door and turned. "Not that I didn't have a dozen opportunities," he continued. "The first night the three of us went to dinner you made a pass at me. You kept fondling my leg under the table." She had taken a couple of steps back into the room. "I was shocked, embarrassed, my best friend's wife." She tossed her coat and purse on the table. "One morning I dropped by to see Art, he was out of town, you said, and you were alone. I started to leave, but you insisted I come in, started to talk, got on your marriage, said it was unhappy, you were going to get a divorce and you started to cry. I tried to comfort you, you took my hand, your robe fell open. I wanted to rush out of the house but you pleaded, grabbed me! I was weak, I'll admit—he'll understand—you're a beautiful woman." Her look was of disbelief, anger, hate, pain! He went on. "When I left that morning I swore I'd never see you again. It was all a mistake, and I was ashamed. But you called me at the office, begged me to see you and I refused. It went on for months. I wanted to tell Art, but didn't, hoping it would stop. That you'd give up." She lunged and slapped him with all her force. And she screamed and he grabbed both of her hands as she tried to claw his face. Twisting her around he pinned her arms and went on. "Then you threatened me. You'd get pregnant, you said, and blame it on me!" She tried to free herself and he tightened his hold. "And I'll make him believe every word of it!" Now her body stiffened and her cries were low, moans, then she sagged and he released her. She didn't move, her back still toward him. The only sounds in the room were those she was stifling. He pitied her, hated what he had to do, wished it could have been otherwise. Why didn't she believe him? Sure, his promise had been a ruse but he might have had a change of heart! And she would have been spared a lot.

Her sobbing stopped, she walked to the table, took a handkerchief out of her purse, blew her nose then turned and faced him. Her eyes were wide, big, blacker than he had ever seen them, one hand gripped the table as if for support.

"There must be ways of getting back at men like you."

He moved toward her.

"Don't touch me!" She shuddered and moved back to the wall.

He stopped a few feet from her. "I just don't want you to do anything you'll be sorry for."

She grabbed her coat and flung it across her arm, started to speak, changed her mind, and slammed the door as she went out.

During the next few days he bought every edition that hit the streets, tuned in the news from the moment he rose in the morning until he fell exhausted at night, listened for Art's car when he pulled up in the morning, waited for his steps on the stairs. There were calmer moments; these things happen all the time and there were few suicides and rarely does a cuckold reach for a gun.

He had just turned off the ten o'clock news a few nights after the meeting with Paula, when the phone rang. Still tense, the ring jangled, was insistent and for a moment he thought of not answering. He rarely received a call at that hour and was sure whoever it was had bad news. It went on ringing, nine, ten times, and he finally swept up the receiver. It was Aunt Annie.

"I'm in trouble, Sam."

"What's wrong?"

"I'll tell you later. Just come down to Lincoln Heights jail. With bail money." Before he could say a word, she turned from the phone and he could hear muffled voices. She was on again.

"Bring a hundred dollars, cash. Hurry, darling." She hung up.
He flung on his clothes and grabbed a roll of bills. The goddamned anarchists! Dante! The Rizzos! God knows who else!
They corrupted her, used her. What in hell did she know? A
couple of months ago she almost married a prince of the Church
and now she was an antichrist. He drove downtown like a mad-
man and then he began to hope; maybe she'd been caught shop-
lifting, people do that impulsively sometimes. Perhaps she had a
fight with a neighbor, she did have a temper, or perhaps, perhaps
what? You're kidding yourself, he thought, you know damn well
what it has got to be. Suppose it got in the papers, with pictures,
him and Aunt Annie leaving the jail. For a moment he thought of
turning around and going home, letting her stay in jail until
morning when he could get a lawyer to handle it and keep his
name out of it. She'd never forgive him.

A bail bondsman slipped him his card at the entrance as Samson went inside and was directed to the desk sargeant. The
charge was assaulting an officer he was told and the bail was a
thousand dollars. The bail bondsman was hovering close now and
he deposited a hundred dollars with the man and after signing all
the papers he was told the prisoner would be out in a few minutes. As he waited, he tried to imagine his aunt attacking a cop
and could not. After about fifteen minutes Aunt Annie appeared,
pale and defiant. As they left the jail he looked about uneasily for
a newspaperman or a photographer and almost cried with relief as
he rushed Aunt Annie to his car without being noticed. For a few
minutes he said nothing and when they cleared the parking lot
and reached North Broadway he turned to her. "All right, what
happened?"

"Didn't they tell you?"

He couldn't keep the anger out of his voice. "No!"

"You don't have to bark."

"What do you expect me to do? Offer you congratulations?"

She was silent for a few moments. "Maybe if you understood
you would. We were demonstrating at the Plaza. Danny was
talking about the Scottsboro Boys and I was handing out pam-

phlets. We had a good crowd gathered and then a cop came up. 'Move on,' he said, roughlike, 'you're blocking traffic.' We had a right to free speech and assembly and we ignored him. The cop started to shove the crowd with his stick and then he pushed Danny off the box he was speaking from. I went up to the big brute and told him what I thought. He pushed me and grabbed the pamphlets. I tried to take them back and he almost knocked me down."

"What did you do then, throw a bomb?"

"Sam, if you ever say that again I'll thrash you, as big as you are."

"All right, all right. What did you do?"

"I had to defend myself. I hit him where it hurts most. With my knee."

"You kicked him in the balls!"

"You're vulgar, Sam!"

"Aunt Annie, how could you?"

"He went down all right and before I knew it another cop grabbed me and took me to jail. It was awful there, Sam. They treat the prisoners like animals, eighty, ninety in a tank. They even fingerprinted me and took my picture."

They reached her house. She put on water for tea, called the Rizzos, told them she was out of jail and was feeling fine. Then she called Dante and told him there was nothing to worry about.

"Some comrade," Samson said, as she hung up. "The cops haul you off to jail and he runs."

"What did you expect him to do, fight the Cossacks with his bare hands? Anyway, Danny does not believe in violence."

"But you do."

"No. I lost my head tonight. It will never happen again."

"A lot of things are never going to happen again if I have anything to do about it. You've gotten yourself involved with dangerous people, Aunt Annie. You know nothing about them. They're using you."

"Dangerous? I never met gentler people in my life. They practice what all the preachers preach and don't live by."

213

He would get at that another time. There were more important things. He would get her a lawyer the first thing in the morning, he told her, but she must understand that his name must be kept out of it at all costs. Maybe if they were lucky the whole thing could be quashed.

"The proper thing to do is go to court and fight it," she said, "because I'm in the right."

"Suppose you lose!" he shouted. "You can go to jail."

"I would lose because the courts hate our kind. And there is no justice. And my work is important. So I must stay free."

"Fine," he said, relieved. "Just let me handle it."

"I will."

The following day he was up before dawn, combing the morning paper. There it was, a small item on a back page. Aunt Annie's name was mentioned and the charge was simple assault. He called the bail bondsman later and made an appointment to see him, got the name of a discreet lawyer who handled cases of this kind and knew his way around the courts. The man had an office on Broadway near the Hall of Justice, told Samson he knew exactly what he was seeking, that the charges would be reduced to disturbing the peace, the fine would be ten dollars, there would not have to be a court appearance, and the legal fee would be five hundred dollars. Samson left the office after leaving a retainer of half the fee with a promise to pay the balance the moment the services were performed. The following day the attorney called to tell him that everything had been taken care of. The only thing on the record was a charge for disturbing the peace and even it would be expunged since it was her first offense. "But she'd better stay the hell away from the Plaza. There's one cop with sore nuts going to be looking for her."

One morning a week later, he heard Jennings pull in with his car and a few moments later he was taking the steps two at a time and before Samson could brace himself he burst into his office. All the signs he had prayed for for days were mixed in Jennings' grin, danced in his eyes and as he paced the room with his head thrown back, Samson expected him to crow. He stopped short and pounded a fist in his hand.

"You'd never believe it!"

"Believe what?"

Art leaned over the desk gripping the edge with both hands as if addressing an audience. "We're going to have a baby. That is Paula and I are going to have a baby!"

Samson poured on congratulations, slapped his back, made the observation he didn't think he had it in him and then took his hand grasping it firmly as he told him how happy he was.

"You know, Sam, at my age you don't think of these things. . . . What I mean is, you think you've had it. . . . Anyway, you know what I mean."

Samson assured him it was no phenomenon, that men can be fertile until they die no matter what age and that he'd better be careful with that pecker when he's poking around in strange places.

"I guess I've been lucky. I hardly use rubbers anymore. But from now on. . . ." He shook his head. "No more chances."

With the pressure of Paula's pregnancy off, Samson set about to find an apartment. The Piedmont, a ten-story building on a Wilshire corner about a mile from the office had been running rental ads in the Los Angeles *Times*. Completed just before the war, it was the only building in the city prior to the thirties that required detailed applications from prospective tenants. Though they still took applications to pacify the older tenants, all the bars were down except to Jews, and a valid signature on a lease with the first and last months' rent deposited took any vacancy available.

He found just what he wanted on the top floor: it had two bedrooms and each had a bath. In addition to a living room there was a full-sized dining room which led to a compact kitchen and a small butler's pantry. The manager, a Mrs. Pruett, who had reached middle-age looking like a movie version of a haughty dowager, showed the rooms and spoke of them as one would of a royal apartment.

"The Pearson's lived here for twelve years. You know them?"

"I know of them," he lied.

"Alice Pearson had the apartment done. The way you see it now."

The walls of the living and dining rooms were of silk brocade paneled with thin plaster moldings of a bud design. The ceilings were dark walnut and the wall brackets and chandeliers in each were crystal. The bedrooms were painted in a leaf green iced with plaster festoons of darker green vines. Only the kitchen was bright as if Alice Pearson had never entered it and left its decoration to a cheerful cook. The place had to be done over. He got six months' free rent on a three-year lease and left a deposit.

He contacted Grace and arranged to meet her for lunch. When he told her of the apartment and asked her to help him with the decoration and furnishings she refused.

"I don't understand," he said. "I admire your taste and need help."

"Sam, your air of innocence is unbecoming."

"I really need help."

"You give me more credit than is due me. It takes a lot of time to furnish a place properly. It took me a year to do my home."

"I'm in no hurry."

"I haven't the time, Sam, please. Go to Sloanes. Get one of their decorators. Tell him what you want. They'll do an excellent job."

"All right. But you'll have to make one promise."

"It depends on what it is."

"That you'll come to see the apartment when it's finished."

"I promise."

He signed the lease the following morning and had a decorator in that afternoon. Samson outlined a budget, asked him to retain the elegance of the apartment with warmer tones. They decided on a combination of English and Spanish period pieces and in spite of the decorator's protests, he insisted on completion in three weeks as a condition of his signing a contract. It was agreed Samson was not to interfere. He would see the apartment only when it was completed.

Mrs. Pruett met him in the lobby the day his personal things were being moved in. The morning before, Sloanes had called to say that everything was ready. He had not entered the apartment since that first day, and any doubts he might have had as to the result were dispelled by the look of approval on Mrs. Pruett's face.

"I must say, Mr. Duke, I did not think that the charm of the Pearson apartment could have been improved."

"Do you like it?"

"I love it. It has grace and beauty. But it's masculine too."

Prepared for little disappointments and compromise, he could not find a piece, an item or an arrangement that he would have touched or exchanged. All the living room overstuffed pieces were high-backed Spanish covered in cut velvet of burnished gold and a thick forest green carpet, tasseled and sculptured, covered the floor. A massive, carved English breakfront covered a wall and there was a fireplace screen medaled with shields and above the mantel a reproduction of Agincourt and there was a fine copy of a Goya and a Velasquez and a coffee table, thick and large, its top resembling a monastery door. His bedroom was maroon and brown with edges of black and the walls were forest green.

He wandered through the rooms, fingered the drapes, ran a hand over the velvet couch, felt the soft carpet beneath his feet, and then eased into a large chair and lit a cigarette. He called the decorator to congratulate him, then dialed Grace. "Just reminding you of a promise," he told her, "to see my apartment when it's ready."

"It's only been a few weeks. You mean you're already in?"

"I pushed hard."

"I did the same and it took me a year."

"When are you coming up to see what can be done in three weeks?"

"I don't know. . . ."
"Dinner tonight?"
"I can't."
"Tomorrow?"
"Why not lunch?"
"Dinner."

There was a long pause. "Make it Thursday. I'll meet you at Perino's at seven."

The meal was a quiet one. She seemed nervous, kept looking at her watch, hardly spoke. He was becoming angry. What was she afraid of? He paid the check and started to leave the table. She did not move, kept her head down and fumbled with the catch on her purse.

"Let's go," he said, trying to sound cheerful.

She looked up.

"What is it, Grace?"

She closed her eyes and shook her head. "I'm sorry," she said, finally looking up at him. "I'm acting like a fool and I know it."

Her praise was genuine, enthusiastic, and as she examined each piece, tried the couch and the chair all her fears seemed to have disappeared.

"It's so lovely," she said, nestling in a corner of the couch as she lit a cigarette. "But I can't believe a decorator did all this. It fits you perfectly."

"I must confess he had a guiding hand."

"I knew you had taste. You see, you didn't need me."

He sat beside her. "That's not true." She squirmed in her seat. "How about a drink? A little cognac I got from the greedy hands of my druggist?" He filled the glasses and proposed a toast. "To fulfillment."

They were in the middle of the second drink and he turned on the radio. She kicked off her shoes when he asked her to dance and her body was tense, almost quivering as it pressed against him. The music stopped and she didn't move, and then he kissed her and her arms went around his neck.

She was lying naked beside him. A beam from the hall light lit the room with a faint glow. They had been resting for about ten minutes. She had given herself grudgingly, tight, tense, unable to let go. The dam hadn't broken and he suspected it would have been overwhelming if it did. Neither of them had said a word. Then she began to speak.

"You're the only man I ever slept with beside my husband." Her voice was low, even, a mumbled confession. "There were times when I was curious, tempted, but it stopped there. I was afraid. I'm still frightened. It's funny. I feel a little shame tonight but no guilt." She brushed his cheek with her lips and rose from the bed. In the beam of light he saw her full figure for the first time. Her hips were a little broad, her legs large and only her breasts were perfectly formed. As she started to dress all his desire returned. He was about to ask her to return to bed when he saw she was crying.

"I'm sorry. I'm a little upset."

Reaching for his robe he snapped on the light. "Let me make some coffee and I'll drive you home."

She came into the kitchen. "I'll prepare it. You get dressed."

The table was set in the little nook. She had found some cheese and crackers and the coffee was poured. They ate in silence. He tried to lighten the mood with a Roosevelt joke he had heard. She smiled dutifully. Then nothing was said for a long time.

"What's troubling you, Grace?"

She shook her head emphatically. "It's not you . . . it's just. . . ." She pushed her chair back and stood up. "I've got to go."

He grabbed her arm as she tried to walk by. "You're going to tell me what's wrong first."

"Please," she said, trying to loosen his grip.

"It's no use. You might as well sit down and talk." Her arm became slack and he led her back to the chair. He filled their cups, she lit a cigarette and sat back. "Start talking, lady." She managed a smile. "That's better."

Lacing her fingers nervously, avoiding his eyes, she crushed the cigarette and reached in her purse for another. He struck a match and held it as the cigarette trembled in her fingers. She searched his face, seemed to be making a decision. Finally, she waved her hands despairingly.

"I don't know where to begin."

He sat without interrupting as she told the story, watched the lovely planes of her face as they shifted with emotion, waited patiently during pauses, discovered depths in her eyes he had never seen.

Her husband like others had pyramided real estate purchases during the twenties. Turning from a law practice he had inherited from his father he applied his talents and connections to syndicating large apartment house buys with friends and clients. By the time the economy started to dive he had a finger in over twenty properties which overoptomistic lenders had mortgaged to the roof. Rents slid, vacancies piled up. It was just an adjustment. Things were going to level off. So he'd milked the good deals and poured them into the lemons and then the game was over and most of the properties weren't worth the mortgages. One by one they went back, some by foreclosure, others by voluntary deed for buttons and the investors forgot all the money he had made for them in the past and acted like he brought on the Depression. She finished and stared at her hands in her lap.

"You're not alone," he finally said. "The whole country is in a squeeze."

She looked up. "It's no comfort."

"At least it's gone, done with. The next move has got to be up."

"That's just it. It isn't over. Gene's been hanging on to the last building. It was the best of the lot and a dozen of our friends are in it. Even my father, for more than he can afford."

"Would I know it?"

"The Columbia."

"On Normandie?"

She nodded. "We bought it in 1928 and put one hundred fifty thousand dollars down. Since then another fifty thousand went in."

He knew the building well.

"We're delinquent on the fist and second. It'll take fifteen thousand dollars to bring them current and give us a little capital to tide us over until things pick up."

"Have you tried borrowing on a third mortgage?"

"They're impossible to get."

"There must be a way if there's enough of an equity."

"There is. Gene is willing to put up the deed as collateral."

"It should be simple then."

"Except for one thing," she said, shaking her head sadly. "The deed can't be recorded."

"Why not?"

"Gene holds it in trust for these people, our friends. He hasn't the heart to tell them how bad things are. They've lost so much already. If they found out it was in another's name. . . ."

Why not take the chance, he thought. If the equity was there he couldn't go wrong. Also, he would make it pay well. And Grace's appreciation would be another consideration.

"What would your husband be willing to do?"

"You might have someone?"

"I might be interested. It's no secret I've loaned money on buildings. It would be strictly business."

"He'd pay the usual ten per cent interest, I guess. And a bonus," she hastened to add. "And if he'd put up the deed as collateral, it would be just as good, wouldn't it?"

He agreed and told her to get him a complete prospectus on the building.

"Suppose I have Gene call you tomorrow and arrange to meet?" He hesitated a moment and she seemed to sense his reluctance.

"I know how you feel about meeting Gene—now. But it would be worse if I handled the transaction alone. Anyway, he knows we met. In fact I told him we played golf a few times."

Botsford called him the first thing in the morning and was in his office before noon. He seemed smaller to Samson as he sat in the chair before the desk, fingering his hat nervously and peering at Samson over the edge of his glasses. Samson went over the figures and asked questions. Botsford admitted the building was forty per cent vacant. "But if I had the money to redecorate and advertise, it could be filled."

Samson didn't question his optimism. His only concern was what would happen if he had to take it over. The building equity was worth at least fifty thousand dollars and if he defaulted and Samson took it over, he could afford to lower the rents and beat anything in the neighborhood.

They agreed on ten per cent interest, a ten-point bonus, and a prepayment penalty. "There's one more thing, Mr. Botsford. I'll need a statement from the holders of the first and second mortgages outlining the terms of their loans."

Botsford's scratchy voice became whiny. "I can get it for you on the first, but the holder of the second is out of town."

"Can't you reach him?"

"I've tried. They said he'd be gone for a month. Hunting someplace." He leaned forward. "Mr. Duke, I must be frank. We can't wait a month, not even a week. The utilities haven't been paid, nor have the salaries. And if we don't bring the loans current immediately they'll start a foreclosure." He rose and leaned over the desk. Samson could see his reflection in his lenses. "I'll give you a letter signed by myself guaranteeing the terms." He straightened up now. "It'll be my personal guarantee."

"I'll see the building today. You'll have my answer in the morning."

He checked the building before noon. It would be a pleasure to own it, he decided. On a hunch he called Ralph Thompson and arranged to meet him for lunch. The moment he mentioned Botsford's name, Ralph started to grin.

"He's hocked for three times more than he's worth," Thompson said. "He's into the bank for ten thousand right now."

"The lying son-of-a-bitch!"

"Have you met his wife?" Something in Samson's face betrayed how well he did know Grace. "You're a member of the club. And it's not exclusive. She's been spreading her collateral all over town."

"Are you sure? About her, I mean?"

"I made the bank loan. I didn't deal with Mr. Botsford."

She took him without mussing a hair. By God, he couldn't help admiring her. "Does her husband know?" he asked.

"He's got to. Anyway, I'm told he can't raise it high enough to pee."

"He must have something. Do you realize what that woman has done to raise money for the team?"

"Maybe she likes it."

He remembered last night and couldn't agree. On the other hand maybe he wasn't her type, too young, hair on his head. "Do you know who holds the second mortgage?"

"Old man Nielson. I know him well."

"What kind of a guy is he?"

"Lives in a downtown hotel which he owns, has an office on Spring Street, is sixty, never married, has no heirs as far as anybody knows. His mother left him a million in the early twenties, ran it up to ten million by now. The Crash didn't even crease one of his dollar bills. He lives on forty dollars a week, only buys paper at big discounts and he can't turn down a profit."

"You sound like you wrote a book about him."

"I could. Anyway, if you're thinking what I think you are, you might be on the right track."

"When did he buy the mortgage?"

"Less than a year ago. We handled the escrow."

"What did he pay for it, Ralph?"

"Escrows are confidential." He added a smile.

Samson knew he was going to tell and decided to make it easy. "Just a guess."

"I'd say, Nielson never bought anything for less than fifty off."

The face value was forty thousand. That meant he picked it up for twenty. If he couldn't turn down a profit, say a quick five thousand, Samson could end up the second mortgage holder and pick up the building for a lot less than he would have dreamed. "Would you call Nielson for me? Let him know I can back up my talk."

An appointment was made for that afternoon. If Nielson was in a selling mood Samson was going to be an angry mortgage holder by morning.

The office was in an old building on Spring Street. Nielson's room—that's all it was—adjoined the toilet at the end of a dark hall. There was no name on the door. Samson hesitated a moment and knocked. A vigorous voice called to him to enter.

Nielson rose from behind a desk, towering over Samson. He was six feet four inches in height and he had the whitest hair, pinkest skin, and his eyes, pale blue, were so light, they blended into the whites and there seemed to be no pupil. His face gave off a phosphorescent cast and his hair shimmered like silk. "Sit down, sit down," he urged as he indicated a wooden armchair.

Samson took the seat and watched as Nielson reached in the pocket of a jacket on a yellow oak coat hanger and pulled out a long thin cigar. Biting the end a little at a time, examining it, he finally rolled it in his mouth wetting it thoroughly before he lit it.

"Now," he said, settling himself behind the desk. "Let's talk." He billowed puffs of smoke in front of his face, eyeing Samson through the screen.

"I'll come directly to the point, Mr. Nielson. You own a second mortgage on the Columbia. If it's for sale, I'm interested in buying it."

Nielson removed the cigar from his mouth, examined the lighted end, and then satisfied with the ash, replaced it and resumed his puffing. Samson took out a cigarette, rolled it around in his fingers, tapped it slowly and lit it. Nielson broke the silence abruptly. "How much will you pay?"

"I have to know a few things first."

Reaching into a file on his desk he whipped out a card and read off it. "The balance is forty thousand even, interest seven per cent paid to June thirtieth this year." He flipped the card over. "All due January, 1933."

"The entire loan?"

"All principal and interest."

So, Botsford lied about that too. He was going to grab his fifteen thousand and walk away from a loan that was due in less than two weeks!

"I didn't realize the loan was almost due. Thought it had a few years to go."

"It's better. You don't renew, the owner can't pay and you end up with the building."

Now he began to question his appraisal of the Columbia. If there was a chance to get the building for the amount of the second why was Nielson willing to sell? He started to frame the question when Nielson interrupted his thoughts.

"I guess you wonder why I might be willing to sell when there's a chance of grabbing the building?"

"As a matter of fact I am wondering."

He leaned back in his chair. "I like paper, any kind of paper. It has priority over everything, can be converted into cash, the ultimate paper which can buy anything. And it doesn't take up any room, you can have millions of dollars of it in a little box and you don't have to deal with tenants and managers and bum leases and leaky roofs and the lot. And it doesn't tie a man down. Satisfied?"

"Satisfied."

"What'll you pay for it?"

"What are you asking?"

He smiled for the first time. "A hundred cents on the dollar."

Samson made a motion to rise. "I'm afraid we can't do business."

"Are you afraid to make an offer?"

"No."

"Insult me, then. Go ahead."

"Twenty thousand. Cash."

Nielson picked up the card and started to finger it. Now he

225

was reading from it and figuring on a pad. "I'll take thirty thousand," he said without looking up.

"Twenty-five thousand and not a cent more," Samson said. "Cash the minute you draw the assignment."

"I'll meet you at Thompson's bank at ten tomorrow morning. Have a cashier's check."

"I'll be there."

Nielson was still figuring on the pad when Samson left.

The next morning Samson paid over the money, rushed downtown, and recorded the assignment. Now he was ready for Mr. and Mrs. Botsford.

Instead of calling Eugene Botsford, telling him he was a crook, and threatening to foreclose, he decided to call Grace. Telling her he made a decision, he insisted on discussing it with her alone.

She appeared at his office within an hour. Elegantly dressed, poise intact, he still found himself viewing her with admiration. If she had come to petition for relief and the circumstances were different, even if she had used him, he might have had some sympathy. But he had been just another worm in a can full of them and he resented it.

From the moment she was seated, it was apparent she knew he had things to discuss other than the details of the loan. There was no intimacy in her tone, no hint of warmth. She plucked off her gloves one finger at a time, feigned great interest in their removal, inspected each then folded them carefully and put them in her purse. There had been no words since their initial greeting. Now she sat back in the chair, sighed almost contentedly, lit a cigarette, crossed her legs and looked up waiting for him to speak. His intention had been to kick out her props gently but now as he watched her, cold and transparent, he changed his mind.

"I inspected the building," he began. "I like it."

She nodded, indicating it was to be expected.

"There's been some discrepencies."

"What do you mean?"

"In your husband's story. And yours."

"What are you suggesting?"

"I'm not suggesting, I'm telling you."

She leaned forward, almost threatening. "Don't take that high horse with me."

"Get off that top rung, Mrs. Botsford. Your husband lied and you lied. You're both a couple of crooks!"

She sprang out of her seat.

"I bought the second mortgage from Nielson this morning. It's due on Monday. What do you intend to do about it?"

"You doublecrosser!"

"I'm filing a foreclosure and putting in a receiver." He stood up. "You'd better get going now. You've a lot to do."

She slammed the door as she left and her heels tapped the stairs like a fusillade.

He filed a foreclosure and petitioned the court for a receiver. It was granted two weeks later. The Botsfords were out but he was still not in possession. Under the terms of the mortgage they had over a year to redeem. Though it was unlikely they would ever come up with the money, their right to do so kept him tied. Also, a receiver's management was costly and inefficient.

A month later the Botsfords were posted at the club. Samson learned their house was under foreclosure and that Ralph Thompson was squeezing them for the loan due at the bank. Armed with this intelligence, Samson called Grace Botsford.

"What do you want?" she demanded.

"I want the deed to the Columbia. I'm willing to pay for it."

"Talk to my husband."

"You can give him my message. I'll give him five thousand for the deed."

"You must be crazy!"

"A week from now I'll give four thousand. In another week it goes down to three." There was a moment's silence. "Then it goes down to two. You'd better talk to him." He hung up.

Three days later, Gene Botsford called and tried to push him to seventy-five hundred. Samson held firm and reminded him that on Monday the price went down to four. The next day Botsford accepted the offer. Samson took over the Columbia for a third of what the equity was worth.

CHAPTER EIGHT

Since her arrest Aunt Annie had been martyred. Her house had become a headquarters, and in and out of it, days and nights, came Communists, Anarchists, and Mutualists, Individualists, and occasional Socialists, all preaching the same ends only disagreeing on the means. Her table was thumped in discussion, the walls reverberated with imprecations, and only on one level did they agree: the Scottsboro Boys must be freed! The imperialists must be stopped! In her parlor petitions were conceived, telegrams were worded, and all night, teams stuffed envelopes and talked of dialectics and surplus value, exploitation, and the white slave. They came from shape-up and factories, the cigarmaker's bench and job hunting. They were Italians and Swedes, from Middle Europe and all of Russia, and melted together, their religions thrown into the pot, they erected a new temple. It was a world that smelled of garlic and fish and stale sweat and it chanted revolution instead of *Te Deum* and implored the workers instead of the old God.

Passion erupting from frustration and continence and a thousand nights of loneliness and as many days of dreams, now poured from Aunt Annie without restraint. It was as if all her life it had been stored for the work that now had to be done. She was everywhere: in the kitchen cooking for ten, rushing copy to a printer, addressing and mailing, and in between devouring pamphlets and books like a neophyte would the *Lives of the Saints*.

Anxious to keep close, Samson had been over to the house a half-dozen times since her arrest, dreading always the distasteful confrontation with her guests. Also, he always had the feeling the authorities would break in at any moment and haul all of them to jail, himself included. If he stayed away, put his aunt out of his life, the movement would strip her clean and not only would he lose what was rightfully his but she would be on his back for life, a dead-broke anarchist probably wanted by the police. So he came, watched, and listened, looking for vulnerabilities with which to turn her direction.

There were times when he would find an opening and implore with reason and she would counter with phrases and dogmas and the others would join in and inundate him. Most of those who came to the house were volunteers, faceless troops like specters in a bad dream. There were regulars however, like Dante and the Rizzos; these he got to know.

One night, an unusually hot evening, with not a breath of air reaching the room from open windows, he dropped in to find the regulars sprawled all over the parlor arguing heatedly. Everyone displayed open collars, rolled-up sleeves, and kicked-off shoes. Only Dante, seeming unmindful of the heat, was fully dressed. Aunt Annie, shuffling about in slippers wearing a light summer dress was refilling a pitcher of lemonade as Mrs. Rizzo, a tiny nervous woman with black hair and eyes and a darkly downed upper lip, arranged glasses and a bowl of fruit on the table. Mr. Rizzo, pulling savagely at one end of a flowing mustache, was wiping the top of an almost bald head with a huge handkerchief. They were engaged in their favorite recreation, rehashing the Sacco-Vanzetti case. Unmindful of the discussion between Dante and Mr. Rizzo, two other men were in a corner near the window arguing hotly. The older man, an ironworker named Kelly who looked like the Katzenjammer Captain—his thick black hair standing straight up like wire on end—was making a point about Governor Fuller, pounding the wall with a massive fist as if the governor was at the receiving end. The other, Arne Proctor, not much older than Samson, with a sharp nose that slashed an intense face from which narrow steel-blue eyes mirrored indignation, appeared to explode as every effort to break in was thwarted by Kelly's uninterruptable rapid-fire speech. Fuming, he left the older man's side with the middle of his sentence dangling and then ending with a grunt of contempt. As Arne headed for the center of the room, Kelly shouted. "You Socialists are all alike! Bourgeois hearts and Marxist tongues!"

Arne shouted back. "Because I don't blame it all on Fuller?"

Kelly clenched his fists. "You're defending him!"

"What about Katzman and Thayer? They're the ones that put them in the chair!"

Kelly was bristling now as he advanced to Arne's side and poked him menacingly. "Fuller could have called it off. The sonofabitch was God!"

Weeks before when Samson had witnessed the first arguments he was certain a fight would ensue, but time after time when he saw their anger at the tips of their tongues and the fierce antagonists leave the flat arm-in-arm, he realized they were rattling scabbards without swords.

Arne brushed past Kelly, poured himself a drink of lemonade, and flopped in a chair.

"Come on," Dante said to Kelly. "You drink, too. Cool off."

Kelly looked at him for a moment, then whirled about, headed for the table and slammed it with his fist. "The bastard should have been shot!"

Mrs. Rizzo stopped fanning herself, held the paper in midair as her husband looked up at Kelly.

"Who should have been shot?"

"Governor Fuller!"

Arne came to the center of the room. "That's the trouble with you. Violence is all you know."

"And what were you banking on? Judge Thayer? Maybe he was gonna have a change of heart? Or that lousy D.A., Katzman?" He spat the name.

"Please, Jack," Aunt Annie said. He shot her a glance and turned back to Arne.

"Or maybe Professor Lowell," he went on. "That two-bit teacher."

"He was a hope, wasn't he?" Arne shouted.

"Huh!" Kelly said with disgust. "His belly was on the ground and his knees were pushing it in a crawl."

"So, what would you have done?" Arne said. "Blow up Massachusetts, the whole Commonwealth, maybe?"

Dante was shaking his head vigorously and broke in. "He's right, Kelly. It's no good to kill." He placed his hand on Kelly's arm. "Bresci killed Umberto and the peasants paid twenty to one. And with Caserio and Vaillant it was the same. We have a pistol, they have a cannon. You kill one man you are assassin, they kill a hundred they are justice."

Kelly tore his hand from Dante's grasp and walked to the open window.

"To fight among ourselves is what they want," Dante went on. "We cannot throw over in a day what they took a thousand years to build." He walked to Kelly's side, placing an arm about his shoulder. "With all my heart I work for that day. But," he shrugged, "you, me, Bartolomeo, Nicola," his hand swept the room, "all of us, we are the first soldiers."

Samson resented his inclusion with the troops and his dislike of Dante was intensified by the strange quality he possessed that prevented him from detesting him as much as he would have wished.

Arne announced his departure.

"Which way you're going?" Kelly asked.

"I'm taking the bus to Jefferson."

"Wait a minute, I'll go with you."

They left still arguing and soon the Rizzos followed. Any hopes Samson had of being alone with Aunt Annie were dashed when she asked Dante if he wished to stay for supper and baited the offer by rattling off a string of enticing cold dishes to which he held up his hands in a gesture of surrender. Samson was included and during the meal the talk was without politics, even pleasant as Dante told tales of the old country, his boyhood and his first days in America. Afterward, they all settled in the parlor. It looked like he was never going to get his aunt alone and now was as good a time as any. He would offer reason and logic to find a perch on the narrow wall she had erected between mysticism and her new religion and it was sound enough he was sure to form a barrier against Dante's rebuttal.

"I don't understand one thing, Aunt Annie," he began. "Do you believe in God?"

"Sure."

"Your friends are atheists."

"There's room for all beliefs."

"They'd destroy the Church if they had the chance."

"Only the evil in it."

"They claim it is all evil."

"Not the teachings of Christ."

"How can you separate Jesus from the Church?"

"The Church has already done so."

"What do you mean?"

"It justifies and upholds everything that Jesus condemned."

Dante sat puffing on a cigar with a bemused look like a teacher admiring his handiwork. Samson switched and turned to the question of government. "Do you believe in it?"

"Absolutely not," Aunt Annie said.

"Why?"

"It stands for disorder and violence."

"Anarchists resort to violence."

"Only to kill a despot."

"So you don't believe in government. How can it be eliminated?"

She shrugged. "I'm not a prophet."

He turned from his aunt and looked at Dante, curled like an idol in Aunt Annie's favorite chair.

"You're the prophet. Tell me, how can you have a society without organized controls?"

For a moment, Dante's calm seemed rippled, then he smoothed it with a smile. "You mean laws?" he asked.

"Of course."

"They are made by the rich man only for himself."

"But they protect everybody."

He shook his head. "Only few. I give example." Samson waited as he wrinkled his brow and looked up at the ceiling, a familiar gesture of his and one that usually preceded a long discourse. Now he settled back in the chair and began. "The law forbids to steal, no?"

Samson agreed.

"If I steal from you I can be arrested. The law punishes me and if possible gives back to you what I steal. If I work for employer and he pays low wages and makes big profit on what I produce, he is taking that which belongs to me."

"But that's not stealing."

"What is difference?"

"If you hold me up with a gun I am compelled to give you my money. You are not compelled to work for anyone."

"That is where you are wrong," Dante insisted. "Say I have a wife and child. I have needs. This is just as powerful as somebody's gun."

"But you are free," Samson protested, "to do anything you wish."

"Ah, freedom!" he exclaimed. "More than all words the most badly used. Am I really free?"

"Our laws guarantee it."

"Such freedom means I have right to do certain things?"

"Correct."

"But it does not mean I can."

Aunt Annie, who had been setting the table, broke in. "You're so right, Danny. It's like giving someone the go-ahead with no gas in the car."

"It's opportunity," Dante went on. "Freedom written down in law books costs too much to buy."

Samson was losing patience. "All right," he said, "so you don't believe in laws. You believe in laissez faire."

His aunt gave him a puzzled look so he explained. "It means let people do as they please. The government should not interfere. The world should go by itself." He looked to Dante for verification and got a nod of his head in agreement. Aunt Annie's expression changed slightly and Samson continued, tracing the origin of that philosophy from its birth in 18th-century France to its application in the present day. Whatever knowledge he might have lacked of the specific use of the economic doctrine and its effect, he tried to hide behind the authoritative tones of names and dates drilled into his head at the university. As he wove his brief, likening the principles of noninterference of the past and present merchants with the similar demands of the Anarchists, Dante sat, eyeing him bemusedly and without interruptions, and Samson began to suspect that his arguments were widening the area of his vulnerability. He rested his case with a loudly declared assertion that the more conservative advocates of free enterprise would find much comfort in the application of the principles Dante defended.

Aunt Annie seemed impressed and questioned Dante with a look which he returned with a smile of assurance before replying to Samson in the patient tone he always employed.

"What you say is true, Sam. But you tell small piece of story."

"What do you mean?"

"The philosophy that things will work out if the government does not interfere, what you call laissez faire, was made for business not for workers. It was born in Industrial Revolution. Factory owners wanted to do as they wish. No laws, no taxes, no restrictions. They were rich and strong. The workers were poor and weak. The man with the gun can live good without law. Permission to carry gun is only law he wants."

"But the demand," Samson said, "was against the government and the landowners, not the workers."

"It was because the workers were weak. They do not threaten the owners of the factory. The landowners were the King and the Church and they were also the government."

"Suppose what you say is true," Samson said. "The laws support the shark against the little fish."

"It is true."

"It seems to me," he went on, reasoning slowly, "that the difference in the species could have come from design and not accident."

Dante looked at him questioningly.

"What I mean," he said, "is that the forces that created man, be it God or whatever you wish, made sardines to be eaten by barracuda, and barracuda by sharks and that the ultimate aim could be the perfection of the shark."

"Where do you read such things?" he said.

"I didn't. It is everywhere for one to see."

"I will suppose now that what you say is true. That nature has created such things. But nature is not always good. There is pestilence that kills, earthquakes that destroy." He had raised his voice, not in anger, but in pain. Then he glanced at Aunt Annie as if seeking support.

"You don't believe these things are right, Sam?" Aunt Annie asked.

He hesitated for a moment. They were both looking at him. It would have been easy to hedge, go along, tell them what they wanted to hear. But the events of the past months loomed before him and for the first time Aunt Annie looked alien and Dante the wedge between them.

"They may be right," he said. "Who are you to say?" She started to interrupt as he went on. "But if they are wrong, they are in the books and no power on earth can tear the pages out."

She looked at him as at a stranger and was about to speak as Dante broke in.

"Such pages, as you call them, have been destroyed."

"Just replaced. The same fist is in the glove."

"Then you believe might is right?"

"Just the winning side."

Dante turned up his hands as Aunt Annie rose. "The heat's got you, Sam."

There was no doubt in his mind when he left that night that Aunt Annie's conversion was complete. Reason was impotent when it tilted with passion. He had surprised himself at the logic he mustered and it made as much an impression as a thistle on a slab of concrete. Well, Aunt Annie could have her crusade and Dante could have Annie, but the financing was going to come from another source.

He waited two days and then called her, said it was urgent she meet him for lunch near his office. He wanted to be sure he got her alone. His plan was simple; he was involved in a big deal, had put every bit of cash he had into it, and was short forty thousand dollars. It would be a loan, he would pay her the same interest as the savings and loan but it would only be for a year and the money would be returned. She could not turn him down and once he got his hands on the cash he would be damned sure it remained there. He hated to lie but it was for her own good and someday she would thank him.

She listened as he made his request and turned him down cold. He pleaded, said he was in trouble and could lose everything, but she would not change her mind. "I don't want my money used for exploitation and speculation."

"What do you think the savings and loan does with it?" He was sorry the minute the words came out.

"I never thought of that. Maybe I'll withdraw it. You're bright, Sam, very bright. You'll work out your problem."

"Suppose I don't."

She shrugged. "Then maybe you'll have to work for a living."

He was about to argue but realized the futility and after he took her to the bus, decided if there was not going to be a pot of gold he was through chasing rainbows. He would see his aunt but her home would be off limits. It was baited for cops and a raid and he was not ever going to be around to be caught in a trap.

CHAPTER NINE

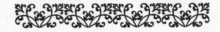

Early in the evening a few days later, the hand of mortality touched Samson Duke and left a lasting print. Within the space of a few minutes Aunt Annie no longer existed, money disappeared along with thoughts of investments, women, dreams, and goals. He was apart from it all as the fear of death occupied every molecule of his brain.

He had been soaking in the tub, contemplating a weekend in Palm Springs. Suddenly, a thunder, not from above but from the earth's guts preceded a violent shake and the building twisted as if trying to break a giant grip. He screamed as the water spilled over the sides and the medicine cabinet flew open and the bottles crashed to the floor. The building's steel whined and the sound of brick, wood, and plaster cracked, and, piercing it all were cries like souls on the way to hell! He was sure the whole building would be shaken loose and he would fall to the street ten stories below and he called out to God as he tried to scramble from the tub and was thrown back and then the heaving stopped and a terrible cacophony of terror filled the air. Not yet certain he would survive or was unhurt or that the monster was only taking a breather he managed finally to get to his feet and step across the floor. Broken glass cut a foot which started to bleed.

Now the building trembled violently again. Wrapping a towel about himself, he reached for the door and found it jammed. Desperate, he pulled with all his strength but it wouldn't budge. He pounded it and cried for help but his voice was lost in a chorus that seemed everywhere. Grabbing the top of the toilet bowl he started to beat the panel of the door. It shattered and sprung open! Still dripping, he grabbed a robe and ran from the apartment. The hall was filled with people dressed and half-dressed, scrambling for the stairs, some crying aloud, others sobbing and all with horror on their faces. The lobby was jammed when he reached it.

People were shouting orders to stay off the streets, to watch out for falling debris. Others stood still, petrified, and a few were on their knees. He ran for the archway separating the lobby from the card room, remembering vaguely reading somewhere that doorways were the safest places during an earthquake. He racked his brain trying to remember everything else he might have learned about quakes; do they erupt singly, or in pairs and what of their frequency, was the first temblor one of many and would there be others? Then he remembered the San Francisco quake and fire. Yes, that was it! The fire did most of the damage. There were no signs of fire, no smoke. He was a little calmer now, relieved. Leaving his position under the archway he joined the milling crowd that packed the lobby. Some, relieved at survival, attempted feeble jokes; others just stood, silent, and one elderly couple still remained crouched under a heavy table huddled close and holding hands. Then came the rumors: five hundred dead, a thousand, buildings in rubble, Long Beach destroyed, a tidal wave. He looked at the clock above the desk—it was twenty after six. Then someone plugged in a radio and a calm voice, too calm, told that the worst was over. There was no reason for panic, but stay off the streets and avoid the Long Beach area.

Certain now that he was safe, other thoughts began to flood his mind. What about the buildings? How badly were they damaged? Rushing to the lobby phone he called each resident manager. There had been only superficial damage, a few broken windows, a fallen parapet at the Columbia. Summoning enough courage to return to the apartment he dressed rapidly and called his aunt. She'd tried to reach him but his phone was out of order. There was no damage to her bungalow and she was in fine spirits. "Maybe a sharp earthquake once in a while is what we need to wake people up."

Leaving the building, he felt brand new; the curtain sure could have gone down for the last time but they gave him an encore. He was even hungry. Rather than stay on the tenth floor in his apartment that night he decided to try the Harvard Boulevard apartment building and sleep in a vacancy on a lower floor. The radio had warned that the settling earth could cause other shakes and he was going to take them close to the ground.

At eight-thirty that night there was another quake, smaller than the first but sharp enough to renew the panic. Samson sustained that one leaning against the Midwood Country Club bar, braving it with a dozen members, all half-crocked.

The morning papers were full of the quake; pictures of debris, lists of dead and missing and reports of looting. Added to the panic was Roosevelt's order closing every bank in the country. When Samson reached his office he found Roy Phillips in the lobby. His eyes were buried deep in layers of puff and the ruptured veins which used to splotch his face now covered it giving a purplish cast to what a few months ago was brick red. "How would you like to own a bank?"

"Not these days."

"The building, not the business. I got a real lead. Pacific National?"

"The one on Wilshire near Vermont?"

Roy nodded. "It's not going to reopen. The president, a guy by the name of Stanley Hudson, is going to have to do a lot of fast talking when the examiners get through."

"What about the property?"

"The building is owned by one Posey Warren, single, address on North Flores. I gotta hunch she and Hudson are pretty close. He's the real owner, she's the dummy."

"How do you know all this?"

"What's the difference, Sam. I know."

Samson pressed for more details.

"There's a first mortgage on the building. If the bank don't reopen that owner's gonna get soft. You might buy it cheap."

Samson told him to dig up everything: the unpaid balance of the mortgage, the name of the holder, and the amount of rent the bank was paying.

By the middle of the week the banks started to reopen and on Thursday he drove to Pacific National and found the doors locked. Roy called that night.

"Hudson killed himself!" he blurted. "Shot clean through the head. At his desk. I gotta see you right away."

He came in waving a newspaper and tossed it on the table. It was the headline, with pictures: Hudson in better days in front of a sprawling house in San Marino with his wife and three kids and one of his office with an arrow pointing to where the body was found.

Roy was pouring himself a drink. "I got everything. But we have to move fast. I didn't think the chump would shoot himself. Now, every sharpshooter in town will be after the property." He set the drink on the desk. "I think I got the jump on them." He took out a small notebook and started to read. "Hudson wasn't the family man the paper says. He bought the property in 1928, put it in Posey's name, then leased it to the bank for twice its rental value. The income must have paid for Posey." He went on with admiration. "He was quite a guy. Paid seventy-five thousand for the property and borrowed that amount from a crooked mortgage company downtown. Paid plenty under the table for it."

"Pretty cute."

"Cuter than you think. He only paid interest on the loan all this time. The sucker that holds it still has the full amount coming."

"Who holds it?"

"Some army jerk. A retired captain."

"How did he get that kind of money?"

"He didn't. His sister died three years ago and he inherited the paper."

Roy went back to his drink, held the glass up to the light, fondled it and drank slowly. The key to the whole deal was getting that mortgage cheap. The deed from Miss Warren could come easily. Samson did some quick figuring. "What's the property worth, Roy?"

"It all depends. If the bank hangs on and starts paying rent it's one thing. It's a white elephant if they move out."

"All right, you're going to pay the captain a visit."

"And do what?"

"Tell him you're a broker. A mortgage broker. Make him an offer for the paper."

"What's my deal?"

"If I get it at my price you get five hundred dollars."

"Oh no," Roy shook his head. "I dug too long for this, Sam. A thousand."

"You must be crazy!"

"I would be if I took less."

"Tell you what. Five hundred if I get the paper and a hundred if I fail. That way you still get something."

Roy smiled. "I'm a gambler too. I don't want a dime if you don't get it. Seven-fifty if you do."

Samson hesitated a brief moment then accepted. "Now, offer the captain fifteen thousand for the mortgage."

"He'll throw me out on my ass!"

"That's what you're getting paid for. All I want you to do is soften him up. I'll do the rest."

"But fifteen thousand. . . . that's only twenty per cent of face!"

"A good place to start."

"Can I do it over the phone?"

"Absolutely not. He might hang up and I want him to hear the whole story. How the bank is never going to open, how they're not paying rent, and how the country's going to the dogs."

Roy reported the following afternoon. "I saw the captain. We talked about the army which he loves and Roosevelt who he hates and we got along great. Then I made the offer and he threw me out."

"What kind of a man is he?"

"He's got a temper. If I were you I'd wait a week before I called and I'd come armed."

Samson waited ten days and made the appointment. To be sure the captain would see him, he made it sound as if he was with the bank. His house, a small bungalow in the south end of town, stood out from all the others on the block like an officer on a parade ground. Its close-cropped dicondra lawn had no trace of devil grass and the white picket fence looked like it had just been painted. The polished brass knocker which brought the captain to the door was a replica of the American eagle and when he greeted Samson he clicked his heels. Samson almost saluted.

"Captain Rieser?"

"Come in, come in," he said, like a command, his smile revealing too-perfect dentures.

Samson followed him through the living room to a small den at the rear of the house. It looked like a room that had been preserved. An ancient Springfield hung high on a wall above a much scarred but highly polished desk; below it a bugle tilted heavenward, a faded blue and gold tassel hanging from its grip. Under it, arranged with the symmetry of cadets on parade, a half-dozen photographed soldiers stared grim-faced into the room, their autographs faded purples and blues. On another wall a map of San Juan Hill flagged with pins separated a photo of Teddy Roosevelt in side-swept hat and one of what could have been Captain Rieser in more glorious days, squinting in the sun. On the desk, flanking *Clausewitz on War* (three volumes), were busts of the master himself and Black Jack Pershing. The only other object on its shiny surface was a small silk flag topped by a golden eagle sticking in the center of an inkstand.

Directing Samson to a chair, the captain stood erect with head high but was unable to conceal a small pot that nestled below his belt like a pumpkin.

"How long were you in the army, captain?"

He seated himself at the desk, arranged Clausewitz, volume one, which had worked itself out of line, swiveled and faced him. "Thirty years. San Juan with General Punston until we captured Aguinaldo and then after Villa with Jack Pershing." He sighed. "Did two more years from 1916 to 1918 but don't count that. Desk job."

Samson shook his head consolingly and he smiled with resignation. "I see you've read Clausewitz," he said, remembering something of the military genius.

"Read him! Over and over again. Greatest tactician of them all. And strategist too," he added, shaking a finger. "Total war! Strike the enemy. All of him, his populace, his territory, and property. Only one nation used it in modern times, the Russians against Napoleon. Only they did it in reverse. Destroyed their own property, sacked their own territory. Brilliant, brilliant!"

Samson steered the conversation. "How long have you owned the mortgage?"

He thought a moment. "About three years. That's when my sister died."

"The bank is in a bad way," he said cautiously.

"That fool, Hudson, killing himself. Only made matters worse."

"They can't be worse. The bank is completely insolvent. It'll take years to unravel the mess." He took a shot in the dark. "I talked to the owner. She hasn't collected rent in months."

"It must be true," Rieser said, almost to himself. "She's way behind in her payments to me."

Now he took a sure shot. "It's that man in the White House," he snapped.

The captain straightened up as if the phrase was a bugle call to action. "Don't mention his name," he hissed, and then delivered a tirade as if bent on destroying "That Man," even suggesting the disease wasn't polio but syphilis. Samson kept shaking his head in agreement. Certain he was convinced their political bonds were alike and they would never reach greater rapport, he decided to get right down to business.

"I have a proposal to make."

Still recovering from his rage, he looked at Samson questioningly.

"I represent buyers of first mortgages."

"I thought you said you were from the bank?"

"You misunderstood. I told you I wanted to see you about the bank property." He watched carefully. Satisfied the captain believed him, he continued. "One of my clients has instructed me to make you an offer for the mortgage."

"Of course, under the circumstances I would be willing to sell," he said. And, after a moment, "But why would they want to buy it?" he asked suspiciously.

Samson smiled as to a fellow conspirator with a coup in sight. "They don't believe as you and I. They think That Man will bring back prosperity." He shrugged. "I'm just an agent. I follow clients' orders." He figured the captain was as soft as he was ever going to be. "I can offer you twenty thousand cash."

For a moment Rieser was stunned, appeared as if he hadn't heard, then muttered, "I'll burn it first." Then he shouted. "Tell that to your client!"

Samson got up and placed his card in the center of the desk. "In case you change your mind, captain." Rieser was muttering to himself as Samson left.

When he called Roy the following morning and reported what had happened, Roy felt they might be getting to the captain.

"I'll wait a week," Samson said. "If he doesn't call, I'll nudge him." Rieser did call and offered to take thirty thousand for the paper. Samson told him he didn't think there was a chance but would talk to his client. He kept Rieser hanging with a waiting game. After a week, Rieser called again. He was down to twenty-five thousand before Samson opened his mouth, and they settled for twenty-two thousand five hundred. At Thompson's bank where the assignments were drawn, Samson presented Rieser the check. "I'm taking it in my name," Samson said. "In trust for my client."

Rieser winked at Samson knowingly as he pocketed the money. "If you're a betting man, you'd run that up to some big money by taking the odds on Socialism by the end of this year. That man and his government, they're taking over everything." He shook Samson's hand and they had a private laugh.

Posey Warren was smarter than the captain, more suspicious. She questioned him thoroughly before she consented to see him. Samson told her he now owned the mortgage, wanted to discuss its delinquency, and thought they might work out something. She tried to draw him out further over the phone but he insisted on a personal meeting.

He expected to see a more mature woman and was pleasantly surprised to find a woman near his age when he entered the apartment. Though her nose was a little broad and her lips too thin, her eyes, widespread and blue, narrowed orientally above high cheek bones dominating her face so that all of its imperfections were soon unnoticed. The finest parts of her were contoured in a lounging pajama. As he followed her into the room, which was furnished expensively, he almost regretted the unpleasant task ahead.

"As I mentioned on the phone, I now own the mortgage on your property. Recorded it yesterday."

"Then you know I'm delinquent."

"So is the bank. They haven't paid their rent in months. Furthermore it'll be months before they resume. If they ever do."

"I'm sure things will get straightened out, Mr. Duke."

"Things will never get straightened out, Mrs. Warren. The bank is busted, cleaned out by Mr. Hudson. If the depositors end up with a dime on the dollar they'll be lucky. I'm here to make you a proposition."

She looked at him suspiciously.

"Your equity is worthless," he went on. "You owe seventy-five thousand dollars on the property. It isn't worth half that."

First she was shocked, then he saw fear and then a shrewd look.

"Why are you here then? Why don't you foreclose?"

"If necessary I will. But foreclosures take time."

All the fear was there again. She spoke slowly as if trying to control her voice. "What do you want?"

"I'll buy your deed."

He watched and waited as she framed the question. "What will you pay for it?"

He didn't hesitate. "Two hundred dollars."

She got up without a word, walked to the door and opened it. "Get out!"

He didn't move.

"Mr. Duke, if you don't leave this minute I'll see to it you're thrown out!"

He walked to the door, brushed her aside and slammed it shut. "No more games," he said. "And don't play the lady with me! Your boyfriend was a crook." She was working hard to control her tears. "The bank leased the property for twice its value for years. So far, the examiners know nothing of your tie with Hudson. If I have to tell them I will." There were a few tears now. "In fact," he said, a little kindly now, "it might be a good idea for you to leave town before any investigation gets into full swing."

"Leave town with two hundred dollars? Go where?"

"I don't know, Mrs. Warren."

"You're rotten," she interrupted. Her composure seemed to return. "Whatever Mr. Hudson did was unintentional. If the market didn't crash he would have never been in trouble. But you . . ." she shuddered. "Why, you're . . . you're contemptible!"

He dropped his card on the coffee table. "Think it over," he said, "and call me. By Monday."

She had no choice and he knew it. The fact that the building was worth less than she owed was one thing, and if that was not persuasive his threat to implicate her with fraud would surely make up her mind. It was just a question of how much and he was prepared to raise his offer to a thousand dollars. She called him on Monday, asked for an appointment and made it very clear she had a counter proposal she was sure would interest him. He arranged a luncheon at the club for the meeting.

She was ushered into the dining room a half hour late. His anger at waiting, which had determined him to stick fast to his original offer, dissolved the moment he saw her. Smartly dressed in a silk suit, she was strikingly beautiful.

They skirted talk of business during the meal, the conversation flitting from golf to the earthquake, a comment on the new administration (she thought Roosevelt was on the right track), legal beer, and the end of Prohibition. It would have been hard to believe she was playing with her last chips. She was so calm he began to suspect he had missed an angle and she was holding an ace. As the waiter cleared the table and served coffee she leaned back and lit a cigarette.

"I made a few inquiries," she began. He watched her as she searched his face. He managed a confident smile. "If I don't give you the deed it will take you thirteen months from the time you file a foreclosure to get possession. You'll have to put in a receiver and they cost money." Now there wasn't a hint of a smile. "And they manage things badly."

"I'm in no hurry."

"I don't believe that, Mr. Duke."

He shrugged.

"Also, I'm not afraid of your threat." He started to protest. "Not that I think you're incapable of it," she continued, ignoring his gesture. "It's just that carrying it out will hurt you as well as me. Implicating me with what you choose to call Mr. Hudson's schemes might cause an investigation. It could jeopardize the foreclosure, delay it."

There was truth in what she was saying and he could sense she knew he was aware of it. "All right. Let's assume for a moment you're right. What do you want?"

She removed a slip of paper from her purse on which he saw a list of figures. "Now then," she said, "it's just a matter of mathematics. A foreclosure including legal fees, the cost of a receiver and other expenses will run in the neighborhood of six thousand dollars." She folded the paper neatly and returned it to her purse. "That does not include loss of income or whatever other use you have in mind for the building."

"I'll assume your figures are correct."

"They're really low, Mr. Duke." She smiled. This time with a little warmth. He found himself returning her smile before he realized they had not yet made a deal. Lowering his gaze he reached for a cigarette. She waited until he lit it.

"I'm only asking for a fair price. A fifty-fifty split. I want three thousand dollars for the deed."

"What are your plans?" he said, ignoring her proposal.

"Plans?"

"When and if we make a deal."

She thought a moment. "I don't know yet. Why do you ask?"

He shrugged. "I thought maybe you'd be looking for work."

"Not right away. I have a few things to settle."

His first thought after her offer was to cut her down to twenty-five hundred, maybe two thousand. But now he felt certain she would not budge, and it would only hurt what he hoped to be future relations. "I'm a little short of cash," he began. "I'll give you three thousand. One thousand now and a hundred a month until the balance is paid."

She thought a moment. "I'll take the thousand down. But I want two hundred a month."

"You've got a deal," he said, extending his hand. "I'll have the deed drawn and we can meet at my bank."

"I'll want a note for the balance."

"You'll get it."

She got up to leave. "When will I hear from you?"

Why delay, he thought. A deal was made and the sooner it closed the quicker they might become friends. "Why not finish it now? We can go right to the bank."

She looked at her watch. "That'll be fine. But I must be home by four."

"Just one favor. I always celebrate when I acquire a building. How about dinner tonight?"

"What have I to celebrate?" she said angrily.

"Just think if someone else bought that mortgage. No deal, just a foreclosure. And you'd end up with nothing. In a way it's a victory for you too." She just looked at him. "Come on," he pleaded. "Give me a chance to prove I'm not as contemptible as you think."

"Let's go to the bank first," she said, sweeping up her things. "Then I'll see."

At the bank she signed the deed. He handed her his check and after arranging to have the instrument recorded they left.

"Now, about the dinner," he said, as they headed for her car.

"Call me later. I don't know yet."

He did, towards evening, and she turned him down and kept him waiting for a week before she consented to see him. When he arrived at her apartment he found boxes stacked all over the room and half the furniture gone. She was dressed and ready to go out the door.

"Breaking up house?"

"Just cutting down the size."

As they drove to the restaurant he asked where she was moving.

"I took a furnished apartment on Gramercy Place."

"I wish I had known. I own a few buildings. Nice ones."

"I wasn't looking for a nice building. Just an inexpensive one."

They drove in silence. He thought about his first two meetings with her and the different impressions he got. In her apartment the day they met he saw a classy hooker, at the club luncheon she impressed him with the smartness of her appearance and the skill with which she handled the transaction. Tonight there was another side, her independence, the ability to make an adjustment. He had a hunch there were other sides, enough to rope a banker.

During the meal she talked about Roosevelt, the new confidence since he was voted in, and the first bit of optimism since the stock market led the country down the drain. He agreed but insisted the country had hit bottom, that the only move was up and that Hoover would have been driven to do the same.

"You're wrong. Hoover was stupid. Worse, he was blind."

He tried to steer the conversation to herself, her personal life but she avoided it at first and he began to talk about himself, embellishing his background with a few feathers he had not used before. It opened her up and she got to her story, emphasizing the differences in their backgrounds.

Her father came from Germany to Omaha where he had an uncle who ran a small butcher shop. Starting in his uncle's shop, cleaning and delivering, he learned butchering from sawdusting the floor to carving beef.

"My mother was German too. Came from a little village in Prussia." Her voice softened and she continued. "She was sent like a package. They pinned an envelope on her with her name and destination on it and instructions in case she got lost." Posey sighed. "She was fourteen, cousins in Omaha waited for her eagerly. They picked her up at the station, took her home and that night fed her well as they pumped her about the old country. The next day she began working as their maid. That's where my father met her. He 'took to her, liked her ways,' he would tell us later." She puffed on her cigarette. "In five years my mother had three babies. I'm the youngest. My sisters married. To butchers. My one brother-in-law was the best beef cutter-upper my father had in the shop. The other one could twist a chicken's neck with a flick of the wrist."

"I can see why you left home."

"The Depression hit. There was no money. People watched pennies and Safeway got the business. My father hung on until he lost every cent. Then he got a job in another shop and my sisters moved in with their husbands and four children. We had a big old frame house and my mother became a maid again. I got a job in a five-and-dime and went to school at night. By the time I saved bus fare to Chicago I had learned shorthand and typing."

"How long did you stay in Chicago?"

"Long enough to run out of money, not find a job, and meet a fast talker. We got married. A few days later I knew I made a mistake. A month later I left him. I kept his name, the only thing he had that was worth while. Mine was guttural and gurgly."

"When did you come to Los Angeles?"

"That's your last question, Mr. Duke."

"Sam. . . ."

She smiled. "I came here two and a half years ago." She left him at the door that night, easily getting around the foot he tried as a wedge. They had luncheons and more dinners and a Sunday brunch and did not get closer than a hand-squeeze. Sure she was interested, each of their visits seeming to chip away at the glacier she was encased in. He decided to make no more moves. If he had established enough interest she would be after him and if not. . . . well, he was through chasing.

CHAPTER TEN

The following week Aunt Annie called to tell him she had sold her house and wanted him to look over the escrow instructions before she signed them.

"What made you sell the house? You loved it. And why didn't you consult me?"

"There was nothing to consult. I no longer want to be a land-owner."

"Damnit, Aunt Annie, even a Bolshevik is entitled to a house."

"Will you help me or not?"

"I'll be over tonight."

He argued for an hour, but it was no use, checked the papers and she signed them. The buyer was getting his own financing and she was coming out of the deal with four thousand in cash.

"Don't go yet, Sam. There's a couple of other things."

He was damn sure he would rather not know what they were as she led him back into the room. "Please sit down," she said, her face beginning to flush. He was prepared for anything. "Danny and I are going to be together."

"You mean you're getting married!"

For a moment she looked at him without saying a word and the shock at his reaction turned to anger and she exploded. "What if I was? Is there anything wrong?"

"No, it's just that. . . ."

Before he could continue she was poking him with her finger as he backed away and she followed him around the room. "It's just what! Maybe an "Eyetalian" isn't good enough for a fine Irish lady! Maybe that slob Harry Baldwin would have been better!"

"I didn't say. . . ."

She was ignoring him and her hands were waving. "That fine, whisky-drinking Irishman!"

"All right," he said, holding up his hands in a gesture of surrender. "When is the wedding?"

She faced him with hands firmly on her hips. "There isn't going to be any. We're going to live together like man and wife. He's a fine man. That's enough." She lowered her voice and turned her head away. "There's a wonderful feeling between us."

"What about the law? And the Church?"

"The law is a contract. There's no need to bind the right man and woman in writing. As for the Church," she shrugged. "I am no longer religious." She looked at him appealing for understanding. Then she took his hand and squeezed it gently. "Wish me luck, Sam."

"Of course," he said, realizing the futility of opposition. He offered congratulations and gave her a warm hug.

She sighed with relief and spoke excitedly of her plans. "We'll need an apartment and that's the other thing I want to talk to you about."

"Where do you want to live?" he asked, hoping it was in an area where he did not own a building.

"Anywhere near a bus. So Danny can get to work and I can be near my meetings. Close to Wilshire Boulevard would be best."

Every building he owned was within a few blocks of the Boulevard. He rummaged his brain frantically for any excuse and could think of nothing that had a ring of sincerity and finally decided to deal with the truth. He had laid a foundation for big plans he told her, was a member of an important club, had begun to build a reputation and they made an agreement that he would not interfere with her life and she was not to interfere with his. And moving into one of his buildings, living with a man to whom she was not legally married could wreck everything he was trying to build.

"I just thought," she said, "if I was going to give money to a landlord it might as well be you."

"I would love to have you in one of my buildings," he lied. "Wouldn't even charge you rent. But you've got to understand my position."

Her face brightened. "It would be nice not to have to pay rent. We're going to try to live on what Danny makes. Suppose we move in one of your cheaper buildings and nobody knows we are related. I swear I'll tell no one. It will help a lot, Sam."

"But how can I explain you're not paying rent?"

"I'll pay the rent. You just give me the money each month."

He was about to protest further when he realized that her denying their relationship could insure against future involvements. There could be other illegal meetings, arrests, God knows what and he could be kept clean. And he knew she would keep her word.

"All right," he finally said. "But I want one thing understood. No meetings in the apartment. That, I won't tolerate." She agreed and he gave her the address of a building he owned on South Catalina Street. "It's a furnished building," he went on. "You'll have to do something about your furniture."

"I'm selling everything, Sam. I don't want possessions."

She had shipped everything she had owned, treasured, across the country and now it was gone, turned into cash, and he shivered when he thought of what was going to happen to the money. Before he left that night he tried again to borrow the bulk of her cash, insisting that he was still under pressure, would have to resort to loan sharks, pay outrageous rates of interest, and that the loan would not only help him out of a tight spot but insure her future as well. Her future was taken care of, she insisted, her needs were little and he must know by now that profit without labor was a dirty word. Then he asked outright how much she was giving to the cause and she told him it was very little, most of it was loans, returnable, she said with the confidence of a banker.

There was a little relief when he left. After all she lived modestly and it could be that his panicked thoughts exaggerated the sums she might be giving away. How much could pamphlet printing cost and mailing and an occasional rental of a hall? And how long could the lousy Scottsboro case last?

Nearly a month after he had acquired the bank property a deal presented itself, forcing a decision he had been postponing. It was a question of taking a big leap and now he decided to jump.

There was no question that real estate would be available at his price and on his terms for a long time. The shock-state of the sellers—individuals and institutions—was so great that months of economic sunshine, maybe years, would be required for them to forget the long black night. They knew only foreclosures and vacancies, unemployment and breadlines, failures and suicides, and ahead was nothing but a politician's hollow promise. All their objective thinking had long ago been destroyed by panic. The cry was "bail out," sit on the buck, and wait to see what would happen. They were easy to deal with.

And there were buyers about, not many, but enough; those who got cooler as the going got rougher. It only took a guy who could add to figure out that the right real estate at these prices was the best investment to be had. So, he had to get to these people and buy so low he could sell them wholesale and get the merchandise and selling sources under his control.

He had a plan and the bank property put him a leg up but he was undecided until Roy Phillips brought him a deal that made him move. Seven buildings he had, over two hundred units from an owner whose confidence had flipped.

"Only this time," he said, standing in front of Samson's desk, "you're taking me in."

"What do you mean?"

Roy leaned over the desk now, excited. Samson had not seen him talk about real estate like this before. "These buildings are clean, every one of them. And top locations. Did you ever see such financing? Forty thousand down for the whole lot! A twenty-year first and they'll take back a fifty-thousand second. I tell you there's a hundred thousand profit in this deal!" He was sweating and breathing hard. "I'll kick back my commission, you put up the dough and I'll do the work. We split fifty-fifty on profits." He watched and waited for Samson to speak.

"Let me think it over."

"Sam, this deal's gonna be gone tomorrow. There are a dozen guys on the phone right now."

"Forty thousand is a lot of cash."

"Just give me a five-thousand deposit. I'll get a sixty-day escrow."

He went over the set-ups carefully. If the buildings were in the condition Roy described, he would have to go. "I'll see them all this afternoon," he said. "Be back here at five o'clock."

They were better than Roy had said. He did not believe Roy could make the deal. Drawing up an offer he gave him a deposit, asked for a ninety-day escrow, and after Roy left, he called Thompson.

"Ralph, I need a loan."

"What kind?"

"On my bank property."

"Please, Sam, not that building. It's a one-purpose deal. And who's going to open a new bank?"

"One purpose, hell! It's going to be the busiest real-estate office in town. Anyway, I need thirty thousand."

"You must be crazy! You paid less than that."

"Who told you?"

"You did."

"You misunderstood me. I bought a seventy-five-thousand first mortgage on that building. Anyway," he interrupted as Thompson started to protest, "get an appraiser down. Tell him I want forty thousand. Then you can cut me down."

"You're wasting your time, Sam. But if you really mean it, I'll go through the motions. Call me in a couple of days."

If the offer was accepted, he would get the money somehow. And what a headquarters the bank would make! It had Grecian columns flanking the entrance with massive glass doors laced with bronze. And on each door at eye level, metal placques depicting an eagle on top of a draped flag and in a half-circle below, the word "INTEGRITY." He would do nothing with the front, just shine the metal and wash the columns. Inside would be simple; tear out the tellers' cages and build small private offices in their place. Stanley Hudson's office would be his, large and paneled; all it needed was new carpeting and a new name on the door. What a beginning and what a foundation and he dreamed and piled stories on until it was ten high and his office on top and everything under his would belong to him and he would be able to see half the city and the pieces of it he owned!

His soaring thoughts were interrupted as Art Jennings walked in. Since Paula's pregnancy Art had fired his young secretary, replaced her with one fiftyish and efficient and with the exception of an occasional drink at the office he seemed devoted to temperance and fidelity. Not anxious to discuss morning-sickness, a pregnant woman's bloom, or a middle-aged man's plans for a son, Samson had been avoiding him as much as possible.

"Funny how time drags sometimes," Art began. "Here it is only May. Two more months to go."

"Two more months for what?" he said, knowing damn well what Jennings was talking about.

"The baby! It's due in July."

"How's Paula?"

"You'd never believe it. She hardly looks pregnant."

For some reason he found it difficult to remember how she did look. The part of him that had concentrated on forgetting her had done a good job. There were times when he thought about the child, whether it would be a boy or a girl and what it would look like. It could even have his old nose. Lately he had not thought about it at all. "What have you been working on, Art?"

Jennings' face clouded. "Things have been a little rough. I don't know what's happened. Seems everybody's waiting to see what that maniac in the White House is going to do," he concluded.

Samson was about to enlighten him with some of his thinking and then decided not to educate him. "I may be moving, Art. Nothing personal. I bought that bank building. I'm thinking of converting it into offices."

"Aren't you better off renting it to the bank?"

"They're busted. At best they'll only stay a few months."

"It's a good location," Art conceded. "But what are you going to do with all that space?"

Samson decided to sound him out. "Make offices. Just for real-estate brokers. It'll give them a solid gold front and the rent will be cheap."

Jennings thought a moment. "You may be right. Certainly better than an old house. Maybe I'll even move in."

"Are you serious?"

"My lease expires this year."

"You can renew it, can't you?"

"I guess I can, but. . . ." He shrugged. "I don't know. I'm getting a little tired of being a landlord."

"I'd like to have you, Art."

"Let's think about it."

After Jennings left, he gave it a lot of thought. Why not? Maybe he could get all of them in: Roy, Ward, even O'Connell and Ritchie. He'd have the merchandise and could not collect a sharper bunch to sell it. What wouldn't they give for a desk or a private office with a respectable front? He grabbed a piece of paper and drew the bank's floor plan from memory. He would drop the ceiling on one side and install private offices. It looked like there would be room for six maybe seven and on the other side he could get a dozen desks. At fifty a month they would stand in line for the offices and for half that there would be no trouble renting the desks. He would have an income and a captive sales force. By God, he'd have the best setup in town! And without a nickel investment. If Thompson got him the thirty-thousand loan it would pay for the building and every cent needed for renovating. It looked too good so he figured again. It came out right.

All he needed now was to secure those seven buildings. He looked at his watch. It was only four, Roy wasn't due for an hour. The phone rang. It was Posey.

"How about taking me to dinner tonight?" Not even a hello. Just like that.

He hesitated a moment. Why run the first time she snaps her fingers? "I'll have to call you back," he said. "I have an appointment at five and don't know how long I'll be tied up."

"I'll be home," she said. "I don't eat until seven anyway."

Roy came in a little before five, his face flushed and smiling. "I got it signed. It's a counter offer with hardly a change. The price and down payment are the same. All they want is a ten-thousand balloon on the second in six months."

"Someone's got to come up with it."

"Don't worry. We'll sell enough to make it."

It did worry him. It was a little more pressure than he wanted. Also, he did not want to sell any of the buildings before six months to be able to take a capital gain.

"We'll just sell a couple," Roy said. "The regular tax isn't too high."

"It's higher than I want to pay."

Roy sat in Samson's chair and did some figuring. His face was still flushed but he wasn't smiling. "Suppose I come up with half," he said, finally.

"Suppose you can't."

"I'll have it. Or I'll get it."

"Get one thing straight." Samson looked at him squarely. "We'll have a written agreement. Nothing is sold for six months. At that time if you don't come up with your five thousand you're washed out."

He hesitated a moment. "How about a little leeway? Say, thirty days?"

"Not an hour, Roy. We've got a ninety-day escrow. You've got six months after that. If I have to put up the ten thousand myself I might have to take in a partner. It's that way or no deal."

"I'll get it," Roy said, handing him the agreement. "Initial the changes."

Samson checked the changes, signed, and handed it to Roy. He put it in his pocket and started to rub his hands. "Now, how about a little celebration, pal?"

"I'm not over the last one, remember?"

"Aw, Sam. You're not the forgiving kind."

"Not the forgetting kind. Thanks anyway. But I've got a date."

"Suppose I get a girl and we join up?"

"This is private," he said, leading Roy to the door. "Just get a good night's sleep and open that escrow in the morning."

It was five-thirty when he called Posey. "I'm free for dinner. Why don't you grab a taxi and come to my apartment?" She accepted without hesitation and he rushed home to prepare.

The moment Samson saw her he got the feeling the parlor games were over. Instead of her usual smartness that veered toward conservatism she was decked out tartly. Everything was cut low and as tight as fashion would permit, her face was made up more for stage lighting than for the living room and her perfume was encompassing.

"Here's a bill," she said, handing him a slip of paper.

"For what?"

"Delivery. Cab fare."

He handed her a five-dollar bill.

"I haven't change."

"Keep it."

She tucked it in her purse and came into the room. "I knew you'd have good taste," she said, looking about.

"I had a little help from a decorator. Would you care to see the rest?"

He took her through the apartment, she made a point of admiring the bedroom and they returned to the living room. "How about a drink?"

"Bourbon, if you have it."

He could not help admiring the manner in which she handled each occasion they had been together. Of all her postures this was the one he liked best. It was real, relaxed. They had another drink and he suggested dinner.

"It's a shame to leave this lovely place," she said. "If you had anything I'd whip it up."

"I wish I had known."

"Next time," she said, smiling, "you'll know."

Delighted at the promise, he suggested they return after dinner for a cognac. At the door she brushed her lips against his cheek and took his hand. Driving to the restaurant, he was baffled at the change that had come over her. During the meal he did the listening, little talking, feeling his way, looking for a clue. The answer came after the meal, over coffee. She had lit a cigarette and kept looking at him with an amused smile.

"What's so funny?"

"Don't be angry," she said, still laughing. She crushed her cigarette, moved closer and took his hand. "I'm just enjoying your confusion."

"I'm glad I'm amusing."

"You're wondering what came over me. Why I've changed. It's simple. I feel a strong physical attraction toward you. In spite of the fact you were contemptible," she added quickly. "It became more intense every time we were together." He moved closer. "I knew you were a louse, still think you are." She ignored his protest and continued. "I knew you were attracted to me." He nodded. "So," she said, "I had to make a decision."

"And what did you decide?"

She was not smiling now. Her eyes were on him, intense. "I called today against my better judgment. Because I needed someone. Does that frighten you?"

"Let's go to my place for that cognac," he said, managing to find his voice.

She sat close as they drove home, her hand playing up the length of his leg. The moment they entered the apartment she threw herself into his arms. She pressed and kissed and nicked his ear, slid her hand to his crotch and then headed for the bedroom.

The early morning light streaked through the blinds painting a lattice of silver on the wall. The only sound in the room was his heartbeat. He was lying on his back unable to see her. Only the warmth of her body told him she was beside him as he slowly picked up the threads of his thoughts and he remembered crawling into bed and her body, warm and yielding, her kisses all over him and her tongue, wet and soft and her hands, the smell of her and the feather hair and pleasure sounds, all of it pieces of a mosaic finally beautiful and done. Now he turned and watched her sleep. She was on her side and a tiny curl was spun about her ear, her lips were just parted and her lashes long and straight rested on her high cheeks like dark lace.

The bars on the wall widened as the morning light grew brighter. He reached for his watch. It was a little after seven. Quietly, he rose, went into the kitchen, put up a pot of coffee, then got the morning paper from the hall. He was reading in the living room when he heard a stir from the bedroom. Entering, he saw her standing at the window where she had opened the blind. She did not notice him at first and was looking out at the sky with arms outstretched. For a moment he did not say a word.

Then he broke the silence. "Good morning."

She turned abruptly and smiled. "Isn't it beautiful?" she said, and then came toward him, opened his robe and buried herself in his arms.

She made breakfast and they sat over coffee until almost nine o'clock.

"I have to go," he finally said. "Stay as long as you wish, I'll call you later."

He thought about her all day, called her in the afternoon, and arranged to see her for dinner. She spent every night with him during the following weeks and Samson felt more contented than he had ever been. Instead of a distraction, hindering his work, she infused him with energy he never knew he possessed.

The bank was put on notice to vacate by the end of June and Samson hired an architect to redesign the interior. Instead of using a contractor he decided to do the renovating himself with a supervising architect. Everything was prepared to start the day the bank moved out. Ralph Thompson came through with a loan. The bank was reluctant, wanted to keep it down to twenty thousand but Ralph pushed them up to twenty-seven thousand five hundred. It paid for the captain's mortgage, Posey's deed, the commission to Roy Phillips, and left almost enough to finish the job.

By this time he had floor plans and sketches of the interior to show other prospective tenants. Art Jennings decided to come in, and with the exception of Ward, the others in Jennings' building joined him. Since Jennings' lease did not expire until October, Samson agreed to take over the rent payments until then.

Realizing the enormity of his undertaking—the bank building, the purchase of the seven buildings together with what he already had—he grabbed every rein, and with the exception of time spent with Posey was on the job day and night. His days were spent executing the plans he spent long nights drafting. Soon he would own a dozen buildings and they would have to buck the trend. The city was full of vacancies, his apartments would have to be rented; the economy was still floundering, his finances would have to avoid thin ice. Though they were still in escrow, Delaney and he interviewed the seven managers, decided to get rid of all of them and start with a crew with no preconceived ideas. He discovered long ago that those without a job, hungrier than those working, were more eager and receptive. They interviewed nearly fifty applicants before the managers were selected. Rules were laid down; they insisted on no deviation and made it clear that every job was probationary. Delaney's talent now had a showcase. Unsmiling, and with a low but firm tone, he set the rules to each manager hired and spelled them in the simplest terms: their only interest was to keep the buildings full, rent to those able to pay. The tenant had to maintain a quiet apartment, other than that he could fornicate and drink with whomever he pleased, make bathtub gin or run a brothel. They had no right to tell a man how to live, he would go on, and end by stating that a man's home was his castle, pronouncing the cliché with solemnity. Some of the applicants were shocked and a few walked out but they managed to cull seven who took Delaney's message with the credulity of novices.

The bank moved out on the second of July. On the day after the Independence Day holiday, the work began. They had a crew during the day, installed lights, and put a shift on at night. Tearing everything out only took a few days, and by the end of the second week all the rough framing was installed. Working from the floor plans, Samson soon began to rent. The word was swift and he filled the private offices within a few weeks and rented half the desks. Roy and Art Jennings leased two of the offices and O'Connell and Ritchie took a third. He kept one for Delaney, whose supervisorial job made it necessary to take him out of managing and keep him at his side. The remaining three were leased to a friend of Ralph Thompson's who dealt in large homes, a mortgage man and a broker in his early thirties married to a woman of sixty who gave him an allowance and permitted him to wander on a long leash. Samson Duke could not have been more pleased: he would be surrounded by some of the best men in the business and would be able to pick at the best of their business.

He had not seen Aunt Annie and Dante since they moved into the building on Catalina Street. She had called once, thanked him for the apartment, told him they were very comfortable, and urged him to drop by whenever he was in the neighborhood. He made time one afternoon and found her alone seated at a table addressing envelopes for a mailing.

The small apartment was cluttered, Dante's possessions adding to the confusion. Hundreds of pamphlets, books, and tracts lined a makeshift bookshelf. Large posters and pictures of Marx and Lenin covered the living room wall and in the bedroom behind the bed a mural-sized poster with a picture of a predatory white standing over the chained Scottsboro Boys, dominated the room. He shuddered when he thought of what the maid might tell the manager when she did the weekly cleaning. His only hope was that she never heard of the case and that Marx and Engels were taken for a couple of dead relatives. His first impression after talking to Aunt Annie was that her ardor had cooled. Encouraged, he began to test his assumption only to discover that what appeared as a lessening of enthusiasm was total exhaustion. She had been working day and night on the case and what before had been the fanaticism of a recent convert was now the dedication of a visionary. Even her appearance had changed. Without the makeup she had been in the habit of using all her life, her face appeared gaunt and colorless. Her eyes, a bit sunken, peered with intensity, no longer alive with dancing flecks. She was very happy, she told him; Dante had brought beauty into her life and her work had made it purposeful. Eager to tell her about his work, his plans for the new building; even about Posey, fill in some of the voids their relationship had contracted, reestablish the harmony he yearned for, he began by saying he was contemplating a major move of his business. She asked no questions, seemed to look through him and whatever zest he contemplated in the telling fizzled as she started to stuff the envelopes she had been addressing. Now it was no longer anger he felt or frustration but a strange sadness. For a while he said nothing and watched her work, as her fingers flew and her head was lowered, her eyes intent. Now his thoughts hurdled the years and he remembered a frightened skinny kid holding a bloody handkerchief to a nose and Aunt Annie's lap with his head in it as her fingers held a cold compress and her consolation and warm breast and then all the days given for him; Steeplechase and Luna Park and the Dodger games and cut-rate tickets at Gray's and the thousand socks she darned, the pants she patched, the trips to the country, the Pierce Arrow bike, the nights she barely slept through his chicken pox, scarlet fever, and mumps. He belonged to her and she was all he had. Couldn't she realize Dante was a stranger? That she was only a small part of his mad design? Would all the years they had lived so close be sacrificed for a dead-broke cigarmaker peddling an insane tract?

She looked up and smiled, a little of the old light in her eyes as if she had been reading his thoughts. "If you can stay, Danny will be home in an hour. Maybe we can have supper together."

It would have to be some other time, he told her and at the door her embrace lingered as if she too had remembered the past.

His business was becoming too complicated to run by the seat of his pants. It was all right to run a building or two from a desk, keep the figures in a notebook, and hope that Uncle Sam would not take a second look at your return. He had been pocketing a lot of the rents, reporting a little more than half of what he had been collecting, keeping the records in his office. The manager's sheets were picked up at the end of each month so that it would not be possible for them to account for more than thirty days' business at a time. Delaney's accounts were handled the same way; it would be foolish to let him in on any swindle—a fired and disgruntled employee could easily rationalize informing as a patriotic duty, and end up with part of the take besides.

Though he had no intention of discontinuing his skimming operations, he had to make sure the secret remained his. If any future tax return was questioned, he wanted the best representation. On Ralph Thompson's recommendation he contacted Tipton, Forbes, and Temple, a New York accounting firm with offices in every major city. They had the government's respect, Ralph advised, and there wasn't a trick of tax avoidance they did not know how to perform. Their main office was in downtown Los Angeles and they had an office in Beverly Hills, where Martin Tipton made his headquarters. Combining accountancy with business management they were the largest auditors and consultants for the top movie people.

When he entered Tipton's office for his appointment he got an arm about his shoulder and a firm handshake. The office walls were paneled in rich walnut, the desk wood matched, so did every piece in the room. The color of the carpeting was duplicated in the drapes, a brass desk set was complimented by brass wall fixtures, lamps and a portable bar topped with the wood of the walls. Mr. Tipton was matched as well. His hair was as white as his shirt, a baby blue tie was as azure as his eyes and a pair of sapphire cuff links peeked from the sleeves of a blue suit that was a shade darker. He offered Samson a cigar which he refused, a cigarette which he accepted, then sat back, still smiling, displaying an unusually regular set of the whitest teeth Samson had ever seen.

"It's beautiful," Samson said, scanning the room.

"A friend of mine did it. A set designer at Metro."

"Ralph told me you handle a lot of movie people."

"We have our share, but we do a lot of real estate from this end. Our downtown office gets the manufacturing and retail business."

As Samson explained his needs, Tipton made notes on a large pad and in spite of his flamboyancy, Samson could tell by his questions that he knew his business.

"You're going to be faced with one problem," Tipton said, when Samson finished. "The question of taking capital gains. Uncle Sam frowns on brokers taking capital gains on the sale of real estate. Oh, you might get away with one or two a year. But that's all. Yet from what you tell me there'll be many more."

He had never given it any thought and it made a big difference. If all his profits were to be declared as regular income, he could end up working for the government. "What can be done?" he asked.

"Let me give it some thought. We'll have to set up something that will act as a precedent for all future deals. If it doesn't hold up, you'll be in trouble." He stood up and Samson prepared to leave.

"When do you want to see me?"

"It'll take a few days. I want to go to the law books, but I also want to talk to a friend at the revenue office."

Tipton called, a few days later, and they met again at his office. He was decked out in blue and white again, the shade of blue a little deeper, which seemed to add a darker shade to his eyes.

"I think I have a few answers," he said, removing a sheaf of papers from a folder. "First thing you'll have to do is to give up your real-estate broker's license. Go out of the brokerage business. You said you weren't interested in commissions. As long as you keep that license they can kick out those capital gains."

"What else?"

Tipton rested his elbows on the desk and threaded his fingers. "We must create an image. One that makes it appear that buying and selling real estate is not your regular business. Just a sideline. First, I suggest you form two corporations. One holds title to buildings you keep for income. This will create the façade of an investor. The second corporation will handle the buying and selling. You'll be an employee in both and draw salaries."

"It sounds reasonable. But what assurances have I?"

Tipton smiled. "I can't give you a guarantee, but I can tell you this. If you are called for an audit, I think I'd have enough to whip them."

"All right, Mr. Tipton, when can we start?"

"The moment we agree on my fee."

The figure he gave for setting up the two corporations through their legal department, for a bookkeeping system and a monthly audit seemed fair. Samson accepted and Tipton called in his secretary and dictated a letter of intent. While they waited, he stripped the formality, insisted Samson use his first name, and told him a little bit about himself.

"I spent twenty-five years on Wall Street. If somebody told me a few years back I'd be living in Beverly Hills and liking it I would have said they were crazy."

"When did you open your offices here?"

"About fifteen years ago. Our clients started coming out and we needed an office. I'd make the trip once or twice a year, take a cab from the station to the Ambassador, conduct my business and shoot back. It was provincial—cow country, I thought. There was the Brown Derby, Bernstein's Fish Grotto, and open country. Every time I got back to New York I'd want to kneel and kiss the pavement."

Then he told Samson what brought him out. "It was my daughter. She married a young man from California. At first my wife and I took it philosophically. We visited her once a year. It didn't fill the void but it helped. Then we had a grandchild and that did it. I rationalized, indulged in sophistry and finally came to the conclusion that the West Coast office couldn't get along without me. Then," he said, smiling, "my suits got looser, my lapels wider and my collar tabs longer. I changed from oxford gray to blue serge and finally to this." He stepped back as if to model. "And I like it," he said, grinning. "I guess the ham in me was just under the skin." He laughed out loud. "You should see my partners' faces when I get to New York. Anyway, I love it out here now, the glamour and beautiful women," he added, winking. "And movie people are a helluva lot more colorful than the tab collar bunch."

The secretary returned with the letter which Samson signed and after promising to have dinner one night in the near future he left.

He hired an interior designer to work with the architect, acquainted him with his needs, told him to submit sketches and samples, selected stationery, decided on an opening date of August fifteenth, ordered invitations for a cocktail party, and placed an ad for a secretary-bookkeeper. The calls flooded his office and by the end of the week he had interviewed over thirty women. Ruth Bennett, inches from forty, angular and unattractive, gave him the impression of being a dedicated machine. An expert stenographer and bookkeeper with title company experience, she appeared to be the best of the lot and pleaded for the job. "I'm divorced and have a teen-age daughter. I need this job."

He hired her to start August first and then briefed her on his operation. She took notes as he spoke and offered to come in a few days earlier without pay, and before she left made it clear she never watched a clock, had nothing to do evenings, and could be available for work at any time. He was delighted with his choice.

On the last day of July, Samson was working late. Shortly before nine o'clock Art Jennings came charging in, roaring the news like a trumpeting bull.

"I saw your light. I just came from the hospital. It's a girl!" He was unshaven, his collar was unbuttoned and he was breathing heavily.

"You'd better sit down."

"She labored eighteen hours . . . it was awful. You should see her . . . the baby, that is . . . looks like Paula . . . maybe my mouth . . . anyway she's beautiful." He reached for a cigarette, lit a match, couldn't find the end, took the cigarette out of his mouth, crushed it in the ashtray, removed another from his pack, dangled it from the corner of his mouth and grinned at Samson foolishly.

Samson felt a little of the excitement, thought about the infant, wondered what part of it was like him, thought about the nose and for a few moments felt a surge of frustration and a little dismay. He quickly put it out of his mind, looked at Art, wondering how he would act and what he would say if he knew the truth. Then he thought of Paula, in the hospital cradling the child, his child, perhaps giving her a breast, and a wave of tenderness such as he never felt for her overcame him. Then he drove it all from his mind. It was over and done and Art was the father and it was legal and a fact and nothing that would ever be said or done would change it. "What are you going to name her?"

"Carla. After Paula's mother."

"A pretty name, Art." Then he thought about a gift and asked what the baby needed.

"She's got everything. I've been buying stuff for weeks. And my mother-in-law sent enough for a dozen grandchildren."

"I'll think of something." He poured a couple of drinks, they toasted the event, and Art left. He called a florist, told him to send a large basket of flowers to the hospital, then wrote a note in which he enclosed a check for a hundred dollars. It read:

Dear Paula:
I was delighted to learn of the birth of your baby daughter and that you and the child are doing well. Though we haven't had the opportunity of seeing each other during the past few months, Art kept me constantly informed. The joys and pain of birth belong to a woman; a man is only a by-stander. I sincerely hope that all the pain is in the past and that the future holds only happiness for you and your little girl. Please consider me a friend and do not hesitate to call upon me at any time you feel I can assist in any way. Enclosed is a small sum to start little Carla's account.

My best wishes,
Samson Duke

Though he hated to reopen a wound he felt to ignore the birth of the child would be worse. Also, his business relations with Art could be closely tied and there would be times when there would be contact with Paula. When he mailed the letter that night he felt a great relief. The birth of the child had ended the critical possibility that Paula would reveal the truth.

He sent out five hundred invitations to the cocktail party and it seemed that everybody came and brought a friend. By eight in the evening, an hour after the affair was to end, nobody had made a move to leave. The caterer ran out of food twice, had to fill in from a local delicatessen, and Delaney tracked down the boot-legger for another load.

Samson moved from group to group making an effort to greet everyone. As he made his way about the room, he heard bits of talk, an orchestration of superlatives about the office and himself, references to his taste, his genius, his prominent family and even his good looks. He was back-slapped, hand-shaked and patted, smiled at, and kissed, his ego getting enough bolstering for a millennium. Of all the compliments those concerning his looks pleased him most. They could laugh at his taste, ignore his genius, and make his Duke a Dukins but nothing would ever again alter his face. The nose fit a duke's and the jaw was a general's and the eyes no longer converged toward the bridge but were deep-set and there was the fine head to top it all. He felt like a little man who grew inches overnight, no longer needing to look up. How he wanted Aunt Annie to see all this! He had been tempted to invite her, exact her promise to say nothing but finally decided not to chance it. She might insist on bringing Dante, and they would be as conspicious as a pair of foxes in with chickens.

Posey arrived and rapidly became the core of a group of men. Martin Tipton came in late. Dressed in black that set off his white hair, he stood out wherever he was in the room. He came up to Samson with a drink in his hand, grabbed his arm and took him to a corner. "Who is she?" he said, pointing to Posey.

"A friend of mine."

"How good a friend?" He was staring at her trying to draw a response from across the room.

"A good friend."

"I'd like to meet her."

"Wait here." Samson went over to Posey and in a few moments eased her from the group. "Someone wants to meet you. He's my tax consultant. Very important." He steered her across the room. Tipton started his smile the moment he caught Posey's eye and by the time they reached his side it was all over his face as he acknowledged the introduction with a slight bow.

"I didn't mean to take you from your friends."

"It was a rescue."

At that point, Al Lifton arrived accompanied by a shorter, older man Samson supposed to be his father-in-law, Harry Finkelstein. This was a contact he had been wanting for a long time. He detached himself from Posey and Tipton, moved to the door, and greeted Lifton.

"I'll bet you're Mr. Finkelstein," he said, extending a hand to the older man.

"You won the bet."

"I'm Samson Duke."

"Who else?"

Lifton seemed to be looking for an escape, spied someone he knew, grunted an excuse and drifted away. Samson took the older man's arm and drew him aside. "I've been wanting to meet you."

Finkelstein's face was perfectly round, the skin of the bald head separated from it by a row of deep wrinkles. When he spoke his eyes were wide and animated and then they would squint, almost closing, as if he were trying to peer inside your head anticipating your reply. "Why should you want to meet me?"

"Al's spoken about you often."

He looked in Lifton's direction, scowling. "I can imagine."

"How do you like the offices?" he asked.

"For offices it's fine."

Samson couldn't think of a reply and asked if he wanted a drink.

"I don't drink after I eat, and I already ate."

"We'll be settled in a few days. I want you to drop in. Maybe we can do business."

He squinted at Samson, seemed to smile and drifted into the crowd. Samson returned to where he had left Tipton and Posey but they were gone. He scanned the room and finally spotted them coming out of one of the private offices. Tipton was talking and Posey was laughing with an animation Samson had not seen in her before. He started in their direction but Delaney headed him off.

"We're running out of everything. What'll I do?"

"Nothing. This bunch has had enough. Pretty soon they'll forget why they came and who gave the party." He told the caterer to start cleaning up, saw to it that the bartenders stopped pouring drinks, then took a stand at the entrance. A few guests began to drift toward the door and Samson shouted out the goodbyes. The start was all it needed; in less than half an hour nearly everybody had gone.

Martin Tipton was in Samson's office talking earnestly with Posey when he walked in on them. He was sitting in Samson's chair, tilted backward, his eyes on the ceiling as he seemed to be pontificating. Posey, caught in attention, was in the chair beside him.

"What's going on?" Samson put enough warmth and friendliness into it to take the edge off his concern. Martin stopped talking, tilted the chair upright and Posey turned to Samson.

"We're talking politics, Sam. I swear it."

They were both so defensive he decided to change the subject. "Well, the party's over," he said. He looked at his watch. "It's about time. I thought they'd never leave."

"It's the free booze," Martin said, getting up. "It always keeps them."

"It's been a pleasure," Posey said, extending her hand as he started to leave.

"Unexpected for me," he said, keeping her hand as they walked to the door.

As Samson and Posey drove to the apartment, she reviewed the party, commented on the large turnout, questioned him about certain people she'd met, ignored his curt answers at first, but then pointedly released the hold she had on his hand and slid to her side of the car.

"You son-of-a-bitch! You drag me away from a group, insist I meet a man, tell me he is important to you, and now you're furious because I was pleasant to him."

"Pleasant! You were holding hands when I was looking. God knows what you were doing when I wasn't around."

"Go ahead. Keep it up. Show me how petty and small you can be." Her arms were folded across her chest and she was staring straight ahead.

"Petty! Small! There you were, right under my nose. . . ."

"Doing what!" she said, glaring at him. "Having an intelligent conversation with your friend! Probably the only one you have with any sense. We were talking politics. On which we happen to agree."

He snorted. "Who are you kidding? You mean Martin's a New Dealer?"

"He sure is. And for reasons you wouldn't understand. Anyway, I've had enough of this. You can drive me home."

"Oh, no. We're going to the apartment. I'll listen. I've got an open mind."

"It's as closed as any I've known."

"Try me," he said, pulling up in front of the building.

"Really, Sam, I'm tired." She didn't move. "I'd like to go home."

He began to realize his suspicion and anger were childish. Anyway, he wanted her with him that night, needed her, and had no intention of letting her go.

"I'm sorry," he said, taking her hand. "I've acted like a fool."

She looked at him for a moment. "I guess I should be complimented. Your being jealous." She shook her head. "I didn't think you had it in you. I thought you were insulated against everything. Maybe you *are* human."

"If that was meant to be a compliment, I resent it." She hadn't moved. "Come on," he said. "Let's go upstairs." There was a brief moment of hesitation and she got out of the car. On the way up neither said a word. They entered the apartment and were still silent. She removed her jacket absently, poured herself a drink and settled on the couch still not talking.

"That head of yours is full," he said. "You look like you made a discovery."

"Just a decision."

He waited for her to continue.

"I've decided to go to work. Mr. Tipton offered me a job."

"He didn't waste any time."

She ignored the remark. "He asked me what I was doing and I told him, nothing. He asked me what I could do and I said I was a top secretary. So, he offered me a job."

Samson had a hunch Tipton liked to chase, saw it was not going to be easy with Posey, then served the job and what went with it. Ordinarily Samson would have relied on his ability to compete. But Martin Tipton was bright and urbane, and, in spite of his age, an attractive man. An obligation for a job added to his charm could be more than he would want to contend with.

"Good salary?" he asked.

"Enough to live on."

"How much?"

"Two hundred a month."

"That's a lot of money these days. Secretaries are putting in full time for less than half that. Good ones."

Posey lit a cigarette and said nothing.

"I don't understand you," he said.

She looked up questioningly.

"All of a sudden you decide you want to work. Just like that. Why didn't you mention it to me? I might have done something."

"Made me your private secretary?"

"You know I can't do that."

"Why not? I'm capable."

"It wouldn't work. It has to be strictly business."

"I'll probably accept Mr. Tipton's job. It will be strictly business."

"I've got an idea. I'll give you a job. Not in my office, but it'll be a job. A real one." He was reaching out but he didn't care. "The salary will be the same and in a way you'll be your own boss."

"Sam, you don't have to. Our relationship won't change."

He wasn't going to give it a chance. "No, I mean it. You can start anytime you wish. I was thinking of hiring someone," he lied. "And I'm sure you can do the work as good as anyone."

"What kind of work?"

"I've got the ownership books of every building in the area. You're to contact every owner by phone, find out if his property is for sale and get all the information. If you run into half a dozen buys a year it'll pay off. You can work from your apartment. You might have to contact some of the owners at night. Other than that, your hours will be your own. Is it a deal?"

"You're sure I can do it?"

"Absolutely."

"You're not doing this to keep me away from Tipton?"

"Why should I?"

"Maybe you like me."

"Of course I like you, don't twist things. Do you want the job or not?"

"I want it. I had all intentions of going to work soon. For you or Tipton or someone else. But not for seventy-five or a hundred a month. And one more thing, to keep the record straight. A month before Mr. Hudson died I started looking for work. We were finished. For a long time it was pleasant. Stanley was an interesting man, we needed each other. Then it began to change and toward the end I began to feel like a piece of merchandise. It wasn't his fault, or mine for that matter, it was just that these arrangements . . . well, you know what I mean."

It looked like he had her figured wrong and was not sure he liked the new image as well. He had taken it for granted that the time would come when he would pick up all the tabs. He meant to discuss it with her but was not sure whether he wanted her to move in or maintain a separate apartment. Now, it seemed the decision was not his. He told her he understood, admired her for the decision, and would put her to work the first of the following week.

It was a month before the clack and clatter of everybody moving in and his own organizing became the sweet hum of a good machine. Delaney had been everywhere—moving furniture, driving managers, expediting and smoothing—all with the imprecating and cajoling of a skinner driving a huge team. Ruth Bennett proved more efficient and eager than her promise. She maintained a system evolved by the Tipton office that kept him informed of every detail of each building up to the end of business each day. It was rare for her to leave the office before seven or eight each evening and he would find her at her desk even on mornings when he checked in before eight. His biggest problem and the one most time consuming was the job he could trust to no one: keeping a duplicate set of the rent records of all the buildings, which he stored at his apartment. He would make the rounds, collect the rents from the managers, skim the top, deposit the balance, and then return to his apartment and make up the rent reports that were to be turned in to Mrs. Bennett. The details were maddening since it involved showing vacancies where none existed and a constant juggling of figures. Up until the time he opened the office and hired Mrs. Bennett he had been taking around two thousand dollars a month off the top. The figure was too large to ignore and when he discovered that Delaney, who checked every report he brought in, treated each vacancy as a personal affront and climbed on the managers' backs he realized he must have discovered his game and was keeping his mouth shut. His choice was now clear; either he stop stealing from Uncle Sam or take Delaney into his confidence. Taking a long look at the figures, calculating the future potential he decided to make arrangements with Delaney, and requested a meeting at his apartment. Although he had a plan that would give some assurance of loyalty from Delaney, he was still aware of risks. However, the pot was worth the chance.

Since he introduced Delaney to the conservative clothing sold at Pesteres, Delaney acquired an incongruity that fitted him like a silk hat on a dunce. Gripped between the set planes of a square jaw and jutting above his bull neck was a long briar pipe which he kept stuffing and puffing without end and rarely removed from his mouth. With it he also developed the pipe smoker's thoughtful expression. The affectation would not have bothered Samson except that his taste ran to a mixture of tobacco whose stink permeated and cloyed and reminded one of his presence hours after he would leave the room.

Puffing on the pipe with vertical lines of introspection knitted between his brows Delaney mumbled a greeting between his teeth as he entered the apartment. Samson got down to business.

"How's your health, Jack?"

"My health? Fine, I guess. Why?"

"I was talking to an insurance man the other day. He's got a plan for employees. Key men," he added.

He shrugged. "What do I need insurance for? I got nobody except a couple of aunts and a cousin somewhere."

"Not that kind. One that'll pay you."

"Something like an annuity?"

"That's right."

"I don't want to spend any money."

"It won't cost you a cent. It'll be a gift from me. Sort of a bonus."

"You don't have to do that, Sam."

"I want to." Delaney started to protest and he shut him off. "I'm going to buy you a twenty-thousand-dollar, fifteen-year annuity policy. You'll still be young and that twenty grand'll come in handy. However, in case you die before it comes due I become the beneficiary."

"Ain't it kinda dangerous," Delaney smiled, "if I'm worth twenty thousand to you dead?"

"You're worth ten times that to me alive. Of course, if you quit before it comes due you get nothing."

"Suppose I get fired?"

Samson put as much sincerity into his voice as he could. "I'm going to need you more as time goes on. Anyway, you've nothing to lose. It's a gift. There'll still be bonuses and raises."

"Gee, Sam, I'm sorry. For the way I sounded, I mean. Thanks." He smiled gratefully. "Was there anything else?" he said, preparing to leave.

"No." Samson followed him to the door. "Oh, yes, there is something. Sit down for a few minutes." Delaney returned to the room. "There's no reason for Uncle Sam to be my partner in everything. I decided to take a few rent dollars off the top for sort of pocket money." If Delaney already knew it there was no sign of it on his face. "When you get the reports check with me on vacancies before you call the managers." He slapped his back. "Okay?"

"Of course. I don't blame you. Everybody's doing it. And when you figure what the crooks in Washington are doing with the money . . ."

"That's the way I feel."

"Don't worry," Delaney said at the door. "I'll handle it." The pipe was back in his mouth and he looked thoughtful. He removed it slowly. "It might be a good idea if this was between you and me. Mrs. Bennett oughtn't to know."

"Under no circumstances is she to know."

"She won't." He gave Samson a reassuring slap on the back and left.

Samson was a little disappointed. The idea of the policy brought little enthusiasm. But time was on his side and though it might appear meaningless now, as the premiums piled up and the years went by, the hook would sink in and the twenty thousand would start looking bigger and might one day become a fat cat.

Anxious to show Aunt Annie the new building, he chose an evening when Dante worked late, picked her up and drove her to the office. This was an opportunity to narrow their rift and take one more crack at her insularity. If what he had accomplished was not proof of the opportunities of a free man in a free society, all future incantations would be futile. Encouraged by her exclamations as they toured the outer offices, he ushered her into his, seated her, and took the chair behind the desk. He watched as her eyes traveled the paneled walls, examined the furniture and finally rested on his.

"Well, what do you think of it?" he asked.

"You must be very rich."

"Not yet, but I'm going to be." He leaned forward intently. "It's what I've been trying to tell you, Aunt Annie. People with imagination and the will to work prosper in this society. Even in a depression, look what I've done." Then he went on to tell her that he had dreams that were being turned into reality and that hers, beautiful as they might be, were good in print and oratory but had no relation to the true world. She listened as he went on about the unchangeable nature of man and then she shook her head vigorously and broke in. "Man's nature is the product of his environment."

"That's what I'm talking about," he interrupted. "That's part of your dream and sounds good but isn't true."

She ignored him. "My dreams are for all men, yours are for a single man."

Forcing a smile, he guided her out of the building and drove her home. She asked him to dinner for the following evening emphasizing the fact that he had not seen Dante for some time and he accepted.

Whatever strength and passion Aunt Annie possessed seemed to have been drained from Dante. After the dinner that night when the three of them were seated in the living room, even Dante became the target for her zeal.

"Why don't you strike?" she demanded.

"For what?" he asked with surprise.

"You work ten hours a day."

"It's piecework. I get paid for what I do."

"The hours are too long," she insisted.

"I could work less."

"Then you'll make less."

"That's right."

"You should make the same for eight hours."

"Of course I should. But Rodriguez can't pay it. Rodriguez is a little man. He employs three cigarmakers, works fourteen hours a day himself, and does not even make wages."

But to Aunt Annie, Rodriguez was a boss. "If he can't pay decent wages, let him get out of the business," she stormed.

Samson said nothing as Dante started to protest like a tired old prophet unable to keep up the pace. Then she accused him of being a Mutualist and flung every lesson he had taught to his face. He rallied and then no longer able to resist, lit a cigar, sank further into his big chair, and closed his eyes. As Samson watched he realized that his aunt was like a behemoth awakening from a long sleep who rose and tumbled everything on its back. The essays of Emma Goldman were the Missal and Kropotkin had written her Bible and Bakunin the Sermon on the Mount.

By the time he left, she had served tea, her anger had cooled, and she was standing behind Dante's chair stroking his hair.

A week later she called Samson demanding to see him immediately. He rushed over to find her angrier than he had ever seen her, waving a piece of paper above her head.

"You're so corrupted you'll even do this to me!"

He grabbed the paper from her hands. It was a notice to vacate within thirty days signed by Delaney. "How could you think I would do this?" he demanded. "I have a supervisor, he runs the buildings. Anyway, what reason did he give?"

"He didn't give any but I squeezed it out of the manager. We're undesirable was all she said. Anyway, you can imagine what she means."

He calmed her down, told her to ignore the notice, rushed back to the office and called Delaney in. He did not know what to do. Aunt Annie had to stay but how could he explain it to Delaney without revealing she was his aunt?

They were dangerous Reds, that was all Delaney said, sucking his pipe. The maid had reported them to the manager. There were meetings going on all night, people coming and going and the walls of the apartment were plastered with all kinds of posters.

"I went in when they were gone. You should have seen the place. Pictures of foreign-looking guys all over and one was a bunch of niggers with a dirty picture of a white man."

"The woman called me," Samson said. "Demanded an explanation, said she was going to turn it over to an attorney. I don't want any trouble, Jack, not this kind. I went over to see her. She said she never held a meeting, friends just visited and that she had a right to hang anything she wanted on her walls. Anyway, she promised to keep visitors down to a couple at a time." As he spoke Delaney's look of surprise told him he wasn't convincing.

"But these people are dangerous, Sam. We ought to report them."

"And get involved? Don't you dare."

Delaney shrugged. "Okay."

The moment he left, Samson called his aunt. She could tear up the notice, he told her, but if she wanted to hold meetings she would have to hire a hall; he did not mind giving her an apartment free but if it meant bringing the authorities in she would have to fight her revolution in another building. She slammed the receiver when he finished and he sat back exhausted and closed his eyes. If he had to kick her out he would do it. She would have to listen to reason; he would find her another apartment and pay the rent. She had to understand! They made a bargain, no interference in each others' lives and she was going to live up to it. And he thought Harry Baldwin was a threat, the church a specter . . . what a joke! Compared to this, Father Keenan was the Guardian Angel, Baldwin a prince, and the Church a benefactor. Even undertakers die and Harry Baldwin could have left his aunt a bundle after the Church siphoned off its share. And a good Catholic surely found no sin in making a buck. He could have borrowed from his aunt, invested her money, done anything he damned pleased. And where would it go now even if it remained intact? For revolution! Well, there were courts, wills were busted and he could depend on a judge.

He had an early dinner with Posey and rushed over to Catalina Street. The voices coming through her door as he stood before her apartment confirmed the worst of his fears. They were all there, Dante and his aunt, the Rizzos, Arne Proescher, and Kelly and all talking stopped when he entered as every pair of eyes were upon him like on an enemy who just stole into camp. Aunt Annie broke the silence, greeted him, took his arm, hustled him into the kitchen and closed the door.

"This is no meeting," she said facing him squarely. "These people are my friends."

"They're also the friends of world revolution, the I.W.W. The Scottsboro Boys and Sacco-Vanzetti not to mention Emma Goldman, Kropotkin, and all the other damn fools."

"If that's the way you feel. . . ."

She turned to leave and he took her arm. "That's the way you made me feel. We made a bargain. Remember? You live your life but you let me live mine. Well, you're doing everything in your power to destroy mine. If the authorities ever break down that door and find out you're my aunt it will destroy everything I am trying to build." He gripped both of her arms. "Look, Aunt Annie, I want everything between us to be as it always was but I can't buy your philosophy. Don't you understand it's as distasteful to me as mine is to you?" As he released her she looked at him as if she was seeing him for the first time.

"I'll move. I am sure there is a landlord in town more tolerant of other's ideas."

He ignored the sarcasm. "I'll pay the rent, whatever it is."

"No thanks." She opened the door and he followed her into the room. His impulse was to get out and never see any of them again but there was contempt and defiance in their attitude as they stared and he decided to toss out caution. God knows they had upset his life, his plans, and driven his aunt from him. Well, he had a few things to say and he was dealing himself in. Pouring himself a cup of coffee from a pot on the table he took a seat and lit a cigarette. If he was going to destroy whatever remained of his welcome in his aunt's home it was going to be in ringing tones. They began to talk again, he watched silently, waited, soon they ignored him and then after a long discourse by Kelly he jumped in with a quote from Herbert Spencer. As an addenda he attached a few well-remembered phrases from Nietzsche's relation to a condemnation of democracy and the idealization of the superman and the torch hit the powder-keg. Even Dante exploded, upsetting his usual calm.

"Spencer was without heart. The coldest man that ever lived. How can you quote him?"

Kelly jumped from his seat, looked at him menacingly and roared. "And Nietzsche! He was insane, hated the world!"

Samson did not know where to start. Arne Proescher, who had walked into the kitchen, shouted, "What do you expect from a goddamn landlord!"

"You can't believe these things?" Dante said.

"Sure I believe them," he answered defiantly. He was damned tired of their puny revolutions, sick to death of their contempt and determined once for all to destroy all their theories with facts. He demanded to be heard and as they gathered around he marshaled everything he could remember from the writings of the two great men. Defending them as realists, with logical minds and a passion for order, something they wouldn't understand he added, he expounded on the survival of the fittest, not as a means to destroy the unendowed but as the logical goal of man to weed and kill and finally breed the best. He insisted that if man constantly sought means to improve the lower animal, strove to propagate a better plant, why should he aspire less for himself. Then he attacked their dream of a society as a community of ants and bees, destructive of initiative and man's right to free choice. When he chose strength instead of altruism and pride in place of humility and asserted that equality was an unnatural condition for selection and survival, Kelly could not constrain himself any longer and broke in, his face twisted with rage.

"Don't you dare compare man with an animal!"

"Or a potato plant," Arne added.

"Man has intelligence," Dante added. "He feels pain, sorrow."

Now, Mr. Rizzo leaped from his seat, pushed Arne aside and

stood over Samson. "Maybe you wanna' put man in a pen like a bull and bring him a cow?"

"That's not what I said."

"It sure in hell is!" Kelly shouted. "Breed, you said. Weed and kill."

He realized they had taken out of context everything that was easy to distort and was about to reply when his aunt stepped in.

"That's enough," she said. "Leave Sam alone. He believes what he believes."

He did not know whether she had interceded to defend him or write him off. A week later, she sent him a note telling him she moved and enclosed her new address, an apartment house on Burlington.

CHAPTER ELEVEN

B y the end of September he closed the deal on the purchase of the seven buildings with Roy Phillips. A month before he'd arranged with the sellers to install new managers so that by the time he took over, the apartments would be operating under Delaney's direction. Now, Mrs. Bennett's work was piled high and he was forced to hire a young girl to assist her. In addition to the bookkeeping and correspondence, he had been sending out extensive mailings to a long list of brokers on the properties, inviting their cooperation. Though he had not been getting much business from the brokers in the office, the income from their space paid the monthly installments on the loan and all the salaries. Considering the state of affairs and the anguished cries everywhere his operation was successful. Even his investment in Posey paid off with the purchase and immediate resale of a small apartment house she had dug up. That one deal paid her salary for a full year.

Though they were seeing each other as often as before, he sensed a change in her that was difficult to define and so subtle that he began to suspect it was caused more by his anxiety than her attitude. He knew Martin Tipton was being attentive to her. Posey denied ever having dinner with him, but they had lunched and she'd been impressed. Accountants come easy and under ordinary circumstances he would have bounced Tipton, but his line was in for big fish and Tipton swam with the school. Some day his account would be worthwhile but now it was small by their standards and to lose him would mean little. So he watched and waited and made every effort to play the game in a way that would please Posey most. Sticking to the rules, he called frequently, never failed to tell her how much he cared, bought her gifts and made few demands. Apparently it was not working. One evening they returned to the apartment after dinner, had their usual drink before going to bed. He had removed his tie and started to unbutton his shirt when she jumped up and grabbed her coat.

"Keep your shirt on and take me home."

"What's gotten into you?"

"I've had enough. I'm sick of this. Dinner, a drink, and to bed."

"That's what you wanted. You said it yourself. And we're great in there!" he shouted, pointing to the bedroom.

"All right. That's what I did want. But not anymore. There are other things."

"What other things?"

"You wouldn't understand."

"I guess, Martin Tipton understands."

"As a matter of fact, he does!" she shouted.

He laughed and she started to run from the room. Grabbing her near the door he whirled her back and on to the couch. "Read the label on the can before you open it! He's married. Remember? All you'll get from him is a lot of intellectual palaver, dinners where he can't be seen, and a quick lay in a motel."

She jumped up and pushed him aside.

"And he'll tell you he doesn't love his wife anymore and maybe he'll get a divorce." She was standing in front of him, her hands working furiously, and he was certain she was going to sock him. He took a step backward and she sank to the couch. For a moment he said nothing and when she sat up and reached for her handkerchief he sat down beside her and touched her shoulder.

"I'm sorry," he muttered. "It's just that I can't lose you. We were getting along fine. I never made any promises. . . . I never pretended."

She blew her nose and kept her back to him. He tried to take her hand but she drew it away. She got up, put on her coat and turned to him.

"Please, Sam, take me home."

He drove her to her door and she left without a word. Suddenly he felt alone, abandoned, cut away, like the last meeting with Aunt Annie. Unlike Gloria who was an animal and Paula who was looking to escape, Posey gave a little more than she took and, more than any person he had known with the exception of Aunt Annie, made him feel he was liked in spite of the bitter pieces that went into the pot.

He tossed in bed that night and could not get her out of his mind. She was no fool and after stumbling in and out of a marriage, bitter at her role with Hudson, she would settle only for a home and love. Their disagreement would blow over, he was sure, and they would go on for awhile—but not for long. Soon he would be faced with the decision. And he was not ready, knew it, and fell asleep wondering how to keep her without giving her what she wanted.

When a week passed and he did not hear from her, he finally called on the pretext of business. Posey made her report as if nothing happened and he asked her to dinner. She put him off for that day but agreed for the following night. They spent it as they did in the past, no reference was made to the night of the argument, but the evening was strained. In the morning she did not join him for breakfast but remained in bed. When he left for the office the fear of losing her became alive, real, and he knew he had to prevent it.

It was a month since he received the note from Aunt Annie telling him she had moved. Early one morning he received a call from Dante. He had to see him immediately, the cigarmaker said, it was urgent and Samson arranged to meet him at a downtown restaurant.

Dante was in a small booth when he arrived, the sadness of his face accentuated by a gray stubble. They ordered coffee and Dante told him that he was very worried about Aunt Annie—she was exhausted, could not sleep nights, was very nervous, and refused to see a doctor. "She works like ten, Sam. All day, half the night. She's on picket line, she write letters, there is no time for rest. Our house is never empty, people all the time. For them she cooks but she does not eat." He shook his head sadly. "I know what you think. I know you do not like me. You blame me, but I do not care. I have deep feeling for Annie." He placed his hand on Samson's arm. "Your aunt is like saint. I plead with her to see doctor, to take rest but she does not listen." He was fighting back tears. "You are closest to her, perhaps she will listen to you. I plead with you to see her."

He wanted to tell Dante what he really thought, that the day his aunt met him was cursed, and if he really loved her he would pack up and leave and give her a chance to return to sanity. But the cigarmaker's concern was too real, his pain too evident and Samson realized it was too late; Aunt Annie's passion was no longer a minor infection but a galloping disease. He promised to look in on her and after parting from Dante, drove to the apartment.

She was alone and though it was only a little over a month since he had seen her he was shocked at her appearance. Her face was haggard, her eyes dull; she looked old. Her greeting was warmer than any of the past months.

He sat beside her on the couch. "You don't look well," he began.

She brushed a wisp of hair that had strayed to her face and forced a smile. "I'm fine. Just a little tired."

He looked around the apartment which was strewn and mussed with neglect. "Have you been to a doctor?"

"There's nothing wrong, really."

"Maybe he can give you something. To pep you up. A tonic, or yeast."

"I take yeast every day. I feel like a sponge cake." They both laughed and he asked about Dante.

"He's working hard, dear man. I don't know what I'd do without him. Anyway how are you?"

"Very busy. Feeling good."

She sat erect and looked at him. "You know you're really handsome, Sam." It was said with the surprise of a new discovery. She touched his arm. "I guess you were right about doing the nose."

"Maybe I'm right about a lot of things."

"Please, not now." A lock of hair fell forward again and she did not bother to touch it.

"All right, but I've a few other things to say. You've got to take time off. A vacation. Maybe a trip to New York. You can see friends. Anything, but you've got to get away." She had been studying his face and he got the feeling she did not hear a word he said. "Have you been listening to me?"

"Every word."

"What are you going to do about it?"

"I'll think about it, Sam." She started for the kitchen. "How about a cup of tea?"

They sat over the brew and hardly spoke and he began to get the feeling that something else, more important than her work was going on. As he talked there was little response. He asked her questions and she only nodded and when a lock fell over her face again and he brushed it up and she did not move, he could no longer contain himself.

"Damnit, Aunt Annie, what is wrong!"

She almost dropped the cup as she spilled tea over the table. "What's the matter with you, Sam!" she demanded angrily.

"What's the matter with me! It's you. You won't talk. You aren't listening. You look like hell. And you won't see a doctor."

For a moment she said nothing as she wiped the mess, then she turned to him. "There's nothing wrong. I did go to a doctor. I'm just beat, that's all."

"What did he say?"

" 'Take it easy,' he said. 'Get more rest.' You're being silly, Sam. Stop worrying."

When he stood to leave, she held him at arms length and her hair was now brushed back off her face and a bit of the old look was in her eyes. He felt better then, made her promise to slow down, and promised to call in a few days.

In December, Posey and he were invited to a party Martin Tipton was giving to celebrate the end of Prohibition. It was the night of repeal and the whole nation was getting ready to slake a long thirst. The hotels and taverns were stocked up, affairs were being given everywhere, and for days in anticipation of the event the talk was of nothing else as if the Depression and all of its meanness would be washed away by the ocean of booze.

He picked up Posey at her apartment. Their relationship had been tolerable, tenuous, hanging to a ledge that was narrowing. He had a hunch she was still seeing Tipton but made a point of never bringing it up and she never discussed it.

Though Martin and he had talked many times of his coming to dinner this was to be the first visit to Tipton's home and he was looking forward to it. There were sure to be a lot of important movie people there, some who might do him good, and he was anxious for Posey to see Mrs. Tipton. The physical evidence of her existence might in some way make Tipton less desirable and attainable.

The home was located on an oval level overlooking the Beverly Hills Hotel. A courtyard large enough to park a dozen cars surrounded the entrance, which was strung with lights alternating between empty bottles of famous brands of liquor, wines, and tiny beer kegs. In the center of a large entry hall they were greeted by a gibbet from which Andrew Volstead hung in effigy. Crowds from the rooms on both sides spilled into the hall. Martin, followed by a petite gray-haired woman, exquisitely dressed in a long gown, pushed their way through the guests and met them at the door. Tipton took Posey's hand and introduced them.

"We finally meet, Mr. Duke," Mrs. Tipton said, looking him over critically. She turned to Posey: "I'm so glad you were able to come." A maid took their coats and Martin led them into the living room.

"You'll have to introduce yourselves," he said, looking around in despair. "There's too many now and I can't remember half the names."

There were perhaps seventy-five persons in the rooms, dressed in casual clothes and evening attire; one man wore a sweater and was tieless, one young woman wore slacks. A group had gathered around the piano where a man was beating out the latest tunes. Along one wall a table was set with hors d'oeuvres and beside it two bartenders with vests and shirtbands, sporting handlebar mustaches, poured the drinks. Two couples were dancing on a tiny patch of floor and groups were clustered everywhere spilling out to the patio and around the pool.

Posey wandered from Samson's side and he scanned the room. Though the home's architecture was New Orleans Colonial with lacy iron lattices and balcony façades the interior was a combination of French chateau and Hollywood modern. It looked like Mrs. Tipton had clung to the past and Martin had imposed his new self. There were tapestry drapes and a modern breakfront, graceful drum tables and low ottomans and the large Oriental rug that covered the floor was edged with throw rugs of modern design. On the walls he noticed a Klee and a Picasso separating a Fragonard. No doubt the Tiptons had compromised.

A butler and maid wove through the rooms carrying trays of drinks and Mrs. Tipton flitted everywhere. He tried to imagine the face without lines and sag and the eyes which now appeared glazed under the makeup. Her nose was fine and her lips well formed and the neck, now stringy, must have been graceful and though her figure was spare it could at one time have been delicate and curvy. She must have been a beauty, he concluded.

Though she chatted with a group and moved on, her eyes followed her husband as if if he disappeared from sight, she would lose him. Tipton was standing in a corner talking earnestly with a woman who appeared to be in her late thirties, dark-haired and dramatically profiled, who gesticulated with wide sweeps of a long cigarette holder which she held loosely in her hand. Tipton caught his eye and beckoned to him. Samson reached the other side of the room and the moment the woman turned to him full-faced he recognized her as a motion picture star whose name he could not recall. Martin placed an arm about his shoulder.

"Joan, I'd like you to meet a friend of mine. Joan Pennington, Sam Duke." She smiled, drawing her lips back slowly revealing two rows of perfectly capped teeth.

"Martin has been telling me about you, Mr. Duke."

Tipton was poised for a getaway. "That's right," he said, looking over his shoulder across the room. "I told Joan you were in real estate. She has a house in Palm Springs." He patted Samson's arm and escaped. Miss Pennington shifted her holder, took his arm and drew him closer into the corner as if to hide him from further intrusion. Standing next to her he discovered that what had looked to be thirtyish from across the room was on closer inspection an attempt to hide fifty.

"Martin told me you buy real estate," she said, still clinging to his arm.

"Occasionally."

"I have a home in Palm Springs for which I have no further use. I wish to sell it."

"I buy only apartment houses. Why not try a broker in Palm Springs?"

"They're asleep, Mr. Duke. Like the Indians there." She waved her holder again. "I wouldn't let them near it."

He was sure she had tried them all. Now he was angry at Martin, palming her off as he did, and was anxious to get away. She relaxed her hold on his arm, and he turned to wave to an imaginary person across the room. "Has Martin the particulars?" he said, edging away.

"He's my business manager."

"I'll contact him in the morning, Miss Pennington. I'll see what I can do." He left her without looking back. Joining a group of which Posey was a part, he shouldered his way in. They were talking shop; rushes and cutting, camera angles, and seemed to be tearing a script apart. One man, tall, unkempt, with loose large joints fitted into a baggy suit and a mane of hair which he kept combing with his hand, had their attention.

"I had to rewrite every line of the script as I shot. Believe me I should get screen credit."

Another man, small, with thick glasses and a bald head, kept shaking his head violently. "Josh is right," he finally exploded. "I don't know how the studio bought it in the first place. Green has no conception of the craft." Samson took Posey by the arm and drew her away.

They picked up two drinks and joined the group around the piano. The music was louder now and the singing less harmonious. A few more couples were on the dance floor and all about the room the tempo seemed to rise. Finally there was a chorus of voices and a group rushed to the entry hall.

"It's Harry and Rita! They would make an entrance . . . look at them . . . I knew it . . . they're always on."

Samson recognized immediately two of the biggest screen stars of the day, costumed for the occasion and well on the way. Harry Taylor was gotten up like an old soak, reddened nose, tie askew, mussed and baggy pants. His companion, Rita Carlton, had an equally red nose, wrinkled black stockings, broken shoes, and a hat tilted crazily on her head. They were surrounded and dragged into the room. Harry rushed to the piano, pushed the player off the bench, and started to play as Rita vaulted to the top of the instrument and began to sing in a simulated whisky voice. Martin joined in and Mrs. Tipton forced a smile while playing nervously with a handkerchief. Others in the room moved away from the group about the piano like a crowd backing away from possible violence.

He nudged Posey. "They're certainly interesting, aren't they?"

"Sam, you're an old man. I have a hunch you never had any fun in your life."

"Do you call this fun?"

"Sure it is. What's wrong with letting go?"

He whispered in her ear. "It's great with the right party . . . alone."

"That's not what I'm talking about."

He was about to reply when Mrs. Tipton joined them. "The buffet is ready in the dining room."

The table was spread with lobster and shrimp, casseroles of hot dishes, relishes, and salads. Carrying out the motif of the party, the two wooden caskets formed a centerpiece with tiny figures of Volstead and Carrie Nation, whose hatchet hung from her neck like a crucifix. By the time Samson and Posey had filled plates, a line began to circle the table. They carried their dishes to a corner of the living room and were joined by another couple, a junior partner in Martin's firm and his wife. They talked about real estate and its future and for a few moments it began to seem to Samson that the evening would be worthwhile. But then he saw Joan Pennington approach balancing a drink and still wielding a cigarette. She was drunk and approached swaying so that he leaped up and grabbed her, leading her to a seat.

"I'm all right," she said, peevishly. "I'm perfectly fine."

She crossed her legs theatrically almost toppling from the chair, straightened up and with head held high eyed him for a moment as if deciding whether it was worthwhile to address him. Then, condescendingly and with as much poise as her condition would allow she spoke. "I want you to understand I'm not anxious to sell my house."

"I understand."

Her chin dropped and her eyes closed. Raising her head with an effort and forcing her eyes to open she went on. "Just because I haven't worked in a while I don't want people to think. . . ."

Her voice trailed off and he reached for her arm as she started to fall off the chair. Spying Martin with a group, he caught his eye and motioned to him.

"I think Miss Pennington needs help," he said, as Martin approached.

Lifting her gently from the chair, Martin led her to the hall where Samson saw him talking to a young man whom Samson had seen with her earlier. A moment later her escort half-carried her to the door. Tipton returned, apologized to the others and took Samson aside.

"I didn't mean to wish her on you. She's an old client I inherited. She's got nothing left but a pile of pawn tickets and a couple of rings. I do want to talk to you about the house. In the morning."

Posey was huddled with three or four people and he wandered out to the terrace. A row of poplars ringed the edge of the grounds, still, unmoving, like silent sentinels. Far in the distance was a crisscross of city lights and to his right a disheveled line of eucalyptus swished in the breeze. On the other side a high wall covered with thick vines of Algerian ivy completed the enclosure. The oval pool in the center, green tiled and lighted, shimmered. It was chilly; there was no one about and he lit a cigarette. Someone had closed the door leading to the house and the sounds from the room were reduced to a hum.

He thought about Tipton and the Pennington woman and the bunch inside and then about the men in his office and all the moths here and everywhere flapping their wings at the few candles that stood like obelisks. Roy and Art and even Ralph Thompson were the little guys but Martin was different; big ideas, big house, big business. Tipton was way ahead but not as far as Samson Duke was going to get. He flipped his cigarette and heard the door open. Posey stood in the entrance.

"You look like the lord of the manor."

"It's just like I was feeling."

"Well, your lady's tired. How about taking me home."

Calling Martin Tipton the following morning to thank him for the evening, Samson was asked to lunch. They arranged to meet in Tipton's office.

"You should have stayed, Sam," he said. "The thing lasted until three."

"I would have. Posey was tired and insisted on going home."

"She looked beautiful last night."

"You have a charming wife, Martin."

"Thanks. Now, I want to talk to you about Joan Pennington's house. She built it in the early twenties when her money was coming in barrels. Spared nothing, imported tiles from Spain, brought over a mosaicist from Madrid to work a full year on one wall, a fireplace and an Olympic-sized pool. Each piece of furniture was custom-made. There are some fine rugs and a tapestry centuries old."

"What'll I do with a house in Palm Springs?"

"Suppose you can buy it right?"

"What's right?"

"Cheap enough for you to want to see it."

"Fill me in on price, terms, everything, before I make the trip."

Martin rang his secretary. "Bring the Pennington file. The one on the Palm Springs house.

"Joan hasn't worked in three years," he explained as they waited. "She's washed up. I'm trying to salvage something. She's already lost an apartment house and a home in the hills. Palm Springs is all she's got." The secretary came in with a legal-sized folder. Samson waited as Tipton went through it, jotting figures on a pad. "This is it," he said, leaning back and reading from notes. "There's a first and a second, both delinquent, and a chattel mortgage on the furnishings also past due."

"What are the amounts?"

"State Bank has a twenty thousand first. All due."

"Will they renew?"

"For a substantial buyer."

"How about the second?"

"One of our clients has it. It's for eight thousand. He'll discount it for fifty per cent."

"And the chattel?"

"That's a little rough, Sam. Pennington dealt with a hockshop operation. There's about six thousand due and they want every cent." He tossed the notes on the desk and sighed. "She put nearly a hundred thousand into the house and pool. God knows what went into the furnishings. Frankly, I don't know what it's worth, but there must be an equity."

"I'll look, Martin, but it's to be strictly business. I'm not sentimental about old actresses."

"Fair enough. I promised her I'd get you to look. I'll submit any offer you're willing to make."

After arrangements were made for Samson to pick up the key at a local real-estate office, he and Posey drove to Palm Springs the following weekend. It was the height of the desert season, and he looked forward to getting away. Also, Martin's description of the house had intrigued him. If it made sense on paper, he was prepared to make an offer. It would be ideal for entertaining, he was sure he could deduct it as a business expense, and a house in the desert might be an inducement to take more time from work.

They left after an early breakfast, negotiated the usually congested downtown area before the crowds, limped through Garvey Avenue lined with the one-story stucco store buildings that appeared cut from dirty papier-mâché, their façades scarred with chipped and painted signs, picked up a little speed through El Monte and Covina before descending to the little valley in which Pomona nestled with palm-lined streets and fine lawns fronting the New-England-style homes. Though the two-lane highway was narrow and often rutted, the drive from Pomona on was pleasant.

It was a winey, winter day, the higher peaks in the east were powdered with an early snow and when they reached Banning, Mt. San Gorgonio glistened with white crystals from its middle to its two-mile height. Descending to the floor of the desert, the hills turned purple and pink and the village of Palm Springs, green and palm dotted, sparkled in sandy waste. It was noon and the sun was straight up as they pulled in front of the real-estate office. Samson got the key and they drove to the center of town and had lunch in an outdoor restaurant near the Desert Inn. Samson had removed his coat and tie, relaxed in the sun and consulted a city map as they waited for their orders to be filled. Posey sat watching the passersby, puffing lazily on a cigarette. "I hope you buy the house. It's so lovely here, so delicious, warm, and peaceful, so cut off from everything."

"Let's hope there's an equity."

The house was on a street called Tachevah, some ten blocks east of Palm Canyon. As they pulled up before a white stucco wall that surrounded it, all they could see was a minaret jutting from a profusion of spiny cactus and other tropicals. On the wall by the entrance in curled Arabic lettering, peeled, and faded blue, were the words, *La Casa de la Estrella.*

"The house of the star," Samson translated.

Miss Pennington was one for monograms and had the building marked as well. A weather vane, whitened by bird droppings, tilted from the roof, its half-moon encircling the words La Estrella.

"I've got a feeling we're in for a lot of ghosts," Posey said as Samson struggled with the lock on the elaborately carved door. It creaked open like a prop in a horror movie. They entered a large entry hall, tiled and domed with scimitars, crescents, and minarets in colored glass. To the right, a living room sprawled, filled with velvet-covered couches, deep-downed and tasseled, scattered ottomans and heavy dark-stained furniture. Under it all was an Oriental carpet of a hundred hues. A panoply covered most of the wall opposite the fireplace, its deep yellows and blues and golden threads forming a high steeple with a suggestion of a grand mufti in its tower looking down on a courtyard, and in the background a yellow sun, half-hidden by dark blue hills completed the tapestry. They stood for a moment not speaking. Posey reached for the cord of a heavy damask drape, pulled it and brought sunlight flooding the room, its beam swarming with dust.

"I guess Miss Pennington never lived in a real world," Posey said. "My God, look at that!" She pointed to the fireplace which had been hit by the rays of light. Hanging over it was a large painting, an image of the owner in other times, garbed as a houri, looking over the room with the possessive air of a favorite in a Mohammedan paradise.

"How would you like to do this place over?" he said.

"Could we ever get rid of the ghosts?"

"Maybe we'll keep them. Brighten them up."

"Let's see the rest," she said, taking his hand.

From the living room a long hall traveled the length of one wing containing five bedrooms, each with a Spanish tiled bath, the layout not unlike a crib in an expensive whorehouse. They were completely furnished, baroque and expensive down to the bedding and silk spreads.

"This can be lived with," Posey said. "It's a little rich but goes with the architecture. But not that living room." She shook her head.

"Not as bad as you think," Samson said. "If we get rid of the tapestry and ditch Miss Pennington, throw out a few daggers and crescents it might work. The furniture is expensive and still good. All it needs are dusting and a shine."

The house was U-shaped and in the other wing they found the dining room with a long oaken table and a dozen carved high-backed chairs, a pantry, kitchen and helps' quarters. It was stocked with everything: dishes and silverware, linens and bedding, crystalware and pots, and in the pantry they found a cupboard filled with bottles of wine. There was a closetful of clothes in the master bedroom and the dresser drawers were packed.

Posey fingered a marabou-trimmed negligee. "It's like she didn't have time to pack."

"Let's go see the grounds." The patio, closed in by a row of ragged eugina boxhedge, was an overgrowth of tropicals in the center of which was a clover-leaf pool lined with a conglomerate design of Moorish symbols. It was empty except for a slimy layer of algae, bugs, and sand. They returned to the house.

"Open all the drapes," he said, "and a few windows. Let's try something." He stood on a chair, removed the painting over the fireplace and then the panoply from the other wall. Now, with the windows open and the light pouring in, the room with all its colors was almost gay in tone. The dust was thick everywhere and they noticed for the first time the fine tiles of the floor, the rich ornamentation of the fireplace and the exquisitely wrought fixtures. The ceiling beams were hand-painted, needing only scrubbing to bring out their colors.

"What do you think of it now?" Samson said.

"I guess all it has is a dirty face."

"I'm beginning to like it. I don't know what I'd change."

"It's exotic, anyway."

"Let's close up. I've seen enough."

It was almost nightfall when they returned to Los Angeles. Samson had been doing arithmetic all the way. Palm Springs was dead. They were giving houses away, but none like this, and though it needed a complete going-over, it was well located on a large lot and built like a fortress. The bank would have to rewrite the loan on his terms. He would offer the holder of the second mortgage twenty-five cents on the dollar, and take his chances with the sharks who held the chattel on the furniture. As for Miss Pennington, anything he'd offer would be charitable. Foreclosure was her only alternative.

He got Tipton on the phone and softened him.

"When did you see the house last, Martin?"

"Two, three years ago. Quite a place, isn't it?"

"It's in shambles. Take a fortune to make it livable. I don't like it, but Posey thinks it has possibilities."

She jumped from the couch and tried to grab the phone. He pushed her away. "She thinks it's a challenge. Anyway, here's what I'll do." Posey stalked angrily from the room. "The bank will have to rewrite the loan. Twenty years at four-and-a-half per cent."

"I think they'll do it," Tipton said.

"I'll give your client two thousand for his second."

"That's only twenty-five cents on the dollar, Sam!"

"If he wants more, let him take over and pay off the furniture, too."

"All right," Tipton said. "I'll talk to him. What else?"

"I'll take care of the chattel. As for Miss Pennington's equity . . . there isn't any."

"And how do you expect to get the deed? By gift?"

"If you weren't involved, I'd buy the first and wipe everybody out. In the name of charity and our relationship I'll give Miss Pennington a thousand dollars for her deed." And then he added, "Believe me, she has no equity. I'm sure every broker in Palm Springs peddled it."

"I'll make the offer. It won't be easy, but I'll do it."

"Everything stays but her personal clothing and the painting of herself."

Tipton chuckled. "I remember that one. It's pretty awful."

Posey returned to the room as he hung up. "I don't know what that house is worth," she said. "Whether you're stealing it or not. But I resent your lying and using me."

"You've got to romance a deal."

"I've a good mind to call Martin up and tell him the truth."

"What's the truth, Posey? Don't you think it has possibilities?"

"Sure I do."

"But what?"

"That's not why you're buying it."

"How do you know?"

"Because I know you, Sam."

"The fact is, I don't know what in hell the place is worth. You can buy all of Palm Springs for a nickel on the dollar. The house is interesting and challenging and I like your taste and think you'll do a job with it." She was softening now. "I may have to hang on a long time before I get my money out, let alone a profit. It's not an investment, it's for fun. And I can use a little."

"Did Martin think he could work it out?"

"I'm sure it's the only offer she's had."

"What about the man who holds the second?"

"He would have moved in a long time ago if he had the capital."

They talked about plans for the house over dinner. If he got the property, Posey was to move in and supervise everything. She would stay on until the job was finished and he would come down for weekends.

"First thing I'll do is get a crew in and clean, just clean. God knows what we'll find under the filth. Then I'll get a gardener, cut the growth, plant grass. And the pool, what about the pool?"

"It'll have to be cleaned, maybe with an acid. The mosaic underneath must be beautiful."

"And the woods of all that furniture. Can you imagine what it will look like shined and polished?"

By the time they went to bed she was so excited about the house she was obsessed with the fear he would not get it.

Martin worked fast. The following afternoon he called to tell Samson he had worked out his end of the deal. "Joan took it pretty hard, but realized she had no choice. She doesn't want to go back into the house. You're to ship her clothes and the painting to her apartment."

"How about the holder of the second?"

"He groaned and accepted."

"I'll get in touch with the bank right away."

"See a guy by the name of Bert Frank. He's been handling the deal."

When he met Mr. Frank in his office the following morning and told him the purpose of his visit, his reception to his proposal added to Miss Pennington's and the holder of the second, made Samson suspect his appraisal of the house. Mr. Frank agreed to rewrite the loan on Samson's terms, did not ask for a financial statement, and almost embraced him when he left.

The holders of the chattel mortgage on the furniture were tougher. Samson called at their office, a shack on Washington Boulevard near downtown L.A., where they handled salary and auto loans as well as on furniture. He sat down with a small bald-headed man who kept playing with a pencil as he eyed Samson with distrust. After giving him the loan number Samson waited as the man fingered a thick file and pulled out a card.

"You say you're buying the property?" he asked suspiciously.

"That's right. But I don't want the furnishings. You can move them out any time you wish. The sooner the better."

"Let's see," he said. "She owes us four thousand plus nearly two thousand in interest."

"I'm not concerned with that."

He consulted the card again. "There's some valuable stuff there. Fine furniture and a Persian rug." He looked up. "Are you sure you don't want it?"

"It's junk. I could use a piece or two, that's all."

He kept looking at Samson, tapping the pencil on the desk like a telegrapher sending a message. "If we sell the stuff for less than we got on it, Miss Pennington will get slapped with a deficiency judgment."

"That's her problem. Anyway, you're betting on a dead horse. She's a broken down actress who hasn't worked for years. All you'll ever squeeze out of her is a fifth of gin." He got up to leave. He knew she had been delinquent for nearly a year and was sure they had tried everything to collect. She had nothing and they knew it. He was almost out the door when the man called him back.

"Wait a minute." Samson turned around but stood at the door. "Come in, sit down, sit down."

"What is it?" he said, without moving.

"The furniture belongs with that house. I know. I appraised it when we made the loan. Maybe we can do business."

"But I don't like the furniture."

His smile was sickly. "Would you like it at a price?"

Samson hesitated a moment, pretended to be giving it some thought, then shook his head negatively.

"Anything is a buy at the right price, mister."

"What's the right price?" Samson asked.

"Sit down," he said, managing a smile. "Let me put a pencil to a piece of paper." Samson returned to the seat and the man started to figure. "There's fifty-nine hundred and eighty dollars due. Nineteen hundred eighty is interest." He made a magnanimous gesture with a wave of his hand. "I'll cut the interest in half."

Samson got up, did not say a word, and headed for the door.

"Wait!"

"Look, you're wasting my time. If you cut the whole figure in half I still wouldn't be interested."

"You mean three thousand!"

"That's right."

He slapped the desk with the palm of his hand like an auctioneer. "Mr. Duke, you give me thirty-five hundred dollars and you bought yourself a houseful of furniture!"

Now Samson was close to where he wanted to get. "I'll talk to my wife. She's the one who has to live with it."

He called after Samson as he left. "My offer is good until tomorrow noon."

Let him sweat a day then offer three thousand, he decided. Late the following day, he made his proposal. The man screamed into the phone and turned Samson down. "Okay," Samson said. "I want that furniture out of there in one week or I charge for storage." He hung up. Fifteen minutes later the man called and accepted the three thousand. Samson took title to the house on the day before Christmas. Posey and he camped in it during the holiday week. Then he left it in her hands and returned to Los Angeles.

There was an offer signed up on the Columbia apartment building waiting for him when he got to the office on Monday. The offer involved a trade for a loft building on Santee Street in the downtown area and although he signed the acceptance he included a couple of loopholes he could crawl through. The deal looked too good; it warranted a closer look. They offered thirty-five thousand cash for the equity in the Columbia, which gave him a small profit, plus an equity in the ten-story loft building over a first mortgage of two hundred thousand. This was valued at seventy-five thousand. However, the building was less than half occupied and its tenants were small businessmen on a month-to-month basis. Samson accepted the deal subject to his approval of the building and tenants within thirty days.

After inspecting the property it became obvious to him that the deal would only make sense if he could find a tenant for the whole thing. Remembering that Martin Tipton mentioned a close connection with a California state senator, he contacted Tipton and arranged a meeting. The best potential customer was the county, the state, or federal government, and if an agency of any of them was looking for space, there could be a chance. Armed with photographs of the building, layouts of typical floorplans, and mechanical installations, Samson met with Tipton the following day.

"I'm not looking for special favors," he said, "I've got all or part of ten floors with ten thousand square feet per floor. I'll be able to rent it cheaper than anything in town."

"Senator Ebberly considers everything a special favor."

"That's the kind of man I like to do business with."

"He's a scrawny, sanctimonious sonofabitch, Sam. Used to be a Fundamentalist minister, a soul saver with a mellifluous voice that rings with sincerity and purrs. He's got the country all sewed up. Biblebelters, right wingers, big business, and crackpots, he's got them all. And if they aren't writing checks for him at election time, they're out in the precincts, ringing doorbells for him."

"Does he still preach?"

"Now and then. Likes to keep his hand in the old fire and brimstone. But most of all, Sam, he thinks like a whore. That goes a long way in politics. And he's in with George Turner. Between those two, they run the county, and maybe even the state."

"Who is Turner?"

"He's a lawyer who doesn't practice law, owns a couple of insurance companies in which he is not active, is probably the most powerful politician in the state, and has never run for an office nor held one. He knows every hand that's reaching out and there's not a thing he wouldn't do for a payoff except one. He hands out judgeships, even federal ones occasionally, and that's where he's holy. A man's got to have the qualifications. Turner has even fought others' appointments and kept a lot of shysters off the bench.

"Interesting guy."

"He is."

"How well do you know Ebberly?"

"Met him in New York about ten years ago. A client of ours out here was in trouble. Ebberly took care of it. Over the years there were other things. He works fast and smooth and when it's done there's never a ripple."

"How well do you know Turner?"

"We're old friends. Drinking buddies. We have a love affair with the Irish poets and the prose-makers too."

"I expect a lot, Martin. From the senator, perhaps from Turner, and from you. The deal's fat and I can afford to pay. And I don't expect you to work for nothing."

"You're a client," he said, smiling.

"This is between you and me."

"Let's see what happens first. It's possible I can't do a thing."

He left Tipton the material, gave him the figures on the rent and told him that whatever was done had to be consummated within thirty days.

Tipton called him that afternoon.

"Ebberly's in Sacramento. He's coming down in two weeks for a hearing in Riverside."

"How about my going to Sacramento?"

"It won't be necessary. I'm sending him all the material. He wants me to send another set to George Turner's office. Get it to me as soon as you can."

Samson had the material delivered that afternoon, but it was a week before he heard from Tipton, who finally called to say Turner had seen the building and would discuss it with Ebberly the following week.

"Does it look solid. Or was he just being polite?"

Martin laughed. "He's never been polite in his life. He said he had an idea. Wanted to discuss it with the senator."

A thought occurred to him and he called Posey in Palm Springs. "How's the work going?"

"I had an army here today. The gardener, the poolman, two maids, and a window washer. I never saw so much sand and dust in my life."

"When will the grounds be finished, and the pool?"

"The gardener is through, planted the grass today. The pool will take a few days. The heater and filter need repairs and the cleaning is going slow."

"What about the house?"

"The drapes and spreads are out being cleaned . . . they're sending a man on the furniture tomorrow."

"Suppose I brought a party of six or eight. Think you can take care of them for a weekend?"

"When?"

"Weekend after this. About ten days."

"I guess so. Everything should be ready. Who are they?"

He told her it was all tentative, that it was to be a business conference and he'd supply details later. Now he called Martin Tipton. "You said Ebberly will be in Riverside next week."

"That's what he reported, Sam."

"The Palm Springs house will be ready. Do you think it's possible to get Ebberly and Turner down for the weekend? They can bring their wives. I'd like to have you and Mrs. Tipton as well."

"I can ask them, Sam, but I don't think this is a necessary gesture. I made it clear to them that you'd be appreciative. They understood."

"A little entertainment never hurts, especially a weekend. Besides, I'd like to get to know them. There'll be other things."

Martin paused for a warning beat. "Before I ask, you ought to know. If Turner's in a drinking mood, he could be hard to handle. He has long dry periods, then he soaks it in. And his wife, Inez, she's never completely dry, but at least she's a quiet drunk.

"George Turner's a big one," Tipton laughed. "He weighs over three hundred pounds."

"Fat doesn't frighten me," Samson said. "Bring 'em on."

"Okay, Sam, I'll ask. All they can do is refuse. I'll be free, but don't count on Sylvia; she hates the desert."

Tipton called Samson the following Monday to say that the invitation had been given. Ebberly and Turner were not yet sure they could make it, and they'd confirm by the end of the week.

"That won't leave me much notice," Samson complained.

"Best I could do, Sam."

"I'll get ready, just in case.

He phoned Posey, decided not to tell her it was only tentative, suggested she stock the house with all the essentials, including liquor, and asked her to line up some servants.

"How will you explain me to your guests? Maybe the senator's wife will object to consorting with a mistress."

"You'll be a guest like everyone else. We'll have separate rooms."

"Thanks a lot, Sam."

"Well, what do you want me to do?"

"Maybe someday, you'll get the idea."

He groaned. "This is a fine time to bring that up."

"Can you think of a better time?"

"Look, I need you for this weekend. I don't deny it. You know the house, I don't. Will you please come, just this once?"

She finally consented. "But I'm telling you this, I'm playing the role straight. If the wives are offended, it will be up to you to smooth their feathers."

There was nothing to do but accept on her terms and hope that

Mrs. Ebberly's sanctimony was as phony as her husband's. On reflection, it seemed unlikely that men like the senator and George Turner would be influenced by their wives.

On Thursday morning Martin Tipton phoned Samson to report that the Ebberly's and the Turners had accepted with alacrity.

"When will they arrive?"

"Sometime Friday."

Restless that evening and overcome with a loneliness he had not experienced for a long while, he decided to drop in on Aunt Annie. When Dante admitted him, the room was in a semidarkness, lighted only by a small lamp, and when Samson entered, Dante cautioned him with a whisper as he led him into the kitchen and closed the door. Despair had bitten into his face. He looked as though he had not shaved for days, and when he spoke, there was a tremor in his voice. "She is sleeping."

"Is she sick?"

Dante nodded.

"Has she seen a doctor?"

"Today. There was X-rays. Other tests."

"Why didn't you call me?"

She told me not to. Made me promise. 'Do not worry Sam,' she said." Tears were brimming in his eyes and he wiped them with a sleeve. "I thought I wait until I get results from doctor tomorrow."

"She told me she went to the doctor a month ago."

Dante gestured helplessly. "Who knows? I pleaded. It is only now that she went. The pain is too great."

"Where is the pain?"

He pressed his abdomen with both hands and dropped them to his sides.

"Maybe it is nothing," Samson said. "Like an appendix."

He shook his head. "It is no little thing."

"Is that what the doctor said?"

"Yes. Tomorrow he will tell me everything."

Samson opened the door and started for the bedroom. Dante

stopped him. "Let me see if she is asleep." He tiptoed to her door, opened it carefully, and after poking his head inside, beckoned. "Annie," he called softly. "Sam is here."

The room was almost dark, lighted only by a beam from the hall. He could see her head stir on the pillow and her arms rise slowly as he approached. She reached for him as he sat on the edge of the bed and drew him to her murmuring his name. Then she released him and sank to the pillow as Dante switched on the bedside lamp. It had only been a few weeks since he had seen her last and though he now suspected the worst was not prepared for what he saw. Her eyes, larger than ever in a shrunken face, stared without life and her skin dried and yellowed, covered the fine bones and wrinkled like old tissue around her once full throat. Her freckles looked green and the gay spots that once danced in her eyes were dirty brown specks. He took a hand and cupped it in his palms as she raised the other to his face.

"Sam." She attempted a smile.

He raised her hand to his lips and then placed it under the covers. He looked up at Dante and saw he was crying. He wanted to console her, tell her that he loved and needed her but all he was able to do was to stroke her forehead with a trembling hand. She turned her head toward Dante, who hastily brushed his tears and pulled a chair beside the bed. "Is there anything, Annie?"

"Supper. Has Sam had supper?"

"I just finished," he said, grateful for words to break his silence. She smiled weakly and closed her eyes and in a moment seemed off in a peaceful sleep. He rose from the bed as Dante turned out the light and followed him out of the room.

"Why didn't you tell me?" he demanded. "I would have had another doctor. A consultation."

"What was there to tell. Last week she was on picket line. Only few days ago I find pills, all kinds, for pain."

"I don't understand," Samson said. "I was here a few weeks ago. She seemed fine . . . a little tired, but. . . ." He waved a hand helplessly. "Not like this."

Dante stood in the middle of the room, slumped like an old man. "Sometimes it happens fast . . . very fast, doctor said."

"How about an operation?"

"Tomorrow he will let me know." He placed a hand on Samson's shoulder. "Either way, Sam, she will die. There is no cure for cancer. Not this kind." He looked at him for a moment, grabbed him in a tight embrace and sobbed. Samson led him to a chair and in a little while he seemed calmed. He began to speak.

"All my life I have many dreams. When I met your aunt was the best one come true. Soon it will be over." He looked past Samson toward Aunt Annie's room. "Some place I read that all life is pain. Happiness is the little times when pain leaves. Since I know Annie it has been all happiness."

As he listened to Dante he tried to grasp what her death would mean. He was independent and a grown man and there was Posey and his work kept him occupied day and night but it seemed that something else, perhaps more important was slipping away. Her existence had been taken for granted, sometimes ignored, occasionally abused, but it was always there, a bulwark on which he knew he could always lean. In spite of all his efforts to break away, leave her for a world in which she would seem to have no place, there would always be a bridge. And he needed it. Not as much as when he was a kid and crossed it every day, but for that time whenever it was when he wanted affection that was not paid for, love that could not be bought, for the skinny kid with the hooked nose as well as for the grown man. She was love and now the insurance was going to be cancelled.

Dante sighed deeply and walked to the kitchen. "Do you want supper?" he asked. "There is something to warm."

"No," Samson said. "Is there anything I can do?"

"There is nothing. A nurse comes twice a day. She gives shots for pain."

He felt guilty about leaving town the following morning but what could he do? And what difference would his being there make to Aunt Annie. "I'm leaving town tomorrow for a couple of days," he said. "I hate to go but it cannot be helped."

"I understand."
"I will call, keep in touch."

He had Delaney stop the car in Pomona so that he could call Dante. The doctor had ruled out surgery as a hopeless procedure that would only compound her suffering. There would be shots for pain and friends would help Dante watch around the clock.
"How long does he think Aunt Annie will go on?"
"It could be any time. No longer than a few days."
He fought to put Aunt Annie out of his mind for the rest of the trip and by the time they arrived in Palm Springs the problems of the weekend ahead occupied him.
The house had been transformed. The outside wall which had been streaked and stained with bird-shit was painted a gleaming white, the small courtyard in front was trimmed and manicured, and the front door, its weatherbeaten façade scraped and shined, revealed a multicolored design of flowers and plumes. Inside, all the colors had been released from the grime, the musty odor was gone, the windows sparkled, and through the glass door that led to the rear of the grounds they could see fresh young grass sprouting between palms, jacaranda, and the spindly ocotillo so native to the desert. Posey followed as they toured the house, openly expressing admiration.
"You performed a miracle," Samson said.
"Just work and your money."
"You should have seen it," he said, turning to Tipton. "You would have never believed it."
"It wasn't that bad, Martin. Everything was here as you see it. Just covered with dirt."
Martin looked at Samson and back to her. "Sam said the place was in shambles."
"It was. Posey's being modest, that's all."
"Let me show you the pool," Posey said. "No wonder that Spanish artist spent six months on it."
The filtered water was as clear as crystal and there wasn't a

ripple on the surface. The scene on the panoply which was removed from the living room wall had been duplicated on the bottom of the pool in mosaic tile with the addition of dozens of color-
fully dressed figures, camels, and horses, a turreted wall and a
gate with a drawbridge. Along the sides were a series of banners
and shields in reds and blacks against the blue background.

"It's certainly busy," Martin said.

"Somehow fits with everything else," Posey said.

"You've done a magnificent job," Samson said, putting an arm
around her. "I'd never have believed it."

"I would have," Martin said. "You underestimate her."

"Maybe I do. Anyway, when do you think the guests will arrive?"

"Anytime between now and five."

"We'd better plan the sleeping arrangements." He decided
that the senator and his wife would have the master bedroom, the
Turners the one next to it. When he suggested that Posey, Tipton, and he each take one of the three remaining rooms, she made
no comment.

Delaney was examining a bar which Samson had not noticed
before in a corner of the living room. It was black lacquered with
a brass footrail and was equipped with four stools.

"I bought it yesterday," Posey said. "Figured politicians like to
drink."

"Did you buy any liquor?"

"Plenty."

Martin went in to change and Delaney was unpacking in one
of the servants' rooms; Posey turned to Samson.

"I'd love a walk. There's a beautiful golf course a few blocks
up. It's usually deserted in the afternoon."

It was that time of the day when the poolsides were crowded
and those less inclined to sun were napping in preparation for the
long cocktail hour. A middle-aged couple walking along Indian
Avenue were the only ones about. They were dressed in resort
togs, and were going at a rapid pace. The man's face tilted toward
the sun as his short tanned legs propelled him like mahogany pis-

tons. The woman, a large pastel-colored purse banging at her side, was in a half-run to keep up.

Posey laughed. "Do you think she's chasing him?"

"Don't they all?"

"Sam, some day you're going to turn around and find nobody there."

The sun was hitting the mountain peak and would soon be gone. The rocky sides of San Jacinto were beginning to turn purple and pink and to the east, still bathed in bright light, the mountains glowed with pastels. They took off their shoes and started on the course. Posey had his hand and they headed for a clump of trees at the edge of the first green. Her tanned face and throat contrasting with a snowy blouse, and her hair combed loose and shining reminded him of a kid as she romped ahead pulling him. They reached a bench under a tree.

"Let's sit here."

For a few minutes his mind was drained of all thought of the weekend ahead. A bird left the cool limb of a pepper tree and a moment later another followed, singing gaily like a lover in pursuit and just above them a gentle wind rustled a bough and a tiny quail soared until it was a speck. Suddenly the wind rose and everything began to move like a changing tableau, the branches swaying to the rhythm of the breeze and in the distance the trees that lined the course began to stir as if awakening to a dance. Posey's eyes were half-closed and her head tilted back. As he watched he realized his resistance to marriage could weaken. The whole of their relationship was balanced precariously; Posey was pushing hard to legalize her role and one day she could turn her back on him if he refused. It wasn't only the community property laws that concerned him, though cutting a pie in half to unravel a knot was not to be desired; it was the act of surrendering, giving up the freedom a man had to have to move and maneuver. If only they could go on without changes.

She opened her eyes and looked at him. "I wish we could have been alone this weekend."

"It would have been nice." He looked at his watch. "We better get back."

When they reached the house a new La Salle was parked in the driveway.

"I should have been here to greet them."

"Don't worry. Martin is skillful."

Senator Ebberly and George Turner looked like Laurel and Hardy. Turner, perched on a seat at the bar, his haunches looking like giant sausages as they ballooned his pants, lacked only the comic mustache and derby to double for the impatient-voiced comedian. Senator Ebberly, standing at his side balancing a drink, spindly-legged in walking shorts, a pasty face acknowledging the introduction, needed only the bewildered expression of the comic to step into his role. Both Turner and Delaney, who was behind the bar, wore open-at-the-throat shirts splashed with a Hawaiian design, looked like touring Elks in a Middle East bazaar.

"Sorry I wasn't here to greet you gentlemen," Samson said.

Ebberly waved a hand. "Forget it. We were well taken care of. Delaney here saw to that," he said, waving his drink.

"Where are the ladies?" Posey asked.

"They were tired. Thought they'd take a nap," Martin said.

"Why don't you join us, Duke," Turner said, waving him over. "Your man here," he went on, jerking a thumb in the direction of Delaney, "mixes a better grog than they do at The Outrigger. Here," he said, handing his glass to Jack. "Fix another. More rum this time."

"I'll have a scotch and soda, Jack." Samson said.

"I'll leave you gentlemen," Posey said, backing out of the room. "The pool looks inviting."

Samson took a seat beside George Turner. He was gulping his fresh drink and Samson began to wonder whether he would be sober enough during the weekend to talk business. Turner's drinking seemed to have no effect on his conversation, which

touched on the desert which he seemed to know well, the Stav-
isky scandal, and the execution of van der Lubbe for the Reichstag fire, on all of which he appeared to be well informed and ar-
ticulate.

"Those Communists will stop at nothing," Ebberly put in.
"Why, the Reichstag is like our house and senate."

"They worked fast," Turner said. "The Nazis, I mean. They
nabbed this Dutch Communist, tried him, and lopped his head off.
No horsing around."

"You can say what you want," Ebberly said, "about Hitler and
Mussolini, but they get things done."

Martin shook his head. "I like our way better. The decision
isn't up to one man."

"You're right," Ebberly said. "But we haven't got those Communist bastards to deal with. They understand one thing—violence."

Rather than get involved in further political discussion Samson
excused himself, said he was going in for a quick dip and left.
Posey was sunning on a rubber raft in the center of the pool
when he joined her. Swimming a few lengths, he got out and
sprawled on a lounge. A few minutes later she sat beside him.

"Looks like a jolly weekend," she said, removing her cap. "I
wonder what their wives are like?"

"It's business and only one weekend. There'll be others. For
pleasure."

"Your Mr. Turner is revolting. Must weigh three hundred and
fifty pounds. And the senator . . . he's the pastiest man I ever
saw."

"You don't have to handle them. Just be pleasant."

She got up. "I'll go in and change."

He wanted to get Martin alone before he got into any further
conversations with the two men. As he was about to enter the
house Martin came through the door.

"I want to talk to you," he said, as Martin sat down beside him.

"First let me say something," Martin said. "I don't know Delaney's capacity. But if he tries to keep up with Turner he'll go out like a light. I've seen George drink a day and a night and stay on his feet."

"I'll talk to him. In the meantime I want to know a few things. Do I discuss the deal with Ebberly or is it Turner?"

"All Ebberly does is make out the checks," Martin said. "George signs them."

"Then Turner is the guy I go after."

"He's the guy, but you'll have to talk to him when he's sober. He came in drunk. Ebberly told me he has been drinking since yesterday. It can go on for a week." Tipton shrugged. "I told you, Sam. George is either very wet or bone dry."

"Ebberly must have some authority. I'll just have to talk to him."

"I talked to him already," Tipton said. "He said the rent's right and the State is considering it. When I tried to press him he clammed up and walked to the bar. Look, Sam, I had my doubts about the idea of this weekend. You wanted it." Tipton shrugged. "Might as well get drunk and join the fun."

Samson walked through the side entrance to his bedroom, waited for Posey and they went into the living room together. Everyone was talking at once as they entered. They were greeted loudly by Delaney, and Samson could see he was drunk. Martin met them at the entrance and escorted them into the room. Neither the senator or Turner had moved, Ebberly still standing at the bar, leaning on it now as he gripped his drink, and Turner perched on the stool, his fat covering the sides. They were introduced to Mrs. Turner who was buried in a corner of the high-backed couch, her drink clutched in both hands and held close like a child holding a toy she had been asked to give up. She acknowledged the introduction with a mutter and went on drinking. Mrs. Ebberly greeted them loudly from across the room and came toward them with both hands extended.

"So nice meeting you both," she said. "Martin has told us so much about you."

"It's nice to meet you, Mrs. Ebberly," Posey said.

"Look," Mrs. Ebberly said, "Let's use first names. After all, we'll practically be living together." She laughed as if tickled with the idea. "Call me Doris."

"This is Posey and my name is Sam."

"Posey . . . what a lovely name." She pointed to the senator. "That's Howard." He shook his head. "And George." Turner didn't move. She ignored Delaney and led them to the couch. "This is Inez."

This time, Mrs. Turner rose and extended her hand. "Hello, Posey." She smiled at Samson and weaved her way to the bar. She was tiny. Slightly over five feet tall, flat-assed and high-breasted and barely a hundred pounds. He looked over at Turner as Inez approached the bar, her little behind undulating, and wondered how they did it.

"What'll you have?" Delaney shouted to Inez. Samson caught his eye and Delaney grinned.

"Fix me another. The same," she said drunkenly, holding her glass as she stood beside Turner, whose hand reached down and cupped her ass. She squirmed away to the other side.

"The stuff sure goes down easy," the senator said as Inez elbowed to his side.

Samson sipped his drink slowly, keeping an eye on Delaney as Ebberly's voice, resonant, campaign style, commented on the U.S. recognition of the Soviet Union. "I don't understand it, giving those murderers respectability."

Martin Tipton joined in. "President Roosevelt doesn't like the Russians. He's taking a long-range view, that's all."

Turner set his drink down and slammed the bar with his fist. "Long range? He's the most nearsighted bastard we ever had in Washington. We should be backing the Germans, not the Russians. Build them up, let them arm." He took a long pull from his drink, dropped his chin, and stared at the floor.

"The Germans can take care of the Russians," Ebberly said. "If we let them."

"We have to play it smart," Turner said, coming to life. "Play it smart," he repeated, his slack mouth barely releasing the words.

"That's right," the senator agreed, setting his glass on the bar as he ran his tongue over his lips as if swabbing them for a speech. "I'm not a diplomat, but I do know this: the Germans are our kind of people. They know how to fight. If the lines are drawn and push comes to shove, I want them on our side." He looked about, as if expecting applause.

Samson switched the conversation. "It's getting cooler," he said. "Why don't we move out to the patio. Jack can set the bar up outside."

Everyone rose except Turner. Samson took Posey aside. "What are the arrangements for dinner?"

"I'm having it catered. Give me an hour's notice."

"You might as well do it now. If they drink too much more, they won't be able to eat."

Delaney had set up the bar on a table and Doris Ebberly was instructing him how to mix her drink. "Just a pinch of rum and the rest can be Coke."

Inez Turner sat cradling a drink, her eyes on Delaney. He seemed unable to avoid her stare and she smiled as she continued to look at him over the rim of her glass.

George Turner came through the patio door. Samson had not seen him except in a sitting position and now, on his feet and walking, he looked even more grotesque. With legs apart to give his thighs room to move, and with arms akimbo supported by his fat, he waddled toward them, mopping his face with a huge handkerchief, his open shirt revealing huge hairy breasts that jiggled with each step. "It's cooler," he said, sweat running down all the folds of his face and gathering in the flesh of his neck. "Here, help me," he said gruffly, standing before a sturdy lounge. Martin and Samson helped him ease into it. They left him and joined the others, and as he sat, puffing and wheezing, mopping his face, he looked like an aged pachyderm deserted by the herd.

Inez was now standing next to Delaney, whispering to him. His face was a silly grin. Samson grabbed Martin's arm and towed him to the other side of the swimming pool. "Mrs. Turner is getting out of hand. I'm worried. And the damn weekend is just beginning. Turner's blind now, but when he sobers up. . . . Do me a favor," he whispered a plea, "and get Mrs. Turner away from Delaney. I have to talk to him."

"I guess you'd better. They're ready to play footsie." Tipton left Samson, approached Inez Turner, took her by the arm, and forcibly strolled with her toward the Ebberlys. Samson beckoned to Delaney, who followed him into the house unsteadily, his eyes glazed. Falling into a chair, he looked up at Samson like a child about to be scolded.

"You're drunk."

Delaney nodded.

"And you're waving your cock at Mrs. Turner."

"It isn't me. It's her. I never seen the likes of it. I can't get away from her."

Samson grabbed his shoulders and shook him. "You're not trying! I've been watching you." He let go and pushed him against the sofa. His head rolled to one side. He slapped his face and straightened it up. "Listen to me carefully. Not another drink. Not one. And stay away from Mrs. Turner. Do you hear!"

Delaney kept shaking his head. "Maybe I'd better leave," he mumbled. "She won't let me alone."

He pulled him to his feet. "I need you here. Throw some cold water on your face, get out there and stay away from the booze." He staggered toward the kitchen and Samson returned to the patio. The sun had slipped beyond the horizon and pale blue shadows shrouded the desert. The senator and his wife were seated with Turner and Martin, and Posey and Inez were at the bar. Posey got up and took him aside.

"At this rate there'll be an orgy before the night's over. And I don't like it," she added angrily.

"I don't know what you're talking aout."

"Yes you do. And so does Martin. Mrs. Turner's drunk but she's still able to talk. And she gave me an earful." She gripped his arm. "Either get rid of Delaney or put that nymphomaniac to bed. Or I'm leaving!" She ran into the house. He rushed after her and caught her in the hall. Just then the doorbell rang. It was the caterers. "I'll do anything," he pleaded. "Just stay."

"I'll see things through dinner, that's all. If you think and if Martin thinks I enjoy this you're both crazy." She told the caterers to set things up in the patio, gave instructions to the maid and turned back to Samson. "Now listen to me. I slaved for weeks to get this house in shape. And you have me open it to a fat drunk, his tramp wife and a sleazy politician." Samson started to interrupt and she raised her voice. "I don't know what you and Martin are getting out of these people. But I know what I'm getting. Room and board!"

"Look," he pleaded, "I'll make it up to you."

"You can't make this up to me."

"Nothing has really happened. Just a little flirtation. Maybe Turner is a little drunk. Delaney too. Is it so bad?"

She was quieter now. "You don't understand, Sam. I don't mind drunks and I don't mind flirting or fornication and you know it. It's just that I like to pick my companions." She turned from him, followed the waiter to the patio and announced dinner.

It was a buffet: cold meats and salads, jumbo shrimp and pâté, chafing dishes containing meat balls, little frankfurters and tamales, and a selection of cheeses. Everyone gathered around the table and filled his plate. Martin piled one and set it before Turner.

Delaney came from the house, looked a little steadier, and avoided Samson's glances. He got behind the bar to make a drink that Turner called for. The Ebberlys were at a table by themselves, huddled over their food talking in low tones. Posey was directing the maid, and Samson joined Martin, seated next to Turner, who was washing down the food with huge drafts of beer. It was dark now and Samson turned on the patio and pool lights. Posey took her plate and joined the Ebberlys and Delaney was eating at the bar. Near the pool light a cluster of moths danced and a breeze came up, rustling the palm fronds. Soon, the meal was over and the tables cleared and the caterer brought out a half-dozen brandies, an urn of coffee, and left. Delaney set chairs and a small table around Turner's lounge and kept the coffee cups and liquor glasses filled.

The conversation drifted from California brandy, defended by the senator, to the latest William Powell—Myrna Loy movie to the Dow-Jones averages and then to Hitler and the Nazis. This last seemed to rouse Turner, who started to squirm in his seat, reached out his hands and was assisted to his feet by Delaney and Martin. He undid his belt, pulled and straightened his twisted shirt, then reached down inside his pants and fingered around as if everything had been displaced. Now, apparently more comfortable, he turned and faced the group, all of his lethargy gone as he loudly defended the German leader.

"He's pulling the country together. He'll have every German working in a year."

"That's more than we can say," Ebberly put in.

"I happen to think Roosevelt is doing a good job," Posey said. "Certainly better than Hoover."

"You have a right to your opinion," Turner said coldly. He returned to the lounge with a groan.

"Hoover really didn't have a chance, Mrs. Warren," Ebberly said.

Posey looked at Samson and smiled as if enjoying his discomfort. "Really, senator, you know better than that. He had three years after the crash. He did nothing."

"And what do you think is being done now?" Turner said. "We have more unemployed than ever."

Samson looked at Martin, he smiled reassuringly and stood up. "No politics," he said, holding up his hands. Rule of the house. Am I right, Sam?"

"Firm rule."

Turner called to Delaney. "How about another one of those drinks."

Delaney and Inez drifted back to the bar, he started to mix the drink and she giggled drunkenly. Turner was watching them, his face without expression. Now, Delaney and Inez were huddled so close their heads were almost touching. Samson was about to do something to break it up when Posey called out.

"Jack, how about a drink? Scotch and soda." Delaney straightened up and reached for a glass. "Make it a double," she said. Samson looked at her. Posey rarely touched a drink after dinner. Delaney brought it to her, almost staggering, and avoiding Samson's look, returned to the bar.

The caterer came out to the patio and Posey got up. "We have to settle," she said.

Samson followed them into the house and wrote the caterer a check and after he left, Posey turned to Samson. "What happens now? Does Inez go with Jack? And what about Doris and the senator? Is she going to be given to Turner?" She was blazing with anger. "And what about me? Am I for Martin!"

"Let me have that drink," he said, reaching for the glass. Posey held on with both hands. "All right," he said. "Get drunk. That's what this party needs. Another drunk."

She closed her eyes and downed the entire drink. "Leave me alone." She started for the patio.

He caught her hand. "You'll get sick."

"Don't you worry," she slurred, waving a finger under his nose. "How about some music? Where's the radio? Let's dance." She picked up the portable from the table and carried it to the patio almost falling over as she stooped to plug it into a socket. Tuning in dance music, she pulled Samson to the center of the patio and fell into his arms. He circled with her a few times and led her to a chair. She jumped up the moment he left her and walked to the bar and poured another drink. Rather than make a scene he ignored her, hoping the last shot would knock her on her ass.

Martin Tipton approached her. "How about a dance?"

Her eyes narrowed cunningly. She raised her arms and dropped them into place as his arm circled her waist and he led her to the center of the patio.

The senator got up, stretched and looked at his wife. "We've had a long day," he said. "Think we'll turn in."

"I am tired," Mrs. Ebberly said.

By this time, Martin had led Posey from the patio into the house. He returned in a few minutes. "Mrs. Warren's off to bed," he explained. "It's been a long day for her." Nobody seemed to care. Delaney and Inez were still at the bar; Samson could see he was too drunk to reason with, and Turner was dozing with his face buried deep in its fat.

"Let's get Turner to bed," he whispered to Martin, tactfully shaking the huge man. Turner's face emerged from the folds, the fat now hanging far below his chin. He pushed Martin aside and shouted. "Fix me another, you Irish bastard!"

Delaney straightened up, hesitated a moment, then slowly began to mix the drink. Samson grabbed it from him and handed it to Turner. The music was still playing. Delaney came from behind the bar, lifted Inez from the stool with an arm about her waist, looked at Samson defiantly, swept her to the center and started to dance. They pressed close, her leg thrust between his thighs, and remained in one spot rocking in a dip. Turner stood up holding his drink and watched them without expression. Samson called to Delaney softly hoping some area of his brain would respond. He kept dipping without a change in rhythm. Turner waddled to the bar and poured himself a drink, mixing it carelessly, splashing it over the counter. Samson realized now that his only hope was for one of them to pass out before Inez got what she was after.

Now, Turner mixed two drinks, took them back to the lounge, fell into it and began swaying clumsily to the music. Samson mixed himself a stiff one, walked to the far corner of the grounds, turned his back to the others and looked out into the night. An almost half-moon hung in the sky like a fat sickle, silvering the desert floor, a siren wailed in the distance and a coyote howled, then a gust of wind whipped across the grounds bending the long-stemmed plants and it was gone and everything was still. Suddenly he realized he had forgotten about Aunt Annie. Avoiding the patio, he went around the side of the house into the kitchen and dialed on the extension phone. Annie was sleeping longer, conscious less, Dante told him, and when Samson said he would make every effort to get there the following night or the latest on Sunday he was told it would make no difference because he was sure she would not last through the night.

He had to see her before she went. She must know he'd been there at the end. He could be in Los Angeles in three hours, spend some time with her and be back by morning.

He headed for the patio wishing for a miracle, that it would be deserted, that nobody had been there at all and it was a bad dream. Martin was standing in the shadows, Delaney and Inez were locked in each other's arms barely moving to the music and Turner sat gripping a bottle of rum from which he drank as he watched, his head sinking further into his neck. Finally, the bottle slipped from his fingers, rolled along the tiles to the center of the floor and stopped as it reached Delaney's feet. Samson motioned to Martin and they dragged Turner through the patio to the house where they rolled him on the bed, pulled off his shoes, and covered him with a blanket. Out in the hall, he grabbed Martin's arm. "I don't know how we're doing it, but this party is breaking up tomorrow morning."

"I wouldn't worry too much. I think George is too drunk to know what's going on."

"But what about the Ebberlys, they're not blind."

"They wouldn't dare open their mouths."

"What a mistake. What a mistake!" Samson repeated. "I can blow the deal, I gotta fire Delaney and Posey's ready to leave me."

"I'll talk to her in the morning."

"Don't bother. I will."

Martin shrugged and looked at his watch. "I guess I'll turn in."

"What about them . . . out there?" Samson said, pointing to the patio.

"Leave them alone, Sam. Go to bed. What else can you do?" Martin left and a moment later, Samson heard steps behind him. Delaney was on tiptoe, reeling and coming through the door. Samson rushed to him, took Delaney by the arm. Delaney pushed him with such force that Samson almost fell backward, then he snapped the switch dousing the patio lights and staggered outside. Sam saw him pick up Inez and carry her toward the far end of the swimming pool. He watched as they began to undress, the pool lights silhouetting them. Inez stripped first and slid into the water as Delaney struggled with his shoes, then joined her. Now Samson could see nothing except an occasional bobbing of a head. Rushing out of the house, he went around the back of the lot and found a spot behind the wall from where he could see everything that went on in the pool, his real concern with one or both of them drowning. He shivered and watched, determined not to move from the spot until they were safely out of the water.

It looked like the first part of the game was to be good clean sport. Inez, who proved to be an excellent swimmer, cut the water gracefully with a fine stroke, keeping Delaney, who was in pursuit, far back as he thrashed clumsily and then rolled over on his back. She would swim under him, pinch his ass or grab his balls. Delaney would bellow as he rolled over and go after her again. A little more thrashing and he was on his back—floating seemed to be his specialty—and she would begin all over again. The last time she stayed under longer and instead of crying out Delaney closed his eyes and to his disgust Samson saw his prick getting hard until it stuck straight up. Her mission accomplished, Inez came to the surface. Now she swam to his side, tried to get in his arms, he started to sink as he reached out for her and ended up in a dead man's float, with the white cheeks of his big ass sticking up and the only thing visible on the surface of the water. Inez was down and under again and though he could not see what she was doing evidently it was giving the slob pleasure, because he did not move. For a brief moment he hoped he'd drown even if it cost him the deal.

Inez came to the surface, swam to the shallow end of the pool and stood up. Her breasts were tiny and except for large brown nipples could have been a boy's. By now, Delaney was at her side and they locked in an embrace. He wanted to leave, knew what was coming, but the possibility of a drowning kept him at his post. After all, they were drunk, dead drunk, and though Inez swam well, Delaney had to struggle to stay afloat and the big ox could go under and he was sure she would not have the strength to save him.

Delaney was into her now and her legs were wrapped around him linked at the ankles near his neck. He grabbed her ass with both hands, pushed with his legs against the side of the pool and they floated to the center. They went under and stayed down so long Samson was about to climb the wall and jump in when she came up at the shallow end and his head bobbed to the surface seconds later. He looked about, spied her and started in her direction. She scrambled out of the pool, grabbed her dress and ran for a patch of grass near the large jacaranda and flung herself to the ground. Delaney climbed out and as he went after her Samson was shocked to see he still had a hard-on. Disgusted, he leaned against the wall, lit a cigarette and looked out on the desert. If only he could be sure they would not return to the pool he could leave, and hope that in the morning everybody awoke in their own bed.

Samson looked at his watch, it was midnight, later than he thought. And he was exhausted, more than he had realized. So much had happened in the few hours it did not seem possible he had left Los Angeles that morning. He flicked his cigarette and peered over the wall. At first he could not see a thing, and, just when he thought his watch was over he heard a noise that sounded like a mewl, and tracing it, saw the two of them rolled under the jacaranda. Delaney was stretched on his back and Inez was at his feet with her head down working up to his thigh and higher and then her mouth had his cock and the sounds became louder and he stopped looking and then heard Delaney moan.

Soon there were no sounds. It was cold, he had enough, they could do as they pleased now, freeze to death, he didn't care. Making his way to the front of the house he entered the hall. As he was about to make his way across the living room he saw De-laney and Inez walking across the patio toward the house. Ducking into a dark corner he watched as they came inside and headed in the direction of Delaney's room.

At three o'clock in the morning he pulled up in front of Aunt Annie's apartment, making the drive from Palm Springs in an hour less than usual. By now his fatigue was so overpowering only his thoughts seemed alive. Dante, the Rizzos, a woman he had never seen before, and a man he knew only as Gerson, were in the living room as he entered. They looked at him like a group of conspirators come upon by a stranger. Only Mrs. Rizzo greeted him as the others prepared to leave as if his appearance was the signal to clear the room. They shuffled out, he heard Mrs. Rizzo give instructions about food saying that her husband would return later in the morning.

"How is she?" Samson asked as they left.

Dante shook his head sadly and headed for the bedroom beckoning Samson to follow. A night light cast a pale beam, barely lighting Aunt Annie's face and a small fan set up on a table beside the bed hummed like a moth, whisking a strand of hair on her forehead. Samson stood at the foot of the bed as Dante leaned over Aunt Annie placing an ear near her mouth. Then he kissed her cheek gently and straightened up. He left the room, Samson followed, leaving the door open.

"Sometimes she call out," Dante explained.

For a long while they sat and neither said a word. They took turns at watching Aunt Annie. Dante got up, went into the kitchen, returned with a pot of coffee, went to the window and stared out. Samson remembered how Aunt Annie looked the night Harry Baldwin came to celebrate, gay and pretty in the new dress and the flowered hat Baldwin had removed with a flourish from the big box. It was frightening, he thought, how happiness could be close to the edge of tragedy and knew nothing of its existence. He speculated for the dozenth time on what would have happened if Baldwin never got that call, if his letter to the bishop had never been sent. Since she met Dante, he had consoled himself as he matched the Church against Dante and his anarchy. Now he knew he had rationalized to smother his remorse. It was nearly four o'clock when they heard her cry out. Rushing into the bedroom they saw an eyelid move and suddenly she twisted her head and her mouth shot open and trembled as she sucked for air. Her chest began to convulse, and as she fought, the last of her life became a noise in her throat. He prayed for her to go, wanted it done! Dante took her hand in his, buried his head in the covers and cried aloud. She fought free from his hold and her arms began to flail helplessly. Samson wanted to rush from the room, out of the apartment into the street. But he could not move, just watched, choked on tears as he cried her name. Then, all her movements stopped and Dante raised his head slowly from the covers. Her mouth was wide open and her eyes half-shut. Still on his knees beside the bed, Dante kissed her on the forehead and with shaking hands closed her lids. He rose, stumbled out of the room as Samson went to her side and looked at her face for a long time. He began to sob uncontrollably and ran out of the room. Dante was placing the call to the undertaker.

"What about the funeral?" Samson asked as he hung up.

"Annie had wishes about it."

"What were they?"

Dante went to the buffet and removed an envelope from the drawer. "They are in here. She told me when she gave it." He handed Samson the envelope and slumped into a chair covering his face with his hands, sobbing without control. Samson fingered the envelope, the face was blank and it was sealed. He placed it on the buffet and poured a cup of coffee. Sure that the document contained a will as well as instructions for burial, all the fears that had been pushed aside for months now filled his head. Would Dante be given the document containing her last wishes if he was not to get everything? They were like man and wife! No, he decided, she would not do it . . . he was like her own son, she loved him, told him so a thousand times! She had only given it to Dante because he was there and she knew she was ill. He was relieved, angered at himself for his doubts. Anyway, he would know soon, would open it the moment her body was removed.

It was almost dawn when the body was wrapped in canvas and carried out. Fighting to keep awake, aching with grief, and fearful of what was awaiting him in Palm Springs, he doused his face with cold water, downed a hot cup of coffee, and took the envelope from the buffet. As he opened it he felt Dante's eyes on him.

It was a holographic will, a few lines in her hand, dated a few weeks before. He started to read it aloud. After a statement about a sound mind and a free will it went on to say that all her assets were in cash deposited with Pacific Savings and Loan Association and what remained after the expenses of her terminal illness and burial were to be entrusted to Dante Marcotulli to be used as he saw fit to continue the work to which she was devoted. All her personal things were to be given to Mrs. Rizzo.

> To my nephew, Samson Duke, who has no need of my money, I give a pair of diamond earrings that were my sister's, and the memory of my love that I shared with him always. I do not believe in God but in the teachings of Jesus Christ. I want no priest and no religious ceremony and only friends to be at my funeral. I wish it to be held at a hall or even a room and I want cremation.

That was all. On less than a page, signed and dated. It took all his control to finish the reading and as he folded it and placed it on the table he was so choked with rage that for a moment he was unable to speak. Sensing it, Dante moved nervously in his seat.

"You knew what was in this," Samson said.

He shook his head. "I heard it first time tonight."

"But you knew what was in it."

"No. She told me give it first to you when she was gone."

He was pounding the table. "But you discussed it!"

Dante stood up and faced him. "We never talked about money."

"Sure. You never talked about money. You got it without talking! Let me tell you something," he said, shaking a warning finger. "That money belongs to me!"

Dante grabbed his hand and held it in a viselike grip. "You listen," he said evenly, and for the first time since Samson had known him he saw hatred in his face. "I do not want this argument . . . not now. But I cannot keep in longer what I have to say." Samson twisted from his grip and fell back into a seat. Dante stood over him. "Not once have we agreed. It was only because of Annie we were friends. All my life I fight your kind. After this I wish never to see you again."

Samson jumped from the seat, toppling the chair. "You'll see me," he said, starting from the room. "You'll see my lawyer!"

"Wait!" Dante commanded. He rushed from the room and returned in a few moments waving a little book which he flung on the table. "This is Annie's bank book. Look at it."

Samson grabbed it and turned to the last entry. It was for a little over two thousand dollars. Flipping back the pages and tabulating quickly he saw withdrawals for the past year totaling nearly forty thousand dollars.

He whirled on Dante. "This money . . . who got it? Where did it go!"

Dante started toward him, his face twisted with fury; Samson backed away and clenched his fists. Suddenly, Dante closed his eyes, his shoulders sagged and his arms fell limp to his sides. He opened his eyes and looked at Samson, all the anger gone from his face.

"Please sit down," he said, softly. "And listen." Samson remained standing.

"Perhaps it is difficult for you to understand," Dante began. "You must try."

"I understand plenty."

He went on as if Samson had not said a word. "What I am telling you is the truth. We lived, Annie and me, on what I made. I never touched a penny."

"Then what happened to it?"

"She gave it for what she believed. To everybody. For everything."

"You mean for your goddamn revolution!" he shouted, picking up the bank book and waving it in his face. "Forty thousand dol-

lars for lousy niggers and a bunch of bums who spend a lifetime
sitting on their ass doing nothing but talking—just talking—about
changing the world because they haven't got the guts to live in it
the way it is!"

"Don't talk like that, Sam."

"I'll talk anyway I want! That money was mine . . . every
cent of it! And if my aunt never met you it would still be here!
Maybe she'd be here, too!"

He backed away as Dante moved toward him. "You better
go," he said, shaking his head. "You better go."

As he looked at him, standing straight with clenched fists, a
stranger who he really never knew, a lousy savior to whom she
reached out when she cut loose from the Church, he began to
sense the futility. There was nothing more to fight for. Aunt
Annie had done what he always feared and whether it was the
sure hand of the Church, or a grubby paw, it made no difference
. . . the money was gone.

Dante stood poised now, with legs spread and fists half-raised.
"You better go," he repeated.

"All right," he said. "I'll go."

Dante lowered his arms and his whole frame slumped.

"There is something of Aunt Annie's I want," Samson said.

"Take what you wish."

"Arrange the funeral. Like she wanted. I'll call tomorrow."

He left him standing and went into her room. He found what
he wanted on top of the dresser. It was a framed picture of him
and Aunt Annie, the only one they ever took together, standing
in front of the Jersey farmhouse not long after his mother died.
He slipped it in his pocket and rummaged through the dresser
drawers. Underneath a pile of her undergarments was the other
thing, an old candy box, a special gift she once received in which
she kept the few valuables she possessed. He found his mother's
earrings among the beads and cheap pins. Taking a last look at
the room, he left.

Driving back to Palm Springs he could barely keep his eyes
open, talked aloud to stay awake and as he got closer to the desert,
his thoughts leaped from what he left behind to what lay ahead

and he felt crushed between disaster and catastrophe. At first he lulled himself, thought of Turner lying beside a fucked-out Inez who miraculously crawled in before he awakened. And a sober Posey reconciled and understanding, determined to make the weekend a success. Delaney, now contrite would be cautious for the rest of his stay bringing a third act curtain and a happy end. But as he left Banning and began the descent to the desert the picture flipped and the house was swarming with reporters and police and Delaney lay dead or maybe it was Turner or both as Inez, drunk, confessed her infidelity as flash bulbs popped and reporters rushed to the phone.

There was not a soul about as he let himself in. Tiptoeing down the long hall he put his ear to Turner's door, heard loud snoring, tested for sounds from Delaney's room, heard nothing, reached his room and collapsed on the bed and in moments was asleep.

He awoke at noon, laid on his back a few moments running over the events of the day before, slipped out of bed, showered and began to dress, preparing himself for whatever he had to face. Posey would be gone, the Turners too, or maybe fat George was still sleeping it off and Delaney and Inez could have skipped for a week of fancy fucking or could be at it now in Delaney's room or . . . what the hell! So he'd lose the damn deal. As he was about to leave the room he saw an envelope at the foot of his door. Inside was a note scrawled in Delaney's writing.

Dear Sam:
I know I'm fired. I'm taking an early bus back to town. I got Mrs. Turner back in her husband's room. He didn't wake up. I'm sorry.

Jack

So, the bastard sobered up and had enough brains to deliver the bitch where she belonged! Now, if Inez keeps her mouth shut he might squeak through.

The senator, Doris and Posey were having coffee on the patio. It was a brilliant day, the sky cloudless, the sun was well over the mountains in the east and the valley was already warm. The senator was dressed in shorts, Doris had on a flared white skirt, her hair was drawn back and she wore a white visor. She looked like a middle-aged Helen Wills. Posey greeted him cheerfully with no sign of a hangover or a hint of belligerence.

"How could you sleep so late?"

"It's such a fine day," Mrs. Ebberly said, looking up at the sky.

"It's going to be hot," the senator added.

"Where are the others?" Samson asked.

"Martin took the car to town," Posey said. "I guess the others are sleeping."

He told them about Delaney. "We got a call early this morning," he said. "One of our managers walked out. Jack had to go in to take over." Posey looked at him and he knew she didn't believe a word he said. She rose and entered the house and the Ebberlys went for a walk. Samson called Dante, who told him the funeral was to be on Monday in a hall downtown. No reference was made to their earlier argument. He took the address and returned to the patio. A few minutes later Martin returned and joined him.

"What happened to Delaney and Inez?" Martin asked.

"I got lucky. Inez ended up in her own bed and Delaney left for L.A." Then he told Martin about the note.

"Turner still sleeping?" Martin asked.

"They both are. I hope they stay tucked in until they leave."

"They'll get thirsty and wake up."

"How in hell does he function?"

"He'll stay dry for months."

Posey appeared dressed for a swim. Martin eyed her figure as she walked by. After she swam a few lengths of the pool she came over for a towel.

"Here, let me," Martin said. He grabbed the towel and began drying her, legs first, all the way up, then her back. When she turned around, he patted and dried her shoulders.

"You'd be nice to have around after a bath," she said.

"He'd love that," Samson said.

Martin held up his hand defensively. "I was just being helpful."

"Sam has other charms," Posey said. "Little things are not important to him."

He overlooked her remark, aware that he could not beat Martin at the game with churlishness. "When do you think they'll all leave tomorrow?" he asked Martin.

"When Turner gets over his morning hangover."

"How in hell do we entertain them until then?"

"The senator plays gin rummy."

"I don't."

"Then I'll take his money. You can tend bar."

"What do I do?" Posey asked.

"Entertain Doris."

"Thanks. We've had a few discussions. She's emptied her head."

"Why don't you fill it with what you know," Martin said.

"I think I will. She needs a little political education."

When the Ebberlys returned, Samson took the senator's arm and guided him to a table beyond the pool. "It's been so hectic," he began, "didn't have a chance to ask what you thought about the Santee building."

"Good building."

He decided not to be evasive, put it to him straight. "Do you think the State could use all or part of it?"

"A survey is being conducted. We're checking comparables." The senator was looking over Samson's shoulder in the direction of Tipton. "Martin," he called out. "How about some gin rummy?"

"Fine," Tipton replied. The senator left Samson without another word and joined Martin at a table on the patio. To hell with it, Samson thought, Ebberly was about as communicative as a fakir in a trance, probably never saw the damn building and would not make a decision until George Turner got off his fat ass and started pushing the right buttons. He was certain now that the weekend was a mistake, a grave error in fact; if the deal was on the right track it had all the grease it needed from Tipton's promise of a payoff. And maybe it's never a good idea for payors to meet payees.

It wasn't until three o'clock before the Turners appeared. Inez came first, greeted everyone, and after a swim returned to the room to reappear a half-hour later, followed by Turner, who, in spite of his rumpled appearance looked more alive than at any time the day before.

"How about breakfast?" Samson asked.

"Something to open the eye first," Turner said.

"Anything you want."

"Where's Mr. Delaney?" Inez asked.

"Had to go back to town."

She looked surprised, started to say something, seemed to change her mind and went to the bar as Samson led Turner to a table under an umbrella. Returning with two rum drinks, Inez gave one to Turner, downed hers, and poured a cup of coffee. Turner finished his second drink and ordered breakfast from the maid, his body twitching as with delight, his eyes gleaming as he called for melon first, then eggs—three—with a thick slice of ham and a stack of cakes, plenty of syrup and butter, toast, and a pot of coffee. When the food came, Turner attacked the meal, piled in mouthfuls and never took his eyes off the food except to cast an occasional side glance like a dog over a plate who fears it might be snatched from him. Finished, he settled back, his hands hanging loosely, his eyes closed like an addict who just had a fix. Inez wandered from the table, Turner opened his eyes and turned to Samson.

"Where you from, Duke?" he asked, looking at him as if seeing him for the first time.

"New York City."

"That's my home town. Came out here in 1908. Arrived on my twenty-first birthday."

Samson calculated swiftly, shocked that Turner was only forty-four. Then he hunted for traces of his real age, tried to picture the face without fat, the eyes without dullness, and the nose before it was a blob. He could find no evidence Turner had ever been young. Turner went on, told how Los Angeles was then. "So damn lovely! All sprawling and the sweet smell of orange blossoms, orange groves to the town's edge. Pastel tinted bungalows huddled on palm-lined streets, night-blooming jasmine. Jesus, you wanted to sing! And clean streets. No smoke. You could wear a white shirt for a week. Snow-crested mountains even in spring and after Manhattan, dirty and old, it was like a fresh, sweet-smelling baby."

His lips, buried deep, twisted in a sad smile. Then he went on about youth with its sap and hope and how, soon one runs dry and the other is lost. The sun passed over the umbrella's edge and blazed on them. Turner started to sweat. Now the animation that had been in his voice and had somehow etched itself into the grayish hide of his face disappeared and his eyes seemed to retreat deep into their sockets. A fat tongue ran the course of his lips.

"I'm dry. How about a drink? Rum and Coke and a dash of lemon."

By eight that night the sun had whipped the Ebberlys and the booze had put the Turners out. The senator and Doris excused themselves and went off to their room. George Turner staggered and passed out in his room an hour before Inez was sleeping it off on a chaise in the patio. Samson carried her to the bedroom, deposited her next to Turner and as he left saw her nestle against his bulk like a tiny cub.

"Well, I hope you two made your deal," Posey said when Samson joined her and Martin in the patio. "I'm off to bed, and I'll want to get away right after breakfast."

"You can leave early," Martin said after she'd left. "I'll wait for Turner and Ebberly. Just show me how to close the house."

Posey was at him the minute they pulled away the following morning. "I'm all through playing hostess, Sam."

"I had no idea it would turn out this way."

"You miss my point. I'm not going to be your hostess for anyone. No more girlfriend without portfolio, to be used whenever a need arises." He started to protest but she ignored him. "That goes for your other needs, Mr. Duke."

"What's gotten into you?"

She swung around and faced him. "A little sense. I've had a few weeks in the desert to think things over. It's been fun being with you. I don't deny it. But that's no longer enough." Her tone was cold, matter-of-fact; it was not an emotional outburst that would disappear. It looked like the moment for the big promise. And being vague would not work now. She was plugged in, always seemed to know what he was thinking, and many times, when he would tell her something, putting into it all the sincerity he could, her look, a half-smile told him she had seen the lie. It was a two-way line and he was reading her now and she was putting out a feeler. He began to speak carefully.

"I can understand your feelings. You have a right to know where you stand."

"Do you? Have I?"

"Of course. And I don't blame you." She lit a cigarette and slid to the edge of the seat. "I know how important marriage is for a woman," he went on. "But it's important for a man too." He could feel her eyes on him. "My feelings for you are deeper than for any woman I've ever known. Every day the ties get stronger. If you want to wait," he shrugged, "speculate . . . it's up to you." He wasn't looking at her, had his eyes on the road, and then heard her laugh, low first, then he turned and her head was thrown back and she was laughing aloud.

"What's so damn funny!"

"You!" She pointed at him and laughed again. "You should have seen your face when you made that speech. It had a halo around it. But I didn't believe a word. Like the top of your head was off and I could see every lie twisted around that brain before it came out on that sugar-coated tongue."

"I meant every word," he said solemnly.

"Come on, don't be so serious. It's only a game and you know it. You enjoy me. We're good in bed. But when you marry it's going to be part of a deal."

"You're wrong."

"I wish I was. Anyway," she sighed, "all this talk is academic. You're not going to marry me and I'm not sure I'd accept if you asked. So let's leave it."

"Leave it how?"

"The way it's been. Except I'm putting myself on record. I'm not your girl."

She had read him correctly. Underlying his thoughts was the conviction he would let her go if marriage was the alternative. When that time came it would be difficult, she was twisted around him and getting loose would be painful. There would be memories; their thighs touching after loving, close even then, the sound of their breathing diminishing, languid, reposed, dangling between wakefulness and a dream. There were the long evenings before bed, the private dinners, the anticipating, the touching each other with their eyes, invisible tentacles of feather and fire, the game before their night. He looked at her face, it had softened a bit as if she knew his thoughts.

"Don't you think you're being hasty?" he said.

"I'm a good waiter, Sam. But you're too patient."

He drove on in silence. When they reached her apartment she refused to let him take her bags and left him at the curb.

The hall on Ninth Street had been carved out of a couple of stores in a dirty brick building with apartments upstairs. It was rented jointly by a group of left-wing organizations and its walls were plastered with their poster art; hollow-eyed workers dragging chains being pursued by fat plutocrats with striped pants and silk hats, heroic workers walking hand in hand with a sun over the horizon and pictures of Sacco and Vanzetti and facsimiles of their letters and the Scottsboro Boys and on the rear wall of a platform a dozen pictures of their heroes hung beneath a draped American flag. Aunt Annie's closed casket, its ends resting on two chairs, was in the center of the stage.

About forty persons occupying folding chairs that had been set up on both sides of the room and separated by a narrow aisle, were in the hall when he arrived. Many of the faces were familiar and though they watched when he walked down the aisle, only a few nodded greeting. His grief was almost forgotten as a wave of resentment and hostility overcame him while he made his way to the front row and found a seat among the close friends. Seated next to Mrs. Rizzo, who greeted him with a warm squeeze of the hand, he looked about to receive cold stares from many others and a barely perceptible nod from Dante. He looked up at the coffin and tried to shut out everything else and fill his thoughts with Aunt Annie's face, young and alive. Deep inside, however, was rage as he realized that even in death he was forced to feel like a stranger. It seemed if she could rise and speak a final word, he would be ignored, and the last of her presence would spend itself on a cry to rally to some goal, some struggle.

By noon, the hall was almost filled and the ceremony began. Dante rose, walked to the front, and turned to the audience. His tall frame, looking more gaunt than ever, was bent from more grief than he could sustain. "All my life, I have met many fine people," he began. "Workers in the cause we fight for. Some have fought for a lifetime, some twenty, thirty years. Annie came to us late in her life. But in the short time she was with us, she did what most of us could not do in our whole lives. Her heart was the grandest I ever knew. I loved her very much." He began to sob, stopped speaking, removed a handkerchief from an inside pocket, and blew his nose. There was not another sound in the hall as they waited. "I will miss her because she was my life," he went on, "and all of you and what you believe will suffer much because Annie is no longer here. She fought, she worked, until it was no longer possible for her to go on." He lifted his head as if to continue, then, no longer able to contain a flow of tears, he covered his face with the handkerchief and walked from the platform.

Kelly followed Dante to the front of the room and then Arne and they talked of her inspiration and her courage and of the empty rank that would never be filled. Mrs. Rizzo's turn came but after moments of sobbing she broke down and had to be led to her seat without having said a word. Samson wanted to rush to the front and say something—anything—say that he too was part of her life—the most important part, but found himself unable to move. It was as if he stood in the wings waiting to go on, only to realize he had the lines of another play.

A curtain parted at the side of the stage and a man walked solemnly to a lectern beside the coffin. He recognized him at once as the man, Gerson, who he had seen last on the day of Aunt Annie's death. Gripping the sides of the wooden stand, he looked over the audience for a few moments like an actor waiting for the proper moment. The poorly lighted stage cast shadows over his pugnacious face, highlighted by a broken nose and a rugged jaw, cameoing the beaten features. As he started to speak Samson realized he was the dialectician—the Grand Mufti. He read a poem, talked about the revolution, referred to Aunt Annie as a soldier, and, weaving a tract with the eulogy, ended with a declaration that Aunt Annie's memory would be served best if all continued the work to which she was devoted.

There were loud sobs as Gerson finished, the undertaker emerged from a parted curtain, announced the service was over, wiped a sweaty hand with a wrinkled handkerchief, ran a finger round his starched collar, the crowd rose, scraped their chairs, and began to shuffle out. As he turned and followed and realized that Aunt Annie would soon be ashes, a loneliness overcame him with a force he had never known and tears came without control.

He reached the sidewalk in front of the hall to find groups gathered, speaking in muffled tones. He started to make his way through when he felt a hand on his shoulder. Turning, he saw Dante's face, drawn with grief, his large eyes shot with tears.

"There will be friends at the flat," he began. "All afternoon. Maybe you will want to come."

He hesitated a moment. There was nothing there for him, not even a memory he wanted to preserve. "I don't think I'll be there."

Dante started to say something and then shook his head. "All right, Sam, then it's goodbye now." He extended his hand.

"Goodbye," he said, turned and walked off and could feel Dante's eyes upon him. He did not look back and never saw him again.

He wanted to be alone. It was as if with enough concentration he could communicate with her, let her know his feelings; her mark upon him was indelible, the estrangement of the past year no measure of what he felt, the love she gave him was all he ever had, that without it his bitterness could not have been borne.

He drove to Griffith Park, found a spot hidden by trees, propped himself against a wild oak, and closed his eyes. His fingers dug into the cool earth and he heard the cry of a jay and the sounds of cicadas and felt an ant crawl on his hand. He remembered picking wild strawberries with his Aunt Annie near a pond about a mile from the farm. She had caught up her apron and they were filling it like a sack and after an hour in the hot summer sun he tore off his clothes and jumped in bare-ass as she sat on the bank shouting encouragement as he struggled to swim. That night she'd let him stay up late, waiting for the jam to cool, and she'd let him paraffin the jar tops.

Sliding to the grass he pressed his cheek to the cool sod and her image appeared. She was smiling happily, her hair an auburn crown, her dancing eyes were upon him and he saw her fine throat and the curve of her full breast and the tapered fingers of a graceful hand and then he saw a flame, dancing at first like a dervish, then it spread and her hair disappeared and her head became a torch, her eyes no longer could see and she soon was a live coal and he fought to find her features as they crumbled in the inferno! "Why cremation," he cried out, "why did she wish it!" He rolled over, buried his face in the grass and pounded the earth with his fists. Then the image disappeared and he turned on his back, looked up at sky patches shining through the trees. But it returned again and again all that afternoon, then began to fade like the dying licks of a flame. Struggling to his feet he left the park and drove home. All that night he tossed and struggled with his grief, dozing off just before dawn, finally awakening with the memory of his aunt beginning to fade.

CHAPTER TWELVE

Samson called Martin daily for ten days after returning from the Palm Springs weekend only to be told that no decision had been reached by Ebberly or Turner regarding the lease to the State of the Santee building. In the meantime, the seller of the Santee building was pressuring Duke to approve the tenants and the lease thereby eliminating the contingency in the deal, threatening to cancel the escrow on the expiration of the thirty-day period. There were three days left to the deadline and Samson rushed to Tipton's office.

"I've got to have an answer. What'll it take to move Turner and Ebberly off the dime?"

"I don't know. George tells me it looks favorable. But certain tape must be cut."

"Did you discuss the payoff with him?"

"Never do. The bill comes with the favor."

"What do you think it'll be?"

Martin shrugged. "Maybe five thousand each. In cash."

Samson leaned forward. "Do me a favor. Meet with Turner,

Ebberly, or maybe both. Tell them there's ten grand apiece in it for each. But I must have a letter of commitment within forty-eight hours." At the door he turned. "If you make the deal there'll be five thousand in it for you."

The following day Martin Tipton called. "I made the offer as you proposed. I'm glad you weren't in our fat friend's office when I told him how generous you were going to be."

"He turned it down!"

"No. The letter you were after was on his desk waiting to be delivered."

"You've got it?"

"Right here."

"Then what's wrong?"

"You jumped the gun. Our friend was ready to deliver the thing for half your offer." Tipton was chuckling as he hung up.

Samson was in Tipton's office within the hour, read the letter which was in a contractual form, called the escrow with instructions to proceed with the closing of the deal and then reached Delaney. Contrite and subdued after his return from Palm Springs, the manager had slobbered his gratitude at not being fired. He was instructed to inventory the furnishings on the apartment house being traded for the Santee building, prepare a rent statement and notices to vacate for the tenants in the downtown building. Now Samson turned to Martin Tipton.

"When you found out they were willing to do it for five thousand apiece you could have suggested they split the difference."

"That's exactly what I did suggest. But then George made an astute observation. You were very shrewd, he said, and knew the value of the State as a tenant in your building, better than he."

Samson managed a smile. "It was worth it. Also, it pays to have someone in your debt. I'll have the money here next week." He was at the door when Martin stopped him.

"I have a favor."

"Anything."

For a moment Tipton hesitated as if he changed his mind.

Then he began. "I don't want to play games behind your back.
I've been seeing Posey."

Samson made every effort to hide his anger. Since Palm
Springs he had only seen her two or three times and then only for
dinner. On other nights when he called she was not at home.

Martin continued. "It's dirty dealing. I know. But I'm in love
with her. It's more than a fair fight, Sam. I'm married and you're
not. And I'm not ready to divorce my wife."

He wondered where Martin made his headway. Could it have
been in Palm Springs? Is that why Posey pounced on him the
moment they left that day? He lit a cigarette nervously.

"It isn't up to me. Posey isn't one to be handed over."

"I know that. But she doesn't want to be pulled apart either.
Look, we're friends, and I don't want anything to interfere. If
you tell me to lay off I will. On the other hand, if you're willing
to let me try and leave it up to her, well. . . ."

Why not, he thought. Why break up a contact when he can
keep it and Posey too? And if there was going to be competition,
what's better than a married man? He might be reluctant, but he
was free, unattached, not tied to a marriage of over thirty years.
And compared to him, Martin was a father, not a lover. Sure,
why not.

"Don't think I'm giving her up," he said. "It's just that she has
a right to choose."

"I knew you'd feel that way. One thing," he said, as he walked
Samson to the door an arm about his shoulder. "Everything
counts. Do your damndest. I'm in this for keeps." Wasting no
time, he called Posey, told her he had two tickets to a play at the
El Capitan, and suggested a supper afterward. She accepted,
sounded more pleasant than she had for weeks, and he began to
think that Martin's moving in might prove the deciding factor in
his own relations with her. First, there was the age difference, and
charm, wit and urbanity notwithstanding, you couldn't get it up
at middle-fifty like at middle-twenty. And there were no encores.
Posey was physical, liked her ass and wasn't likely to trade it for

fascinating conversation in dark corners of out-of-the-way restaurants. And he was a fish that might be hooked while Tipton wasn't eligible to get into the tank.

Mrs. Bennett came in as he was going through the morning mail. "There's something you wanted me to remind you of," she said, consulting her book. "A balloon payment on a second,trust deed. It's due in ten days."

He checked the calendar and realized it was almost six months since they closed the deal on the seven buildings. "Is Roy Phillips in his office?"

"Yes."

"Send him in."

Roy came in shaking his head. "I know. I know," he said. "The payment is due next week. Don't think I haven't been trying. I've been everywhere and haven't been able to raise a cent."

"What am I supposed to do? Lay it all out?"

"You could, you know. For thirty days. I'll have it then."

"I'm not going to lay it out. First of all, I'm short. If you don't come up with your end I'll have to borrow."

"You mean you'd wash me out? Like that?" He snapped his fingers.

"Like that."

"But the sale of one building will get us off the hook."

"Then sell one."

"You know it can't be done in time."

"I'm sorry."

"If you'll endorse my note at the bank, Ralph will lend it to me."

"He won't," Samson lied. "I'm into the bank now for more than they wanted to lend."

Roy was leaning over the desk, hovering over him, his veins were fiery, his breath foul with last night's binge, his eyes watery. "Jesus, give me a break. I'll get it!" He leaned over farther, his breath was all over Samson now. "Everybody's broke. But I talked to a few people, friends. I've offered them half my profits."

"Then there's nothing to worry about," Samson said, rising to get away from him. "You'll probably have it."

Roy followed him as he walked to the door. "But I might need a few days. A few extra days, Sam!"

He was sick of him, his whining, the stink of him. "When we made the deal I was very clear. And I haven't changed my mind."

Phillips looked at him for a moment then rushed out. Samson called Ralph Thompson.

"Roy Phillips might want me to endorse a note for a loan. I don't want to. Told him I'm loaned up." Thompson promised to handle it.

"Roy Phillips came to see me last week," Posey said when he picked her up that evening. "He wanted to borrow some money. That is, he wanted me to put up money on a deal. Said he's in it with you."

"Just forget it. It's too risky."

She shook her head. "God knows, he's always got a hangover. But I never saw him like the other day. He was shaking all over."

"The booze is killing him." He changed the subject. "Is it too early to ask you what you're doing after supper tonight?"

"I'm going to bed."

"Alone?"

"Perhaps."

She came home with him that night and Tipton slipped into last place. He was certain her abstinence during the past few weeks had been total. In the morning she brought up Roy Phillips again, pressing him for details. He told her about the deal, emphasizing the risk by saying that the five thousand he needed the following week was only the beginning of his obligation, that if the buildings did not carry themselves he would have to come up with his share of the deficit.

"I don't want you to gamble your last dollar," he added.

"Looks like a good gamble. You're in it."

"My position is different and you know it. Anyway, I'm sick

and tired of Roy's whimpering. He knew what the deal was when we went in and I warned him there would be no extension."

"You can't blame him for trying. He told me there's a potential profit of a hundred thousand dollars in the deal."

"That's an alcoholic dream. It's going to be a long haul. Might take a few years to sell all the buildings and if I'm lucky there'll be a fraction of that."

"Don't you think you ought to give him a little more time? After all, he has enough problems. And he is your friend."

"I have nothing to do with his problems. He had those long before I met him. And he's not my friend. He squeezed me on every deal until he thought he had me dry. With him it's strictly business. And that's the way it's going to be with me."

"He's been going all over town, Sam. Seeing other brokers, people you know, and telling them the story. I don't imagine he's doing you any good."

"Look, the name of the game is money and they all know it."

She shook her head and shrugged. Nothing more was said.

When he reached the office that morning, Roy was waiting for him.

"I found a way to raise the money," he said.

"How?"

"Yesterday I took Harry Finkelstein for a ride and showed him all the buildings. He said he'd be happy to make a third. He'd even go to twenty thousand if we wanted. Let's take it, Sam. You've got to borrow the money anyway. He'll make it straight interest for two years. By that time I'll have the buildings sold and everyone will be paid off."

"Beside an arm and a leg what else does Mr. Finkelstein want?"

"So, he's expensive. What difference does it make? The deal can stand it." He was in front of Samson's desk, gripping the edge. Saliva had oozed from the corners of his mouth and just under an eye the cheek ticked.

"Sit down," Samson said. "And for Christ's sake pull yourself together. You act like if you lose this deal there'll never be another."

"I've been counting on it." He sat down. "Maybe there never will be another," he said.

"I'm not going to borrow the money from Finkelstein. I'll go out of business before I pay his kind of usury."

"I tell you what," Roy said. "Charge everything out of my end, bonus, interest, everything. It won't cost you a cent."

"Thanks. The buildings are in my name. I'll have to sign the note. What happens if nothing is sold when it's due? Who'll have to come up with the money then? And before I ask for an extension from that kike I'd shoot myself." The look on Roy's face turned to despair. "The deal stands as is," Samson went on. "You've got until next Thursday and that's that." He walked out of the room and left Roy slumped in the chair.

Art Jennings was entering the building through the front door followed by Paula carrying the baby. "You've never seen her, have you?" Art said, as Samson came over and tweaked the infant clumsily. Paula shifted the position of the baby so that it faced him squarely. She acknowledged his greeting with a bare nod. He made all the exclamations of admiration and found himself looking for some testimony in the baby's face to the part he played. Her eyes were dark, almost black, Paula's eyes, and the flawless baby skin was creamed ivory and the lower lip pouted, curling over a tiny pompon chin. He looked for a sign of his old nose but the infant's was a button. She could be a little bit of him but nowhere was a trace of Jennings. He stepped closer, reached out, and poked her belly gently, uttered a silly sound, found himself making faces and got her to smile. Paula shifted so the baby's back was to him. By this time Mrs. Bennett appeared and was joined by a couple of men from the office. He stood on the edge of the circle as they expressed their admiration, looked in Paula's direction, saw that she had been watching him. There was a look of triumph in her face and he got the feeling she was paid in full.

The baby was beautiful and all he could do was touch it. They all moved into Art's office and he returned to his. Roy had left and he closed the door. He turned to the work on his desk.

There was more in his personal account than he thought and with funds in the building accounts he could make the payment with comfort. He felt sorry for Roy; on the other hand there was no doubt in his mind that if they were switched Roy would gobble the opportunity.

Roy did not show up at the office for the next few days. Thursday rolled around and Samson sent a registered letter to Roy's house notifying him he had exercised his rights under the terms of their agreement and that he was no longer a participant in the deal. Then he had Mrs. Bennett make setups on the buildings and mail them to the brokers.

In the meantime, Roy had vanished. His wife called, told him Roy had not been home for days, was drunk when she saw him last. Now she feared something had happened. Roy had disappeared in the past but he always called after a day or two. "He was worried about some deal, Mr. Duke. He wouldn't tell me the details except that it was a big one, important. He kept repeating, 'I'm going down the drain, I'm going down the drain.' "

On Sunday, Posey and he drove down the coast and had lunch in Laguna. It was the first time he had seen her since the night of the theater. The little tensions were not present that day. Maybe Martin was coming out second best. Whatever the reason, he found her amiable, pleasant. Skirting any subject on which they might clash, he courted her with compliments and by the time they arrived at his apartment at the end of the day they were tuned in.

There was an urgent message from Delaney pinned to his door.

"They found Roy Phillips," Delaney said when Samson reached him on the phone. "He's dead."

Posey was watching as he tried to keep any sign of shock from his face. "What happened?" he asked.

"It looks like he killed himself. He left a note. They found him in a room on San Pedro Street. The landlady smelled the stink. Must have been dead a long time."

There was no use pretending any longer. Posey was looking at him as if she had heard every word.

"Who told you all this?"

"Ruth Bennett called. Roy's wife has been trying to reach you all day."

He hung up and Posey didn't take her eyes off him. "It's about Roy Phillips," she said. "He's dead, isn't he?"

"The fool killed himself."

"You're angry at him, aren't you? He ruined your day, destroyed the cozy evening you planned." He made a move toward her. "He told me how he pleaded and you wouldn't give an inch!" She was backing away from him. "He told me there was a fortune in the deal and that you were stealing his share! I didn't believe him . . . he was a drunk, I said to myself . . . raving." She grabbed her coat, started for the door and turned. "Now I know it was true. Every word of it!"

He leaped across the room, grabbed her arm and spun her onto the couch. She tried to get up and he pushed her back. "Maybe in his booze-filled brain it was true—but goddamnit that isn't reality! Reality is when he was all grown up and didn't top five feet! When his kid grew up and looked down on him when he was twelve! And when he realized that the kid was blond and had blue eyes and looked like a six-foot captain his wife shacked up with in San Diego!"

Her face filled with horror. She kept shaking her head. "You're worse than I thought. Worse!"

"He told me the whole story. One night when he was drunk in my apartment. He had to knock himself off. It was on his schedule. Do you think a sane man would kill himself over one deal?"

"You knew all this," she said, "and you still pressured him."

"I wouldn't call that pressure."

"You wouldn't." She got up and ran out of the apartment.

There was no doubt now that underlying all her feelings toward him was resentment, bitterness, maybe hate; that maybe she never forgot the building she lost and all it took was this . . . a trigger. Well, it was out now, there could be no more pretense and if they ever got together again she would have to take the first step and it would be on his terms. The phone rang, he reached for it and stopped. He did not want to talk to anyone, surely not to Roy's wife. Not tonight. He poured a stiff drink and the phone still rang and he started to leave the apartment and it was still ringing when he went out the door.

Roy's death was the topic when he reached the office the following morning. Art Jennings draped an arm about his shoulder, almost consolingly, as if the death had a meaning for him the others did not share. He shook his arm off angrily, went into his office and buzzed Mrs. Bennett.

"What did Mrs. Phillips say when she called you?"

"She was hysterical. All she kept saying was, 'I've got to reach Mr. Duke,' over and over. I asked if there was anything I could do and she kept saying she had to see you."

"Hold my calls." He dialed Roy's number.

A man answered and he asked for Mrs. Phillips. "This is Mr. Duke," he began.

"Mr. Duke!" She began to sob and he waited. "I've got to see you. There was a note." Her voice was more controlled now. "Can I come to your office?"

That was the last thing he wanted. "I'll come to your place. In an hour." Every damn thing Roy did was messy. Whether it was living or dying. What could be more unpleasant than trying to console the widow of a broke drunk. But there was nothing he could do and he sure in hell didn't want her in the office.

The apartment was in a four-flat on New Hampshire. He was admitted by elderly woman who kept fingering a crumpled handkerchief with which she dabbed her eyes. A tall boy with blond hair darted from the room down a long hall that led off the dining room. Mrs. Phillips was sitting on the edge of the couch staring at her hands, which were limp, palms up, in her lap. He had seen her once before on the night of the office opening and remembered thinking then how young she looked, pretty, petite, almost like a kid on her first high heels.

"I'll be going now, dear," the old lady said. "Call if you need me."

He took the chair near Mrs. Phillips and looked at her. She appeared shriveled as she sat with lowered head, reached in her pocket and pulled out a crumpled piece of paper and handed it to him. It was scrawled in pencil. He smoothed it out.

Dearest:

Right now the devils are gone and the rats and snakes. It's quiet, but not for long. They'll be back and I can't stand it anymore. Go see Sam Duke, he owes me a lot of money. Enough for expenses for you and the boy. I've always loved you. Forgive me.

The signature was barely legible. He folded the note and handed it back to her.

"The coroner called about the arrangements. I haven't any money."

"I'll take care of everything. Roy did have some money coming. When I sold some buildings. Two thousand dollars. You won't have to wait. I'll take care of the funeral and send you a check for the difference."

"Roy never told me about his business. He kept everything to himself." Her voice trailed off. He got up and she followed him to the door. She put a hand on his arm. "I hated to call you but I had nobody else. And the note. . . ."

"It's perfectly all right. He had it coming."

He returned to the office, called the coroner, was told the body would be turned over the following day, and made arrangements for the funeral. Sending Delaney down to select the casket, he told him to get the cheapest one, had him pick up the clothes from Roy's apartment and deliver them to the undertaker. The funeral was held at noon on Wednesday at the Hollywood Cemetery. He mingled with the crowd of about fifty persons, offered a few words of consolation to the widow after the service and as he left saw Posey entering a car with one of the men in the office.

Rather than see Mrs. Phillips again he mailed her a check for sixteen hundred dollars itemizing the four hundred dollar funeral expense. It was finished now, his contribution to Roy's wife was charity, two thousand dollars more than he had coming and he was damn sure if Roy held the checkbook and he had died in that room a spray of flowers would have been sent to potter's field and a note with a hundred bucks to his weeping widow. All the do-gooders he ever met were broke, ready to slice another's melon, and themselves shelling out nothing but bleeding hearts, tears, and advice. Even Posey. Did she forget that when they dealt she squeezed out the last possible buck for her deed? And where would he be if he didn't play for keeps? Maybe still working for Bob Kinder, ringing doorbells, carting around Mrs. Ginsburgs, or worse, still collecting tenement rents in New York waiting for his boss to die so he could get a promotion. If Aunt Annie would have lived longer she would have been broke, living in a slum on what Dante brought home from a cigarmaker's bench, laughed at as a sucker by all the do-good bastards that trimmed her of everything she had. Oh no, once they find the soft spots they stick it in and you're drained. And you get a pat on the back and told you're a nice guy. Maybe Posey wants to be liked and a few of the others, but it's a luxury he could live without. As for love, even that can be bought, or a damn good facsimile and it can last a lot longer than a heart throb on an empty stomach or under a leaky roof.

A few days after the funeral a messenger delivered the owner-ship books Posey had been working with and a statement of the money owed her. He mailed her a check the same day. Though he knew he would miss her he was certain that the pain would grow less and one day her image would become as faint as a healed scratch.

CHAPTER THIRTEEN

It was only when Posey and he parted that he realized how much time he'd spent with her. Now he filled the hours with work he'd neglected. Each evening he returned to the office after dinner, checked Delaney's reports and Mrs. Bennett's books. He was going to make sure Delaney would never be tempted, and bookkeepers have been known to bilk the boss. On weekends he checked the ads and ran down the deals. The brochures he mailed to brokers proved so successful he enlarged the list and by the end of the summer sold all but two of the packages he'd bought through Roy Phillips. He acquired a few more buildings through the men in the office who were all scrambling now to submit deals to him. He expanded the office staff, getting an assistant for Ruth Bennett to keep her on top of the important details, and had Delaney organize his own maintenance department.

The problem was obtaining merchandise. With the uncertainty of the economy, bogged down with unemployment, snarled by bureaucratic tape and an aborting NRA, aggravated by Hitler's grabs, the murder of Dollfuss, and the assassinations in

Russia, the jockeying and shifting of the European powers, he realized there was enough powder laying around to blow an empire to hell let alone the little realm of his own. It was time to draw down, not go for too many passes unless it was with someone else's money. The insurance companies were coming to him now, and the banks, and he discovered that a deal could be made with no down payment, that every hand was out, and that a buck here, a case of booze there, a weekend in Palm Springs with or without girls, a golf bag, a set of clubs, even a couple of tickets to a show was all one needed. It was easy, almost too easy and he began to wonder if there was a trap others saw that he did not. No, they were trapped, not he, dragged down with wives and kids and petty pleasures, that a piece of ass and the time it took was more important than a good listing, a sale, that scrambling for a buck was relatively easy but that the big money took plotting, concentration, and the biggest chunk of one's time.

Determined to put no more of his own cash in any deal, he turned to Harry Finkelstein when a building came along that required a down-payment. Not long after the cocktail party celebrating the opening of his office he met with Harry Finkelstein. They fenced like two old pros and Samson decided that Finkelstein could only be had on reasonable terms if he was baited and teased. He asked for a small second mortgage loan from the older man, paid him his exorbitant asking fees, and, a few weeks later paid off the loan. Exultant at receiving a bonus for so short a loan, Finkelstein began calling or stopping by Samson's office.

Samson borrowed again and then a third time, paying both loans off long before maturity. Then, one day he told Finkelstein he had another source of money at much lower rates and could no longer do business with him.

"How much lower?" Finkelstein asked.

"Ten per cent per annum, five points for one year and no payoff penalty."

"I don't believe it, Sam."

"It's true, Harry."

Finkelstein left that day, wished Samson luck with his new

connection, and didn't show up for three weeks. When he finally came, on the pretext of wishing to use the phone, he grudgingly agreed to meet the terms Samson had outlined, provided Duke include a payoff penalty of two points.

"All right, Harry. It's a deal. Only because you give me good service." Now Finkelstein would come to the office every day like a peddler making his rounds, squat, bald, squinty, rubbing his hands. Samson gave him his bonuses in cash, borrowed every cent he needed to buy a building and gave him a second mortgage as security. An arrangement was made that the building was the sole security, there was to be no personal liability. In the beginning Finkelstein balked and whined, walked out, came back, wheedled a fatter bonus and left with a sly smile. Where else could Finkelstein get the action he gave him and at two per cent a month on his money and half of that in cash? Within a year he was Samson's partner in a dozen deals and did not realize he was taking all the risks for a thin slice of the profits. By now Samson had a ticket on every horse in the race and could not lose. And they were all free. If the market went up he would have the profits, if it went down Finkelstein and the insurance companies and banks would be the ones looking for tenants.

The space available to him in the office grew tight and he began to take over the desks, move out the brokers. By the end of the year he decided to convert the entire building to his own use. There were two bookkeepers beside the assistant to Ruth Bennett, a man in charge of maintenance, a flunky for Delaney, and a stenographer. A room was needed for mimeographing and files and space for expansion. Also he found out that the brokers were stealing some of the listings before they reached his desk. It was no longer necessary to keep a sales force captured. His business was like a clearing house and he was contacted by every broker in the west part of town.

On the day he gave everyone notices to move, Art Jennings came in to see him. During the past year Art had lost a couple of big deals and seemed to have run out of steam. In spite of the fact that they had been in the same office Samson made their encounters brief. Jennings wasn't doing well and Samson knew it. Ralph Thompson reported rumors that Art was thinking of selling his membership in the club. As he stood before the desk, heavier-jowled and puffier, Samson saw all the years totaled. The impeccable tailoring no longer hid his gut. His mustache, painted and perfectly trimmed, only accentuated the mouth lines and slightly shriveled lips, the matching color of his hair seemed artificial and his eyes, smaller and more piggish were almost the color of the pale green flesh that creped in bags beneath them.

"You got a minute?" He tried to smile—a flash—it disappeared as if the effort was too much.

"Sure, sit down."

He remained standing, popped a cigarette from a pack and lit it nervously. "You know, Sam," he said, pacing and trying to put a lift into his voice, "I've been giving it a lot of thought since we got the moving notices. What difference does it make how the money comes in? It's what it all adds up to at the end of the year that counts." He stopped in front of the desk, gripped the edge, and leaned forward. "You need somebody here like me. This thing has gotten too big for one man to handle. You need sort of a . . . sort of a vice president." Now he smiled. He became enthusiastic. "Deals are coming in every day. Buildings to look at, offers, trades to run down. One man can't do it all. He'd have to have two heads and another pair of feet." He laughed, then became serious. "I like it here, Sam, and I want to stay. I've got a proposition and I think it's fair. All the way around."

Now he sat down. "You know I know the business." Samson nodded. "Well, I'll check the deals. The ones you haven't time for. Even Harry Finkelstein. You've got a lot of things with him. I can handle that Jew. I've known him for twenty years. Better than you do, Sam, believe me. You need a right-hand man and I can fill the bill. I want a little draw, say seventy-five a week. The rest will come out of the deals I handle. Say, one per cent. And the draw will be against it." He sat back now, smiling, even with his eyes. He looked happy.

Samson's first thought was to turn him down. Why get tied to a loser? But there was some truth in what Art said; he was too busy, had been passing up deals, and Art knew the business, had connections too and if he could buy all that for seventy-five a week it was worth a shot. "Naturally, I want time to think it over, Art," he said. "But it sounds right. I'll let you know in the morning."

He grabbed Samson's hand, shook it hard, slapped his back, and walked out of the room.

After he accepted Jennings' terms, he was amazed at what the lousy seventy-five a week bought. The stuff that hit his desk now was sifted; only the brokers with deals that made sense were allowed to see him. The others, the stumblebums, were handled by Art in the outer office. Samson found time he needed for the insurance companies, banks, even a round of golf once a week. Soon, Jennings was earning three times the weekly guarantee, working harder than he ever had. Each week he would grab that seventy-five dollar check, fold it and slip it into his money clip with a grin. It was his insurance, the jazzing he needed for confidence, the filler-in when deals are months apart and you're a front-runner, a little too old to come from behind. Anyway, it was working and if he ever ran down, out of steam, couldn't produce, he could never say Samson hadn't given him a chance.

The shadows of war that flashed and disappeared now emerged from the cover of diplomatic jargon, secret preparation, and within a period of a few months, Hitler's army booted themselves into the Rhineland, Mussolini's air force battered Ethiopia as his troops swarmed over the land, and the Communists grabbed the Spanish peninsula after a riotous election and a threat of military revolt. Britain seemed more interested in who the new king was going to marry. France mouthed nonentities in the halls of the League. By the end of March the Germans endorsed Hitler by all but one per cent of the vote. A few weeks later, when the Italians marched into Addis Ababa, the League of Nations' sanctions proved as effective as a whisper in a hurricane. The talking time was over: Hitler and Mussolini proved that force was what it took.

Practically everyone at the club was pulling for the Fuehrer-Duce team. The Germans looked like a good bet to stop the Russians cold, something neither France nor Britain was able to do, and Italy dished out fascism with pomp and flair, making it palatable to all except a few Reds, had people working, whipped into line, and every damn train in Italy ran on schedule. Compared to the fumbling and bungling of Roosevelt's Washington, the Germans and Italians, run by an elite, were showing the way to a world that had stumbled too long without strong leadership. At the club, Samson joined ranks with those who maintained silence, avoided the claque led by Teddy Hofstedter, who openly committed himself to an oligarchy.

That summer was convention time, and after Landon won the nomination, Samson consented to head the Ways and Means Committee, even though he was certain every dollar would be on a loser. Roosevelt had put everybody on his team: the working slob got back his beer and booze, government handouts and fireside chats, the intellectual was dragged from the ivy halls and poor pay to Washington's glitter and cushy jobs, and even businessmen, still groping through the debris, took no chances and beat the drum.

With Art Jennings assisting, Samson raised more money than he did in the 1932 election and even managed to siphon enough of the funds to boost Ebberly, who was up for re-election, by way of establishing some credit with a sure thing. Hope died fast at the club on election night, lasting only through the returns from Maine and Vermont. Even the optimists left the blackboard for the bar before ten o'clock.

Tired of the pretense and display of enthusiasm he never felt, and sick of the depression that pervaded the rooms, he attempted to slip out of the door when Art Jennings, who had been drinking all afternoon, grabbed his arm and towed him toward a corner. His face was flushed, red as meat, and his eyes, barely focused, seemed to swim in their sockets like phlegm. Samson waited as he ran a puffed tongue over his lips.

"I meant to talk to you before . . . anyway with the election and all. . . ." His brow knitted in concentration and his eyes found Samson's face. "My daughter from my first marriage is coming out from Boston. I told you about Beck."

Samson vaguely remembered the story. "When did you see her last?" he asked.

"Nearly ten years ago. She must have been sixteen then. But I've written to her. From time to time."

Samson patted his back and started to leave. "Well I guess you'll be anxious to see her."

"Wait!" he almost shouted. Samson stopped. "I need help, Sam. Beck and I, we're sort of strangers. I can't bring her to the house. He grinned foolishly. "Paula . . . that is . . . she's even younger than Beck. You know how it is back in Boston. They just don't understand." He grabbed his lapel. "I'm meeting her at the train tomorrow night. She's staying at the Ambassador. It's going to be tough the first night. I thought I'd take her to dinner. I don't want to be alone."

"Where in the hell do I fit in?"

"I need someone with me. Please."

"When is she arriving?"

"Six-thirty. Let me call you at the apartment when I arrange for dinner."

He tried to remember everything Art had told him about her as he drove home; his meeting her mother when he worked at the restaurant near Harvard, knocking her up, her parents insisting on a marriage on their terms, the mother's death when the child was an infant, and Art turning the baby over to the grandparents. They were rich and influential and the girl's mother was an only child. Maybe she was attractive. As he crawled into bed that night he remembered he forgot to ask if she was married.

They met in the restaurant's bar at eight o'clock. Samson arrived first and ordered a drink. As Jennings and his daughter approached in the dim light which blacked out Art's jowl and sag he was amazed at their resemblance. Only their bearing was different, his slightly stooped, hers erect, almost imperious, like one trained to walk through public rooms. They were introduced and led to their table. Now in the light he saw she was tall and a little hippy with long reddish hair bunned at the back of her neck, had the green of Art's eyes but not the gray, which blended with the clustered freckles that spread across her nose and top of her cheeks ending in faded swirls around her eyes. For a few moments she ignored them both as she removed her gloves slowly, casting glances about the restaurant. Finally, she placed them in her purse, snapped it, and turned toward Samson. Her eyes were greener than he first thought and her lips fuller, sensuous. Unlike Art, whose agitation was now displayed by a lighted match searching for the end of his cigarette, Beck managed hers in the manner of a thoroughbred, head high, rigid, a ripple the only sign of her turbulence. If the evening was to be tolerable it was going to be up to him. Samson began cautiously. "Is this your first trip to California?"

"Yes." Now she smiled and her teeth were large but well formed.

Art lowered his head and poked the ash in the tray as if to burrow a hole in which to bury himself. Then he raised his head and tried a smile, she met his eyes, held them a moment without expression and turned back to Samson.

"How long do you plan to stay?" Samson asked.

"Beck's plans are indefinite," Art said.

"They're not at all. I'll be in Los Angeles a few days, then I'm going to Santa Barbara to stay with friends. A week or two and I'll be going home."

"It's too bad," Samson said. "There's a lot to see in our city. I was hoping to show some of it to you."

"You're very kind. But I doubt I'll have the time."

"Your first trip." Art shrugged. "I thought you'd spend more time."

"I must get back," she snapped. She picked up the menu. "Do you mind if we order?"

They buried their heads behind the bills of fare as if they were shields. Drinks were ordered and then the meal, and in the long silences between the desultory conversation, what would otherwise have been unbearable strain was relieved somewhat by the mechanics of eating. Her talk was restricted to polite replies. Art ventured a few meek inquiries and Samson supplied the bulk of the meager remarks with the broadest of observations. He insisted on paying the check, his small contribution to her welcome to the city, he explained, and by the time they left it was decided he would drive her to the hotel. Art arranged to meet her for breakfast and left.

Driving down Wilshire in silence, something about her manner, attitude, the tilt of her head, gave him the feeling the distance between them was a chasm. It could only be cleared by a leap.

"You're rude," he began.

She turned sharply, her look of surprise shaded with indignation and disbelief. She opened her mouth as if to speak and he went on.

"You sit there like you're being chauffeured."

"You're very sensitive, Mr. Duke. I didn't think I'd be called upon to amuse you."

"I wasn't expecting entertainment. Just an acknowledgment of my existence. You were my guest for dinner. I am driving you home."

"Mr. Duke, I didn't ask you to take me to dinner. Couldn't understand your being there in the first place. As for taking me home, that was your idea."

They stopped at the hotel parking lot. He shut off the motor and turned toward her. Instead of reaching for the door handle which he half expected her to do she turned in her seat, folded her arms, and looked at him. "You obviously have something on your mind, Mr. Duke. You might as well say it for I doubt we shall ever meet again."

"I have, but the car is not the place to talk. There's a bar in the hotel. Will you have an after-dinner drink?"

"I suppose I can use one."

Except for a few people seated at the piano bar watching, sad-eyed, as the player, a stout woman, sequined and spangled, improvised tunes, the room was empty. They found a corner table, ordered brandy alexanders and for awhile neither spoke. In the dim light the freckles high on her cheeks blurred into shadows accentuating a glow in her eyes. He watched her hands, long and tapered, the fingers ivory sticks in the gloom, as they played nervously about the table, finally sought her purse from which she removed a pack of cigarettes. They lit up and the drinks arrived.

"As to dinner," he began. "My being there was a favor to your father. He asked me to join you." He smiled, "To be more accurate he pleaded with me."

"No doubt he told you why he didn't wish to be alone with me? All the intimate details of our lives?" She crushed her cigarette angrily, pushed aside the tray, downed her drink and ordered another.

"Only that your mother died when you were an infant. And that he's seen you a few times over the years."

"Three times to be exact. Anyway, I'm sorry we used up your evening." She started to rise.

"You ordered another drink. And I haven't finished."

"Please hurry. I've had a long day."

"What began as a chore turned into a delightful evening. In spite of your rudeness," he added hastily. "I never thought anyone could resemble Art and be so lovely."

"I guess I'd be ungracious if I didn't thank you. Thank you, Mr. Duke." Her drink arrived and she sipped it slowly, appeared oblivious to Duke's presence as she listened to the piano player who was beating out a medley of ragtime tunes. He watched, saw her eyes struggle slightly to focus, a corner of her mouth crease to a hint of a smile as she began to tap the rhythm of the music on the table. Now that she was beginning to unbend, the brandy unstiffening some of that New England starch, he found himself beginning to enjoy her company for the first time that evening. She downed her drink, fumbled for a cigarette as he ordered another round. By the time she was midway through the third drink she began to ask about Art, his wife, the child, his position in business, and complained that she knew little about him.

He passed over Paula lightly, told her about the child, that Art was associated with him, and made it clear they were not partners. By this time he began to feel the drinks and the effect on Beck was evident in her efforts to keep her head from rolling to the side. Sober enough to realize they had enough, he paid the check and escorted her to the elevator.

It was before nine when he phoned her, but she had already left the hotel. At noon, Art poked his head in his office, entered, followed by Beck.

"If you told me you were so important I would have treated you differently," she said, looking over the office and nodding her approval.

"I wanted to be sure you weren't after my money."

Art was grinning. "Beck told me you went for a drink after you left me."

"Drinks," Beck said. "I almost had to be put to bed."

"You did very well. I'm beginning to think the stories about prim New Englanders are sheer propaganda."

Art excused himself. "I have to make a call. I'll be right back."

She sat on the edge of the desk and studied him for a moment. "You're not much older than I." Her face was whimsical now. "Did you inherit your money or make it by sheer ruthlessness?"

"It's all a front." He looked at his watch. "It's lunchtime. Will you join me?"

"I was going to skip a meal. God knows I should," she said, slapping her thigh.

"Have a cup of coffee. And I'll tell you the story of my life."

They asked Art to join them but he pleaded an appointment. Samson almost expected him to wink, slap his back and wish him luck.

After lunch they drove up and through the hills stopping along the way. The city was different from its top with its meadows of lush green, the red tile mosaic, the oil wells crawling the humps of the hills, all of it spilling from the mountains to the west, festooned by its coastline and the sea. Beck lingered at every piece of jutting land they stopped at, walking to its edge and with arms open as if gathering it in, would throw her head back and rhapsodize. They walked to a tip of a finger from which their eyes swept everything from downtown to Catalina. He stood close behind her and when she turned abruptly to exclaim their faces almost touched. For a brief moment their eyes met, then she stepped back.

"All of it," she exclaimed, turning to the city again. "It's so new, washed. It's like it wasn't here last night, was just born."

"It is new, Beck." It was the first time he used her name. "New York, Boston, and the rest, they're old and dirty, can never be scrubbed clean." She nodded. "Why don't you take the time, see more of this? We have a desert and higher mountains and great valleys. Do you know we can feed the nation from the crops of San Joaquin?"

"Maybe I will."

By the time they returned to the hotel she had told him a little about herself: "I graduated from Radcliffe a few years ago, majored in sociology, did work in a Boston settlement house and edited manuscripts for some of my former profs in my spare time."

Her grandmother died the year before, the estate was just settled and the old house was up for sale. "The executor insists I live in it until it's sold. Says it's easier to dispose of a home that's occupied. God knows it's difficult enough to sell large homes these days. In the meantime I'm living there by myself. It's lonely."

That night, during dinner, she told him she'd decided to extend her stay. She consented to his driving her to Santa Barbara. He drove her the following Sunday, they had lunch at the El

Paseo and he returned to Los Angeles. She was to be gone a couple of weeks and he tackled the work that had accumulated during her stay.

Now he began to examine the possibilities of marriage. He was twenty-eight, could afford the luxury of selection, and it was becoming increasingly apparent that marriage, in spite of its burdens, provided advantages. Once married, a game with a Paula or a Posey is just that, and promises of marriage overt or implied are rarely solicited or given. Actually, if one is inclined toward variety, marriage is the best protection. Regardless of the transgression, be it for a day or a week, one must return home to a wife. The single man must make a commitment, the married man isn't expected to. Also, bachelors are suspect, if not envied, and are resented by wives as kindlers of their husband's discontent.

Though Beck did not have Paula's beauty or Posey's chemistry, her qualifications outdistanced the others. Mingled with his thoughts was Beck's money. Why deny its advantages? Though he was certain it was considerable he decided to clear the point before he made commitments.

He bought an extensive report from Dun and Bradstreet and by the time Beck returned from Santa Barbara any doubts he might have had about the size of her estate were dispelled. Not only was the inheritance larger than he thought, it also had the advantage of liquidity. With the exception of the residence in Boston and a cottage on the Cape, everything was tied up in cash, municipal bonds, and preferred stocks.

She returned late on a Sunday night two weeks later. Early the following morning she called him and he detected an air of expectancy in her voice. "I hope I didn't wake you."

"I'm an early riser."

"Do you take ladies to breakfast?"

"I'll be right over."

Her greeting was almost effusive. She took his hand and led him to the coffee shop.

"I'm beginning to feel you're glad to see me," he said as they were seated.

"I've just spent two weeks, breakfast, lunch, and dinner, walks and talks, every waking hour, with the most insufferable bore I have ever met."

"Your friend?"

"Her husband. Poor Helen. With her money one would imagine she could have gotten anybody. She's attractive too. I don't understand it." She shook her head. "He's twenty years older than she, walks on his toes to reach her height, wears a corset I'm sure and talks of nothing but Bismarck, duelling scars, and Heidelberg."

"A German."

"Friedrich Blomberg-Holstein. Maybe that's it. She wanted a hyphenated name. She met him in Germany a few years ago, they corresponded, she imported him and they were married. He hasn't worked a day, devotes himself to body building and drinking. Every morning he's in the pool, which he keeps unheated, for his *kalt planche,* turns up for breakfast still blue, and downs a *schnapps.* Then the Victrola starts. Siegfried, de Gotterdamerang, and the operas, all day long. I can write the scores by heart." She shuddered. "Anyway, it's good to be back. Good to see you."

Things were going better than he had hoped. He decided to leap, forget preliminaries. If she was going to stay on what he was about to suggest would be appealing; on the other hand if she had decided to leave this would be the time to change her mind. Her smile was reassuring.

"I cleaned up my work. I'm taking sort of a vacation until after the first of the year. There's a lot of Southern California I haven't seen; the coastline down to San Diego, Arrowhead, Idyllwild, some of the hidden valleys and Catalina. I have a house in Palm Springs. I plan to spend Christmas week there and leave after New Year's." He spread his hands. "I'm inviting you for all or part of the next three weeks."

"I'd love it. But I'm not sure about Christmas. There are friends back home and . . . well, it's gay in Boston that time of the year and I'm usually with them."

"That's the trouble with you New Englanders . . . tradition.

How about pioneering? The desert in December is beautiful. Oh yes, there'll be other guests . . . chaperones."

"It isn't that, Sam . . . it's just. . . . Let's see what happens," she finally said.

They were together a good deal during the next few weeks: a trip to San Diego for the day, Lake Arrowhead, even the boat trip to Santa Catalina Island. His conduct was constrained, he wasn't taking any chances. There were times when he would hold her hand and gently increase the pressure only to feel her withdraw. He was in no hurry. In place of physical attraction, he found discussions of art, music, and the theater stimulating and informative, welcomed her sensitivity to his moods and thoroughly enjoyed a mild disposition which bore no resemblance to the first night of their meeting. It was only when Art's name came up that a cloud descended on her warmth and gaiety like a shroud. He began to sense that her resentment toward Art transcended his image and encompassed other men as well. Even her grandfather was mentioned as a "martinet," this without a smile, and her grandmother was an "old dear."

Though he had no interest in mending her rift with Art there was no doubt that his association with him could affect her interest in himself. If no ground was found on which she and Art could stand he would have to make a choice and though discarding Art would be painless it would be better if she forgave her father. Art needed him as a son-in-law, would feel his security more assured and even if his influence upon her would be meager, it might be the little Samson would need to complete his plans. He wanted her and wasn't going to lose out for failing to play the percentages.

A week before Christmas, Beck decided to stay and spend the holidays in Palm Springs. He could think of no couple more urbane and acceptable than the Tiptons.

"I know it's a bad time of the year, Martin, but I'm in a spot. It isn't only a chaperone I need. Beck's intelligent, educated. You and Sylvia are perfect. I couldn't just have anyone."

"You sound pretty serious about this girl."

"As serious as I've ever been."

"I'll see what I can do."

Tipton talked to Sylvia and they consented. However, they would have to return for a New Year's party, he said.

He approached Beck about her father. Art had joined them for dinner a couple of times since that first night and it seemed she was beginning to thaw. She asked about Carla and when he whipped out a picture she raved in the proper manner, making no references to Paula who had posed with the child. Samson was not sure Paula would accept the invitation even if Beck consented but felt compelled to extend it. He began to have the feeling that Beck was looking for a form of conciliation, if not complete, at least one that would make their being together more comfortable.

"There'll be another couple," Samson said. "But somehow I'd feel guilty if I didn't ask Art and Paula."

"It's a good idea. I shouldn't resent the wife. She's done nothing to me. And ask them to bring the child."

He couldn't make it, Art said when Samson extended the invitation the following day.

"Why not?"

"Paula's mother is due from Mexico City. She'll be with us a few weeks. Much as I'd like to come, I can't leave."

Samson was about to invite the mother and decided against it. Then he suggested they all get together after the holidays and before Beck returned home. Art beamed, thought it a great idea, started to leave, changed his mind, and after shutting the door to the office, leaned over the desk smiling confidentially.

"I want you to know I'm happy about what's going on." Samson looked at him with feigned surprise. "Between you and Beck." He laid a hand on Samson's shoulder. "I hope it comes off. I never thought of you as a son-in-law." Now he jabbed his arm and winked. "Couldn't ask for a better one."

"You're jumping to conclusions."

"She's a great girl. Fine family too. Not my part," he hastened to add.

"I agree. But your mind is running ahead of events."

"And she couldn't do better either." He jabbed again, grinned, winked, and left.

Martin and Sylvia performed as if they were rehearsed, his eulogies were so extravagant Samson found himself displaying modesty he never knew he possessed. Martin spoke of his energy and imagination, his faith in the city and the scope of his operation. As for the future, his fancy took off and Samson became the most dynamic real-estate operator in the state. His protests were brushed off as humility. Sylvia Tipton was the matchmaker in classic form. When Samson spoke she beamed and shook her head admiringly, her response to Beck was equally laudable and her references were embroidered with "you two," "ideal couple," and she worked "made for each other" to a frazzle. Samson could understand Sylvia's actions, a woman's instinct to secure a sister, but Martin had him baffled until he cornered him one morning.

"You're everything I said you are, Sam. And you're going to live up to my predictions. And," he smiled, "I'd like to see you married."

"Why?"

"I've been seeing Posey. With you married, I don't think she'll ever speak to you again."

"She sees *you* and you're married."

"But she gave you up when you were single. Anyway," he said, patting Samson's back, "Beck's a lovely girl. Don't pass her up."

By the end of the week the efforts of the Tiptons reached the point where another gesture, another word could have turned the serious play into a farce. Samson sensed it like he could sense the moment to close a deal, when he knew that one more word, the expression of another thought, could unravel everything. Beck felt it too because the minute they all drove off she flopped in a chair, closed her eyes, and with arms hanging limp, heaved a sigh. Samson stood watching her, she opened her eyes, looked at him, they started to smile and then both laughed without control.

"Oh . . . I never heard the likes of it!" Beck said. "Could everything they said about you be true? And me! Witty, charming, cultured, even beautiful." She wiped her eyes.

"They sounded like press-agents," he said, flopping in the chair beside her.

She started in again, laughing so hard she bent over double. Caught by the infection he joined in and for a few minutes they laughed and stopped, looked at each other and started over again. They finally subsided and he went into the house and brought out cold drinks. Beck had fixed her face, sat in the same limp position smoking a cigarette and staring out into the desert.

"I made a reservation for dinner," he said. "The restaurant is having a 'Gala New Year's Eve at the Sands. Fun and Favors. Come as you are.' Might be fun."

"Sounds like it. Can I wear a sweater and skirt?"

"Sure. They'll be in everything from pants to evening gowns. And there'll be Hawaiian shirts to tuxedos."

"That's one of the things about California. The informality. Back home we're hidebound by tradition. We're insular. And you see it all around you, even at the university. Everything is old and worshiped. It's like . . . it's like the old ivy clings and chokes."

"And becomes twisted."

"You're right. Anyway, I'm untangling now and I like it."

They took a walk in downtown Palm Springs. He bought her a floppy straw hat, showed her the golf course, and by the time they returned, the winter sun had dipped behind the mountain, bringing on an evening chill. He lit the pile of logs in the fireplace and as they sat on the couch watching the flames, they hardly spoke. As Samson watched her staring into the fire, he was certain her thoughts were on the trip home and the decision to return and the conditions under which it could be made easier. She was almost his age. The specter of being thirty and a spinster could be chilling and there was no other man or he would know, and though she might do better, he was a damn good prospect and if he put himself on a platter and handed it to her it would be hard to turn him down. The dilemma was to overcome whatever problems that kept her single so long. No doubt there were things about her he did not know and he was going to make every effort to find them out before she left.

The fire had gone down; he fed it a couple of logs, returned to the couch and reached for her hand. She gave it listlessly.

"You leave the day after tomorrow," he said. "It isn't much time. There is something I want to say."

She squeezed his hand and let it go. "Not now, Sam. Please."

"Now is the time. We're hours from a new year . . . a good time to talk about a new life."

"That's just it. A new life means the end of the old. It's a big decision. And . . . I haven't had enough time to think." She looked at him pleadingly.

He tried to draw her toward him. She squirmed away. He pretended to be hurt and she reached out and touched him.

"Sam, dear. It has nothing to do with you. It's me. There are things I can't explain. Not now. Give me time."

He forced her to face him. "I must tell you that I love you. And I never felt this way before."

She lowered her eyes. "I thought I felt this way once and was mistaken." She looked up. "Now it's happened again. I want to be sure . . . must be. It's been fast, and is so close. Don't you see? I have to get away, feel it from a distance." She smiled. "Without your charming presence, Sam, your enchanting desert night, the wonderful drives and the sea. I want a long hard look at it in the light of a dreary Boston day."

He had gone far enough, made his point. "Agreed," he said, jumping up. "How about a drink on that?" She nodded. "There's one thing," he said. "If my image begins to fade in that dreary Boston of yours, promise to let me know. I'll pack my wand, pin a desert star on the end and fly back to enchant you."

"I promise."

They entered the restaurant and the maitre d', Phil, whose patronage he bought a long time ago with fat tips, bowed them to a corner table from which they could see the entire room. Phil's bogus smile, more forced than usual, lacked the spurious warmth that always adorned it. However, he did take time for polite inquiries and suggestions. "I think you have the best table, Mr. Duke." Then he offered the confidential information reserved for favored clientele. Samson expected him to look over his shoulder as he bent forward and whispered. "Stay with the steaks tonight."

Samson thanked him, slipped the usual fee for such attention into his palm, and ordered drinks.

"Maitre d's are the same all over," Beck commented as he left. "They even have the same expression."

"I never want to know what they're really thinking."

The drinks were served and as they sipped them they surveyed the room. Tables were beginning to fill, paper hats, streamers and noise-makers were being distributed and the undercurrent of forced gaiety was becoming evident. Some wore serious faces as if contemplating the residuals of a bad year, others, already drunk, were shouting to friends across the room whipping themselves into the high spirits the occasion demanded.

"I wasn't sure when you said people would wear everything," Beck said. "I thought I was being daring. But look at them."

There were slacks and mink coats, dress suits and evening gowns and one couple wore tennis shoes and sweaters. They ordered a second drink and he asked Beck if she was ready for dinner.

"I'd rather wait. I'm enjoying this." She looked at her watch. "It's not ten yet."

"We better go easy on the drinks then. I don't want you to start the New Year with a hangover."

"I don't get them. Good constitution. Thanks, anyway." She leaned over and pecked his cheek.

By eleven o'clock they had finished their fourth drink and ordered the food. The tempo of the room had increased; what had been a hum of voices was becoming a crescendo. The tables were jammed, customers stood two and three deep at the bar and the drunks around the piano, all in a different key, were drowning out the efforts of the player. Beck, flushed and sweaty, was leaning heavily against him, pressing his thigh with hers and teasing him with handclasps and wet kisses. He had hoped the food would sober her but she insisted on wine with dinner and by the time they finished, a little before midnight, she rose to go to the ladies' room, swayed and would have fallen if he hadn't grabbed her. He escorted her and waited outside the door. Just after midnight she came out, her pale face accentuated by the freckles, and she was clutching a handkerchief with which she dabbed her eyes. The welcome to the New Year was in full swing, all the lights had been dimmed, couples were wrapped in each other's arms, sour notes of Auld Lang Syne filled the room, and there were tears and laughter, shrill, moaning, like the babble of a delirium and then a net full of balloons was released from the ceiling and a hundred hands shot up grasping. Beck flung her arms around his neck, found his mouth, and pressed tightly closed lips against his, and then for an instant, as if it were a scream, she opened her mouth wide, forced her tongue into his and then released him and fled to the table. He followed, wiping the sweat that had drenched her hands and still smelling the vomit from her breath. Half-carrying her, he managed to get her back to the house and to bed. She slept late the following day and did not appear until noon. He had breakfasted, read the morning paper, and was sitting in the patio. She came out with a hand pressed to her forehead.

"Happy New Year!"

"Not so loud."

"Hangover?"

She nodded.

"Coffee?"

"A pot of it."

She finished a full cup before she said a word.

"How much did I drink last night?"

"Plenty. You went out like a light."

"What happened?"

"I carried you out of the restaurant. Over my shoulder like a sack. Then I got you to bed and you looked so desirable I took advantage of you."

"Be serious. I know I made a fool of myself. And I am sorry." She kept shaking her head. "I don't understand. It's never happened before. I don't remember a thing after I got up to go to the ladies' room."

"Blessed are the drunk."

"Was I that bad?"

He laughed. "You were delightful. Very affectionate. Which was a pleasure, I may add."

"I'll never be that way again. I promise."

"Affectionate?"

"You're pulling my leg."

"How about breakfast? You'll feel better. Then we can tidy up and head back to town."

They reached her hotel late that afternoon and found a message from Art. He wanted Beck to meet Paula and the baby before she left town, and arranged for all of them to go to dinner that night.

"I don't feel up to it," she said when she hung up. "But I guess it can't be avoided."

"It'll be easier than you think. Paula is friendly and your little sister is a beauty."

"It's funny. I just don't think of Carla as a sister." She was silent for a moment. "It's hard to believe . . . a sister." She put a hand on his arm. "It was a better trip than I expected. Even if there would have been no family."

"Now let's make some plans," he said. "Your train leaves at eight tomorrow night. I'll give you time to pack, pick you up for lunch, spend the afternoon with you, then an early dinner and to the depot. There's something I want to show you before you leave."

"What is it?"

"A surprise."

The following day she told him about the dinner the night before as they wound through Laurel Canyon headed for Mulholland Drive. Carla was more beautiful than in the photo and Paula who was one of the loveliest women she had ever seen, couldn't understand her accepting her father, found her to be as friendly as Samson had said and the evening ended on a note exceeding her hopes.

"I must not live with the past. My father was a scoundrel. But I guess there were circumstances. And he was very young when he met my mother."

He turned off Mulholland Drive and climbed a vast knoll. Beck jumped out of the car and ran to the edge. From where she stood, there was a three-hundred-sixty-degree-view sweeping from the ocean to the northern mountains, the skyline of the city and the San Fernando Valley. She took it all in then turned to him, her eyes wide with wonder.

"Sam, it's the loveliest sight I've ever seen!"

"I'm thinking of buying it. In fact, I just made up my mind."

"What will you do with it?"

"Build a home."

"Oh, Sam!"

"I'll need a little help. Maybe on your next trip you'll give me a hand. Sort of help me lay it out."

All the way down the mountain she did not say a word. He helped her with the packing, they piled everything into the car and drove downtown. They had dinner at Bernstein's Sea Food Grotto and were at the train station by seven. The train opened shortly and they went to her compartment. She had spoken very little since they left the hills that afternoon, her conversation during dinner avoided anything personal, revolved around train schedules, the arrival in Boston, the difference in time, dining car hours and the strange fact that Pullman porters are called George. It was chatter, the noise one makes to muzzle thoughts.

The train's departure was announced. At the last call she took his hand and followed him to the platform. He took her in his arms, felt her press against him and then push him away. He was off the train now and she was on the steps.

"You'll write?" she asked.

"There'll be a letter waiting for you."

The train began to move and she waved and he stood there until she was out of sight.

She answered all his letters by return mail. At the beginning her letters were long and descriptive, a detailed account of a day at her work, a visit to her old school, the theater and ballet, a recommendation of a new book. He responded with the purchase of the mountain top, plans for the house, and a word about her being missed. By the beginning of spring her letters were more frequent and intimate; the house was still unsold, seemed emptier and larger each day, how beautiful the desert must be at this time of the year and the sight from the hills and she missed it all and him too. Then she called one night and they talked for an hour, babbling all the things their letters had skirted. She told him her nights were long and without sleep, she had never been more sure of anything, was closing the house, this time for good, and would be out on the next train.

Although he never discussed her with Art, Jennings seemed up-to-date when he collared Samson a few days before she was to arrive. "I just heard from Beck," he said, and gave him a wink. "Understand she's due on Thursday and that you're going to meet her."

"She's due at six-thirty. You can be there."

Art chuckled. "Not on your life, my boy."

"Listen. Beck is shy, a little fearful. I wish to God you wouldn't take so much for granted. She doesn't like to be pushed. And neither do I."

"I'm sorry." But Jennings was grinning.

She got off the train carrying a small traveling bag, looked slimmer, younger, almost beautiful. He started walking toward her. She saw him, dropped her bag, and ran into his arms. Her lips were warm, soft, and yielding. As they drove to the hotel she did not take her eyes off him, would reach for his hand, stroke it, lean forward, and kiss his cheek, then settle back and look at him again. When they reached the room, he ordered drinks while she washed up and changed.

"No more separations," he said, holding up his glass.

"Not permanent ones."

"You look younger, lovelier," he said, setting the glass down. She spun around and ran her hands down her hips. "I'm not beautiful. But I am slimmer. Diet and pining. I missed you."

"No more than I missed you."

"Did you, Sam?" she said, coming up to him. "Did you really?"

He gave her his answer with the tenderest look he could muster and followed it with a long kiss.

They talked about plans during a long dinner. Her stay was to be indefinite. She would return to Boston in a month or so and if the house wasn't sold it was to be closed. With the exception of a few personal things and favorite pieces of furniture, everything was to remain. He told her about the house on the hill; the architect was waiting for final approval of the plans. Samson wanted her to go over them. "The drawings are in the apartment. How about seeing them tonight?"

There were nearly two dozen sheets of prints and specifications and an artist's rendering in color of the front elevation. She exclaimed when he showed them to her. "It's like a castle."

"Start on the plans. I'll put up some coffee."

They were spread on the table when he returned and she was poring over them. "I've never read a set of plans."

He showed her how to determine room sizes, explained the detail sheets and specifications, and she began to make notes. The living room was too large she thought; people live outdoors so much in California, and the pool was large enough for the public, and the bedrooms were perfect, the master, king-sized and the guest rooms cozy, and she loved the kitchen, big as that of an inn and the specifications intrigued her: Spanish tile and oak, wrought iron and planked floors and doors thick and carved and the balconies reminded her of mantillas and mandolins and guitars. It wasn't real, she said, only gingerbread, and she was going to awaken in a dreary room in a Victorian house on a gloomy Boston street. They drank coffee and sat up half the night, talking furniture, decoration, landscaping, and drapery. It was after three when he finally rolled up the plans.

"It's a dream," she said. "But won't it be too expensive?"

"Not as much as you think. I'll contract it myself. Material is cheap and labor three-four dollars a day and a box lunch."

"When will you start?"

"Do you approve the plans?"

She looked at her notes, tore them slowly into small pieces and put them in the ashtray. "There are my objections."

"Then I'll give the architect the go-ahead. He can finish them in a week. It'll take another week for a permit and we're on our way. How about us, our plans?"

"When I return to Boston it'll be to wind things up."

Two weeks later he had a crew digging the foundation. Beck was on the job every day, Delaney acted as foreman, and Samson supervised everything. By the time she was ready to leave the framing was completed and the plasterers started to wrap. They purchased furniture, selected rugs and drapes, and estimated the completion date for the first week of September. Beck was to return not later than the middle of August, be in on the finish, have it furnished and equipped and they were to be married. It was to be a small wedding, in a minister's study with Art, Paula, and the Tiptons as guests. The night before she left, Samson arranged a dinner in a private dining room at the hotel. It was to be a surprise for Beck. He called Martin and Sylvia, and caught Art in the office.

"It's so short notice. I'll have to call Paula. We'll need a baby sitter."

"Let me call her," Samson said. "I want to extend the invitation."

He was coming into the family and it was time to know where they stood. They had not been alone since the scene in his apartment and if her bitterness had become malignant it would express itself in private conversation. She answered the phone and there was a moment's silence when she recognized his voice. He inquired about Carla and told her the reason for the call.

"I suppose we'll have to come," she said.

"Can't you forget?"

"I don't want to talk about it. Art and I will be there. Goodbye." There were no accusations or threats. It was much as he could hope for.

Beck entered the room, saw the others, and covered him with a flurry of kisses dampening his face with tears. She composed herself, made a pretty speech of welcome. He formalized their engagement with a few words, presented her with a ring, and opened the champagne. There were toasts from everyone, even from Paula, who rose, hoisted her glass, looked directly at Beck, and wished her luck. Maturity had added to her beauty and for a few fleeting moments Samson felt a pang of regret.

Beck returned by the middle of August. She'd sold the furniture but not the house. Her personal items were shipped, and with the exception of the cottage on the Cape, which she decided to keep, she left nothing but her investments and the roots that dangled from her memories. By the end of the month the furniture was moved in and they engaged a housekeeper, Mrs. Weber, a middle-aged squat chunk of German efficiency.

They were married on a Sunday in the study of a Presbyterian minister and left on their honeymoon. The plan was to motor up the coast to San Francisco. It was to be only for a week; Beck could not wait to get into the house and he was anxious to return to his desk.

Reaching the Santa Barbara Biltmore in the early evening, he engaged a suite with an ocean view, and after changing to comfortable clothes they took a walk about the grounds. Beck wanted to call her friend, Helen, but he urged her not to, suggesting she might insist on seeing them. He had no desire to spend his wedding night discussing Teutonic heroes with her husband. They finally returned to their rooms where he changed into pajamas and a robe. Beck remained in her street clothes.

He ordered dinner and champagne sent to the room, and suggested Beck make herself more comfortable, but she paced and smoked, talked about his childhood and hers, went to the can, frittered with her hair before the mirror, avoided looking at him and stalled. It wasn't that he was anxious, if anything it was curiosity. He would have been content to offer her any state of celibacy she wanted but was afraid that anything short of an ardent display on a wedding night would be unjudicious. However, she talked without stopping, as if to halt would be the signal for him to advance. They had been speaking about his childhood and he was having a helluva time remembering the lies he had told her.

"When did your mother die, Sam?"

"I was four."

"What was she like?"

"You don't remember much at four. She was pretty, I know. I've seen pictures." Then he described Aunt Annie.

"How about your father?"

He told her he died when he was twenty hoping it confirmed his previous story. When she asked for a description he imagined himself at age forty and rattled it off. By the time she forced him to run through aunts and cousins and an uncle or two he had enough.

"That's enough autobiography. Let's drink the champagne before it gets warm. And the dinner will be up any minute."

"I'm not really hungry. You're rushing things."

"We've had a long day. And we're due to leave the first thing in the morning. We should get some sleep."

From then on she was silent, answered in monosyllables, forced smiles in response to his attentions, ate the meal like one condemned. He wanted to shake her, tell her she was a grown woman. Then he looked at her face, it was full of fear and it dawned on him that she might still be a virgin. In spite of her age, she had been sheltered, her mother's route into marriage must have been known to her and her grandparents probably hovered over her like Salem elders. By the time the dishes were removed it was ten o'clock. She was at the window, staring out and puffing a cigarette. They had to get into bed that night and his patience was ended.

"Come here," he said, "I want to talk to you."

She sat down, clasped her hands in her lap and stared ahead. "There's nothing to be afraid of. If you don't want me to touch you, say so. I'll understand."

Avoiding his face she began to speak. "I've only been intimate with two other men. With one, the affair lasted a couple of months. And the other . . . one night." She looked up at him. "Neither experiences were pleasurable." She turned away. "In fact they were ghastly." He thought she was going to cry but she caught herself and went on. "I am afraid of not pleasing you. Afraid of your disappointment more than anything else."

"That's funny," he said. "I have the same fear." She searched his face for confirmation. He made every effort to conceal the lie.

She knelt beside him and put her head in his lap. He stroked her hair. "I never thought a man could be kind. My grandfather never kissed me. Not once I can remember. If he was pleased he would pat my head, call me good girl, like I was a prized animal that had won a ribbon in a show. He treated grandmother worse, like she was an unwanted guest he couldn't get rid of." She raised her head from his lap and seated herself on the floor beside him. "Sometimes for days they would barely speak." She shuddered. "I'd pray he wouldn't come home. And there were nights when I would hear grandmother cry in her room." She shook her head. "I don't understand why she stood for it. Why she didn't leave him. I'd rather die than live her life. It's horrible to say, but the only time she seemed happy was after he passed away."

They finally got to bed. The champagne, warmth of her body, and mere closeness of a woman began to have its effect. Her back was toward him, he ran his hand over her behind, it was round and firm and he became excited. Now he had a hard-on and moved toward her, her body tensed and she moved away. He waited a few moments and tried again. This time he groped for her breast and she twisted out of his grasp. All the desire left him and he rolled to his side of the bed. She didn't stir, and soon the sound of her breathing evened and he knew she was pretending to be asleep. He began to get drowsy, thought of his first night with Posey and started to doze.

On their second night, at a hotel in Carmel, she came to him without asking, treating it as bravely as one would a trip to a dentist. She pleaded for time and understanding and he assured her that his only desire was to please her and that obsession with sex was not one of his problems. He would give her as much or as little as she wanted, he decided, and when it became necessary he would find comfort elsewhere. He left her alone for the next few nights and her relief was evident. She strived in all other areas to please him and he found her stimulating and amiable.

The house was filled with flowers and gifts when they returned, all with messages, from the Tiptons, Art and Paula, and the office staff. On Monday morning he reached his desk with a burst of energy that seemed to have stored up.

Their marriage could not have fitted better. He found the key to harmony very quickly and after a couple of months his bedroom antics were confined to a pat on the ass and a goodnight kiss. When they bought their furniture, Beck selected twin beds without consultation and if their sterile sex life were producing problems they were not evident in Beck's behavior. She seemed happy and content, grateful in fact, and it became no longer necessary for him to join her in bed to assure her of his feelings. There were occasions, only when she was drunk, when she would come to him and he would perform. These sessions were brief and unpleasant and he never knew whether she was doing a duty or satisfying a need. Whatever the reasons, they were never discussed and he did no further questioning. Otherwise their life ran smoothly and under Beck's guidance, Mrs. Weber ran the house like a fine hotel. The price of Mrs. Weber's efficiency was her insistence on autonomy and since her management was flawless, they had no reason to resent the cost. Between shopping with Sylvia Tipton, bridge or golf at the club, and a day or two as a hospital volunteer, Beck's time was so consumed that Mrs. Weber became indispensable.

His contacts at the club began to broaden; Beck managed to lure some of the more important members to their home, always collecting a compatible group interested in real estate or finance. Since most of her contacts were through the wives, and she knew little of the husbands, she always consulted him in preparing a guest list. One evening she asked about Clarke Jones, a bachelor Samson had seen frequently at the club but with whom he had never had a closer relationship than sharing a foursome. Jones was on the border of fifty, had an annoying habit of continually sucking on a pipe as he looked thoughtfully over an aquiline nose from a pair of narrow-set eyes. Samson heard he lived alone with an old-maid sister in a large home in Hancock Park and had connections with a Midwestern insurance company whose properties he was liquidating. He was delighted to have Jones, and was curious about Beck's interest in him.

"It's for Sylvia . . . that is, a friend of hers. Mimi Rutherford. You might have heard me mention her. She's been divorced for over a year. And . . . well, she's looking."

"She might take one look at him and get sore," Samson suggested.

"Not Mimi. She's anxious."

It was arranged and not long after Mimi was trotted in for inspection, in fact before they sat down to dinner, it was obvious that Clarke Jones made his decision. He sat next to her but ignored her completely, kept a conversation going with Samson across the table and after the meal escaped to the library where he dragged him and closed the door. He sank into a leather chair with a sigh, lit his pipe, made a pointed remark about his commitment to the single life and began to discuss business. Since building the house Samson realized that land and construction costs were so low it was possible to develop a brand new project for very little more than the price tags on old buildings. The problem was financing, and though the banks were still shy, able to depend on income from other sources, the insurance companies whose main income had always been from real-estate financing were timidly coming back into the market. However, he wasn't interested in the conventional loan which amounted to around 60 per cent of the cost of the project, but on sums that would cover the entire cost of construction and part if not all of the land. Now he tested his ideas on Jones.

"You represent Rocky Mountain Life . . . the real-estate liquidation part. How's their cash position?"

"Healthy."

"Would they be interested in making loans on apartment houses? New construction?"

"Not a chance, Sam. They made millions of dollars' worth of farm loans in San Joaquin, Imperial, and Orange County. Practically all foreclosed. They wouldn't dream of another loan until most of the land was disposed of."

Samson knew that some of the laws demanded that insurance companies dispose of real-estate holdings within five years of acquisition. Other companies owned buildings that brought some income, but Jones's company owned farms whose crops didn't bring in enough to pay the freight to the market and in many instances were left to rot in the fields.

"Suppose they could put their money out on loans and dispose of their land at the same time?"

"Good loans?"

"Solid."

"If you've got that one figured out, Duke . . . well, you can write your own ticket."

"I think I have. Let's take a hypothetical situation. Let us suppose your company has a piece of land on their books that costs them twenty thousand dollars but is really worth ten. I apply for a hundred-thousand-dollar loan on a building to be built. And I agree to accept eighty thousand in cash and the piece of land and give them back a mortgage for the hundred thousand."

Jones put his pipe down. He knitted his brows and his eyes seemed to touch his nose. "Let me understand. As part of the hundred thousand loan you would accept land worth ten and take it for twenty?"

"That's right."

"Which means you would actually be paying a ten thousand bonus to get the loan."

"Right again."

Jones's pipe went out and he relit it. "And the company would eventually realize the full amount they have in the land. . . ."

"Correct. And every piece of land they tie into a loan will bring them back their original cost. No loss."

"I can see the advantage to the company. Provided the loans are secure. But how do you come out? How can you afford to pay such large bonuses?"

"My ability to buy land cheap and my knowledge of how to build below the market make it possible for the project to absorb the high loan cost. I'll expect the company would have to make a little concession and not be too conservative on their appraisals, so I can end up with enough cash on each deal to make the project equitable. But as far as security is concerned," Samson went on, "let me tell you this. There hasn't been a new building built since 1930. Most of the housing available is ten to twenty years old. New apartments will clean out the old buildings and at rents that are competitive. There will be a negligible vacancy factor. The loans will be safe."

"It makes sense, Duke. I'll drop a note to the home office in St. Louis."

Samson wasn't sure he absorbed everything and a note to the office was not what he wanted. "Do any of the executives ever come out here?" he pressed.

"I'm expecting the president next month. He's my brother-in-law, you know."

"There are some refinements I haven't worked out yet. Why not forget the note. By the time your brother-in-law gets here I'll have the package complete." Jones promised to call him the moment he knew the date of his arrival.

In the meantime Samson wasn't going to wait, nor did he want to be dependent on one company. He had Ruth Bennett make up a list of all the smaller life insurance companies who had offices in Los Angeles and started to make the rounds. After a half-dozen calls that ran from flat turndowns to vague promises, he found one company whose agent, Owen Potter, questioned him carefully and told him that State Life of West Texas had a man on the coast during the twenties who loaded them with loans that had gone sour. "They have a lopsided portfolio and they're looking for a deal," Potter said.

"We own ranches and farms from Santa Barbara to San Diego. Orange and lemon groves, some grapefruit, walnuts and plain dry farming. And we've plenty of money for new loans. Suppose you write up everything you told me, and I'll shoot it to Dallas."

Samson prepared a prospectus, included the details of his present operation, bank and other references and had it in Potter's hands the following day. A week later he received a call from Potter. A meeting was arranged for the following Monday with the company's president who was coming in from Texas.

Expecting someone tall and rangy, booted with hardly urbane he was taken by surprise when he met Fines Cady in State Life's offices. Before him was a short, delicately made man, meticulously dressed, with a narrow face etched like the lines in a pine plank, topped by a full head of hair, thick and black, that stood up like quills. Next to him, Owen Potter, who was almost as short, but round, bald, and puffy, reminded him of a cushion. Cady offered him a cigarette from a gold case, tapped his thoughtfully and began to talk.

"Owen sketched your deal and I read your prospectus. Give me more details."

Samson went over the story carefully, said he planned a series of furnished and unfurnished apartment houses, as many as they would finance, told of his background and present position, that he could provide a satisfactory financial statement and other references. "This is not a one-shot deal," Samson emphasized. He talked about thousands of units, enough loans to eat up a big chunk of the land State Life was holding.

"We would be interested in furnished apartments only," Cady said. "Los Angeles is a suitcase town. They'll rent easier. What can you bring them in for, furniture and all?"

"No matter who sharpens the pencil out here they can't bring it in for less than three-seventy to four dollars a square foot including land and furniture, but I can do it for three gentlemen. I'm a helluva buyer of land. I know every hungry material house and subcontractor in town and can buy labor by the pound. My operation will be efficient, lean. I don't want to be penalized for this. I want to be paid for it. I want to borrow three dollars a foot."

"That means you'll have no money in the deal."

"Yes I will. I'm willing to take up to twenty per cent of all my loans in land. It'll come in at half its worth. That means on every hundred thousand I'll take twenty in land. And there might be other loan expenses," he said, putting out a feeler.

Cady took a pad from Potter's desk and started to figure. He tore off the sheet, looked at it for a few moments and tossed it on the desk. "We're pretty close. We've been going to sixty per cent on a four-dollar cost. If you want a hundred per cent of three and will take twenty per cent in land we'll only have to pinch our boots a little to squeeze it in."

"What's the next step?" Samson added.

"I want to think it over. I'll be in town for a few days, maybe a week. You'll hear from me before I leave."

The following morning Cady came to his office unannounced. He wore a double-breasted suit, a tab shirt, and a tiny bud in his lapel. He stood at the door, his manner almost diffident.

"I should have called. But I was in the neighborhood."

"Delighted to see you."

"I won't be long." He removed some papers from his pocket. "Look them over," he said. "It's a list of our smaller ranches. Mostly in Orange County. The prices are a little soft. Not much."

There were three sheets with information on about thirty pieces. Most were in oranges, a few walnut groves and a hundred acres of grapefruit in Coachella Valley.

"I thought you might have time to look a few of them over while I'm here."

Though he had no desire to spend a few days checking properties without the assurance of a deal, Samson had the feeling Cady was closer to working things out than he indicated. He looked at the list again.

"I'll check a few in Fullerton, Anaheim, and Santa Ana. It should give me an idea."

Cady nodded, lit a cigarette and looked about the room, his gaze stopping at a picture Beck had given him of herself not long after the wedding.

"Your wife?"

"Brand new. Been married less than a year."

"I married early. Was still an undergraduate."

"Where did you go to school?"

"University of Texas and two years at Columbia. I thought of law at one time. The war came along and I got caught up. Spent a year in the army and . . . well you know how it is. Once you leave school it's hard to go back. My father's business was spread out, he said he needed someone at his side he could trust." He smiled wryly. "So, I went into things, Texas style; ranching, wild-catting, and speculating. Then the crash put an end to it all and now I'm a prosaic insurance man."

"Not prosaic, Mr. Cady." Cady smiled. "Is State Life a mutual or stock company?"

"Stock company. Unlisted and privately held. When we picked up the pieces after the crash we found the only thing left worthwhile was a few thousand shares of State Life. It's funny. It was one of those investments one makes for grandchildren or to cash in some day for a trip. Now it had to be put to work for all of us. Anyway, we picked up enough proxies to move in."

"You sure did a job. Most smaller companies have sick real estate and no cash."

"Do you believe in luck?"

"Luck's important. But some people get breaks and do nothing with them."

"I mean pure dumb luck."

Samson agreed it existed.

"We foreclosed on four thousand acres near a little town in west Texas. The loan should never have been made in the first place. We were in it for thirty dollars an acre. There was enough water to keep a hundred head. The rest was bone dry earth and sage." He chuckled. "If one were to look for a corner of America to sweep all the dirt, this was it. Land around it was being offered for five dollars an acre and less and there were no takers. We couldn't give it away and wrote it off. About three years later a man walked into my office. The Texas type you see in the movies; boots, big hat, grubby and drawly. He looked at the ranch, he told me, it wasn't much but he was a "country boy" and thinking of a little farming. At first I wasn't suspicious but when the act became too professional, when he reached in a faded vest for a toothpick and started in on his teeth, butchered the language more than necessary and began to pick his nose, I looked him over carefully. He forgot to rub the shine off his manicure. So I stalled him and sent a geologist to the four thousand acres." Now Cady leaned forward and punctuated each word by tapping his finger on the desk. "The oil was so close to the surface a dog could have smelled it." He sat back. "That's dumb luck."

The morning wore on, Samson told them to hold his calls, they talked about the situation in Europe which Cady thought would lead to war, the future of real estate which they both agreed would come into its own in the event of a conflict. He questioned Samson about himself and Samson gave his patent answers and by the time Cady rose to leave he began to get the feeling his visit was not entirely in the line of business. He was at the door, turned, hesitated a moment and came back to the desk.

"Potter, my man here, is new in L.A., doesn't know his way around." It came without hesitation. "I wonder where a man can have some fun in this town?"

Samson started to think of the better restaurants, bars and then it dawned on him what Cady wanted.

"I sort of feel like relaxing," Cady continued. "Back home, everybody knows you."

Samson thought of Delaney. He could dig up whatever Cady wanted.

"Where are you staying?"

"I have a suite at the Gaylord. It's big enough for a party if you can join me."

"It'll be a pleasure." He could do with a good tussle.

Cady was grinning. "I knew I came to the right place." Samson reached for the phone and got Delaney.

When he told him what he wanted, Delaney said they had enough hookers in the building to supply a platoon. "Just give me the specifications."

Samson covered the mouthpiece. "He can get anything you want."

Cady's expression and tone was as serious as one would expect from a man selecting a thoroughbred. "Young as possible, pretty and a good body. A very good body," he repeated.

Cady gave Samson his apartment number. He doubled the order and told Delaney to have the girls there at six o'clock. They arranged for him to be at the apartment at five-thirty and Cady left.

Samson called Beck, told her he had a man in from Dallas, had to entertain him and would be home late. When she suggested he bring Cady to the house, he told her he wore boots and a big hat, was grubby and grimy, hashed the language, and the only thing civilized about him was a highly polished manicure that fit him like satin pumps on a pig. Not only would he enjoy the needed therapeutics but he had the feeling that Cady had made a favorable decision on the deal. To make sure that Cady's obligation went beyond the arrangements he called Delaney and told him to pick up the tab for the girls and to impress upon them that if either one took a dime from Cady they would be turned in.

"They're gonna cost a lot of dough, Sam. They got a minimum even if they don't spend the night."

Samson had a hunch the minimum was going to be used up and they would be working overtime.

The girls arrived at six. By eight o'clock, they were all loaded. Cady took his pick and was off to the bedroom leaving Samson the oldest who was twenty and worked him over on the living room couch. An hour later Cady came out of the bedroom roaring drunk and stark naked, dragging the girl and calling for a switch. He appeared obsessed, looked at Samson almost without recognition, grabbed his girl and hustled her off to the bedroom slapping her ass and shouting obscenities. Sobered a bit by the spectacle, Samson poured another drink and after a few minutes was back on the couch. It took her nearly an hour to turn him off and then he dozed. He was awakened by loud voices from the bedroom. The room was dark and he was alone. Pulling on his pants he went to the door which was partially open. With the aid of moonlight he saw the three of them on the bed, bodies twisted like worms in a can, grunting and squealing like animals. He closed the door, dressed, and left the apartment.

Cady could not get enough. During the next three days, Delaney kept him supplied. The cost was running up but Samson didn't care, because by the time he ran out of what was keeping him going he was certain the only thing that could kill their deal was for every one of his wells to run dry. Late in the afternoon of the day following their party he received the first call. Cady's speech was careless. He slurred, he drawled, Samson got the impression that what he was saying came from a part of him trappings and breeding only disguised and that Mr. Cady had a load on his back. And he was drunk. "This is your buddy, Fines."

"How are you doing, pal?"

"Great, great! But I ran out . . . that is, they ran out. They don't make them like they do in Texas . . . ha, ha, ha. Boy, what a night! You got a couple more around? Big tits this time . . . big tits. Yessir, tits." It sounded like he dropped the phone.

"Are you all right?"

"Never better, buddy boy. Never better."

"Have you eaten?"

"Eaten? Eaten what? Ha, ha, ha. Sure I've eaten."

"Suppose I come over," Samson said. "In the meantime take a cold shower and then we'll make arrangements."

Cady was in his robe and drinking when he got there. The apartment was a mess, bedroom pillows on the living room floor, sheets, covers, and cushions strewn everywhere, filled ashtrays and a couple of broken glasses and last night's dinner smelly garbage on a tray. Samson got him in the shower and by the time he came out looking amazingly fresh Samson had the place straightened up.

"We had a night, didn't we, Sam?" Cady proceeded to pour himself a drink. Samson noticed three empty bottles beside the one he was pouring from and suggested it might be a good idea to taper off.

"I never taper off," he said, holding the glass high. "I just quit." He downed the drink. "Now," he said, rubbing his hands. "Did you call for the girls?"

"Are you sure you want them?"

"Sam," he said, coming up to him and dropping his hands on his shoulders, "I'm a faucet that don't get turned on too often. Once on, it stays until it runs dry. Call the girls."

"Okay." He picked up the phone and reached Delaney.

"What did your friend do to those dames?" Delaney said.

"Never mind that. I want another, same address."

Cady grabbed the phone. "Make it two, friend. And be sure they have big tits." He handed Samson the phone and grinned.

"Was he kidding?" Delaney asked.

"You heard him."

"Wait a minute, wait a minute," Cady said. "Hold it." He covered the receiver. "Tell your man I'll call him direct. Maybe tomorrow. I won't have to bother you."

He gave Delaney the instruction, told him to keep them coming and hung up. Cady took his arm, led him to the door, opened it, slapped his back and almost pushed him out. "If you're going to be visiting me, don't forget to knock." He roared.

"If you need anything just call."

"I got everything I want."

He did not hear from Cady until Friday but all during the next few days, Delaney kept him informed with bulletins; he had sent up two more pair, would run out of decent merchandise, Samson was stuck for over two hundred and he sure wanted to meet that man before he left town and shake his hand. Just before noon on Friday, Cady called. All the mildness and manners were back in his voice, he spoke as if the last time they talked was at the meeting in his office, asked if he had a chance to see any of the land and suggested they get together for an early dinner that night since he was returning to Dallas on a nine o'clock train. Samson had taken off a day, seen a few of the ranches, told him so and they arranged to meet.

During the meal Cady spoke only of business, said he decided to go ahead on a couple of deals, would make no commitment on an extensive program, but if things went well there would be unlimited money at Samson's disposal. He could not ask for more, told Cady so and said he would contact him the moment he had a package ready to go. The meal was over, and there had not been a word, not even a hint of what had occupied Cady during the past few days. The incident was too obvious to be ignored; on the other hand the fact it had been skirted so completely could mean that like social diseases and the family idiot it was not to be talked about. However, he was saving it for last, for the few minutes left before he had to make his train, a good excuse to touch upon it without comment and run. They were waiting for the check.

"There isn't much time. I have something to say so please don't interrupt me." Samson nodded. "First of all, thanks for the party."

"It was a pleasure."

"I'll make it up." He lit a cigarette. "I work hard in my business. I'm like a train that can't get off the track, going full steam because they're piling on the coal, and then once in a while, not often, the throttle is too wide, the pressure too much. . . ." He waved a hand. "So, I jump the track."

Samson said he understood, said he felt that way himself at times and that as far as he was concerned it never happened. Just before Cady left he handed Samson an envelope for Delaney. He knew it contained money and protested.

"Give it to him. He earned it."

Samson waited on the platform and watched his slight figure until it disappeared into the train.

Land was being given away, a lot, an acre, it made no difference; it was the ass end, the last thing anyone wanted with every piece of improved real estate going begging. Samson picked up a piece on Clinton in Hollywood big enough for eighty units, for nine thousand dollars. It was covered with trees, palms, eucalyptus, and a few peppers. They were old ones, big-trunked and too expensive to remove so he instructed the architect to design the building so they would fit into patios, line the drive and shade some of the west and south exposures. He wanted everything completed in a couple of weeks, even if he worked day and night. Within a month he had plans and specifications, a cost breakdown and every dollar of the cost added up. He put the money where it showed, called for the cheapest plumbing and wiring, the minimum requirements on framing, used concrete slab on the ground floors and pine on the upper story, there wasn't a foot of hardwood in the building, the kitchen cabinets were metal, and the only "number one" lumber in the building was on the façade. It came in under two-ninety a square foot including everything, better than he expected but not as cheap as he knew it could be done. The subs still had a little left in them to be squeezed and the carpet man made it clear he was ready to sharpen his pencil to a stub.

The over-all building contained forty thousand square feet, the carports sixteen, the total cost ran to $130,000. He padded it, represented it as one-forty, asked for a larger allowance for the carports, and delivered the package to Potter's office. With it he included an economic breakdown showing rent schedule and expenses predicated on current prices and came up with a total evaluation of the finished project of just under $200,000. Potter went over everything carefully, asked a few questions and just before Samson left told him it would be in the mail that night and he would hear from him within a couple of weeks.

A day before he went to see Potter he received a call from Clarke Jones telling him he was expecting his brother-in-law and would get them together when he arrived. When they finally met it was evident he was cut out differently than Cady. Typically Midwest, he looked like a faded photograph of a preacher with his collar turned front. After their first meeting in Samson's office where he explained his plan he decided to get him to the house for dinner. This bird was tough, looked at him suspiciously every time he made a statement, with an accompanying grunt that seemed to add a note to his disbelief. Samson's inclination was to lay out his proposal, have him take it or leave it, but he could not afford the luxury. Of all the companies he contacted, only Clarke Jones and Cady's showed interest and even if Texas came through he did not want to be at the mercy of one source. Anyway, if Mr. Norman Hotchkiss had a part of him that could be warmed, a home-cooked meal and a charming hostess might do the trick. He would be delighted, he said. Samson asked Clarke Jones to join them and arranged it for the following night.

After a pleasant dinner during which Beck managed to keep Hotchkiss smiling with amusing anecdotes of her college days they adjourned to the library where she poured coffee, laid out the brandy and prepared to leave.

"You don't have to go on my account, Mrs. Duke," Hotchkiss said.

Beck looked to Samson for a sign.

"I'm discussing a new project with Mr. Hotchkiss," he said. "It might interest you, Beck."

"It's time I learned some of the mysteries of your business."

"It's your business too," Hotchkiss said. "I understand you have community property laws in California. The wife owns half of everything." It seemed amusing to him and he laughed.

"Is that true, Sam?"

"Absolutely."

"Then I will stay. Protect my interests." They all laughed and the discussion began. It seemed that Mr. Hotchkiss' caution was dictated by fear. Unlike Cady, who owned controlling interest in his company, he was an employee, and though president, was subject to the censure and control of a board.

"I'm really a trustee," he explained. "All I can do is recommend. The final decisions are made by the loan committee."

Samson brought the duplicates of the package submitted to Potter, showed him the plans, specifications and other papers, explained the loan was being considered by another company but that since it was typical of what he was doing it was a good sample of what to expect.

"How much of a loan are you looking for?" he asked.

He lied. "A hundred fifty thousand."

"You understand if we decide to go into loans of this kind there will have to be independent appraisals and verifications of cost breakdowns."

When he left that evening he told Samson he would hear from him within a few days. After they had gone, Beck questioned him about the details of the deal, evidencing more interest in his affairs than ever before. When she asked about the community property laws, he explained that everything earned by husband or wife during a marriage was the property of both.

"What about assets one has before marriage?"

"That's separate property."

"It all seems so unfair."

"Why?"

"You're risking what you had, gambling to make large sums in which I share equally and my money is safely invested and bringing so little."

"I'm not complaining, darling. You keep it that way."

By the end of the week he received a call from Clarke Jones telling him that Hotchkiss was interested. Samson would be sent a list of the land they owned in Southern California and to call him the moment he had something to submit. On the following Monday, Potter called telling him he had a wire of commitment from Texas and was ready to open an escrow. The only thing to be decided was the selection of the ranch that was going into the deal. Samson picked a grove in Riverside, twenty acres of prime Valencia oranges with a good house that approximated twenty per cent of the loan. He contacted a broker in the area and told him to sell it immediately at the best available price. He got an offer which he accepted that brought more than half of what he had taken it in for and he tied the sale escrow in with his escrow with State Life.

There was no question he had the formula, would no longer be dependent on the market for merchandise, could create his own, new and modern, and at a cost the old buildings could not compete with. As long as Cady and Hotchkiss and other companies like theirs came up with loans, his production could be unlimited. Thousands of units could be built with a minimum of his own capital.

His business would have to be reorganized; the old properties eventually disposed of, room made for an architect and draftsmen. Direct factory connections for furniture and mill contacts for carpeting would have to be developed, middle and secondary men eliminated. There would be work crews to dig up and cheap subs and he had to option land, all he could find, for as little as possible. Once he got started and the word got around there would be others in the game. But he had the first jump and if it was long enough he could be out front and never headed off.

Within a month he had the eighty units on Clinton under construction and a hundred-unit deal ready for submission to Clarke Jones. He came to Samson's office and spent an hour going over the plans and cost breakdown carefully.

"How does it look?" Samson asked.

"It looks good. How much do you want?"

He asked for a larger amount than he expected to get, a sum that would take him out and leave a little. Jones didn't balk, made a sucking noise with his pipe, checked the figures again and sat back.

"What do I do now?" Samson said. "Submit it to the home office or to their local appraiser?"

"Oh, I'll handle it. And I'm the appraiser."

Samson told him he was sure they could work together.

"There's one little item, Sam. Norman didn't like to talk about it." He smiled. "He leaves those things to me."

Samson knew the bite was coming and was a little surprised. Hotchkiss didn't look like a man with a hand out. Jones removed the pipe from his mouth, set it carefully on the tray, toyed nervously with a cufflink and then faced him with all the determination he could manage.

"I can almost guarantee every loan . . . within reason, that is. Norman doesn't just recommend deals to the committee. He tells them and they stamp it. However, there is going to have to be participation."

Samson wanted to look pleased, tried a smile. "Go on."

"After all, you'll end up with practically nothing in these deals. So, I want a deed to ten per cent of the ownership above the loan." He was watching Samson carefully now.

"It's a pretty stiff bonus, isn't it? On top of the land I'm taking?"

"I don't think so. You're not giving any of your capital. Just a little piece of the profits. And if I'm in with Norman, you can imagine how hard we'll be working for the partnership."

He could not ask for a better arrangement and knew it. But to accept the size of the cut without opposition would make it look too easy. He wanted Jones to feel he squeezed him for all he could. When he offered five per cent, Jones didn't budge. He upped it to seven and a half and Jones just shook his head.

"There must be some compromise," Samson protested.

"That's just it. There isn't. My instructions come from Norman. I couldn't accept a per cent less. He wouldn't understand."

"Well, if that's the case," Samson said, with resignation, "I guess I have no choice."

"I'm afraid not."

They made their deal. Jones was going to form a separate corporation with his sister as sole stockholder for the purpose of taking title to his interest in the buildings. He had a list of the land the insurance company owned with him. Selecting one that represented about twenty per cent, he told Samson he had a friend who had seen it and might pay sixty per cent of the asking price. "My friend usually buys what I recommend."

Samson could not understand his offer. Jones surely knew he was prepared to cash out any of the land for one-half of the asking price. He did not have to wonder long.

"This is a separate deal, Sam. You don't have to accept it. If you do, however, I expect the usual commission."

"How can I turn it down," he said, throwing an arm about Jones's shoulder as he got up to go.

It only remained for him to complete his reorganization, liquidate, change his staff and mode of operation. Delaney was already on the building job, taking over the superintendency like a sergeant would a platoon. Tipton's office had set up the books for the building corporation and there was only the sale of the old buildings. He called in Art Jennings.

Now, with the architect and draftsmen ready to move in, another building to start, and others to follow he was forced to tell Jennings his plans. He did not want it hinted there might not be a job for him in his new setup. First of all he still needed him, surely until the last of the old buildings were disposed of. Also if he got the idea he was going out there might be the temptation to start something on his own. In spite of the fact that Art and Beck were getting along well, he had no intention of padding his payroll with deadwood.

"What's going on around here?" Jennings said. "It looks like we're going into something big."

He explained his plan, gave no details, said it was still a test but that his cash position was such that it was necessary to dispose of the buildings they had on hand.

"If it works, I'll be in the building business. And I don't believe in spreading out too thin. If it doesn't . . . well, the old buildings will still be around."

"We're doing so well. Why can't we handle both?"

"I haven't the money or the time."

"I've got all the time in the world. I can take the old operation off your hands. As for the money, did you ever think of talking to Beck? She must have plenty. And I'm sure it's laying around doing nothing."

"I wouldn't dream of it," he said indignantly. "I'm in a crap game and you know it. Anything can happen. They can be shooting at each other all over the world any day. And with it every building equity can disappear." He got up from behind the desk and started to pace. "Beck's money is hers. Safe, solid." He turned on Jennings. "How can you even suggest it?"

"I'm sorry, I . . . well, I just thought that . . . ." He looked at the anger in Samson's face. "Forget it, Sam, forget it."

"I will. Now let's get down to business. Order a new batch of brochures on everything but this building and the one occupied by the State. I want five thousand. Ruth Bennett has the brokers' list. If there aren't enough names add to it. I want them in the mail by the end of the month." Art started to leave. "Wait a minute. Keep all this under your hat. I'm not looking for competition." At the door he put his hand on Jennings' shoulder. "I'm sorry I got sore . . . about Beck's money, I mean. It just struck me . . . well it rubbed me wrong."

"I guess I shouldn't have mentioned it."

By September he had six hundred units completed and under construction, an inventory of land for an additional five hundred, and sold all but two of the old buildings. In spite of the fact that scary war headlines toppled the stock market and some investors were running for cover he kept going. He had nothing to lose, had a free ride for the jackpot, the sale of his old buildings loaded him with cash and State Life and Rocky Mountain were taking all the risks.

After Munich, he got a call from Cady and Hotchkiss—they were worried they said. Maybe he should slow down. The war talk sounded too real. Samson convinced them the problem was getting enough built before it started. With a war on, all peacetime construction might stop. The longer the war, the better off they would be. Apartments could be like gold. He urged Cady to come to Los Angeles, see the finished buildings, and note the low rate of vacancies. Cady spent two days; they toured the buildings, checked some of Samson's optioned land, and came to an agreement. Samson wanted straight loans now, no land; the bonuses were too high. For longer terms and lower interest, he agreed to accept less money.

"There was never a surer thing," he told Cady. "If we get into war, building has got to stop. Eventually every apartment will fill and we'll be running at a hundred per cent occupancy."

"What if there is no war?"

"Not a chance."

With Clarke Jones it was easier. He was sitting on his ass, Rocky Mountain's money wasn't his, and Samson could make him rich. He made the same deal with Jones: no more land, all money, and easier interest on the loans.

He had a year, he figured, maybe two, that was all. Any of the fires Hitler was neglecting, Mussolini was starting on his own, and the Japanese were heating things up in Asia. His goal was at least twenty-five hundred units before the lid dropped. The government was already on his back, protesting his capital gains, claiming he was a dealer, not an investor and after a series of meetings with Tipton, it was agreed he would be better off hanging on.

"They're not going to stand still for it, Sam," Tipton told him. "I had a battle on your last return. Don't sell for awhile. A year or maybe two. Then we might find an angle."

He was putting in twelve hours a day, seven days a week, would see Beck for a dinner, an occasional breakfast, their conversation was brief and he had not touched her for months. She had given up the hospital work, was playing golf every day and now her drinking went through lunch to cocktails before dinner. Also, she was seeing a lot of Paula, thought her "very sweet," had her take up golf and they were always at the club.

The opportunity he was waiting for came unexpectedly one night when he came home early and found her waiting for him. A week earlier he had a session with Art Jennings and it was agreed he would wind up the month and leave. His last dozen checks had just been for his guarantee, the new operation had knocked him out of the box, he was rummaging for deals like a beggar and realized he hit the bottom of the pile.

They had finished dinner and Beck found him in the library.

"I had a proposition today, Sam. Can I talk to you?"

"From a man?" he said, hardly concealing his sarcasm.

She looked at him, ignored the remark, lit a cigarette nervously and went on.

"From my father."

"What did he want?"

"I understand you're letting him go. You didn't tell me."

"By mutual agreement. My operation has changed. He no longer fits in."

"Anyway he wants me to furnish money for some deals."

"What kind of deals?"

"It's a little vague. It has something to do with buying apartment houses, fixing them up, and selling them. I guess I'm to put up the money and share the profits."

"I won't let you touch it. Those days are over. And I resent his coming to you."

"Why? He has a right to ask."

"I have a better right and didn't. I've been working on short capital, still am. My money comes from loan sharks at exorbitant rates. Why do you think I've been putting in long days and nights? It's because I'm being squeezed, racking my brains, twisting and turning. Don't you think I can use capital?"

"Then why didn't you ask? You know I have money."

"I don't know how much you have and don't care. It's yours and I don't want to touch it."

"That's silly. You told me half of what you make is mine. Why shouldn't I contribute?"

"So far, I've managed without it. It's been difficult, God knows," he said, shaking his head. "But somehow I'll work it out."

"I have a lot to make up to you, Sam," she said. "I may be a fool but I'm not blind. I know what's happening and I hate myself for it. But I can't help it. I'm trying very hard. Do you understand?"

"Of course I do, darling. And I've a lot of patience."

She searched his face for a moment, she smiled affectionately. "Now," she said, "if you'll get me a nice tall drink, scotch and a little soda, I want to talk business."

She took a long pull from the glass and cradled the drink in her lap. "We never discussed it but I have a lot of money. Over three hundred thousand in bonds and other things. And there's the house on the Cape. The money is earning me practically nothing. Maybe three per cent."

"That really is very little," he agreed.

"I want you to use it. As much as you wish. I can write to my lawyer immediately."

He shook his head. "I must refuse."

"You can't refuse. You must see my position. I want to be part of . . . well more a part of the marriage. Anyway, I'm sure it'll be well invested."

He protested more, feebly. She was adamant and he finally agreed. "On certain conditions, however. I'll take only what I need. Right now it's about a hundred thousand. It's possible I'll never need more. Your money will have to be protected and there's only one way."

"I'm not concerned about that."

"But I am. My assets now are about three-quarters of a million. You can verify it with Martin Tipton." Her face registered absurdity at the suggestion. "That may even be a conservative figure. Everything is in my name and in the name of corporations I own." She finished her drink and signaled for another. He joined her this time. "I propose we make identical wills leaving everything we have to each other." He waited a moment for the suggestion to sink in. "I have no one else in the world but a couple of old aunts who have more than I." He took her hand. "You're really all I have."

She looked at him and he could see the liquor had taken effect; she was struggling to evaluate what he had said. "Why not sleep on it and we'll decide in the morning."

She slept late the following day. Instead of leaving as usual he kept in contact with the office until she came down to breakfast. Finally, over coffee he picked up their conversation.

"I thought about it, Sam and I want to go ahead. There are just a couple of reservations. I want to leave a little fund for my college, to set up a scholarship. Say, ten thousand dollars. And the house on the Cape. Grandmother and I spent summers there alone. I want it for Carla."

"I think it's a wonderful gesture."

"Also, I want to leave her some money. Enough for college and a good start. Twenty-five thousand dollars."

They agreed to have the wills drawn, she promised to contact her lawyer immediately and then brought up Art. "We can't let him down. He's got Paula and the child—it wouldn't be right. Can't you find something for him?"

Art would be sure to come back to Beck if he didn't do something. Samson did not want him back in his business, snooping around, particularly after Beck's money was in it. And he knew that a job—any kind—one that you find for poor relatives was something Art would not accept. He still belonged to the club, lived and dressed well, and wasn't old and tired enough to give it all up without a fight. Samson was sure Art resented his success and when he found out where Beck's money was going his bitterness could be compounded. There was nothing he could do, but he figured Art could be had cheap and it would be foolish not to pay the price. He promised Beck he would see to it that Art got back in business, on his own, with any help he needed.

"Art is capable," he told her. "Don't worry."

"I'll leave it up to you."

"Oh, yes. Our plans, the wills and the money. I'd rather you didn't discuss it with anyone."

Art didn't waste any time. He must have seen Beck that day and caught Samson in the office later that evening after everyone had gone. His hat was in his hand and he looked whipped.

"Beck told you I talked to her. I hope you don't think I was going behind your back."

"She's your daughter. You have a right."

"Yeah." He found a chair, looked at him for a few moments, started to speak, hesitated, and then, feeling sorry for him Samson began.

"You can make it on your own and I'm willing to help. But I want Beck out of it." Jennings shook his head. "You know apartment houses, older ones, as well as anyone in town. Get set in an office. I want you to buy and sell, I'll put up the money—up to twenty-five thousand dollars. That's what you'll have to play with. Title goes in my name and we'll split fifty-fifty."

"You won't be sorry, Sam. With that kind of backing I can't miss."

"There's one thing. You buy nothing unless I okay it. The sales are up to you provided there's a profit."

"It's a deal," he said, smiling now. "I'll find a desk somewhere. It's all I'll need. And I'll be digging." He was on his feet. "You wait and see, we'll build it up. By God, Sam, it'll be a pyramid!"

After he left Samson made a mental note to be sure his office handled all the books and rent collections.

During the next few weeks Samson worked closer to home, managed to have breakfast with Beck each morning, spent the dinner hour with her, even took her out a couple of times and on two occasions joined her for a round of golf. Her game was almost as good as his; she drove a long ball and was hard to beat around the greens. On his second round with her he was surprised to see Paula coming up to join them. He found himself walking with the caddy during most of the game as they toured the fairways huddled in conversation. Though Paula was pleasant, she only talked to him when it related to the game and by the time it was over he felt like a stranger they had picked up to fill in. Afterward they gathered at the bar and though he knew Beck had been drinking more lately he was shocked at the amount she consumed. Paula, who barely finished a drink when they were together, kept up, and by the time they left the two of them were huddled and giggly and needed help to the car.

After a series of letters and telephone calls between Beck and her attorney, the hundred thousand dollars arrived with a letter of caution. The wills were prepared and after having them signed and witnessed together with an agreement that neither could be changed without the other's consent, Samson deposited them in a box at the bank.

The pot was full with all the steam he needed to keep a boil. He had cash and credit, a bead on the target and zing, and a pocket full of bullets. He figured a war was a certainty and with it prosperity for those with enough sense to stay out and work the home front. They let the line too loose on Hitler and he took up the slack and like a dog tired of bones he was after the whole animal. Russia was the bait that Hitler dangled and France and England with Uncle Sam nodding consent, were waiting for the Germans to devour it. What a gambit! Fatten the Fatherland with a few countries, toss in some Jews and midst shouts of "aggression," mingle immobility, indecision, and neutrality, let the panzers cross the rivers and plains straight to Russia's heart. And we could watch it all, and so could France and England and the others, and with Russia's defeat and Germany's exhaustion there would be an end to the Commies and Hitler would have to turn to us not to conquer but for help. There was no doubt that the Germans would win; they had the most modern army in Europe, better than the French, their tank divisions were superb, and even Lindbergh said they had the greatest military air fleet in the world. Although he hated to side with Teddy Hofstedter, Samson found himself in agreement after a long discussion one night when Hofstedter had cornered him at the club. First he agreed with Samson that the U.S. and her buddies were doing everything possible to promote a war between Germany and the Russians.

"And don't think Hitler doesn't know it. There are things going on I tell you." He looked confidential. "Sure the Germans had a beef—Versailles and all that—but it's not the issue anymore. And we know it. The Red bastards are out to conquer Europe and then the world. And the only thing that can stop them is the German army and we know that too. I tell you, Sam, the Aryan world is going to wake up some day and realize that Hitler had more foresight, more understanding than any leader in a thousand years."

Samson could have agreed with him with more comfort if he didn't shout and wear that goddamn mustache. "How do we know he won't turn on us when he's finished off the Russians?"

"Why should he? We're his kind. . . . Didn't he offer to deal with us, and the English and the French?"

"What about the Italians?"

"He had no choice. We turned him down. It was expeditious." Hofstedter leaned forward and lowered his voice. "I can assure you when the right moment comes the wops will be put in place. And you can say the same thing about the Japs." He sat up. "You know damn well what he thinks of those mongrels."

If we would stay out of it, keep hands off, Hofstedter was sure Hitler would be marching in Red Square a month after his armies crossed the border. Then Europe would be cut up, each piece would have autonomy with German supervision, a partnership would be formed with the West and then the Japs would be put in their place.

"Let's face it, Sam, the real menace is the colored races. But first we have to purify ourselves, weed out the half-castes, the Slavs, the Poles—hell they're half mongolians—and the half-nigger Italians and Greeks. Then we'll be ready."

It was a grand plan Samson told him, and hoped it worked, but whether it did or not, any doubts he had about a war were dispelled that night. What difference did it make whether Hitler invaded Russia or turned on France, or Stalin jumped them both; the drums have been beating too long, the forces were rallied, cannons were being geared for lack of argument, the lathes were spinning bullets and soon the breadlines would thin and the factories fill and men would be taught how to die. The snowball was on top and ready to roll and that's the way it was and always would be.

CHAPTER FOURTEEN

Art Jennings proposed the purchase of three buildings during the next couple of months and after inspecting them Samson realized he was floundering like a fish brought to deck. It was not only the absurdity of the deals that disturbed him but his insistence that Samson's eye was not on the market and a hint that prejudice had played a part in his decisions. Samson found valid arguments for his reasons but ran against a wall of sulking postures, derision, and bombastic blasts that resembled a state of paranoia. He tried patience, encouragement, and a few hundred dollars in advance, but when he found out Art was golfing at the club and boozing it at the bar he closed the purse and ignored his calls. Jennings finally reached him through Beck, who got the message from Paula, and he got it all one night when he returned home to find Beck too drunk to stand, slumped in a chair as she eyed him malevolently over the edge of a tall glass. By God, he thought as he watched her, she looks exactly like Art! Her face had begun to puff and her eyes seemed smaller. If she needed a shave she could pass. She waved the glass threateningly. "What have you done to my father!"

"What the hell are you talking about!"

"Don't use that language with me," she slurred. She tried to rise and fell back in the chair. Now she narrowed her eyes and shook a warning finger. "I know what you did . . . and don't lie. You kicked him out, that's what! And after he taught you the business, made you what you are." Her hand dropped and she looked in the glass as if searching for more words.

Watching her, he could not conceal his disgust, wanted to grab and shake her, tell her she was a drunk, a frigid one at that, and he was sick of her goddamn hangovers and the fact that she only spread her legs to pee! But she was too drunk. His words would be like smoke in a wind. If there was ever going to be a resolution it was going to be on his terms when he wished.

He grabbed her arms, lifted her from the chair and shook her. "You're drunk!" He shook her again. "Do you hear!" Her look was dazed, as if she was seeing him for the first time that night, as if all that had been said was dissolved by the fumes in her head. She dragged her feet as he led her upstairs and she passed out on the bed.

Downstairs, he poured himself a drink and began to pace the room. Mrs. Weber had gone to bed. Whatever dinner there was had to be prepared and he was in no mood for reheated dishes or cold meat and he suddenly had the urge to get out of the house, from the over-filled ashtray next to Beck's chair, her stained glass, the damn smell of her! He realized how alone he had been all these months, that Beck had been like a stranger in a dorm, a prisoner in the next cot and that he wanted the warm belly of a woman, the feel of a breast, a hot willing cunt! And then he thought of Posey.

The last time he saw her had been at Roy Phillips' funeral. God, he wanted her now—needed her! Martin Tipton was still seeing her, had gotten her a job in an office downtown and confessed they were only friends. Samson looked at his watch; it was only eight-thirty. Why not call her? All she could do is laugh, insult him, and hang up. On the other hand, perhaps she would ask him over if only to gloat, and then throw him out. Even that was better than nothing. He had to see her.

Her name was in the book and he placed the call. At first she was friendly as if the shock of his voice had obliterated her feelings of animosity. Then, when he asked her if he could come over, that night, she laughed.

"Are you serious?"

"I was never more serious."

"Where's your wife?"

"She's out."

"So you want to sneak up here. What for?"

"To see you. To talk to you."

"We've nothing to talk about."

"We may have, Posey. It's been a long time since we've seen each other. You've never been out of my thoughts."

She laughed aloud.

"I deserve that," he said, "but it's true."

"You lie as well as ever, Sam."

"I don't expect you to believe me. Just see me, let me talk to you."

"I'm tired, Sam. Maybe some other time."

With that opening, he pleaded. "Please see me tonight. I'll promise to leave before ten."

There was a long pause. "All right. But for a very short time."

She greeted him with a puzzled smile, took his coat, and led him to the living room. It was warm and tastefully done. He recognized some of the furniture she had when they first met. For a few moments he looked at her as she stood with folded arms in the center of the room and watched him, appraising. It was the look that always penetrated his deceit and found the huddled truth. Guile would be useless and he knew it. What about the truth, all of it?

He asked about her job, the state of her health, displaying every bit of concern he could muster. Martin had gotten her a position in a lawyer's office, she enjoyed the work, got good pay and was very happy. And she meant it, he could tell; there was a serenity about her she never possessed which seemed reflected in the room, in the warm subdued colors, in the glow of the lamps, the haunting face in a Rivera print, and rows of books in gay jackets.

He knew he could never begin where they left off. He had to start all over and the rules were going to be different. When she didn't offer him a drink, he talked on, probed, tried to find out if there was another man, talked about the impending war, about Hitler, remembered her feelings, dropped it, and then when he realized his conversation was tangled and snarled, evaded everything he had come to see her about, he stopped abruptly as the smile that had been gathering on her face broke into a laugh. He lowered his eyes and stared at his hands.

"All right, Sam," she said. "It's getting late and I do have to go to bed."

He lit a cigarette and sat back, feeling relaxed and calmer than he had been in a long time; like a man who had wrestled with all alternatives and suddenly knew he selected the right one.

"I came," he began, "because instead of forgetting you as I once thought I could, you kept coming on until you were there all the time."

"I don't believe you." She snapped it.

"I also came here because I wanted to take you to bed. Now I know it's impossible," he hastened to add.

"What about your wife?"

"What difference does it make?"

"A lot, to me."

There was no turning back. And he didn't want to. The fact that she had not ordered him out by now was enough. If she was willing to listen there was hope and she was going to get the whole damn truth.

"I made a mistake," he said. "I might have had a chance to marry you and I didn't. I married a woman for her money, because I didn't believe in love, didn't know what it was until I lost it." He waited a moment and then went on. "My wife wears dresses and high heels, silks and perfumes. But it's a masquerade, because that's where her femininity stops. She's cold, frigid . . . never melts. I'm telling things I've never breathed to a soul . . . things I find difficult to accept myself."

"I'm sorry, Sam."

"That's not all. She drinks. Right now she's lying in bed, dead drunk. Tomorrow morning there'll be a hangover and she'll start over again." He finished and she didn't say a word, just kept looking at him. "I want another chance," he finally said. "On your terms, whatever they are."

She shook her head. "There are no terms, there is no chance. I gave you up when you were single. Not because you wouldn't marry me. . . . I'm not sure I would have had you. Because of what you are . . . what you still may be."

He leaned forward in the seat as if to close the gap between them. "I have changed. The lesson was hard but I learned it. If I would have known a year ago what I know today there would be no marriage." Her eyes seemed to soften—it was a sign of hope— an opening. "Just give me a chance."

"It wasn't easy leaving you, Sam. The ache was there a long time. I'm over it."

"Now can be a new beginning. You'll see it'll be different."

"It is different. You've got a wife." She got up. "No, Sam. I won't go through it again. It isn't worth it. I don't think you're worth it." She reached for his coat. "You'd better go."

He took the coat and her hand. "Suppose I get a divorce?"

"Call me when you do."

"In the meantime, let me see you. Once in awhile." They were at the door. He tried to kiss her, she turned her face, clung to him a moment and pushed him away.

"Please go!"

He went out the door.

He slept in the guest room that night. The next morning he left early, instructing Mrs. Weber to call him at the office the moment Beck stirred. There were a few things that had to be settled that day and he had no intention of competing with a bellyful of booze. He wanted her clear-headed, right after breakfast, as sober as she ever got. He got the call at ten o'clock and rushed home. Beck was in the breakfast room sipping coffee, wrapped in a robe, her hair loose and looking like hell.

"What are you doing home at this hour?" she demanded.

"You were too drunk to talk to last night."

"Huh." She lit a cigarette, inhaled, choked, coughed, took another drag, crushed it and swallowed the last of the coffee.

"You said a lot of things that weren't true about me and your father. They need straightening out."

She jumped up, almost upsetting the chair. "What things! That you used him, he served his purpose and you threw him out!" She ran from the room almost slipping on the hall tiles, into the living room where she wheeled on him as he followed and shook a warning finger. "I know you. And I know what you're after!"

It was worse than he thought. Someone had been talking to her and it wasn't Art; it was Paula! The resentment was still there, maybe bigger, festering. He had to be careful. Meeting Beck's fury head-on could blow everything to hell. He did not say a word, seated himself in a chair, and watched her as he lit a cigarette and waited for her to pour out everything. But she was finished, spent. She wrapped her robe around herself tighter, shivered, and collapsed on the couch. Her head was thrown back and her eyes closed and a hand hung limp over the side.

He waited a few minutes. "Beck," he called softly. She stirred and opened her eyes. "There's a lot to talk about. Things are tangled." She was looking at him now, but without hate, like a spanked child who wants to be stroked. He went up to her and touched her hair. "I've taken the day off. Why don't you shower and freshen up. We'll take a drive to the ocean—down the coast maybe—have lunch and spend the day."

She started to speak, shook her head and made her way upstairs.

They drove south along the coast, lunched at Laguna, walked along the beach, strolled through the shops, and returned home. All during the day she listened and hardly spoke. He made up his mind to confirm part of what she hurled at him about Art. Telling her how kind Art was to him when they first met, teaching him the fine points of the business, introducing him to important people, watching over him like he would a son, he traced the ensuing years carefully. He understood the torment Art was going through, but it happened to many men, could be his own lot some day and when he changed the course of his business and Art did not fit in he consented to Beck's wish, which was also his, and offered to back Art in his own deals. But now the market was changed; deals were not easy to find and he had loaned Art money and would have given him more. When he discovered he wasn't working, was hanging around the club, drinking, he thought he needed a jolt to bring him back and though it hurt he decided to be firm until Art came to his senses. Sure that Paula had been the source of her information he went on to say it was only natural for a man to blame someone else when explaining his failure to his wife.

Beck understood, she finally said, was sorry about the outburst. When she began to chastise herself for her drinking, her feeble performance as a wife, he told her that adjustment to marriage was difficult and there must be compromise, forgiveness, and above all patience and that he would make every effort for them to succeed. It was worth it because he loved her.

That night she did not drink and they went to bed early. Showered and perfumed, she doused the lights and came to him. He handled her with all the perception he possessed, his lips cruised from the lobe of an ear to a nipple to every crevice and back to her lips, she would moan and relax then cry out and tense. One moment her fingers would feather him, the next dig into his flesh, she tongued him and bit him, pressed against him and pushed him away and then for the first time since they married she grabbed his prick. He rolled her over and slipped it in. At first she swiveled her ass then, with a cry, she stopped and as he kept on pumping he felt her stiffen and by the time he poured it into her she was as still as a corpse.

From that night on, Beck would not allow him to touch her.

When he would attempt to kiss her, she would offer her cheek and on one or two occasions when he thought he might crawl into her bed she turned on her side and buried her head in the covers. At first he made advances for the sake of harmony, when he discovered their relationship was better served by total abstinence he substituted cordiality and good humor.

In the meantime he contacted Art and told him he needed someone to work with Delaney, knew of no one more capable and whom he could trust and put him on the payroll at a hundred a week. This was three times the going rate for stumblebums and Art accepted it with such slobbering gratitude Samson thought he was going to douse his hand with kisses. For him it was an insurance policy and cheap. He instructed Delaney to use Art without seeming to order him around and keep him in a jacket and tie and with clean hands.

With the new arrangement in his home came a bonus he could not have hoped for. In the past, whenever he was to be detained he would call Beck, explain the nature of his engagement, and tell her the approximate time to expect him. It was foolish, she now explained, he wasn't a child and did not have to call her. By the same reasoning she informed him she did not want to feel constrained. If she was not at home when expected he was not to be concerned.

He had not neglected Posey. Hounding her with a week of calls after the evening at her apartment, he finally got her to lunch. She was distant, cold, but there was an opening and he knew it. There were flowers delivered to her desk every morning, notes tucked inside gifts, then a dinner, then another, and when they were together he barely touched her, tantalized, teased her until one night when they returned from dinner and he pecked her cheek at the door and prepared to leave she took his arm and led him back to the room.

It was better than it had ever been. Whatever their differences they were evened up in bed. He kept up the shower of gifts, insisted on paying her rent, bought her a new car, raised her standard of living too high for her to ever afford it without him.

As for the future? He loved her; as far as he was concerned they were as good as married. His wife was an arrangement, a corporation that would some day be liquidated. There were arguments, of course, periods when Posey was depressed, tired of hiding, but there were weekends at Palm Springs, trips to San Francisco, a whole week once at Coronado, and plans, all kinds, Hawaii and Mexico and someday—soon—he would show her New York and then Europe . . . if there was no war.

And Beck was now content. He did not touch her, never asked where she had been, let her drink without complaint, saw to it she got to bed when she was drunk, paid the bills, and supported her father. Everything was oiled smooth. Posey, though chafing at times, could hardly be considered discontent and though Art was getting a hundred a week for twenty-five dollars' work, any alternative would bring on complications. He was pensioned, on the shelf, easy to watch. He had a small office where Delaney kept him busy with paperwork, used him to run to the bank, deliver documents, and, on rare occasions, Samson had him look into a piece of land that had been submitted. The size of him was cut and with it his pride.

By the end of 1940 Samson had close to two thousand units finished or under construction representing a total value of six million dollars in which his equity roughed out at a million. So well had they been financed that his cash investment in all was less than a hundred thousand dollars. There was a lot at stake now, more than he had ever imagined, and when the Selective Service Act was instituted and he had to register for the draft he made a careful study of the situation and proceeded with plans to keep on the home front.

So-called "defense plants" were springing up everywhere, vacant stores and backyard garages were converted into machine shops, guys with two hundred bucks and a steady hand were going into business, the aircraft plants were building assembly lines, the tooling for war had begun. They weren't taking men

his age yet—it was a peacetime army—for defense; no boy would
be sent overseas the president said and so forth. . . . War or not,
overseas or at home, the army meant a uniform and it took you
out of circulation. The place to be was out, making things a war
used up and selling it for as much as you could get. In the army
cooks became clerks and clerks became tank commanders and
sometimes even generals and there were gravediggers too. There
were many ways to dodge the draft, some brought shame, others
honor, presidential citations, and a million bucks. He was only
nine years old at the outbreak of World War I, but he remembered casualty lists and war millionaires, the Marne and Chateau
Thierry and burgeoning industry. And when the war was over
the rich slacker was twice blessed when he gave a man with a
stump a job. Samuel Johnson once said that patriotism was the last
refuge of a scoundrel but he was talking of a different brand. During a war patriotism was a deadly blunder.

The first thing Samson did was to contact Howard Ebberly.
He met the senator in his Los Angeles office, freshened his memory concerning the cash he had funneled into his campaign, and
then questioned him. He wanted all the information he could be
given about the draft, who they were going to take, and who
might get a deferment. He made it very clear that the only reason
he came to see him was that he wanted to do his duty and be sure
his talents were not dissipated in a position that could be filled by
a clod.

"They might take me in the army and have me shoveling
horseshit or digging graves. They do that, you know."

"How about a desk job . . . in Washington. Or maybe in
L.A.?"

"That's just it. At best I'd be a clerk. And God knows they
have enough of those around. Listen, Howard," he said, with all
the patriotic fervor he could pitch, "I want to help my country. If
I have to do my duty on the home front, then damnit I'll give up
the glory."

Ebberly asked him the number and location of his draft board.

"I think Charley Simpson is on that one. He lives in the neighborhood and I know he heads a board. I'll talk to him."

"Remember," Samson said, as he left. "I don't want any favors. Just information."

He got the information the next day.

"Charley's your man all right. They won't be taking men your age for awhile. Maybe never. Unless we get into a war. He also told me they're going to lay off men in essential industries. They'll take married men with children first."

That was all he wanted to know. Now he went to see Tipton. Martin covered his disappointment about the resumption of Samson's relationship with Posey with a good-natured observation that Posey's rejection confirmed his good taste, a young woman worth pursuing would have better sense than to play with a man who rolled over the side of fifty.

With Martin he was candid. "I had to register for the draft. And I don't want to end up a buck private in the army. I want to buy a defense plant."

Tipton laughed.

"What's so funny?"

"Three other clients are looking for the same thing. An actors' agent, a stockbroker, and an attorney. Looks like there won't be enough of them to go around."

"How would you like to be bugled out of a cot at dawn and have some asshole with two or three stripes on his arm screaming at you before breakfast?"

"I wouldn't like it. But war is hell, remember? And Mr. Hitler can't be talked to anymore, he's got to be shot at. If some of you didn't think he was a funny man with a mustache and others that he was a savior this wouldn't have happened. There was a time he could have been stopped with a slingshot. Now it's going to take everything we've got, and England and France, and God knows who else."

"That's just it, Martin. It's going to take everything we've got, including married men without children age thirty-two."

"Tell me, don't you think there are such things as just wars? Don't you realize if Germany takes over Europe we're next?"

"I don't think Hitler's going to take over Europe. And if he does there's an ocean separating us. Anyway, that's not my immediate concern. There'll be plenty of itching suckers in line to sign up. There always have been. I don't like soldiering, don't like orders shouted at me, lousy food, lumpy beds; I like to sleep late, go to bed when I damn please and I like living. Now, what do you suggest?"

It looked like Martin was going to try one more recruiting pitch, then he smiled wryly. "All right, get your defense plant."

"Any ideas?"

"Try an ad. Put it in the *Times* classified. Money to invest in machine shop, defense plant. Something like that. You'll get answers."

He put a box ad in the following day and within two weeks received over a hundred replies. He weeded through the letters, checked half a dozen and ended up talking to the most likely prospect in a plant on Robertson Boulevard. It seemed to have everything he wanted: small, but still big enough to have landed a contract with Douglas for some magnesium parts, adequate equipment, room for expansion, and a hungry owner with big dreams, a head full of tools and dies and hands that could tear down anything and put it together blindfolded. Jack Gilbert was thirty, he told Samson, had a fused hip, was 4F and was tooled up for the duration. They were seated in a glass-enclosed crib that served as his office from which he could watch every worker without rising from his chair.

"The help you get these days. . . ." He shook his head. "You gotta watch them like a hawk."

"What did you make before you got into aeroplane parts?" Samson asked.

"A little bit of everything. Rebuilt transmissions, rear ends, made a few parts for a local washing-machine company. Did a little tool and die work too." He held up his hands and spread his fingers. "They can do anything," he said, looking at them admiringly. "With the right tools I could do surgery on a fly."

They toured the shop, he explained the machines, caressed them like pets, showed Samson the tool room, wiped his hands on some waste, and returned to the office.

"I'm running twelve hours a day now," he said. "Soon it'll be twenty-four. I need more machines and a building for them. The shack next door is for rent. It'll take two big turrets and a half-dozen engine lathes. And there's room for storage."

Samson asked about his rent, the length of his lease, cash position, and accounts receivable. He had two years on his lease and an option for five more and as his receivables grew his cash position became weaker.

"I can hock my accounts but it costs too much. Anyway, that'll only take the pressure off for awhile. I want to buy more machines and take the place next door. I think this is just beginning. We're in for a long war. What do you think, Mr. Duke?"

Samson agreed and they got down to specifics. The book value of the plant was twenty-five thousand dollars on which he owed five. He wanted an investor to put up an equal sum plus an amount to match the accounts receivable, out of which he would clear the debts and create a fifty-fifty partnership.

"Would you be active?" he asked.

Not to be active would not go well with the draft board. He told Gilbert he would have to be on the payroll, act as controller, but that the work would be done in his own office where he expected him to send daily reports. The salary could be small.

"I draw a hundred and fifty a week now plus a little for expenses," Gilbert said. "It may sound like a lot, but I'm always here. Put in sixteen, eighteen hours a day."

He had Martin's office send a man down to check the books and found them sound. The deal was made. The business was to be incorporated, each was to receive fifty per cent of the stock. They were to draw profits moderately and only after a reserve was built up. And Gilbert was to make all decisions.

"It isn't that I want to be the boss," Gilbert explained as they sat in Tipton's office before signing the papers. "It's just that I built this from a bench lathe in my garage. It's like you raised a kid."

They signed the documents, agreed that Martin's office would do the auditing, and then he invited Gilbert to lunch.

"You have no idea how big this thing can get," he told Samson over coffee. "It's just a question of getting help, the machines and the space for them. There's talk that Douglas is going to hire thousands more. Lockheed, too. I can get all the orders I want. But I got to deliver on time and the parts must fall in the tolerance. Now it's easy, but later on it'll be stuff within one-ten thousandths. Engine lathe work, highly precision. Maybe tools and dies. That'll be big money."

He not only bought insurance against the draft, he thought as he left Gilbert, it looked like the business could pay all the premiums and leave a bundle besides.

CHAPTER FIFTEEN

Only those who lived in fantasy and politicians speaking for home consumption talked of the United States not getting into the war. Roosevelt called for war production on a twenty-four-hour, seven-day-a-week basis. New army camps were being built, others reactivated, and recruits poured into them by the thousands. With the talk of price ceilings, priorities for nonessential goods including building materials, Samson decided to pull out of construction and diversify. As the last of his buildings were being completed, he called in Delaney, who seemed to have acquired a veneer to go with the responsibilities Samson had given him and the money that went with it.

"I think you're right, Sam," he said, as they huddled over the figures of the last building. "The material houses are getting independent and I'm losing men to the war plants. Our pay is good, but the buggers are looking for deferments." His jaw was always squared now even when the pipe wasn't stuck in it.

"Finish the building and we'll quit. Then I want you back to supervising the managers. How much help will you need?"

He developed a habit of speaking slowly as if every utterance was preceded by profound thought. Samson had to wait until he lit the damn pipe. "I'll need the maintenance crew and one man. A flunkey."

"Fire everybody else when the building is finished. Now send Ruth Bennett in."

He told her of his plans and asked her how much help she would need when he closed the building business.

"I can handle everything with two girls."

"We'll have twenty-five hundred units and the books for the machine shop."

"I've been doing the Gilbert books on the weekend. Don't worry, Mr. Duke, I can handle it."

"All right. But give yourself a raise. Fifty a month starting the first."

"Really, it isn't necessary."

"Take it and don't argue. By the way, how's your daughter?"

Ruth Bennett beamed. "She's at U.C.L.A. Going to be a teacher. Without this job, steady and all, I don't know how I would have managed."

He came out from behind the desk and draped an arm about her shoulder. "I'm glad I was able to afford you."

"You'll never be sorry." She had a handkerchief out now and began dabbing.

"Now get to work."

He remained at his desk the rest of the afternoon going over his holdings, computing his income, adding cash and other assets. With a ten per cent vacancy factor the apartments would net over twenty-five thousand a month after all expenses and mortgage payments. There was other income too, from loans, dividends on stocks, and other interest. His assets including the money from Beck's estate exceeded two million and with the money piling up it would increase every day. The war could bring inflation and by the end of it his equities could increase three or four times in value, the cash he had to play with—over a half million now—could double or more by the time peace came.

And the defense plant—it could be the biggest bonanza of all. Beck was his only problem. What would she do if she found out about Posey? He was certain she knew he was chasing around but suppose the other woman had a name, an identity? He never knew what she was thinking. In the mornings she would be nursing a hangover, too sick to talk, and at other times whenever he got home, early evening or late at night, she was drunk. Round the clock, never a letup, starting before noon and ending when she was out on her feet. Many times he would find her on the bed, fully clothed and snoring like an animal. And it seemed that Paula was with her every day. Paula had a maid now and could leave the child and he would find her there in the evening, around the pool during the day and on occasion she would sleep over. Would she talk some day when they'd be boozing and her brain was in a fog and her bitterness got on top and spilled?

He had to avoid a divorce. He would be cut like chop meat, divvied-up. More than half his assets were earned since they married and would be difficult to conceal.

That night he went home early, determined to spend more time with Beck. She liked golf, he would play with her more often; she played bridge, he would learn the game, and though she loved the theater he hadn't taken her in months. She was not home when he arrived. He had Mrs. Weber keep the dinner warm until eight o'clock when he finally sat down alone. At nine o'clock he called the club. She left an hour ago the doorman said.

"Was she alone?"

"Mrs. Jennings was with her."

An hour later the phone rang. It was Paula, babbling, crying. "We've been in an accident! Beck's hurt!"

"How bad?"

"I don't know," she wailed. "We're at the Good Samaritan."

He couldn't get another thing out of her and hung up. Paula was sitting in the hospital room when he arrived. Her shoes were off, her stockings torn; she had an arm bandaged and scratches over her face. Beck was lying on the bed, asleep it seemed, her lip and one eye swollen. A gash snaked across her nose.

He rang for the nurse and was told that Beck would be all right, was just bruised and had a couple of broken ribs. Then the nurse took him aside.

"There's a policeman downstairs, Mr. Duke. You had better see him."

He was in the waiting room and read from a pad. "Speeding and drunk driving. Ran over the curb and into a pole. I should have taken them to Georgia Street Receiving but it happened right across from here." He waved the pad. "There'll be drunk driving charges, Mr. Duke."

Samson gave him his card, thanked him, and told him they would be available.

He stayed with Beck until she awoke, opened the good eye, looked around the room, saw him and moaned. He went to her side. "You're going to be all right. Is there much pain?" She nodded and he called the nurse. After giving Beck a sedative, the nurse suggested he leave. "She'll probably sleep until morning. Why don't you return then."

He called his lawyer in the morning, gave him the information, was told not to worry and went to the hospital. Beck was sitting up in bed. The eye was blue and the lip looked like a blob of uncooked dough. She touched her face gingerly and she began to sob. "What a mess I made . . . of myself—of everything."

"It'll heal. You'll never know you were in an accident."

"It isn't only that," she blubbered, but she couldn't go on.

"Don't try to talk. I know it's difficult."

"How's Paula?" she asked.

"Just a few scratches and a torn pair of stockings."

"When I think of what could have happened . . ." Beck shuddered.

"Don't think about anything. Just rest. The doctor said you can go home tomorrow. In a couple of weeks you'll be as good as new."

She closed her eyes and in a few minutes was snoring gently. He left word that he would return later in the afternoon, then rushed off for an appointment with Teddy Hofstedter. The market was jittery, had been for a year, there was little volume and the blue chips had stalled. Most of his stock investments were in motors, steel, and utilities, sure things for the long haul. He had been playing around with a few dogs for amusement more than anything else and felt the time had come to dump them and look into the war babies. Hofstedter was to have a list prepared.

Teddy had shaved off his silly mustache and combed his hair straight back right after Hitler and Stalin made their pact. There was no more talk of "wermacht" and "stukas," words he had uttered in pure German and when there was talk of war around the club he remained silent. Though Samson had no use for him personally, Hofstedter had the German trait for thoroughness and his knowledge of the market had kept him out in front.

"Here they are," he said, handing Samson a list. "No guarantees, mind you, but everyone is geared for defense. They'll grow as long as the war lasts. Some are selling at ten times and a couple at eight and everyone has a backlog that'll keep them going for a year."

Samson looked over the names carefully. There were aircraft and parts companies, some electronics, a clothing firm, and a munitions manufacturer.

"They'll never pay dividends," he went on. "Every dollar of profit will go into expansion."

"What about peace? Suppose the war ends?"

Hofstedter shrugged. "It's a guess. They're a good buy now. Some of these companies can triple their production in a year. If peace comes, it'll be a dirty word. Then you get out."

Samson was sure the "word" wouldn't be around for a long time. Relying on Hofstedter's suggestions he selected six of the stocks and gave him the order to buy at the current market. Hofstedter called for the latest quotations and tallied the order. "It'll be around a hundred thousand dollars."

"I'll leave a check."

"Margin?"

"Cash. I don't like your interest rates."

"It's a lot of money, Sam."

"It's on a favorite."

"May I offer a suggestion?"

"Sure, go ahead."

"My judgment's been good." Samson nodded. "Things are tricky now. Sometimes we get things long before it hits the ticker. Let me be the judge of when to sell. There wouldn't be time for a phone call."

Samson agreed, with the understanding he be notified immediately.

Beck was more cheerful when he returned that afternoon. She had taken some food and though the eye looked worse, the swelling on the lip had gone down.

"I saw myself in the mirror," she said as he came in. "How can you stand the sight of me?"

"It's a good sight. You're alive. It could have been otherwise." He brought her flowers and magazines, sat with her for an hour, and left after making arrangements to pick her up at checkout time the following day.

He went to see Posey that night and told her what happened. Her face was expressionless as he described the accident and Beck's condition; she just listened, didn't say a word. Then she turned on him.

"I hate myself. Hate everything I'm doing, everything I'm thinking."

"What are you talking about?"

"Don't pretend. You're never going to get a divorce and I know it." She ignored him as he tried to interrupt. "So, what am I waiting for? For your wife to die!"

"Posey!"

"Oh, stop it! I watched you tonight when you described the accident. There was disappointment in your voice. 'Just bruised and a few broken ribs.' You would have been happy if it was fatal, wouldn't you? Well, I would have been happy too. That's the truth! And that's why I despise myself. I don't know your wife. She's never done me any harm. For all I know she's a nice woman. Probably too damn good for you!"

"Too good for me! She's kicked me out of her bed and she drinks all day long."

She was standing close to him, her eyes wild. "Why—don't—you—divorce—her!"

"Because I haven't the heart to."

"You? *You* haven't the heart!" Now she was laughing without control and when he tried to touch her, stop her, she brushed him aside and kept it up. Suddenly she stopped. "Your heart is custom-made for it. You know why you won't divorce her and so do I. It's because of the money." She spat it. "You married her for it and now you won't divorce her for the same reason!"

"I've given you everything you've wanted, bought you things you never dreamed of having, paid your rent, the car you're driving is a gift, even that dress you're wearing came out of my pocket."

"You bought me too cheap. Now I'm through. Do you hear! Get out!" She ran from the room and slammed the door.

He started to run after her, then stopped. The pressure had been too great. Why continue it? He could deny nothing, just offer palliatives that would wear off like aspirin. To have to lie to and cheat a wife was enough; adding a mistress, contentious, volatile, and suspicious was too much. The course was too rocky, the rewards inadequate. It was just as well this way. He left the apartment and headed home. He'd forget her, for a while anyway.

He brought Beck home from the hospital the following morning and spent the day with her. Paula came over to visit in the afternoon and it was decided she and Beck would spend a week or so at the Palm Springs house the moment Beck felt a little stronger.

"At least I can keep out of sight until the eye heals," Beck said.

"Maybe I'll bring Carla," Paula suggested.

It was a good idea he told them and said he would have Delaney drive them down. "It's a long ride and you're jittery."

Beck was away two weeks and returned on a Sunday. It was a warm summer day and he was lounging around the pool going over Ruth Bennett's latest reports on the machine shop. The plant was running three shifts, orders were backlogged until the end of the year, and Jack Gilbert was dickering for a vacant lot in the rear for further expansion. It looked like there was going to be a Christmas bonus, he mentioned in a memo, an amount equal to his total investment.

Samson was thinking about peacetime industrial expansion, demand for new products, and the rebuilding. A week before, Hitler, with most of Europe mopped up, marched into Russia and some experts thought he would have the country in a month. We would be in it any day he was sure, and the real struggle would begin. In the meantime, the continent was being systematically destroyed and when the war was over there would be little left, and win or lose the U.S. would have to rebuild and feed the world. If Germany conquered Britain before we got in too deep he was certain we would make peace. The Atlantic Ocean was a big leap and neither power could cross it with enough arms and men to conquer the other. So, the world would be divided and the mark and the dollar would be the medium of exchange and business would go on as usual. Look at history and charter the course, money talked and power grabbed, and they had one language and no country.

So deeply was he engrossed he did not notice Beck who stood in the doorway watching him.

"You're lost," she said.

He jumped. "I didn't expect you so early. Let me look at you," he said, as she turned for inspection. "You look wonderful. What have you done?"

"Salads and sun and no liquor. Sam, I feel wonderful. I guess I needed the jolt of the accident to wake me up. It was getting pretty bad, wasn't it? The drinking, I mean."

"It was, Beck. Also, my attorney had a helluva time with the drunk driving citation. He got it quashed but almost didn't make it. If there's a next time there won't be a chance." Then he smiled. "Anyway, you look great."

She did look good. The loss of weight added planes to her face and with the exception of a faint discoloration about the eye, was as good as new.

"How are the ribs?"

"Fine. They're still taped, but no pain." She eyed him critically. "You look tired. Been working hard?"

"I've been busy. There'll be a letup though. We're finishing the last building."

"What about the army, Sam? I mean, do you think they'll take you?"

"When they get around to old men, they will." He did not tell her about the defense plant and thought he would keep it quiet for awhile.

She got up and stretched her arms heavenward, wriggled her fingers and looked at their tips. "I've never felt better in my life," she said, twirling a couple of times and settling down beside him. "I want to do something about it. Sort of celebrate."

"What?"

"We've never had a house-warming. Let's give a party, a big one. The weather is ideal, we can serve outside. I'd like to have Martin and Sylvia, Paula and my father. There's a few from the club, and you can invite business contacts and maybe Mr. Delaney and Ruth Bennett. What do you say?"

"It's a swell idea."

She picked a Saturday a month away, grabbed a pencil, and began to make a list. They spent an hour going over names and agreed on fifty. He included Ebberly and Turner, was sure Delaney would stay clear of Inez and put him on the list, Clarke Jones, Hofstedter, and a half-dozen others.

"I'll take care of everything," Beck said. "You've enough to do. Let's see," she said, excitedly. "There'll be invitations, decorations for the garden, the caterer . . . oh, yes, music. A little band for dancing." She rattled on, made notes, looked up phone numbers, and addresses, called Paula, told her about the plans bubbling like a teenager discussing a date. That night they had an early dinner, went to a movie, and got home around midnight.

He did not know what to expect when they went to bed. Once, during the movie she had taken his hand but it seemed like an unconscious act. So far, there had not been a gesture or look to suggest a change in her habits. They undressed, she got into her bed, turned off the light, and said goodnight.

During the next few weeks he found himself involved with the excitement Beck had generated around the party. She enlarged the guest list, ordered a bigger band, lanterns for the pool area, and favors for the guests. Mrs. Weber got a new outfit—starched cap and all—there was to be a butler in tails and a couple of young men to park the cars. It wouldn't be a party, but a ball, Beck's debut. Or, perhaps a clearance. The cause of the accident was gossiped about at the club and he imagined the select cadre was concerned. Anyway, he was delighted with the change that came over her, and if giving up booze was not replaced with a need to perform in bed he could contemplate a long marriage without unpleasant tasks.

Paula arrived at the house early on the day before the affair to help Beck with the final touches. Coming home that evening, he was about to enter the house when the door flung open and Paula ran past him sobbing violently, sped to her car and streaked down the hill. As he came into the hall he saw Mrs. Weber escape to the kitchen and close the door. All the fears he had were confirmed when he reached the living room. Beck was sprawled on the couch, her hand clutched a tall glass that rested on the carpet, a half-empty bottle of liquor and a split of soda was on the table next to a cigarette spinning smoke from the tray like a signal.

For an instant he was stunned, then all the fury and distaste he had ever felt balled up inside like a cocked missile. With a cry of rage he ran to the couch, grabbed the drink from her hand and flung it against the wall. Then he pulled her from the prone position, sat her up, slapped and shook her, and dragged her to her feet.

"You drunken bitch!" he shouted. "Just one more day! You

couldn't wait one more day!" She was dead weight as he held her up, her head rolled and her eyes were lost in their sockets. He slapped her again, she opened her eyes, looked at him and then spat full in his face. At that moment he could have beaten her to a pulp but remembered the party, that too much had been done, that an excuse for a last-minute cancellation would be just that, an excuse, and even the real reason would be mild compared to the poison that would drip from the wagging tongues. Well, by God, there was going to be a party and Beck was going to be at that door greeting the guests, elegant and charming and cold sober if he had to work on her all night and guard her all day! He flung her over his shoulder like a sack and carried her upstairs.

Disgusted with the sight and smell of her but fearful of letting her out of his sight he did not leave her all night. He awoke early and stole downstairs to corner Mrs. Weber in the kitchen. Sure that she had taken sides as housekeepers generally do, he had not paid enough attention to her to know where she stood. He suspected her sympathies were with Beck—their contact was closer —they would occasionally huddle and talk and even joke at times. When he greeted her as she sat at the kitchen table sipping coffee she jumped up and the look on her face indicated she knew what he was after.

"I want to talk to you," he said. She nodded. He came directly to the point. "What happened here yesterday afternoon, Mrs. Weber? There's no time for games."

She looked at the door leading to the service porch as if it offered a means of escape, looked back at him and just shook her head. "Nothing really happened. Your wife and Mrs. Jennings were in the living room talking. I guess they had some disagreement. They did raise their voices."

"How long had they been drinking?"

"I don't know. Maybe an hour or two."

Then he asked if she heard anything they said, she swore she didn't, never listened in, and then her lips clamped tight and her look became defiant and he knew damn well her mouth would remain shut.

"All right. Clean the mess in the living room and I want every bottle of liquor in the house locked in the cabinet. Then give me the key."

She started to scurry from the room, then stopped. She sucked in her lower lip and clamped her teeth on it, a habit she had to keep from uttering something she wanted to say but was afraid to. Then she blurted.

"I got to say something."

"Sure, Mrs. Weber."

"I don't think Mrs. Duke and Mrs. Jennings are good for each other."

He took her hand and led her to a chair. She was comfortable now, her hands in her lap, ready to talk. "Yes. You see the fight yesterday was not the first time. Mrs. Jennings used to come over a lot, before the accident, that is, and . . . well, there used to be a lot of fights. Pretty bad ones."

"Do you know what they were about?" he asked casually.

Mrs. Weber smiled. "I never listen," she said. Samson dismissed her. She wasn't going to say anything more. Not now.

But what could Beck and Paula possibly squabble about? The baby? No. Beck would have confronted him at once. Was it about money? Was Paula begging for Art and herself? No, Beck was generous. He thought of other things, but they made no sense or did not ring true and he made his way upstairs confused and certain he did not have the answer.

After he showered, dressed, and returned to the room, Beck began to stir. First it was a groan, then she twisted in bed, then her eyes opened and she looked up at the ceiling. When he was sure she was wide awake he walked to the side of the bed. "Do you remember what happened?"

She kept staring at the ceiling. "I know what happened."

"Everything?"

"Everything."

"Then we can get right down to essentials. Over seventy-five people are coming here tonight. It was your idea, your party. It's going on . . . as scheduled. And you're not going to touch a drop, smell a cork, until the last of them leave. Do you understand?"

She nodded.

"I don't know whether your drinking caused the fight or whether it was the other way around. I don't care. But I'll tell you this, if you want to kill yourself there are easier ways. Boozing is long and painful."

He left her struggling to get out of bed and went downstairs. After some food and a pot of coffee, she seemed better, sober, almost herself and went about the final arrangements for the party. They barely spoke all afternoon and though she appeared contrite, at times he also detected a new note of coldness, defiance. It was as if she had turned a corner and they had lost contact.

The guests were due at eight o'clock and about an hour before, as he was going upstairs to dress, he heard her on the phone. She was talking to Paula, softly, apologizing it seemed, and when she joined him in the bedroom he saw a smile trace her face for the first time that day.

Only Beck's face stood out clearly that night, the others were fuzzy and dim, their sounds monosyllabic. He moved among the guests with a fixed smile, patted a shoulder, complimented, flattered, never lingered, wove through and by the time everyone arrived, managed to enact an acceptable role of a host. So intense was his concern about Beck that the blurry visages of all the others left him only with impressions of forms and shapes, blobs of color and truncated speech. To Teddy Hofstedter's exultation at Hitler's break with Stalin, he managed a nod to a ready smile. Clarke Jones, waving a pipe, got a slap on the back when he brought up the healthy state of their real estate with an appreciative wink. And when Martin Tipton arrived, a fluff of white above his favorite blue, his hand waved across the room and then

Paula, later than the others—black monochrome—relieved only by the pale olive of a face. He saw George Turner, a bulge where he stood with Inez a sliver at his side. As the room filled, the talk became a jabber, then a din, and the music began and a blaring saxophone added to the cacophony. Beck, tall, elegant, her hair piled high, glided across the room, avoided his gaze, smiled greetings with hardly concealed grimness. The garden doors were opened, the orchestra moved outside and the dancers spilled out to the patio and soon their colors whirled like pinwheels. Those inside knotted into groups and their words became a hum. Then he remembered and looked for Delaney and saw him talking to Ralph Thompson and Inez Turner in another part of the room. For a moment he lost Beck and then found her, head above the others, talking in a corner with Paula and Sylvia Tipton. He got his first drink of the evening, and it hit his belly like hot flannel, spread and warmed. As he toured the room along the edges of the gathered groups, the talk was war, Smolensk and Moscow, blitzkrieg and panzers. Someone said it was as good as over. Others weren't sure. Another quoted from Senator Truman who said we ought to help whichever side is losing and let them kill each other off. He moved away as Hofstedter damned the senator and began a speech.

Outside, it was a waltz and the couples were close and the flickering lantern lights jerked shadows like puppets and then the music stopped and he saw Beck talking to the leader and dinner was announced. Soon the house emptied and chairs scraped and the waiters moved deftly and the patio was filled with the noise of eating. The table was arranged in a hugh L with Beck at the toe and his place at the top. He watched her from where he sat; she was no longer grim as she tossed her head and laughed. Wine was poured, glasses clinked, dishes clattered. The main course was served, everybody seemed to be talking at once, drowning out a violin which had begun to play.

A chill wind came up and after dinner everyone moved inside. The bar was stacked four deep again, there was brandy and liquors and there were groups again, smaller and louder, in the library and hall as well as the main room. Art Jennings was proclaiming, flushed and loud, dusting off "the good old days." Paula was talking to Martin and watching her husband with disgust as Beck came to her side, slipped an arm around her waist and whispered in her ear. Paula smiled, turned her back on Art, and resumed her conversation with Martin as Beck moved away. He had not said a word to her all evening. Now he approached her. She waited for him grimly and after he thanked her for "laying off" and complimented her for the success of the evening, she turned and walked away without a word.

The crowd had thinned, one batch left as soon after dinner as they could with grace, the less hardy drinkers started an exodus around eleven and after dismissing the help he stacked the bar in the living room for the boozers, the bachelors who had no place to go, and the couples who did but couldn't bear the thought of being there alone.

Now he relaxed. The Turners were in position, George was sunk in a chair and dazed, Inez took over a corner of the bar and just stared into her glass, a half-dozen drunks gathered around the piano where Clarke Jones banged away as three or four couples balancing drinks weaved on the floor. Art Jennings was still at it in the library, this time wearying his listeners with real-estate talk of the twenties and Teddy Hofstedter was plotting the Russian campaign on the back of an envelope to a group around the couch. Ralph Thompson was asleep in a corner chair next to a drink that had fallen from his hands.

It looked like those remaining were dug in. He decided to change into more comfortable clothes and wait for the opportunity to ease them out one by one. The bedroom door was slightly ajar, a soft light shone through the crack and as he was about to enter he heard the murmur of voices. At first he hesitated, thought some of the women were tidying up, then he opened the door cautiously. He stood on the threshold and looked around. At first he did not see anyone, then a drape moved at the far end of the room. Beck and Paula were standing in front of it, so close they were like one, and he slipped out silently as Beck cupped Paula's face in her hands and planted a kiss on her lips.

He ran downstairs. The party had entered a new phase, unrestrained now, a couple of the wives were giving a solo exhibition in the center of the floor, others circled them clapping hands; Hofstedter and his group were around the bar and as he rushed out the front door for air, time to think, he saw Inez in the hall, arms spread, turning to the music like a somnambulist.

CHAPTER SIXTEEN

During the next few months Beck and he saw little of one another. When his schedule brought him home early she managed to be away and after familiarizing himself with her routine, sleeping until noon, then coffee and the first drinks, days at the club, then cocktails and disappearing, he arranged his own affairs to keep their meetings brief.

At first, she concocted stories, left notes. Later she did not bother. After he started sleeping in the spare bedroom, they often did not see each other for days.

His first reaction after the night of the party was to confront her with what he had discovered, demand a showdown and a divorce. Then he realized the folly of it. Pride wasn't going to top good sense. Their marriage was dead, that was certain. The question now was how to bury it. He could go on this way indefinitely, but could she? According to Art, Paula was never home, neglected the child, and had defied him a couple of times when she rolled in late and drunk. He would wait, he thought, until the sight of him was more than she could stand and then there would be no haggling, just his terms to cut her loose.

She spent Thanksgiving at the Palm Springs house with Paula and little Carla. A few days after she returned he came home early not expecting to find her and looking forward to a quiet evening alone. Of late, when poor planning brought them together she would tank up fast and crawl up to bed to sleep it off. This evening, however, she appeared sober and even friendly as she greeted him. "Are you staying home for dinner?"

He nodded.

During the meal they hardly spoke and when he rose from the table she asked him to stay.

She was fidgeting with a fork drawing designs on the cloth and did not look up. "I guess we both have a lot of things on our minds," she began. "The fact is our marriage has failed."

"It's floundering," he smiled, "but it hasn't failed. Oh, it needs bolstering, it . . . well, adjustments are difficult."

"I've tried, Sam. It can't work."

He walked around the table, stood behind her and put his hands on her shoulders. "It means a lot to me, our marriage. I'm willing to endure anything before I throw it away."

She twisted out of his grasp. "It's no use. I can't go on."

For a few moments he said nothing. Then he walked around the table and faced her. "You'll have to go on. I don't want a divorce."

"Why?"

"I told you. This marriage is important to me. I want to give it every chance."

"Sam, you don't understand!" Her eyes were boring into his trying to tell him the thing she wouldn't dare utter. He held them for a moment and then said very slowly. "I *do* understand. But I prefer to wait." With that he left the room as she buried her head in her arms.

He spent the following Saturday night with a hooker and returned home after midnight, exhausted, aching for bed. Beck was not home, her space in the garage was empty. Since their discussion a week before she had been drinking more than ever, staggering in at all hours and they had not met. In spite of his fatigue he could not sleep, tossed for a couple of hours and at about two o'clock heard her car screech to a stop in the driveway. A few minutes later the front door slammed and he waited for her steps. Minutes went by and he crept out of bed and went out into the hall. The light was on downstairs and he heard the tinkling of a glass. Then he heard her. The sounds she was making were not cries, but moans as if every tear dried up and only the anguish remained. He left his door slightly ajar, returned to bed, and waited. Soon she was on the steps and he listened as she seemed to be dragging herself slowly, her sounds now a wail. In her room with the door shut the sounds continued, muffled. He rolled over and soon fell asleep.

Rising Sunday morning, still tired, he decided to cancel a golf date and spend the day lounging about. It was one of those delightful December days, so clear that the view from the patio was infinite. It was warm enough for outdoor eating and even a swim. So perfect was it for languishing that he hoped for no calls or visitors, a day of idleness. Beck would not be up until noon, and after last night's binge might remain in her room longer. He swam the pool a dozen times and then took a hot shower while Mrs. Weber prepared to serve him breakfast in the patio. On a lounge and sunning as he glanced idly through the morning papers he felt more relaxed than he had in months. Soon he became drowsy, half-dozed, awoke, and went off again his thoughts floating lazily. Aunt Annie's face appeared; it was in the beginning on the Jersey farm and he thought how beautiful she was, how her hair shone like polished copper, and how her eyes danced with a joy she never really had. He tried to picture her face the day she died but it eluded him, and then it appeared and he saw her hair dirtied with gray, fanned out on the pillow like a withered crown. And Dante's head lifted from the bed as he released her lifeless hand and left him alone in the room as he walked out crying like a child. All Samson could remember were his eyes, black and burning, and the stooped shoulders from the cigarmakers' bench. If only they could be here, both of them, to see what their hated world offered. What was their utopia compared to this?

It was after two when Samson opened his eyes. He was hungry, found Mrs. Weber in her room. After he asked her to prepare some sandwiches, he inquired if Beck had come down. She told him there wasn't a sound from her room, that she was probably still sleeping. After lunch he went over some papers, picked up a book and started to read, left it and dozed again. He was awakened by the shrill ring of the phone. He grabbed the patio extension. It was Art Jennings.

"Did you hear the news?" he shouted.

"What news?"

"The Jap bastards. They bombed us! Sunk the whole goddamn fleet. Killed thousands!"

"Will you calm down!" he demanded.

"Calm down hell! Turn on the radio!"

He ran inside and switched it on, sure that Art's account was colored with the usual license he took with facts and was shocked to find he had not exaggerated. There were things to do, he hardly knew where to start, and just as he was about to reach for the phone he heard a piercing scream, looked up and saw Mrs. Weber on the stairs and grabbed her. She was still screaming.

"Stop it and tell me what's wrong!"

She couldn't talk, spittle oozed from the corners of her mouth, her tongue thrashed about like a mute's and her eyes were wide and bulged as she jabbed her hand in the direction of Beck's room. He released her and ran to the open door, stumbled over a pile of clothes in the center of the floor and saw Beck sprawled across the bed. A leg dangled from the edge, she was nude from the waist up, her hair had fallen from the pins across her mouth and covered one eye and her hand covered a breast. As he approached the bed he thought he saw her move, was about to drag her, shake her out of a drunken sleep and he saw the movement again and it was a strand of hair whipped by a gust from an open window. Then he reached her side, brushed the hair from her face and felt its ice and saw that her mouth was wide open and her eyes were staring at the ceiling. He lifted her leg to the bed and it was cold, all of her was cold, and he closed the eyes but could not shut the mouth and after covering her with a blanket looked about the room. He found the bottle of pills—there was one left—and then he searched the top of the dresser, her desk, the tables beside the bed and there was no note. The phone was ringing again and he rushed downstairs. Mrs. Weber was sobbing into the receiver and when he grabbed it the party hung up.

"Who was it!"

"Mrs. Jennings. When I told her she just screamed and dropped the receiver."

"Go to your room," he ordered. "Don't answer the phone or talk to anyone!"

He called the doctor and then Martin and told him what happened.

"Call Ebberly, Turner, anyone you know. Get to the coroner. I don't want this in the papers. I don't want any publicity!"

The radio was still blaring the news: *"It has been reported that subs have been sighted off the Santa Barbara coast! The Coast Guard and planes have been alerted! Cabinet meeting called for eight-thirty this evening! Roundup of all Japanese by F.B.I. . . . !"* He switched it off. He had to be calm, think. . . . Beck was gone now and what he did or did not do would make no difference. There would be talk, all kinds, but as long as it was kept out of the papers he didn't care. Let them speculate, say what they damned pleased, everybody knew she was a drunk and alcoholics died every day.

He crossed the room and grabbed the phone. He didn't want Art there or Paula. He didn't want a wake.

Art answered. "Paula told me. She's hysterical."

"Keep her there. I'll call you later." The minute he hung up, Martin called.

"It's all arranged." He gave him the name of a North Hollywood mortuary. "Have them take the body there. I talked to the coroner. He'll have the autopsy done tomorrow. There'll be no publicity."

The doctor arrived and he took him upstairs. After a quick examination he called the mortuary and then the coroner.

"They'll be here within a half an hour. Do you want me to wait?"

"It won't be necessary. Just tell me the procedure."

"The coroner's office will send out a doctor to do an autopsy. Then the body is turned over for private rites."

They came in a panel truck and removed Beck's body on a stretcher covered with a sheet. They drove off and he called Mrs. Weber. Still dazed, she sat in her chair and stared. He had enough to do, didn't want her around.

"Take a few days off. I'll call you when I need you."

She packed her things and he called a cab. After she left he took the phone off the hook. He wanted no calls, no interruptions. He tried to feel some grief but there was none.

It was in the deck. If it hadn't been pills, it would have been booze or another accident. She just couldn't handle it . . . switching to women. His wedding night—God, he should have known! Well, she was gone now.

Pouring a stiff drink he turned on the radio. It was full of the war, there was talk of invasion, evacuating the coast and more about sighting Japanese subs, people were leaving Los Angeles in droves, there was panic. He called Delaney, told him about Beck, told him to say nothing after listening to his message of condolence and arranged to meet him in the office the first thing in the morning.

"People are leaving the city," he said. "We're going to lose a lot of tenants. Call the managers and get a report." Then he got Teddy Hofstedter.

"What do you think of the news?" he asked.

"They were still talking in Washington. Nomura and that other one! It was hypnotism, Asiatic style. We were being put to sleep."

"We're awake now. What about the market tomorrow?"

"It should be way off. Maybe for a week or two."

"What should I do?"

"Sit on everything."

He reached Jack Gilbert at the plant. Gilbert said he wished there were more than twenty-four hours in a day. They were working round the clock and it was just the beginning.

1945

CHAPTER SEVENTEEN

H e could see all the city from where he stood. It was the time
of the day he loved most, the sun dipping, everything bathed in
pure light. Like when dawn peeks in the east and the horizon is
streaked and all emerges from the dark. His apartment was on top
of the Chateau Baroque, a building he'd purchased three years before, a few months after Beck's death. It was just above the Sunset
Strip on a level plot, shielded by rows of poplars surrounding the
gardens and pool area. It was pleasant living really; his neighbors
minded their business and a separate elevator to his suite assured
him complete privacy. His apartment contained ten rooms, was
designed for the original owner-builder who left it in 1935 for a
federal prison after he was nabbed for fleecing in bogus stocks.
The man had excellent taste and in addition to some of the main
pieces which Samson retained he was loath to part with a portrait
of the former occupant which hung over the fireplace in the library. Done in a Renaissance style with warm skin tones emerging from a dark background, his predecessor stared sagely in the

garb of a Medici. The image, Samson told himself, was a constant reminder that you do not steal without a license.

It was getting dark, a cool ocean breeze swept the terrace, and he went inside. Martin Tipton and Jack Delaney were due after dinner for a meeting Samson called after the news of the Japanese surrender was flashed over the wires the day before. Pouring a drink, he splashed it with soda and carried it into the kitchen. Alex Bautista, who ran his house with the aid of a day maid, was pouring over the *Racing Form*. In his middle forties with sad eyes of a mare and jowls that sagged like a hound's, Alex moved about the house in a slow gait and Samson always expected him to sniff. The only time he was animated was when he talked to the book-maker, his main contact with the outside world and the cause of his constant insolvency. In exchange for Samson tolerating his gambling he performed his duties faithfully, was a fine cook, and watched the household expenses with the concern of a peasant. On occasion he drove for Samson and always kept the car shined like a hearse. His total absorption with the various racetracks made him impervious to everything else about him. He saw and heard nothing. He looked up from the *Racing Form* which was covered with his calculations.

"How are you doing?" Samson asked.

"Pretty good, pretty good." That meant his losses were light.

"I'm dining alone tonight. I won't need you later. You can take the car."

On his nights off Alex went downtown, to the Million Dollar Theater, where he took in a stage show and the Spanish-language double feature. In fact, that's all he ever did, except on the days he went to the local tracks.

"Thank you, Mr. Duke. Maybe I'll go to a movie. I'll make a pot of coffee and have cold cuts if you want some later."

Samson ate dinner on a small side terrace that was covered and shielded from the wind. Lighting a cigar, he thought about the evening ahead. He had his own ideas, but it never hurt to pick a brain. He would not give a nickel for all of Martin's political ideas, bleeding heart that he was, but the accountant had eyes for loopholes, particularly in the tax laws, and could make a book of them look like a brick of Swiss cheese. In addition to Martin's office handling his auditing and counseling, Samson made use of their legal department, particularly the services of Walt Covington. Only out of law school a few years, Covington graduated at the top of his class, made Law Review, and had every large firm in the country bidding for his services. Martin had landed him with a paid-in-full trip to Los Angeles the summer he took the bar exam, an apartment at Malibu, and, when Martin found out that Covington only took his eyes from a law book to look at a woman, he had them lined up at the beach. Walt was a little guy, five-four, a hundred-ten, eyes always squinting behind thick glasses; altogether an unimpressive looking gent. But his mind was honed and between his knowledge of the law and Tipton's experience Samson could be sure that Uncle Sam never owed him a dime. Though he paid well for the services he received and was assured of the best they had to offer, Samson liked a little insurance. So, during the war when urban lots and raw acreage dipped to near-Depression levels, he poured over a million in cash into land in Los Angeles and Orange Counties and saw to it that Tipton and Covington came in on a couple of deals.

For a brief period after Beck died, Martin and Samson barely spoke; business was conducted through Walt. Samson had campaigned hard and resumed his relationship with Posey, but she quickly gave the ultimatum: marriage or nothing. At first he went along, even talked about plans for the future. But he stalled and Posey finally wrung the confession that he wanted to wait—indefinitely. She tossed Samson out and Martin moved in. Duke was furious, told him so, and did not speak to him for months. Not long after, Posey met her man, an attorney in the office where she worked. After they were married, Martin and Samson made peace as they commiserated one night over a couple of fifths, decided they were brothers, and Posey was the best thing that got away.

Until a few months before, he hit and ran. For awhile it was a good game, therapeutic, and he played it with zest. Added to the large contingent Hollywood normally lured, were those who flocked to California to work in defense industries; the army had gobbled the young men and the lucky civilians had their pick. He sampled secretaries and professionals, a riveter and a waitress, would-be actresses and once, a colored whore. Finally he realized he had been getting the dessert without the meal, and one night when he rolled off a belly and lay awake in the dark he was startled and then shocked; he had forgotten the name of the woman he had just laid and his mind had to leap back and trace the events of the evening before she could be identified. Four nights in a row he had slept with a different one, the conversation leading to the sack had been the same, their flesh felt the same. Their passions were a spark and he wanted a flame. For a month he did not touch another woman and then one night he met Lee Marlowe at a party at Martin's house. She was a successful Broadway actress who had moved to California to fulfill a four-picture contract.

Divorced from a New York director, Lee Marlowe lived in a rented home in Brentwood with her five-year-old daughter and a maid. Samson took her to lunch, ran it through cocktails, then dinner, and by the time he drove her home, it was evident they connected. It was not only her looks that attracted him—a perky, Peter Pan face and a graceful body with promising lines; it was also her "no nonsense" attitudes that had a primitive quality. He felt an ease he had not experienced with another woman. She was a lot like Posey, even less inhibited, had a career, money, and no desire to rush into marriage. They were together constantly, in touch with each other every day. As far as he knew she saw no other men.

Tipton and Delaney were due any minute and as he was about to set up the liquor, the phone rang. It was Lee.

"How about coming over? Clara's off."

"I'm having a meeting at the house. I'm afraid it'll be too late."

"Call me later. I'll be up."

Tipton and Delaney arrived a little after eight, Martin was in a hurry, he said, with guests at home. He fixed himself a drink as

Jack Delaney sat on the sofa, puffing his pipe, composed as a sage. During the years he'd put on considerable weight, thickening all over, from his puffed-up cheeks, which half buried his eyes, to his behind which matched an enormous belly. Martin, on the other hand, had grown lean, his neck wrinkled and stringy, his face lined like a file.

Martin slid into a chair balancing his drink. "Why the urgent meeting?"

"Anything wrong?" Delaney asked.

"Everything's right. Except the war's over."

"But it was just over yesterday," Martin said. "The last guys who died aren't cold yet. And Sunday's a day of rest. Don't you remember?"

Samson ignored him. "There's going to be building—everything. Homes, apartments, commercial. I got the land. Just want to swap a few ideas."

Delaney knit his brows and clamped his jaws tightly, gripped the pipe with his teeth, a signal that he was thinking. Martin held his glass up to the light turning it as if examining its contents. Neither said a word.

Martin took a long drink and set the glass on the table beside him. "You know what I think? I think you're crazy."

"Thanks."

"All right," Martin said. "Maybe you're not crazy, maybe I'm just tired. But can you tell me why a man worth millions, single, no dependents, has to work? Let alone the first thing in the morning?"

"Cut out the philosophy."

Martin shrugged as Delaney smoothed his brow and removed the pipe from his mouth. "I think the thing to do," Delaney said, "is to sit back for awhile and see how things shape up. There are a lot of adjustments from war to peace," he offered.

Samson ignored him and turned to Tipton. "What are your ideas about building, Martin? Organization, structure, tax traps."

"I don't see what you can do tomorrow, next week or next

month. There are going to be changes. Even the tax laws will be modified."

"Suppose I go into the building business. Form another corporation. Will I be able to take capital gains?"

"It'll depend on the size of your venture. If it's big, you won't have a chance." He looked at his watch. "I've got to go. Don't know why in hell you dragged me here in the first place."

"I've been sitting on my ass four years. I'll go crazy if I don't begin to move."

Martin was at the door. "I know what you're looking for. I'll fill in Walt and we'll meet in a day or two." He was out of the apartment before Samson could say another word.

Delaney was making a sandwich and Samson poured himself a drink. "You'd think I was working for him," he said angrily.

"He did say he had guests," Delaney said, "and it *is* Sunday."

"It's Sunday after the war." Then he talked over the apartment house holdings. Delaney answered with grunts as he chomped on the huge sandwich and guzzled from a can of beer. The cream was off the depreciation, Samson told him, and he wanted to sell a few buildings a year until they were all disposed of. However, he would wait until the rent ceilings were lifted. Higher income would mean higher prices.

"What about capital gains?" Delaney managed between swallows.

"What about them?"

"Martin always said you can't take too many in any one year. We own fifty-three buildings."

"We'll sell some and trade others. I'll have to take chances. There's damn little depreciation left. It's all income now. And I'm working for Mister Sam not Uncle Sam."

Delaney managed to hoist himself out of the chair by nine-thirty and left. Samson called Teddy Hofstedter, made an appointment for the following day and then called Lee.

"The meeting broke up earlier than I thought."

"Come on over."

As the taxi wound down Sunset he thought about the evening

ahead. It wasn't often they had the house to themselves. During the school year, her daughter Laura was with her and though the child was only five she was a restless thing and one never knew when she would crawl out of bed and wander about. One night when he was into Lee and stroking like mad he was tapped on his bare ass. Little Laura was beside the bed demanding to know the name of the game. It took an agonizing half-hour before they diverted her long enough, they hoped, to erase the scene from her mind. The next day Lee had a lock installed on her bedroom door. And if it wasn't Laura it was the maid, Clara, a fat Negro woman, a chuckler and grinner whose private thoughts were always evident on her large black face. After the incident with Laura he insisted they do their fucking in his apartment, agreeing to send Alex away for the night. They tried it a few times but Lee always insisted on going home afterward to be on hand when Laura went off to nursery school. And she hated to leave a warm bed so it was back to her locked bedroom door. Anyway, tonight was going to be perfect, he thought, and it would be another month before the damn kid returned from New York.

The house was a sprawling bungalow on Carmelina, set back from the street hidden by foliage. Lee was at the door as he paid off the cab and greeted her. She wore a housecoat, carelessly tied, half a tit exposed, and when he embraced her, running his hands over her ass he could feel nothing on underneath. After a long kiss she pushed him away, brushed a stray lock with a sweeping gesture and arched her back theatrically, movements instilled at one time or another he imagined, by a series of directors.

"Slow down, lover," she said.

"No time to waste," he said circling her waist and leading her into the house and toward the bar. "Clara can pop out from behind a drape at any moment with that damn cackle of hers. Why don't you get rid of her? Get someone deaf and dumb."

She was pouring his martini. "Never. She's wonderful with Laura. And I like her laugh. It's cheery in the morning. You don't know what it's like to have to be on a set ready to work at seven. I'm up at five, mean and cross, and Clara smooths me out." She poured herself a drink and they both settled on the couch. The lights had been turned low, the hi-fi was playing softly; Lee had prepared the set. She was curled at the opposite end of the couch, her coat was open and her legs were drawn up in a manner that gave him a view of all her thigh and a peek of hair at the crotch. Peering at him over the edge of her glass she reached up and turned on the lamp beside her.

"What are you doing that for?"

"You got hurry written all over your face. You'll be rushing the second act curtain."

"Then sit up like a lady and hide that beautiful pussy."

She stood up, wrapped the gown around herself, secured it with a flourish and returned to the couch. Seated primly she talked about her next picture, the leading man who she was sure was a switch-hitter if not a fag, the director, the argument about billing, the deficiencies of her agent, that every picture was referred to as a package and that talent in Hollywood was just merchandise, canned and sold. He had heard it all before from her and her friends, excoriations, loud damnations when they were working and the money was rolling in and when they were securely contracted, all of them reducing their tirades to bleats when they needed a job. He allowed her to pour it out, run down, without interruption, and without reminding her that she had been after her agent for weeks to extend her contract, that she made more from one picture than from a half-dozen plays, that he knew damn well she loved the money more than art, and that Broadway was not offering much of either. But he was not about to enter into a discussion which was academic anyway and mar what looked to be a perfect night. She finished, heaving with emotion and puffing furiously on her cigarette. He reached over and patted her hand consolingly.

"Just one more picture and you'll be able to return to the stage."

"It'll be liberation." She swung around and crushed the cigarette in the ashtray. Her gown opened and she made no effort to secure it. He slipped his hand between her thighs, his face still displaying evidence of concern. She pressed her legs together preventing his hand from moving up, her signal she wasn't ready, had a few more things to say. He had been through the game dozens of times. The pattern was usually the same but the lines were different and she liked to talk to the last possible moment. "You don't know what it's like," she went on. "Take after take until you're ready to scream. And no audience. Just hot lights and big snaky wires all over the place." She relaxed her legs a bit, he inched up and she closed down again. "A play is different. There are people out in front, you can hear them breathe. It's like you're connected to them by something invisible." He murmured an agreement as she unzipped his fly and grabbed his cock. Her legs spread a little more and he reached her crotch and began to finger it. He knew she would go on until he felt some lubricity. "You don't know what it's like, Sam, to sense a reaction to your art. To be able to move people." She had his joint out now and was stroking it. He kicked off his shoes and started to unbutton his shirt with his free hand as they both squirmed to hold their positions. She had a hold on him now like a grip on an axe handle and he was fingering her like mad. "Anyway, darling, one more picture and I'm through." Unable to wriggle out of his pants he rose, kicked them off and stood beside the couch naked. His cock was out straight; she sat up and as he came toward her she grabbed and kissed it. Then she delivered her last line. "Believe me, it'll be joy to get back to Broadway." Sinking to the couch his hand flew to her crotch and he knew she was ready. She twisted out of her robe, they rolled to the floor her hand still on his cock which she guided to her mouth as he swiveled and buried his face in her crotch. At times like this when they had whole nights undisturbed they would follow the identical routine; going down, a rest period, more martinis, a simulated chase in the pool where he would nab her at the shallow end, they would drift and fuck, then to bed and once again in the morning standing in the shower.

After breakfast he returned to his apartment, changed, and headed for the office, the scent of Lee all about him.

As he drove down Wilshire his thoughts turned to the defense plant. They made enormous profits during the war, pocketing large sums even after government renegotiation and the excess profits taxes. A few months before when it looked like the war was nearing an end he suggested cutting down but Gilbert resisted. When Samson suggested that the government, pouring billions into defense, made every show a hit and that a highly competitive peacetime economy would require retrenching and new planning, he scoffed. The fool had educated hands, Samson figured, but his mind was not equipped for the problems that were ahead. And Samson had no intention of stepping in and running things. Anyway, he was getting out before the fat disappeared and all they had to divide was the bones. He made a mental note of seeing Gilbert as soon as possible.

Ruth Bennett greeted him with her usual look of concern and appraisal. Since Beck's death, her maternal instincts manifested themselves in searching questions about his health, lectures on smoking, drinking, and late hours. There were times he found himself lying to her like a kid to a pestering parent and he was getting sick of it. She was a health food and vitamin freak, a devout Christian Scientist, and if there was not a sermon of Mary Baker Eddy's greeting him on his desk he would find a jar of dried prunes (no sugar), a slab of unprocessed cheese, even a dozen fertile eggs. For Christmas the year before she had delivered to his apartment a huge box containing whole-grain, nonhydrogenated nut butter, cold pressed oils, all varieties of organic fruits and vegetables, and a dozen different jars of vitamins and minerals.

She irritated the hell out of him and if it wasn't for the fact she was faithful and knew the apartment house business thoroughly, he would have gotten rid of her long ago. Well, it would not be long now, he thought as he pulled up to the rear of the office; by the time most of the apartment buildings were liquidated she would go.

Usually he would enter through the parking lot and go directly to his office, clean up unfinished business of the day before and

then call her in. Only if there was something urgent did she contact him before he buzzed. This morning she was waiting for
him, her cold appraisal evident as if she was looking for a new
wrinkle, as she handed him a note.

"She called three times in the last hour. I guess it must be important."

He took the message and went into his office. It was from
Paula Jennings. Her voice was crisp and businesslike when he
reached her.

"I must see you right away."

"Anything wrong?"

"We'll talk about it."

He agreed to meet Paula at his apartment at five. All their
meetings since Beck's death had been strained and unpleasant. A
month after the funeral Paula had divorced Art, whom he
promptly fired. Paula's decree netted her single status but not a
dime. When she came to Samson after running out of cash, told
him she could not get a cent from Art for child support, and reminded him that Carla was his, he agreed to help. He made a condition that he be permitted to see Carla from time to time. It was
agreed and his monthly checks to her were generous. After a few
months, she got a job in the decorating department of W & J
Sloane and a year later came to him for a loan. She had an opportunity to buy into a partnership with an established decorator
who needed capital. She offered Samson an interest in the business but he refused, gave her the money as a gift, feeling it might
insure his visitation rights with Carla. He saw little Carla a day
each week and now that day was as important as any. The child
was twelve, as lovely as her mother, more delicately featured, and
having no contact with Art for years, Samson became father,
guardian, and confidant. As the child drew closer to him, Paula's
resentment increased, causing a breach between her and Carla.
Though he made every effort to enhance her devotion without in
any overt way denigrating her mother, days without chastise-
ment, movies and swimming in his pool, gifts and dinners and
promises for the future, Carla's unhappiness at home was begin-

ning to shred the little that existed of his relationship with Paula. Certain now that Paula wanted to see him about Carla, he was determined that whatever Paula demanded he would not alter his relationship with the child.

He called Jack Gilbert, made an appointment to see him at the plant in an hour, checked the market, and rang for Ruth Bennett. She sat down in the chair in the usual way, stiff-backed on the edge, and gave him the usual appraising look. Her daily lectures were short, a sentence or two followed by a patient smile but those on Monday morning had to cover a weekend and were longer, detailed, always ending with an admonishing finger and a saddened look.

"I know just what you're going to say. I look like a big nonorganic blob!"

"Mr. Duke, I wasn't."

"Don't lie!"

"I wasn't lying."

"It's your concern about my health that's making an old man out of me before my time. You know what you are, Miss Bennett? A computer for an undertaker!" She plucked a handkerchief from her sleeve and stifled a sob. "You keep *reminding* me I'm growing older . . . adding up the wrinkles, keeping tab on my color!" The handkerchief was over her mouth now as if stifling a scream. He was getting back at her for all those morning lecturers he sloughed off in silence. "Let me tell you a few things, Miss Bennett. I get my grains from Scotch, my starches and oils from greasy fried potatoes, and my exercise in bed with women." He stood up. "Lots of them!" She swept up her book and fled from the room. He felt good, damn sorry he didn't take her on years before.

He made a couple of calls, was about to leave for the appointment with Gilbert when the door opened and Ruth Bennett poked her head through. He ordered her in and she began to speak, her eyes staring at the floor.

"If you want me to leave, Mr. Duke. . . ."

"I don't want you to leave. Just let me deteriorate in my own way. I'm not the yogurt type or the whole-grain type and I hate brown sugar." She flicked out the handkerchief again. He went up to her and patted her shoulder. "What do you say we forget it?" She nodded and as he started to leave grabbed his hand and he was sure she was going to carry it to her lips as he slid it from her grasp. "I have a few appointments on the outside. I'll be at the plant and then at my apartment."

With the acquisitions they made during the war, the plant sprawled all over Robertson Boulevard. The original building now only housed the offices and the tool and die department; a half-dozen additional buildings contained the production equipment and warehousing. Gilbert enlarged his private office, paneled the room and furnished it expensively. The walls were covered with colored photos of every type of airplane the company supplied parts for and the most prominent display was an enlarged photograph of Jack Gilbert standing beside an old engine lathe in the garage of his home. Dressed in greasy coveralls and sporting a cheap haircut he looked like a valve grinder in a two-bit filling station. The picture was captioned, "The Founder."

Familiarity long ago replaced Gilbert's once formal condescending manner. Just about the time their assets crawled near the million mark and he shed coveralls for a business suit, a beat-up jalopy for a Cadillac and exchanged a cramped apartment for a two-story home in Beverly Hills, he dropped the mister, greeting Duke by his first name and a sound slap on the back. In fact, it was at his house-warming that Duke was forced to attend together with a crew of machinists and their plain wives that he first called him Sam. Gilbert was drunk that night, perspiry, smelly drunk, and after managing to spit it out the first time he "Sammed" him all over the place until Duke bowed out as gracefully as he could at a disrespectable early hour. The palsy relationship did not take, and since then, whatever little there ever was of their rapport had worn thin. For a long time he tried to throw his dull self and duller fat wife into the pot and after Samson's repeated rejection of the offering he unskillfully concealed his feelings beneath a layer of belligerence.

Gilbert was up to his usual game as Samson walked into the office, seated behind his desk and ignoring him as he made computations on a pad. That day as always he kept at it a full minute before he acknowledged his presence. Samson never believed in frontal attack, always liked to flank, but Gilbert's grin, smirky and insolent, touched off the powder long before he intended to use it.

"I've had enough of the business and more than enough of you." Gilbert was still grinning but there was no mirth in his eyes. "You're going to buy me out, Jack." There was no grin now; hostility masked Gilbert's face. And there was confusion—surprise. He ground his cigarette in the tray, twisting it slowly, his knuckles white as he seemed to be giving himself time to think. Then he looked up, his malevolence on full display.

"I ain't buying you out until I'm damn good and ready. Maybe never."

Duke was grinning now, enjoying every moment. "You had better listen carefully," he said. "Because I'm not going to repeat. This plant is going to be appraised, every piece of machinery in it, the inventory, the accounts receivable, all the real estate. We are going to add it up and deduct the accounts payable. And then you're going to go out and raise the cash and give me a check for one-half of the net assets." He sat back and watched Gilbert's face twist through shock, anger, and cunning.

"And what if I refuse?"

"I'll file a suit for partition. The court will put the business on the block. And with the war over defense plants are a dime a dozen. Only secondhand machine dealers will be bidding and they don't pay a nickel for goodwill."

"You'll be cutting your own throat, Sam."

"Just yours, Jack. I got twenty times my investment out of this plant. And it kept me out of the army. I don't need it anymore.

But you do." Gilbert's fear was smeared over his face. "Without it you'll be back in that garage," Samson went on, jerking his thumb to the picture on the wall.

Gilbert stood up, towering, as if the posture would add force to his words. "You can't wash a man out, there are laws. And you don't frighten me. Do you hear?" He came from behind the desk and stood beside Samson. "I worked all my life for this," he said, clenching a fist and pounding it in his hand. "And I'm not going to let a lousy draft dodger take it away from me! I'll go to court— I'll tell the judge . . . the papers. . . . I'll tell how you lied about the amount of time you put in working, that you did nothing, that you just bought into the plant to stay out of the army. I'll ruin you!" Both his fists were clenched and Samson stood up.

"You'll ruin nobody but yourself. If I lied about the time I put in the plant you verified it. And I've got a million dollars' worth of war bonds to prove my patriotism and a plaque from the Hollywood Canteen for my contributions and a certificate from the blood bank. What have you got to show for your war efforts? A Cadillac, a Beverly Hills house, and a fat bank account. I think you'll keep your mouth shut."

"You're a bastard!"

"The war looked like it was over with months ago," Samson went on, ignoring the remark. "I said, pull your horns in, cut down. Get ready for a sensible peacetime operation. But you kept on expanding, buying more machines, eating up the reserves." Gilbert retreated behind the desk and flung himself in the chair as Samson continued. "You're a tycoon now, an industrialist. Well, let me tell you something," he said leaning over the desk. "You're nothing but a lousy mechanic and the town is crawling with them. And if it wasn't for the war you'd still be in that garage eating beans." Gilbert started to interrupt but Samson shouted him down. "You listen until I'm finished! I haven't a thing to lose by going into court and auctioning it off. Because you're an asshole and the business is going broke and I don't intend to be around picking up pieces!"

"What makes you think I wasn't making plans?"

"What kind of plans?"

"For peacetime conversion."

"Buying more machines, adding help. Do you call that peacetime conversion?"

"That was months ago. The war was still on. Nobody knew how long it was going to last."

"Everybody knew, except you. Germany was finished and an idiot knew that Japan was nearing the end."

"But nobody knew about the bomb. If it wasn't for the bomb the war could have gone on for a year. Even Truman said so."

Samson knew Gilbert was soft now, getting where he wanted him. "Look, Jack, maybe the bomb did end the war a year sooner. Maybe I haven't the temperament for this business. You love those machines out there. They're alive to you. To me they're complicated pieces of steel at the end of an electric plug. And I'm sure there's going to be peacetime contracts. Plenty of them. I'm a real-estate man; this isn't my business and I want to get out of it. I tell you what I'll do. Get those appraisals, arrive at a fair market value of the entire business. I don't need the cash. I'll take a down payment. Say a third. The rest you can pay off. I'll give you a year, eighteen months." He thrust out his hand and after a moment's hesitation, Gilbert grabbed it. "Is it a deal?" Gilbert nodded.

Before Samson left, Gilbert promised to have everything prepared within a few weeks and he followed him to the door and patted Samson's back as he walked out.

He could not have made a better deal, Samson thought as he headed for Paula and his apartment. The real estate was paid for and he knew it would appraise for at least $150,000. And right now the machines would appraise fairly high, there had been a shortage of them right up until V-J Day and it might take months, he figured, until it was realized they would be a glut on the peacetime market. His guess was that the total evaluation including accounts receivable would near the half-million mark. The only thing that worried him was whether Gilbert would last long enough to pay him off.

Paula was waiting for him when he arrived at his apartment. She was on the terrace cradling a drink and he watched her for a few moments before she turned and greeted him. He had not seen her for a few months and realized she was more beautiful than when they first met. She had allowed gray swirls of her hair to remain untouched giving her face a softness which enhanced her maturity. In spite of the fact he knew she was having an affair with an attorney by the name of Ann Schneider, a tweed-suited bull-dyke who he had met at her shop a few times and who seemed to dominate her completely, he still could not conceive of her passing up nights they had years ago for a tussle in bed with a woman. She came into the living room and matched his smile with an icy look.

He nodded and followed her as she settled in a chair and lit a cigarette.

"What do you want to see me about?" he asked, taking a seat opposite her.

He guessed she had her speech prepared because she launched it without hesitation.

"I've obeyed every rule in the book, followed every instinct a good mother should have. For years I have always managed to be home when Carla returned from school. I've interested myself in everything she's involved in, allowed her privacy whenever she wanted it. She has her own room, radio, all the clothes she needs." He watched her, nodded at the appropriate moments, did not say a word as she went on. Instead of raising her voice she lowered it now as if the tone would curb her anger. "She's never left the house in the morning without a breakfast I prepared. I never struck her." She was lighting a fresh cigarette now from the one she had been puffing. Alex walked into the room.

"Good evening, Mr. Duke. Can I get you anything?"

"Nothing. I'll call if I need you."

"Fix me another drink," Paula said. She stared out the window as she waited. He wondered what in hell she was getting at. Alex brought the drink and left, closing the door. Samson waited as she took a long swallow before he spoke.

"Nobody denies you've been a good mother."

"Then why does my daughter cringe when I kiss her? Squirm from my arms when I try to put them around her?" Now she raised her voice. "She'll sit at a dinner table staring at her plate without a word and rush to her room the minute the meal is over." He shrugged. All her control was gone now as she slammed her drink on the table. "I'll tell you why she acts this way. One day a week she's with you and her mind is poisoned! You'll deny it, I know. But you're a liar!" She swept the drink from the table and downed it.

"And you're blaming it all on me."

"You're damn right, I am." She jumped up. "But I'm putting a stop to it. You're not seeing her anymore."

He waited a moment to cool before he spoke. "Did it ever occur to you," he began, "that this thing you're talking about was brought about by your actions? Not mine."

"It's a lie and you know it." She was back in the chair nervously lighting a cigarette.

"Carla's not a baby anymore. Furthermore, she's bright. And she knows everything that's going on. Fag friends, lesbians. What do you expect the child to think?"

"What does she know about it? You planted those thoughts."

He jumped up. "I've never said a word, not even hinted. Your partner is a pansy. You're surrounded by them. And your friend, that woman—she's as feminine as a truck driver. What in hell do you expect Carla to think!"

She was on her feet, shouting. "I'm not here to discuss my friends!" She swept up her purse, gloves, and whirled on him. "If Carla doesn't change, if this alienation continues, you're never going to see her again." She started for the door and Samson grabbed her. "If you try that, I'll tell her everything. About you and that Schneider creep and what you both are."

She twisted from his grasp. "If you do I'll kill you." She was out of the room before he could say another word.

For the rest of the week he waited nervously for Sunday. It was his custom to call Paula every Sunday morning and arrange to pick up Carla. Usually he would call around ten, pick up the child before noon and keep her until after dinner. He rose early that morning and called a little after nine. Paula answered, he told her he wanted to get an earlier start and wondered if he could pick up Carla by ten. She was cold but consented and when he reached the front of the building, Carla was waiting. She was radiant, snuggled up close to him as he drove, chattered endlessly, firing the usual questions.

"Where are we going first?"

"To the apartment. Alex will make us a second breakfast."

"Gee, that's keen. Then where?"

"We'll swim and sit around the pool awhile."

"Then what?"

"We'll take in a movie."

"Which one?" she asked, excitedly.

"Any one you want."

"Alan Ladd's in one at the Chinese. He's keen. And Van Johnson."

"Both in the same picture?"

"No," she said disappointedly.

"You'll have to make a choice."

"Can't we see them both, Uncle Sam?"

"I'm afraid not."

She sighed. "Alan Ladd's cute. But Van Johnson makes you want to swoon. Do you like freckles? I mean on a boy," she hastened to add.

"I guess I do."

"I'm crazy about them. On some boys, that is. Let's go to the Van Johnson movie."

He watched as she leaped from the car and sped ahead of him. Her sloppy cashmere sweater hung far below her waist and as she ran she kept pushing up the long sleeves which kept crawling over her hands. Everytime he was with her he looked for a hint of a crooked nose, little eyes, saw neither and marveled she was his. Nature was kind after all, compensated, molded fairies from gnomes, brought forth flowers from a twisted bush. He never felt as close to anyone, except Aunt Annie before she tried to save the world. Of course there was Posey, Lee, even Paula for awhile, but it was different. He always got the feeling they needed him, not wanted him. Carla's response was spontaneous, uncalculated, a pure reaction to something that emanated from him that was the finest feeling he ever had. He wanted to give to her all she could consume, wanted nothing in return except the sight of her joy, a look of love when they were together, one of sadness when they parted. Nothing was going to keep him from her, not Paula, any law or circumstance. She was the only thing alive that held title to his flesh.

Alex made her favorite dish, crisp waffles swimming in blueberry syrup. They ate on the terrace with the hot sun warming their backs. Afterwards she roamed the apartment, a habit every week, seeking something he might have acquired. She knew every inch of the place, even called his attention when a piece of furniture was moved. By noon they were down at the pool, had it all to themselves and after an hour of sunning and swimming came upstairs. She spied Alex in the kitchen working over her brown and white saddle shoes with cleaning fluid and let out a scream as she snatched them from his lap.

"Why did you do it?" she cried out. "They're supposed to be dirty. It took me weeks to get them that way." His sad eyes appealed to Samson; there was bewilderment—hurt.

"Alex was just being kind," he explained.

"I know," Carla said, examining the shoes carefully. "But he should have asked. Look at this one," she said, holding up a shoe. "It's practically clean!" When Alex, who only half understood, offered to dirty it up, Carla explained that the dirt had to be accumulated and not applied and that now she would have to work on it all over again. As they left the room, Alex whipped out the *Racing Form*, still shaking his head.

After the Van Johnson movie, during which she ran the gamut from scream-stifling to moaning, she sat quietly beside him as they drove back to the apartment. She always took an overnight case with her on their days together in which she carried her dress-up clothes for dinner. Though he had fixed up a bedroom for her, allowed her to select the furniture, had it equipped with her own phonograph and favorite records as well as every frill to delight a young girl, she only slept in it once during the years. That was on a weekend when Paula went away and had no one else to leave her with. Otherwise he was forbidden to have her overnight. She went to her room to change while he freshened up. She was dressed and ready and sitting next to Alex at the kitchen table completely absorbed as he explained to her the merits of the thoroughbreds he had selected for the next day's card. Jumping up when Samson entered she took his arm and they headed for Musso's. It was her favorite restaurant, the waiters knew her and the chef usually added something special to her main dish. Still filled with the experience of the movie she dramatized scene after scene as they drove to the restaurant. By the time they ordered she seemed released from the movie's spell and turned to him with a serious expression. "Do you think my mother is beautiful, Uncle Sam?"

He hesitated for a moment, wondered what she was leading up to. "Yes, I do."

"But she never goes out."

"I'm sure she does."

"With men, I mean."

The waiter came with the first dish and he tackled it without answering. Anything he would say could be quoted or misquoted by Carla in an argument with her mother. If she was going to find out about Paula it was not going to be through him. He continued to eat hoping she would switch the subject but she went on.

"My girlfriend, Thelma Cowen, her mother is divorced and she goes out on dates all the time. And you should see her. She isn't even pretty."

"Your mother works hard. She's tired at night."

"But she goes out, Uncle Sam. A lot. With that Ann Schneider. And her partner, Ronnie, goes along. Do you know him?"

"I met him."

"I like him. He's cute. But he's always with the two of them. Mother and Ann, I mean. He never takes mother out alone." She stopped eating, traced the cloth with her fork. He switched the subject.

"I got a great idea for next Sunday," he said. "We'll go to Catalina."

"On the boat?"

"We'll fly over and take the boat back."

They spent the rest of the dinner talking about the trip. He explained to her about the small seaplanes that fly to the island, talked about the glass-bottomed boat and the trip around the island and she did not mention Paula for the rest of the evening. It was a close call and he was not going to be trapped again. Carla had sniffed the trail and it was not going to be long before she found the body. Something had to be done and he had an idea and Paula was going to hear from him in the morning.

He purposely had Paula meet him at a restaurant, certain her breeding would not allow her to raise her voice in public. But as their discussion became more intense and her efforts at control reduced her tone to modulated wrath, her face, aided by all the hatred she could muster in her eyes, contorted with such malevolence that she was unrecognizable. He realized her loathing of him was so great there was nothing he could ever do, no act he would ever perform that would enable them to relate from a posture of nonbelligerence. And now he was sure she would make effort to break any hold he might have on Carla.

The waiter removed their unfinished plates. Paula seemed to calm down for a moment as she reached for a cigarette. He lit it for her and resumed the conversation carefully.

"All I did was make a suggestion."

"Thanks."

He ignored her sarcasm. "She's at an impressionable age.

Maybe when she's older she'll understand. But right now, like I said, she should be out of the house. Lots of girls go away to private schools."

"I know. My parents sent me to one and what did it get me?"

"That was different. You left your country as well as your home."

"It was no different," she said angrily.

"Look, Paula. You either let me send Carla away to school or switch back to men. I won't have her living in that atmosphere!"

"*You* won't have her! You denied her a real father for years. And now when you have nothing but your filthy money you're trying to steal her. Well you won't!" She started to gather her things, her voice rose, people began to stare. "Carla stays with me," she said, lowering her voice. "And I warn you. Stay away." She got up and ran out of the restaurant.

For a month he was not permitted to see Carla and then she showed up at his apartment, refused to return home unless she was allowed to see him regularly. Paula had no choice and after a heated telephone conversation consented to resuming the weekly visits. The child had to get out of the house, go away to school; there was nothing he could do at the moment. But she was pulling away; nothing could prevent the break.

CHAPTER EIGHTEEN

He sat facing the view from Martin Tipton's office, his eye tracing the sharply defined hills above Sunset until he found the Florentine turret of the Chateau Baroque. The day was so clear a pair of binoculars could have picked up Alex through the window, hunched over his *Racing Form*.

For the past minutes, Martin had been talking to a client and was making no attempt to hide his annoyance. The white hair he prized was yellowing, the meticulous blue dress no longer seemed to blend. Accompanying his impatience was the staccato tap of a pencil on a legal pad, increasing with intensity. Finally, Tipton flung the pencil on to the desk and shouted into the phone. "Then do as you damn please!" He slammed the receiver and turned to Walt Covington. "That was John Gardner. You handle him from now on. I'm sick of two-bit actors." He faced Samson. "He's supporting two ex-wives, three children, hasn't a dime, he's getting married again, and wants to make an offer on a house in Beverly Hills."

Covington was seated in a high-backed chair in his usual position: legs crossed with a toe hooked behind his calf, looking like a thing tightly wound ready to spring. "Where did he call from?" Covington asked.

"From the real-estate office."

"He can't issue a check without our signature. He'll call back. I'll talk to him." Tipton sighed wearily and turned to Samson.

"You're impossible at times, but at least you can afford it." He ran his fingers through his hair. "All right . . . what were we talking about?"

"My ass is flat from sitting. The war ended fifteen months ago and you're still telling me to wait."

"That's right."

Samson tried Covington. "You said you were working on a building idea."

The lawyer unwound his legs and leaned forward. "There's a little risk but I think it'll work." He outlined the plan in his droning nasal tone. "Find a competent builder who will form a limited partnership, become the general partner, and do the actual construction. Sell a parcel of land to the syndicate, take half-cash down and participate as a limited partner with the difference between the selling price and the down payment. The general partner takes all the risks and assumes the liabilities. You will operate from an invulnerable position. When each project is completed the partnership is dissolved and the limited partners can take capital gains."

"How do you know the government will allow capital gains?" Martin asked.

"I don't. There's no ruling on it. May never be. But when and if they rule against it I don't think they'll make it retroactive. Anyway, that's the chance."

"Where does this builder get the down payment for my land?"

"There's money around. Syndicates are being formed every day."

"How are the profits divided?"

"The limited partners get from fifty to sixty per cent. It depends on the deal you make."

"The big risk is if the houses don't sell," Martin said.

"With the GI's coming back and no-down payment government financing, they'll be waiting in line," Samson said. Walt's idea sounded good, something to dig into. Before he left that day he cornered Covington in his office.

"There's a matter, Walt. A domestic thing. Martin doesn't have to know." Covington twisted up in his chair. "There's a child. She's thirteen, you might call me her guardian. Her mother and I have known each other for a long time. The child is attached to me and unhappy at home. Two or three times during the past year she left, bag and baggage, and came to my apartment pleading for me to take her in. Naturally I sent her back home. I'm worried she'll do something desperate."

"What about the mother? Is she married? Divorced?"

"Divorced. The father hasn't been in contact with the child for years." He hesitated, wondered how much he could tell him. "Look Walt, this has got to be lawyer-client relationship."

Covington barely curved his lips in a smile and raised his right hand. "Give it to me from the beginning."

Samson told him the mother had been married to a close friend and associate. When she divorced and the husband left town the mother had turned to him for financial help. Now five years later he'd become very attached to the child.

Covington leaned back in the chair, linked his fingers, and cracked his knuckles. For a moment he said nothing. "What do you want to know?" he finally said.

"The child dislikes her mother. She's unhappy at home. She's attached to me. Is there any way of getting her legally?"

"You must be kidding."

"The mother is a lesbian."

"Is that all?"

"What do you mean, is that all?" Samson said angrily.

"Just what it implied." He leaned forward. "If the mother was a lesbian, held up a few banks, *and* took dope, I'd say the court might relieve her of custody. But you wouldn't get her. She's got a natural father. He gets first choice. And he'd have to be pretty rotten for the court not to grant him custody. You'll never get the child legally. Forget it."

"But the child's unhappy."

Covington stood up, arched his back, stretched all of his sixty-four inches. "All kids are unhappy. Especially at that age. They resent parents. I hated mine and you probably hated yours. As for the lesbian bit, maybe the kid'll never find out. If she does," he shrugged, "it's a fact of life."

He was sorry he consulted with Covington. The answer should have been obvious and Covington's head had a compartment that stored everything.

There were two urgent calls from Jack Gilbert waiting for him when he reached his office. It was almost a year since Gilbert bought him out and the going was rough. He had given Samson a chunk of cash down and a loan back on the real estate secured by a chattel mortgage on the equipment. He was fumbling the peacetime conversion, had a skeleton crew working and was three months delinquent on his obligation to Samson. When Samson returned his call, Gilbert insisted on seeing him.

"I'm busy," Samson lied. "We can discuss it on the phone."

"It's too important," Gilbert pleaded. "Let me run down now."

Samson consented reluctantly. It was so much easier to turn one down over the phone. It seemed like a few minutes when Ruth Bennett buzzed to say that Gilbert was waiting. He decided to have him cool his steam as he placed a call to Fines Cady. It had been months since he had seen the Texan and knew he was due for a trip to L.A. for his periodic visit to the local office and some fun. He wanted to pick that well-organized brain and discuss Covington's idea. He would be out in a week, Cady said, needed a day or two in town for business and suggested they hole up at the Palm Springs house for a few days for a little "wenching." Samson hadn't shot at something new, since he'd met Lee, two years before. Maybe a fresh deck would turn up a trump. Also, he was not so sure Lee wasn't playing the game with a hidden card. He heard too many stories about what went on at out-of-the-city locations. He began to thumb through his book looking for numbers and realized they were two years old. He would call Delaney who knew every dame available in their buildings and would have a week to fill the order.

When Jack Gilbert walked in he looked frayed. New face lines and an unpressed appearance showed there was no joy in his living. He told his story too rapidly as if anxious to reach the point of his plea and dispense with the unpleasantness as soon as possible. He had contracts pending, large ones, to manufacture parts for a garbage disposal company, a dishwasher plant. Lockheed and Douglas were also prospects. Samson nodded and said nothing as Gilbert lit a cigarette, took two or three deep puffs, and got down to the facts.

"I'm gonna need some capital. For payroll and retooling. About fifty thousand dollars. I tried to get a second trust deed loan on the building but can't. You've got to help me out, Sam." His lips were dry, his tongue swabbing them.

"I'm not a moneylender." He was certain Gilbert knew he was lying.

Gilbert leaned forward, his hands gripping the edge of the desk. "You don't have to lend me money. I can place a new first trust deed loan on the building for about a hundred and fifty. I'll give you a hundred thousand on account of what I owe you and you can take the balance in a second trust deed. That'll give me the fifty I need." Now he made no pretense at pleading. "Sam, it's all I need to get me out of a mess and get going again."

If he let Gilbert go down the drain he would have to foreclose and would end up with the building and equipment. The building was worth every bit of the amount Gilbert owed but it would take months to take possession and God knows how long to dispose of. So, if he accepted he would get a hundred thousand in cash and be a good guy. And he did feel sorry for the poor son-of-a-bitch.

"How about your house?" he asked.

"Hocked."

"How bad?"

"An insurance company loan for twenty-five."

There was not much of an equity but something. "I'll do it," he finally said. He thought Gilbert was going to slobber. "But I want a second on the house as additional security and the chattel stays on the equipment."

Gilbert was smiling, some of the wrinkles seemed to disappear. "You won't be sorry, Sam, you'll see. You'll get it all back, every penny." He was on his feet, at the door. "God bless you."

After he left, Samson dictated a letter to Gilbert outlining their agreement, gave him two weeks to get the deal into escrow, and told Ruth Bennett to mail it registered, return receipt requested. It was in the record now and if he could not come up with the loan, Samson made it very clear there would be a foreclosure and no further conversation.

Fines Cady never seemed to change. He looked no different than when Samson met him ten years before. The little gray he had then was now touched up and if anything he looked younger. Samson did not know what went on under that skin but if Cady's manifestations were any criterion it had to be established that using a body prevented atrophy. He swam, golfed, and played handball and Samson watched him work through a half-dozen sets of tennis and drinking gave his liver a workout and in bed he inspired incredibility. The energy his body plant developed generated steam to spare: with Cady driving, his company had swallowed a half-dozen others and was now operating in ten states. Though he always enjoyed being with Cady, whom he considered a protean man, a pragmatist as well as a dreamer, Cady's presence gave him a feeling of inferiority. He felt himself stripped of all the layers with which he had lacquered his image over the years, and he saw the immutable evidence of his birth, the old nose, the lies. On the other hand Cady seemed to communicate with him without descending and Samson reasoned that his own state of mind erected a hurdle his friend did not see.

He cleared the decks for a week, inspected and briefed the two dames Delaney had selected, and waited at his apartment on Sunday until Cady called. The Texan was flying his own plane, a Beechcraft Bonanza. He was to arrive at the Santa Monica airport during the late afternoon.

That morning, Samson picked Carla up, explained to her they would have to forsake dinner that night and after an early matinee they returned to the apartment. She seemed listless, depressed, and when he tried to probe she withdrew and he decided to leave her alone. She would pour it out when she felt like it, always did. It wasn't going to last much longer, her living in that house and sooner or later Paula would realize that if Carla was not sent away to school she would lose her altogether. When he received the call from Fines telling him he had just landed and was on his way, he sent Carla home with Alex promising her a full day and evening the following Sunday.

Fines bounced in an hour later, went for the bar, poured himself a straight scotch, and flopped on the couch.

"Almost didn't make it. Hit a crosswind over Tucson that had me bobbing." Then he grinned. "What did you line up?"

"Two dolls. I interviewed them yesterday."

"Interviewed them?"

"Delaney lined them up. I sure wasn't going to rely on his taste."

"What's mine like?"

"You can have your pick. Since you go for big tits, she's blonde. Very pretty . . . nineteen-twenty."

"What are they supposed to do beside whoring?"

"Actresses. In between roles at present. Anyway we're paying dress-extra fees. Fifty-five dollars a day for the pair and all they can eat. I said there might be a bonus."

"I hope you weren't looking for bargains. Sounds cheap."

"It was the asking price."

"Tell you what," he said, his face lighting up. "Suppose I call them. Have them come over tonight. Sort of a preview."

"They might be busy, I told them to be ready for Tuesday afternoon or Wednesday."

"Busy! I want them rested up, dried out. Come on, Sam, my boy," he said, slapping his back. "Get them on the phone."

Samson dialed and Fines grabbed the receiver as a voice answered. "Look honey, this is Fines Cady. Since you and your friend are going to spend a few days with us don't you think we all ought to meet?" He listened for a moment and his face broke into a smile. "That's right, tonight." Samson could hear her voice as Fines reached for his drink and drained it. "The same rate honey. Union scale and all you can eat." Now he laughed aloud. "Sure, baby." He handed the phone to Samson. "Give them the address and tell them how to get here." As he gave her the instructions Cady waltzed around the room holding his glass high in the air.

"They'll be here in an hour," Samson said, hanging up.

"Good. That'll give me time to clean up."

"What about dinner?"

"First we'll look over the dames. If they check out we'll call Chasen's and have them send it up." He danced out of the room. "I'm going in for a shower," he announced.

Fines returned to the living room looking refreshed and relaxed. Samson wanted his thoughts on the plan he discussed with Covington and decided to pin him down before the drinking and whoring commenced. He outlined the idea as Cady settled comfortably cradling a drink.

They discussed the millions of men being mustered out, the plant conversions, the rush for the first new cars since 1941 and the shortages of durable goods. Money was plentiful with nothing to buy and every show was a hit. There was a little madness in the land, Fines thought, the war already forgotten and the things men died for and a new one was on the way; the "cold war" declared so eloquently by Churchill in Fulton, Missouri, and old enemies were becoming allies, former friends suspect and there was the atom, the weapons it would power and very few people seemed to care. Fines was serious now, his drink remained untouched as he leaned forward in his seat, unsmiling, intense.

"When I was in college I wanted no part of the so-called real world. I dreamed, idealized, thought of entering the ministry." Samson smiled. "It's the truth, I even made inquiries at the School of Divinity. Then it was going to be criminal law and I even thought of social work. But when the crash came and my family nearly went down the drain all the stardust disappeared. People were rotten I found out. Play the game to survive. The evidence is everywhere. Billions in black-market cash when boys were dying for a few bucks a month. I've been all over the country during the past year, to the fun cities, the luxury spots, and there you see it in fur salons, jewelry shops, and swank hotels. Well-dressed men with their wives or chippie girl friends peeling the coin off in hundred-dollar bills. And the little slob is no different. Do you know, Sam, the majority of people in this country hated to see the war end? It gave them overtime and double-time, red-neck bums who never wore shoes were hauling in a hundred a week." He reached for the drink and sipped it thoughtfully. "You ask about building," he went on. "How can one miss? There hasn't been any construction to speak of since the late twenties. Since then we've had a thirty-million population increase. And the civilian army is coming back with big eyes and hard-ons and they'll be rushing into marriage and that'll mean homes and apartments." He leaned back. "Our companies, Sam, are prepared to finance any housing tracts in the states we operate with all the capital the law allows. Particularly with the government insuring our loans. Sure go in. Get good legal advice on taxes and jump."

Samson elaborated on his plans and then offered Cady a piece of whatever action in which he became involved. As a partner, the syndicate would be certain of the best available financing and he surely owed him something for past favors.

They toasted the coming boom, capital gains, and by the time they got around to the girls the buzzer rang. Fines rubbed his hands, put a grin on his face, and stood in the hall before the elevator waiting for the door to open.

Fines seemed to share Samson's appraisal and ushered "big tits" into the room with a courtly flourish. She called herself Pris. Samson's went by the name of Angie, which seemed to fit her

jet-black hair, matching eyes and olive skin. She reminded him of
Paula. By the time they disposed of their wraps, Fines had Pris on
the couch with his arm about her shoulder.

"Do you believe in love, Pris?"

"Uhuh."

"At first sight, I mean."

"I guess so."

"Well I'm in love." He turned to Samson. "I want to thank
you from the bottom of my heart for making it possible for me to
meet Pris."

The girls started behind and never caught up. They did not
leave the apartment that night, Fines called his office the following morning told them not to expect him until the end of the
week, and when Alex arrived with the car that afternoon he
hustled them into the big sedan, Samson drove to their apartment,
they filled a suitcase and the four headed for Palm Springs. During the trip both girls kept conversation alive, detailing the problems of launching an acting career, the expenses of a wardrobe, of
acting and voice coaches, the unpleasantness of handouts demanded by casting directors and producers. Seated in the front
with Samson, Angie emphasized the blonde's remarks by ex-
claiming, "so right" after each diatribe on the perils of Hollywood as Fines worked over Pris in the rear seat grunting affirma-
tions in a voice that did not seem connected to his body as he
rummaged in her pants and brassiere. Pris tried comments on real
estate, the oil and insurance business, larding her remarks with
outrageous clichés as the car sped to the desert. When they
reached the house Fines leaped from the car waving the pants and
brassiere like a banner.

They had the girls clean the accumulation of sand the desert
winds had swept into the house and went to the village to shop.
Loaded with provisions they returned and Fines called a conference. Mounting a table, grinning, he addressed them in the patio.

"Here's the script, girls. We don't leave the house during our stay. There's food and drink galore, no time out for doing dishes or making beds, no talk of business, show business or otherwise," he added with a glance at Samson. "Just eating and sleeping, fucking and sucking with a dash of scotch in between."

From that moment on, Cady cavorted like a satyr. He got drunk and stayed drunk, walked about naked even at mealtime and insisted that Pris follow suit, went down on her after dinner as Samson and Angie were on dessert, crept into Samson's room later that evening and tickled his ass with a feather duster as he was banging away, roared with laughter as Samson chased him through the house to the pool where he jumped in, Samson following, and then leaped out, heading for Samson's bedroom where he locked himself in with Angie for an hour. Afterwards he sat up drinking half the night and the following morning Samson, hoping to find Cady sleeping off a drunk, found him instead on a lounge on the patio with Pris, writhing in an embrace as Angie sat nearby reading a magazine. Duke left the patio, pretended to call his office, returned and told them he had to be back in Los Angeles as soon as possible, would leave the car, take the plane and the house was theirs as long as they wished. Another day and he and Fines would never speak to each other again. The bastard accumulated lust; the next time he unzipped his fly, Samson was not going to be within sight.

By the end of the week, Fines Cady returned from Palm Springs looking a little haggard. No mention was made of the girls, his business side turned on as they huddled in Samson's office and went over the building program. He suggested a builder by the name of Allan Hinds with whom he had done business.

"He's conscientious, knows construction and I'd trust him with my last dollar."

"Has he any money?"

"Not a dime. He's too honest. You raise the front money, get the financing, give him the land and he'll turn out the best house the dollar will buy."

Samson contacted Hinds the day after Cady returned to Texas, was impressed with his knowledge of the business, told him to stand by and then contacted Harry Finkelstein who still hung around his office "for old times sake." Though he no longer had use for the old man there was something about him he admired. Finkelstein made it the hard way; not only was he a Jew, but he looked like one, talked like one, and there surely wasn't a time in his life when he wasn't taken for one. In spite of it all he didn't strike out. And in all of Samson's dealings with him in the past he found his word reliable. There were times when he had given it in haste and a night's sleep proved it unwise but he never reneged. Samson knew that Finkelstein was active in his temple, whose Brotherhood included some of the wealthiest Jews in town. They were always sniffing for deals and if Finkelstein would go they would follow.

Finkelstein had shriveled over the years, never seated himself or rose from a chair without an oi-vey, but his mind was as sharp as the first day they met.

Samson waited until he eased himself into the chair, groaned, stuck a cigarette in a long holder he fancied, lit it with a trembling hand, inhaled deeply, and settled back with a sigh. "Like a horse with a broken leg they should shoot me," he said.

"You got a hundred thousand miles on you yet, Harry."

"To go where?"

"How would you like a piece of a deal without putting up any money?"

"Who do I have to rob?"

"Not a soul. I have a proposition that is so foolproof the rabbi at your temple can recommend it."

"I wouldn't be surprised."

Samson went on and outlined the deal, spoke of the building boom that was imminent, the government financing, the shortage of homes and the fact that the moment the house was sold you were bailed out on the loan with a profit.

"Your temple is loaded with people looking for investments. I'll put the package together, you raise the front money, and get ten per cent off the top."

At first there was a sign of interest, his eyes lit a bit, then he turned in the chair, winced, and held up his hand.

"It's not for me, Sam. My wife is gone, may she rest in peace. If my grandchildren are bums they'll never have to work. If I lift one little finger to leave my lousy son-in-law more money I should be struck by lightning."

"Would Al be interested?"

"Huh. The only thing that interests him is when my funeral is." He removed the cigarette from the holder, crushed it, blew the smoke from the holder and placed it carefully in his pocket. Samson rose to indicate the meeting was at an end.

"Wait," Finkelstein said. "Maybe I got somebody." He seemed to be sorting his thoughts and then began. "There is a young man by the name of Phil Matlin," he went on, "who has money of his own, tremendous drive, and who is looking for a deal."

"What do you know about him?"

"I know if I was the boss from an army I wouldn't let him in. From a buck private he made a fortune. If I went into business I'd make him a general." Confidentially he told Samson that Matlin, who was in his late twenties, was unable to beat the draft but managed to make the army pay. Landing with the second wave on the Normandy beach he somehow survived and by the time the smoke cleared had organized a black-market ring that netted him over a hundred thousand dollars before the army released him after he suffered injuries in an automobile accident somewhere in France. He was a member of Finkelstein's temple, was considered a war hero by the Brotherhood who knew nothing of the source of his fortune and a young man to "watch." Before the war he was a draftsman, knew enough about building to sound intelligent. Gossiping further, Finkelstein told Duke that Matlin married the daughter of the temple president, a retired jeweler, who gave the couple a home in Beverly Hills for a wedding present. He concluded bitterly that Matlin turned out like all sons-in-law and was cheating on his wife and then added philosophically that when a daughter is not a beauty a father's got to settle.

"For you he'll go good, Sam," he said as he left. "You don't have to get married."

Finkelstein's description of Phil Matlin was adequate but superficial. Calling Samson for an appointment, he arrived at the Chateau Baroque after dinner a few days later and by midnight had overcome all the disadvantages of his first impression. Bouncing out of the elevator, Samson beheld a figure not much bigger than Roy Phillips', chewing on a huge cigar, swinging his hand like a roundhouse as he gripped Samson's, proclaiming his pleasure at the meeting in a loud voice, taking in the room with darting eyes as if he was casing it and then flopping into a chair and calling for a drink.

"I really need it, Mr. Duke," he said as Samson handed him a tall scotch and soda. "Been on the go since six o'clock this morning. That goddamn army bugled me out of the cot at dawn and I haven't been able to sleep late since." He took a long swallow, smacked his lips, set the drink on the table and looked around the room again. "You sure have a nice place here, Mr. Duke. This is the way to live." As he whipped out a lighter and applied it to his cold cigar, puffing furiously, Samson decided to let him talk. He tried to envision anyone placing confidence in this coarse little man and did not think it possible. On the other hand anyone who could make a fortune as a private first class must have more than meets the eye.

As Matlin went on speaking it became apparent that Harry Finkelstein had filled him in on Samson's background. His voice a clamor, he proclaimed his admiration, flattered and eulogized, punctuating his words with vigorous head-shaking, broad sweeps of his arms, clenched fists, commenting that he had known of Samson for a long time, had been wanting to meet him and that Finkelstein's suggestion that he call had been an answer to a prayer.

"I'm honest, Mr. Duke," he said with a pious look, "I say what I feel. You and I can do business together. I know it. And I'm here for that chance."

"Did Harry tell you what I had in mind?"

"Just that it had something to do with the building business." As Duke outlined his plan, Matlin did not interrupt, registering his reaction with body movement. By the time Samson was finished it was evident that Matlin understood and was in agreement with everything that had been said.

"I tell you what, Mr. Duke. There's a lot of talk around and it's cheap. Show me the land, tell me how much money the deal takes, and give me thirty days. I guarantee if the money isn't ready in a trust account it means the town's dried up."

Duke told him he had a hundred acres in Garden Grove, that the price was three thousand dollars an acre, that he wanted half in cash and would come in for the other half with the limited partners. Allan Hinds, the builder, was to get twenty per cent of the profits. Matlin was to get ten per cent for raising the money, and the limited partners were to split the balance. They discussed available financing, the type of house to be built, and the organizing of a sales force. Matlin offered to do more than just raise the front money for his cut; he would arrange the F.H.A. loans and put together a sales force. As he left, Samson said he would think it over. He was certain he would go ahead with Matlin, but a little sweat would do no harm.

The following day he made his deal with Allan Hinds. They agreed to use Duke's offices temporarily and Hinds was instructed to line up an architect. Walt Covington was already working on the form of the limited partnership and by the time Samson returned home that evening he experienced an excitement absent since the beginning of the war. The money made during the conflict had a different feel; his hand was not in the defense plant nor did it guide the stock market. The muscle he had formerly used was slack, there had been nothing to prove and less to do. It was a new game now and he had a hunch it was going to be a big one and he could not wait to wade in.

The following morning Phil Matlin was waiting in his reception room and followed him into his office. Without saying a word he tossed a bank book on Samson's desk showing a fifty-thousand dollar deposit in a trust account.

"Just in case you had doubts, Mr. Duke. There's one-third of what we need," he said, pointing to the book. "And it only took a phone call. The word's gotten around. I'll bet by the time I get to the temple tonight they'll be waiting in line." He was shifting the fat cigar from one side of his mouth to the other and grinning.

"How can people put up money when they don't know what it's for?"

"They're investing in me."

Samson smiled and extended his hand. "All right. We have a deal." Matlin grabbed his hand in both of his and pumped it hard. "Just give the orders, partner."

"My attorney is drawing the documents. Hinds, the builder, will order the engineering so we can file for the subdivision. It'll take a few months before we can start with the street improvements and building. In the meantime you can check with the F.H.A. Consider this your office, there's a desk outside and a phone."

Every time schedule was shattered by Phil Matlin's energy and drive. He hounded the architect, tormented the engineer, judicious greasing turned state officials in charge of subdivisions into office boys and while other contractors took their turn in line he flanked the ends and roared out in front. Not satisfied with the service he was getting at the local F.H.A. office he went to Washington and returned with his loan applications on top of the pile. With Matlin's hunger in the pot, Samson was certain it would be kept boiling and though he held the strings he gave the younger man all the slack he wished. The construction began before the streets were in and by the summer of 1947, a few days after the models were completed and the houses put on the market, all were sold.

Restless, undisciplined, and alienated from her mother, Carla had moved out of the house a half-dozen times within a period of two months, spent the night at Samson's apartment only to be dragged back the following day. At first, Paula responded with rage and threats, accused Samson of encouraging the child. But when Carla left one day, did not show up at Samson's and, instead, spent a night with a girl friend without calling Paula, it was finally decided to send her to a boarding school. Martin Tipton recommended one in Massachusetts, not far from Martha's Vineyard. Carla agreed to enroll provided Samson promised to visit her at least twice a year. She refused to have Paula take her to the station. Samson, accompanied by Lee Marlowe, picked her up a week before the commencement of the new semester. As they drove downtown with Carla between them, Carla clung to Samson's arm tearfully, exacting his promise to call and write often as well as visit during his trips to the East.

"Her mother must hate you," Lee remarked as the train pulled out and they walked to the car.

"I'm sure she hates herself. I had nothing to do with it."

"You'll never prove it to me."

"What are you talking about?"

"If you could see yourself when you're with that child . . ."

"I've known her since she's an infant. Her father was a louse and deserted her. I could afford it so I helped out. Actually we're relatives. You know that my first wife was her half-sister."

"All right, brother-in-law, drive on."

He had no wish to discuss it further and for a while they drove in silence. Lately he had been detecting an undercurrent of irritability in all of their conversations. Only when they lay together with all thoughts other than an impending orgasm nonexistent did he feel the closeness of their early relationship. There was no talk of marriage, but Lee would often talk about the fact that her daughter had a part-time father, deplore Samson's lack of interest in the child, and, one evening, reported that Laura asked her if Samson was not her other daddy. He ignored that remark and though she did not pursue it further she sent him home early without the usual wind-up in her locked bedroom. It was when he criticized her friends that her rancor became more manifest. Even when she would deliver a tirade against them for their superficiality, his agreement would turn her against him and she would flay him for his insensitivity to the arts. The arguments were usually more intense after he spent an evening with them and was forced to listen to what he considered their childish prattle about their make-believe world. Tonight he was headed to another of the dinner parties she put on so often and was determined to keep his mouth shut. If only they would talk about other things beside the little world in which they played their games. Well, perhaps they would leave in time for him to have a go at Lee before he went home.

Dropping Lee at her home he drove to his apartment, changed clothes, fortified himself with a couple of drinks, and returned to Brentwood to find the guests all assembled.

The evening spent itself in a usual course: the actors grimaced and gesticulated, the writers pontificated, the director mused with an air of aloofness. Everybody got drunk. The conversation switched from themselves to the cold war, Gandhi's fast—evolved with overtones of Communist sympathies from all present—and by the time the last of them staggered out, Samson sat sipping a brandy his contained rage mirrored in his eyes as Lee returned to the room and exploded.

"I will not tolerate rudeness to my guests!" She was on the fireplace pedestal, one arm draped on the mantel, glaring at him.

"What did I do?" he protested.

"Your contempt was evident by your silence," she said descending from the pedestal.

"There was nothing I had to say."

"Doesn't anything interest you besides making money? There's a big world out there," she said, with a sweep of her arm.

"Art, creativity, politics. . . ." She took a cigarette, lit it with a trembling hand, poured a drink of brandy, fell into a chair and stared ahead.

Her rage that night seemed to spring from deeper wells and he was certain that his attitude toward her guests was an excuse. The fear he had of losing her, which in the past he attributed to his insecurity, now became real and he proceeded with caution.

"If I was rude it was unintentional. I know little of art and perhaps I am not creative. I have nothing to contribute on these matters. As for politics . . . well, you know where I stand. You've accused me of red-baiting your friends before and I thought it best to keep my mouth shut." He watched her carefully, her face began to soften. "Why don't we forget it?"

She started to reply, then shook her head. "I'll forget it." She rose. "I'm very tired, Sam." The finality in her tone was too evident.

As he drove home, going over the events and conversations of the evening, despising himself for his docility, the fear of losing Lee dissolved in the fury that swept him. What do these people know about life? What have their responsibilities ever been other than to their egos and vanities? Two-bit actors, half-assed writers, loaded one day, broke the next, borrowing, living above their means, mooching and chiseling between jobs. And their left-wing politics. Chomping on filets and guzzling Courvoisier while they bleed for the proletariat. He wondered how they would talk if they had a balance in the bank and a paid-up car. As for Lee, she was never happier than when she picked up a few points in the market or he took her in on a deal. They were all full of shit, he concluded. The only difference between himself and the entire bunch was that he was honest and named the game.

CHAPTER NINETEEN

B y the time the second subdivision financed by Phil Matlin
was built and sold, Duke realized that the demand for new homes
eliminated any risk for him. Allan Hinds proved to be as capable
as Fines Cady promised, a sales organization was available, and a
little legwork was all that was needed to package a deal. He
owned the land, F.H.A. funds were unlimited, the profits were
enormous, and it made no sense for him to continue the arrangement with Phil Matlin, who had served a purpose during the pioneering period, when wrinkles had to be tackled and ironed out.
Everything was smooth now, one could not miss and Samson
called on Walt Covington. He decided to go into the building
business himself, hire Hinds on a fee basis to do the contracting
and make his arrangements with a sales organization. And all of it
could be operated with a couple of secretaries out of his office.

Covington listened as he outlined the plan. "You'll be making a
lot of money for Uncle Sam," he concluded. "You'll never get
away with capital gains."

494

"Suppose we form a separate corporation for each project? And dissolve it when we sell out?"

"They'll never allow it. Every nickel will be regular income."

"Suppose I establish another business? Then building can be a sideline."

"That other business will have to be damn big to make the construction business a sideline."

"Let me worry about it. In the meantime I'm dickering for a big hotel on the beach. It's a white elephant, but I can get in for a few years' prepaid interest as a down payment and think I can make it carry itself. The depreciation should give me over three hundred thousand dollars operating loss each year."

Covington shrugged. "That's only peanuts. You're talking about making millions."

"There are other deals like it around. I'm looking at one in New York next week. A sale and a leaseback. If it stacks up it should show a couple hundred thousand paper loss."

It was decided that separate corporations would be constructed for each project, they would hope that the government would allow capital gains when they were dissolved and that for insurance, Samson would shelter his income from building with as much paper loss as he could accumulate from depreciation on other buildings.

Matlin could not conceal his disappointment when Samson told him of his plans.

"We could become the biggest builders in the state, Sam."

"We don't need each other. There's going to be a few hundred thousand homes built in California in the next few years. Enough for a hundred builders."

"How much land have you got left?" Matlin asked.

"More than I need."

Matlin got up and paced, all of his body in motion. "Look, I know the business. You know I can raise money." He stopped at Duke's desk. "Sell me some land with no down payment. I'll pay you off within two years on every project and pay a premium price for the terms." He was tense, eager, holding his breath.

Why not? Samson thought. Now, Matlin was seasoned, knew the ropes, every shortcut and turn in the road. He could only miss if the entire economy sagged and that was not in sight. And when one bought land with nothing down the price was high. "Let's start with forty acres I got in Pomona. The price is four thousand an acre, no down, and subordination." He could almost hear the tumult in Matlin's brain, there was a smile on the younger man's lips but his eyes were cold.

"Isn't the price a little high? There's stuff kicking around the area for twenty-five hundred."

"My land is prime."

"But Pomona's Pomona."

"That's the price, Phil. If I don't get it now," he shrugged, "in a year they'll be begging for it."

"Have you got a plot map?"

Ruth Bennett brought in the map and Matlin said he would see the land and discuss it further.

"I'll be in New York next week. Let me know when I get back."

The plane lofted, in minutes was over the sea, banked sharply and headed east. He had an appointment to inspect the building the following morning, would look at a few comparables afterwards and conclude with a meeting with the broker. He had no intention of making an offer while in New York, would express enough interest to solicit the broker's pursuit and wait until the seller got hungry.

He had not seen Carla for nearly a year. She had remained in New England during the first summer away, preferring to spend the holiday at a friend's home on the Cape rather than with Paula, who had objected strenuously but was finally forced to consent. At first, Carla's letters were cool as if punishing him for their separation. Then the tones changed and she filled pages with enthusiasm about the school and her new friends and her last few letters were pleas for his visit. Arrangements had been made for her to take a few days off from school, he reserved a two-bedroom suite at the Warwick and planned to spend the balance of the trip showing her the sights. The business trip was an excuse he confessed, the separation from Carla had left a void that neither preoccupation with business nor Lee's ministrations had filled. All his life his relations with others excepting Aunt Annie had a transiency, bound together with feeble threads that broke when self-interest began to wither. In the rare moments when he permitted his thoughts to vault far into the future even to the end of his life and he totaled the residuals of all his efforts, Carla emerged as his only nonelusive treasure. She would marry he was sure and her children also would be his, their very existence added vines that would bind them all together. Carla and whoever she brought into the world would be the only evidence of his flesh. As for Paula, her perversion was abdicating her role and he would wait for that day when her position would be completely vacated. And he would always be near to fill every void as it appeared.

He spent the following day inspecting the property, making comparisons and consulting with the broker. Unlike the setups handed out by Los Angeles brokers, the prospectus mailed to him by the New York agent was conservatively composed. The building looked better than it did on paper. Samson evidenced his interest and told the broker he would think it over and get in touch with him after he returned to L.A. That night, he returned early, excited at thoughts of seeing Carla the following day.

The next morning he ate a large breakfast in the hotel dining room, and by noon was at Grand Central impatiently awaiting the arrival of Carla's train. He tried to picture her a year older, imagined a Paula at fifteen, lovelier, perhaps taller, larger-eyed and gayer, but when the gates opened and he saw her walking toward him all his conceptions paled. She was full-grown, her head was high as she approached him with long graceful strides, her face was haloed with a thick black sheen that matched the dark depths of her eyes and flowed to the back of her neck tied loosely with a white silk bow. He swept her in his arms, held her close, put her from him, surveyed her, took her in his arms again and led her from the terminal before either said a word.

At the baggage stand he finally spoke. "You've grown. You're a young lady."

She hugged his arm, her look tender as her eyes searched his face. "You haven't changed, Uncle Sam. Just as handsome and dashing as ever. I'm so happy to be with you."

In the taxi, still clinging to his arm she loosed a barrage that reminded him of their meetings on the Sundays he would have her for the day.

"I've only been to New York once for a weekend. There's so much to see. What have you planned, Uncle Sam? Can you spend much time with me? I want to see a play and go to a fine restaurant and Central Park and the Metropolitan Museum. . . . Fifth Avenue, the shops. . . . I have two new dresses with me and high heels. . . . the girls at school died with envy. . . . Oh, Uncle Sam," she went on throwing her arms about his neck, "I missed you so."

His business was finished, he would be with her until she returned to school, he told her, they would see a play every night and there would be dinners and shopping and a boat ride around Manhattan and the top of the Empire State, all would be hers to see from the Battery to Central Park.

As he waited in the sitting room of the suite for her to change, answering her chattering questions as she shouted through the half-open door, he was swept with a feeling of tenderness he had never experienced. The next few days had to be all Carla's, every moment minted for her pleasure and joy, he wanted nothing for himself but to see her happy. Any other compensation would diminish the gift he wanted to give. They would see the plays she chose, eat where she wished, trudge through the park, explore the city until his feet were sore, go to sleep when she wished and if necessary get going with the dawn.

By the time they were back at Grand Central having their last cup of coffee together as they awaited her departure on the eight o'clock train, he discovered that New York proffered a face for the young and that only an unquenchable determination to please propelled his tired fat. She had set the pace of their holiday and he had followed gallantly; little sleep (one had to be insane to sleep in Manhattan, she had said), wearying walks, jolting taxis, matinees, and eight-thirty curtains, late suppers, breakfast at dawn, shopping tours and the hard marble floors of the Metropolitan. As he watched her sipping her coffee mournfully he felt a need for the first time to tell her the truth. What joy there would be if he could add to their relationship the knowledge that would bind them forever. She was his daughter but to her he was only a benefactor who would one day be replaced by a closer tie and he was certain to become a fond memory, a pseudo uncle, a fill-in when a father was needed.

At the gate she lifted her face, he kissed her gently on the lips, her eyes filled as she turned abruptly and ran toward the train.

CHAPTER TWENTY

The building boom surpassed dreams of the optimists. New tracts opened at dawn to block-long lines of prospective buyers queued all night to get someone to take their down payments. Land prices zoomed, construction workers peddled themselves to highest bidders, materials found their way to jobs through a black market, shopping centers sprung up at the edge of tracts, and ex-carpenters, now contractors, were driving Cadillacs with telephones. The two-thousand-dollar acre went to five and ten and then to fifteen; hundreds prowled the outskirts looking for land to build as suburbia spread west in the San Fernando Valley, east in the San Gabriel Valley, north to the foothills, and up the sides of mountains. The money for loans flowed from banks, insurance companies, and savings and loans associations, and Uncle Sam backed it with a guarantee. Syndicates were formed and oversubscribed; everybody was standing in line. To know a builder was to have the best friend in town.

By the time Samson Duke finished his fourth tract, completed over a thousand homes, setting aside the commercial land for a shopping development, he decided to leave the game. The real profit was in the land. Let the others scrounge for skilled workers, bleed in the black market, fight with the F.H.A., the building inspectors, and the Department of Subdivisions. His own construction added to what he had sold to Phil Matlin only consumed about five hundred acres. He had two thousand left in the San Fernando Valley, Orange County, the hot spots. Land was expendable and builders knew it and by God he would make them bid.

With the exception of a few buildings that still retained depreciation fat and the clear land, his assets were tied up in securities, trust deeds, and an enormous amount of cash all of which could be managed by a competent secretary. In the summer of 1950, just after the start of the Korean War, he made his move. Everything old would go; there would be a new office, new setting and horizons, a renewal of vigor. Ruth Bennett was nearing sixty, the signs of her age a constant reminder of his over-forty status. She had been thinking of retiring she told him when he disclosed his plans; her daughter was married, lived in San Diego, and there were two grandchildren she wanted to be near. After a session during which she alternated between slobbering gratitude and shrill praise it was decided she would stay until he found new offices and made the move. Jack Delaney received the news with more composure. He was getting on, he said—sixty-two—had a neat pile fattened recently by the annuity policy set up for him years before, and plans.

"Sam, you forced me to do something I wanted to do but didn't have the guts."

"What's that?"

"There's a little widow up in Oxnard. Used to be married to a navy man. We've been sort of talking about getting tied-up. But with me working down here and her living up there taking care of some property she has, well, it was an excuse to stall." His eyes were on Duke but he did not seem to be talking to him. "I guess when a man reaches a certain age he gets a little scared. Getting old and being alone." His eyes lit up. "Ruby, that's her name, is pretty young yet. Somewhere in the forties. She likes to do things, all kinds, and I figure an old horse needs driving to keep going." If it was all right, he would leave at the end of the month.

Now that the decision was made and the move begun, Samson felt like he was shedding an old skin and couldn't wait to wriggle free. With the exception of large pieces of real estate held for tax shelters only, all of his assets would be tied up in the best inventory of all, cash and its equivalent. It always had a market, was a first lien on everything and a vault full of it could be engineered by one brain. Renting a suite of offices in Beverly Hills, he furnished it lavishly and by the fall of the year had leased the old bank building to a mortgage company, retired Delaney and Mrs. Bennett, and began to interview secretaries. He wanted one young he told the employment agency, in her twenties, competent and she had to be attractive. The salary he promised was high and by God he wanted something good to look at. Mrs. Bennett offered to remain on until he hired someone but he would not consider it; he wanted none of her appraisals or assessments. He borrowed a bookkeeper from Tipton and started the interviews. By the end of two weeks he ran through twenty applicants, and was about to conclude that good tits and legs and a pretty face did not go with ninety words a minute and a knowledge of bookkeeping, when a young woman was ushered into his office at the end of a day. The measurements were perfect, the hair was red, dyed for certain but a match for green eyes and smooth white skin that set off soft lips below a small nose. And he liked her walk as she crossed the room, head high, handed him a card with her name and took the seat before his desk.

"Sherry Larsen," he read aloud, put the card on the desk and watched her as she surveyed the room displaying a profile that matched the loveliness of her full face. "Tell me about your experience," he continued.

"I've had nine years. Typing, shorthand and bookkeeping. Started when I was nineteen. My typing is perfect, I can take a letter as fast as one can dictate."

"How about bookkeeping?"

"I understand you're in real estate. That's why the agency sent me. My last job was with Western Escrow Company. I handled all their books, made out their closing statements."

"Why did you leave?"

"The salary was too low and they wouldn't give me a raise." She lit a cigarette, took a deep drag and then continued. "Look, Mr. Duke, I know you're a busy man and must have interviewed a lot of girls. I know what you want and I can fill the bill." She hesitated a moment and continued. "I want a certain kind of a job and a decent salary. I'm not broke and can wait until I find it. The salary you offer is fine for a start and I'm looking for a position in a one-woman office. This may sound immodest, but you'll be making a mistake if you pass me up." She smiled for the first time.

"Are you married? Any children?"

"Divorced. No children or invalid mothers to take care of. I don't like to work overtime but when it's necessary I will."

"Do you live alone?" The moment the words were out he regretted them. He was looking for competent help, not a piece of tail. If there was a bonus later, well and good, but he did not want to give her the impression that a piece of ass once in awhile would compensate for goofing on the job.

She smiled. "I live alone, Mr. Duke."

"When can you start?"

"Monday morning would be fine."

"Miss Becker in the outer office is here temporarily. She will spend as much time as necessary to show you the files and the bookkeeping. If any questions come up after she leaves you can contact her at my accountant's office." He rose and extended his hand. She took it and he held her hand as he continued. "If you're as qualified as you say there will be no problems." He released her hand. "The bookkeeping will be simple," he said, as he escorted her to the door. "But there'll be a lot of correspondence. The hours are nine to six with an hour for lunch. On days your desk is cleared by five you can leave. If your work piles and you're needed after six I expect you to stay on."

By the end of the following week her speed in taking his dictation and letter-perfect transcribing made him realize that Ruth
Bennett put in long hours to compensate for a lack of efficiency.
Sherry Larsen was good to look at, she smelled good, her skirts fit
tight, her ass was round, and she didn't lumber in and out of a
room; she made his office a place for pleasure as well as work.

The old business was dumped, together with Ruth Bennett and
Jack Delaney. Phil Matlin and his investors were scrambling on
their own, a whole new field was wide open—the money business—and Duke set out.

From a conversation in the locker room of the club he learned
that Universal Savings and Loan Association of Beverly Hills was
for sale. A few phone calls and a Dun and Bradstreet's report elicited the information that the company was family held, conservatively run, with small assets, and a valuable charter. Further prob-
ing informed him that Ben Hardin, a one-time actors' agent who
was now in the mortgage business had optioned all of the stock
and was beating the bushes for investors.

Hardin was easy to reach, had heard of Duke, he said, and
would be happy to discuss the deal. During the meeting in Duke's
office he displayed the histrionics of Lee Marlowe and mixed it
with the body movements of Phil Matlin, adding a flair that
seemed to emanate from an enormous vanity and ego. About
Duke's age with a crop of prematurely gray hair topping a classic
profile, he gave the appearance of Hollywood's version of a vote-
getting politician. After minutes of pacing and jaw-jutting, loud
assertions and demands, insistence of the invulnerability of his position, he was persuaded to take the seat before Duke's desk.

"With three months to go you'll probably raise all the needed
capital," Duke began. "But you'll be dealing with dozens of investors, each with his own accountant, many with an attorney.
By the time you satisfy everyone you'll have a deal, an ulcer, and
a coronary."

"You're wrong. I've got something good and everyone I've
talked to knows it."

"Fifty partners can drive you crazy, Hardin. I've had them. Anyway, I can offer a bonus the others can't."

"Bonuses can be expensive."

"Not mine. Because I'll be padding my own account as well as yours."

Hardin yanked out a cigar, lit it, puffed it furiously and then settled back. He seemed calmer, like a squawking infant given a pacifier. "What about the bonuses."

"I have the unlimited capital needed for expansion, a contact in Sacramento for additional charters, and a vast knowledge of real estate available when needed. You can be the boss, run the whole thing, Hardin. I'm willing to be a limited partner. I just want the right to put my nose in and make suggestions."

Hardin rose and began to move about the room, slower this time, speaking as he moved, emphasizing with a hand that chopped and swept. "I'll make you the offer. It's not open to counter proposals. I have an option on the stock for $300,000. It's worth double," he chopped. "Right now. Today. You put up the money, all of it. I get half the stock which I'll put up as collateral for my share. I'm the boss, we consult, that's all."

"Can I see a balance sheet? P and L statements?"

Hardin grinned. "For the last twenty years. You won't believe it. It's Fort Knox, the Bank of England. All the ink is black. There was never a Depression, never a foreclosure. He took the cigar from his mouth and leaned over the desk. "With Universal's record we'll get a dozen charters. The public will gobble the stock like chickens a sack of corn."

Within a week they made their deal and a month later took over the Association. They went through the personnel like locusts and within ninety days not an old employee remained, all of them fired, their brains picked clean. Samson brought a half a million of his own as a deposit, tapped Martin Tipton and Covington for a chunk, insisted on a hundred-thousand deposit from Hofstedter who made it squealing, solicited everyone he knew not missing Lee Marlowe and Sherry Larsen and with an additional million and a half in deposits, went to Sacramento to call on George Turner.

Though he managed to keep in touch with the politician with Christmas gifts, occasional notes and an appropriate letter of condolence when his wife Inez died, he had not seen him in a couple of years. Martin Tipton had mentioned that the loss of Inez had been devastating but Duke was not prepared for the shriveled replica of Turner's former mountainous self. His once fat face sagged in folds, the triple chin was hanging gray flesh and the eyes, without life, peered suspiciously from a cavern surrounded by brown wrinkled skin. His clothes hung like Charlie Chaplin's rags. During the meeting he barely spoke, utilizing shrugs, head-shaking, eyebrows, hands, and occasional grunts. It was as if there was nothing worthy of comment, that he disliked repetition, and long ago had said everything he had on his mind.

He wanted to open a new branch of Universal Savings and Loan as soon as possible, Samson told him, and needed a sub-charter. There was sufficient capitalization increase, they had a piece of land optioned on Sunset Boulevard for a location, and all they needed was the grease to move.

"If you can conform to all regulations it's simple," Turner said.

"How simple?"

"Fifty thousand in cash. Delivered here in used bills."

"That's a lot of money, George."

"There's a lot of hands out. It's a lot of favor." He half-rose as if to signify the meeting was at an end. Samson smiled quickly, pulled out a wallet and withdrew a wad of bills which he placed on the desk.

"A deposit." Turner swept up the bills, crumbling them as they were jammed into his pocket. "I'll have the balance on delivery," Samson said.

"No C.O.D.'s. All the money in advance."

"Suppose something goes wrong?"

"There's a hundred applications for charters for each one granted. I'm the only man who can guarantee delivery. The only thing you can stumble over would be my dead body. Bring in all the money and pray for my good health."

The charter was delivered and by the end of the year they got yet another and opened a branch in the San Fernando Valley. Now, small banks were beginning to spring up everywhere. The public gobbled the stock which rose far out of proportion to the earnings. Everybody was buying the future, there was going to be all up and no down, the country was headed for inflation, committed to it; cash was a dirty word and only a fool hung on to it. Samson Duke, with huge sums to deposit in a new bank, boosting it off the ground, found himself courted by the promoters and soon became a director and stockholder of a dozen banks. A multimillion dollar statement and a million in cash brought him in on the ground floor and paid for a loud voice in management. He would keep his deposit in long enough to solidify his position, latch on to founder's stock at bargain prices and then shift the funds as needed to repeat the process. Some of the bank stock was held in his own name, others in the name of corporations he controlled. Through his directorships he managed to get on loan committees and then he hit upon a plan and rushed to see Walt Covington about its implementation.

"I think it's foolproof," he explained to the attorney. "But I want another head to be sure." Covington listened with half closed eyes, the top of his head inches below the high-backed chair as he swiveled slowly back and forth stopping occasionally to lean forward and make a note. "I've been making loans and collecting bonuses. The percentage of my return is dependent upon the length of the loan. The shorter the period the bigger the return. Listen to this, Walt," he said, unable to contain a broad smile. "I make a fifty-thousand loan on a piece of real estate. It's for one year. I charge five maybe ten points bonus. Suppose I can turn around immediately and sell that loan and only give away a point or two?"

"A good supposition," Covington said. "If you can find a sucker."

"That's it, I control a dozen suckers. I just want to know if they can bite back."

"You don't mean to unload them to Universal and the banks?" Covington asked.

"Unload's the wrong word. I mean to sell it to them, add to their portfolio. I want to know the risks, Walt. Is it legal?"

"It's legal but damned unethical. If a loan goes sour and the bank takes a bump you'll have to talk fast to explain away a conflict of interest." He straightened up and leaned across the desk. "It'll leave you wide open."

"Suppose I sell them with recourse, guarantee them."

"That's different. But you'll be the sucker. There'll be contingent liabilities on a ton of paper."

"A small risk. Money is going to get cheaper for the rest of our lives. We're doomed to inflation. And if it ever goes the other way, breadlines and apple peddlers, there'll be a new government with a different face. Maybe Lenin's picture will be on a dollar bill."

Circulating the word that he had unlimited funds for loans, Duke got submissions from brokers from Malibu to downtown. Soon he was making two, three loans a week, big ones, construction first, interim financing, and first trust deeds on prime land, all short term packing big bonuses. Distributing them carefully among the banks and Universal he soon was placing about a hundred thousand dollars' worth a week, giving away a point or two, and pocketing the difference.

His drive was matched by Hardin who remained at his desk in Universal Savings and Loan's main office eighteen hours a day. By the time they opened the third branch the Association's deposits zoomed to fifty million and they began preparing a prospectus for a public issue. They ran the maze of the Securities Exchange Commission without a hitch and by the time the fourth branch was under construction the stock hit the public, was gobbled up in hours and Duke's and Hardin's holdings multiplied geometrically.

The game ate time like a hog. An eight-hour day was always tight and Sherry Larsen never left the office before seven. There was Saturday work too and an occasional Sunday, all of which was done in the library of Samson's apartment. At first, Sherry brought pad and pencil, a professional manner in office dress. Warmer days brought casual clothes, breaks for a swim and cocktail hours. Sherry's cool unemotional detachment seemed to hold out promise for an uncomplicated arrangement. And lately, Lee Marlowe was boiling over more frequently, seemed to be taking longer stints on out-of-town locations. Their bouts in bed when they did occur seemed less relished and more constrained. The constant proximity to Sherry began to produce heat and one night as he lay in bed thinking about her he found himself fingering a hard-on. The following day he gave her a raise in salary, the third since she was hired, and told her she would be needed for the weekend. Alex was ordered out and told not to return until Monday.

Sherry arrived early Saturday morning carrying a small bag in which she usually packed her bathing suit, removed a dress, underthings and a pair of shoes which she placed in the closet.

"I hope you don't mind," she said as he watched her unpack. "I'm meeting a girl friend after work."

"I was hoping you'd have dinner with me," he blurted.

"I need a little notice."

He looked at his watch. "It's nine o'clock. Dinner at eight. That's eleven hours."

She looked at him a long moment without expression, then a smile touched a corner of her lips. "I'll call my friend." He left the room as she dialed returning a few minutes later with the work file.

"Dinner?"

"At eight."

They stabbed at work all morning, he dictated mechanically,

her letters came out of the machine with errors and omissions, they stopped for coffee two or three times, there was a tenseness like between opponents before a bout. Though he had been observing her for months, wondered if the breasts were real or rubbered, the thighs as soft as he imagined the ass round or faked, it was an appraisal without the savour of anticipating the imminent. They stopped for lunch; he opened a bottle of wine and they never got back to work. There was a swim and a hot shower a little romping and a fuck all done as if it had been rehearsed.

He lay beside her as she dozed, breathing gently. He thought about Lee, the complicated maneuvers, the lines of dialogue before the act which ended up a small part of a big scene. Sometimes he felt like a minor player upstaged by a star. With Sherry it had been simple; perfect chemistry, a short prologue, a hard prick, a wet cunt, and one long act. And her body, all of it round and firm; better than the label on the package. By God he was relaxed, he thought—drained—she knew when to move and when to stop, to squeeze and release, built his load behind a dam before she opened the locks. It was superb—artistry—with a purity of its own.

She stirred and he turned toward her, they wrapped around each other face to face, her lips touched his—so soft—her mouth opened and he felt her breath, her tongue, musk mixed with perfume, his hand ran the velvet of her ass, she twisted gently, his cock was hard and hot again—so miraculously soon—and he rolled her over and rammed it in. Now she was asleep, the day was wearing out, the gray light of evening shrouded the room and he closed his eyes. When he awoke the room was barely lit by the hall light's beam, he heard a rustle, turned and watched as Sherry struggled into a slip, reached for a garter, and strapped a hose.

"What time is it?"

"Almost eight."

"I slept for hours."

"We both did. I just got up."

He twisted out of the covers and stood beside the bed, her back was toward him as she faced him in the mirror. "I knew this was going to happen, Boss," she began. "The day you hired me I knew it." He waited. She strapped the other hose and turned to face him. "And it was good like I knew it would be." He nodded as she stepped into her dress, zipped the side and straightened up. "Put something on, Boss." He slipped into a robe and followed her into the living room. Standing at the window with her back toward him, she lit a cigarette and began to speak. "I found out a long time ago that most things are better said—quick. There's no misunderstandings." She turned. "Can I have a little bourbon and water, Boss?"

"Sam . . ."

"Boss . . ."

He shrugged, poured her drink, one for himself and settled in a chair as she stood over him.

"I don't want to lose my job." He started to interrupt but she went on. "I like the work and the pay. There's nobody to support me—yet." She flopped in a chair across the room, pulled at the drink, set it down and looked at him, seemed to hesitate as if deciding to continue. He took the moment.

"You'll always have a job."

She smiled a little sadly and went on. "Boss, you know nothing about me. Never asked. I began to work when I was nineteen. That's when I got married. My husband just started medical school. We were broke. I had a dream, a doctor's wife, and. . . . well, he studied and I worked. Six years. Typing all day, cocktail waitress at night. It paid the rent, bought clothes, food, books and tuition." He took her extended glass and refilled it. "It's funny," she went on, "you dream, build on it, pad it, soon you have a house on a knoll overlooking the Bay—we lived in San Francisco —and kids and you're a doctor's wife and the rest of your life is mapped. All you've got to do is live it nice and easy. Then things begin to happen that you don't want to believe because you don't want to lose your dream. Anyway, my doctor stayed out nights, we fought, he lied, and a year before he was to start his practice he left me."

"Another woman?"

"A rich one. She got him all made. Ready to go. Opened a swell office for him. She has the house and the kids."

"I'm sorry, Sherry."

"I'm not. Obviously he was a louse." She looked at her watch. "It's getting late. Why don't you shower and dress? I'd like to go to dinner."

The evening was over and there were no misunderstandings. Her lines were out and husband number two was going to be rich; Samson was a catch but would never be bagged, she enjoyed tussling with him too much to turn it down, their chemistry had a lot of glue and was better than love and lies. She knew about Lee Marlowe and did not care, made it clear when she got a nibble on another line she would shake Samson loose. He found it difficult to contain his elation; she was a gold bond in reserve with no contingent liabilities. She spent the weekend at his apartment, they played in the bed on the couch and floor, there were smells and touch and sounds, discovery; it was all without words.

CHAPTER TWENTY-ONE

Samson dialed Paula's number then hung up quickly. How in hell could he tell her that her daughter wanted to come out for the summer vacation on the condition that she stay with him? How could he permit Carla to visit L.A. and find her mother living with Ann Schneider, who had moved her Cuban heels under their double bed, never let Paula out of her sight, and fondled her man-like regardless of who was in the room?

He picked up the phone and dialed again. It had to be resolved and the sooner the better. He was calling about a letter he had received from Carla, he said, thought it should be discussed and asked if she would meet at his office or apartment.

"We'll meet at my house this time," Paula said coldly.

"Suit yourself."

"I'll be home all evening."

The house was a small bungalow done over in Regency style with a shingled mansard roof, ornamental iron trellis, and shuttered windows. The area, a half-dozen block compound just south of Sunset Boulevard, had been taken over by homosexuals and was known as Fairyland. With imagination and excellent taste the small community had been transformed from rows of boxlike California bungalows to small chalets, Italian villas, English cottages, and modern townhouses. A huge white French poodle greeted him in the entry hall as Ann Schneider opened the door. Decked with a rhinestone collar and a blue ribbon, the animal reared, gripped his shoulders with his front paws and before Duke could squirm aside, was up against him simulating a dry fuck.

"Get down, Beau!" Ann commanded. The dog leaped aside, danced into the living room as Samson followed. Shouting further orders, Ann managed to get the animal settled in a corner quivering and wailing. "He's not used to strangers," she said, waving Samson to a seat. "Paula is showering. She'll be in shortly." She extended a hand. "May I see the letter?" He started to withdraw it from his pocket and stopped.

"I'd rather give it to Paula."

Ann shrugged, seated herself, lit a cigarette, picked up a magazine, turned the pages idly, and ignored him. He had only seen Ann Schneider two or three times before. They had never exchanged more than a dozen words, their mutual dislike without qualification. He examined her carefully now, looking for evidence of her masculinity and with the exception of a simple wool skirt and a mannish shirt saw nothing that would separate her from her sisters. What the hell made them that way . . . trade the real thing for a dildo? He had seen pictures of them—six-, seven-inch rubber pricks, crafted to scale, a perpetual hard-on cold as brass balls. Ann Schneider crossed her legs, he got a flash of bare thigh, his mind's eye traveled to her crotch and he saw her striding a broom, a strapped-on cock sticking straight out not far below hanging tits. What a sight, he thought, controlled a smile as the dog left the corner of the room, whirled and leaped on Paula who had entered from the hall. Ann dragged the animal into the kitchen, closed the door and returned as Paula began to read the letter. Finishing, she handed it to Ann who read it hurriedly and then turned on Duke.

"You surely don't plan on having Carla stay with you?"

He ignored her and addressed Paula. "She can't stay with me. What do we do?"

"I'm writing her," Paula said. "She's coming out this summer. And she's staying with me."

"In this house?"

"What's wrong with this house?" Ann said.

"You know damn well what's wrong." They were all on their feet now in the center of the room, the dog began to dance around them like a fighter looking for an opening.

"Don't bother with him, Ann," Paula interceded. She was brushed aside as Ann approached him closer. "Let me tell you something, Mr. Duke, before you leave, which will be in a minute." Beau was snapping at his feet. "You've done all the dirty work you're going to do. That girl is coming here this summer. And if you do anything to stop her, she'll learn enough about you to turn you out as a leper. Now get out!" The dog had the cuff of his trouser, Paula pulled him off by the collar as he strained, yelling and leaping, Ann ran to the front door and opened it. "Get out!" He rushed from the house and she slammed the door.

What a fool he had been, he thought as he drove blindly heading for his apartment. For years, every contact with Paula had ended this way; hardly veiled civility then the explosion and the pouring out of hate. He did not know how, not yet, but by God, Carla was not going to set foot in that house. A young, fresh, more beautiful edition of her mother, he was certain Ann Schneider would be after her in no time. Almost side-swiping a parked car on Doheny Road he pulled to the curb, shut off the engine and waited until he began to calm and his thoughts became tempered with reason. Paula would write that letter, it would promise an exciting summer, be a gentle plea, motherly. Though he was certain Carla would not respond, he was taking no chances, would come up with bigger, more luscious bait. Starting the car, he headed home.

He went over each detail of the plan carefully before he placed the call to Carla the following day.

"Did you receive my letter?" Carla asked the moment she heard his voice.

"I got it yesterday. I went to see your mother."

"Why?"

"I had to. She'd never stand for your coming out here and not staying with her."

"I'll be eighteen next week, Uncle Sam. I don't need her permission."

"It's academic anyway. I plan to be in Europe most of the summer." Now he took the one chance. "Of course if you want to come out anyway and stay in my apartment alone. . . ."

"I want to be with you."

"Then it's simple. There are dozens of student European tours. Sign up on one and I'll be able to meet you over there. But you must write your mother immediately and tell her of your change in plans. Don't mention that I'm coming over."

"Why do we have to lie, Uncle Sam?"

"Because I don't want to hurt your mother. Please do as I say."

She would write the letter, she said, and then asked when he was coming to New York. It had been nearly a year since they had seen each other and summer was so far away.

"I have so much to tell you. I graduate this June, you know. And I've been accepted at Wellesley. Please come soon."

Why not? He wanted to see her and he needed a change. "Can you get away for a long weekend?"

"Of course!"

"I'll make arrangements and call you back."

Let Paula match that lure, he thought as he hung up. And if Carla's letter reached her before she had a chance to write, he might never be suspected.

His plane arrived late and Carla was waiting for him in the lobby of the Warwick. The moment she rushed into his arms, kissing his mouth, his cheeks, clinging to him, a fine perfume encompassing, and he held her at arm's length and her eyes held his, he realized the accommodations he arranged for would be unsuitable. There was something about her that challenged, warned, and he left her and changed the two-bedroom suite he had reserved, for separate rooms—unconnecting. How could anyone change so much in a year, he marveled as they rode the elevator to their floor? She did not question the arrangements, different from all his other visits and he half-suspected she shared his thoughts. Disturbed at his excitement he arranged to meet her in the lobby after cleaning up.

They found a small French restaurant on 56th Street where she ordered her first cocktail with him, puffed languidly on a cigarette, watching him bemusedly as he tried to avoid her eyes. They talked about the European trip. It was to be for two months, chaperoned, but she would be able to slip away and be with him. She did not write Paula, she told him, but called and everything was settled, her mother seemed satisfied; they even ended their conversation on a pleasant note. He was not to worry, she added, there was not a hint of his meeting her in Europe. A bottle of wine she insisted on ordering with dinner flushed her cheeks, peals of her laughter rang from their table— half-hysteria he wondered—then she quieted, seemed to steal her glances at him, he felt warmed by the wine and then began to sweat. He had to end it—that moment—she was delicious—a stranger—he must be mad! Barking at the waiter for the check he paid it hurriedly, rushed her out of the restaurant, they walked silently to the hotel, her arm linked in his. He had to get away—to his room—think! Pleading exhaustion and promising an early breakfast together he left her at the door to her room with a peck on the cheek.

He locked his door, opened the window wide, looked out over the city, breathed the cool night air. He drank too much, that was all and he was exhausted, tomorrow morning everything would be different—like it really was. You cross a country in hours, rush from a late plane, no rest, drinks and food in a poorly ventilated restaurant with a woman who was a girl and the wine has fumes and the perfume—everything is fuzzy—you're not thinking. Can I be so drunk! He kicked off his shoes, flopped on the bed and buried his face in the pillow.

The ring was insistent, a clang that matched the pounding in his head, he rolled over and picked up the phone. His mouth was cotton, his head was full of lint, his collar was tight, his belt pressed, her voice was crisp.

"First call for breakfast."

"Meet you in the lobby." The sound of his voice summoned his brain. Cold shower, shave, dress . . . start all over . . . sanity. The shower head needled—cleared his head—the razor ran his face without a nick, the lotion stung and he smelled the spice. It was all real now as he dressed, the night before a fantasy. She was not in the lobby, he took a seat facing the elevators and waited. He tried to train his thoughts on mapping the next few days: seeing a few brokers, even shopping on his own, but there was only her face, the figure he dared not appraise the night before and the way she looked at him. And his own damn excitement. Jesus, God, he could not wait to lay eyes on her! Every time the elevator hit the lobby he couldn't wait for the door to open. He tried to build a barrier against his tumult. . . . *she's my daughter, I've changed her dirty pants, wiped her running nose, led her by a tiny hand!* The pounding in his chest was now a beat in his head, the elevator door opened, he jumped up as she ran to him kissed him full on the mouth, took his arm and led him to the dining room off the lobby.

She insisted on sitting next to him at a corner table instead of across and he felt her thigh press against him as he mumbled his order and inched away. Now she seemed to withdraw, there were moments of long silences, lingering looks as if they were strangers who just met, assessing, treading carefully. By the time they finished breakfast he managed to ease the tension, bring to the surface the bubbling excitement she always evidenced on her previous trips to New York. They would see the shows, buy clothes for her trip; a new set of luggage and dine in a list of restaurants she had compiled.

For the next few days he made every effort to contain the forces that flailed at all of his attempts to hide the feelings that ripped at his guts. Dining in Jim Downey's, one of Carla's favorite restaurants, the night before he was to leave, he ran into a real-estate broker he knew who was alone at the bar. Anxious to be alone with Carla on the one hand, but constantly fearing the moment when the fragile façade he had erected to hide his feelings would be swept aside, he was almost relieved when the broker, Frank Evans, asked to join them for dinner. Older than Duke, but witty and urbane, he slid into the booth and after the introduction to Carla, never took his eyes off her, nor stopped talking to her, ignoring Samson who found himself fighting an outburst of jealous rage. The man was old, there was sag and wrinkles and gray, damnit the skin creped, the fingers were claws. Don't touch her, do you hear! The night would not end. Evans rhapsodized, eulogized. Dinner and wine, then a walk from Eighth Avenue to St. Patrick's and Carla held their hands squeezing his and looking at Evans and her hips were swinging and the breasts bounced against her pink blouse. . . . In his room he stalked and finally undressed, burying himself, his thoughts, under the blankets.

She went to the airport with him, her train was not leaving until hours later, and she made it clear as he entered the ramp. "I'll be waiting for you in Paris. . . . Samson."

Was there not anything in genes that communicated? As the plane strained toward the Coast his thoughts fought back to the night Paula told him she was pregnant, he tried to remember her words, her look; was it a lie to dump Art Jennings and latch on to him? Jennings was contemptible, her marriage an ugly trap and he could have been the route for escape. Suppose he did find out for certain that he was taken in, made a fool of all these years? Then what? Carla was only eighteen. He was old enough to be her father and he acted and felt that way all these years and now. . . . What did happen? She made the advances from the moment they embraced in the lobby of the Warwick and then she flirted, teased, beguiled, and he fought, but not for long. But why was it necessary, she was his daughter. . . . Wasn't she? As hard as he tried not to, he fantasized and his thoughts riding with terror brought Carla to him as a woman, not a daughter, not a child and he felt engulfed with a feeling of love he had never experienced—

and desire. Perhaps if he combed the past, ran down every clue, pressed Paula, demanded, he might get the confession that she lied. And what about Art Jennings?

By the time the plane's wheels touched the field at Los Angeles his mind was made up. There could be no work, no thought for anything else. Alighting from the plane he bought a ticket for the next flight to Las Vegas, checked into the Flamingo and placed a call to Art Jennings. He had not seen him since they parted years before, heard he had been doing well in real estate, had married again—a young dancer. Art greeted him with a friendliness he did not expect, would be delighted to see him he said and they arranged for supper within the hour. Apparently the high desert air and a young wife was agreeable. When Jennings met him in the lobby he looked younger, trimmer than Duke had ever seen him. Draping an arm around Duke's shoulder, Jennings led him to the dining room where he was greeted by the captain who led them to a corner booth.

"The usual, Mr. Jennings?"

"Canadian and water, Frank." He turned to Duke who ordered scotch and soda and handed them the menu. "You order, Sam," Jennings said. "I'll drink along." As Duke looked over the menu, Jennings went on. "Sometimes you don't know whether you're getting the back of a hand or a shove in the right direction. When you kicked me out I hated your guts. No hard feelings, Sam. You did me a favor. I was through in L.A. and didn't want to admit it." He was grinning, his eyes laughing. "This town is new, booming and I'm in the middle of it. And I got the best wife I ever had."

By the time Duke was on his coffee, Jennings was on his fourth drink, a double, each drink brought a toast to the "good old days" and a pat on the back. He would never get Jennings' tongue that loose again.

"What I don't understand, Art, is the fact that . . . well you never made any attempt to see your daughter. She's a beautiful young lady."

"Paula poisoned the kid's mind."

"She's your daughter. You could have made an attempt."

"I didn't have a dime. At the beginning I didn't have fare to L.A. And now, what the hell. How can I explain a nineteen-year-old wife to an eighteen-year-old daughter?" He slapped Duke's back and ordered another drink.

Jennings seemed to be reaching a point where another drink could lay him out. It had to be now. Duke said it—smiling—accompanied it with a friendly pat. "You big ox, sometimes I think you've been shooting blanks for years."

At first, Jennings looked bewildered, then he smiled, and finally laughed out loud. "You must be kidding."

"The way you acted toward Carla. There were times I thought she wasn't yours." It was out, could bring anger, self-defense, but maybe confirmation. Duke watched him carefully, Jennings was concentrating hard as if searching for something. Then he began to talk. "I got a million of those things in my jism, always had. You'd never believe it, Sam, but even today . . . I always had to have rubbers stashed everywhere." His chin lowered to his chest and he straightened up and looked at Duke. "Would you believe every time I tore off a piece without a raincoat the broad got knocked up? It's true. It happened with Beck's mother and a dozen others. I should've had a doctor on the payroll. Always when I was drunk—I didn't give a damn—took a chance." The waiter brought the drink, he emptied half, set it down, and stared ahead. "Paula never wanted kids. We weren't getting along. Never did. She always made me use rubbers, wouldn't use the woman's thing. I know Carla's mine." His speech was halting. Duke leaned forward devouring every word. "We hadn't had each other for a long time, me and Paula. One night I came home drunk, horny as hell. There she was, loaded herself, been drinking wine all afternoon. Well, I guess she needed a stack. It was bing, bang, on the living room floor." He started to laugh. "She woke up sober and started to douche. Didn't stop for a week. I guess it was like trying to wash the salt out of the ocean."

He finished his drink and stood up gripping the table for support. "I gotta pick up my wife. She's finished the two o'clock show." Samson had him by the arm and led him from the room.

"What happened after that night, Art?"

"With Paula?"

"Yes."

"That's when Carla came into the picture."

Samson couldn't wait to get him in a cab, be alone, go over every word he heard. Rushing to his room, he locked the door, did a turn, another, pirouetted again. "She lied!" he shouted. "The bitch lied!" What a sucker he had been. What a fool! How could he have allowed himself to be taken in by such a cheap trick? It was over now, the lie uncovered like vermin under a rock. He could not wait for morning, to get back to town and to Paula.

Taking the first plane to L.A. he got to his apartment, freshened up and by nine o'clock was ready to call. She had to see him, he would work it somehow, and alone, without Ann Schneider. The moment she heard his voice he sensed she was going to hang up.

"Paula, listen to me. . . ." Silence. "I'm sorry about what happened at your house. I apologize." No reply. "I have to see you. It's about Carla. I just returned from New York and saw her." He waited and she finally spoke.

"What about Carla?"

"I won't discuss it over the phone. Just meet me. Anywhere."

There was a long pause. "I won't come to your apartment."

"How about my office? Late in the afternoon. I'll let my secretary go. We'll be alone." He gave her the address and she promised to be there at four.

Going through a pile of urgent work he sent Sherry home at three-thirty and then sat and watched the clock. Paula came a little after four, he closed the door of his private office, turned and faced her. He began by telling her about Carla, how well she looked, her excitement about the trip to Europe, her entrance to Wellesley in the fall. Embellishing the account with as many details as he could think of he finally stopped. There was a long silence.

"Is this what you wanted to see me about?" she finally said.

"Part of it."

"Now tell me the other part."

He launched into the account of his meeting with Art Jennings, repeated every word he could remember of their conversation, left out nothing. All during the speech she just sat looking at him without expression, without comment. Now he waited. She reached in her purse, withdrew a mirror, examined herself, brushed a stray hair, returned the mirror, snapped the purse shut and looked at him. She was smiling.

"Well?" he said.

"What difference does it make now?"

"A lot of difference. If Carla isn't my daughter, I should know it."

"How would it change things?"

"I'm middle-aged, Paula. I have no plans to marry. Every blood relative I had is gone. Carla is the only one . . . if you can prove she's my daughter."

"What are you suggesting?"

"That one day she can be the richest girl in town."

"How can I prove it?"

"By convincing me that Art lied yesterday."

She was calm, pleasant, smiling. "How can I do that? Won't it be my word against his?"

"Yes. And I'll be the judge." Now he leaned forward, intent. "We'll go to Vegas. You and me. The three of us will have it out. I'll get his story again and then I'll want to hear yours."

Her gloves were out of her purse, the pack of cigarettes went in, the purse snapped shut. She stood up. "Aren't you afraid?"

"Of what?"

"What Mr. Jennings might do when he finds out you were sleeping with his wife. . . . when you were his best friend?"

"I'm willing to take a chance."

She was at the door and turned, her calm was gone and the

smile. "You never stoop lower than I know you're capable of. If I could be sure Carla was not yours I would be the happiest woman on earth."

He ran to the door, blocked it as she retreated into the room. "Maybe she isn't. Maybe Art was right!"

"He was. I spent an hour in the shower after. And I was with you the night before . . . and the day after!" She rushed to the door, slammed it behind her.

He spent the summer in anguish. He detailed every arrangement for meeting Carla in Europe, then he cabled excuses for delay and when he finally wired that he was not able to come she replied with letters and cables, angry, frustrated, all with overtones of love.

He turned to Lee Marlowe for comfort, but the fire was petering out. In desperation he asked her to marry him one night when they were lying beside her pool after their usual aquatics.

"Marriage will wreck a good relationship." She delivered the cliché with an indulgent smile. When she left for La Jolla to do a play, he turned to Sherry Larsen, whose ministrations, as efficient as ever, were sustenance not substance.

By the end of August, a week before Carla was to return, he received a call from Rome, and midst sputters and howls was able to determine that she expected him to meet her in New York before she returned to school. Not to go after avoiding Europe was unthinkable. He would go to New York, blame business on the stymied European trip, temper their relationship, ease it to sanity.

His face was dressed with a paternal smile, an arm was extended, she ducked, ignored the smile, slid under the wing, looked up at him for an instant, kissed and pressed against him whispering, "Samson, Oh, Samson . . ." He felt her belly and thighs, gripped her . . . disengaged, towed her from the ramp.

Every manifestation of excitement he ever felt for a woman was there. Carla's arm was around his waist, squeezing, hugging, there was no pretense, none of the subtleties of their last meeting . . . they were being engulfed and he wasn't doing a damn thing! They were through customs, in the cab, her hand had his, squeezing, they were seated close . . . by God he had to tell her the truth . . . there could be no more delay! But what was the truth? How in hell could he tell Carla he was her father if he was not? Her name was Jennings; Art was her father. Could he tell her that he cuckolded the man she thought to be her father? Carla raised his hand and pressed the back of it with soft lips, then she released it, caressed his thigh, he pushed to the corner of the seat, she was against him, her mouth found his ear. . . . "I am in love with you, darling Samson." Her lips brushed his ear, down his cheek, the back of his hand again. There was no answer, no solution. There was so little time, no time. His mind raced over the day Paula first told him she was pregnant, their later talks, Art's tale in Las Vegas, and the final meeting with Paula in his office.

He pushed Carla from him roughly. "You've got to stop this. I'm old enough to be your father." She looked surprised, then hurt, slid to the other end of the cab. He felt in control now, went on with more confidence. "You're like a daughter to me. You will always be like a daughter." Now he pleaded, "Don't make it difficult. Don't destroy that." Her warmth was gone, the tender look, the hurt had turned to anger. She was silent, the lover sulking after a quarrel. When the cab reached the hotel, Samson followed her into the lobby, and registered for both of them. He left her at the door of her room without a word.

Later, when he called her to arrange for dinner, she pleaded fatigue, said she would see him in the morning and hung up before he could reply. Vastly relieved at not having to see her that night he dined alone at the 21. He lurched to his room long after midnight, collapsed in bed dead drunk, sleeping until nearly noon of the following day. When he called Carla's room, he was told she checked out and had left a note in his box. He ordered breakfast and had the note sent up, tore open the envelope.

Dearest:

By the time you read this I will be on my way back to school. It would have been unbearable to see you again on this trip under these circumstances. I can understand your feelings but you must understand mine. My trip to Europe was made as a consequence of your promise to join me. I would not have gone otherwise. It was clear to me then and clearer now why you did not come. My love for you could not exist without some response and though there was no expression I sensed your true feelings on your last trip. I do not know what I shall do nor how it will end but do know that neither time nor distance is a healer.

> With all my love,
> Carla

He reread the note then tore it to bits. Now it was very clear: he must not see her for a long time, nor communicate with her.

Reserving a seat on the earliest available plane to L.A., he called Alex to meet him at the airport.

CHAPTER TWENTY-TWO

During the next few months he heard frequently from Carla, telephone calls and short notes, all without hysteria, calm declarations done as carefully thought-out initial maneuvers of a long campaign. He handled all of their communications without a trace of commitment. However, in spite of his negative responses, when they spoke or when he answered her letters he spent long hours during days and sleepless nights thinking about her in a manner that terrified him. They must stay apart, that's all there was to it.

His work load proved an able assist. Between the banking business, mortgage loans, and the burgeoning Universal Savings and Loan there were few hours during a week when his mind was unoccupied.

Although Ben Hardin's energies produced more than Duke ever hoped for, the ex-agent's manias ran counter with their rising fortunes. His car was chauffeur-driven, he issued orders from a multibuttoned intercom system built into a desk that rose on a dais at the end of a forty-foot-long office whose walls were muraled with photos of Ben Hardin at ground-breaking ceremonies, the entrance to a new building, at the Los Angeles Stock Exchange, the day Universal went public, photostated news clippings preserved in plastic; a graphic life of the Association's president. His visage was never absent, for in a corner a larger-than-life bust done in the marble manner of the noble Romans depicted Hardin's equally noble profile and mane. Not content with projecting his image upon every aspect of Universal, Hardin ventured into the community at large, burrowed into political campaigns, emerged on TV shows and at banquet tables arm in arm with the candidate. Not content with regular press releases during which he pontificated on the present and future of savings and loans, he made the talk-show circuit discoursing on the pill, modern art, teeny-boppers, and psychedelic drugs. Duke found himself spending more and more time at the Association's offices making every effort to cap the flow of Hardin's rhetoric. Hardin defended himself strenuously, pointed to the growth of the business, attributing it to the constant publicity he was mustering. Realizing that Hardin was intractable, Duke decided to keep the lid on as much as he could and wait for an opportunity to pry Hardin loose and toss him on his ass. He made it his business to be present at loan committee meetings, and at one of them an application from Phil Matlin was submitted and recommended by Hardin. It was for a three-million-dollar second trust deed loan on the Westside Country Club, comprising 180 acres.

Hardin was pressing hard as he presented it to the committee. "It's the largest piece of urban land held by one entity," his voice boomed. He wielded a huge cigar like a scepter. "The loan's a little tricky. We've got to curve around a few regulations. Matlin's got other security. I can get additional trust deeds on a dozen of his properties."

"But it's a second," someone protested.

"There's a ten-point bonus," Hardin said. "Three hundred thousand."

"How long does he want it for?" another asked.

"Just eighteen months. Do you realize what it means?" Hardin was striding the room now, puffing, gesticulating, jaw-jutting. "Ten per cent interest, a prepayment penalty, *and* the points." He stopped the pacing, slid into his chair. "We make seven hundred fifty thousand profit." He threw down the pencil. "In eighteen months."

"What's he paying for the property?" Samson asked.

"Thirty-five million."

"What are the terms?"

"The owners are carrying back thirty million, interest only at six per cent for five years."

"So if we lend him three million he'll only be in it for two plus the points. That means we'll be in over ninety per cent of his cost."

"Never mind his cost, Sam. He's been sniffing at the deal for years. He's a member of the club. There's been dissension, fights, half the members are not paying dues, they want out." Hardin produced a sheaf of papers from his case. "I have three appraisals here. One of ours and two independent." He shuffled the papers. "One independent comes in at forty-two million, the other at forty-two million five. I told our appraiser to knock it down, be conservative as hell. Here," he handed Samson the paper. "He came in with forty-one million."

Samson passed the sheet around, the five other members looked it over silently and for a few moments nobody said a word. Hardin was watching them, chewing his cigar savagely. Samson said nothing, kept shaking his head negatively, determined that the Association was not going to make that loan. But he waited for the others, ready to join the chorus and turn it down. The loan committee was dominated by Hardin, Duke, and Ira Sommers, an ex-president of the Bank of America whose early training left him on the conservative side. Once Sommers made up his mind he was intractable and the others, a doctor, two attorneys, and an accountant usually followed his suit. It was an agreed policy that all loans over a hundred thousand must be approved unanimously. If Sommers went along, Duke decided to vote it down, but he was anxious for the negation to come from the ex-banker. The moment Sommers began to move his head from side to side slowly it was a sure sign that Phil Matlin had some more shopping to do. Hardin saw the sign before Sommers opened his mouth.

"It's the most lucrative piece of business we've ever had submitted. We can't turn it down." Sommers' head was shaking vigorously. Hardin leaned over the table, pointing his cigar at Sommers. "Ira, you've got to have some imagination."

"I have, Ben. And a conscience. I can't recommend the loan." Hardin looked at the others, they were smiling agreement, he turned to Samson as if to appeal, hesitated a moment, jammed the cigar in his mouth and rushed from the room.

"You did right, Ira," Samson said, patting his shoulder. "Ben gets carried away. Sometimes he forgets he's dealing with public money."

Duke waited a week before he called Phil Matlin, certain that he had applied to other institutions for the loan. If it had not already been committed, Matlin would be as soft as Samson wanted him. Savings and Loans were usually at the end of the line because of their exorbitant charges and if Matlin had come to Universal in the first place, he must have been everywhere.

"How did you know about it?" Matlin asked when Samson reached him by phone.

"I'm on the loan committee at Universal."

"They're idiots. It's the safest loan they ever had submitted."

"That's exactly what I said. Anyway, drop by. Let's talk about it."

Matlin was in Duke's office in an hour. Armed with plot plans, topographical maps, area studies, and projections; he seemed nimble as ever in spite of the fact that he had put on considerable weight since Samson had seen him two years before.

Moving about the room like a dancer, stopping to make a point with a sweeping arm, raising his voice for additional emphasis, lowering it and narrowing his eyes as he confided, Matlin revealed his plans. "Sam, I'm going to build a city. Office building, apartments, a hotel, a theater. There'll be nothing like it west of Chicago . . . maybe in the country. It's all in here," he went on, poking his head. "Soon it'll be on paper. Then it's going up."

They spent the entire afternoon together. Samson questioned, probed; Matlin recited with passion. Spent, he finally collapsed in a chair. "Will you make the loan?"

"Let me think about it overnight. There's a lot to consider on, Phil." Matlin appeared so exhausted he did not seem to be reacting. It was as if he had pitched the deal a dozen times, always failed, had done it again that afternoon mechanically and was certain of another rejection. He groaned as Duke went on. "I like you, Phil. I don't want to see you make a mistake. And I don't want to make one. A year and a half is a short time. What if you can't get your financing?"

Matlin shot up, aroused. "But I can!"

"All right. Leave everything with me. Also the list of the other properties you're willing to put up as security. I won't leave you dangling. You'll get an answer in the morning."

Samson spent most of the night going over the figures and documents and by morning was certain the loan was secure and would be a bonanza if Matlin defaulted.

When Matlin arrived at Duke's office the following day he was handed a letter of commitment. It called for acceptance or rejection within twenty-four hours. Reading it over carefully he was silent for a long moment. He looked at Duke, "You want fifteen points?"

"$450,000."

"It's got to be added to the loan. I need the three million net."

"You'll have to raise it, Phil."

"I can't."

Samson believed him and moved to the concession he was prepared to make. "Get half. I'll raise the loan two twenty-five."

Matlin took out a pencil, did some figuring. His mouth

worked, he was taking deep breaths, he tore the sheet from the pad and crumbled it. "Are you ready to go?" Samson nodded. "Why does the four-fifty have to be cash under the table?"

Samson smiled patiently. "There are laws, Phil. You know that. Usury. Treble damages."

"I'll never sue and you know it. Anyway, what in hell are you going to do with all that cash?"

"It's a problem. But there's no other way. With insurance, that is."

Matlin looked at him for a long moment as if seeking a sign that might promise a concession. Samson's smile hung tight, his eyes were blank. "How do you want to handle the money?"

"I want it in hundred-dollar bills. When you have it we'll count it together and put it in a suitcase. Before that, every document will be signed and ready to record, except my escrow instructions. We'll go to the escrow together with the suitcase. I'll sign the instructions, there will be a special recording, confirmed over the phone." He spread his hands, smiled. "You leave the bank with my check and I carry out the suitcase."

A fifteen-day escrow was opened, the clerk worked nights, weekends, all the documents were drawn, executed, and sent to the title company to be ready for a special recording. Matlin lugged a suitcase to Samson's office on the morning of the day the deal was to close. It did not take long to count the cash: forty-five bundles, each containing a hundred hundred-dollar bills. Though curious as to how Matlin gathered together so much cash, he refrained from inquiring. Matlin seemed in a great hurry, took Samson's arm and led him from the room, his farewell to something precious was too painful to sustain longer than necessary. They drove to the bank, the suitcase between them, not a word exchanged. Duke signed the escrow instructions, the title company was called, and instructed to record. During the hour it took for confirmation neither man left the booth, the bag nestling on the floor between them. The clerk had prepared the closing statement, the check was drawn, ready for signature and a little after eleven the title company called. The deal had been recorded. Phil Matlin folded the check, placed it in his wallet and followed Samson and the suitcase out of the bank.

"Can I drive you to your car?" Samson asked.

"I'd rather take a cab." Samson shrugged and started to leave as Matlin grabbed his arm. "I have something to tell you." For a brief moment he looked squarely at Duke who felt his own gaze waver. "To begin with," he went on, "I happen to know you weren't pulling for me during the loan committee meeting at Universal." Samson was about to protest. Matlin's look deflected the lie. "You set me up that afternoon and a week later called me for the kill." The bag was getting heavy and Samson set it down on the sidewalk. "You added five points in cash to what I could afford to pay."

Samson reached for the bag. "If you want to make a speech it'll have to be some other time. I'm in a hurry."

"I'm almost through. I just want to tell you I've done business with the meanest men in this town . . . Jews and Gentiles. The hardest Jew I ever met had a soft spot in him somewhere . . . he had a conscience, a soul. Things your kind are without." He turned to go, hesitated and faced Samson again. "You made me proud to be a Jew." He was halfway across the street before Samson could move.

He picked up the bag and headed for his car. The little kike, crawling on his belly, begging, then crying. And *he* talks about a conscience, him . . . running a black market, fucking the army, the government, and the G.I.'s. The bag's heft which he shifted to his other hand reminded him of its contents: fifteen, maybe twenty pounds of cash, more money than most saw in a lifetime. He had made cash under the table deals before, five thousand, ten, but never like this. Most of it had gone into his box at the bank, the biggest they had to rent and as he got into his car he realized his overfilled box could not contain the bundles of bills. He started for his office and then steered for his apartment. It would be safer there until he decided where it was to be deposited.

Alex was in the kitchen, the breakfast dishes stacked and un-washed, a marked *Racing Form* spread over the table. Duke was sure the beds were unmade.

"I didn't expect . . ." Alex began.

"Never mind. Here." He handed him a twenty dollar bill. "Take the day off and the night." He didn't want him around with all that cash in the house. Alex was a snooper and one never knew. It was enough cash to buy him a racetrack. Alex gathered up the *Form* and walked to the sink.

"I'll leave after the dishes."

After he left, Samson called his office, told Sherry he would not return that day, checked all the doors and windows and opened the bag. Benjamin Franklin never looked better, all forty-five hundred engravings of his fat contented face, every one a note guaranteed by Uncle Sam and payable on demand. He could write a check for fifty thousand of these bills, more if necessary, but somehow it was different, figures, digits, entries in a check-book or a ledger . . . not like this, coin reduced to its purest form.

He fixed a scotch and soda, sat, sipped it slowly, his eyes on the open bag on the coffee table. Certain things only could be bought with cash: crooked politicians, senators, congressmen, maybe even a Supreme Court Justice. He had enough to buy a state leg-islature and part of the Congress. He poured another drink, a double and felt even better. Now he remembered his favorite tale, read when he was a kid, Edmund Dantes, in the grotto on the Isle of Monte Cristo, after his escape from the Chateau d'If, fingering the gold and precious stones, crying aloud, "the world is mine!" Reaching his hand into the bag he removed a package of bills, ripped the binder and fingered the notes allowing them to fall to the floor. He could not buy the world but there was little in it he couldn't have. He thought of Carla, for an instant, shut her out of his mind and poured another drink. On his feet now, he held the glass aloft, toasting. Nobody knew how far he had come, his past was sealed off. Aunt Annie would have known. He toasted him-self. He felt hungry, made a sandwich, a pot of coffee, ate in the living room and began to sober up. He fixed another scotch and settled on the couch.

It's funny, he thought, nobody ever asked about his past. Even Lee, it was like she didn't give a damn. All she knew was that he was raised in Brooklyn, never asked about his father or mother or whether he had sisters or brothers. Anyway, what could he tell her if she asked? The truth had been varnished with so many layers it had been painted out. He kicked off his shoes, stretched out on the couch, and felt himself drop off to sleep.

When he awoke it was night. He felt rested, relaxed, no sign of a hangover. It was one of those days, he thought, he could drink without letup and it was all glow and no pain. Fixing a drink he walked to the window; the lights were on now all over the city, puffed up stars, bigger than the heaven's specks and more real. Then he thought about the cash, realized it would have to be kept in the apartment for the night and began to rummage for a safe place. It would be safe, he was sure, but one never knew, why take chances? He removed the bills from the bag, divided it up and hid it in four different places. If anyone laid hands on part of the loot they sure in hell would not look further.

After a shower and shave he felt more alive, excited. The deal called for a celebration! He thought of Sherry and then Lee. He had not seen Lee for a couple of weeks, had not talked to her on the phone. By God, he would see her that night, bring her a gift she would never forget and maybe it would be like old times.

What a surprise! He would drive over, they would go out to dinner and come back to his apartment. Dressing carefully he went into the kitchen and found what he was looking for. Alex had a stand that looked like a tree with metal arms on which he hung cups. Removing it from the cupboard he brought it into the living room and stuck a dozen hundred dollar bills on the protruding arms. Lee had everything, but not a money tree! Wrapping it carefully, excited at the prospect of the evening he left the apartment and drove to Brentwood.

Maybe it was a good idea after all, marrying Lee that is. . . . there was a lot they had going, and it had nothing to do with her economic security . . . she had a career, money . . . sure she turned him down, but it was the way he asked . . . like an invitation to enter a contract. . . . it wasn't wooey or gooey. And he was getting there. . . . Forty-five ain't springtime, there were signs of creaks and squeaks. Funny, how clear things get sometimes when you're drunk. Well, tonight that scotch was like truth serum with a jigger of courage. Carla had to forget him and a marriage to Lee would do it. And he could never make a better match; a prominent actress, still young and beautiful, great in the sack when she was tuned . . . things had not been going too well lately but maybe it was because he had quit the romancing, took her for granted. This time there would not be a suggestion for a premarital agreement . . . a simple proposal, no strings. He took the turns on Sunset Boulevard with screeching tires, began to sing aloud, almost passed her house, cut into her driveway sharply and nearly ran into a small sports car parked in front of the door. Maybe she had a guest? No matter, he would wait until they were alone, maybe ask her when they got to his apartment. Scrambling from the car, clutching the money tree he took the three steps leading to the door with a leap and rang the bell. He was humming a tune when the door opened. Lee was framed in the entrance, a tall figure in the shadows in back of her.

"I should have called," he said, half-questioningly.

"No, it's all right, Sam." There was a moment's hesitation. "Come in."

He would give her the gift later when they were alone, he thought, as he placed it on the table in the hall and followed Lee and the man into the living room. She turned gracefully and handled the introduction.

"John Arley, Sam Duke." Samson forced a smile as the man shook his hand vigorously, they all walked to the center of the room and stood silently like actors waiting for a cue. Samson took Arley in swiftly; tall, handsome, that goddamn actor's voice. . . . young. "John's opposite me in my new film," Lee delivered. "Mmm," Samson managed to get out. "Are you in the business, Mr. Duke?" Lee came in before he could answer, linking her arm in his. "Sam's a financier, real estate." He nodded as Lee began moving with precision, linking her other arm in Arley's and leading both men toward the bar. "Will you fix us a drink, John?" Arley was behind the bar. "What'll it be?" "My usual, dear, very dry," Lee said. He needed a pickup, quick. "Scotch, straight," Samson said.

How long had she known him, he thought? The sonofabitch seemed at home, like there was a vacancy and he moved in. He downed the drink, placed the shot glass on the bar, tapped it like a message and Arley filled it. He had not seen her as often lately, business gobbled his time, does that mean she had a right to screw around? Aah, he was only imagining, that was all. He downed the shot of scotch and wanted another, with soda this time. Something to hold and sip. Better not ask, just sorta' get behind the bar and pour it himself. Christ, they'd think he was getting drunk! Lee had John's hand and was leading him from the bar, calling over her shoulder. "Join us when you've fixed your drink, Sam. And bring the peanuts." Two jiggers but plenty of soda, they'll think the drink's long and weak. He eased from behind the bar carefully, the corner of his eye caught the money tree on the table in the hall. Wait till she sees that.

There was music from somewhere and Lee and John were in the center of the room dancing—tight, close—swaying to the rhythm, hardly moving. "Where's Laura?" he ventured. He didn't give a shit, it was something to say. "She's at a girl friend's for the night," Lee said over her shoulder. Some of the drink missed his mouth as he took a swig, dribbled over his chin, he wiped it with the back of his hand, felt himself sway and grabbed the back of a chair. She had a lot of nerve, dancing with this guy, close like she was slipping it to him. And right in front of him! Might as well get it over with. "Lee. . . ." Over her shoulder. "Yes, Sam?" He set the drink down. "I hate to break it up but I thought you and I would go to dinner." He was smiling now, looking at John, a friendly goodbye. The dancers separated, looked at one another and John advanced. "It'll have to be another time, sport." He was smiling—friendly. "Lee and I are booked." Courage and truth was in that bottle. "Look, Jack, I've important things to say to the lady." Lee was headed between them like a referee. Arley brushed her aside and a formidable finger was pushing Samson from the room. "You'll have to talk to her after breakfast, friend." Samson saw the part in his hair, it split an arrangement that curled and flowed to the back, he gripped Lee's favorite lamp, a Nubian supporting a shade, his fingers gripped the waist and he swung for Arley's head. The actor danced aside, aimed a left at Samson's head, it was a feint, Samson dropped the lamp, his hands went up in defense and a fist crashed just below his sternum and his knees buckled as he clawed for air and went down. Lee was screaming as Samson crawled to the front door, found the knob and twisted it open. He was outside, the door slammed shut, it was a little easier to breathe and he staggered to his car. "You bitch, you'll pay, do you hear!" Screaming tires rounded the turns, puffing to fill his lungs, he began to sob and did not stop until he reached his apartment. He poured a drink, spilled half on the bar, brought the glass to his lips. The smell made him sick and he ran to the bathroom fell on his knees over the toilet and vomited, each gag bringing on an excruciating pain. His head was splitting as he pushed himself to his feet, each breath brought a sharp jolt to his sternum. He downed aspirin, made it to the bedroom, and collapsed on the bed.

The ringing would not stop. It jingled and jangled in his head and every sound was the blow of a sledge. Half-awake, he twisted, cried out in pain and groped for the phone.

"Sam, it's Lee, are you all right?"

He mumbled a response.

"I am sorry about what happened, Sam. But you were drunk." He just wanted to sleep. Why don't they leave him alone? Lee was still talking, he did not understand, finally he mumbled. "In the morning, in the morning," and hung up the phone.

His head seemed apart from him, something screwed on to torture and the light from an early morning sun stabbed as he opened his eyes. As he rose from the bed he cried out, the pain in his chest, intense. It was a little after seven, less than twenty-four hours since he left the bank with the money. Moving gingerly, he made the rounds, found the money where he had hidden it, then he put on a pot of coffee, drew a hot bath, and sank into the tub. Closing his eyes he relaxed, the heat felt good, maybe it would take away some of the pain. First, he would go to the bank, rent their largest box, and get rid of the money. Then a doctor and if he was okay, nothing broken, he would have it out with Miss Marlowe; fucking around with a two-bit actor . . . if that was the crud she wanted, she wasn't good enough for him. And by God, he would let her know it!

Then he remembered her call. She did say she was sorry, and he had been drunk. Maybe he was wrong, the actor might just be a friend? If it were true he sure screwed it up, and on the night he was going to ask her to marry him. He got out of the tub. The pain had lessened and he began to dry himself. He wanted last night to be a mistake; his mistake. Lee meant more to him than he had imagined, she had given him pleasure for a long time, a thousand hours would have been lonely without her and if they drifted apart lately it had been his fault; he had been coasting. Maybe what happened last night was a good thing, it could have been a warning that he had run out of residuals.

The sharp edge of the pain in his chest dulled and he decided to forget the doctor. If anything was broken, a hot bath could not have taken away the pain. Gathering together the cash, he placed it in the suitcase and left for the bank. With the money safely stored in the vault and the key to the box dangling from his chain he drove to his office. He would call Lee immediately and see her for lunch and if calm, sober assessment of her relationship with the actor was correct, he would propose to her on the spot. Her response to his call was warm and friendly; she could not make it for lunch but would meet him for cocktails.

He sent two dozen roses to her house, rushed to Donavan and Seaman's picked a pear-shaped diamond engagement ring on consignment packed in silk and purple velvet which nestled in his breast pocket. He was at Perino's promptly at six carrying a beribboned orchid in a plastic box. By God, he'd blitz her!

She met him in the bar carrying one of his roses which she handed to him. She removed the orchid from the box and laid it on the bar.

"They were lovely and thoughtful," she said, "especially after last night."

"I'm sorry about last night. I was drunk. I owe your friend an apology." He reached for her hand.

Her fingers laid against his without response. "I met John in La Jolla. He was opposite me in the play."

"I'm sure I'll get to know him better."

They sipped their drinks.

"You'll like him, Sam."

"I'm sure I will." He gulped his martini and ordered another. She fingered the orchid. "I was jealous," he laughed. "Funny, you're losing something . . . then for the first time you want it bad."

She withdrew her hand from his and he reached in his pocket and removed the ring. She eyed the box and covered it with her hand.

"Don't, Sam, don't say anything more until you hear me out." *Hear me Lee, I never said it to a woman before but I'm saying it now! How can I make you believe I love you, that I'm lonely, that I need you?* He opened the box and plucked the ring from its nest. Taking her hand he fumbled for her finger, but she clenched her fist.

"It's too late, Sam. You missed your cues." She rose from the stool. "I'm not in love with you, Sam."

"Arley?"

"We're going to be married after the picture."

"I can't make you change your mind?"

She shook her head.

He lifted his drink. "Well, here's to your happiness."

Still standing, she sipped her drink, reached into her purse and withdrew a packet of bills. "Your gift was generous but I can't accept it."

"Keep it. A wedding present."

She slipped it into his pocket. "I have to go." She was out of the bar before he could say another word.

He placed the ring carefully in the box and set it on the bar beside the orchid. Then he ordered another drink.

Turning south on Western Avenue he headed for Gardena. Oh, how Aunt Annie looked at him that day as the cab headed for her home and she talked excitedly about the city, the sun and her hands warming him as her fingers tapped out her love! At Vernon and Western he stopped at a bar. A double scotch, straight. The beer drinkers looked up and then down into their glasses. Someone slid a coin into the juke box. It blared, its multicolored lighted belly heaving to the tune. He began to feel sick and then was out in the cool night air. Past the drugstore two blocks and a left then three houses on the right and he shut the motor and snapped off the lights. The bungalow looked smaller than he remembered, the lawn unruly with weeds, the jacaranda weighted by neglect, almost hiding the lighted window that was muted by a ravely shade.

Samson vaulted the fence, stumbled, found his feet and reached the side of the house. He circled the house and everything was drawn, the garden jungled with weeds. He smelled damp wood and rotten leaves. A dog whined, then yelped and he ran through the growth, scaled the tiny fence and reached his car.

From the moment the thought appeared, a flash at first, submerging, reappearing and nagging, he knew what the decision was going to be. Now he was hungry, realized he had not eaten all that day. Stopping at a restaurant he gorged on steak and potatoes, cups of coffee, his head cleared, he was sober and he drove to his apartment. Alex was asleep at the kitchen table, his head cradled on an arm over the marked sheets of the *Racing Form*.

"Wake up," Samson said, shaking him. "I'm leaving for New

York. . . . tonight. Lay out my things." Alex shuffled out of the room.

Securing a seat on the midnight flight, he called Sherry, told her he would be gone for a week, would be at the Warwick. He would spend a day or two on business, then call Carla. Her message was still clear and now his answer was ready.

Making the rounds of his New York properties took a day. Carla's reponse to his call was rapturous and by the time he arrived at the station to meet her train he arranged reservations for dinners, picked up tickets for the shows and her suite was decked with flowers. She rushed to his arms, her lips found his mouth, cruised his cheek. He felt their softness on his neck. She would not let go, he had to pry her loose like ivy off a wall.

All his fear was gone, he was light-headed, gay, and as they walked arm-in-arm from the station he felt the beginnings of a hard-on. The moment they got into the cab she was on him. Slipping her leg between his she began to grind against him, his hands cupped her behind, her tongue was in his ear, trailed the side of his neck, her mouth covered his, then she trembled violently, rolled off him sobbing at his side as he finished coming in his pants.

They checked into the hotel and went to their separate suites. As he groomed and dressed carefully preparing himself for the evening thoughts began to pelt the barricade he had erected in his mind. To hell with it! To hell with everyone, Paula included. Never had he felt more sure of a woman, been less lonely, more wanted and loved. There had to be a solution. As for the trick that Paula played, the lie, the classic gambit to hook a man. . . . well, only a sucker took that bait. He was that. No more.

Carla was radiant when he entered her suite. With the exception of the few words exchanged at their greeting little had been said between them. Now, as if to caption the picture of their wild ride from the station, she poured it out, hugged his arm as she led him to the couch and plopped beside him.

"Darling, don't say a thing. Listen. I prayed for today and

knew it would happen. I fell in love with you years ago. It was on your first trip to visit me. My diary is full of it. I'll show it to you some day." She stroked his hand. "I know the problems. You're more than twice my age, I've been like a daughter." He winced. "Mother will be furious, I know she dislikes you. Let her. I'm of age . . . she can do nothing." She rose and whirled, her hands above her head, plucking from the sky. "I feel so much I can burst." She wheeled, planted a kiss on his mouth. "I'll finish the year at college and then come to you. My head is full of the letter I'll write mother. She'll have to understand."

"Carla, let me say something. I feel everything you do. There are problems. They must be resolved. We have three, four days together. I want time to think. You need time." She began to protest. . . . then she smiled.

"All right, darling."

"Let me tell you what I've planned," he said. There were reservations in restaurants she had never visited, a fistful of the hardest-to-get tickets to shows, no rough-riding cabs, a chauffeured limousine for the duration of their stay. In a few minutes she was ready to leave, they had a drink at the hotel bar and were driven to the restaurant. The evening wore on, the qualitative change in their relationship became more real. Evidence of her beauty was everywhere; in the eyes of men and women they encountered, even elicited a couple of appreciative whistles. What other genes she might possess were smothered by her Latin heritage. Her skin was tinted, more so than Paula's. It glowed like polished obsidian, her eyes were Aztec black and when he looked at her throat he remembered the first time he met Paula as she descended the step to Art Jennings' office on the night so long ago. How it flowed without a ripple to a full breast that peeked from a low-cut dress. . . . Carla's breasts were fuller and as she walked ahead entering the hotel at the end of the evening he saw long sensual legs without the bow Paula always tried to hide. Mingled with relief was disappointment as Carla pecked him goodnight and left at the door of her suite. All during the evening she appeared restrained, held his hand but never got closer. It was better . . . how could one think with a pounding head and heart and a hard-on in his pants?

Her game was evident the morning of the last day they were to be together. Gay and excited at the tour of the city she refrained from overtures and once when he tried to take her in his arms she twisted free. He began to wonder if she had a change of heart, whether close examination, day and night contact had revealed creaks and cracks, lines and jowl. Second thoughts were more objective; maybe he flunked the test.

They sat across from each other at breakfast, she began to amuse herself.

"You're not eating." He was toying with his fruit cup.

"I'm not hungry." He pushed the dish aside.

"I'm famished." She devoured a melon.

He fumbled. "Carla, I. . . ."

"Yes. . . . ?" Her eyes lit, a look questioned.

"I'm confused . . . that is . . . well the first day . . . damnit darling, you know what I mean. . . ."

She reached for his hand, squeezed it as she spoke. "You said you wanted time to think. Remember?"

He nodded. "And I wanted to give you time."

She rose from her seat and slid next to him, her hand on his leg, sliding, caressing. "I've thought of little else for two years."

All his doubts disappeared by the end of the day. They walked along Fifth Avenue hand-in-hand, she rode smack up against him in the rear of the limousine, at lunch she had him hemmed in a corner booth, the fire that had been banked for days was raked and he was beginning to feel the heat. She coddled a drink as he guzzled three martinis at The Plaza Bar, time was encapsulated in the moment, the past was obliterated, the future was not born. They had enough of restaurants, crowds, the city. She agreed that dinner in his suite was ideal for a farewell, he bought an orchid and pinned it to her lapel, they rode the elevator with hot hands clasped and in his room he switched to scotch and by the time the ordered dinner arrived and the waiter spun the wine bottle in the cooler and left, the room was the world, Carla's eyes the light, her body the warmth and her touch the beat.

From a long way off he heard the toot of a horn, then a roar, first soft then louder, sounds of an angry sea . . . his head was a carbuncle bigger than his body, any movement and it would burst. Don't move. Try to think! The sounds were traffic and it must be day and he was naked in his bed.

Fragments of thoughts began to move about the raw flesh of his brain; they established the hotel, the bed, the room. He tried to move again and cried out in pain. Perhaps he could move his body without changing the position of his head. He slid to the edge of the bed, started to rise, fell back, and for moments did not move. He opened his eyes. A sliver of light from the edge of the drape speared the room. He rolled to the side of the bed, found the floor with wobbly feet and made his way to the bathroom. In the mirror his face stared back, every year he had racked up engraved; the dulled eyes, the mouth lines that bit deep, the creped bags that bunched under the lids, the thinning hair peaked at the temples and going gray. Swallowing aspirin he got in the shower, took it ice cold and with a towel wrapped about his middle returned to the room and opened the drape. His jacket and pants were a crumpled pile on the chair, his shirt was on the dresser, his shoes were in the middle of the room. In the living room half-eaten food was strewn over plates, an empty wine bottle rested in the bucket, two others were on the table, one overturned, and Carla's coat hung over the back of a chair. He went to the bar, poured a stiff drink of scotch, downed it and flopped in a chair. His head began to clear, things were coming back and as he stared at the littered table he began to remember. They came up the elevator holding hands; he was a little drunk, there was more to drink and he ordered dinner sent up . . . caviar, Chateaubriand for two and vintage wine. He remembered music. They danced, pressed together in the middle of the room, swaying, barely moving, her hair black strands of silk, her perfume overwhelming. Then what? He beat his head. Then what? They were on the couch . . . but it must have been after the supper was sent up because there was a toast with the wine, and then? He was too tense, trying too hard, maybe if he relaxed it would all come back. He ordered dinner. They danced, the couch, the toast . . . what happened then? He was in the middle of the room, holding a glass high . . . it was brandy, yes they had sent up brandy, and he was saying something, proclaiming . . . It was all he could recall. Once before this had happened to him; he had blacked-out after a night's binge and the next day when they told him what he had done, what had happened, he did not believe a word they said, was sure they were pulling his leg.

Rushing out of the room he fell on the bed and buried his head in the pillow, Carla's perfume was all about him, he sniffed the sheets, it was there, and then he began to examine the bed; long black strands of hair were everywhere. God, she must have undressed him, crawled in with him. He grabbed the phone and called her room, she answered sleepily. "Good morning, darling. What time is it?"

"It's ten o'clock." He was shouting.

"I've such a headache."

She was drunk too. Maybe she forgot, won't remember—"I'll have some coffee sent up."

Her voice was clearer now. "Don't. I'd rather have it with you. Meet you in the lobby in half an hour." She hung up.

Looking fresh and glowing as she got off the elevator, she took his arm and they went into the dining room. Not a word was mentioned of the evening before and by the time they were on the last of their coffee he could stand it no longer.

"About last night . . . I guess I made a fool of myself."

She smiled. "You were drunk, darling . . . but lovable." She laughed. "We were both drunk. Do you know how much I had? I kept count. Two martinis at The Plaza, another in the room and all that wine. . . . I must have drunk a bottle by myself."

Was it possible the worst did not happen? She said she was drunk. Maybe she crawled in the bed to sleep it off while he was in the other room? And then got up and went to her own room? Or maybe he fucked her and wasn't even conscious!

He must have been insane to think that Paula would consent to a marriage. It could not be too late, he had to get out of it somehow. Rising abruptly he looked at his watch.

"We'll have to go. Your train leaves in a couple of hours. I have business calls to make. My plane leaves at three." He was out of the restaurant nearing the lobby, she followed.

"I'm packed, darling. Let me go with you."

"You can't. These are business calls." He was deliberately cold, curt, and sensed her confusion. They were in the elevator, reached her floor. "I'll meet you in the lobby in an hour and we'll drive to the station."

They sat in opposite corners of the limousine as they drove, not a word had been spoken. He was staring out the window, dared not meet her eyes, she finally spoke.

"What's happened? What have I done?"

"I'm a selfish man, Carla." He was still looking out the window. "I've lived alone a long time. I like it. I intend keeping it that way." Now he turned. Her head was bowed, a handkerchief dabbing her eyes. He began to feel anger at her, at himself. "We haven't been thinking clearly. Our heads were in a bucket and our feet a mile off the ground. Damnit, when we hit that ground it'll hurt. Christ, can't you see!" They had reached the station. She just looked at him, nodding her head in bewilderment. Then she murmured. "Don't take me to the train," and rushed out of the automobile without looking back.

CHAPTER TWENTY-THREE

The enormity of what he had done—the flight to New York, meeting Carla at the train, the scene in the cab, and their last night—was heavy on him, but more disturbing was his reluctance to end the relationship. Time and reason told him that Lee's rejection, self-pity, loneliness, depression, and a river of booze had driven him to New York. What an anesthesia! Well, he was sober now, and sane. If he overcame every other obstacle, one loomed, terrifying, spectral, and Paula's wrath could be homicidal. He must stay away, not communicate, and hope that Carla's hurt was so deep her love for him would lose to pride.

At first he tackled each morning's mail fearing the sight of an envelope with her large sweeping hand, trembled every time Sherry informed him of a New York call. But after two months he found himself waiting for the mail, looking for the letter, and grabbing every long-distance call with hope.

If Sherry Larsen suspected his malaise she probably attributed it to the announcement in the press and radio a few weeks before of Lee's marriage to John Arley. Samson had been seeing Sherry twice a week; Alex would be sent away for the night, supper would be sent up. After meager conversation, it was to bed to play mechanical tricks. The first time she turned down his invitation he gave it no thought. When she refused a weekend invitation to the Palm Springs house, claiming a friend's wedding in San Francisco, he half-suspected she was lying. When she finally consented to come to his apartment one evening and after dinner began to squirm as he ran his hand over her ass, claimed she had a headache and was going home, he exploded. "What's gotten into you!"

"I have to tell you, Boss." She found a chair across the room and waited until he settled on the couch. "I met a man. . . ."

"Go on. . . ."

"It's real, Boss. I'm in love, I mean."

"When did all this happen?"

"I met him a few months ago. At first it was . . . well, it was for fun." She caught his eye. "You should know about that." His look wavered. "On my lonely nights I couldn't call you. Could I?" He had no answer. "I spent last weekend with him. I lied about San Francisco."

"And you fell in love?"

"It wasn't that simple. I must have loved him the day we met. But I was scared. You can understand that, Boss."

"Damnit, don't call me Boss!"

"All right, Sam."

"When do you quit?"

"I'm not. You'll have to fire me."

"You're not going to get married?"

"In a month or two."

"And you're going to continue working?"

"I'll have to."

He leaned forward. "Don't tell me you're going to marry a poor slob?"

"He's finishing law school. Then there'll be the bar and two or three years as a clerk. I'll have to help out."

Damnit, she was beginning to look good to him now. Something you take for granted, you begin to lose it, somebody else wants it. Like it was with Posey, Lee and others. Why shouldn't he have a chance? Sure, he treated her like a delivered package, but it was the way she wanted. She said so herself. He was on his feet, standing before her. "You took a beating from a doctor and got dumped when he made the grade. What makes you think you might not wind up the ex-wife of an up-and-coming attorney?" He reached for her hand. "What makes you think this guy is different?"

"He's different."

He poured a drink and for a few moments neither said a word. He finally said, "Lawyers are a dime a dozen, the town is full of them. They're not like doctors, they haven't got a monopoly. What'll it get you?"

"What have I got now?"

"I know I haven't treated you . . . well, maybe I haven't romanced you. But that's the way you wanted it. You told me. Love was for peasants. You wanted to marry a man with money. Lots of it. Sure I have money, but I'm not the marrying kind. You know I'm not the marrying kind, Sherry?" She nodded. "Don't rush. Look around. With me at least you're free to find a better deal."

"I don't want to be free. I want to be tied up, involved, mixed in somebody else's life. Maybe knowing you taught me. When we first met I admired you, I still do. I began to fall in love with you and when I realized how hopeless it was I talked myself out of it. It was easy, Sam. You never threw a coal on the fire. At the beginning, sex with you was great."

"It's still great."

"It isn't, and you know it." She began to gather her things. She was at the door. "Do I still have a job?"

"Of course, of course." He let her go without another word.

There was a stillness in the apartment, like the walls were battened, the cracks caulked. In the past when Alex took his two weeks in Mexico, making the rounds of relatives, it was a relief. A maid cleaned every day, left before Samson came home, he took his meals out, and afterwards the apartment was without other's steps, eyes, ears. Now the silence was imposed, a hard lid to pry. Martin Tipton was busy when he called the night before, would be tied up all week. Walt Covington was a computer and Jack Delaney's hookers had no faces. Dinner at the club followed by brandy at the bar could only cull a drunk. Ben Hardin could only make it for lunch, Sherry dodged cocktails on Thursday, and on Friday night after dinner alone, Samson called Teddy Hofstedter. He would be delighted to come over, the broker said. When Samson hung up he realized it was the first time he had invited Hofstedter, that every visit had been unheralded and unwelcome. He was at the apartment in half an hour, and greeted Samson with his usual ebullience, a posture he displayed for few people. Samson waited for his hand which always sprung like a rapier thrust, and gripped the sausage fingers. The Hitler mustache was long ago replaced by a high clipped haircut which made him look like a pulpy Junker. They tackled a bottle of scotch, there was a glow, they ran through averages, short interest, touched on the commodities and by the time the bottle was half-drained their collars were loosened, Hofstedter was sprawled on the couch rubbing a roll of fat that bulged over his belt as Samson refilled their glasses and settled in a chair. After a moment's silence, Hofstedter switched the conversation abruptly.

"How is it you never remarried, Sam?"

Duke found it difficult to hide his surprise. In all the years he'd known Hofstedter he'd never heard him discuss anything that did not relate to the stock market or politics. Teddy was on an elbow, looking at Samson intently.

"Never found the right woman." Samson said.

"Are there such things?"

"I guess so."

Hofstedter settled on his back again, folded his arms across his chest, his sagging jowls and bristling hair making him resemble Hindenburg laid out. "I've never married."

"I guess if you remain single beyond a certain age it's hard to tie yourself to a woman," Samson ventured.

"A man doesn't tie himself, Sam. He gets tied. Women are deceptive, 'Bound in matrimony' is not merely a figure of speech. Women pretend to suffer in childbirth, the fruits of which are the strongest bond. From there, they keep the man wriggling for freedom until his last breath." This came with all the venom he usually reserved for Communists, do-gooders, and bureaucrats. When Hofstedter finished he was sitting up, almost heaving with the effort, then he settled back and for a moment closed his eyes. Finally, he rose, weaved to the bar, poured a drink and took the chair next to Samson pulling it up so close their knees almost touched.

"I almost married once." He shuddered. "Was to be a church wedding. A big one. My mother arranged everything," he said bitterly.

"What was she like?" Samson asked.

"She was like my mother. They banded together like thieves."

"What did she look like, I mean?"

He took a moment as if not wishing to describe her superficially. "She had little eyes, like green raisins stuck in a big face with a big nose and a wide mouth. The rest of her was flat." He halted, drained the last of his drink, twisted his face with disgust as if the bitter drink reminded him of her image.

Duke was beginning to feel dizzy, Teddy's voice, as he went on, seemed far away.

"The courtship was swift. Hortense, that was her name, must have prepared herself for a long time." The name tickled Samson, seemed to fit her description and he laughed aloud, Teddy stopped talking, looked at Samson then joined in as if he had read Duke's thoughts and they roared until the broker got up, staggered to the bar, refilled their glasses and returned to his chair. Tapping Samson's knee to punctuate he continued. "They visited us a half-dozen times over a few months. One day my mother invited them to spend a week with us. She made no bones about it, said Hortense would make a fine wife. I told her I couldn't be less interested."

"How did it happen?"

Teddy smiled. "Almost happen." He was patting Samson's knee. "One afternoon I escaped to my bedroom. Left them all in the living room. It was a hot day and I took off my shirt and flopped on the bed. I must have dozed because I didn't hear Hortense come in. There she was standing before the bed. She sat beside me on the bed smelling of some sweet scent." Samson was finding it difficult to concentrate as Teddy went on. "Within seconds her skillful hands were all over me and before I knew what was happening she had gotten what she came for."

"You mean she got fucked?"

"You can call it that."

"Damnit man, what do you call it? I like to call a fuck a fuck."

"All right, she got fucked." He whispered, uttered the vulgarism. He had never heard Hofstedter utter a foul word and by God, he squeezed it out of him. As he continued to laugh, Teddy kept patting his knee as if to pacify him. "The following day my mother cornered me and with mock horror which immediately cooled to understanding, told me she knew. The bitch told her mother who in turn ran to mine with the tale. From then on they had it easy. I couldn't look any of them in the face. Mr. Meedy, Hortense's father, followed me with his eyes like an executioner. By the last day of the visit my goose was put up to be cooked. Hortense walked about the house with head held high as if one day she would be delivered of a prince. By the time they left arrangements had been made."

Samson's head had cleared a little, Teddy got up, walked to the back of Samson's chair, a hand rested on Samson's shoulder. "I wanted to run away, then reason told me it would be folly. But I was going to get out of that marriage. At first I pleaded with my mother for understanding. She would have none of it. She said I had to right the wrong dealt under her roof." He returned to his chair, pulled it up so close that their knees were touching. Leaning forward, he began to speak, his voice a plea for understanding. "I'm to tell you something I never told a soul."

All of a sudden he looked strange to Samson, as he gripped his knee with trembling hands. "I know you'll understand, Sam," he said. The hand loosened on the knee, remained a caress. "I couldn't marry this girl," he almost whispered. "I couldn't marry any girl." He searched his face and Samson returned the look with the least expression he could muster. For a fleeting moment a look of hesitancy clouded Teddy's face and then it cleared. "I couldn't tell this to my mother. She wouldn't understand."

Almost sober now, he realized that Teddy was very drunk. The thought that kept nagging him did not seem real. As he crossed his legs to deflect the broker's hand, Teddy moved closer. "I waited a week and then left the house for a whole day. When I returned that night I told my mother I had been to a doctor. I told her Hortense had given me a disease." Discarding all pretense he gripped Samson's thighs. "You understand why I had to do it, Sam?" Duke tried to rise but Hofstedter's hands held him like a vise. "Please . . . give me a chance. You're so attractive!"

Duke rose with a roar and sent Hofstedter sprawling. "So that's what it's been all these years. That's why I've never seen you with a woman!" The broker was on his knees before the chair, his head buried in his arms, his frame shook with sobs. "I don't care what you are," Duke went on. "You can suck cocks, take it up your ass! But to proposition me!" Hofstedter started to his feet, did not look at Samson as he gathered his things. At the elevator he turned and faced Samson's glare.

"I'm sorry, Sam . . . I didn't know . . . I thought. . . ."

"You thought, what!" Samson reached for a glass and flung it at the broker, it crashed against the wall as the elevator door opened and Hofstedter escaped.

Duke rushed into the bedroom, rummaged through a drawer and came up with a small notebook. He found the list: Vicki, Stacy, Kelly—no last names, just phone numbers and a notation to mention Jack Delaney. But it was a year since he called any of them, when Fines Cady was in town, and a whore's phone number was as temporary as a hard-on. But there was one, he remembered, months before, when Lee was out of town, Alex was away, he was alone and the apartment wasn't friendly. She was good, by God—she was the one who brought the vibrator. What in hell was her name? Where did he put her phone number? She was a real-estate woman for an office on The Strip and fucking was a sideline between deals. She had given him her card. He almost shouted for joy as he found it and placed the call. A sleepy voice answered.

"Terry?"

"Who's this?"

"Sam Duke. Jack Delaney's friend."

"I'm sorry, mister, I'm in bed."

"Look, you remember me. I live in The Chateau Baroque. The penthouse."

"I can't see you tonight."

"Can you give me a number? Have you got a friend?"

She told him to hang on. He was going to get laid that night if he had to hunt one up in a bar, if he had to wake Jack Delaney in Oxnard! Damnit, from now he was going to have a list, up-to-date, on tap! She came back on the phone.

"Call Hollywood 4000. Ask for Helen."

"What's she like?"

"She's a blonde."

"But what's she like?"

"She's just what you're looking for."

"Give me another one. Just in case."

"You really got hot nuts. All right, wait a minute." A few moments. "Call the same number. It's an exchange. Ask for Kim. She's a redhead. Ask for her first. She isn't cheap but you'll get your money's worth."

Kim said she was expecting a friend, would be finished in a half-hour, could be there by eleven.

He resumed his drinking and watched the clock. By the time she arrived he was glowing like a coal. By God, she looked good, he thought as she stepped out of the elevator. Had a bit of class.

Her eyes were green, there was a hint of freckles, could be a real redhead he figured. Her coat was off, he handed her a drink and ran a hand over her ass. She reached for his crotch.

"You're primed, Mr. Duke. If I blow on that it'll pop off."

He started to undress. "Take off your clothes."

"Here in the living room?"

"That's right." He wasn't going to rush things. March her up and down in front of him, get an eyeful. And when they got in that bedroom he was going to fuck her until she hollered.

"Look, Mr. Duke, I'm good in there," she said pointing to the bedroom. "Even fancy. But I don't go in for anything but the straight stuff."

He stepped out of his clothes, she climbed out of her dress, unhooked her brassiere, revealed small breasts half covered with dark brown nipples—a disappointment—but when she took off her shorts and turned before him, arms extended, the long, well-padded legs and great round ass more than compensated for the deficient tits. They stood at the bar, thighs touching, sipping their drinks. His hands were all over her, found her cunt, his finger went in, she grabbed his cock and he felt it grow. Now he liked her breasts, there was something virginal about them and the hair around her box was red by God! Not as bright as her hair but red nevertheless. She didn't look like a whore, looked as refined as any of them; Posey, Lee, even Beck, the whole lot of them. They were standing belly to belly, his hands were on her ass, she was grinding slowly, looking up at him smiling, a little girl's smile, he bent down to kiss her and she averted her head . . . whores don't kiss, he remembered, and then he remembered the friend she had before she came, the cock she probably sucked, the wet deck . . . but what difference does it make. . . . she was drinking scotch, it was a sterilizer and anyway he wanted to kiss her. Then she gave him her mouth, wide open, soft lips, smooth tongue . . . all women were whores, only some got licenses from a preacher, the state; who could sit and judge? Now they were on the bed, her tongue was in his ear, gently nipped the lobe, how good it felt on his neck, he shivered when it lingered on his nipple, began to feel a gathering in his groin when it flew over the head of his prick to lick his balls. Not that way, he wasn't going to come that way, he was going to roll her over and ram it in and she was never going to forget that prick! Now it was in, everything inside her seemed to rush to meet it, her ass began to swivel, she was moaning—by God, now she let go little screams—"Ai," she came out with, she was getting it like she never had before, a whore getting fucked like she never had before! Her legs were high on his back, he drew back and rammed it in, she was calling for it now, "more baby, MORE!, fuck me, fuck me, aah, aah!" she was on top now sitting on his cock riding him like a mustang and then he let it go—a gusher!

He woke up in the middle of the night and found her gone. For the moment he was angry. He'd paid her for the whole night. Then he felt a wave of relief. What do you say to a hooker after she's used?

The letters started to arrive from Carla. The first was a short note, warm and friendly, without a word about what happened. It told of hard work at study, loneliness, concern for his well-being. It was a door-opener, a start from scratch. He answered it in the same manner and tone and received a reply by return mail; a little yearning now, more endearing salutations, his rational thoughts kept telling him to look for reproof, rejection, but his hopes soared each time he tore open an envelope. By the end of spring there were no pretenses, her letters grew longer, her patience shorter, she could not wait for the end of school so that she could come to the coast and they could be together. By playing the game—corresponding, he had acquiesced, how could he tell her not to come and what was going to happen when Paula found out as she surely would? It was almost with relief that he faced a crisis with Universal and Ben Hardin.

The first sign of trouble was a visit a month before by a man who identified himself as an investigator for the House Committee on Un-American Activities. The man's attitude when he sat in Duke's office puffing on a pipe, was casual, his references to Ben Hardin oblique. He was certain Duke knew of the Committee's work, he drawled, they were forced to run down every lead, most were from crackpots, people with grudges. They had to be careful not to hurt innocent persons and Ben Hardin's name came up in such a manner, he was sure it meant nothing, in fact might even be another with a similar name. Then he asked if there were any attitudes or conversations with Hardin that might indicate implication with Commies. When Duke assured him there were not, the man left with a caution not to say a word to Hardin, that the whole thing was surely a case of mistaken identity or the finger of a crank. However, when the man returned accompanied by an assistant who questioned Duke from a sheaf of notes it became evident the trail waas warm. The moment they left, Duke was on his way to Universal. He rushed by the receptionist, the secretary, the marble bust, fell into a chair before the desk as Hardin, on the phone, looked at him questioningly, lingered in conversation and hung up. Duke waited as Hardin reached for a cigar, lit it slowly, rolled it, looked at the first ash, shoved it in his mouth and leaned back. It was hard to believe that Hardin ever knew a Commie, let alone was one of them. He lived like a potentate, strutted like a Roman senator, and wouldn't share the air he exhaled. But, why take chances? He removed the investigator's card from a pocket and flung it on the desk.

"What's this all about, Ben?"

Hardin looked at the card without picking it up, the end of the cigar became a live coal as he puffed furiously, the smoke almost screening his face. He swiveled his chair and with his back to Duke began to talk.

"Did you ever do stupid things when you were young?"

"A few times."

Hardin spun his chair slowly. "I am going to give it to you straight, Sam, just the way it was. When it's 1935 and you're twenty-one years old delivering packages in lower Manhattan for twelve dollars a week wearing out a pair of shoes with soles a half-inch thick every thirty days, filling up on Automat beans and you see guys leaving plush offices and stepping into limousines you begin to hate . . . you begin to think."

"So, it was a depression. Fifty million people were sweating then."

He ignored Duke. "I lived at the 'Y'. A lousy room with a window on a shaft. The whole building smelled of dirty sneakers and disinfectant."

"You just got me right here, Ben." Duke laid a hand on his heart. "Stop the bullshit and come to the point."

"All right. It's simple. I met a girl. She had her own apartment, two rooms not one. She had a stove to cook and there were curtains on the window and a rug. She started taking me to meetings. I swear I didn't know what they were talking about. I would have followed her to hell rather than lose her."

"They were Commie meetings?"

"I guess so."

"What do you mean, you guess so. . . . Were they or weren't they?"

"Yes."

"Then what happened?"

"Well, I guess I joined the party."

Duke leaped from his seat. "You guess you joined! You mean you don't know?" He was shaking a fist. "Damn right you knew. And there's a lot of other things you know you're not telling. Let me tell you something. I don't care what you did or what you were . . . or still are for that matter. All I know is that if the word got out that the president of Universal Savings and Loan was once a Communist there'd be a run on us like we had a disease! And the stock—yours and mine—we could wipe our ass with it." He advanced toward the desk his arm extended, finger jabbing. "You're going to resign, Ben. Call it ill-health, retirement; call it any damn thing you want. But you're out!"

Hardin was on his feet, shouting. "If you think I'm going to give up all this because of a witchhunt, you're crazy!"

"A witchhunt! Do you call digging Commie rats out of a hole a witchhunt? Plotting to overthrow the government—force and violence—that's what you were doing!"

"It's a goddamn lie! We had meetings, we talked, discussed a little Marx, Lenin—it was all academic."

"You lied before and you're lying now. A minute ago you said you didn't know what they were talking about. Now it's Marx, Lenin, maybe when it all comes out you were a commissar. You better tell me the whole story. I'll get it anyway."

Hardin returned to his seat. Duke stood before the desk. It was worse than he thought, maybe resigning wouldn't do any good. By God, he was going to get the truth, every bit of it and then talk to the investigators. Something had to be done. The Savings and Loan was at stake. "Give it all to me, Ben."

"I came to Hollywood, got into the agency business. Everybody was a pinko. If you didn't join them you were out in the cold. So, I went to a few meetings, put up a front. That was all, I swear."

Duke took a seat and lit a cigar. For moments neither spoke. If that was all, if Hardin was telling the truth, maybe it wasn't so bad. You don't kill a guy for what he was and it looked like Hardin wasn't much. They just had to keep it under cover. "What did they tell you, Ben—the investigators—what do they want to do?"

"They're coming to see me in the morning."

"What time?"

"Ten o'clock."

"I'll be here."

Hardin started to protest, then shrugged.

Duke went directly to Martin Tipton's office, rounded up Walt Covington and closeted himself with the two men.

"What can be done?" he asked after telling them the whole story.

"I'd never believe it of Ben Hardin," Tipton commented.

"Damnit, you sound like you admire him?"

"In a way I do."

"Oh, shit!" He turned to Covington. "You make some sense."

"There's a lawyer in town. He sorta operates the underground railroad from Hollywood to closed hearings in Washington."

"What do you mean?"

"You pay him a fee, he puts you in touch with the right people in D.C. You grease a few palms and get a secret hearing. You spill your guts for the record and they close the book."

"How do you know about this?" Martin asked.

"I had friends. They hit paydirt in Hollywood and went red. They wanted to tell all without kleig lights. I did some snooping and dug this lawyer up.

"What's his name?"

"Arthur Gantner. His office is in the Roosevelt building."

Duke wrote the name in his notebook and left.

The following morning the investigators came directly to the point. They knew that Hardin was no longer a Communist, but they needed information for their files. A loyal American should cooperate. All they wanted was a few names, former cellmates, leaders. Ben Hardin sat through the meeting and barely said a word. When the men rose to leave, Duke thanked them and led them to the door. "Mr. Hardin will be in touch with you, gentlemen."

Then he told Hardin about Arthur Gantner, wrote his name and address on a slip of paper. "Don't waste any time, Ben," he said, and left.

He did not hear from Hardin for days, his calls to him were not returned, and one afternoon Samson entered his office and found Ben Hardin waiting in the reception room. For an instant he did not recognize him; he was sunk in a chair, looked old, the slick gray mane was awry and the horn-rimmed glasses constantly whipped on and off, used only to read, rested in place. He followed Duke into the office and in the brighter light, the mouth lines, bitten deep, showed through a beard growth and a half-chewed cigar dangled limp from the corner of his lips.

"Did you see Gantner?"

"Yes." Almost a whisper.

"What did he say?"

"It's simple—cost a lot of money—but it's simple."

"So what's wrong?"

"Sam, I gotta tell them the name of everybody I ever knew—men, women—friends."

"What difference does it make? Give them a few names."

"It doesn't work that way. Gantner told me. They want a lot of names. They give me a list—people I don't even know."

"Then name them, damnit! What are they, a lousy bunch of reds!"

"But some of these people are still my friends. They work in pictures. They'll be blacklisted."

"Listen to me, Ben, you haven't got a choice. You give them what they want in private or they'll blast you in public."

Hardin straightened up. "Suppose I tell them nothing in a public hearing? Tell them to go to hell."

"The fifth amendment?"

"That's right."

Duke was out from behind the desk, standing over Hardin. "If you do that I'll wipe you out. I'll run Universal's stock down to peanuts and buy you out with the shells. You'll be out of a job—you'll never get a job. Not even in the agency business. Put your friends in your position. What would they do for you? Not a goddamn thing."

"I'm not so sure."

"Well I am! I've had enough. This is Friday. I'm giving you until the end of the day on Monday. If you don't make the arrangements with Gantner there's going to be a board meeting on Tuesday and you're going out on your ass! And then I'm calling a press conference. Can you see the headlines? Ex-red fired from post at Universal Savings and Loan! By God, it might even be good for the business."

Hardin rose wearily. "All right. I'll see Gantner on Monday. But I want to tell you something for the record. I've been nasty, done a lot of things I'm ashamed of, but what I'm about to do puts me as low as I ever got."

"Okay. So you're ashamed of yourself."

Hardin was back from Washington within a week, refused to tell Duke any of the details except that he gave them what they wanted and got a clean bill. Also that Gantner's fee was five thousand and that it took another twenty thousand in cash to pave the way in the Capital. Hardin was going to bear watching, the record book in Washington sometimes got into strange hands he found out; there were leaks and he was sure Hardin knew it. When you're sitting on a bomb you live a lot—and fast—and you don't wait for annuities but grab the cash. There were going to be eyes on Hardin, every loan application was going to be studied, no more committee meetings rushed between noon and a one o'clock lunch.

In the middle of June, Carla called. Whatever had been left restrained in her letters poured over the wire. How does one prepare for an execution he wondered as he hung up? All the things he should have said now rushed through his mind, he picked up the receiver to call her back then replaced it. What was the use? They were over the dam, Carla was coming out and Paula would know.

He arrived at the airport to meet Carla and found Paula at the gate. He looked at her and she gave no message; a glance, bare recognition, and her back as they waited. The plane's arrival was announced, in a few moments Carla seemed to eject, pecked her mother, and ran to his arms. He tried to evade her, managed to give her a cheek, push her to arm's length. Paula was ignored, her invitation to Carla to stay at her home declined with firmness.

"I'm going to a hotel. I have a reservation."

They were waiting for the baggage. He had to get her alone before she could talk to Paula. "The hotel is on the way to my office. I'll drop Carla off."

"I'll take her," Paula said.

"No, Mother." She pecked Paula's cheek as Samson picked up her bag. "I'll call you later." He was dragging her toward the car afraid to look back.

As they sped to the hotel, Carla snuggled close and he shouldered her aside, she said she loved him, he did not reply, she said she knew he loved her, he turned and faced her.

"You've made a mistake."

"You're lying, Sam. You know why I'm here. You didn't tell me not to come. Forget your stupid ideas about age."

"Age? This is latent adolescence, compounded by incurable romanticism aided and abetted by middle-age senility. Listen to me, Carla. I'm not in love with you and we're not going to get married. And your mother is to hear nothing of this nonsense."

"Mother's no fool. I'm sure she knows."

"Then I'll straighten her out."

Carla changed the subject, talked about her school, the things she was going to do in Los Angeles, the friends she wished to see. By the time they pulled in front of the hotel he realized all his protestations had been ignored. They arranged to meet that night for dinner.

All during the evening he emphasized, punctuated, pounded; she laughed, thought it a good performance, said that his willingness to sacrifice in spite of his love only made her love him more. He gave up, dodged her for a couple of days and tried again. This time he suggested there was someone else.

"Sam, I don't believe you." She appeared worried for the first time, there was no smile, no mischief in her face. They were having lunch at the Brown Derby in Beverly Hills, her conversation had vaulted the wedding, was dealing with the redecoration of his apartment.

"It's true, Carla. I didn't want to tell you before."

"Who is she?"

"I can't tell you."

There was relief, a trace of a smile. "There is no other woman."

"There is."

"Then why can't you tell me who she is?"

"She's in the process of getting a divorce. My name must not enter into it. There are children." He cut deep. "One is your age." Now she searched his face, riveted on his eyes looking for the lie. He tried to compose an expression of sincerity and compassion. "I've known her for a long time."

"You're in love?"

"Yes."

She looked at the table, toyed with the cup. "What about New York—your last trip?"

"We were drunk." She looked up, for an instant he wanted to confess the lie, take her in his arms and damn the consequences. She was on her feet, fumbling with her purse, slid from the booth and ran from the restaurant.

All that afternoon he paced his office unable to work, to think, her face before him, the look that could turn from hurt to hate. He was going to lose her—the little love that might have been his, the love of a daughter was gone. He left the office and started to walk home. The sun was up, not yet finished with the long summer day, a breeze that cooled the nights blew gently from the west as he trudged, head down, along Wilshire toward Doheny. Doubts that in the past had flashed through his mind like shooting stars only to be lost in a dark corner of his brain began to assail him. He had mapped the road ages ago, his eye on the top of a mountain. Nothing had gone wrong, everything according to plan, goals were reached—disappeared and he zoomed to a new plateau; the sky was the limit. But the heavens were infinite. It was a climb now up Doheny toward Sunset, he began to puff, slowed his pace. Halfway he had to stop and rest. Looking ahead he saw the Chateau Baroque high above the Strip, its tower jutting against the darkening sky. He should have taken the car, was a fool to have walked, the last quarter mile was a goat trail. He remembered taking the hill at a fast clip, ran it once, there was never strain, breath to spare—it was years ago. Was there a limit to power, wealth—was the trail a circle? Suppose one found a spot along the way and leveled out? But, what about the game? Do you quit when you've read the deck, know every turn of the card? Nothing stands still, and if you do not go up you go down. This he could control; the size of a pot, when to draw, when to stand pat, when to bet. It was his game. There was another where all you did was ante; time dried up the flesh, furrowed the face, hardened the routes through which life was pumped, bent and shrunk and finally put you away.

By the time he had his third drink on the terrace, the relaxer after two warmups, his thoughts had waded through the marshes of remorse and were not toying about the edges of fear. Suppose Paula did not accept the Oedipal syndrome, a young girl's affinity for the older man, the father image, the protector, the lover? What if Carla confessed, documented the days they spent in New York, the night in his suite? He wasn't going to speculate. . . . Carla had to be convinced it was a mistake, to pursue it further would aggravate hopelessness. He had been mad; middle-age was a disease that occasioned temporary manifestations of insanity. Damnit, it was logical but what had logic to do with a young girl loving a father who isn't sure he is her father? More drinks and no dinner, stumbling to bed wrapping the blanket like a membrane . . . sleep.

The phone jangled. Paula's voice was level, cool. He was to come over—it was a command. It was seven in the morning, somehow he had managed to sleep through the night. He wondered how much she knew? Her voice had no anger—was weary —resigned. By the time he reached her house he made up his mind to say little—react—there could be no mistakes.

He saw the evidence in Paula's face; sleeplessness had smudged under her eyes, wide and darting like after viewing a specter. It was soon evident that Carla had told her nothing. Paula questioned him and then studied his face as he answered. Now that he knew the facts he felt in command, calmed, worked the theme of immature romanticism, the oedipal, made up quotes from Freud ending beside Paula on the couch patting her hand reassuringly.

"We'll work it out. Together." The last word sounded false. Her hand slid from his. "What I mean," he hastened to add, "is that I'll do anything necessary. Whatever you think should be done."

"I was with her all day yesterday." She smiled bitterly. "She was nice to me. Confided like to a friend."

"I told her there was another woman. That we were waiting for her divorce. Would marry."

"Is it true?"

Might as well lie. "Yes."

"She doesn't believe it. Says you're lying because you think it's for her own good."

"She'll have to be convinced. Look, Paula, I'll dodge her—indefinitely. But get her away. Out of the city."

"She won't go."

"Then I'll go. I can't leave my business all summer but I can arrange to be away a good part of the time. By fall you should be able to convince her that the whole thing was a mistake. Then maybe a trip—to Europe—around the world. It'll be my gift."

For the next two weeks he managed to elude Carla. She called at the office, the apartment, before dawn and after midnight, wrote letters, left notes, he checked out of the apartment into a hotel, kept in contact with his office by phone and finally fled the city by the end of June. He returned to his office after Labor Day to find a message from Carla dated early August, read a note she had posted in the middle of the same month—cold, cryptic—a farewell. Paula's phone was disconnected. He drove to the house, found it occupied by a couple who informed him they had purchased it a month before. Ann Schneider's office supplied the information that she had left the city and her forwarding address was a post office box at Martha's Vineyard. He wrote, received no reply, tried the phone and found no listing, sent a wire and wrote again and a week later received a letter from Paula. The campaign was a success beyond her hopes. His impression on Carla was fading like an old laundry mark and if he loved his daughter he'd play dead. Months went by and he heard nothing, then, driven by curiosity as well as a desire to know if she was well he hired an investigator who snooped and sniffed and called in his report: the three women lived in Beck's old cottage and if the local wagging tongues were to be believed, they had perfected a *ménage à trois*.

CHAPTER TWENTY-FOUR

Until a few years before, he had felt indestructible; the only occasions he had to call on a doctor were for a prescription for flu and shots for a trip. But when aches and slowdown called for yearly checkups he shopped the market and settled for Joe Engle. Martin Tipton had used him for years. Find an internist, a gifted diagnostician, Martin had said. Lie to your wife, your friends, throw curves at partners, but level to the man in charge of blood pressure and cholesterol, a hard artery or calcification.

The first time he visited Dr. Engle he was grilled for an hour about his past before he submitted to an intensive examination; he studied the plasticized diplomas: Cornell University Medical School, Fellow in Internal Medicine, Phi Beta Kappa. He left the office feeling as secure as a baby who had emptied a breast. Engle's stethoscope was an antenna, his fingers delicate tendrils, and best of all, one could read the diagnosis in the frank gray eyes. By God, if he had a tumor or white cells were running wild he wanted to know it before creditors, partners, or undertakers and Joe Engle's eyes couldn't cover up. There were other credentials;

a Jew never got to medical school with B's and Joe Engle had a list of patients with long experience in buying the best.

When the symptoms first appeared, Samson brushed them like a fly—three, maybe four scotches before dinner, wine with the steak and brandy with the coffee and after . . . and a hard-on's a muscle and booze a depressant. It began the summer he ran away from Carla, at first he attributed it to nerves and tension, but when he returned to town, rustled up Kim, tossed her two hundred and she earned the pay and his pecker hung like a worm, he called Joe Engle and set up the appointment.

"Maybe I'm tired, Joe," he said, as they sat in the consultation room. "I can't get it up. No matter how I try." He was looking at the doctor's face for encouragement, understanding, a cure. Dr. Engle smiled.

"We'll take a look."

In the examination room the doctor examined his cock—no expression—had him cough as he fingered under his testicles, took his blood pressure, tested his reflexes and then in the proper position slid a rubber-gloved finger in the rectum and probed.

"Well?"

Joe Engle removed the glove, tossed it in a receptacle. "Get dressed. I'll see you in the office."

Seated before the desk, Samson examined Engle's face for a clue.

"There's nothing wrong," the doctor began. "Pathological, that is. Prostate's normal, healthy. Any pressure lately?"

"Nothing more than usual."

Engle sat back, laced his fingers and propped his head. "Emotional distress can cause these things. It happens to younger men. At our time in life it's part of the middle-age syndrome."

"But does it last? Jesus, to go through the rest of my life without a hard-on . . ." Engle was smiling. "It's not funny." The doctor's grin broadened, he started to laugh. "Go ahead, enjoy yourself. Maybe a soft cock's funny. When it's hanging between someone else's legs."

"I'm sorry, Sam." He was serious now. "We all go through this."

"I don't mind going through it. If there's an end to the road."

"There's an end. Solve the problem that caused it."

"What problem?"

"I don't know, Sam. I'm not a psychiatrist. Impotency can be caused by frustration, guilt, anxiety. And a few dozen things in the unconscious."

"What do I do?"

"Solve your problems alone or get help."

"An analyst?"

"Maybe."

"Not me."

Engle shrugged. He started to write on a prescription pad. "I'm going to give you a stimulant. It might work. In the meantime I want a urine and blood specimen. The nurse will take it. Try this," he said, handing Samson the prescription. "If I find anything wrong after the test I'll call you."

Samson called the next day, was told the tests were negative, if the medicine didn't work he should seek other help. Prone on a couch. Coughing up to a lousy analyst lapping it like a voyeur. Not for him! He'd met these bums: Martin Tipton collected them and Lee Marlowe. Hovering at cocktail parties, brush mustached, some bearded, trailing their wives like hounds, sniffing and pontificating with looks, shrugs, and lean uttering, they devoured, and dished their words at a buck a yard. He wasn't buying their brand.

The problem was as old as the bat and balls, the Greeks never hit the couch and there was a Renaissance without Freud. He had seen a dozen people go the route; years at a hundred or two a week, in the end with the same limp only dragging a crutch. The few that made the grade only swapped hats, trading insecurity for slavery, while paying the master fat fees. By God, if the time came when he would need an analyst to keep him on the track he'd leave the train. All he needed was a fresh start. The right woman.

The closest thing to what now he was certain was needed was a Sherry Larsen; physical rapport, enough ingredients to make things sticky but not binding. Sherry had been married now for over a year. His few attempts at reviving her interest brought threats to quit and ultimatums. He gave up, content to make use of the only talent she was willing to proffer: efficient handling of his affairs and total trust. He decided to wait, stop pushing, stay away from women altogether for a while, save it up. When the right one came along, ripe, waiting to fall he would be there. No more reaching for the high branches. In the meantime his energy could be preserved for the more important things: a business that was burgeoning. New plans. Dreams.

Though he had not heard from Phil Matlin since the day he collected the cash, the talk was that Matlin was having a rough time getting his project off the ground. He had been peddling plans and projections to a dozen insurance companies seeking re-financing and if the gossip had credulity, Matlin would be coming around for an extension. He came on schedule: sixty days after the loan was due, a week after a dozen calls for an appointment and a forty-five minute wait in Duke's reception room. He entered the office, refused a seat, stood before Samson's desk, bristled like a cock on a vane.

"I need a ninety-day extension, Sam," he said, as he unrolled a half-dozen sheets and spread them on the desk. There were renderings and preliminary floor plans, studies and specifications, projections of income and expense. The first unit was to contain twin office towers, a regional shopping center, and a couple of apartment houses. Matlin seemed to forget why he was there, talked about the project with the fervor of a coach between halves. Duke said nothing. The memory of their last meeting was fresh. Taste it, roll it on your tongue, smack your lips! It wasn't a thing to be swallowed hastily. Matlin's head was high. Godamnit his jaw was thrust. Play with it, twist it down, bring the kike to his knees! Then do business. Matlin finished, began to roll the sheets. Duke said nothing, waited until the rubberbands were in place and the little man seemed to fall into the seat beside the desk.

"Well, Sam?"

"I counted on the money. Need it."

"You won't get it sooner by squeezing. A foreclosure takes months."

"It's another game."

Matlin's words sounded cracked like they were scraped off a dry throat. "We got along, Sam. Made a lot of money together. The last time at the bank, you could hardly blame me." He was on the edge of the seat now, the words were coming fast. "We can joint-venture the whole thing. I'll put up my equity against your loan, take a proportionate interest. We'll do the thing together." There was enthusiasm again, a broad smile, he reached for the large rolled sheet, snapped off the band and started to unroll it.

"I understand the deal. I don't want partners."

The smile was gone, all the papers were carefully placed in the briefcase, the lock snapped and Matlin looked up. "I don't want trouble, Sam. Let's work it out."

"I made a loan, it's past due. Pay it up or I foreclose."

"You got four hundred and fifty thousand! In cash, under the table. Every dollar was usurious."

Samson rose. "Get out. You're all alike. In a pinch you crawl and squirm." Matlin did not move. "I said get out!"

Matlin whipped a hand across the desk and grabbed the front of Duke's shirt, twisted until Samson felt his chin pressing against the wood. The hand was like a clamp, he could not move, Matlin was over him shouting in his ear. "Your ancestors were barbarians when mine were kings! Do you hear?" The grip tightened, Samson's nose was on the wood, the pressure was more than he could bear; he grabbed the edge of the desk, turned it over, felt a blow on the side of his jaw, fell back, saw Sherry rush into the room as Matlin grabbed his case and ran out.

The following day he filed a notice of default on the loan and a week later received a phone call from an attorney.

"I'm James McMahon." The name was as familiar as aspirin. He'd hold out for a ten-thousand dollar retainer and take a case free; he defended murderers and swindlers, fought for corporations and Communists and never ran out of the money. When McMahon suggested they meet and talk, Samson's first impulse was to refer him to Walt Covington, but there was something in McMahon's tone that suggested a preliminary might be preferable to a main event. He would be happy to meet in Samson's office, McMahon said, and they arranged for the following afternoon.

McMahon was tall and straight, an Ivy League suit hung without a bulge, pale blue eyes beneath a high forehead topped by thin blond hair showed no hint of guile, a warm smile dressed by a fine row of too-perfect dentures revealed a pair of dimples that softened an angular face. He seated himself before Samson's desk with great care, crossed his legs, arranged the crease of his pants, and settled back.

"I've heard a lot about you, Mr. Duke," he began. "Wanted to meet you for a long time."

It could be like sitting before a loaded gun, Samson figured . . . give a watch and a purse and save your life. If Phil Matlin became a "cause," the papers would pick it up . . . radio and television. . . . McMahon was a star . . . he had a public. Toss a few to the kitty and rake in the pot. McMahon had to be looking for salvage.

"I've wanted to meet you too. Kinda' hoped it would be under different circumstances."

"This is really a social visit. I'm going to say a lot of things a lawyer shouldn't before a potential opponent." He tapped a cigarette and lit it slowly. "Certain cases should never be reduced to a written complaint, never reach a courtroom. This situation, for instance. . . ." The smile was broad, looked genuine. "You received $450,000 in cash . . . incredible!"

"Mr. McMahon, you're talking riddles . . . anyway, this visit may be social to you but as far as I'm concerned you're a lawyer working overtime. Write it out and send it to my attorney."

"Wait." McMahon held up a hand. "I'll do that. But let's talk about the script." He dragged and crushed the cigarette, smiled and settled back. "I like a fight when there can be a clear decision. But I hate to get mauled in a draw. It's like this: my client had an appointment to meet you at the escrow and he only had a week to prepare. He cleaned out a hundred twenty thousand dollars from four savings accounts, took it all in cash. Borrowed fifty thousand on stock, cashed the check, took cash. Two hundred and eighty thousand in addition he tapped from friends, relatives, a loan at the bank, hocked jewels . . . it was all turned into cash. Then he kept his appointment."

Samson rose. "See my lawyer, Mr. McMahon."

"I will, I will, but hear me out." Samson hesitated and sat down. "He claims he gave it to you in a suitcase. You deny it." The lawyer shrugged. "Maybe we can prove it, maybe we can't. Maybe we can locate the cash." He leaned forward, a finger threatened. "Boxes have been located and opened." He smiled. "Juries are unpredictable . . . emotional . . . they're people. Innocent men are convicted every day on circumstantial evidence. Now, suppose you lose and appeal. . . . Think of it, Mr. Duke. I get an injunction on the foreclosure, the appeal takes months, maybe years." He tapped a cigarette and lit it, puffed a cloud. "My client has nothing to lose."

Samson fought the impulse to order McMahon out.

"I've been blackmailed before, Mr. McMahon."

There was no trace of a smile. "Matlin put up a half a dozen apartment houses as additional security for this loan. He's willing to drop the hundred and eighty acres. But that's all. . . . Release the other collateral and we'll be friends. You get the land— Matlin's dream." He rose like an obelisk. "If you don't I can promise a ride through the courts that'll make a bronco's back seem like a billowy cloud." He swept up his case and left the room.

A week before the redemption period elapsed Samson signed a

document releasing the properties put up as additional collateral and secured a deed in lieu of foreclosure on the country club property. With it came the renderings and studies, plans and reports, all the pieces of Phil Matlin's city.

When he called Fines Cady he embroidered the invitation. "How would you like to make a million bucks while you're gettin' laid?"

"Never mind the money."

"Hop a plane and bring your checkbook."

He brought Kim to the airport.

"It's twenty dollars an hour. Keep track and give me the tab."

"It's a hundred dollars minimum, Sam."

"If you can last, you're good for a grand."

"He's as good as dead."

Fines bounced as he got off the plane, took Kim's arm, called over his shoulder to Samson.

"Your taste is improving."

On the evening of the third day, Kim called. "You owe me a thousand dollars and a vacation."

"Where's Fines?"

"In heaven."

Fines was at Samson's office the following morning.

"I'm in love with a whore and it's your fault."

"You can take her home. Let's get down to business."

"You mean I was being buttered-up for a touch?"

"Not a touch. A gift. Look." He spread out the plot plan, the renderings, projections. "What you and I have been working up to all our lives. A city—contained, integrated. A fortune—a monument. It's like leaving a pyramid." He was flipping the pages of the plans. "We'll make Beverly Hills a suburb," he glowed, "Brentwood a village," he crowed. "Look at it!"

Cady began to examine the documents like a curator, made notes, looked up. "My first impression is that you're nuts." He rolled the papers and stuffed them in his case. "I'll look them over," he said. "See you tomorrow."

They were seated across Samson's desk the following morning.
"What's the arithmetic?" Cady asked. "On the land?"

"A hundred eighty acres. Thirty million first. Interest only at six per cent. All due in three years. The equity costs me three million."

"You'll never get the deal off the ground in time. What'll you do when the loan comes due?"

"Refinance."

"Who in hell is going to make a thirty million loan on vacant land?"

"I've a few bucks, Fines. And I'm counting on you."

"Insurance companies can't loan on vacant land. And I'm getting old. The deal's a long haul."

"It isn't, Fines. By the time that loan is due I'll have commitments on a dozen buildings; commercial, apartments, shopping centers. Can't you see? Look. . . ." He was around the desk, an arm was about Cady's shoulder, a finger was on the plans, jabbing. "It's a new city, tenants will be waiting in line . . . triple A's will gobble the space, apartments will rent off plans . . . a view of the ocean and the entire city . . . there'll be condominiums, theaters. . . ." He straightened up and walked to the window, his hand swept the panorama. "Everything you see now will be second-rate."

"I don't buy it, Sam. I smell slowdown. It's in the cards. I don't want a package like this when it comes."

"Package! A hundred eighty acres of urban land . . . pissing distance from a great city. There isn't any more!"

"Maybe you're right. But like I said, I'm getting old. Anyway I've got enough and so have you. There are other games. Travel, whatever romance I can handle, then a rocking chair with a view and . . . memories." He went up to Samson and touched his arm. "Forget it. It's too big for one man. The land is good, sell it. I know a dozen corporations who would snap it up. They've got public funds to spend."

"I'm going to build this city, Fines. It's the only important thing in my life."

Cady shrugged. "Good luck, but don't come to me in a year or two for a loan or a hand. I'm getting ready to close my books, get out of the business, turn it over. And when I do it's final."

Martin Tipton's office was now a machine; Tipton came in a few times a week to push the buttons, Walt Covington was around to repair the breaks. Samson's account was a symbol on a computer, his monthly statements looked like they had been printed by a chicken's foot and pecked. When he finally settled in a chair before Tipton's desk after waiting three days for an appointment he exploded.

"Damnit, if I'm going to get printed and punched by a machine, what in hell do I need you for!"

"To shift the gears."

"If it's a joke, I'm not laughing. I need advice, help. And not from a smart-ass punching buttons."

Tipton smiled. "To tell you the truth I hate the goddamn things myself. I used to be for progress, now I'm not so sure."

Samson was unrolling papers, spread them out on Tipton's desk. "You know the country club land . . . the 180 acres?" Martin nodded. "I own it. I need loans, contacts with every insurance company you know." He outlined his plans, spread all of Matlin's papers on the desk. "The interest is running me a million eight a year. I got to get off the ground—fast. I have an architect. He's starting on plans for two office buildings, renderings on an apartment house and a condominium. In a few months I'll have something to show. In the meantime I need loan commitments; they can be verbal but I need a start." Tipton went over the figures, made notes on a pad as Samson went on. "Martin, it's like when I first got started. Days are too short—I can't wait to get up. It's a dream I tell you. Except when I wake it's true." Tipton asked a few questions, scribbled on the pad, pushed it aside.

"It can be a nightmare, Sam."

"What do you mean?"

"It's too big for any one man." He leaned forward, spoke softly. "Sell the land and take the profit. Or syndicate it."

"You must have been talking to Fines Cady."

"I haven't seen him in a year."

"Well I have. And he's old. Maybe you're there too."

"Maybe we both know when to quit." Duke started to gather up the papers. "When will you have enough, Sam?"

The papers were folded, rolled and put away. Samson stood up.

"What's enough?"

"When you're no longer the smartest kid on the block. When you can't add a column of figures in your head . . . dollar signs become a blur. When the zeros in your bank book go off the page. It's a different game today, Sam. There are kids out there," Tipton pointed, "in my office—fresh out of school, degrees in things you and I never heard of. Their heads are full of figures, and machines to add them up. You're an old horse pulling a buggy."

"Just you watch this old horse. I'll build those buildings while the machines are still figuring if it can be done! Get me a list of every insurance company you know. The names of the men who write the checks. Send them letters. Tell them who I am. I'll be in touch with them." He walked to the door and turned. "I'm going ahead, Martin. If you're a friend you'll help."

"The letters will go out this week. I wish you luck."

Within a month, Samson toured New York, rode to Boston, Hartford, New Haven. Doors opened and slammed shut. Some insurance companies thought the project premature. Where there was interest there was also fear of putting so much money in one area. Others wanted leases before they would commit. They were blind! Wait until he got it rolling, majors waiting to sign leases, big corporations fighting for whole floors. They'd come begging to make loans. By God, it would be on his terms!

He contacted Martin Tipton's New York office and arranged a meeting. Tipton, Forbes and Temples' offices were in a stubborn little building on a sliver of a lot on Broad Street. Flanked by two skyscrapers after the firm refused to joint venture with either of the owners, the four-story structure looked like a rotted stump. Joseph Temple managed to maintain his person and the interior of the offices in strict conformity to the building's façade. Samson had met him years before on one of his infrequent trips to the West Coast. He oozed a provincialism peculiar to New Yorkers. Everything worthwhile was in Manhattan, why leave it? San Francisco, a little New York? And who runs the hotel in Los Angeles? He could not understand how Martin lived in Los Angeles, a converted desert. But Temple had contacts, solid as Manhattan's rock and Samson was going to pry them loose.

As he sat in Temple's office, dark with age (and lack of light—it looked out on a shaft) he carefully picked his way using prejudices as signposts.

"I need a group, a company with vision." Lay the bullshit, thick and bold. Temple had tunnel vision. "The money is here, Mr. Temple, and the brains. I want to build a city." He smiled. Temple was warmed up, offered Duke a cigar, told his secretary to hold his calls, sat back. Samson talked about his plans slowly, softly, contained with effort all the enthusiasm that would have bubbled like froth and by the time he finished, Temple was examining drawings, layouts and figures.

"Maybe that's what Los Angeles needs," he finally said. "The beginning of a real city."

"It could not have been put better, Mr. Temple."

"Ever hear of Atlantic States Holding Corporation?" he asked abruptly. "They're listed."

"Aren't they mainly in railroads?"

"Oil and steel too," Temple said. "I happen to know they're looking into real estate developments."

"Mortgage loans?"

"They feel the money is in development. That's the way I feel."

"Where are you staying?"

"The Plaza."

"I'll call in the morning."

Temple called before he showered the next morning. "I set up an appointment with Atlantic. They're at Number One Broadway. See you there at noon."

They were waiting for him when he arrived, Joseph Temple and an Armstrong, Jones and Tuttle all framed by walnut walls covered with New York skyline prints. Samson made his pitch, keyed it low. They listened—not a word until he was through.

"We're interested in land development," Armstrong said.

"Los Angeles is far away," Tuttle put in.

Jones nodded and Joe Temple picked it up.

"It's an enormous project, Sam. It'll take time to study."

"How long?"

"Weeks," Armstrong said. "You'll get an answer."

"I'm returning to the coast tonight. Call me if you're interested." He left with the assurance that he would be contacted.

He paced Dr. Engle's office, flipped the pages of *Time* and *Look,* was about to demand admittance when the receptionist called his name. Engle was seated in his consultation room hefting a paper weight like a shot-putter.

"Go ahead, throw it," Samson said as he flopped into the seat before the desk. "If you can't cure a patient, kill him."

"Kill you?" Engle laughed. "You're an annuity."

"Very funny."

"You were making the jokes."

"All right. Blood pressure normal. Cardiogram like a sixteen-year-old. Prostate a pleasure to feel. No blood sugar problem. Reflexes like a tennis player. How do you account for the fact that I wrestle in bed, Venus dingles my pecker and I piddle like a kid? And don't tell me it's in my head."

Engle dropped the weight and leaned forward. "Sam, a head's a piece of meat like the rest of you. Except, we know less about it than your liver, heart, or guts. If you want, I'll go through it again; cardiogram, blood tests, urinalysis, stick a rubber finger up your ass, send you a bill and a clearance. Your brain got ten thousand messages and you were shooting replies from the time you started to breathe. I'm a doctor, not a telegrapher."

"Joe, I need help."

"I told you where to find it."

"Not an analyst!"

"Why?"

"Doc, it's got to be physical. When I lay in bed and can't sleep and my heart is pounding like it wants to get out . . . did you ever feel the blood running through the pipes? And everything gets tickled except where it counts, like rusted plumbing? It can't come from my head."

"Everything else checks out, Sam."

"God—damn—it! Everything *you* know!"

Engle banged the desk. "Maybe you wanted to fuck your mother. Maybe you got buggered by a boyfriend! Maybe all cunts are your mother's. Maybe every ass is a boy's! Do you want me to go on, enumerate the possibilities? Where you slipped and fell? When you didn't do what you wanted, when you knew damn well you shouldn't do it in the first place! Jesus, Sam, can't you see how complicated it can be? I examined you up to your ears. Get a doctor who can carry the monkey or make it on your own." Engle reached for his phone. "Harriet, I'm taking calls." He rose from his chair. "I've an office full." He left the consultation room and called over his shoulder, "I can't help anymore."

He should not have listened to Martin Tipton in the first place. Joe Engle was a plumber not a doctor. The town was full of good men. Beverly Hills was a medical center, the best brains were up for sale and all the money to pay for it. He was on his third drink, the terrace was cool as the sun dipped and the fog swept from the sea. Psychoanalysis. A fancy name for a referral fee. He staggered to the telephone and called Walt Covington. "Who's your doctor?"

"Just like that?"

"Like that."

"John Addington. Corns to cancer."

"Any good?"

"Harvard. Johns Hopkins. Beverly Hills."

"Where is he located?"

"Roxbury Drive. His number's in the book. What's wrong, Sam?"

"I got a headache. Talk to you later."

Dr. Addington's office was soothing; flocked wallpaper and spy prints, a student lamp on a table of wormy chestnut, a nurse to lead him from the sanctuary to a consultation room where Dr. Addington rose from behind a desk extending a hand.

"Please be seated, Mr. Duke."

They talked for an hour without interruption. What an agenda! He had never experienced it before. Childhood diseases, sleeping habits, eating habits, sex life, exercise if any, type and frequency. How do you piss and how do you shit, consistency of stool—color—night sweats, nausea, stomach gas, headaches and your parents—are they alive? if not what did they die of and at what age? (he lied) as the doctor went on, making notes, filling pages.

"I reserve two, sometimes three hours for a new patient." Dr. Addington sat back. "I hope you're not in a hurry."

Samson nodded consent.

The human body was complicated machinery, the doctor explained. He removed his horn-rimmed glasses, cleaned them thoughtfully as he elaborated.

"Mechanics spend more time on a carburetor and a sticky valve than doctors take with a patient." He replaced the glasses which enlarged the frank blue eyes. "I'm not criticizing my colleagues. There are not enough doctors to go around, patients are lined up like on an assembly line. They must be cared for." He smiled. "There are doctors—a few—who cannot work this way. I've limited my practice—twenty-five patients, maybe thirty—no more." His fingers combed a shock of prematurely gray hair. "Would you believe it consumes ten, twelve hours a day?" Samson nodded his belief. "Everyone has a right to medical care," he smiled. "Including the rich. If a man can afford the services of a private physician he has a right. My patients pay me an annual fee. Some I see as often as once a month, others less frequently."

"It's like paying a doctor to stay well. Like they say the Chinese do."

For an hour and a half he was tapped and listened to, reamed and viewed, there were machines and blood samples, he filled a bottle with urine and Addington smeared a spot of his feces from the tip of a rubber glove to a glass slide. Instructed to dress, he returned to the consultation room where Dr. Addington was consulting his notes and finally looked up. "I'll have the lab tests in a few days. Everything else appears normal."

"How about the prostate?"

"The prostate?"

"There's a problem, doctor."

Addington smiled. "The prostate could use a little stimulation."

"Stimulation?"

"Massage. I want you here two or three times a week. It'll take a minute. But I think it'll bring results."

"I've been having trouble getting an erection." Addington made a note. "For a long time."

"How long?"

"A few months," he lied.

Addington rose, rounded the desk and placed an arm around Duke's shoulder. "Middle-age sluggishness, that's all, Mr. Duke. We'll have you perked up in no time. Make an appointment with Miss Olson. Let's start with three times a week until we get results." He led Samson from the room.

He had been to a dozen doctors in his lifetime, none had impressed him like Addington. He was getting on the roster.

"How about my signing up, Doctor?"

"Think about it. Let's get the results of your tests."

"I'll see you next week."

The following Thursday, Duke sat across Addington's desk. The doctor smiled like a judge handing out a prize.

"Everything is like you're forty not fifty: blood, urine, cholesterol . . . and we're going to keep it that way. We'll have the prostate operating like a tuned carburetor. But I need your help."

"I'll do anything."

Addington scribbled on a pad. "Take these three times a day, one after each meal. A mild sedative, relaxer."

"What are they?"

"Phenobarbital, quarter grain, very mild. And I want you here three times a week for the massage. Take the pressure off, don't test it for awhile.

"How do I enroll?"

"Miss Olson will discuss my fee."

The nurse's office was tiny, a small desk and two chairs. Her voice was low pitched, it was like getting signed up to an exclusive club.

"Doctor Addington told me to squeeze you in. His fee is one thousand dollars a month, which includes everything, visits as often as you like, all lab tests, house calls." Addington was going to have a finger on his pulse and another up his ass and Harvard and Johns Hopkins turned out the best. Samson slept the night through for the first time in months.

During the following weeks letters began to arrive from New York; copies of notes from Temple to Atlantic States Holding Corporation, replies from Armstrong, a note from Tuttle, requests for more facts. He mailed maps and more studies, topography, population studies, vacancy factors, rental rates, percentage of occupancy, local building costs. They responded with calls for aerial photos, engineering and geological reports. Samson worked eighteen hours a day, prodding, pushing the architect, Tipton's office and the engineer. Sherry Larsen was kept late every night for two weeks and quit.

"You can't quit now!" he screamed as she stood before the desk after calmly announcing her retirement. "You've everything at your fingertips. I need you."

"You don't need anybody, Sam."

"Just another month—or two. The deal will be wrapped up by then. There'll be a bonus—big one." He smiled.

"Not another week. I'll call an agency. What do you want? Young and pretty, competent and plain? Tell me." He was out from behind the desk, had her hand, pleaded, whined. "Just sixty more days, Sherry." She slipped her hand from his.

"A week to break in a new girl. That's all." She left the room.

He started to follow then went to the desk and grabbed the phone. "Can I call you at home if we need a file, information?"

"Sure, call."

"Get the agency. Young, pretty *and* competent. You know what I want. You interview, pick a couple of the best, and I'll make the final decision."

"Salary?"

"Seven hundred a month."

"That's more than I'm getting."

"She'll earn it." He heard her swear as she hung up. Fuck her! If she wanted to spend the rest of her life cooking for a shyster lawyer, washing his dirty shorts, and maybe someday wiping snot from a couple of brats, let her! After all he'd done for her. He'd get a secretary, a better one; the town was lousy with them. For that extra salary he could parlay a winner in the office to a fast ride in bed. The massages were beginning to show results; since Dr. Addington's finger went to work he felt more tickle than he had in years.

Sherry rang. "The agency will start the girls coming tomorrow. You're going to do the interviewing, and you'd better hire a girl fast. I'm leaving by the end of the week."

They started to come the next morning, a half-hour apart; tall and short, blonde and dark hair, from twenty to early thirty, good shorthand, bad typing, great legs, bad tits and by four when he was ready to offer Sherry a thousand a month and no overtime the right height, age, tits and legs walked in. She transcribed his dictation on the machine with a rat-a-tat-tat, flicked the paper from the roller and handed it to him. No mistakes and done in a flash. He looked over her résumé. Jan Schwartz, twenty-five, six years experience; insurance company, saving and loan and land developer. And single, no children. Jewish, he was sure. A change of luck.

"When can you start?"

"Immediately."

He called Sherry. "I've hired Miss Schwartz. She's starting now."

At the end of the day on Friday, Samson handed Sherry a thousand-dollar check in addition to her pay. She looked at it for a long time, finally settled in the chair before his desk.

"What's wrong?"

She nodded. "Nothing."

"What do you think of Miss Schwartz?"

"She'll work out fine. Why did you do it . . . this," she said, holding up the check.

"Back pay. You know how it is. Nobody is appreciated until they're gone."

She rose, went to his side, and kissed him gently on the mouth. "We had the recipe, Sam, and you balled it up. It could have been great. Goodbye. . . ." She rushed from the room.

He shut the door, took the phone off the hook and sat for a long while. An overwhelming feeling of self-pity came over him. What does one look for in a woman? Attractiveness, the right disposition, the smell you like, the feel, being wanted and wanting, the morning over coffee, eyes locked exchanging messages of the night. . . . Jesus, what else? It was all there and he'd let it go . . . again.

A moment later the phone rang. "Mr. Temple calling from New York, Mr. Duke."

"I'm coming out on Monday, Sam. Armstrong and Tuttle will be with me."

By the end of the week he had them all over the land, flew it in a helicopter, consulted with the architect and engineer, went over the figures with Tipton and their Los Angeles lawyer and accountant. By the time they were ready to leave, the deal appeared settled. Joe Temple promised him a written proposal within ten days.

Samson rushed from Tipton's office, squeezed in a massage at Dr. Addington's, and got back to his office just before Jan Schwartz was ready to leave. What a week! It looked like the time to celebrate and now was as right as any to let Jan know about her other duties.

Pushing himself wearily from bed, Duke made his way to the terrace. The sun had just come up, the early morning dampness chilled as he clutched the robe to his throat. In the distance, Catalina floated in the mist, the Palos Verdes peninsula jutted, her face pocked like a Seurat and below, Sunset Boulevard stretched and snaked around palms and tiled roofs ducked under eucalyptus and peppers and disappeared. He breathed deeply, drank cold air, kept barring insistent thoughts until they spilled over. "Miss Schwartz—Jan—dinner tonight? Something to celebrate." Candlelight and martinis, Alex gone. Steaks from Chasen's and wine. Brandy on the terrace and willing, willing lips, eager to please. Oh, soft nipples tipping firm breasts. The good feel, the good smell of cunt. *oooh! aaah!* ready—*fuck daddy fuck meeeee!* pump and groan, sweat, moan, cry out roll off, finger a limp dick. "Sorry, Jan, sorry, it's one of those nights—forgive me." No more words as she dresses silently and is sent home in a cab.

He staggered into the kitchen, put on a pot of coffee, and ran to the shower. Maybe Engle was right, Addington's finger a placebo, the casualty in his crotch shot down from his head. Maybe he ran the string? Everybody can't keep getting it up until they die; some men give out at forty. Some hearts give out at fifty, others don't quit until everything around it dries and cracks. There are thirty-year kidneys and eighty-year livers. A guy will have arteries of rubber and another puffs and huffs with dried macaroni. But *he* was healthy! Didn't Addington say *he* was healthy? Stepping out of the shower he rubbed himself briskly, looked down at his cock perched above his balls, a button disconnected from the juice.

By the time he reached the office he decided he would give Addington another month. From Jan Schwartz there was not a hint of the night, it was as if she wiped the slate for a clean start. Grateful, he went about his business determined to forget the "goddamn thing" until his balls rang the bell.

A week later Joe Temple called; the board met, approved the deal, they wanted to discuss purchase price and terms.

"Purchase price?"

"Joint ventures are against their policy, Sam. No partners. They're prepared to buy the land. It'll be a helluva profit." Atlantic States was conservative, about as venturesome as a shotgun in a chicken coop, if they wanted to buy the land there would be a dozen others in line. To hell with all of them. Joint-venture or he'd go alone.

"I'm not interested in selling. I'll be a partner or no deal."

"Think about it for a few days, Sam.

"The answer is no. Let them think it over."

"It's a buy out or no deal. They made it clear."

"No deal. Goodbye." Before the morning was over, Martin Tipton called.

"I talked to Joe Temple. Why not reconsider?"

"The property is not for sale."

"You can't handle it alone. It needs corporate funds. Manpower. You need an organization to build a city. Sam, your rocker's tipping. Meet me for lunch, let me call Joe and tell him to withhold your refusal."

"Martin's right," Covington put in. "Why not sell, take the profit and run?"

Now he knew the difference between the men and the boys. Covington and Tipton. A little man with a high gloss rubbed on with a Harvard sheepskin, an old man afraid to look ahead. The world was filled with them; two passes and they drag down. To beat the game one needed a long-distance eye for leverage and guts. Huh! Puny dreams—shit in their blood. He almost wanted to shout it!

"You're old, Martin. You roar, can't bite—and you," he turned to Covington, "you're just a mascot." Covington uncoiled in his chair. "Listen, both of you. . . . I didn't come here for advice. That city is going to be built—by me. I don't want shaky hands handling the books. If I'm bleeding and you can't stand the sight, get the hell out!" Tipton nodded in Covington's direction, the lawyer rose and left the room. Samson lit a cigar, flung the match to the floor. Tipton spoke softly.

"You're right, I'm old. Maybe you get sentimental, become honest with age. I think you're making a big mistake, but I've been wrong. I don't understand why you drive. Who's there to leave it to? There's a lot I don't understand, about you, about myself, about everything." He was at Samson's side, a hand on his arm. "I'll do what I can." He patted Samson's arm and left the room.

Words, rhetoric, phrases. At game. Parcheesi. Monopoly. Drinking from a breast until feet don't wobble. A piggyback ride until you're able to walk. Kick their crutches and they fall on their ass. What were your dreams, Martin? Out of college, step into the firm, marry Sylvia—legacy—a soft seat until the end of the ride . . . arrangements . . . wills and cash, trust funds—a cushion under your bottom until you're laid away. Dreams are made in darkness and if you never see the night there is no yearning for the day.

days. All his pleas for a one-year renewal were denied and the Bank of the Pacific was the last stop. They were given his financial statement a week before and though he was certain the loan would not be turned down, having been assured by Martin Tipton who had talked to a member of the board, he was apprehensive about the terms that would be imposed. Land loans were difficult to secure, the smaller banks, those on whose boards he served, passed them up and the giants like Pacific worked a borrower over knowing damn well they were the end of the line.

He was ushered into a conference room—introduced to five men who were the board, and told that his urgency had been noted. He would get their decision by the following day.

The chairman reviewed the loan, questioned him about some items on his statement and the queries began from the others.

"You need a thirty-million-dollar payoff. The loan applied for is for fifteen. How do you propose to raise the balance?"

"It's available now, in cash."

A young fat one with a perspiry bald dome and a narrow nose that supported over-sized horn-rimmed glasses. "How does one raise that much cash?" A quick smile—on and off.

He couldn't tell them that he had been to every loan shark in town, paid the huge bonuses with which he was so familiar, and in addition paid out nearly all of the cash he had been nursing from the haul taken from Phil Matlin a few years before. He smiled back. "I always have four or five million available—my statement reflects that. The balance came from loans on other real estate—firsts and seconds." The fat one sat back.

From an older man, near sixty, with a booze-blotched face and a shock of snow white hair. In a gentle tone. (Maybe some soften when they grow older.) "We can only make a three-year loan, Mr. Duke. Where do you plan to get the money when it's due?"

"I have a development ready to go," he lied. "Construction loans and takeouts. Should be able to pay the bank off within a year or eighteen months."

A nervous little man, sucking a cold cigar appeared impatient. "Are the commitments in writing?"

"I've never needed that," he lied again. "I've been building for thirty years, borrowed hundreds of millions. All on handshakes. Call Fines Cady. He heads State Life of West Texas. My money is coming from them." He was certain that Cady would back him up. Made a mental note to call him the moment he got back to his office.

"Mr. Duke." The chairman spoke. He was young, not more than thirty-five, Samson figured . . . how in hell do they get on top at that age? "Please understand that we do not question the security. Nor your ability to perform when the loan comes due. However, we're a public entity, governed by banking laws and policy. Bank examiners frown on land loans at best. They can only be justified by adequate security and profit to the bank."

"Let's talk about that profit," the last man spoke. All during the conversation he had been making notes on a pad. Now he tore off the sheet and sat back, apparently the one selected or volunteered for delivering the shaft. He looked like a minnow: small head, narrow shoulders bound by an Ivy League suit, delicate woman hands that played with the yellow sheet. By God he looked like Walt Covington. "If we make the loan, the terms are as follows," he looked up. "There cannot be any deviations, Mr. Duke." His eyes went back to the paper as if he dared not meet Samson's stare. "Fifteen million, three-year due date, interest only monthly at eight per cent per annum, ninety-day prepayment penalty." He placed the paper on the desk and faced Dupe. "Three points."

Samson calculated quickly. He had hoped for a two-point bonus and seven per cent interest; on the other hand the ninety-day prepayment penalty was a pleasant surprise—he had expected six months—and the fact that they waived amortization for the life of the loan took a lot of pressure off.

"Isn't eight per cent a little high?" The five men shook their heads. "All right, I'll buy that. Don't you think with all the security two points would be justified?"

"Not to the bank examiner," the chairman put in.

"Nor to the bank," another said.

He looked all of them over; there wasn't an encouraging face in the lot. "I'd like to think it over for a day." He was eager to accept the loan, then and there, not take chances. But if there was one among them who felt he had accepted too readily and could have been pushed harder he did not want to give him a chance for another shot. He got up to shake hands all around; they rose as one, told them they would have his answer in the morning.

Back in the office he called Fines Cady. "Sam, your goddamn project is going to ruin me. How in hell could you tell them I gave you a commitment? I can't lie if they call."

"You've lied a thousand times. And it was only verbal I told them. You can always change your mind. Jesus, Fines, you've got to back me up."

Cady finally agreed after warning Duke never to put that kind of heat on him again. "If you fall on your face and they call for that commitment I'm stuck with fraud."

"They'll never call."

The following morning he accepted the loan. Due to its size Bank of the Pacific divided it with two other banks. The escrow was opened and within thirty days the deal recorded.

The loan gave him three years, not much time. The city was still in his head, buildings reached to the sky in dreams, arithmetic dizzied . . . zeroes into infinity. But insurance companies were myopic, bankers blind, they had computers but no imagination. By God, if they couldn't see he would give them something to touch, feel. He cleared every detail from his desk; Tipton's office to manage every building, the bank to collect on the loans he held, and Jan to stiff-arm every broker, every promoter every little dreamer. There was only one project.

He poured through books by Wright, Stone, de Mies; simplicity, economy, function . . . it was the basic theme. De Mies summed it—"less is more." Samson wasn't sure what it meant but it seemed to paraphrase what they all said.

He met with his architect. "Nothing freaky, experimental. Give them Wright and Stone plus a conventional touch. People have got to understand."

John Holland had been hired when Duke acquired the land, did the renderings, speculated, charging only for cost.

"What do you want, Sam? More elevations, floor plans? I've done a dozen."

"Scrap them. We start from scratch."

"Fine. Twenty-five dollars an hour and costs."

"Okay, punch the clock. Now listen. A hundred eighty acres —rectangular." He took out a sheet of paper. "Eight office buildings—limit height—four thirty-story towers, apartments—a regional shopping center—a theater, miniature center—one-story, stucco, tiled roofs, California style and in the middle, John, a hotel, modern but Greek as high as the zoning allows and broad boulevards and fountains and load it with sculpture and big trees. Put it all on paper—landscaping, sidewalks and curbs, street lights and parking."

"Everything?"

"Every detail. Then I want it modeled—in scale."

"Sam, you're talking about a lot of money."

"Get it done."

Holland was badgered and pushed—nights and weekends— and in less than ninety days a scaled model, a city in plastic was erected on a huge platform in a room adjoining Samson's office. The street lights were real, so were the signs, windows lit at the press of a button, fountains sparkled with light and even the automobile headlights could be turned on and off.

A press conference was called, the model was photographed, and accompanied the lead article in the Sunday edition of the Real Estate section of the Los Angeles *Times.* For days his phone rang; leasing agents looking for jobs, contractors and subs, satellite tenants anxious for space, dozens of real-estate brokers. Then came the letters, some from out of the state, all wanting to get "in"—maintenance companies and window washers, Otis elevators and Westinghouse even a brochure from ALCOA describing aluminum modules. But nobody with a loan: a promise to finance.

Reprinting the article, he enclosed it with the prospectus and a covering letter and mailed it to over a hundred large corporations whose current performances indicated an interest in a large real-estate venture. A month passed, then two, not even a polite inquiry. Tipton proposed a limited partnership, called a meeting of clients: doctors, lawyers, actors and others in the industry. He was quizzed and cross-examined, questions flew and he got up, walked out, rushed to Addington's office.

"Look at this!" he said, flipping open the lid of a pillbox. "White ones to slow me down, pink ones to speed me up, red ones to put me to sleep. I can't take it any more! The pains are real—in my chest, under my arm—and the headaches. . . . Christ, Doc, if I have a bad heart and my pressure is up, don't lie!"

"You haven't got a bad heart—yet. And your pressure is still normal, but it won't be for long. If you don't get away, for a long time—forget your business—everything you're imagining will become real. And that's a prediction." He gave him a shot. "I'm knocking you out. Go home, get some sleep, and call me in the morning."

It was almost noon when he awoke, Alex handed him a batch of messages. There were three calls from Martin Tipton. Feeling better than he had in weeks he had a leisurely breakfast and decided to spend the day at home.

"I'm not taking calls, Alex. From anyone."

"Mr. Tipton?"

"Particularly, Mr. Tipton."

In the late afternoon, Martin walked in. "You should hide," he began. "You made a fool out of me and a bigger one of yourself." He fell into a chair. "Get me a drink, a stiff one." Sipping it he looked up at Duke who had not said a word. "Say something. Something rational for a change."

"I'm going to sell the land."

He sighed with relief. "You're not crazy."

"I'm giving myself another month. If nothing develops the land goes."

"Why torture yourself any longer? Call Joe. His people are still interested. I'll bet he can have a check in a week."

"Another month. I've got to give myself another month." He took Martin by the arm. "Please, finish the drink and leave me alone." At the door Martin turned.

"I'd advise you to keep your word, Sam. There's more at stake than you think."

"I know what's at stake. Now go."

A week later he got a nibble, then a big bite, and a few days afterwards he was on a plane to New York. International Industries Ltd., a British-based American controlled conglomerate with headquarters in London received the prospectus and wanted to talk. He met with the New York officers, calls were made to London, a second meeting was held, then a third and then the American director, an engineer and comptroller flew to Los Angeles. There, Duke, showed them the land, the plastic model, refined the figures with Tipton's aid and after a couple of days he was informed that a meeting to discuss details had been set up in London for the following week. Pleading with Martin Tipton he got him to agree to accompany him and they checked in at The Dorchester a day before the scheduled meeting. All the tensions of the past months seemed to have disappeared, the energy that had never failed him before returned, he ordered drinks, opened the window on the park, shouted to Martin who was unpacking in the adjoining room.

"I knew I'd do it! The deal's as good as made. They had my figures and brochure two months ago. You can be sure they checked it out before they contacted me. These talks aren't preliminary, Martin, they're gestures. Their minds are made up. It's just a question of the arithmetic."

Tipton entered the room. "Don't be so cocky. Corporations this size move slowly. You can bet these talks are preliminary."

"You can bet," he mocked. "You've always taken the devil's

role, Martin." He laughed and slapped the older man's back. "Come on, you old fart, freshen up. We're going to do the town —and don't be negative about that."

They ran out of steam by ten o'clock and though he grumbled when Martin insisted on dragging him home he couldn't wait to fall into bed.

The series of meetings lasted a week at International's offices on Marylbone Road; morning teas and then lunch. Weak gin and roast beef, more tea, sandwiches, warm ale or stout, back to The Dorchester, off to the theater, Soho for dinner, brandy in a Belgravia flat, a walk through St. James, a breath of air, then to bed. Then a night at Hampstead Heath, London villa style: heather and a little forest. A house with a name and a limousine to The Prospect of Whitby with a cold Thames spray and warm beer and rugby players' dirty ditties.

"Sam, we're being softened up," Martin said, collapsing on the bed after the fourth day. "Now I know how the British Empire survived—cold air and warm beer—a combination to produce anesthesia . . . and charm. Let's get a good night's sleep and attack."

On the morning of the fifth day the officers of International propositioned. A separate corporation would be formed to be called International Properties which would become a subsidiary of the parent corporation. The parent company will commit itself to lend I.P. up to forty-five million; fifteen million immediately to pay off the bank loan, working capital, and equity financing as needed. The land to be put into the deal for forty million. Duke to receive shares in the company for the amount of his equity in relationship to the total investment. The stock would not be negotiable. The parent company to take back a first mortgage on the property, the amount to be increased as money is advanced. The first buildings to be built for cash, to be financed through insurance companies when completed and leased, which funds are then to be used to recover the loan to the subsidiary company. All monies advanced by the parent company to be repaid in five years. International controls at all times. Duke, the minority stockholder, must abide by all decisions. Five years is too short a time, Duke protested, and they agreed on seven.

"I'll need time to think it over, gentlemen," Duke said as he rose to address his hosts. They shook hands, slapped backs and said they would await his answer.

"They put up the money, sure, but your equity is their cushion," Martin argued as they flew over the Pole. "Sell them the land, Sam. Take the money and run. You can be wiped clean."

"I'll run. With them. Martin, the beer clogged your brain."

"If you want to turn fifteen million from a fat goose into a thin equity, it's your goose."

A week later, Samson called New York with the message; it's a deal on the condition that the project be named "Duke City." They liked the name, International replied, and would start drawing the papers. For over a month, documents flew the ocean, . Covington approved a point, vetoed another. International's attorneys were no less constrained. Samson fled to Palm Springs, tried the sun, the white pills, and the red. Headaches pounded, chest pains stabbed; Jan Schwartz joined him with a notebook and a nightgown.

Walter Covington called in the early part of September.

"Every wrinkle's ironed out. The papers are drawn and ready to sign. They've agreed to fly to the Coast. Signing ceremony, press conference, the works. It'll be good publicity."

At noon on Friday the principals gathered around the model of Duke City. Flashbulbs went off, they signed in Duke's office, more pictures taken, then the press ran to the booze, the rooms filled with people, voices and tobacco smoke. Samson was grinning and patting backs, the voices were blending into a roar, faces began to blur, he motioned to Martin who took his arm and led him into the hall.

"Drive me home—quick. . . ."

"What's wrong?"

"It's nothing. Just dizzy. Take me home."

There was not a word between them on the ride. The terrace was cool. Duke removed his tie, opened his collar, was breathing deeply. "Thanks, Martin. I'm better now. Let's go inside."

"How about calling your doctor?"

"No need." He collapsed in a chair and closed his eyes. "I guess I put every bit of energy saved into this. Like a long-distance runner at the finish line." He opened his eyes and smiled. "Maybe I'm getting old."

"All the fuel's gone, Sam. You better refill."

"Maybe I'll go to the desert for a few days."

"That won't wet the bottom of the tank. You've an enormous project ahead. You need a long rest, a complete change of environment, no telephones, deals, lectures from me. You need new faces, new scenery, even different air to breathe. How about an ocean voyage, through the Canal to Europe? Two, three weeks on the sea. It's the best advice I've ever given you, Sam."

"I haven't got the strength to argue, you devil. I'll make the arrangements in the morning."

"I'll make them today. Get in bed and take the phone off the hook.

A week later he sailed from San Pedro, kept to his cabin for days, emerging for the first time when the ship docked at Acapulco. He stayed aboard, strolled the deck, ate alone and returned to his cabin. He realized for the first time how far he had extended himself. All during the years it had been climb, a plateau, consolidate and another hill, he was like a plane refueled in midair, determined to go on until the motor conked before it landed. For months, maybe years the messages had been coming clear: headaches and chest pains, tortured hours without sleep, impotency, his engines whirred and blocked everything. Not any more, he was in neutral until the trip was finished.

CHAPTER TWENTY-SIX

Early in the morning of the second day out of New York, more relaxed than he had felt for months, he descended to the cabin class deck, strolled for a turn and settled at the rail. The ship rolled gently in a hospitable sea, in the east the sun seemed little troubled in lighting the sky, the mist fled before the rays, it was already warm. He turned and saw a woman sharing the rail a few feet away. The shadows hid her face, he saw only her profile, she was humming softly, about her seemed an aura of serenity and composure.

"Good morning." He felt clumsy.

"Isn't it lovely?"

He drew closer, beyond the shadows. "This is the time of day I love most." He agreed. "It's sad that people sleep and miss the dawn."

"Yes."

"Did you board in New York?"

"Los Angeles."

"You've been on board two weeks. How I envy you."

They circled the deck, her arm in his as the last of the mist disappeared and the sun took over the sky. They were at the stern rail watching the wake when she asked his name.

"Samson. . . . Samson Duke."

"What a lovely name." He had never been told this before.

"And yours . . . ?"

"Martha Halliday."

He joined her for breakfast, missed her at lunch, and found her at dinner. By the second day he'd abandoned first class to return only late at night to sleep—full of wonderment. He had never met anyone so tranquil—composed—and it was without a trace of lethargy, resignation, all of it flowed as natural as water from a mountain spring. She was like a cool hand. They took long walks, lolled in deck chairs wrapped to their chins, dined leisurely, and talked.

By the end of the third day among many things he learned that she was the widow of a professor who died two years before, had a grown daughter recently married who lived in New York, and that she had been to Europe many times and knew it well. In exchange he told her little about himself, except that he was a widower, childless, and was in the real-estate business in Los Angeles. She spoke about her husband with no bitterness at his early death, the wonderful years they spent together. His marriage had beauty too, Samson told her, and though not long lasting left memories he would always cherish. They were in the bar sipping a predinner drink, she reached out her hand in sympathy, touched his, squeezed his fingers and withdrew. It was the first time they had touched—flesh to flesh—and he was overcome at the sensation it produced. Every plan he might have had for a European stay was cancelled. There was no need to see the people at International, they did not know he was going to be in London and as for Tipton's suggestions—he was sure Martha had better ones. They were very simple, he found out as they shared a train compartment on the ride from Plymouth to London.

"I only have two weeks. I learned long ago not to try to cover Europe in fourteen days. It will be a few days in London and then

Venice. Since I visited it a few years before I dreamed of going back. Oh, Sam, the poets were so right about Venice. Have you seen it?"

"No. Would you mind a newcomer gawking at your side?"

"I'd be delighted. I will be staying at a small hotel near St. Marks. When you arrive you can call me. It'll be fun."

When you're winning you don't drag down but double-up. "Where are you staying in London?"

"A little pension on Albion Street. I've stayed there before. It's charming."

"I made no reservations. Didn't think it necessary off season. Do you think they'd have an extra room?"

"We'll find out." She smiled and reached for his hand.

They called from Victoria Station and were told a room was available. His was on the floor above Martha's. It did have the charm she mentioned, but none of the conveniences he abandoned when he cancelled the suite he had reserved at The Dorchester. The bath was down the hall and a chamber pot was on a stand and added to the chintz drapes, glass curtains, patch rug and brass bed, it brought him back to Aunt Annie's bedroom on the Jersey farm. He had not thought about her for a long time and now, somehow, not only the room but Martha reminded him of his aunt when she was young. There was something he could not define about Martha and Aunt Annie—a resemblance. It wasn't hair or eyes—Martha was blonde and her eyes were blue—it was an attitude, a posture, maybe a philosophy. Aunt Annie possessed a tranquility too—in the early days before the meeting with Dante; it might not have been as self-assured as Martha's, might have been a residual of resignation, but its effect on others was the same. He made a mental note to tell Martha about his aunt some day.

He unpacked, cleaned up as best he could and went down to Martha's room. It was near dinnertime and though it was full pension and meals were included he was determined to dine that night in an intimate booth and not at a boarding house table. She was on the last touches when he came in, motioned him to a seat as she applied lipstick.

"You must do me a favor, Martha," he began.

"You sound so serious," she said, dropping the compact into her purse and taking a seat on the edge of the bed. Though he had marveled at her unbelievable complexion, a shade of white with the delicate patina of ancient marble from the forehead to the neck, all even in tone and only contrasted by the blue of her eyes, he was not prepared for the skin tones of the flesh he now saw as her skirt crawled and he got a glimpse of her thighs. He began to feel the faint beginnings of all the sensations of the past. She must have sensed his preoccupation and pulled the skirt down.

"I am serious," he went on. "To be frank I planned to stay at a much more expensive hotel."

"Why didn't you, Sam? I would if I could afford it."

"We'll discuss that at another time," he smiled. "In the meantime I'm spending far less than I anticipated and I insist on your sharing the windfall. Will you dine with me tonight—in a lovely restaurant in a quiet booth—our first night in London?"

She laughed. "You put it so well, how can I refuse."

"Any suggestions?"

"Restaurants?"

"Yes."

"There is a place. Near Soho. I dined there once years ago. But it's expensive, Sam."

He rose and extended his arm. "Please do not spare me. Let's go."

They had been sitting all evening in a small booth, their thighs constantly in touch. Never had he experienced as much of a thrill with as little provocation. Her looks at him, the touch of her hand, the tremor when he touched the length of her leg. God, he wanted her that night, was sure he could produce, but not in the pension on a broken-down bed. He took her hand.

"I've never seen the English countryside."

"It's exquisite."

"Let me rent a car for a few days. Come along and show it to me."

She only hesitated for an instant. "All right, Sam."

Dreading the left-handed driving, he wanted to rent a car and a chauffeur, but it would invade their privacy and he wasn't ready to put his affluence on display. Maybe he could peddle himself without a penthouse and Cadillac, a country club and a desert home. The chances were that Martha was not interested in jangles and spangles but he would never have to guess; she would have to take him on before she opened the whole package. Rising early, he packed, rented a car and had it at the curb by the time she came in for breakfast.

"Good morning." She gave him her hand as he led her to the table. "It's early. I didn't think you'd be up."

"Up and ready. The car's in front and my bags are packed." He spread a map on the table. "Here's Britain, take any road." He watched as her finger traced, her brow furrowed, two fine lines on Carrara marble. He was sure she was forty—at least—he marveled at her face—no lines, sag, or blemish; an open window to interior serenity. And the sweet flesh of the body is better preserved than a face; his juices bubbled and thumped. She looked up.

"We only have two or three days. The Shakespeare country is beautiful, and Oxford, you'll love it. . . ."

Within an hour they were out of London. He quickly became accustomed to driving on the "wrong" side and relaxed. Rain threatened from the moment they left but somehow the sun managed its struggle with the clouds and bright patches of its light shone on the meadows, rolling hills and steepled roofs in the tiny villages. He only sensed the wondrous beauty of all they passed. It was almost subliminal as his thoughts dwelled in the excitement of his anticipation and his eyes left Martha's face only to keep to the road. They stopped at a tiny inn at Henley, lunched by the river, walked around the town, and continued on their way. By the time they toured Oxford, visited a few of the colleges, it was the end of the day and his thoughts turned to plans for the night. She remembered a small inn outside of Banbury, she said, it was only twenty-five miles and on the road to Stratford. For the first time it struck him that her consent to travel with him might not have implied the use of a single room. He started to pose the question—put it to her directly—one room or two? Give her a choice and he would surely sleep alone. He wasn't about to push the odds.

It was easier than he thought! a double room, Mr. and Mrs. S. Duke, U.S.A. no request for passports. Martha glowing like a bride, the bags deposited, a slight bow for the tip and they were alone. He clasped her hand and they stood in the middle of the room. A fat mattress on a cherrywood poster, a dormer window looking out over a meadow, a low rocker and a high-backed chair and a pitcher on a sideboard. She looked at him and was smiling; it was tender, also a brave smile. He raised her hand to his lips, kissed the palm.

"Why don't we unpack, darling? It was the first time he had addressed her in that manner. "Then we can have dinner, retire early, and be on the road at dawn."

She went into the bathroom, closed the door; he removed the few necessary things from his suitcase, slipped a pair of pajamas under a pillow and Martha returned to the room. Seating herself on the window she pulled the curtain aside and looked out.

"Some things change so slowly, others transform before your eyes. I stayed at this inn before, Sam, dear. Our room, my husband's and mine, was down the hall. Nothing that I see from this window is different from what I saw years ago. The trees aged but who can tell, the cobblestones have added a few years to their centuries, everything else—the houses, the shop fronts, have had a little more beating from the weather. My life changed overnight." She dropped the curtain, walked to where he was standing and took both of his hands. "Overnight, Sam—everything that had been real became memories. Most were beautiful and I'll always have them. But I'm alive, darling, and I'm feeling again, something real, and I'm glad it's happening in this place—with you." Her lips were softer, more tender than any he had ever touched, a hand caressed his neck another drew him closer, his hand slid to her buttock—oh sweet ass! So round and firm, their lips were still pressed, her mouth opened and a darting tongue found his, he managed a hand on her breast and they fell to the bed and then for the first time he felt in his groin the stirrings of a dead volcano—he wanted to cry for joy fall to his knees and kiss her feet and then he realized that all the inferno below had not raised a hackle on his cock! He released her abruptly and rolled on his back; she lay beside him and neither said a word. Tell her the truth! That you're impotent, at least be honest, don't let her take the blame. He turned to her, to blurt it—she placed a finger on his lips.

She whispered. "I don't want you to say anything." She rose from the bed. "Let's undress," she said, and began to unzip her blouse. The day had ended, only a faint light streaked the horizon, he pulled the drapes, the room was in darkness as he removed his clothes and crawled into bed. Slowly he began to explore; all the promises came to life like a score in the hands of a conductor—skin—soft to the eye, silk to the touch, the curves he saw leaped to life and the tempo, that of a tom-tom or a cymbal or a drum, ended with the sound of a trumpet all beginning with a violin's bow—sweet, soft until the whole ended in a crescendo. It was a long feast. They would lie, their bodies barely touching, her hands coursing his thigh. Endearments murmured as his blood gathered in the long-limp prick, big—bigger than it ever had become as she guided it to her whispering, spreading her legs, slipping it in and gyrating until he was totally drained. That night there was never enough, areas of eroticism never tapped before, stored for his lifetime, exploded in expression. Oh, Martha! I kiss your cunt, the lips are of a goddess, the perfume angel's musk delicious to my tongue as you lick and lip my godhead!

They awoke at dawn, he pulled the drapes and in the new light her hair flowed on the pillow like gold, her eyes took on sky color and sea, and her nipples were pink crests on tea roses. And he slipped her gift, throbbing and hard into her warm cunt and what had been dust flowed into her.

For the next two weeks he was transported, earth was the springboard to heaven, a boat on the Avon River was a barque on the Nile, he was a prince in Venice and Martha was a queen, the Grand Canal was their sea and the Square of St. Marks was surrounded by their palace and cathedral. Rarely letting go her hand they walked the narrow streets, turned corners to marvel at Byzantine squares, Renaissance palazzios, Gothic splendor, they crossed a piece of the Adriatic to Lido and walked the beach, spent an afternoon in Peggy Guggenheim's gardens with Picasso, Matisse, and Klee, and at night they toasted at Harry's bar where Martha told him of Americans—some now ghosts—who wrote poetry and prose, pouring Harry's liquor over their wounds as they wailed an expatriate's lament.

He could not believe his good fortune. From Martha sprang a fountain of elixirs: magic for the soul, the mind, and the body. Some mornings he would lie awake watching her still asleep, her gentle breathing barely perceptible. No part of her moved; she looked like a goddess done by the hand of a master. Then she would awaken slowly, drowsily, there would be the instant to set time and place and then she would turn to him with a smile, reach out a hand and draw him to her. And the precious, conscious hours would begin again; long hours of love-making, more than he had been able to sustain in a lifetime, walks through ancient streets, palms pressed, aperitifs at cafes under the warm Italian sun, and always about them the treasures of a noble people preserved by sacrifice and fierce pride. Then the night would come —sensuous, exhausting—and sleep.

They boarded the plane at London for the trip home. Not once during the two weeks had a word been uttered about the future, now he searched his mind for a way to continue their relationship.

Clearing customs he took her to her apartment in the west

eighties, left for The Plaza while she unpacked and rested. That
night they dined in the hotel dining room and it was as if they
had descended from a cloud and had feet firmly planted on the
ground. At evening's end he suggested he return to her apartment for the night, she refused gently, pleading weariness.

"Remember the time lapse, Sam. It's five in the morning in
London. And that means for us. Please dear," she patted his hand.
"Give me a chance to catch up."

He barely disguised his disappointment as they drove to her
home in a cab. At the door (she did not invite him in) he outlined
plans for the following day. "We'll meet for breakfast, have lunch
and dinner, then the theater. Just tell me what you want to see."

"Sam. . . ." a restraining hand was on his arm. "I've been
gone over three weeks. There are things I must do. I haven't seen
my daughter, there are chores—a thousand things. Oh, Sam," she
traced his face with her fingers as if to wipe off the pain. "We'll
see each other soon. In a few days."

What could he say? What right did he have to possess her?
Was it possible that it was finished for her, a shipboard romance,
catalyst to two whirling dizzy weeks? Her husband had been
dead for two years. She was a woman. He might well have been
the first man to get to her since her husband's death. But no, it
wasn't a game with Martha, never could be. He must accept what
she told him; she has to see her daughter and there were chores
she said and a thousand things.

He phoned in the middle of the following morning and there
was no answer. All day long he kept trying, a call every hour, his
frustration finally turning to anger which by evening became
sickening fear. Where was she? Jesus, didn't she know how he
felt? Didn't she realize that the only reason he'd remained in New
York was to see her? He had an office waiting for him. Architects—a city! He kept calling, through the dinner hour, had food
sent up and kept at it until he heard her voice at the other end just
before midnight.

"I've been calling all day, since early this morning. You knew I
would call, if you had to leave why didn't you call me?" It all

came out—in a bunch, before she could say a word. Then there was a long silence. Her voice was cool, controlled when she finally spoke.

"I don't know why you're angry, Sam. I told you I had things to do." Now an edge was added to her tone. "I didn't think I had to report to you. In fact I was certain you had things to attend to."

"I'm sorry, Martha. I've acted like a fool. It's just that I have nothing to do in New York. I'm only staying on to see you. Maybe I misunderstood—a lot of things."

"Perhaps I did too, dear. Please come for breakfast. And we'll spend the day together."

The table was set when he arrived and she greeted him in a flowered housecoat. When he took her in his arms she responded as he had hoped and they sat down to eat. On their second cup of coffee she began.

"Just listen, Sam, until I finish. I have had a lot of happiness in my life—but also tragedy. To me, neither pleasure nor pain has been transitory, they keep clinging to my thoughts, my dreams. My beautiful memories are fading and the hurt is growing less. All this has taken a long time. I'm a practical woman, dear. I don't want to suffer." She stopped for a moment and refilled their cups, went on, reaching for his hand. "What has happened between us has been beautiful to me. If it ends here," she smiled, shrugged, "I have no regrets. It'll be on a delightful note."

"Martha, this is the beginning, not the end. I have plans for us. That's why I've stayed on. To discuss them. I want you to come to Los Angeles."

"I can't make a trip now." Visiting him in Los Angeles had other implications she went on to say and she was not interested in rushing into anything. Also, she wanted time to think; a shipboard was magic, an English countryside was an enchantment, and Venice was make-believe.

"When will you come?"

"Soon."

He pleaded for a date, she refused to commit herself, he threatened not to leave until she did.

"All right. I'll be out before the end of the year."

They had dinner that night and he left on the morning plane for Los Angeles. It was the end of September, there was October and November, at least sixty days before he would see her again.

When he reached his office he realized he had been out of contact with it since the day he left and had not thought about it from the moment he met Martha on the deck of the boat. It was some sort of a victory, he figured; he had never lost touch with his office for more than twenty-four hours. The work was piled, mail was stacked on his desk, messages covered a couple of sheets, the urgent ones lined in red. Jan looked particularly pretty that morning as she sat before his desk, notebook in hand, wearing a Peter Pan collar—crisp—circling the top of a tailored navy suit that hugged her breast and waist. She inquired about his trip, commented that he looked more rested and relaxed than she had ever seen and adding that he was missed. This was all done in the manner she reserved for the office—terse, clipped, only a hint of a smile. She exuded efficiency that morning and as he listened and watched he remembered the night he tried with her and failed; her skill, passion and patience and his button-sized prick and dead balls! Looking at her he became excited, wondered what would happen now. Was it Martha's magic, a rare chemistry that was needed to release his potency? Was he cured, or was she the only brand to which he could respond? It was important, he had to know—now—that night.

"There's so much to go over, Jan. I'll be tied up all day. How about dinner tonight?"

She smiled—"I'd love it."

The moment she left he called Alex and instructed him to take the night off. It was going to be dinner in his apartment and Jan was going to be in for a surprise.

He dialed her number first at six A.M. Los Angeles time, nine o'clock in New York, and there was no answer; during the next three hours he tried the number a hundred times he was sure, at times twice in a minute. Between calls he drank a pot of coffee, ignored the phone when it rang, sent Alex away when he came in, told him not to return until the following day; nobody must see him, he had to be alone with his humiliation. When he downed one pill and a second an hour later he realized they were the first in over a month. Martha, answer your phone! His phone rang, kept on, would not stop, he picked up the receiver savagely. "Who is it?" A small voice. "It's Jan, Mr. Duke. I. . . . I just wanted to be sure you were all right." "I'm fine. Won't be in today." He slammed the receiver. Kindness, concern, goddamn patience; that's what it was—her understanding! If she'd crawl in the sack, give him a good shot, pack him in and run when he didn't get it up—that was one thing. One could blame it on speed, timing, you don't always get the brass ring the first time around. But she worked on him long enough to bring back the dead—just short of artificial respiration—and by the time it looked like his pecker wasn't crippled but dead her own steam ran up. . . . He groaned as he remembered. . . . "Sam, darling, I gotta come . . . please, PLEASE! Down there—kiss it baby, kiss!" What could he do, she earned it. Down his head went and in seconds it was like his face got caught in a storm. She must have been grateful because she left in the middle of the night without waking him. He grabbed the bottle and poured half a glass, the first before-breakfast drink he ever had. Then he dialed New York again and Martha answered. It was even in her voice —he actually felt the damn thing come to life. . . . God, what was it? "Martha, it's me, I miss you." She laughed. "You just left." She had a power. "It seems like a month. Anyway, darling, how are you?" She said she was fine.

"How about dropping everything and coming out . . . now?"

"Sam?"

"Thought I'd try." They talked for fifteen minutes, it took him that long to become reassured and he only hung up after the third time he asked if she missed him and was answered in the affirmative. He felt better but could not face the office. He called Jan, told her to gather the papers on his desk and send them to the apartment by messenger. Nobody knew he was back, not even Martin Tipton; he needed a couple of days to get organized, and the privacy of the apartment was what he needed.

Only a little of the spade-work had been done while he had been gone. International's architects, a New York firm with offices in Los Angeles had conferred with John Holland who reported to Duke on the Monday following his return.

"They're being nice, professional courtesy and all that. But we're a continent apart—and a decade or two."

"What do you mean?"

"In the East they play it safe; the Chrysler building worked and so did Pan Am so why take a chance. Out here everything is new. It wasn't too long ago when the biggest building was an adobe hut. I hate to sound corny, but we have to create, not imitate. Practically every advanced idea in architecture in recent years came out of the West—mainly California. They're nice guys, Sam, and I'll try to work with them. But I don't think I'll last."

"Your design's great. Those Eastern architects must listen!"

A week later, Holland quit. He sent a memo to Duke. "They listened and never replied." He enclosed a bill for services to date. Samson called Covington who called New York, the message was relayed to London and the answer was back on Duke's desk within a week. "Regret Holland's quitting—stop—our architects inform everything on schedule." Samson rushed to Covington's office waving the cable.

"Line twenty-six, Sam, page seventeen," he started to read. "All plans, specifications subject to the approval of the party of the first part." He put the agreement on the desk. "And that goes for financing, tenants, down to the color of the Kotex container in the ladies john. If you like Holland's work have him design you a house. . . ." Samson sputtered, Covington listened. "I'm sure you're right aesthetically. But you're a silent partner, Sam."

By the end of November preliminary drawings for the first two buildings were on the boards with construction to commence in six months. It was to be twin thirteen-story office buildings, totally speculated; not a tenant signed up. There was no question; International had the key to the "city" and he couldn't pick the lock. Let it get started, buildings under way, leases signed—then he would step in. He might be a minority stockholder, but by God they had rights too!

In the meantime his calls to Martha were more frequent and by the first week in December he pressed her for a definite date.

"It's near the end of before the end of the year."

"I'm spending Christmas with my daughter." He arranged to pick her up at the airport on the evening of the day after Christmas.

The bungalow he reserved at the Beverly Hills Hotel was hidden by palms, bougainvillea covered the entrance with a burst of purple and a pepper tree spread green lace about the windows. By God, the apartment in the eighties was going to look like a stable! He stocked the refrigerator with cheeses and smoked meats, champagne and patés and on every surface was a vase of roses. It was going to be a total campaign—all of his affluence garlanded with his love.

If there were any doubts in his mind, the sight of her at the airport destroyed them; the look of her was enough, the way she shifted her weight when she walked—almost an undulation—and finally her touch and feel and smell. With an arm about her waist he led her to the car after picking up her bags and they headed for the hotel.

"I made a reservation at the Beverly Hills. It's quiet and not far from my place. You'll like it."

By the time she walked through the suite slowly, examined the bedroom, living room, kitchen and dining area he knew he had

blundered. Instead of the pleasantly surprised look he had anticipated there was a puzzlement and then concern as she turned to
him.

"What does all this cost, Sam?"

"It doesn't make any difference," he said.

"It makes a lot of difference to me."

"You're my guest. If propriety would have permitted you
would have come to my home. Anyway," his arm swept the
room, "I can afford all this. Allow me the pleasure."

Her look softened, she went up to him, kissed him gently and
led him to the couch. "I know I'm going to sound ungracious.
You're been very thoughtful, all this is lovely." She seemed to be
searching for words. "It might be difficult for you to understand,
but . . . what I'm trying to say, dear, is that I have definite feelings about luxuries I cannot afford. First of all they're not important to me. Also I have a fetish about independence. I insist upon
paying for my own room, Sam, and I surely cannot afford this.
Please get me the least expensive room they have." She would not
bend, finally agreed to spend the one night in the suite only after
he arranged for her to be moved to a cheaper room the following
morning.

"What about the champagne?"

"We'll drink that now," she said, heading for the kitchen.
"And you can take home the leftover goodies. In the meantime
I'm hungry and thirsty."

By the middle of the evening after they had consumed the second bottle of champagne and half the hors d'oeuvres, decided
against going out for dinner, and she had retired to change into a
dressing gown, his good humor had returned together with the
long absent hard-on. In bed, all he had dreamed of came alive and
by the time he left, drunk and drained, he pranced as he made his
way to his car and drove to the apartment singing at the top of his
lungs.

Up at dawn, he waited impatiently until the middle of the
morning before he called. "I hope you haven't had breakfast," he
sang out.

"I haven't been able to move. What was in that champagne?"

"French sunshine. I'm coming right over."

He instructed Alex to prepare his best breakfast, rushed to the hotel, and returned with her to his apartment. The sun had been up early, the terrace was warm, and Alex had the food spread on the table, waiting. After a quick tour of the apartment, her cries of delight like a child opening gifts, they settled on the terrace. A westerly breeze opened a corridor of sky through the smog so that a sliver of the sea could be seen from where they sat.

"Oh, Sam! It's like a fairyland. Why didn't you tell me you had such a lovely place?"

He started to grin. "Luxuries aren't important." She smiled and soon they were laughing aloud.

By the time they reached their coffee he began to tell her about the "city." This trip was going to tell her everything about him, everything he wanted her to know, and surely about his affluence. She was bound to be impressed. Her exclamations when she saw the apartment were clear manifestations that her protests could be residuals of intellectual snobbery.

"It's going to be the largest single urban development in the country, Martha. There will be everything from office buildings to theaters. Wait until you see the site. It's a golf course now; a hundred eighty rolling acres in the prettiest part of the city."

During the next two weeks he managed to be with Martha constantly, conducting his affairs from her room, his apartment, the telephone in his car, and, on one weekend, from the home in Palm Springs. She started to probe, dig into his past, boyhood, youth, family.

His answers were brief, fragmented—abstractions designed to blunt a thrust for detail; a broken home, shunted from private school to private school, the early death of parents and the rearing by an aunt, gentle and loving who died in his arms long ago. It was when she questioned him about his career that he became eloquent. Touring the city he brought her to his cornerstones; the old house on Wilshire where he started with Art Jennings, the first apartment house on Ingraham where he met Jack Delaney; the bank building, a dozen others, housing tracts and sprawling acres, even the home he built for Beck. Encouraged by her questioning he became carried away by his history, swept aside the barriers, and with her he relived his victories; the cunning with which he acquired the bank building—his first big step—the acquisition of fifty apartment houses before the war and the housing shortage, the war plant with Gordon, shrewd purchasing of stocks and then the building boom for which he was well prepared with hundreds of acres of vacant land bought at depressed prices.

It was at the Palm Springs home, where they spent her last weekend sunning and swimming, that he began to sense a coolness. At first he attributed it to his insecurity but when she began to speak about her husband, the happiness of her marriage, the pattern of their life, music and the theater, simple pleasures, emphasizing that values were the yardstick not cost, it became apparent that they had been traveling different roads. He began to sense that the fabric of their relationship was unraveling. What a fool he'd been. Bragged and blustered, inflated a flagging ego into a fragile balloon.

As they headed for home and her last night in Los Angeles he said little, chose what he said with care, listened mostly as she talked about her plans. She had applied for a teaching position at a private school in New York, would begin the following semester, was looking forward to it as well as to a grandchild that was on the way. It all had a note of finality. Could she have taken their affair so casually? A few tussles in the sack, a trip to the coast for an encore? Jesus, for him this was the beginning! They'd have dinner in his apartment—the two of them—he would do some fast talking. They left the table and were sipping brandy in the living room. He had been sitting next to her on the couch, now rose and began to pace.

"I don't know how to begin." He hesitated, drained the

brandy, set the glass on the table and faced her. "I've made a thousand deals in my life . . . they all seemed important—now— making you understand how I feel is the most important thing that can happen to me."

"Sam, I. . . ."

"I can't believe that what has happened between us was—well, something casual."

"Casual? You're the only man I've been with since my husband died."

He sat beside her and took her hand. "I love you, Martha. I know what love is for the first time." She reached out and stroked his cheek. "Marry me. Give up the teaching. We'll live out here and you can visit your daughter and new grandchild whenever you wish. They can visit us." He had a grip on both of her hands, felt her try to pull away. She was slipping, he had to hang on, all of the things he wanted to say and how he wanted to say them were forgotten, his thoughts piled up and poured out. "You can have everything you've ever dreamed of—homes, cars, servants, travel—financial security—for you—your daughter. There'll be a premarital agreement."

She was on her feet laughing. "Sam, you must be joking."

"I'm not!"

"All right. Put it in writing and I'll have my lawyer look it over."

"Your lawyer . . . ?"

"Of course. You want me on consignment. If we're going to make a deal I want it to be legal."

"Martha, I'm serious."

"So am I." She was still laughing.

He looked at her, the smile had left her face, there was still a trace of merriment in her eyes. "All right. You won't regret it. It'll be generous." He was at her side, took her hand. "You're not angry?"

"Why should I be? You made an offer. Now drive me to my hotel." She gathered her things and was at the door.

In the car neither said a word, at the entrance he extended a hand. "Goodnight, Martha. I'll be by in the morning and take you to the airport." She nodded and left.

The following morning she was gone, checked out. The clerk handed him a note.

Dear Sam:
   Your offer has been considered and turned down. Sorry.

Goodbye,
Martha

His despair dissolved into anger. If she wants a poor slob, let her have one. There wasn't a woman alive who wouldn't jump at the offer he'd made. By God, she was smack in the middle of middle-age. From then on the years tear you apart in double-time. To hell with her!

He struggled for a month; a scotch at eleven and two cocktails before lunch, fuzzy until six, a sweat at the club and then a rub and one for the drive home and on the terrace he would smooth out, doze, and then the long nights would begin. Seconals lost their bite, nembutals knocked him out until dawn and then the steep climb through the hours of the day. One night after battling sleeplessness until after three he finally dropped off to be awakened by a sharp pain in his chest. For minutes he lay still, afraid to breathe or move, then, as the pain persisted he called out for Alex who came shuffling in struggling with a robe.

"Call Doctor Addington. His name is in the book. Quick!" As Alex fumbled with the book and began to dial the pain left Duke's chest and he broke out in a sweat. Now he tried to remember all he knew about coronaries. Was the pain steady or did it come and go? Did it have to occur in the heart area or could it attack anywhere? A shooting pain down the left arm . . . did there have to be a pain down the arm? He grabbed the phone as Alex reached Addington. "Get here quick!" There was no pain now but his body was drenched with sweat. Alex stood, watching dumbly, like a frightened animal, confused, waiting to be directed. Samson closed his eyes. "Get me a towel, a glass of water." God, he was thirsty. "Hurry." He pulled the covers about himself as his body began to shake with chills. Alex returned, dried Duke's body and then covered him with an extra blanket and took a seat beside the bed. The chills began to subside, he became overcome with languor, then drowsiness and he felt himself dropping off to sleep.

Awakening, he heard voices, opened his eyes and watched as Dr. Addington was preparing the portable electrocardiograph on a table beside the bed.

"Hello," he said weakly. Addington turned, and without a word began to explore his chest with the stethoscope, listened intently, turned him over, examined his back and then stood up.

"Any more pain?"

"No."

He took his blood pressure, then he shoved a thermometer in his mouth. "I'm sure you didn't have a heart attack. We'll take a cardiogram anyway." In a few minutes the click of the machine was the only sound in the room, Alex left and the doctor began to study the graph. After a few minutes he turned off the machine and took a seat beside the bed.

"There's nothing wrong. With your heart, that is. How many pills did you take tonight?"

"A couple."

"How much did you have to drink?"

"I don't know. A few."

"You've got a fever. There's a slight congestion in your chest. I'll leave a prescription. But that's not your problem."

"What about the pains in my chest?"

"Tension. I'm sure of it. I've given you a pill to sleep and another to relax. They're crutches, they don't cure. And they don't mix with liquor." He got up. "I'm warning you. If your nerves break down it'll be a long way back." He wrote out a prescription, said he would call later, and left.

The pale light of dawn was beginning to show through the drapes, he heard the faint hum of the elevator, the door open and close and then all was still. Addington was dead serious. He had always taken his complaints lightly, brushed them off. Maybe that was why he continued to go to him—there was never panic, always assurance; his bellyaches were never cancer, headaches never caused by tumors or high blood pressure and chest pains never had organic origin. But not now. Addington was making a prediction: a one-way ticket for a nervous breakdown. He could eliminate the business pressures, let International carry the load. If the time came to refinance and he was washed out he would still have a million left for every finger and toe. But it wasn't business and he knew it. He thrived on that kind of pressure, it was all part of the game he loved, the only one he knew. He closed his eyes and forced Martha's image to appear; her hair was spread on the pillow at the tiny English inn, the scent of her was all about him, the warmth of her body heated his and they came together and during all their days the promise in her eyes, the squeeze of her hand, the lightly brushed kiss was fulfilled again and again in the darkness of their rooms. And there was the first night at the Beverly Hills Hotel—it was so clear—she was lying on the bed, giggly drunk and he buried his head between her thighs, felt the hairs about his face as he licked and kissed until she came, moaning and twitching, calling his name and then they rolled over and her mouth found him. Magic! Sorcery! Oh, Martha can't you forgive—care!

The following Monday he flew to New York and went directly to her apartment unannounced. All during the flight he rehearsed his presentation; she'd been right, he'd pursued money all of his life. But now he realized he was wrong. There were other things, more important. The moment the "city" was on the way he'd quit, they would travel, see the world. The premarital agreement was out; that was the old Duke speaking.

It was late afternoon when he rang her bell. After her first look of surprise she asked him in. At first he talked about the smoothness of his flight, his constant wonder at the airplane, asked about her daughter, she asked him about the weather on the coast, the progress of his building. Each time there was a pause the conversation resumed in more deviate areas. Damn her, she knew why he was there could see his agony! Why doesn't she make it easier? Finally, she looked at her watch. "I've an appointment. Was about to leave."

"Martha, I had to see you, explain. There has been a terrible misunderstanding." She looked at him, excused herself, dialed a number and told the person she would be late.

"Would you care for a drink? Coffee?"

"Nothing."

"All right, Sam. There was a misunderstanding. You feel you've been wronged." He nodded. "Did it ever occur to you that I'm the one who's been hurt?"

"It did. But after you left." Now he delivered his speech, assured her she was right, confessed to being a money grubber all of his life, thanked her for making him see how wrong he had been, painted an exciting life for them both and when he came to the premarital agreement, he thought he added just the touch, lowered his voice and hung his head. "I've never been more ashamed of anything in my life," he concluded. She listened to him patiently, made no comments and he searched her face for a reaction as he was speaking and found it impassive. Now he looked up and waited.

"I believe you, Sam . . . your intentions. I'm not sure you can fulfill them."

"Just give me a chance!"

She went on as if he had not spoken. "The things that men become that make them successful is what I fear."

"Would you love me if I were poor?"

"Perhaps."

"It doesn't make sense. Do you despise money?"

"No."

"I don't understand, I. . . ."

She placed a hand on his arm. "Let me think it all over." She looked at her watch. "I do have to go."

"Let me see you tomorrow?"

"No. You're asking me to make a big decision. I need time."

They left the apartment together, he pleaded again to see her, she refused and left him standing on the curb and after kissing him on the cheek promised to write and got into a cab. He returned to the airport and flew back to Los Angeles.

For a week he did not leave the apartment until after the mail was delivered. A dozen times he picked up the phone, dialed her number, and hung up. What more could he say? Then her letter arrived, short and cordial, thanking him for the offer of marriage and turning him down. He drank the rest of that day, did not leave the apartment, and passed out on his bed.

They were on coffee refills, skidding on two martinis apiece. "You wanna' build a city. . . ."

"Yeah. . . ."

"A phallic symbol."

"Intellectual shit."

Finger pointed. "Sammy. . . ."

"Don't call me that. . . ."

Reverent bow. "Duke. . . . S. Duke. . . . You wanna' fuck the whole world. . . ." warning finger. . . . "You haven't got a big enough hard-on. . . ."

They parted that day more distant than since they met.

Armed with the package—plot plans, aerial photos, economic breakdowns, renderings and projections—Samson toured. Insurance companies in Texas, the Middle West, Connecticut, and New York, a company in Maryland, then Illinois, Utah and then home; where there was interest the conditions were the same: line up major tenants, sign leases. It meant pouring millions into plans and improvements before he could get commitments for space. It was too risky.

During the next couple of months he crossed the country a dozen times, ran every lead down, got vague promises, outright refusals and two more offers to buy. Martin Tipton called and demanded a meeting in his office. Walt Covington was coiled in a large chair and Martin was pacing.

"I've got a few things to say, Sam." He waved a sheet of paper. "Here are figures you should know about. Net income from golf course, thirty thousand a month. Interest on loan on 180 acres is one hundred fifty thousand a month. Taxes twenty-five hundred a month." He held the sheet of paper up to Samson's face. "See this number, the red one? Over a hundred thousand a month in the hole. And in less than eighteen months a thirty million loan comes due." He rounded his desk fell into the chair and shot a warning finger. "You're being chewed—big bites. You can handle it but by the time the loan comes due and you start out to refinance, that land won't look like a city—it'll look like your cemetery plot."

CHAPTER TWENTY-SEVEN

The day after Jan Schwartz received her Christmas bonus she quit. Samson received the notice as she sat before his desk, hands folded in her lap with a lowered head. Her voice was almost a whisper. "I start my new job on Monday."

"You're giving me no notice?"

"I'm sorry."

"But why are you leaving?" The words were out before he had time to think. She looked up, caught his eyes and held them, his gaze started to drift as she began to speak.

"You've been good to me. I'm making less money at the new job. But there's not going to be after hours' work." Her voice rose. "I can't take it any more. . . ." Now she was out of her chair. "You're sick, Mr. Duke. Maybe you need a psychiatrist—maybe something else . . . but you're sick!" She rushed out of the room and a moment later he heard the front door slam.

He remembered their nights together, at least one a week, particularly the more recent; his wild experimentations, oral, anal, her acquiescence, tears, pleadings and her hysterical exits. Shud-

CHAPTER TWENTY-FIVE

The main offices of the Bank of the Pacific were on the top floor of the newest building in Beverly Hills. As he sat in the reception room observing the girl at the switchboard, her hands working like a puppet, her voice shut off by a sliding glass window, he realized it had been years since he had been kept waiting more than a few minutes to see any one. It was a half hour since he had come to the appointment on time and his constant inquiries drew a mechanical smile from the receptionist and an assurance that they would be with him in a few moments.

He pulled out a pillbox, removed a tiny white pellet from a collection of varied sizes and colors, placed it on the back of his tongue and swallowed. The heart flutters and chest pains were due to tension, Addington assured him as he increased the dosage from quarter-grain to one-half and urged him to take it easier. Take it easier! For nearly eighteen months he had beaten on insurance company doors looking for financing. Failing everywhere, he had to turn his energies during the past thirty days toward raising the thirty million that was coming due within ten dering, he remembered their last bout, a few days before. It was in the living room, after dinner, and both were drunk and he began to undress her slowly, kissing each part of her as it was exposed; first one breast, then the other until he rounded her pussy and tackled her anus, undressed, and tried it from the rear. She squirmed free and ran across the room, he bounded after her, tripped over a lamp cord, sprawled against the edge of a chair, catching the blow smack in the middle of his crotch, roared with pain as he grabbed his balls and sat helplessly as she put a coat over her nude body and fled from the apartment. The following morning, as usual, she said nothing. And now she was gone. He reached for the phone and called the agency.

"Do you handle Negro applicants?"

"Yes."

He told of his needs, emphasized that the girl must be attractive and the following day began to interview. Nobody could criticize him for hiring a Negro. There was integration, wasn't there? The third one he talked to seemed to fit the bill; sixty words a minute typing, ninety words on dictation, and she could not be more than twenty. Large brown eyes, lips were not too thick, and if her clothes weren't stuffed with "deceivers," her tits would fit a hand and her ass could be comfortable. He waited a week before he ordered her to his apartment to take care of accumulated work. With overtime pay, of course. They worked all morning and all went well, she refused a cocktail before the lunch, wanted none of the wine. He began to question her about her personal life, her answers were brief, by which time he had finished the wine, was feeling good—damn good—and he decided to get to the business at hand.

"You're very pretty."

For a fleeting moment there was fear in her eyes and then it disappeared.

He smiled. "You're pretty light. Bet there's somebody white in your family." Now he was grinning. She had just applied lipstick and was returning everything to her purse.

"My family is all black."

"Well, white or black . . . races are all alike, people are all alike."

"I guess so."

"You know . . . feelings—emotions."

She rose. "I'd like to finish early. There are things I have to take care of." She headed for the library. He followed her and closed the door. "I guess we can put the rest off until Monday." She had her sweater in her hand, turned to leave and he blocked her at the door. "You're very pretty. How about you and me integrating?" His smile was fixed, her face showed her fear, then he reached out to grab her.

"Take your hands off me."

"I just want to be nice."

"Then step aside."

He reached out, she kicked him in the shin and ran out the door as he danced about in pain. He caught up with her at the elevator as she was pushing the button frantically.

"If you lay a hand on me they'll hear me on Wilshire Boulevard!"

"Please, you misunderstood. . . ."

"Huh! I've been fighting off dirty old men since I was a kid. They talk alike and they smell alike. And you stink like the rest of them." The elevator reached the apartment and she got in. "You better get my check in the mail first thing in the morning."

He hired four more girls before the end of that year and then he quit. It had become good vital statistics, poor typing and shorthand. The last one had the specifications of a winner and the right attitude. Sauntering into his office she plopped into the chair, arranged her skirt in a manner that gave him a free sample, made it clear immediately that she was unencumbered, loved to work, wouldn't even mind a little traveling on the job. He forgot the typing test, hired her on the spot, ignored the quality of her work for the first week and took her to the Palm Springs house for a working weekend. They got drunk the first night, reached the bed with enough steam for a few preliminary passes before they conked out. He opened his eyes just after dawn, felt a strange sensation, grabbed a stiff prick—the first in a year—almost cried for joy as he awoke the girl and rushed to the bathroom to relieve a filled bladder only to pee the hard-on down the drain.

It was almost with relief that he decided to hang up the musket—for a while at least—and tackle a mountain of work that sheer incompetence had caused to accumulate. Putting in a call to an agency for a bookkeeper-stenographer—no age limit—talent the only qualification, he culled a Mrs. Emily Powell from a discarded heap of middle-aged wizards who had lost out in offices all over the city to the generation coming up. Mrs. Powell had been rescued from a spinster's title by a brief marriage ages before. She tackled the work with fervor and within two weeks had his affairs more current than they had been in years. Her orderliness and precision in contrast to what had been going on for a year made him realize the extent to which everything had been neglected. He plunged into work, which soon occupied his thoughts to a point where his pecker problem was filed in a corner of his brain for future consideration.

It had been eighteen months since the golf course was shut down, the bulldozers moved in, and the earth began to be moved. The utilities went underground, the grading was nearly finished when International decided that instead of twin towers for a start they would go with one office building and a twenty-story apartment house and the first phase of a shopping center. Duke protested. This meant new plans, at least a year's delay. His protest was noted, Covington reported after speaking to London, but the original plans would be scrapped, the new ones were already on the boards. Now it was the end of 1962 and a spade had not yet been put in the ground. Didn't they realize that the loan would be due the parent company in 1966, that they were nearly two years behind schedule? He demanded that Covington insist he get an extension—now! He was being premature, they answered. He began to hound the architect, had him on the phone every day, drove to his offices, even pushed the draftsmen. Forty million dollars' worth of land was vacant, wasn't producing a blade of grass, a day's loss of income was staggering while those fucking English were on their asses sipping tea making changes! He should have known better than to deal with fourth-rate people from a fourth-rate nation! He flew to New York and then on to London, paced the floor of his Dorchester suite, waited days for his calls to be answered, a meeting set up.

Then they gathered around a table at International's office and the Englishmen listened; polite, attentive, soft-spoken, even when he shouted and the conference ended, and he was patted, reassured—"old chap, old boy, old man" he was slapped on the back hard—English balls—taken to one club for lunch to another for dinner and driven to his plane in a Rolls.

In the spring of 1963 a steam-shovel took its first bite of dirt and the construction began. The major shopping center tenants had already signed leases, a bank and stock broker had taken the ground floor of the office building but only a couple of the upper floors had been rented. And only one apartment was spoken for; one of four penthouses leased to an aging star. Duke had wanted to set up his own leasing company but International had insisted on turning the job over to Cunningham and Sons, an old-time Los Angeles realty firm vegetating on the fat of an old reputation. There was no longer a Cunningham, no sons, only a son-in-law now sixty, married to an only daughter, holding down a fort that flew a faded flag. Their offices downtown in the Cunningham Building sported yellow-oaked desks, worn carpets, venetian blinds, and a half-dozen salesmen who had grown overripe. Samson hounded Covington who sent communiques and got answers referring to the contract. In desperation, Duke sought tenants, advertised, sent out a mailing, handing them to Cunningham to close the deals. By the end of the year when the structures' skeletons silhouetted the site he managed to lease three full floors of the office building, secured a half-dozen satellites for the shopping center and leased ten apartments. He visited the site several times a day, watched the steel tied and welded, modules craned into place, the concrete poured and long after the working day stopped he would climb the beams test the floor under his feet, the groins out of which the buildings were emerging. Then there were ducts and vents, switches and pipe, plaster and paint and the buildings were being formed, skeletons were being shaped, profiled, and they became suites and shops and by the end of 1964 the first tenants moved in. But their rent did not pay the taxes, interest on the interest which was eating up principal like a tapeworm. Office space was begging, apartments were vacant, and owners were offering concessions; six months' free rent on a three-year lease, pets and kids welcome, Blue Chip stamps, free baby sitters, refrigerators and stoves and beds were thrown in and couches, rent signs were everywhere, signals of distress.

They were calling it a recession. There were no apple sellers or panhandlers, the beggars still had silks, the disease wasn't a plague, just spotty, the high-rollers, go-for-brokes, the pyramiders were getting dumped. The gold coasts were tarnishing; over-built Arizona, California, and Florida where savings and loans poured their funds to builders with dreams and no substance for high interest and points. Build a building, we'll take you out, lend a hundred and ten per cent of cost, the money is pouring in, we gotta put it out. A police action became a war, advisers became soldiers as L.B.J. and a thousand million a month went into Vietnam. The flow of money at home trickled and then stopped. The squeeze was on; the guy without the cushion was out on his ass, thin equities disappeared, the small banks were whimpering and the savings and loans panicked. Samson had loosened his tight hold on Universal a year before, had not seen Hardin for months, kept buying the stock as it plummeted, certain it would recoup. Now it was down to eight from a high of thirty-two a year before. He stormed into Ben Hardin's office after the Savings and Loan Commissioner's office had done an audit and sent him the report.

"Did you see this!" he shouted, waving the document.

"I saw it." Hardin was calm, almost smiling.

"Nineteen per cent of a loan portfolio delinquent; in foreclosure or repossessed! Unfinished buildings, unsold tracts," he was reading from the report, " 'an unjudicious lending policy has caused the Association to take back hundreds of properties whose real market value can be considered substantially less than the Association's cost.' " He flung the report on the desk and shook a fist at Hardin's smiling face. "You've been taking money under the table from your building friends. Don't deny it!"

"I deny it."

"I'll prove it."

Hardin lit a cigar, tilted in his chair and billowed the smoke towards the ceiling. "You're getting out, I want your resignation—now—today. And when I get through with you, you lousy red, you'll be rotting where they all belong!"

Hardin leaned forward, the smile was gone. "Let me tell you what the commissioner didn't put in the report. What he told me this morning. In this office. We're practically insolvent, he said. If the word gets out the depositors will be lining up to withdraw their funds. From other associations as well. So, we're going to have to sell our stock. He has the buyer. Northern Savings and Loan. They know our condition, the facts. The price is to be five dollars a share."

"Five dollars! It closed yesterday over eight."

"Try and get it. If you put your blocks on the market it'll be down to two dollars in as many days. I have nothing to sell."

"You mean to tell me you've been sitting here milking the funds and sold your stock?"

"You're beating a dead horse. I borrowed ten dollars a share from the bank on every share I owned. When it was selling over thirty. They sold me out sixty days ago." He picked up an envelope and handed it to Duke. "My resignation. It's all yours. I'm taking a trip."

"Where are you going?"

"To Geneva."

"You'll never leave the country. I'll have you indicted!"

"All I'm guilty of is bad judgment. The commissioner already agreed. Also, it's poor policy to indict presidents of sick Savings and Loans. There are too many around."

Samson managed to dispose of a few thousand shares at between six and eight before the news of Hardin's resignation and the takeover by Northern was announced. Also he started to liquidate his bank stocks, taking losses on some, breaking even on others. He began to sense a feeling of panic, urgency, for the first time in his life he questioned his judgment, the wisdom of his decisions. He was going to play it safe, for a while at least, until the country returned to sanity. He put all his available cash into low-yield tax-free municipal bonds, started to withdraw from the stock market and liquidate some of his second trust deeds. Maybe the game was different—the rules—changes were geometric, computers could think some said . . . who knew? Maybe even the long-hairs were here to stay and the crew cuts and button-down collars were never coming back. At the club where he spent long hours eating up an evening, his contemporaries had dwindled, sideburns were growing longer, and even Charley, the porter, wore a natural.

He went to his office now to open and answer the mail, spending the balance of the day at the club or the construction job. Alex had quit months before after hitting a daily double at Caliente, returning only to pack his things and return to his home in Mexico. Samson started to replace him, became discouraged after a few interviews, and settled for a woman coming in every day. His evenings now became a patterned ritual: drinks at the club, dinner alone or with an old member, more drinks and home, stoned, to bed, or dinner at the apartment, booze, TV and to bed. On a few occasions he would have a hooker up for the night to take a crack at resurrection only to have the faint hope of the early evening as dead as his cock by morning.

He had been avoiding Martin Tipton for months, conducting his affairs through Covington. The attorney was laconic, barely communicative. He neither lectured nor made predictions. None of his friends were at the club that night and he dreaded facing the evening alone. He called Tipton and pleaded with him to have dinner at his apartment. Though he was shocked at the change in Tipton's appearance when he stepped off the elevator he said nothing. All during the meal the talk was devious, the kind of conversation one has with a seat partner on a plane. When the housekeeper finally left and he and Martin were seated in the living room, Samson finally said "You look like hell. What's wrong?"

For a moment, Martin didn't answer, sat sipping the drink, looking at Samson, his pale blue eyes unblinking in their nest of yellowed flesh. He downed the drink like a toast. "I'm going to die."

"We're all going to die."

"But I know when. I have cancer of the lymph glands. Terminal."

Suddenly he felt close to this man, did not know how to express his horror and muttered, "I'm sorry."

"Don't be." Martin poured another drink and sat back. "There is a time to die. I could go on . . . what would be the purpose? It's a rhetorical question, Sam. Like they say, I'm facing the moment of truth. All our lives we worked, Sam, both of us and after clothes on our backs, warm beds, and food you know what we got? Dried ink on deeds, in bank books . . . compare it to companionship or a kiss from the soul pumped by the heart. Love is what it's all about, Sam. And you know what kind? The sinking, feeling kind, the dizzy-heights kind, the emotional, distressing, slavish—all that—the romantic kind."

"You've had Sylvia, your daughter, grandchildren. I'd trade any day."

"Poor Sylvia. I never loved her and she knew it. My daughter left a long time ago. And to my grandchildren I'm a caricature, one dimensional. And since you said you'd trade, let me tell you something. You had what I wanted. I was in love with Posey, would have left Sylvia in a minute if she would have me. But she was in love with you. You fool, what you gave up."

"If you love someone you take them on their terms."

"What terms? Warm your bed until you find a rich wife? That was it, wasn't it?"

"We broke up before I married Beck, before I met her."

"But those were your rules and Posey knew it. She knew you better than anyone." He smiled. "The fact is, the only reason I have any affection for you—you're hard to like, you know—was that if Posey loved you there had to be something worthwhile under your lousy exterior. Oh, yes. One advantage of knowing you're going to die is that you can say any goddamn thing you wish." He poured a large drink. "You know," he went on, "you gotta live your life like you're an artist who's going to make one painting. Think of that, Sam. What's your mural? No, don't tell me. Let me tell you. God, I'm getting drunk. Haven't felt better in weeks. It's better than cobalt. You're worth millions and haven't any kin. You've outwitted tax collectors and tenants, bankers and borrowers, contractors and suppliers, insurance companies and lawyers. All your life you added up the dollars and ignored the sense. A pun, Sam. Ha, ha! Never made a will—can't give it up. You poor sonofabitch. You got an idea you can take it with you." Martin rose. At the elevator he turned. "Oh, yes, my funeral is going to be private. Nobody is going to have the opportunity to gloat through tears that the stiff is poor Martin Tipton and not themselves." He was in the elevator and going down before Samson could say a word.

He couldn't believe that Martin was going to die—soon. Then he calculated swiftly; when he met Martin they were ten years apart—a hundred and twenty months. Cancer got to a lot of persons between sixty and seventy. Jesus, half the people he knew died of cancer! A hundred and twenty months. It was hard to believe, especially when you think how fast a month goes; one can't think of death. Sure, everybody's got to die. What happens when you get reminders? Like you're close to sixty and you got a bad heart, like your pressure could make a balloon out of an artery . . . like you're Martin Tipton and you got a reservation. . . . Maybe Martin was right about Posey. He poured himself a drink and wondered what their life would have been if he married her. She would be his age now—fifty-eight—pretty old. . . . But his cock was older, it was ninety. He turned on the radio, they were playing a Chopin piano sonata; he liked Chopin, the only composer whose music he recognized, especially his sonatas. He sank in a chair and closed his eyes. The only sense that Martin made was about companionship; it sure in hell gets lonely. Damnit! He jumped up and filled his glass. It was late, he was tired and shuffled off to bed. And he had been thinking a lot about a will, had ideas, nothing definite, but ideas. After a couple of hours he took a second red pill but could not sleep. Love is what it's all about, Martin said, pontificating; the idea was as new as the wheel. The Greeks praised it, Shakespeare played it, the Neanderthals must have chipped it on the walls of the cave. So he loved a woman and she didn't love him back; that was only one kind of love. Love is a noun and a verb, there's falling in love, being in love, giving love and taking love and love is a feast and best of all is making love. Well, he didn't know about Martin, maybe the poor bastard never touched base, maybe Posey was the only woman he ever loved. Too bad my friend. Love can be contracted and expanded, you never saw its versatility. There's love for an hour and for a night, sometimes years, rarely a lifetime. The goddamn pill didn't even make him drowsy. He got out of bed slipped into a robe and walked out on the terrace. The air was damp, he shivered and drew the robe about him. He thought of Martin's appearance that night: the lifeless eyes, the parchment skin, taut over the bones, creped under the eyes, stringed down the neck, all of it like a layer of flake, dead but still hanging on. A wave of self-pity swept over him. In spite of their many disagreements over the years, he was a friend, perhaps his best, he trusted him, he was the only one he ever confided in. There weren't many: Fines, Jack Delaney. He had not talked to Cady in nearly a year and the last time he saw Jack was when he dropped in the office one day on a trip to Los Angeles to congratulate him after the news break on the "city." There weren't many. Friendship. Martin didn't mention that—more enduring maybe, less demanding. Back to bed and under the covers and maybe sleep. You work with what you got, you "do your thing" like they say; he had love and used it up, a fucking plague was taking away his friend, but he had his dream and that golf course was going to be

a city with his name carved into the granite for all to see for a
hundred years!

He tried not to think about Martin, avoided going to the Tipton office, the busy days occupied his mind with other things but
the nights brought his friend's gaunt face to the terrace, the living
room, and, in the darkness of his bedroom it was luminous. He
wanted to visit Tipton, but what was there to say? Talk about the
present, now, and you compound pain. There was no future and
Martin made it clear that the past was a wasteland.

So he didn't call; he received information and delivered messages through Walt Covington and asked to be notified if anything happened. Also, he was having troubles of his own, troubles
of the living. For weeks it was hard to pee—slow start, weak
stream, sometimes just a dribble. At first he ignored it; Jesus why
look for trouble and he was sick and tired of going to doctors. Finally one morning he had a bladder full ready for delivery and
there was no starting. By ten o'clock he was sitting in the office of
a urologist that Dr. Addington recommended, ready to burst.
There was no time to take a history, the doctor's clever finger
massaged the prostate, not a drop was coaxed and he was cathet-
erized. Relieved of the pain but frightened he sat in the consultation room as the doctor droned with questions.

"Been taking any new medicines lately?"

He thought about the pills—but hell, he had been taking them
for years. "No. Nothing new."

Then the doctor asked about drinking habits, smoking habits
and frequency of sex. He wasn't drinking more and smoking less.

"It's been difficult to have an erection."

"How difficult?"

He was going to use comparables, weigh and measure—shit,
you're talking to God! "I can't get a hard-on."

The doctor made a note. "How long has this been going on?"
It had been going on a long time, he told him, a couple of years

maybe more. "It used to be that I'd feel something down there but couldn't get it up. Now there are no messages."

The urologist was thorough, he probed again, fingered the prostate, turned him around, squeezed the head of his cock, and smeared the secretion on a slide. They were back in the consultation room. "You're sure there have been no new drugs, change in habits?"

Samson thought again and shook his head. "Nothing."

"We had better do a urogram. Complete X-ray. We get to see everything."

"What are you looking for?"

"The prostate is enlarged. But not enough to cause this. I want to see the kidneys and bladder."

Before Samson could ask another question, the doctor left the room and the technician took over. After a shot in the arm that made him slightly dizzy and a series of X-rays in a half-dozen positions he was asked to dress and wait in an examining room.

"It'll be about a half-hour," the nurse said.

He leafed through the *New Yorker, Business Week,* and *Life,* fought off visions of living with a kidney machine or slowly dying of cancer—maybe he and Martin would have a double funeral— he found himself being led back to the consultation room shaking and wiping sweaty palms along the sides of his pants. There was another wait. He was no longer analyzing his fears, weighing the pros and cons, figuring the percentages; there was a blockage! It was a question now of whether it was benign or malignant. By the time the doctor walked in he was trembling in the chair.

"Did you see the X-rays?" It was almost a shout. The doctor was smiling, Duke's nerves began to steady, he was examining the urologist's face for another sign—more hope—anything that would free him from the hook on which he was quavering.

"Everything's negative—kidneys, bladder—not a sign of anything." Duke wanted to cry out, kiss the doctor's hand, the pounding in his heart subsided, he felt weak, jellied joy. "The urethra is a tiny canal," the doctor went on, "sensitive, easily irritated. Sometimes distress can cause this condition; nervous tension, emotional problems." Then he explained about the sphincter bladder spasms.

Samson hesitated. "Could impotency cause this?"

"I would say it's possible. But rare. However, if the impotency is psychological, and I have every reason to believe it is in your case, the same forces could be causing the spasms that turn off your water." The doctor's manner changed, his smile was friendly, it was like he removed his gown and faced Samson in mufti. "Maybe if we can coax that thing up and get you laid— well after awhile it might do the trick."

"I'm ready."

"Have you seen a psychiatrist?"

"No."

"I can give you a series of treatments, massage, but I'm sure it would do no good."

Samson left with instructions to sit in a warm bath three times a day, was given a prescription for a sedative and told to consider seeing a psychiatrist.

The warm baths helped; sometimes he would have to sit for half an hour until he was able to empty his bladder in the tub. In between he would stand over the bowl or a urinal for long periods, run the water in a sink think of waterfalls and rivers before he was able to dribble. There were times when his mind was occupied with other things and he was able to urinate with comparative ease. But this did not occur often. After a torturous night when he felt his bladder would burst he called Dr. Addington who recommended a psychiatrist.

Arriving a few minutes before the hour, he waited in a tiny reception room and as his watch pointed to the hour a small man about his own age came in and led him along a narrow hall to his office. The room was fitted out like a comfortable library, the blinds were drawn, the soft light of a lamp lit it all with a warm glow. The doctor was writing: name, address, age, marital status, occupation; then he pushed the pad aside and looked up.

"Now, Mr. Duke, what seems to be bothering you?"

Fighting off suspicion, all his prejudices towards psychiatrists, he told him of his impotency.

"How long has this been going on?"

"Oh, I don't know. A couple of years, maybe three."

"You don't remember when?"

"What do you mean?"

"If a man can't get an erection—well it's sort of a trauma. He sometimes remembers the time it first occurred."

"Well I don't."

"Has it been total?"

"What do you mean?" The doctor smiled.

"Have you had a hard-on since the first time you couldn't get a hard-on? That's what I mean."

"Yes." The doctor looked at him, silent, expectant. "There was one woman."

"Do you want to tell me about it?"

"There's nothing to tell."

The doctor made a note—maybe a doodle. That's what they do, he heard. Sometimes the bastards don't even listen. The doctor looked at the clock, Samson followed his gaze. Twenty minutes of the hour was gone.

"Do you want to talk about anything, Mr. Duke?"

"What do you mean?"

"I ask you a question—you ask what do I mean." He shrugged. "If you want to sit here at forty dollars an hour and tell me nothing—that's your business; if you're waiting for me to talk don't waste my time or yours. I'm paid to listen."

Now the room was so quiet he could hear the hum of the electric clock. He turned from the doctor and stared at the wall. What could he tell this man—this stranger—that from the time he maybe fucked his maybe daughter the whole thing started, that he found a woman who brought him back to life and that he loused it up with contract talk? Did he have to tear it out of his guts at forty dollars an hour? How could he talk about something that he dared not think about? The defenses he had built against Carla's image had become so effective that she rarely entered his thoughts and her face had almost blurred out of existence. Was she to come alive—perhaps to the amusement of this doctor—faker? Half of them were he was certain. Samson rose, stood over the small figure, peeled two twenties from a clip. "Don't bother sending a bill." He looked at the clock. "I got twenty minutes to go. Keep it for a tip."

The things became routine; sitz-baths and the long stance over the can, even the pss, pss sounds he would make like Aunt Annie used to when she was training him to pee. It was like learning how to live with a limp but there would be long periods when his sphincter wasn't jumpy and he would pee with the abandon of a kid melting snow. He had found the key except it did not always work. There was a list of do's and don'ts; make it mechanical, clutter your mind with other things or make it blank and don't approach the john with fear and never think of sex.

Interest rates began to climb with the draft calls and casualties in Vietnam. A new commander promised victory and for the moment, "Westy" seemed a hope, L.B.J. hauled out all the drums but for some reason nobody marched to the tune. Jesus, what was happening! The VC were being knocked out ten to one, saturation bombing in the North, the navy pounded the coast, how in hell do they stand up! Samson was at the "City" every day, all the buildings under construction were nearing completion, tenants were moving in, high costs and tight money had curtailed building, a trend had reversed. There was now a shortage of apartments and office space; a landlord's market was developing. By the beginning of 1966 the office building was nearly all leased, the shopping center was filled and the apartment house had a waiting list. For weeks Samson had been trying to get an expression from International about new construction; he called London, New York, sent wires without a response. By God, if they thought a minority stockholder had no rights they had better read the law! Insisting that Walt Covington accompany him they flew to London and managed to round up the board.

"I know how angry you are," Covington said, as they drove to the meeting. "Cool it. They're the boss. Whatever you get you'll have to wheedle out of them."

"We'll see about that."

They were polite, as always, soft-spoken, courteous, sat around the table like a dozen actors in a drawing-room play. Nobody stepped on a line.

"We've finished a shopping center, office building and an apartment house. We're full. There's a waiting list. Everything we build from now on will be snapped up when we break ground."

"We'd like to wait awhile. Building costs are high," one said.

"Not as high as rents are gonna be."

They looked at one another and the chairman spoke. "That's a matter of opinion."

Covington broke in. "Gentlemen, all indications are that building costs are going higher. Rents will be commensurate. The sooner we get construction going the lower our costs will be."

"That's right," Samson said. "We're in an inflationary spiral and it looks like there's no end."

One of the board spoke, a young one. "Your stock market is down sharply. Your president and Westmoreland claim the war is nearly won." He threw up his hands. "That'll mean a letdown, unemployment, lower prices." The others shook their heads in agreement.

"The president has been wrong before and so has every general we sent to Vietnam," Samson said. "Suppose the war lasts for years?"

"Impossible." Three of them said it in chorus.

All that morning they argued, the Englishmen calm, Samson with desperation. They stopped for their lousy tea and soon they were off to the club for lunch and by the time they returned for an afternoon session, Duke forgot new construction and began to fight for concessions.

"There's forty-five million due by the end of the year. I'd like an extension. Say, a couple of years."

"That's impossible," the chairman said, without hesitation.

"We're a public company," another said. "We can't justify it to our stockholders."

"You're collecting interest, the buildings are profitable. The land is prime. The loan is secure."

"It's against our policy to extend loans," the chairman said.

Samson looked at Covington whose eyes cautioned. "All right, gentlemen. I have another plan. With what we have completed and the remaining land I can get a loan on the entire project for the amount due you. That way you get your money, my investment will remain." He sat back. "You're in for a free ride."

"What would the terms of the loan be?"

"Seven and a half per cent, maybe eight."

The chairman rose. "Suppose we think it over, Mr. Duke. We'll let you know tomorrow." They were all on their feet before Samson could say another word. It was agreed that he would meet with three members of the board the following morning.

"What do you think they'll do?" Samson asked Covington as they drove to the hotel.

"Turn you down."

"How can they? I'm getting them off the hook and they end up with a fat equity with no investment."

"They're trying to get you off the hook without your investment and no equity."

"I can't believe it."

"You better start. I get the impression these gentlemen are cut out of the same tweed of the men who stole for good Queen Vic."

"You're going over our agreement. You've got to find a loophole. By God, there'll be another revolution!"

Returning to the suite, Samson ran for the bathroom and stood over the toilet trying to wheedle a dribble. Returning to the room half-emptied he found Walt hanging up the phone. The attorney's face wore an expression of disbelief, sadness.

"It was the office. Martin just died." Covington went to the window and stared out at the park. Neither man said a word for a long time. Samson poured a drink downed it slowly and finally spoke.

"He was my best friend."

"He was the best friend of a lot of people," Covington said. "We don't have to rush home," he went on. "There is to be no funeral."

"I know."

That night they dined alone, drank heavily, toasted Martin and found it easy to remember good things that he did. Hung over and depressed they made their way to International's offices the following morning. Though the shock of Martin's death had been softened by the months of preparation, the fact that he had ceased to exist produced a trauma he had not anticipated. It was the finality, the end of the slim hope, the consummation of the inevitable prediction for all men. He was not superstitious, he always told himself, mystics cling to a nether world because of the inability to cope with the real world, but he was certain that Martin's death was a herald and that the meeting he was headed for was to be only an exercise.

The chairman recited the decision without an apology. It is against the corporation's policy to borrow money when they had large cash surpluses and under extraordinary circumstances only would they borrow money at the high interest rates Samson suggested. The fact that they would have no money invested is only academic. They did not go into the deal to bail out at the first opportunity but to develop a piece of land in a most complete and intelligent manner.

"So you expect the loan paid when it is due?"

"I'm afraid so."

"And there's to be no more construction at present?"

"Exactly."

All the hostility he felt towards these men, steam that started to build when he first negotiated, now began to gather in his gut roared to his head, pounded in his ears, was about to explode when he felt a grip on his arm as Covington began to propel him from the room, pushed him out the door and down the hall.

"Why didn't you let me tell them what I had to say?" he roared as he wrenched his arm free.

"If you could have seen your face. . . ."

"That smug bastard!"

"Where in hell do you think you'd get if you took a poke at him?"

During the flight home they kept to themselves, the attorney scribbled on a legal pad and Duke spent long intervals nudging a bladder that gave sparingly. He left Covington at the airport and sped home to a warm tub where he finally emptied himself. Early the following morning he was at Covington's desk.

"I have an idea," Covington said. "It might work. Duke City goes public."

"What do you mean?"

"I talked to an underwriter last night. We've got the most valuable piece of urban land in the country. He's sure we can raise a hundred million dollars. International spins off the subsidiary company and it goes public."

"Suppose they refuse?"

"They will. But if we go to the stockholders the board will have a helluva time justifying their position. Let me get a concrete proposal from an underwriter. We'll submit it to International. If they refuse, we try the back door."

Within a month they had a prospectus and shopped around. Though new issues were stumbling, "Duke City" had the appeal. Batten & Osborne agreed to underwrite and Covington and Duke flew to London. A hundred million guaranteed, enough to pay off the loan, fees, reserves and a pie to divide between International and Duke. This time the board laid their cards face up; no spinoff, no new stock issue, the loan comes due, no pay-off and Duke is out.

They managed to get a list of International's and started to run them down. Ten-, twenty-, and hundred-share holders were spread all over Europe, a few lived in the States, the big blocks were either owned or controlled by members of the board of directors.

"There's got to be another way," Samson said at the end of a long day after they had conferred with a half-dozen small shareholders whose holdings did not represent one per cent of the stock. "This could take a lifetime."

"Maybe we blew enough smoke. Let's see the board."

The board listened, said they would consider and the following day agreed to extend the loan for an additional year.

"What's a year!" Samson shouted. "You won't build, won't take an available loan."

"If interest rates go down, we'll accept a loan. If building costs go down we'll build."

"But I tell you they're not going down. They're going up!"

"That is where we disagree, Mr. Duke. And for your sake let us hope we are right."

"What'll I do now?" Samson asked as they left the offices with the agreement to extend.

"Pray for the end of the war—a depression—low-interest unemployment."

Unemployment, low interest, a depression! Jesus that's where he held his breath and plunged, but one swam with minnows then not sharks, and a barracuda was a yard long. Now a giant step crossed a continent not a county and Wilshire Boulevard was bought by the inch not by the mile and you had to own a bank not a banker and if you weren't tied to a can that became a merger welded to an acquisition that became a conglomerate you were a helpless sardine.

CHAPTER TWENTY-EIGHT

During most of the years he held aces and trumps, was an odds-on favorite in every game. Now he was in the back seat, lurching and hurtled, and the driver was hydra-headed, instructed by a comptometer, programmed by calculation devised by the end product of a syndrome. The board of directors of International were spewed from a machine, a loan was coming due and they were going to skin him from his chin to his balls. He began to get the feeling of a duck soaring from a blind into peppered shot. He threaded through the agreement like a snail, crawled around commas and colons, sniffed at ambiguities, filled pages of notes and delivered them to Walt Covington.

"Here's my homework. Go over it carefully. Those bastards will file a notice of default the day after the loan's due. Find every hole in our agreement."

"I think we've enough to enjoin a foreclosure."

"It's not enough. The injunction has got to stand up against a demurrer. We've got to get into the courts, and keep it there.

That land will have weeds a mile high before I get through with those bastards."

Thirty days before the loan was due, Samson received a notice from International. Five weeks later they filed a foreclosure. Covington prepared a forty-page brief leaning heavily on the traditional rights of the minority stockholder, demanded an injunction which was granted by the court. A demurrer was turned down but the court insisted that Duke post a bond. After a frantic search for an insurance company who would write it, one was located who agreed to underwrite it for a half-million-dollar premium.

"It's a lot of money," Covington said, as they met in his office. "We've got thirty days to post the bond. Let me feel them out on a settlement."

"There's one settlement. I get to refinance and the building goes on."

"You know they want to squeeze you out. Let me try for your money back. Maybe with interest."

"The city's going to be built. Nothing less."

"Sam, you must be getting old, losing respect for money. I can't guarantee we'll win this. Sure, we got a good case but I've seen better ones lose. And it could take years."

"Let it. There's a couple of hundred million dollars profit in that deal. And nobody's fucking me out of my share." Duke rose, his bladder was filled, had not been emptied since the night before. "No settlement. I'll talk to you later." He ran out of the office, stood at the urinal, dribbled, and rushed home to a warm bath. Since the affliction he had installed a phone on the wall beside the tub. He called Covington.

"Order the bond immediately."

"Wait a few days. Think it over."

"It's thought over."

Available cash for loans was drying up as the prime rate rose; banks were borrowing money at seven per cent and lending it out at eight and nine, bond issues were begging. Fairly liquid, and with unlimited credit at the banks, Samson investigated the second trust deed market. He had been out of it for a couple of years and decided to call a few of the brokers who had supplied him with loans in the past. The response was overwhelming; apartment house loans, business properties, residences, loans on vacant land, no more arguments about points, name it and make a deal. His initial commitments were gobbled up, he raised the ante, there was no resistance; ten points one year, twenty for two and twenty-five for three, prepayment penalties and acceleration clauses. He tied up with a broker he trusted to deliver the bonuses in cash, borrowed a million dollars from the bank putting up securities as collateral. By this time the only relief he got was in a warm tub, was tired running home to sitz, closed the office in Beverly Hills and had Mrs. Powell come to the apartment three days a week. It was like the Depression days—better—and a galloping inflation would wipe out any mistake. And it looked like the war was going to drag on in spite of L.B.J's vow.

The mortgage business had given him new zest, he forgot "The City" as he planned each day; appraisals before noon and back for a bath and the club for golf. Usually he would have to rush home after a game for the sitz; sometimes he got lucky, pissed in the shower, and was able to remain at the club for drinks and dinner. One evening he left the club after dinner, warmed by the drinks, delighted with an empty bladder and headed for home along Sunset Boulevard. Starting at Laurel Canyon the hippies were clustered at corners, sprawled in parkways, and crawling the sidewalks. At Clark Drive he stopped for a signal when a young girl stepped off the curb, opened the door and slid in the seat beside him. Overcoming his surprise he was about to demand that she get out when the signal changed and her hand grabbed his thigh.

"Please, mister. Just drive me a few blocks."

"What's wrong?"

"A freak on a bad trip been giving me a time."

She was closer to him, her hand had not left his leg, now it was caressing it. Jesus! Raiser of the dead; down deep he felt jumping beans, tiny worms swarming in the halls of his scrotum. . . . Her hand slid from his thigh, flicked the switch on the radio spun the dial and the car filled with rock sounds and jive. She whipped a comb from a purse and ran it through long strands that hugged her face as her body undulated shifting her ass from side to side. *Drive on! don't say a thing, pass Doheny, cruise along the dark part of Sunset–guile–no missteps–balance feathers in a wind!* A tiny skirt edged full thighs as his glance focused on mini-breasts pasted against a multicolored blouse. As the car sped past the Beverly Hills Hotel the road began to twist and they headed west. The music was louder, pounding, insistent, her eyes were closed her arms moving like serpents to a fakir's flute. Questions stumbled in his mind over thoughts, fear and longing vied: underage—God, she couldn't be more than sixteen—they'll be looking for her: parents, cops! Maybe not, there was an army of them, he read it. Floaters from broken homes, out of contact for months and nobody cared. . . . Now the radio cried; a soft ballad began, she seemed to slump, her hand reached for his thigh, inside this time, he was afraid to move, barely breathed—his prick was getting hard!

He whispered. "What's your name?"

"Tally."

"Tally?"

"Would you believe Tallulah? Some actress my father thought was groovy."

"Where does your father live?"

"Santa Ana."

"Is that where you live?"

"No, man."

"Where do you stay?"

"We got a pad in Laurel Canyon—three of us." The ballad was over the music blasted again, her body began to weave. He reached out and let his hand fall on her thigh, she put her hand over his and pressed it against her. He reached the freeway turned south got off on Wilshire and headed east.

"Where do you want to go, Tally?"

She flicked off the radio, slid to the corner of the seat and seemed to be examining him. Now she reached for his hand. "I don't want to go home, if that's what you mean."

"No?"

"What's your name?"

He was about to lie, but blurted it out. "Sam."

"That's groovy. I never knew anyone with that name. You're not very old, are you, Sam?"

"Guess I'm going to be fifty soon."

"You sure don't look it. My father's only forty and he's got no hair and wrinkles. I'm eighteen—almost. Got a cigarette?"

"I'm sorry."

"Shit!"

"I'll get some."

"I'm hungry. Let's go someplace and get a hamburger and Coke."

He headed toward Dolores'. A drive-in was the best place. Nobody he knew ever went there; he could park in the rear and be hidden.

He sat beside her as she wolfed a two-decker hamburger and noisily sipped a Coke. Between bites she would inspect him, run her hand up and down his leg unconcerned with where it rested, reach across and deliver a sharp bite on whatever part of his face was within reach. Finally, gorged and seemingly contented she lit a cigarette, laid her head on the back of the seat as she waited for him to pay the check and the waiter to remove the tray.

He would have to take a chance he figured as he drove toward his apartment. A motel was out of the question and the chances of anyone seeing him enter the building was slim. They entered the penthouse and she cried out.

"Woweee! Is this all yours? I mean, do you live here alone? Are you married?"

"It's all mine, I live here alone and I'm not married."

Now he saw her for the first time in the full light as she ran around the room, bounced on the couch, rushed to the terrace and back to the room where she kicked off her sandals and squatted on the floor. She was taller than he had thought, her full thighs curved to a neat behind and though her eyes were small they were bright blue and fitted well in an angular face that was softened by full lips. He poured himself a stiff drink, hesitated and then offered her one.

"I don't touch it. Haven't got a joint around?" He looked puzzled. "Marijuana—pot."

"I'm sorry."

She reached into her purse and removed a pill. "Got a Coke?" He poured the Coke over ice and handed it to her. She popped the pill in her mouth and sipped the Coke.

"What's that?"

"A diet pill."

"Honey, you don't have to diet."

"Sammy, you're square. Diet pills are an up." She pointed toward the ceiling. She twirled a couple of times, came up to him flung her arms about his waist and pressed with all her strength; he could feel her tiny breasts, her thighs, her arms slackened a bit but she did not move and then came in closer as he felt his prick harden as she pressed against it. Then she pushed him away.

"Where's the head?"

"In there," he said, pointing to the bathroom.

He wanted to shout for joy! Doctors, psychiatrists, what the hell did they know! all he needed was a little love, attention— Christ maybe he would be able to pee again! She returned to the room, popped another pill, swallowed the Coke then took his hand and demanded to be shown the apartment. They toured the rooms, she tried chairs bounced on beds, flicked switches; they returned to the living room and she turned on the radio. The rhythms boomed, he downed another drink, kicked off his shoes, flopped on the couch, she climbed on his lap put her hands about his neck and began to gyrate to the music. Reaching inside her pants his hand cupped her ass she moved faster, her head back and eyes closed. The music became louder he tried to move to the beat her hand reached down and grabbed his crotch, she leaned back lost her balance and they both rolled to the floor. "Let's get zappy, pappy woooeee!" she screamed. Twisting from him, he lumbered after, trapping her on the bed. She squirmed out of her brief things laughing, squealing as he tore at them. From the other room a guitar wailed, a bass thumped, there were drums, he was out of his clothes his prick up; not at twelve o'clock, aimed at heaven, but straight out not hanging in shame. Talleeeee! He buried his head between her thighs, burrowed in, began to lick and kiss, she crossed her legs locked him in place and half-squashed, he lapped and fought to breathe as she screeched and squealed tore his back with nails, grinded and bumped, released him rolled over on top now biting—his neck, an ear, down to his long-dead cock, nipped it he cried out—pain, joy—she spun around sat on his prick and rammed it in! "fuck, pappy, fuck!" she wriggled and he pumped and then it came—a dribble not a jet, and she rode, slid off sobbing, and curled beside him.

He awoke to a purring snore, a touch of velvet on his chest and a warm hand on his belly. His eyes found the illuminated clock. A little after one. Carefully he slid from the bed made his way to the living room poured a long drink and went out to the terrace. A black sky canopied the city lights, a westerly breeze whipped about him as he leaned over the wall. Who made the rules, the age of consent? Maybe it was an edict of Rome or a paragraph in Napoleon's Code, but what had it to do with the size of a breast, pubic hair, or the juice of sex? Consent had to do with people, touch and tremors, not the dust of old laws.

Tally was curled like an embryo when he entered the bedroom. He covered her carefully and watched her sleep in the soft light of the lamp. Why not? A million men married girls her age. He pictured her with hair cut short, groomed and polished and dressed with care, sandals traded for pumps a mini-skirt with mink, maturing as he ages, juicing old joints, firm as he softens and always lovely to look at. And in the meantime, years ahead like tonight, pouring sap like a colt. Consent? A wrinkled father with a bald head, debts and ninety bucks a week; he'd sign a paper like a shot. Removing his robe he climbed into the bed slipped into the curve of her body and closed his eyes.

Barely awake, his mind groped as his hand slid along the sheets reaching for her body. Feeling nothing he crawled from the blanket and an empty bed, looked at the clock—it was after nine—ran to the living room, the terrace, the kitchen and all the rooms. Back in the bedroom he began to examine opened drawers his clothes piled on the floor, remembered his wallet on the dresser, the watch he had placed on the table, his jewel box on a small desk. Everything was emptied; a couple of hundred in cash gone, the Tiffany watch, gold cuff links and a set of diamond studs. It was a gag, she was hiding would spring from a corner and yell "Pappy" rush to his arms and his dream would begin to knit. Now he roamed the rooms like a sleuth, opened closet doors looked behind furniture ran to the terrace back to the kitchen looked behind the drapes and finally slumped on the couch. A hooker, a fucking whore! By God, he'd find her, prowl The Strip and when he did, Oh, when he did! A pressure was building in his bladder—fast—knives were sticking in his gut, he rushed to the bathroom, spun the faucets and began to fill the tub. He slid in, shuddered as his ass touched the still cold bottom. His gut was a balloon—growling—he slid down as the water swirled about him; relax, let go! The pain became more intense, there was a noose inside—tightening, tightening—Jesus let it come! He tore the receiver from the hook on the wall and dialed, there was water all about him, inside, outside. . . . God. Dr. Addington be there! The phone rang once, twice, three times, four, it was the exchange, he hung up remembered the home number, the one for emergencies, dialed and waited for the rings, the pain was curled in his belly crawling to his back reaching out to his chest the phone continued to ring the water roared from the faucet. God let him pee! It began slowly, a drop, a trickle, a squirt, a drop again and a trickle and then it came, a pulsating stream, a gusher from his tortured bowels! He slid the phone onto the hook, closed his eyes and emptied himself into the tub. For a long while he did not move, as the water lapped about his exhausted body, bubbled and swirled and gurgled at the drain. Painfully he rose, turned off the faucet, was about to get out when the phone rang.

"Sam?"

"What is it, Walt?"

"I got a call from International. Their New York lawyer. They want to settle."

"Settle?"

"Maybe your money back, all of it."

"I'm not interested."

"Sam, listen. We can lose. I told you. Get through with them."

"I'll get through. When I can piss all over them!" He hung up the phone and slid back into the tub.